AURORA FLOYD

AURORA FLOYD

Mary Elizabeth Braddon

edited by Richard Nemesvari & Lisa Surridge

broadview literary texts

Canadian Cataloguing in Publication Data

Braddon, M.E. (Mary Elizabeth), 1837-1915
    Aurora Floyd

(Broadview literary texts)
ISBN 1-55111-123-3

I. Nemesvari, Richard Andrew, 1959- . II. Surridge, Lisa A. (Lisa Anne), 1963- .
III. Title. IV. Series.

PR4989.M4A97 1998   823'.8   C97-932505-6

Broadview Press
Post Office Box 1243, Peterborough, Ontario, Canada K9J 7H5

in the United States of America:
3576 California Road, Orchard Park, NY 14127

in the United Kingdom:
B.R.A.D. Book Representation & Distribution Ltd.,
244A, London Road, Hadleigh, Essex SS7 2DE

http://www.broadviewpress.com

Broadview Press gratefully acknowledges the support of the Canada Council, the Ontario Arts Council, and the Ministry of Canadian Heritage.

Text design and composition by George Kirkpatrick

PRINTED IN CANADA

Contents

Acknowledgements

Our grateful thanks to Lisa Power and Diana Rutherford for secretarial assistance; to Susan Keelor, Melinda Maunsell, and Greg Seib for library research and text scanning; to Marie Surridge and Derek Wood for help with translation; to Peter Shillingsburg for technical support and editorial advice; to Richard Onslow of Racing Promotional Literature for information on Victorian flat racing and to the Harry Ransom Humanities Research Center for providing us with a microfilm copy of the first edition of the text. We also acknowledge the work of P.D. Edwards, who was the first modern editor to take on the task of providing scholarly annotations for this novel. We are grateful for the financial support of the University of Victoria President's Committee on Faculty Research and Travel and the St. Francis Xavier University Council for Research. Finally, we would like to thank Jane Strickler for her always insightful comments and suggestions.

Introduction

The "Sensational" Life of M.E. Braddon[1]

In the 1860s English novelists including Mary Elizabeth Braddon, Wilkie Collins, and Charles Reade diverged from contemporary literary practice to create the sensation novel – a genre which, to the dismay of critics, seriously challenged social and cultural ideologies. Sensation fiction was initially perceived as a shockingly new and threatening kind of literature; however, novels like Braddon's *Aurora Floyd* actually emerged out of recently established Victorian institutions such as the penny press and the divorce court. In its fraught relationship with realist fiction, and its presentation of secrecy, detection, and fear of domestic scandal, sensation fiction explored the increasingly prominent class and gender anxieties of the period – anxieties which, in the case of Braddon, were highlighted by her unorthodox personal life.

Braddon was born into an apparently secure middle-class family in 1835.[2] The household possessed a parlour and three servants, these placing it firmly within the respectable ranks of the Victorian bourgeoisie. However, her father Henry, a partner in a firm of solicitors, was careless in both his work and his spending habits, resulting in the family's financial ruin when Braddon was only four years old. Her parents separated, and it was not until many years later that Braddon's mother, Fanny, revealed to her that Henry Braddon had been an unfaithful husband as well as a failed provider.

This rather traumatic early childhood resulted in the appearance of a series of feckless and occasionally destructive fathers in Braddon's fiction, of whom Archibald Floyd is a relatively innocuous example. Although the text of *Aurora Floyd* follows the conventional Victorian device of making Aurora motherless, thus "explaining" her lack of proper socialization, Mr. Floyd is unable to provide real aid to his daughter in any of her dilemmas. A weak, and therefore essentially absent, father requires a strong-willed daughter. This was a lesson Braddon learned, and she both acted on it herself and had her heroines act on it as well.

The other lesson Braddon learned was just how fragile middle-class respectability is without the money to sustain it. Although immediately after her separation Fanny Braddon managed to maintain some of the comforts her family had possessed before her husband's failure, she and her children were forced increasingly to economize, and to move into successively poorer suburbs of London. By the time she turned twenty-two Braddon was determined to change this, to support herself and earn enough to ease her mother's financial difficulties. It was at this point that she took the literally dramatic step of becoming an actress.

In the unpublished memoirs of her early life, *Before the Knowledge of Evil*, Braddon observes that when a girl of good family decided to enter the theatre it was "a thing to be spoken of with bated breath, the lapse of a lost soul, the fall from Porchester Terrace[3] to the bottomless pit," and that her decision "convulsed her family to the most distant cousin."[4] Since actresses and female performers were often associated with prostitutes, such a disreputable occupation was very difficult to live down. After Braddon's relations failed to dissuade her from attempting this rash scheme, their next argument was that the least she could do was to change her name, and thus the stage career of "Mary Seyton" was born. Under this name Braddon performed in a series of plays, usually in supporting roles, and always in smaller towns such as Hull and Brighton. Thus although she was far from a failure, it is clear that Braddon was not moving into leading roles, and that it was unlikely she would receive the invitation to perform in London which was the mark of true theatrical success. She seems to have enjoyed the life of an actress, however, and the opening chapter of *Aurora Floyd* is obviously autobiographical. Her sympathetic portrayal of Eliza Prodder, Aurora's actress mother, and her good-humoured presentation of the provincial stage, shows Braddon suggesting that acting was not necessarily the death-blow to character and morality that many middle-class Victorians assumed. Chapter I can therefore be seen not only as a defence of actors in general, but of the author in particular.

After three years in the theatre it became obvious to Braddon that, although acting provided her with a relatively steady income, it was never going to bring financial security. By this point, however, she was receiving encouragement to pursue a potentially more lucrative line of work as a writer. In late 1859 or early 1860 she had written a comedietta entitled *The Loves of Arcadia*, which was performed at the Strand Theatre in London, and was quite successful.[5] More significant, however, was her meeting with John Gilby, a Yorkshire squire who undoubtedly saw one of her performances and struck up an acquaintance with the young actress. It is Gilby who appears to have offered to support Braddon while she attempted a literary career, and to try and help her get her work published. What is certain is that in 1860 Braddon quit the stage and went to live near Beverley, Yorkshire, Gilby's own town. Robert Lee Wolff speculates that Gilby was trying to bring Braddon closer to his own economic level so that he could eventually offer to marry her, and he insisted that she attempt to write a collection of verse because he thought it would pay better. The high point of this collection was to be a long narrative poem, in Spenserian stanzas, celebrating the exploits of Garibaldi in his efforts to unify Italy, a subject selected by Gilby himself. Unsurprisingly, this less than engaging project came to bore Braddon, and she began working on a novel during the intervals when she wasn't struggling to understand the Neapolitan revolution and the campaign in Sicily. This novel, called *Three Times Dead: or the Secret of the Heath*, was Braddon's first attempt at sensation fiction, and she noted that it was "an infinite relief to turn from Garibaldi and his brothers in arms to the angels and monsters which my own brain had engendered, and which to me seemed more alive."[6]

Braddon dutifully completed *Garibaldi and Other Poems*, as subsidized by Gilby, and although it was published in 1861 it did not cause much of a stir. *Three Times Dead*, published a year earlier, had done little better, and Braddon never received the full fee promised her by her publisher. Unfortunately for Gilby, however, what the novel *did* do was bring its author into contact with Robert Maxwell, a London publisher who was constantly on the lookout for new writers. The original relationship does not seem to have been particularly smooth, since Maxwell first promised Braddon that she could be the editor of his magazine *The Welcome Guest*, and then broke his word. Eventually, however, they resolved their differences, with the result that at the end of 1860 Braddon left Yorkshire for London, and in the first half of

1861 set up a household with Maxwell, leaving Gilby finally and thoroughly in the lurch. Gilby's response is unquestionably that of a disappointed and abandoned suitor, his final bitter letter to Braddon concluding with the comment "I can only feel pity for you not unmingled with contempt, and wonder if you have one redeeming trait in your character."[7] Braddon's life as an actress may not have been particularly eventful, but it certainly ended with a flurry of emotion.

Maxwell could not legally marry Braddon because his wife was still alive, although incarcerated in what the Victorians would have called a madhouse. On most other counts, however, he was a wonderful choice of partner for an aspiring author. Energetic and unrelentingly self-promotional, Maxwell lived in a constant whirl of writing and editing. He also founded and then suspended literary magazines with scarcely a pause in between. One of the first things he did was to reissue *Three Times Dead*, with considerably more publicity than Gilby had managed, under the new and sensational title of *The Trail of the Serpent*. Within a week it had sold 1,000 copies. Braddon's new career was assured.

It was her third full-length novel, however, which made her fortune. *Lady Audley's Secret* began serialization in Maxwell's magazine *Robin Goodfellow* in July of 1861. Unfortunately, the journal lasted only thirteen weeks before being forced to close down, and assuming the story was dead, Braddon abandoned it and began *Aurora Floyd*. As was Maxwell's habit, however, he immediately began a new project entitled the *Sixpenny Magazine*, and popular demand was so great that he re-serialized *Lady Audley's Secret* in it. Braddon completed the text for this journal and it was published in three volumes in 1862 as a runaway best seller. Indeed, the novel was a phenomenon, generating extreme responses from reviewers which naturally helped its sales. Almost instantly Braddon was placed in the middle of the debate about sensation fiction, and the popularity of *Aurora Floyd* coming immediately after *Lady Audley* ensured that she stayed there. But of course this also placed her private life in the glare of public scrutiny, and for a couple living as she and Maxwell were this was more than a little uncomfortable. For a while they attempted to conceal their true relationship, but with the birth of their first child on March 19, 1862, this became impossible. Maxwell's way of attempting to deal with the growing scandal was, in early 1864, to have various newspapers print small announcements stating that the two had married. This, however, turned out to be a serious mistake.

Maxwell's first wife had a brother-in-law named Richard Brinsley Knowles, and he immediately wrote letters denying the possibility of the marriage to every newspaper that had published the announcements. He pointed out not only that his sister-in-law had "borne her husband a large family,"[8] but that she was very much alive. Since Braddon and Maxwell could hardly rebut Knowles' claims, Maxwell's ruse had only increased the adverse publicity surrounding their union. Nonetheless, during this time Braddon signed some of her letters "Mary Maxwell," which suggests she viewed herself as married. And when John Maxwell's wife died in 1874 they made their relationship official less than a month later.

Given these very irregular circumstances it was not difficult for certain reviewers to equate the immorality of Braddon's life with the supposedly immoral tendency of her writings. In everything except name, however, Braddon and Maxwell lived an exemplary Victorian family life. On the proceeds of Braddon's writing they purchased a solidly upper middle-class home in Richmond, where they lived together until Maxwell's death in 1895. She fulfilled all the required tasks of running a household, and as far as can be told was loved by both her own five children and her step-children. Neither Braddon nor Maxwell were engaged in a radical questioning of marriage, but were instead making the best they could of an adverse situation. It is risky, therefore, to see Braddon as completely subversive in her relationship to middle-class mores, despite what some of her critics implied. While her fiction certainly questioned Victorian stereotypes of womanhood through her strong female characters, many of her novels were solidly conventional in their acceptance of duty and the class status quo.

Ironically, given the fierce debate over whether sensation fiction acted to corrupt its readers, Braddon's personal life bore a strong resemblance to that of her contemporary George Eliot, who was viewed as one of the moral arbiters of the age. Like Braddon, Marian Evans was also the partner of a married man, but because as George Eliot she wrote "serious" fiction instead of the merely sensational, she never received the kind of *ad feminam* attacks to which Braddon was subject. Both women had to deal with a certain amount of social ostracism, but Eliot's authority as a writer was never called into question in the same way as Braddon's. This hardly seemed to slow Braddon down as she wrote her novels, edited magazines, kept up a lively correspondence with such literary figures as Edward Bulwer Lytton, and survived into a wealthy and finally respected old age. Nonetheless, the different treatment accorded the two women reveals that sensation fiction in itself was seen as posing some kind of threat. What that threat consisted of can only be understood in its relation with the realist novel that was perceived as the literary norm for fiction by the mid-1800s.

Sensation, Realism, and the Victorian Press

> And yet I sicken again with despondency under the sense that the most carefully written books lie, both outside and inside people's minds, deep undermost in a heap of trash. I suppose the reason my 6/- editions are never on the railway stalls is .... [that they] are not so attractive to the majority as 'The Trail of the Serpent'; still a minority might sometimes buy them if they were there.
>
> George Eliot to John Blackwood, 11 September 1866[9]

That *The Trail of the Serpent* was still selling well enough in 1866 to cause George Eliot such "despondency" was a mark of Braddon's popularity. Significantly, Eliot's obvious distaste for this kind of writing was based on two criteria, one aesthetic and the other more material. By categorizing sensation fiction as "trash" she explicitly dismissed it from the realm of realist art which she had striven so painstakingly to create in *Adam Bede* (1859) and *The Mill on the Floss* (1860). As Patrick Brantlinger puts it, the "development of the sensation novel marks a crisis in the history of literary realism. At the same time that George Eliot was investing the novel with a new philosophical gravity, the sensationalists were breaking down the conventions of realistic fiction."[10] With its roots in the Gothic romances of the turn of the century and the Newgate crime novel of the 1830s, and its echoes of contemporary stage melodrama, sensation fiction was seen by many as a regression, a degrading step backwards which undermined the hard-earned respectability of the Victorian novel. The kind of romanticism it seemed to encourage ran counter to the serious exploration of society which realism held out as both its justification and its artistic goal.

The sensation novel's detractors claimed that, by pandering to the lowest tastes of its audience, to the desire for physical and emotional titillation, it prevented the appreciation of true fictional artistry by literally creating a "diseased appetite" for improper kinds of writing. Sensation fiction also tended to represent sexual irregularities as being behind the frauds, murders, bigamous marriages and other transgressions which drove its plots. This emphasis on criminal action and illicit passion, rather than on character and motive, was seen to indicate that sensationalists did not deserve a place in the front rank of England's authors. And even more unpleasantly, this low form of writing sold in wildly large numbers.

Eliot's letter to Blackwood also reveals an author disappointed in the profit generated by her books. The lucrative market for six-shilling editions, available in railway waiting rooms, and for the even more widely purchased two-shilling yellowback editions of novels, was dominated by sensation writers such as Braddon. It was through these kinds of mass sales that a writer could sustain a large income, and Eliot's unhappiness in having her work supplanted by "trash" cannot have been helped by the fact that it was such highly profitable trash. Indeed, the very profitability of sensation fiction became an argument for its aesthetic rejection. As Lyn Pykett observes, "In the moral panic that surrounded the debate about sensation fiction. . . . [o]ne of the chief objections to [it] was that it was (at least in the opinion of middle-class reviewers) a commodity, produced (and deformed) by market forces, and directed at the appetites of consumers."[11] This argument was clearly an attempt to establish boundaries between high art (as represented by a realist fiction somehow removed from market forces) and low art (as represented by sensation fiction, solely determined by those same forces). Needless to say, such a purity of division was impossible to sustain, but what is interesting is the number of Victorian reviewers eager to support it. Clearly the reviewers described by Pykett felt that something very important was at stake in their defence of "pure" literature, and in order to better understand what they were defending it is necessary to look at a very specific piece of government legislation: the removal, in 1855, of the stamp tax on newspapers.

At first glance this may seem to have little to do with arguments about proper and improper art. But the result of removing this tax was an explosion in the growth of one-penny newspapers, such as the *Daily Telegraph*, whose low price made them available to a large, working-class audience. These papers concentrated much more on reporting crime than did their "upscale" rivals, and they took particular delight in presenting the lapses and scandals of the middle and upper classes. Working-class readers "were thus enabled to read circumstantial accounts of the misdeeds of their social betters, and magnify their iniquities, with the same freedom as the middle classes had always enjoyed in reading about theirs."[12]

The popularity of penny newspapers prepared the way for the popularity of sensation fiction, for both insisted that the potential for crime lurked behind the façade of middle- and upper-class respectability, and both attracted an audience by stripping that façade away. And it was this sharing of content and attitude which so disturbed some contemporary reviewers, because it indicated a "contamination" of the middle-class, realist novel by a lower-class influence. This explains the intensity of the attack on Braddon and other sensationalists: by wilfully breaking down the kinds of distinctions which art is thought to help establish, they threatened to collapse the stratification upon which Victorian society depended. This threat finds its clearest expression in the conclusion of W. Fraser Rae's 1865 article for the *North British Review*, which provides this specific condemnation of Braddon:

> Others before her have written stories of blood and lust, of atrocious crimes and hardened criminals, and these have excited the interest of a very wide circle of readers. But the class that welcomed them was the lowest in the social scale, as well as in mental capacity. To Miss Braddon belongs the credit of having

penned similar stories in easy and correct English, and published them in three volumes in place of issuing them in penny numbers. She may boast, without fear of contradiction, of having temporarily succeeded in making the literature of the Kitchen the favourite reading of the Drawing room.[13]

That anxious "temporarily" in his last sentence reveals Rae's hope that the literary/class distance between Kitchen and Drawing room might, in the future, be safely restored – once the challenge posed by sensation fiction was defeated.

But there was another, even more direct, link between sensation novels and the Victorian press which caused trouble for the defenders of realism. Finally, if all else failed, critics of sensationalism simply accused it of being unbelievable, of creating an unrealistically sordid, extreme portrayal of individuals and society which experience did not support. Yet, in sensationalizing contemporary life, "the novelists paradoxically discovered that they were making fictions out of the stuff that filled the newspapers every day."[14] Charles Reade in particular enjoyed rebutting charges that his stories were fantastical by pointing out the exact newspaper story from which he had taken his plot. And *Aurora Floyd* contained references to two widely reported, sensationally middle-class crimes, the Palmer poisonings and the Road murder, thus implicitly connecting the novel's own fictional murder to these actual homicides. In other words, sensation fiction could argue it was *more* "real" than realism, because it possessed a connection to actual events which realism, as "pure" art, could not match. In its very "impurity," then, the sensational undercut realist fiction's claim to superior truthfulness. Sensation novels subverted realism by exposing the essential artificiality of its conventions, and revealing that the realist novel had no more claim to be a direct representation of experience than any other form of art. Fictions like *Aurora Floyd*, therefore, called into question carefully constructed Victorian hierarchies of literature and class. But more specific elements of sensation fiction, in particular the presentation of detection and the revelation of scandalous behaviour, were equally challenging, and increased the anxieties of those who saw the form as threatening.

Sensation, Detection, and Victorian Scandal

Because it focused on hidden vice and crime, at its core a sensation novel was a novel with a secret. The uncovering of that secret, along with the resolution of the complications it had generated, drove the plot. It is hardly surprising, therefore, that the tension between concealment and detection was often central to this genre. But it is important to remember that, for Victorians, the idea of detection created a certain ambivalence. The Detective Department of Scotland Yard was established in 1842, and its use of plainclothes detectives was worrisome to a British population which, although by mid-century fairly accustomed to the idea of uniformed constables controlling the "criminal classes," was considerably less comfortable about a body of men authorized to investigate respectable middle-class householders. Anthea Trodd summarizes that discomfort nicely when she states

> At one level these problems concern etiquette, uncertainties about the social status of the policeman, and the conversational peculiarities of being interrogated by a kind of higher servant or lower tradesman. More significantly, the encounters betray deep fears about the threat to the world of domestic innocence posed by the new police world of subterfuge and surveillance.[15]

In the 1850s, however, the detective force received some useful public-relations exposure through a series of positive articles published in Charles Dickens' magazine *Household Words*. Dickens and his co-editor W.H. Wills extolled the powers of observation and deduction exhibited by police detectives, and thus not only provided support for Scotland Yard, but also helped establish the idea of the "art of detection." Nonetheless, both Dickens and Wills also portrayed their detectives safely concentrated on thieves, fences, and corrupt servants, never on the middle-class readers who made up their audience. By the 1860s, then, the detective, although somewhat reformed, still had the potential to provoke anxieties about the surveillance of the middle class by its social inferiors. And sensation fiction's use of detectives, professional and amateur, played on these fears in ways which both fascinated and repelled its readers.

Perhaps even more disturbing, however, were the gender anxieties accompanying the detective's power to investigate the middle-class household. The Victorian home was constructed as a feminine space, separate from the public and corrupt (masculine) world of business and intrigue. At the centre of the middle-class home was the "angel in the house," the Victorian ideal of pure womanhood, whose presence, as most explicitly stated in Ruskin's "Of Queens' Gardens," was meant to sanctify the private world of the family:

> [W]ithin [the] house, as ruled by her, unless she herself has sought it, need enter no danger, no temptation, no cause of error or offence. This is the true nature of home – it is the place of Peace; the shelter, not only from all injury, but from all terror, doubt, and division. In so far as it is not this, it is not home; so far as the anxieties of the outer life penetrate into it, and the inconsistently-minded, unknown, unloved, or hostile society of the outer world is allowed . . . to cross the threshold, it ceases to be home . . .[16]

The detective's ability – indeed, his *duty* – to invade the domestic sphere when required, exposed the middle-class home to the very forces (error, doubt, and division) which it was supposed to repel. That a lady could be forced to answer questions, and endure the suspicions of an (often lower-class) intruder into her realm, was clearly shocking. But the real fear was that the "angel in the house" might be no angel at all: as Trodd observes, "Fictions which chose . . . to argue for the criminality of the angel in the house were locating their point of crime at the heart of the Victorian ideology of the home."[17]

The issue of detection centred on the family was given an additional impetus by the Matrimonial Causes Act of 1857. This act greatly relaxed Britain's divorce laws, making it possible for a husband to divorce his wife if he could prove her adultery, and for her to divorce him if she could prove adultery as well as one other serious offence such as violence, desertion, or extreme cruelty. The obvious inequity of the legislation aside, John Sutherland notes that the Act "mobilized a whole new army of amateur and unofficial detectives; namely, the suspicious spouse and his or her agent."[18] The resulting flood of divorce actions provided masses of scandal focusing primarily on the failed domestic arrangements of prominent upper and middle-class families. It is no coincidence, therefore, that in *Aurora Floyd* one of Talbot Bulstrode's great fears about marriage is having his name dragged through the publicity of the divorce court, or that John Mellish's agony over the suspicions surrounding his wife is magnified by the "penny-a-liners" (496) who thrive on reporting innuendo against Aurora. In presenting these concerns, Braddon was simply echoing the worries of her audience, as well as manipulating them to achieve an emotional response. Sensation fiction played on the Victorian fear of scandal, especially scandal concerning women, and in so doing became scandalous itself by suggesting that improper female behaviour not only existed, but was widespread.

In terms of Victorian gender beliefs, therefore, the detective posed a double threat. First of all, he collapsed the wall between public and private spheres, thus revealing how fragile, and perhaps indeed imaginary, that separation was. Second, once the home was opened to investigation, there was the risk that the lady of the house might be revealed not only to possess flaws, but to be deceptive, unfaithful, or actually criminal. Detection was thus a risky occupation because it could expose middle-class domesticity as a false front, and thus call into question the entire gender ideology on which the domestic ideal was based.

Aurora Floyd: The Home Under Seige

> How dreary it all seemed to John Mellish to-night! He wondered how people felt who had no social mystery brooding upon their hearth; no domestic skeleton cowering in their homely cupboard. (357)

In *Lady Audley's Secret*, Braddon shocked Victorian readers when she cast the blond-haired "angel in the house" as bigamist, murderess, and lunatic. The novel also featured an amateur detective torn between revealing the corruption in his revered uncle's home, or preserving this façade while knowing it to be rotten. *Aurora Floyd*, Braddon's follow-up best seller, achieved its sensational impact through similar means: it too questioned assumptions concerning femininity and the purity of the home. This time, Braddon created a heroine whose sexual history, athleticism, and knowledge of "low" manners and people made her antithetical to the chaste and protected Victorian ideal woman. The novel also exposed to scrutiny the "holy circle of the domestic hearth" (195), showing it undermined from within, under seige from without, and betrayed by the woman at its centre, whose uncontrolled passions and promiscuous social connections breach the walls of the domestic "citadel" (195).

Aurora's challenge to the Victorian womanly ideal is represented partly through her love of riding, hunting, and the turf. As H.L. Mansel observed in the *Quarterly Review*, Braddon offered her readers a "fast young lady, full of stable talk, deep in the mysteries of the turf, and familiar with Bell's Life."[19] Aurora's fascination with masculine sports signals her rebellion against female education and acceptable pastimes; her use of stable and riding slang appropriates masculine and lower-class language. Braddon herself stepped out of the conventional feminine sphere in order to write the novel: as Henry James observed, part of the text's sensational appeal lay in its detailed descriptions of "illegitimate" life such as the "names of drinks, the technicalities of the faro-table, the lingo of the turf, the talk natural to a crowd of fast men at supper." Braddon, James wrote, "knows much that ladies are not accustomed to know, but that they are apparently very glad to learn."[20]

But most saliently, Aurora's love of horses links her to a widespread debate on women and riding, especially women and hunting, which arose in the 1850s and early 1860s. These were the years in which the pursuit of fox hunting – associated with the masculine qualities of courage, coolheadedness, and cavalry skill – was increasingly entered by women. Conservative reaction to this phenomenon focused on hunting's inconsistency with middle-class feminine propriety. In April 1854, for example, a letter to *The Field* identified "Six Reasons Why Ladies Should Not Hunt." The writer objected that "[a] lady in the hunting-field is liable to see sights and hear language ... not ... adapted for the drawing room"; "[i]t is not becoming in a gentle and modest Englishwoman to be seen careering across country, surmounting every variety of obstacle that presents itself;" "[g]entlemen cannot observe the courtesies of the drawing-room in the hunting-field;" and that "a lady [who hunts] is unavoidably liable to be seen jostled and mixed up . . . with company which husbands, fathers, and brothers, cannot witness with approbation. . ."[21] The passage reveals contradictory anxieties: first, that the hunting field is not appropriate for women (who belong in the drawing room) because drawing-room courtesies (the hallmarks of gender hierarchy and class division) cannot be maintained in the field. The second – and greater – fear is that women are actively rejecting the domestic space of the drawing room and are showing their aggression by metaphorically "surmounting every variety of obstacle that presents itself." (In *Lady Audley's Secret*, the conservative Robert Audley uses a similar metaphor when he reflects, "That's the consequence of letting a girl follow the hounds. She learns to look at everything in life as she does at six feet of timber or a sunk fence; she goes through the world as she goes across country – straight ahead, and over everything."[22]) Aurora's love of riding thus acts as a kind of shorthand for her rejection of the drawing-room world of chaperoned Victorian femininity, and for her passionate and impulsive (unfeminine) character.

Aurora's love of riding is also linked to her other major violation of feminine mores: her improper sexual passion. Writing in *Blackwood's Magazine* in 1867, Margaret Oliphant objected that sensation novels presented a "very fleshly and unlovely" portrait of the "feminine soul," depicting

> [W]omen who marry their grooms in fits of sensual passion;
> women who pray their lovers to carry them off from husbands
> and homes they hate; women, at the very least of it, who give
> and receive burning kisses and frantic embraces, and live in a
> voluptuous dream . . .[23]

Most contemporary readers would have recognized "women who marry their grooms in fits of sensual passion" as referring to Braddon's *Aurora Floyd*, whose relationship with James Conyers reveals an unladylike passion for a handsome man of inferior class – a man who "sprang from the mire of the streets, like some male Aphrodite rising from the mud" (246), to quote the narrator's scathing assessment of his origins. The heroine's liaison with her father's groom plays on precisely the anxieties suggested by *The Field*: that, among other things, women on horseback will be "jostled and mixed up" with inappropriate (lower-class, male) company. Aurora's sexual relationship with Conyers takes place in a tactful lacuna reminiscent of Gaskell's *Ruth* (1853), but the Victorian convention which associated women's unchaperoned riding with sexual permissiveness, together with the contemporary slang meaning of "ride" to indicate sexual intercourse, meant that when Aurora is absent with the handsome young groom from 2 p.m. to sunset, and returns her thorough-bred chestnut "with heaving and foam-flecked sides" (64), Victorian readers would have understood clearly why the heroine is hurriedly sent off to school. And while Braddon may, as Henry James put it, "[save] the proprieties"[24] by marrying Aurora to Conyers, the fact that this particular sexually suggestive episode occurs outside marriage says little for the heroine's chastity.

Repeated references to Aurora's abundant black hair reinforce the heroine's association with uncontrolled sexual urges. W. Fraser Rae observed that Braddon is obsessed with Aurora's hair, which is variously described as "black," "blue-black," "dead-black," and lastly "purple-black," and as arranged in a "diadem," a "coronet," "serpentine coils," and "blue-black snakes."[25] Again, specific Victorian codes are at work here: according to the conventions of heroine description, dark, abundant, and untrammelled hair represents sexual and emotional volatility. And this strong suggestion of sexual disorder works in tandem with a slew of references linking Aurora with passionate and transgressive women: Cleopatra, Lady Macbeth, Nell Gwynne, Lola Montez, and Charlotte Corday.

Not that dark-haired sexual adventuresses are rare in nineteenth-century literature. But Braddon goes some way towards suggesting that this "Cleopatra with . . . a taste for horseflesh" (80) will make a better wife and mother than her blonde and chaste cousin Lucy, the very embodiment of the Victorian angel. This conservative ideal is described by Talbot Bulstrode, who seeks "some gentle and feminine creature . . . spotless as her own white robes, excelling in all womanly graces and accomplishments, but only exhibiting them in the narrow circle of a home" (86). Braddon makes it clear that Lucy represents the perfection of conventional womanhood: her education and manners are faultless; her emotions are impeccably controlled; she is beautiful, loving, submissive, protected by her mother and ready for the protection of a husband. The text does not criticize Lucy, but undercuts the ideal itself as infantilized, ignorant, hemmed in, and – most damning of all – boring: "There are so many Lucys but so few Auroras" (94).

In contrast, Aurora's education is incomplete (she knows more of *Bell's Life* than of Gibbon); her youthful exuberance has been unpruned; she knows far more than a lady should of dog fanciers, gambling, and masculine sports; she is sexually experienced; and she has been in an unhappy, exploitative, adulterous – and possibly abusive – relationship. Partly, Braddon is responding to the exigencies of plot: as E.S. Dallas observed in *The Gay Science*, if Victorian writers were to place women at the centre of their plots, it was impossible that these heroines could remain pure and refined: "The life of women cannot well be described as a life of action."[26] Braddon puts it another way: "if [Aurora] had been faultless, she could not have been the heroine of this story; for I think some wise man of old remarked, that the perfect women were those who left no histories behind them . . ." (477). Yet Aurora's character not only creates action; she also represents, if not an ideal, then a new type of woman, whose worldly experience, Braddon dares to argue, eventually makes her a more mature and wise partner:

> [S]he did love you, Talbot Bulstrode. . . . She loved you as women only love in their first youth, and as they rarely love the men they ultimately marry. The tree is perhaps all the stronger when these first frail branches are lopped away to give place to strong and spreading arms, beneath which a husband and children may shelter. (185)

This is in direct contrast to the more conventional Victorian view (expressed by Talbot) that a woman's life should be "a white unblemished page" (157). And Braddon went so far as to close the novel with a portrait of her controversial heroine "bending over the cradle of her first-born" (549) – the very picture of conventional motherhood. (As H.L. Mansel observed caustically, "By a fortunate arrangement of nature, . . . the birth of the infant is delayed beyond the usual time, till the groom is really dead and a re-marriage has repaired the irregularity of the bigamy."[27]) Thus while *Aurora Floyd* challenged contemporary views on what an ideal young woman should be, paradoxically it was quite conventional in depicting where that woman's happiness would ultimately lie: not in the stable, but with her husband, home, and children.

While much of the text's sensational impact lay in its controversial heroine and her challenge to the Victorian ideal of womanhood, *Aurora Floyd* also played on contemporary fears concerning the vulnerability of the home. From the moment when John Mellish marries Aurora, his household is threatened from within and without. The most obvious threats are the envious Mrs. Powell and the vicious Steeve Hargraves (the "Softy"), "one for ever brooding discontent and hatred within the holy circle of the domestic hearth; the other plotting ruin and vengeance without the walls of the citadel" (195). Yet it is really Aurora herself who has breached the walls of the domestic "citadel." Mrs. Powell gains power by observing the restless movements of the heroine, who is constantly leaving the domestic sphere in favour of illicit spaces – the grounds during a storm, the park at night, the trainer's lodge. Aurora haunts the thresholds of the house, forever at doors, at gates, at windows. If the home is vulnerable, it is because she refuses to be contained within it.

The most crucial example of Aurora's straying from the home is her cross-class liaison with Conyers. This relationship strikes the very heart of middle-class values. For while Braddon depicts it as possible for men to raise (sufficiently grateful) women up in class status through marriage (as Archibald Floyd lifts Eliza, Talbot Bulstrode lifts Lucy, and John Mellish lifts Aurora), a woman who marries below her station is shown to be degraded. Aurora's relationship with her father's groom thus entails not only sexual unrestraint, but an improper social promiscuity. Marriage may save the sexual proprieties of this liaison, but it cannot legitimate this breach of the class structure. This sense that Aurora's pride (as much as, perhaps, her virginity) has been besmirched is expressed by John Mellish:

> She was his faith and his worship, and it was for her departed
> glory that he wept in this cruel day of shame. The wrong which
> he found so hard to forgive was not her wrong against him; but

that other and more fatal wrong against herself. . . . [I]n his struggle against that sorrowful anger which he felt for her folly, every one of her perfections took up arms upon the side of indignation, and fought against their own mistress. Had she been less beautiful, less queenly, less generous, great and noble, he might have forgiven her that self-inflicted shame more easily. But she was so perfect; and how could she, how could she? (411)

Mellish's middle-class home is thus made insecure by Aurora, who has breached the very class boundaries which define it. It is because of this flaw in the "holy circle of the domestic hearth" (195) that Mrs. Powell and the "Softy" accrue power.

Aurora is also indirectly responsible for the presence of Steeve Hargraves, who is represented as the serpent in her Eden, "a slow, ponderous serpent creeping towards its prey" (256). Yet if Hargraves represents the serpent, it is only because Aurora is Eve.[28] It is her "sin" – her relationship with Conyers – which is the real threat to this middle-class Eden. The text's anxieties concerning this cross-class liaison are merely projected onto Hargraves (a groom, who, like Conyers, has been injured in a riding accident). Aurora's threat to the Mellish home is represented most forcefully in the notorious scene where she whips the "Softy" because he has kicked her dog:

Aurora sprang upon him like a beautiful tigress, and catching the collar of his fustian jacket in her slight hands, rooted him to the spot upon which he stood. . . . Taller than the stable-man by a foot and a half, she towered above him, her cheeks white with rage, her eyes flashing fury, her hat fallen off, and her black hair tumbling about her shoulders, sublime in her passion.

The man crouched beneath the grasp of the imperious creature. . . .

"How dared you!" cried Aurora, – "how dared you hurt him? My poor dog! My poor lame, feeble dog! How dared you to do it? You cowardly dastard! you —— "

She disengaged her right hand from his collar and rained a shower of blows upon his clumsy shoulders with her slender whip; a mere toy, with emeralds set in its golden head, but stinging like a rod of flexible steel in that little hand.

"How dared you!" she repeated again and again, her cheeks changing from white to scarlet in the effort to hold the man with one hand. Her tangled hair had fallen to her waist by this time, and the whip was broken in half a dozen places. (193-94)

In contemporary reviews of the novel, this scene, and not Aurora's more serious crime of bigamy, aroused by far the most anxious and negative responses. It was described by *Fraser's Magazine* as a "fatal mistake"[29] and by the *North British Review* as "wholly untrue to [women's] nature."[30] It was quoted at full length in three major journals (the *Athenaeum*, the *Quarterly Review*, and the *North British Review*) and singled out for commentary in two more (*Fraser's Magazine* and the *Christian Remembrancer*).[31]

The scene seems to have aroused such anxiety because it dramatizes and encapsulates (within the bounds of the estate and in front of John Mellish) all the forces which threaten his home. First, the stable setting, as well as Aurora's riding habit and whip strongly link this episode to the spectre of female rebellion articulated by the hunting debate. Second, Aurora's brutality associates her with unladylike aggression and physicality. Most saliently, however, this appropriation of masculine manner and action, together with repeated references to John Mellish as a henpecked husband, indicate that Aurora threatens to hold the whip hand in her marriage as well as with her servants.

This reading of the scene is reinforced in stage versions of the text, where it is immediately preceded by ones depicting Aurora's domination over her husband. *Aurora Floyd; Or, The Dark Deed in the Wood* opens with Aurora criticizing her husband's stable, bossing his servants about, and telling her husband that he is a "grown-up baby."[32] In *Aurora Floyd: Or, The Banker's Daughter*, she also criticizes John's horse racing, calls him "you tiresome great stupid you," and tells her own father that he doesn't understand what he's talking about. In this version, her father commiserates with John ("I'm afraid you find her a sad tyrant, Mellish"), to which the son-in-law responds: "I say with the man in the story, whose wife used to beat him: – 'It amuses her, and does me no hurt.'"[33] In both stage versions, then, the association of riding paraphernalia with female aggression is reinforced by explicit indications that Aurora inappropriately dominates her husband. This suggests that the beating scene represents as much a confrontation between Aurora and John – concerning gender roles and power in their marriage and in the running of their household – as it does a class confrontation between Aurora and a servant.

While this scene plays out the power struggle in Aurora's second marriage, it is greatly complicated by its connections to her first. As has already been suggested, the "Softy" acts as Conyers' double, his presence in John Mellish's stable embodying Aurora's contamination by her previous liaison. No wonder, then, that Aurora conceives an instinctive loathing for this half-witted servant: like Uriah Heep in *David Copperfield*, Hargraves is compared to a "loathsome member of the reptile race" (229), and like Uriah, he provides a focus and scapegoat for the loathing directed at the lower-class male whose social ambitions take the form of sexual attention towards his employer's daughter. Thus when Aurora beats Hargraves, she not only acts out her aggression in her new marriage, but violently reasserts the class privilege which she forgot in her teenage liaison with Conyers. The scene therefore encapsulates in one sensational episode the forces which threaten the Mellish home: Aurora's unwomanly aggression; her rebellion against the domestic sphere; her lack of proper submission to her husband; and, most crucially, the contagion of her earlier sexual relationship with the stable hand. When Conyers arrives in person at the estate, then, he merely represents the latest and most obvious manifestation of the class contamination which has threatened John Mellish's home since his wedding day. And when he is murdered, the suspicion which falls on Aurora renders explicit the latent anxieties which have long surrounded the "angel" of the Mellish home.

The murder of James Conyers has a double effect on this fiction of the vulnerable home. Most obviously, it introduces a new threat to the household: Joseph Grimstone of Scotland Yard, with his "small gray eyes" (497), "stumpy morsel of lead pencil" (506), "greasy paper" (507), cockney accent, and easy familiarity with gardeners and pawnbrokers. He exemplifies the ambivalent position of the detective as discussed above, suspect because he is not of the middle class and because his methods seem disturbingly close to those of the criminals he pursues. In a passage which was later cut, the first edition articulates this anxiety:

> It is a wondrous provision of Providence that the treachery which would be hateful and horrible in any other man, is considered perfectly legitimate in the man who is employed to hunt out a murderer or a thief. The vile instruments which the criminal employed against his unsuspecting victim are in due time used against himself; and the wretch who laughed at the poor unsuspecting dupe who was trapped to his destruction by *his* lies, is caught in his turn by some shallow deceit, or pitifully hackneyed device, of the paid spy, who has been bribed to lure him to his doom. (524)

In this respect, therefore, Grimstone's appearance represents the climax in the series of escalating threats to the Mellish home, and plays to Victorian anxieties about the intrusion of the detective into the middle-class domestic space.

Yet at the same time the murder of Conyers has the reverse effect: paradoxically, it works to make the home more secure. By shifting from sensation plot into murder mystery, Braddon not only kills off the villain of the piece – Conyers – but ultimately shifts the locus of guilt outside the home, away from the middle class and from her controversial heroine. Superficially, the crisis in John Mellish's marriage would appear to occur when he discovers Aurora's bigamy and flight; in fact, however, this marks the turning point where the tensions in his home begin to be resolved and his authority is restored. For, by seeking Talbot's protection, Aurora symbolically reenters the home even as she leaves it; she turns to the most secure home in the text, the household where the domestic niceties of china teacups and mignonette boxes reflect an underlying patriarchal order in which Lucy is protected by Talbot from moral ambiguities and unpleasantness – even from her disorderly cousin. By turning to Talbot as a "wise judge" and the "arbiter of her future" (440), Aurora confirms her need for male authority and protection. She also turns her secret – the secret which has exposed the Mellish home to investigation and threat from "police-officers and stable-boys" (431) – over into male, upper-class hands. From this moment on, despite the continuing murder investigation, the real anxieties of the text are laid to rest. The Mellish home no longer harbours rebellion and secrecy at its centre. Aurora is now obedient to male authority, nurtured by Lucy, and transparently innocent of the murder: "he [John Mellish] had seen the truth, radiant as the light of inspiration, shining out of her beautiful face" (506).

From this point too, Aurora is increasingly portrayed as Conyers' victim. Her active sexual involvement with Conyers (conveyed, to Mrs. Oliphant's dismay, by Aurora's solitary rides with the dashing young groom) is retroactively defused. In retrospect, the groom is increasingly depicted as a "base-born schemer" (424) and Aurora as "young, inexperienced, and trusting" (449). The blackmail negotiations cement Conyers' association with greed and work to recast his early relationship with Aurora in this exploitative light. It is significant too that Aurora's bigamous marriage to the upper-class Mellish is now seen as her "true" marriage and the legal marriage to the lower-class groom as somehow invalid. "The future is not yours to dispose of," Talbot tells Aurora. "[I]t belongs to *your husband*, John Mellish." To John he recommends: "[G]et a new licence and marry *your wife* for the second time." (443, 439; emphasis added). In each statement, the previous marriage to the groom is ignored. Even the title practices the same sleight of hand – for, as the reader discovers, Aurora is in fact, for most of the text, "Aurora Conyers," not "Aurora Floyd".

As Aurora's power diminishes, Talbot's increases: he becomes the protector of the Mellish home, defending its inhabitants from the "slander" (503) of the popular press. As he explains to Aurora:

[W]hen an event of this kind takes place, it is very difficult to say who may or may not be suspected. Different persons set up different theories: one man writes to a newspaper to declare that, in his opinion, the crime was committed by some person within the house; another man writes as positively to another paper, asserting that the murderer was undoubtedly a stranger. Each man brings forward a mass of suppositious evidence in favour of his own argument, and each thinks a great deal more of proving his own cleverness than of furthering the ends of justice. No shadow of slander must rest upon this house, or upon those who live in it. (503)

In protecting the Mellish home, Talbot is defending his home also: as he reflects, "his name was allied, if only remotely, with that of his wife's cousin; and that the shame which would make the name of Mellish a byword, must also cast some slur upon the escutcheon of the Bulstrodes" (540). Talbot must also guide the detective to the truth. He and John may recognize the innocence shining out of Aurora's face, but it remains for them to convince the less enlightened Grimstone of her blamelessness. In order to protect the home, therefore, Talbot actually invites the detective in – but on his terms, and with Grimstone's attention safely directed to the "guilty" world outside the domestic sphere. Once again, windows are identified as a key locale, but this time because they have allowed the outside in, not vice versa. Instead of focusing on Aurora's guilty entrances and exits by windows and doors, Talbot shifts the investigation towards the "Softy's" opportunities to invade the home and pocket the weapon. Moreover, he mediates between the detective and the lady of the house, making sure that Aurora is never directly subject to interrogation by the police. All questions to her are posed by either Talbot or John: her privacy and security are thus reconstituted. Ironically, then, it is when Aurora is being investigated for murder that she is, for the first time, secure.

The detective plot thus puts to rest the sensational threats posed by the first two volumes of *Aurora Floyd*. The sexually passionate, athletic, rebellious heroine is rendered passive under male authority, and middle-class anxieties are assuaged as Conyers is disposed of, the servant/spy Mrs. Powell is conquered, and the working-class detective's scrutiny is directed away from the home. It is symptomatic of the novel's final conservatism that Grimstone is limited to the minor victory of identifying a brass button. The arrest of the real murderer (who else but the half-witted groom himself?) is achieved by amateurs. Talbot Bulstrode supersedes Grimstone when he combines perspicacity (the ability to read Aurora's shining face) with military skill. He advances on Hargraves "as if he had been educated for Mr. Grimstone's profession" (541). In the ensuing hand-to-hand battle with the

"Softy," the namesake of Sir Walter Raleigh is assisted by the practical and loyal Samuel Prodder. Amateur skill and courage oust not only the criminal, then, but the detective himself.

This final arrest of the "Softy" for the murder of Conyers allays many of the text's anxieties. By pairing Talbot and Samuel Prodder, Braddon produces a pleasing (and conservative) vision of harmonious class hierarchy. By scapegoating Hargraves for the murder, Braddon distances guilt from the middle-class home, while at the same time purifying the text of the last trace of Aurora's cross-class liaison. And finally, by replaying and transforming the earlier whipping of the "Softy" by Aurora, this second beating scene lays to rest the text's sensational threat to gender relations. Hardiness, aggression, and the right to punish are safely restored to male hands. Symbolically, the "whip hand" of the novel has passed firmly back to the male sphere where it belongs.

Notes

1 The information presented in this section derives largely from the only full-scale biography of Braddon to date: Robert Lee Wolff's *Sensational Victorian: The Life and Fiction of Mary Elizabeth Braddon* (New York: Garland Publishing Inc., 1979).

2 In her unpublished memoir, *Before the Knowledge of Evil*, Braddon wrote that she was born in "the year of Queen Victoria's accession" (i.e. 1837). Robert Lee Wolff gives her true birth date as 4 October 1835 (see Wolff 19).

3 Porchester Terrace was in Bayswater, a fashionable area of London developed in the early Victorian period. Its large houses within easy reach of the city became immediately popular with the middle and upper middle classes. Here it stands generally for middle-class respectability.

4 Quoted in Wolff, 45.

5 See Wolff, 75-76.

6 Quoted in Wolff, 82.

7 Quoted in Wolff, 96.

8 Quoted in Wolff, 104.

9 Gordon S. Haight, ed., *The George Eliot Letters*, vol. 4 (New Haven: Yale UP, 1954) 309-10.

10 Patrick Brantlinger, "What is 'Sensational' about the 'Sensation Novel,'" *Nineteenth-Century Fiction* 37:1 (June 1982): 27.

11 Lyn Pykett, *The 'Improper' Feminine: The Women's Sensation Novel and the New Woman Writing* (London: Routledge, 1992) 30.

12 P.D. Edwards, Introduction, *Aurora Floyd*, by Mary Elizabeth Braddon (Oxford: OUP, 1996) ix.

13 See Appendix B.3, 592.

14 Brantlinger, 9.

15 Anthea Trodd, *Domestic Crime in the Victorian Novel* (London: Macmillan, 1989) 12-13.

16 See Appendix A.3, 565.

17 Trodd, 99.

18 John Sutherland, "Wilkie Collins and the Origins of the Sensation Novel," *Dickens Studies Annual*, Vol. 22 (New York: AMS Press, 1991) 244-45.

19 See Appendix B.1, 577.

20 See Appendix B.4, 598.

21 See Appendix A.2, 553-54.

22 Mary Elizabeth Braddon, *Lady Audley's Secret*, ed. David Skilton (Oxford: OUP, 1991) 116.

23 See Appendix B.5, 602.

24 See Appendix B.4, 598.

25 See Appendix B.3, 586-87.

26 E.S. Dallas, *The Gay Science*, 2 vols. (London: Chapman and Hall, 1866) 2: 297.

27 See Appendix B.1, 578.

28 Aurora is also like Eve in possessing forbidden knowledge (about the masculine world of horses, dogs, and the turf) and in her inappropriate assertiveness with respect to her husband. She shows her contrition by falling on her knees in front of the patriarchs (Talbot and Archibald) of her world. Moreover, like Eve, Aurora is punished by being placed under her husband's dominion.

29 "The Popular Novels of the Year," *Fraser's Magazine* 68 (August 1863): 261.

30 See Appendix B.3, 587.

31 This scene may have been inspired by Lola Montez (to whom Aurora is compared in Chapter IV). During Montez' liaison with the King of Bavaria in the 1840s, her dog was one day struck by a tradesman. Montez beat the man with the dog's leather leash, opening several cuts on his face. She also slashed an elderly man with her riding whip because he was blocking her path. *Lola Montez in Bavaria* (1852) (in which Montez played herself) featured a scene in which Montez used a whip against a mob. In real life, she carried a diamond-studded whip around New York, cracking it if she was not served promptly at stores and restaurants. In Australia in 1855, she dressed in male attire and horsewhipped a newspaper editor. See Amanda Darling, *Lola Montez* (New York: Stein and Day, 1972). John Mellish's nickname for Aurora is, of course, "Lolly."

32 C.H. Hazlewood, *Aurora Floyd: Or, The Dark Deed In the Wood* (London: Thomas Hailes Lacy, [1863]) I.i.

33 B. Webster, *Aurora Floyd: Or, The Banker's Daughter* (London: Webster and Co., [1863]) 22-23.

A Note on the Text

Aurora Floyd first appeared as a serialization in the monthly magazine *Temple Bar*, which ran the story in thirteen instalments from January 1862 to January 1863. Braddon then sold for two years the right of publication to the publishing house of Tinsley Brothers, which paid her the substantial fee of £1000. The contract between the parties, now held in the Wolff collection,[1] stipulates that Braddon shall revise the serial "in such wise as she may deem expedient" for its appearance in book form.[2]

Tinsley published a number of three-volume "editions" of the novel, reaching the so-called fifth edition by June of 1863, but these are simply impressions of the first edition with altered title pages. The first actual re-setting of the text is the single-volume edition, issued by Tinsley as the "eighth edition," which appeared towards the end of that same year. Although *Aurora Floyd* was extremely popular, there is little doubt that this multiplicity of "editions" was an advertising ploy used by Tinsley to generate increased demand for the book. With the expiry of this contract the rights to further editions of the novel reverted back to Braddon.

Since, as P.D. Edwards has pointed out, it is unlikely that the manuscript of *Aurora Floyd* has survived,[3] any discussion of this text's evolution must focus on the serial, three-volume first edition, first single-volume edition, and subsequent single-volume editions. The following analysis of variants between these texts is based on computer collations derived using the PC-CASE (Computer Assisted Scholarly Editing) program.

The novel's serialization contains a significant discrepancy which is corrected in the first edition. The last chapter of the June instalment (Chapter XVIII in the present edition) contains the scene in which Aurora and James Conyers confront each other in the lodge by the north gate. With Mrs. Powell and Steeve Hargraves hidden at the window and eavesdropping on the conversation, Conyers demands £10,000 to emigrate to Australia and keep his relationship with Aurora secret. In the next chapter, however, which opens the July instalment, Aurora goes to her father and requests that he advance her the considerably less staggering sum of £2000. This error in continuity is simply left unresolved in the serial, and it requires six revisions in the first edition to correct the problem. It seems likely that Braddon, in considering the situation, concluded that Mr. Floyd would be unlikely to give his daughter £10,000 without some kind of specific explanation, and so the author reduces the bribe to a large but more reasonable amount. This also makes Conyers' later dissatisfaction more understandable, since his cooperation is being purchased relatively cheaply.

Tinsley's three-volume edition of *Aurora Floyd* contains two significant stylistic differences from the *Temple Bar* serialization. First, there is a widescale addition of exclamation marks. In 135 instances an exclamation mark is substituted for some other form of punctuation, while in only 13 instances is an exclamation mark removed. Without the existence of proofs it is impossible to tell whether these alterations were made by Braddon or, as is perhaps more likely, they are the result of Tinsley's compositors altering punctuation in order to suit their own sense of how the text should read. In any case, the addition of 122 exclamation marks increases the emotional pitch of the novel, particularly in its dialogue. The result is to make its tone more melodramatic and, since the first edition is the foundation for all subsequent editions, this increase in sensationalism is retained throughout the text's development.

Further, in 45 instances dialect or slang is substituted for standard English, while in 22 cases the situation is reversed. These changes seem likely to be Braddon's, and the overall pattern is to increase the use of slang and dialect by the Yorkshire servants at Mellish Park, and decrease this usage by their masters. More specifically, Steeve Hargraves' language is lowered by the addition of a significant amount of non-standard diction, while John Mellish's occasional lapses into Yorkshire dialect and "horsey" slang are reduced. This increases the linguistic distance between the propertied characters and those who serve them, thus reinforcing issues of class distinction which are central to the novel.

Braddon also made a large number of substantive revisions to the text which serve the general purpose of tightening up her sentence structures and descriptive passages. Others, however, have more pointed goals, as the following brief examples demonstrate. When Conyers is dismissed from the Floyd household in Chapter II of the serial, and leaves without saying goodbye to the other servants, their response is to describe him as someone "whose absence was no loss to the household." In the first edition, however, he becomes someone "who had always been too high for this business." This change provides an early indication of Conyers' refusal to accept his "proper" place, a character flaw which will attract a large amount of narrative commentary in later chapters.

Talbot Bulstrode's military background is also modified through authorial revision. In the serial we are told that during the Crimean War he commanded a "regiment of foot" when "the heights of Inkermann were won." For the first edition Bulstrode is placed in a "cavalry regiment," and participates when "a memorable and most desperate charge was made against a bristling wall of Russian cannon." Braddon makes the first of her two male protagonists considerably more dashing by promoting him from the infantry to the cavalry, and this allows her the further possibility of associating him directly with the charge of the Light Brigade. This increases the romantic contrast between Talbot and John Mellish, as well as helping to explain Lucy Floyd's intense infatuation with her Cornish hero.

Finally, in Chapter XXV, when Aurora is informed by John that Conyers has been "hurt," her response in the serial is "'He is dead?' she said." In the first edition this becomes "'Is he dead?' she asked." This change causes Aurora to ask a question, rather than make an ambiguous question/statement, and thus more clearly implies her innocence. This is the first of the changes Braddon will make hinting that her heroine does not commit Conyers' murder, a fact which is much less overt in the *Temple Bar* serial.

A collation of the two earliest versions of the novel, therefore, makes it clear that Braddon took seriously the opportunity to revise her text. She uses the first edition to correct any mistakes made in the rush of serial publication, to focus her narrative, and to hone the presentation of her characters.

Tinsley's "eighth edition," the text's first appearance as a single volume, is dated 1864, thus following the common Victorian practice of "post-dating" novels published towards the end of a year. There can be little doubt that the publisher set this version of the novel from the three-volume edition, but collation reveals that the two texts are not identical. For one thing, Tinsley used different printers for the two settings,[4] resulting in different house-stylings. Thus the three-volume *Aurora Floyd* uniformly uses the "z" construction for words such as "victimize," "idolize," and "recognize," while the single-volume uses the "s" construction ("victimise," "idolise," "recognise"). Similarly, the three-volume spelling of "gray" is universally changed to the single-volume spelling of "grey." More importantly for the rhythms of the text, the single-volume version uniformly adds an adverbial comma when describing speech inflections; thus, the first edition's constructions of "said John simply" or "cried Aurora bitterly" become "said John, simply" and "cried Aurora, bitterly." On at least one occasion this difference in punctuation style changes the meaning of the text. In Chapter VIII, when an inebriated John informs Talbot that he should have married Lucy, the first edition reads "'Married whom?' cried *Talbot rather savagely,* shaking off his friend's hot grasp" (emphasis added). The single volúme changes this to "'Married whom?' cried *Talbot, rather savagely* shaking off his friend's hot grasp" (emphasis added). Obviously this comma shift causes "savagely" to modify "shaking" rather than "cried," thus altering the description of Talbot's response.

There are also a number of substantive changes between the Tinsley three-volume and single-volume texts. Several of these are obviously compositor errors. Thus, for example, in Chapter XXX when Aurora finally reveals to Talbot the secret of her marriage to Conyers, the first edition tells us he stares at her "blankly," while the eighth edition reads "blandly," a much less likely reaction. In Chapter XXXVI of the first edition Aurora describes Conyers as "insolent, as he always was." The single-volume changes this to "insolent, as he always was," and while it is doubtless true that Conyers is usually both insolent and insolvent, the context of this statement confirms the correctness of the first edition. Both of these slips are corrected in subsequent versions of the novel.

The significance of this edition cannot, however, simply be dismissed, because by far the majority of substantive changes made in it *are* transferred to the single-volume editions which follow. The first edition's "worth of silver coin" becomes the eighth edition's "worth of coin;" first edition "seams and elbows" becomes eighth edition "sleeves and elbows;" first edition "courier, who conducted" becomes eighth edition "courier, who accompanied;" first edition "concentered" becomes eighth edition "concentrated;" first edition "irrecoverable" becomes eighth edition "irrevocable." Each of these changes, and many like them, appear in the Stereotyped single-volume edition which follows Tinsley's version, and they materially alter the novel's presentation. Again, in the absence of proofs, it is impossible to say whether Braddon was given an opportunity to modify this text, and whether at least some of these alterations are authorial revisions. On the face of it this seems unlikely, since at this point she had no particular stake in the book, and was writing new works at a feverish pace. What *is* likely, however, is that in looking for a text to use as copy for her own single-volume edition of *Aurora Floyd*, to be released after Tinsley's rights expired, Braddon turned to an already existing single-volume version which, as far as she knew, was a reproduction of the first edition. The Tinsley eighth edition is therefore essential in understanding the transmission of the text. It passes on much of its house-styling, including the added adverbial commas, and a large number of substantive changes to the next stage of the novel, which Braddon manifestly *did* revise.

It is no exaggeration to say that the revisions made to the text after it passed out of Tinsley's control are the most significant in its entire development. Possibly Braddon made these changes for some earlier single-volume version, but what is certain is that they were in place by the Stereotyped edition, which in turn was used to print the two-shilling yellowback editions which flooded the cheap-volume market of Victorian, and indeed Edwardian, Britain. This version of the novel, therefore, received the widest distribution of any form of the text.

That the substantive alterations made were authorial is clear from both their type and their scope. Thus, for example, in the first edition much is made in the early chapters of the wound Talbot receives in the Crimea, and the "stiff leg" he suffers as a result. In the Stereotyped edition the twelve references to this wound, spread out over the first twelve chapters, are systematically removed. The kind of detailed reading required to make such a change is unlikely to have been undertaken by anyone except Braddon, and in retrospect her reasoning seems clear. When James Conyers reappears in Aurora's life after the false report of his death, the text constantly emphasizes that he walks with a limp, a limp which symbolically associates him with the deformed hunchback, Steeve Hargraves. Although Talbot is criticized for his overfastidious pride and inability to trust Aurora, Braddon can scarcely have desired that he share the same physical defect as Conyers, and thus become potentially associated with him, and even the "Softy," in the reader's mind. By removing all references to Talbot's leg wound, she ensures that no such confusing ambiguities arise.

Similarly, a crucial modification occurs in Chapter XXII, although it consists of only a single sentence. In the first edition, the scene in which Aurora unexpectedly encounters Steeve Hargraves among John's guns contains the following passage:

> He had this pistol still in his hand when the door was suddenly opened, and Aurora Mellish stood upon the threshold.
> She spoke as she opened the door, almost before she was in the room.

In the Stereotyped edition this is altered to:

> He had this pistol still in his hand when the door was suddenly opened, and Aurora Mellish stood upon the threshold. *The intruder dropped the pistol into the capacious pocket of his fustian jacket as the door opened.*
> Aurora spoke as she opened the door, almost before she was in the room. (emphasis added)

As already noted, Braddon makes Aurora's innocence in Conyers' murder clearer as the text evolves, and this is the key moment in that evolution. The subsequent discovery of this discarded pistol beside the pond may leave John Mellish doubting his wife, but the audience of the Stereotyped edition would have had no such suspicions. This version of the text not only tells us that the "Softy" has both the motive and opportunity to kill Conyers, but also places the murder weapon explicitly in his possession. Any suspense about the novel's heroine being a murderess is, therefore, effectively precluded.

By far the most important change made to the Stereotyped edition, however, has nothing to do with character or plot; it has to do with narrative voice. Fifteen passages of one hundred words or more of the narrator's commentary, some of which are substantially larger, have been removed from the text, along with a significant number of shorter narrative sections. This certainly tightens the presentation of the story, but at the cost of excising the narrator's often telling observations on the action. Since these passages are so lengthy, one example will have to stand as representative. In Chapter XII, after Aurora finally recovers from the shock of Talbot's dissolution of their engagement, the following appears in the serial, first, and eighth editions, but not in the Stereotyped:

> The lovers who die for love in tragedies die in such a vast hurry, that there is generally some mistake or misapprehension about the business, and the tragedy might have been a comedy if the hero or heroine had only waited for a quarter of an hour. If Othello had but lingered a little before smothering his wife, Mistress Emilia might have come in and sworn and protested; and Cassio, with the handkerchief about his leg, might have been in time to set the mind of the valiant Moor at rest, and put the Venetian dog to confusion. How happily Mr. and Mrs. Romeo Montague might have lived and died, thanks to the dear good friar, if the foolish bridegroom had not been in such a hurry to swallow the vile stuff from the apothecary's! And as people are, I hope and believe, a little wiser in real life than they appear to be upon the stage, the worms very rarely get an honest meal off men and women who have died for love.

These ironic observations, debunking those who "die for love," foreshadow and thus reinforce the novel's anti-romantic celebration of John and Aurora's eventual marriage over that of Talbot and Lucy. All the deleted passages are direct addresses to the reader by the narrator, and they are instrumental in guiding her or his response. Their removal, therefore, creates a significant difference between the *Aurora Floyd* read by its original audience in 1863 and 1864, and that experienced by those who came to it later.

This being so, we have selected the three-volume first edition as our copy text. In contrast, the two most recent editions of the novel have reproduced late single-volume versions of the text.[5] But given the questionable revisions introduced into the Tinsley "eighth edition," and the widescale changes to the novel's narration which appear in subsequent versions, it is fair to say that these texts are not the ones which caused such an uproar when the book was initially released. A return to the three-volume edition, therefore, provides the contemporary reader with an opportunity to explore the text which originally so shocked and titillated its Victorian audience, and which solidified Braddon's reputation as queen of the sensation novelists.

Notes

1 The Wolff Collection is located in the Harry Ransom Humanities Research Center at the University of Texas at Austin.
2 See Robert Lee Wolff, *Nineteenth-Century Fiction: A Bibliographical Catalogue Based on the Collection Formed by Robert Lee Wolff*. 5 vols. New York: Garland, 1981.
3 See P.D. Edwards, "M.E. Braddon Manuscripts in Australia," *Notes and Queries* 233 (Sept. 1988), 327.
4 The Tinsley three-volume edition of *Aurora Floyd* was printed by William Clowes and Sons, Stamford Street and Charing Cross, the single-volume edition by Bradbury and Evans, Whitefriars.
5 The 1984 Virago *Aurora Floyd*, now out of print, is a photo-reproduction of an undated John and Robert Maxwell edition. P.D. Edwards' edition for the Oxford World's Classics series (1996) is based on the Stereotyped edition.

Mary Elizabeth Braddon: A Brief Chronology

1835   Born October 4 at 2 Frith Street, Soho Square, London, third child of Henry Braddon and Fanny White

1839   Parents separate due to father's financial failure and infidelity; Braddon and her mother briefly move to Sussex before returning to London and eventually taking lodgings in Hammersmith

1845   Enroled at Dartmouth Lodge, boarding school for girls; withdrawn shortly after due to family's poverty

1857   Becomes actress using stage name "Mary Seyton"; performs in provincial theatre, mainly in Yorkshire

1860   Leaves the stage; publication of *Three Times Dead*, the first of Braddon's eighty novels; meets publisher and editor John Maxwell

1861   Establishes household with Maxwell, but cannot marry him because his first wife is alive and confined in a Dublin insane asylum; Braddon becomes stepmother to Maxwell's five children

1861-62   Begins correspondence with Edward Bulwer Lytton, which continues until his death in 1873; *Lady Audley's Secret* serialized in *Robin Goodfellow*, but remains incomplete when magazine fails; begins writing *Aurora Floyd*; due to public demand, *Lady Audley's Secret* is re-serialized and completed in *Sixpenny Magazine*, and becomes wildly popular

1862   *Lady Audley's Secret* published in three volumes by Tinsley Bros., dedicated to Bulwer Lytton; Braddon bears first of six children by Maxwell

1862-63   *Aurora Floyd* serialized in *Temple Bar* and is immediately successful

1863   *Aurora Floyd* published in three volumes by Tinsley Bros.

1864   Publication of *The Doctor's Wife*, Braddon's adaptation of *Madame Bovary*

1866	*Belgravia Magazine* founded by Maxwell, conducted by Braddon; publication of *The Lady's Mile*, her first piece of non-sensation fiction; Braddon and Maxwell purchase Lichfield House, Richmond, which becomes their permanent residence; Braddon's third child by Maxwell dies in infancy
1868	Death of sister and mother; Braddon suffers nervous collapse complicated by puerperal fever
1873	Writes and stages *Griselda*; efforts as dramatist achieve limited success
1874	Maxwell's wife dies September 5; Braddon and Maxwell marry October 2
1876	*Belgravia Magazine* sold, Braddon resigns as editor; publication of *Joshua Haggard's Daughter*
1878	Founds, edits, and writes for *The Mistletoe Bough*, annual Christmas magazine which continues publication until 1892
1884	Publication of *Ishmael*
1885	Unpublished article "Émile Zola and the Naturalistic School, or Realism in French Literature"
1888	Publication of *The Fatal Three*
1891	Maxwell becomes increasingly ill and eventually an invalid
1895	Death of John Maxwell; Braddon burns many of his letters
1907	Suffers slight stroke; publication of *Dead Love Has Chains*, written in 1904
1913	Attends "moving picture show" of *Aurora Floyd*
1915	Dies February 4
1916	Publication of *Mary*, her last novel

VOLUME I

CHAPTER I.

HOW A RICH BANKER MARRIED AN ACTRESS.

FAINT streaks of crimson glimmer here and there amidst the rich darkness of the Kentish woods. Autumn's red finger has been lightly laid upon the foliage – sparingly, as the artist puts the brighter tints into his picture: but the grandeur of an August sunset blazes upon the peaceful landscape, and lights all into glory.

The encircling woods and wide lawn-like meadows, the still ponds of limpid water, the trim hedges, and the smooth winding roads; undulating hill-tops, melting into the purple distance; labouring men's cottages gleaming white from the surrounding foliage; solitary road-side inns with brown thatched roofs and moss-grown stacks of lop-sided chimneys; noble mansions hiding behind ancestral oaks; tiny Gothic edifices; Swiss and rustic lodges; pillared gates surmounted by escutcheons hewn in stone, and festooned with green wreaths of clustering ivy; village churches and prim school-houses: every object in the fair English prospect is steeped in a luminous haze, as the twilight shadows steal slowly upward from the dim recesses of shady woodland and winding lane, and every outline of the landscape darkens against the deepening crimson of the sky.

Upon the broad *façade* of a mighty red-brick mansion, built in the favourite style of the early Georgian era, the sinking sun lingers long, making gorgeous illumination. The long rows of narrow windows are all a-flame with the red light, and an honest homeward-tramping villager pauses once or twice in the roadway to glance across the smooth width of dewy lawn and tranquil lake, half fearful that there must be something more than natural in the glitter of those windows, and that maybe Maister Floyd's house is a-fire.

The stately red-brick mansion belongs to Maister Floyd, as he is called in the honest *patois* of the Kentish rustics; to Archibald Martin Floyd, of the great banking-house of Floyd, Floyd, and Floyd, Lombard Street, City.

The Kentish rustics know very little of this City banking-house, for Archibald Martin, the senior partner, has long retired from any active share in the business, which is carried on entirely by his nephews, Andrew and Alexander Floyd, both steady, middle-aged men, with families and country houses; both owing their fortune to the rich uncle, who had found places in his counting-house for them some thirty years before, when they were tall, raw-boned, sandy-haired, red-complexioned Scottish youths, fresh from some unpronounceable village north of Aberdeen.

The young gentlemen signed their names McFloyd when they first entered their uncle's counting-house; but they very soon followed that wise relative's example, and dropped the formidable prefix. "We've nae need to tell these sootherran bodies that we're Scotche," Alick remarked to his brother, as he wrote his name for the first time A. Floyd, all short.

The Scottish banking-house had thriven wonderfully in the hospitable English capital. Unprecedented success had waited upon every enterprise undertaken by the old-established and respected firm of Floyd, Floyd, and Floyd. It had been Floyd, Floyd, and Floyd for upwards of a century; for as one member of the house dropped off some greener branch shot out from the old tree; and there had never yet been any need to alter the treble repetition of the well-known name upon the brass plates that adorned the swinging mahogany doors of the banking-house. To this brass plate Archibald Martin Floyd pointed when, some thirty years before the August evening of which I write, he took his raw-boned nephews for the first time across the threshold of his house of business.

"See there, boys," he said; "look at the three names upon that brass plate. Your uncle George is over fifty, and a bachelor, – that's the first name; our first cousin, Stephen Floyd, of Calcutta, is going to sell out of the business before long, – that's the second name; the third is mine, and I'm thirty-seven years of age, remember, boys, and not likely to make a fool of myself by marrying. Your names will be wanted by-and-by to fill the blanks; see that you keep them bright in the mean time; for let so much as one speck rest upon them, and they'll never be fit for that brass plate."

Perhaps the rugged Scottish youths took this lesson to heart, or perhaps honesty was a natural and inborn virtue in the house of Floyd. Be it as it might, neither Alick nor Andrew disgraced their ancestry; and when Stephen Floyd, the East-Indian merchant, sold out, and Uncle George grew tired of business and took to building, as an elderly, bachelor-like hobby, the young men stepped into their relatives' shoes, and took the conduct of the business upon their broad northern shoulders. Upon one point only Archibald Martin Floyd had misled his nephews, and that point regarded himself. Ten years after his address to the young men, at the sober age of seven-and-forty, the banker not only made a fool of himself by marrying, but, if indeed such things are foolish, sank still further from the proud elevation of worldly wisdom, by falling desperately in love with a beautiful but penniless woman, whom he brought home with him after a business-tour through the manufacturing districts,[1] and with but little ceremony introduced to his relations and the county families round his Kentish estate as his newly-wedded wife.

The whole affair was so sudden, that these very county families had scarcely recovered from their surprise at reading a certain paragraph in the left-hand column of the 'Times,' announcing the marriage of "Archibald Martin Floyd, banker, of Lombard Street and Felden Woods, to Eliza, only surviving daughter of Captain Prodder," when the bridegroom's travelling carriage dashed past the Gothic lodge at his gates, along the avenue and under the great stone portico at the side of the house, and Eliza Floyd entered the banker's mansion, nodding good-naturedly to the bewildered servants, marshalled into the hall to receive their new mistress.

The banker's wife was a tall young woman, of about thirty, with a dark complexion, and great flashing black eyes that lit up a face, which might otherwise have been unnoticeable, into the splendour of absolute beauty.

Let the reader recall one of those faces, whose sole loveliness lies in the glorious light of a pair of magnificent eyes, and remember how far they surpass all others in their power of fascination. The same amount of beauty frittered away upon a well-shaped nose, rosy pouting lips, symmetrical forehead, and delicate complexion, would make an

---

1 Industrial areas in the north of England, including Lancashire, Yorkshire, Northumberland, Cheshire, Staffordshire, some areas of the Midlands, and the great manufacturing cities of Liverpool, Manchester, Durham, Birmingham, and Sheffield.

ordinarily lovely woman; but concentrated in one nucleus, in the wondrous lustre of the eyes, it makes a divinity, a Circe. You may meet the first any day of your life; the second, once in a lifetime.

Mr. Floyd introduced his wife to the neighbouring gentry at a dinner-party which he gave soon after the lady's arrival at Felden Woods, as his country seat was called; and this ceremony very briefly despatched, he said no more about his choice either to his neighbours or his relations, who would have been very glad to hear how this unlooked-for marriage had come about, and who hinted the same to the happy bridegroom, but without effect.

Of course this very reticence on the part of Archibald Floyd himself only set the thousand tongues of rumour more busily to work. Round Beckenham and West Wickham, near which villages Felden Woods was situated, there was scarcely any one debased and degraded station of life from which Mrs. Floyd was not reported to have sprung. She had been a factory-girl, and the silly old banker had seen her in the streets of Manchester, with a coloured handkerchief on her head, a coral necklace round her throat, and shoeless and stockingless feet tramping in the mud: he had seen her thus, and had fallen incontinently in love with her, and offered to marry her there and then. She was an actress, and he had seen her on the Manchester stage; nay, lower still, she was some poor performer, decked in dirty white muslin, red-cotton velvet, and spangles, who acted in a canvas booth, with a pityful set of wandering vagabonds and a learned pig. Sometimes they said she was an equestrian, and it was at Astley's,[1] and not in the manufacturing districts, that the banker had first seen her; nay, some there were, ready to swear that they themselves had beheld her leaping through gilded hoops, and dancing the cachuca[2] upon six bare-backed steeds, in that sawdust-strewn arena. There were whispered rumours that were more cruel than these; rumours which I dare not even set down here, for the busy tongues that dealt so mercilessly with the name and fame of Eliza Floyd were not unbarbed by malice. It may be that some of the ladies had personal reasons for their spite against the bride, and that many a waning beauty, in those pleas-

---

1   Astley's Amphitheatre in London featured equestrian entertainments such as staged military campaigns and Shakespeare on horseback.

2   A Spanish solo dance.

ant Kentish mansions, had speculated upon the banker's income, and the advantages attendant upon a union with the owner of Felden Woods.

The daring, disreputable creature, with not even beauty to recommend her, – for the Kentish damsels scrupulously ignored Eliza's wonderful eyes, and were sternly critical with her low forehead, doubtful nose, and rather wide mouth, – the artful, designing minx, at the mature age of nine-and-twenty, with her hair growing nearly down to her eye-brows, had contrived to secure to herself the hand and fortune of the richest man inKent – the man who had been hitherto so impregnable to every assault from bright eyes and rosy lips, that the most indefatigable of manoeuvring mothers had given him up in despair, and ceased to make visionary and Alnaschar-like[1] arrangements of the furniture in Mr. Floyd's great red-brick palace.

The female portion of the community wondered indignantly at the supineness of the two Scotch nephews, and the old bachelor brother, George Floyd. Why did not these people show a little spirit – institute a commission of lunacy, and shut their crazy relative in a madhouse?[2] He deserved it.

The ruined *noblesse* of the Faubourg St.-Germain could not have abused a wealthy Bonapartist with more vigorous rancour[3] than these people employed in their ceaseless babble about the banker's wife. Whatever she did was a new subject for criticism; even at that first dinner-party, though Eliza had no more ventured to interfere with the arrangements of the man-cook and housekeeper than if she had been a visitor at Buckingham Palace, the angry guests found that

---

1 Alnaschar, a pauper in the *Arabian Nights*, gets so involved in dreaming about the wealth he will get from his glass-selling business that he accidentally smashes all the glass. To be "Alnaschar-like" is to count your chickens before they are hatched.

2 The 1850s and 60s saw considerable public agitation over the wrongful imprisonment of sane people in lunatic asylums. Such imprisonments became stock devices of sensation novels like *Lady Audley's Secret*, Wilkie Collins' *The Woman in White* (1860), and Charles Reade's *Hard Cash* (1863).

3 A reference to the ill-feeling of the aristocracy (*noblesse*), displaced and impoverished by the French Revolution, towards the family and supporters of Napoleon Bonaparte, who profited by it. The *Faubourg Saint Germain* is an area originally outside the actual city of Paris in which the homes of many aristocratic families were to be found.

everything had degenerated since "that woman" had entered the house. They hated the successful adventuress, – hated her for her beautiful eyes and her gorgeous jewels, the extravagant gifts of an adoring husband, – hated her for her stately figure and graceful movements, which never betrayed the rumoured obscurity of her origin, – hated her, above all, for her insolence in not appearing in the least afraid of the lofty members of that new circle in which she found herself.

If she had meekly eaten the ample dish of humble-pie which these county families were prepared to set before her, – if she had licked the dust from their aristocratic shoes, courted their patronage, and submitted to be "taken up" by them, – they might perhaps in time have forgiven her. But she did none of this. If they called upon her, well and good; she was frankly and cheerfully glad to see them. They might find her in her gardening-gloves, with rumpled hair and a watering-pot in her hands, busy amongst her conservatories; and she would receive them as serenely as if she had been born in a palace, and accustomed to homage from her very babyhood. Let them be as frigidly polite as they pleased, she was always easy, candid, gay, and good-natured. She would rattle away about her "dear old Archy," as she presumed to call her benefactor and husband; or she would show her guests some new picture he had bought, and would dare – the impudent, ignorant, pretentious creature! – to talk about Art, as if all the high-sounding jargon with which they tried to crush her was as familiar to her as to a Royal Academician. When etiquette demanded her returning these stately visits, she would drive boldly up to her neighbours' doors in a tiny basket-carriage, drawn by one rough pony; for it was a whim of this designing woman to affect simplicity in her tastes, and to abjure all display. She would take all the grandeur she met with as a thing of course, and chatter and laugh, with her flaunting theatrical animation, much to the admiration of misguided young men, who could not see the high-bred charms of her detractors, but who were never tired of talking of Mrs. Floyd's jolly manner and glorious eyes.

I wonder whether poor Eliza Floyd knew all or half the cruel things that were said of her! I shrewdly suspect that she contrived somehow or other to hear them all, and that she rather enjoyed the fun. She had been used to a life of excitement, and Felden Woods might have seemed dull to her but for these ever fresh scandals. She took a malicious delight in the discomfiture of her enemies.

"How badly they must have wanted you for a husband, Archy," she said, "when they hate me so ferociously! Poor portionless old maids, to think that I should snatch their prey from them! I know they think it a hard thing that they can't have me hanged, for marrying a rich man."

But the banker was so deeply wounded when his adored wife repeated to him the gossip which she had heard from her maid, who was a stanch adherent to a kind, easy mistress, that Eliza ever afterwards withheld these reports from him. They amused her; but they stung him to the quick. Proud and sensitive, like almost all very honest and conscientious men, he could not endure that any creature should dare to befoul the name of the woman he loved so tenderly. What was the obscurity from which he had taken her to him? Is a star less bright because it shines on a gutter as well as upon the purple bosom of the midnight sea? Is a virtuous and generous-hearted woman less worthy because you find her making a scanty living out of the only industry she can exercise; and acting Juliet to an audience of factory-hands, who give threepence apiece for the privilege of admiring and applauding her?

Yes, the murder must out; the malicious were not altogether wrong in their conjectures: Eliza Prodder was an actress; and it was on the dirty boards of a second-rate theatre in Lancashire that the wealthy banker had first beheld her. Archibald Floyd nourished a traditional, passive, but sincere admiration for the British Drama. Yes, the *British* Drama; for he had lived in a day when the drama was British, and when 'George Barnwell' and 'Jane Shore' were amongst the favourite works of art of a play-going public. How sad that we should have degenerated since those classic days, and that the graceful story of Milwood and her apprentice-admirer is now so rarely set before us![1]

---

1 Victorian theatre was heavily influenced by continental forms (melodrama was French and German in origin) and by adaptations of continental, especially French, plays. Braddon recalls two popular eighteenth-century British plays: Nicholas Rowe's *The Tragedy of Jane Shore* (1714) and George Lillo's *The London Merchant* (1731), also known as *The History of George Barnwell*. The latter features an apprentice who is lured by his passion for a fallen woman, Millwood, to steal from his master.

Imbued, therefore, with this admiration for the drama, Mr. Floyd, stopping for a night at this second-rate Lancashire town, dropped into the dusty boxes of the theatre to witness the performance of 'Romeo and Juliet;' the heiress of the Capulets being represented by Miss Eliza Percival, alias Prodder.

I do not believe that Miss Percival was a good actress, or that she would ever have become distinguished in her profession; but she had a deep melodious voice, which rolled out the words of her author in a certain rich though rather monotonous music, pleasant to hear; and upon the stage she was very beautiful to look at, for her face lighted up the little theatre better than all the gas that the manager grudged to his scanty audiences.

It was not the fashion in those days to make "sensation" dramas of Shakespeare's plays. There was no 'Hamlet' with the celebrated water-scene, and the Danish prince taking a "header" to save poor weak-witted Ophelia.[1] In the little Lancashire theatre it would have been thought a terrible sin against all canons of dramatic art, had Othello or his Ancient attempted to sit down during any part of the solemn performance. The hope of Denmark was no long-robed Norseman with flowing flaxen hair,[2] but an individual who wore a short rusty black, cotton-velvet garment, shaped like a child's frock, and trimmed with bugles, which dropped off and were trodden upon at intervals throughout the performance. The simple actors held, that tragedy, to be tragedy, must be utterly unlike anything that had ever happened beneath the sun. And Eliza Prodder patiently trod the old and beaten track, far too good-natured, light-hearted, and easy-going a creature to attempt any foolish interference with the crookedness of the times, which she was not born to set right.[3]

---

1   Sensation dramas were melodramatic stage productions with elaborate sets and sensational scenes. An example is Dion Boucicault's *The Colleen Bawn* (1860), which featured a scene in which the heroine, pushed into the water because she will not give up her marriage certificate, is saved from drowning by a poacher. The set featured blue gauze as water; the heroine Eily sank beneath the surface against a backdrop of the Killarney lakes. The *Hamlet* "water scene" imagined here seems to be based on *The Colleen Bawn* and conflates Ophelia with Eily.

2   In 1823, Charles Kemble staged Shakespeare's *King John* at Covent Garden, featuring costumes researched by J.R. Planché. His production started a fashion for historical accuracy of sets and costumes in Shakespeare productions.

3   *Hamlet* (I.v.188-9).

What can I say, then, about her performance of the impassioned Italian girl? She wore white satin and spangles, the spangles sewn upon the dirty hem of her dress, in the firm belief, common to all provincial actresses, that spangles are an antidote to dirt. She was laughing and talking in the white-washed little green-room the very minute before she ran on to the stage to wail for her murdered kinsman and her banished lover. They tell us that Macready began to be Richelieu[1] at three o'clock in the afternoon, and that it was dangerous to approach or to speak to him between that hour and the close of the performance. So dangerous, indeed, that surely none but the daring and misguided gentleman who once met the great tragedian in a dark passage, and gave him "Good morrow, 'Mac,'" would have had the temerity to attempt it. But Miss Percival did not take her profession very deeply to heart; the Lancashire salaries barely paid for the physical wear and tear of early rehearsals and long performances; how then, for that mental exhaustion of the true artist who lives in the character he represents?

The easy-going comedians with whom Eliza acted made friendly remarks to each other on their private affairs in the intervals of the most vengeful discourse; speculated upon the amount of money in the house in audible undertones during the pauses of the scene; and when Hamlet wanted Horatio down at the footlights to ask him if he "marked that,"[2] it was likely enough that the prince's confidant was up the stage telling Polonius of the shameful way in which his landlady stole the tea and sugar.

It was not, therefore, Miss Percival's acting that fascinated the banker. Archibald Floyd knew that she was as bad an actress as ever played the leading tragedy and comedy for five-and-twenty shillings a week. He had seen Miss O'Neil in that very character,[3] and it moved him to a pitying smile as the factory-hands applauded poor Eliza's

---

1   William Charles Macready (1793-1873), eminent Victorian actor-manager, first played the title role of Bulwer Lytton's *Richelieu* at Covent Garden in 1839. This meticulously researched and rehearsed role was to become one of his most famous; before he retired, he played it 71 times in London alone.

2   *Hamlet* (V.i.222).

3   Eliza O'Neill (1791-1872) made her Covent Garden debut in 1814 and had a five-year career of unbroken success before she left the stage to be married. Juliet was one of her most famous roles.

poison scene. But for all this he fell in love with her. It was a repetition of the old story. It was Arthur Pendennis at the little Chatteris theatre bewitched and bewildered by Miss Fotheringay all over again.[1] Only that instead of a fickle, impressionable boy, it was a sober, steady-going business-man of seven-and-forty, who had never felt one thrill of emotion in looking on a woman's face until that night, – until that night, – and from that night the world only held for him one being, and life only had one object. He went the next evening, and the next; and then contrived to scrape acquaintance with some of the actors at a tavern next the theatre. They sponged upon him cruelly, these seedy comedians, and allowed him to pay for unlimited glasses of brandy-and-water, and flattered and cajoled him, and plucked out the heart of his mystery; and then went back to Eliza Percival, and told her that she had dropped into a good thing, for that an old chap with no end of money had fallen over head and ears in love with her, and that if she played her cards well, he would marry her to-morrow. They pointed him out to her through a hole in the green curtain, sitting almost alone in the shabby boxes, waiting for the play to begin, and for her black eyes to shine upon him once more.

Eliza laughed at her conquest; it was only one amongst many such, which had all ended alike, – leading to nothing better than the purchase of a box on her benefit night, or a bouquet left for her at the stage-door. She did not know the power of first love upon a man of seven-and-forty. Before the week was out, Archibald Floyd had made her a solemn offer of marriage.

He had heard a great deal about her from her fellow-performers, and had heard nothing but good. Temptations resisted; insidious proffers of jewels and gewgaws indignantly declined; graceful acts of gentle womanly charity done in secret; independence preserved through all poverty and trial; – they told him a hundred stories of her goodness, that brought the blood to his face with proud and generous emotion. And she herself told him the simple history of her life: told him that she was the daughter of a merchant-captain called Prodder;

---

1   In W.M. Thackeray's *The History of Pendennis* (1850), the naive young Arthur Pendennis falls in love with an Irish provincial actress, Miss Fotheringay (whose real name is Costigan and whose father is a drunkard). He is rescued from this youthful infatuation by his worldly uncle.

that she was born at Liverpool; that she remembered little of her father, who was almost always at sea – nor of a brother, three years older than herself, who quarrelled with his father, the merchant-captain, and ran away, and was never heard of again – nor of her mother, who died when she, Eliza, was four years old. The rest was told in a few words. She was taken into the family of an aunt who kept a grocer's shop in Miss Prodder's native town. She learnt artificial flower-making, and did not take to the business. She went often to the Liverpool theatres, and thought she would like to go upon the stage. Being a daring and energetic young person, she left her aunt's house one day, walked straight to the stage-manager of one of the minor theatres, and asked him to let her appear as Lady Macbeth. The man laughed at her, but told her that, in consideration of her fine figure and black eyes, he would give her fifteen shillings a week to "walk on," as he technically called the business of the ladies who wander on to the stage, sometimes dressed as villagers, sometimes in court costume of calico trimmed with gold, and stare vaguely at whatever may be taking place in the scene. From "walking on," Eliza came to play minor parts, indignantly refused by her superiors; from these she plunged ambitiously into the tragic lead, – and thus for nine years pursued the even tenour of her way; until, close upon her nine-and-twentieth birthday, Fate threw the wealthy banker across her pathway, and in the parish church of a small town in the Potteries[1] the black-eyed actress exchanged the name of Prodder for that of Floyd.

She had accepted the rich man partly because, moved by a sentiment of gratitude for the generous ardour of his affection, she was inclined to like him better than any one else she knew; and partly in accordance with the advice of her theatrical friends, who told her, with more candour than elegance, that she would be a jolly fool to let such a chance escape her; but at the time she gave her hand to Archibald Martin Floyd, she had no idea whatever of the magnitude of the fortune he had invited her to share. He told her that he was a banker, and her active mind immediately evoked the image of the only banker's wife she had ever known: a portly lady, who wore silk gowns, lived in a square stuccoed house with green blinds, kept a

---

[1] The pottery-producing districts of Staffordshire.

cook and housemaid, and took three box-tickets for Miss Percival's benefit.

When, therefore, the doting husband loaded his handsome bride with diamond bracelets and necklaces, and with silks and brocades that were stiff and unmanageable from their very richness, – when he carried her straight from the Potteries to the Isle of Wight, and lodged her in spacious apartments at the best hotel in Ryde, and flung his money here and there, as if he had carried the lamp of Aladdin in his coat-pocket, – Eliza remonstrated with her new master, fearing that his love had driven him mad, and that this alarming extravagance was the first outburst of insanity.

It seemed a repetition of the dear old Burleigh story[1] when Archibald Floyd took his wife into the long picture-gallery at Felden Woods. She clasped her hands for frank womanly joy as she looked at the magnificence about her. She compared herself to the humble bride of the earl, and fell on her knees and did theatrical homage to her lord. "O Archy," she said, "it is all too good for me! I am afraid I shall die of my grandeur, as the poor girl pined away at Burleigh House."

In the full maturity of womanly loveliness, rich in health, freshness, and high spirits, how little could Eliza dream that she would hold even a briefer lease of these costly splendours than the Bride of Burleigh had done before her!

Now the reader, being acquainted with Eliza's antecedents, may perhaps find in them some clue to the insolent ease and well-bred audacity with which Mrs. Floyd treated the second-rate county families, who were bent upon putting her to confusion. She was an actress: for nine years she had lived in that ideal world in which dukes and marquises are as common as butchers and bakers in work-a-day life; in which, indeed, a nobleman is generally a poor mean-spirited individual, who gets the worst of it on every hand, and is contemptuously entreated by the audience on account of his rank. How should she be

---

1 The true story of Sarah Hoggins, a villager who in 1791 married Lord Burleigh, whom she had met in the guise of a landscape painter. In "The Lord of Burleigh" (1842), Tennyson describes how, upon discovering her husband's true rank, she died under "the burthen of an honour/ Unto which she was not born." William Hazlitt and Thomas Moore also published versions of the story.

abashed on entering the drawing-rooms of these Kentish mansions, when for nine years she had walked nightly on to a stage to be the focus of every eye, and to entertain her guests the evening through? Was it likely she was to be over-awed by the Lenfields, who were coachbuilders in Park Lane, or the Miss Manderlys, whose father had made his money by a patent for starch, – she, who had received King Duncan at the gates of her castle, and had sat on a rickety throne dispensing condescending hospitality to the obsequious Thanes at Dunsinane?[1] So, do what they would, they were unable to subdue this base intruder; while, to add to their mortification, it every day became more obvious that Mr. and Mrs. Floyd made one of the happiest couples who had ever worn the bonds of matrimony, and changed them into garlands of roses. If this were a very romantic story, it would be perhaps only proper for Eliza Floyd to pine in her gilded bower, and misapply her energies in weeping for some abandoned lover, deserted in an evil hour of ambitious madness. But as my story is a true one, – not only true in a general sense, but strictly true as to the leading facts which I am about to relate, – and as I could point out, in a certain county, far northward of the lovely Kentish woods, the very house in which the events I shall describe took place, I am bound also to be truthful here, and to set down as a fact that the love which Eliza Floyd bore for her husband was as pure and sincere an affection as ever man need hope to win from the generous heart of a good woman. What share gratitude may have had in that love, I cannot tell. If she lived in a handsome house, and was waited on by attentive and deferential servants; if she ate of delicate dishes, and drank costly wines; if she wore rich dresses and splendid jewels, and lolled on the downy cushions of a carriage, drawn by high-mettled horses, and driven by a coachman with powdered hair; if, wherever she went, all outward semblance of homage was paid to her; if she had but to utter a wish, and, swift as the stroke of some enchanter's wand, that wish was gratified, – she knew that she owed all to her husband, Archibald Floyd; and it may be that she grew not unnaturally to associate him with every advantage

---

1 Eliza has, in other words, played Lady Macbeth. Her daughter, Aurora, will later be compared to Lady Macbeth in a more sinister light, as sharing her domineering character as well as the taint of murder.

she enjoyed, and to love him for the sake of these things. Such a love as this may appear a low and despicable affection when compared to the noble sentiment entertained by the Nancys of modern romance for the Bill Sykeses of their choice;[1] and no doubt Eliza Floyd ought to have felt a sovereign contempt for the man who watched her every whim, who gratified her every caprice, and who loved and honoured her as much, *ci-devant*[2] provincial actress though she was, as he could have done had she descended the steps of the loftiest throne in Christendom to give him her hand.

She was grateful to him, she loved him, and she made him perfectly happy; so happy that the strong-hearted Scotchman was sometimes almost panic-stricken at the contemplation of his own prosperity, and would fall down on his knees and pray that this blessing might not be taken from him; that, if it pleased Providence to afflict him, he might be stripped of every shilling of his wealth, and left penniless, to begin the world anew, – but with her. Alas, it was this blessing, of all others, that he was to lose!

For a year Eliza and her husband lived this happy life at Felden Woods. He wished to take her on the Continent, or to London for the season; but she could not bear to leave her lovely Kentish home. She was happier than the day was long amongst her gardens, and pineries, and graperies, her dogs and horses, and her poor. To these last she seemed an angel, descended from the skies to comfort them. There were cottages from which the prim daughters of the second-rate county families fled, tract in hand, discomfited and abashed by the black looks of the half-starved inmates; but upon whose doorways the shadow of Mrs. Floyd was as the shadow of a priest in a Catholic country – always sacred, yet ever welcome and familiar. She had the trick of making these people like her before she set to work to reform their evil habits. At an early stage of her acquaintance with them, she was as blind to the dirt and disorder of their cottages as she would have been to a shabby carpet in the drawing-room of a poor duchess;

---

1 Eliza Floyd's affection for her loving husband is contrasted to the prostitute Nancy's loyalty to the brutal Bill Sikes in Dickens' *Oliver Twist* (1838). Nancy's loyalty to Sikes was celebrated by Dickens: in his preface, he described it as "the last fair drop of water at the bottom of the weed-choked well."
2 Former.

but by-and-by she would artfully hint at this and that little improvement in the *ménages*[1] of her pensioners, until in less than a month, without having either lectured or offended, she had worked an entire transformation. Mrs. Floyd was frightfully artful in her dealings with these erring peasants. Instead of telling them at once in a candid and Christian-like manner that they were all dirty, degraded, ungrateful, and irreligious, she diplomatized and finessed with them as if she had been canvassing the county. She made the girls regular in their attendance at church by means of new bonnets and smartly bound prayer-books; she kept married men out of the public-houses by bribes of tobacco to smoke at home, and once (oh, horror!) by the gift of a bottle of gin for moderate and social consumption in the family circle. She cured a dirty chimney-piece by the present of a gaudy china vase to its proprietress, and a slovenly hearth by means of a brass fender. She repaired a shrewish temper with a new gown, and patched up a family breach of long standing with a chintz waistcoat. But one brief year after her marriage, – while busy landscape-gardeners were working at the improvements she had planned; while the steady process of reformation was slowly but surely progressing amongst the grateful recipients of her bounty; while the eager tongues of her detractors were still waging war upon her fair fame; while Archibald Floyd rejoiced as he held a baby-daughter in his arms, – without one fore-warning symptom to break the force of the blow, the light slowly faded out of those glorious eyes, never to shine again on this side of eternity, and Archibald Martin Floyd was a widower.

---

1 Housekeeping.

CHAPTER II.

AURORA.

THE child which Eliza Floyd left behind her, when she was so suddenly taken away from all earthly prosperity and happiness, was christened Aurora.[1] The romantic-sounding name had been a fancy of poor Eliza's; and there was no caprice of hers, however trifling, that had not always been sacred with her adoring husband, and that was not doubly sacred now. The actual intensity of the widower's grief was known to no creature in this lower world. His nephews and his nephews' wives paid him pertinacious visits of condolence; nay, one of these nieces by marriage, a good motherly creature, devoted to her husband, insisted on seeing and comforting the stricken man. Heaven knows whether her tenderness did convey any comfort to that shipwrecked soul! She found him like a man who had suffered from a stroke of paralysis, torpid, almost imbecile. Perhaps she took the wisest course that could possibly have been taken. She said little to him upon the subject of his affliction; but visited him frequently, patiently sitting opposite to him for hours at a time, he and she talking of all manner of easy conventional topics, – the state of the country, the weather, a change in the ministry, and such subjects as were so far remote from the grief of his life, that a less careful hand than Mrs. Alexander Floyd's could have scarcely touched upon the broken chords of that ruined instrument, the widower's heart.

It was not until six months after Eliza's death that Mrs. Alexander ventured to utter her name; but when she did speak of her, it was with no solemn hesitation, but tenderly and familiarly, as if she had been accustomed to talk of the dead. She saw at once that she had done right. The time had come for the widower to feel relief in

---

1 Aurora, the Roman goddess of the dawn, is described by Homer as "rosy-fingered" and "saffron-robed." Like her namesake, she has an association with horses: she drives a chariot and pair through the sky with her brother, Helios (the sun). For Victorians, the name Aurora was linked to unconventional women: George Sand (whose real name was Amandine-Aurore Lucille Dupin) and Elizabeth Barrett Browning's heroine, Aurora Leigh.

speaking of the lost one; and from that hour Mrs. Alexander became a favourite with her uncle. Years after, he told her that, even in the sullen torpor of his grief, he had had a dim consciousness that she pitied him, and that she was "a good woman." This good woman came that very evening into the big room, where the banker sat by his lonely hearth, with a baby in her arms, – a pale-faced child, with great wondering black eyes, which stared at the rich man in sombre astonishment; a solemn-faced, ugly baby, which was to grow by-and-by into Aurora Floyd, the heroine of my story.

That pale, black-eyed baby became henceforth the idol of Archibald Martin Floyd, the one object in all this wide universe for which it seemed worth his while to endure life. From the day of his wife's death he had abandoned all active share in the Lombard-Street business, and he had now neither occupation nor delight, save in waiting upon the prattlings and humouring the caprices of this infant daughter. His love for her was a weakness, almost verging upon a madness. Had his nephews been very designing men, they might perhaps have entertained some vague ideas of that commission of lunacy for which the outraged neighbours were so anxious. He grudged the hired nurses their offices of love about the person of his child. He watched them furtively, fearful lest they should be harsh with her. All the ponderous doors in the great house at Felden Woods could not drown the feeblest murmur of that infant voice to those ever-anxious, loving ears.

He watched her growth as a child watches an acorn it hopes to rear to an oak. He repeated her broken baby-syllables till people grew weary of his babble about the child. Of course the end of all this was, that, in the common acceptation of the term, Aurora was spoiled. We do not say a flower is spoiled because it is reared in a hothouse where no breath of heaven can visit it too roughly; but then, certainly, the bright exotic is trimmed and pruned by the gardener's merciless hand, while Aurora shot whither she would, and there was none to lop the wandering branches of that luxuriant nature. She said what she pleased; thought, spoke, acted as she pleased; learned what she pleased; and she grew into a bright impetuous being, affectionate and generous-hearted as her mother, but with some touch of native fire blended in her mould that stamped her as original. It is the common habit of ugly babies to grow into handsome women, and so it was with Aurora Floyd. At seventeen she was twice as beautiful as her mother had been at nine-and-twenty, but with much the same irregular features, lighted up by a pair of eyes that were like the stars of heaven, and by two rows of peerlessly white teeth. You rarely, in looking at her face, could get beyond these eyes and teeth; for they so dazzled and blinded you that they defied you to criticise the doubtful little nose, or the width of the smiling mouth. What if those masses of blue-black hair were brushed away from a forehead too low for the common standard of beauty? A phrenologist[1] would have told you that the head was a noble one; and a sculptor would have added that it was set upon the throat of a Cleopatra.

Miss Floyd knew very little of her poor mother's history. There was a picture in crayons hanging in the banker's sanctum sanctorum which represented Eliza in the full flush of her beauty and prosperity; but the portrait told nothing of the history of its original, and Aurora had never heard of the merchant-captain, the poor Liverpool lodging, the grim aunt who kept a chandler's shop, the artificial flower-making, and the provincial stage. She had never been told that her maternal grandfather's name was Prodder, and that her mother had played Juliet to an audience of factory hands, for the moderate and sometimes uncertain stipend of four-and-twopence a night. The county families accepted and made much of the rich banker's heiress; but they were not slow to say that Aurora was her mother's own daughter, and had the taint of the play-acting and horse-riding, the spangles and the sawdust, strong in her nature. The truth of the matter is, that before Miss Floyd emerged from the nursery she evinced a very decided tendency to become what is called "fast."[2] At six years of age she rejected a doll, and asked for a rocking-horse. At ten she could converse fluently upon the subject of pointers, setters, fox-hounds,

---

1 Person who studies the bumps and depressions of the head as an index to character, on the theory that specific mental faculties are located in particular areas on the surface of the brain. Phrenology was popular in the Victorian period: its adherents included Marx, Hegel, George Eliot, Queen Victoria, and the Brontës.
2 Unrefined in manners; disregardful of propriety. Aurora's interest in riding and the turf, use of racing slang, and general impatience with feminine education associate her with the contemporary "Fast Young Lady" (See Appendix A.1, 551).

harriers, and beagles, though she drove her governess to the verge of despair by persistently forgetting under what Roman emperor Jerusalem was destroyed, and who was legate from the Pope at the time of Catherine of Arragon's divorce. At eleven she talked unreservedly of the horses in the Lenfield stables as a pack of screws;[1] at twelve she contributed her half-crown to a Derby sweepstakes amongst her father's servants, and triumphantly drew the winning horse; and at thirteen she rode across country with her cousin Andrew, who was a member of the Croydon hunt. It was not without grief that the banker watched his daughter's progress in these doubtful accomplishments; but she was so beautiful, so frank and fearless, so generous, affectionate, and true, that he could not bring himself to tell her that she was not all he could desire her to be. If he could have governed or directed that impetuous nature, he would have had her the most refined and elegant, the most perfect and accomplished of her sex; but he could not do this, and he was fain to thank God for her as she was, and to indulge her every whim.

Alexander Floyd's eldest daughter, Lucy, first cousin, once removed, to Aurora, was that young lady's friend and confidante, and came now and then from her father's villa at Fulham to spend a month at Felden Woods. But Lucy Floyd had half a dozen brothers and sisters, and was brought up in a very different manner to the heiress. She was a fair-faced, blue-eyed, rosy-lipped, golden-haired little girl, who thought Felden Woods a paradise upon earth, and Aurora more fortunate than the Princess Royal of England, or Titania, Queen of the Fairies.[2] She was direfully afraid of her cousin's ponies and Newfoundland dogs, and had a firm conviction that sudden death held his throne within a certain radius of a horse's heels; but she loved and admired Aurora, after the manner common to these weaker natures, and accepted Miss Floyd's superb patronage and protection as a thing of course.

The day came when some dark but undefined cloud hovered about the narrow home-circle at Felden Woods. There was a coolness

---

1   Slang: unsound or broken-down horses.
2   The Princess Royal was Victoria (1840-1901), the eldest child of Victoria and Albert. Titania appears in *A Midsummer Night's Dream*.

between the banker and his beloved child. The young lady spent half her time on horseback, scouring the shady lanes round Beckenham, attended only by her groom – a dashing young fellow, chosen by Mr. Floyd on account of his good looks for Aurora's especial service. She dined in her own room after these long, lonely rides, leaving her father to eat his solitary meal in the vast dining-room, which seemed to be fully occupied when she sat in it, and desolately empty without her. The household at Felden Woods long remembered one particular June evening on which the storm burst forth between the father and daughter.

Aurora had been absent from two o'clock in the afternoon until sunset, and the banker paced the long stone terrace with his watch in his hand, the figures on the dial-plate barely distinguishable in the twilight, waiting for his daughter's coming home. He had sent his dinner away untouched; his newspapers lay uncut upon the table, and the household spies, we call servants, told each other how his hand had shaken so violently that he had spilled half a decanter of wine over the polished mahogany in attempting to fill his glass. The housekeeper and her satellites crept into the hall, and looked through the half-glass doors at the anxious watcher on the terrace. The men in the stables talked of "the row," as they called this terrible breach between father and child; and when at last horses' hoofs were heard in the long avenue, and Miss Floyd reined in her thorough-bred chestnut at the foot of the terrace-steps, there was a lurking audience hidden here and there in the evening shadow, eager to hear and see.

But there was very little to gratify these prying eyes and ears. Aurora sprang lightly to the ground before the groom could dismount to assist her, and the chestnut, with heaving and foam-flecked sides, was led off to the stable.

Mr. Floyd watched the groom and the two horses as they disappeared through the great gates leading to the stable-yard, and then said very quietly, "You don't use that animal well, Aurora. A six hours' ride is neither good for her nor for you. Your groom should have known better than to allow it." He led the way into his study, telling his daughter to follow him, and they were closeted together for upwards of an hour.

Early the next morning Miss Floyd's governess departed from Felden Woods, and between breakfast and luncheon the banker paid a visit to the stables, and examined his daughter's favourite chestnut mare, a beautiful filly all bone and muscle, that had been trained for a racer. The animal had strained a sinew, and walked lame. Mr. Floyd sent for his daughter's groom, and paid and dismissed him on the spot. The young fellow made no remonstrance, but went quietly to his quarters, took off his livery, packed a carpet-bag, and walked away from the house without bidding good-bye to his fellow-servants, who resented the affront, and pronounced him a surly brute who had always been too high for this business.

Three days after this, upon the 14th of June, 1856, Mr. Floyd and his daughter left Felden Woods for Paris, where Aurora was placed at a very expensive and exclusive Protestant finishing school, kept by the Demoiselles Lespard, in a stately mansion *entre cour et jardin*[1] in the Rue Saint-Dominique, there to complete her very imperfect education.

For a year and two months Miss Floyd has been away at this Parisian finishing school; it is late in the August of 1857, and again the banker walks upon the long stone terrace in front of the narrow windows of his red-brick mansion, this time waiting for Aurora's arrival from Paris. The servants have expressed considerable wonder at his not crossing the Channel to fetch his daughter, and they think the dignity of the house somewhat lowered by Miss Floyd travelling unattended.

"A poor dear young thing, that knows no more of this wicked world than a blessed baby," said the housekeeper, "all alone amongst a pack of moustachioed Frenchmen!"

Archibald Martin Floyd had grown an old man in one day – that terrible and unexpected day of his wife's death; but even the grief of that bereavement had scarcely seemed to affect him so strongly as the loss of his daughter Aurora during the fourteen months of her absence from Felden Woods.

Perhaps it was that at sixty-five years of age he was less able to bear even a lesser grief; but those who watched him closely, declared that he seemed as much dejected by his daughter's absence as he could well have been by her death. Even now, that he paces up and down

---

1   With its own courtyard and garden (which, in Paris, implied a somewhat luxurious situation).

the broad terrace, with the landscape stretching wide before him, and melting vaguely away under that veil of crimson glory shed upon all things by the sinking sun; even now that he hourly, nay, almost momentarily, expects to clasp his only child in his arms, Archibald Floyd seems rather nervously anxious than joyfully expectant.

He looks again and again at his watch, and pauses in his walk to listen to Beckenham church clock striking eight; his ears are preternaturally alert to every sound, and give him instant warning of carriage-wheels far off upon the wide high-road. All the agitation and anxiety he has felt for the last week has been less than the concentrated fever of this moment. Will it pass on, that carriage, or stop at the lodge-gates? Surely his heart could never beat so loud save by some wondrous magnetism of fatherly love and hope. The carriage stops. He hears the clanking of the gates; the crimson-tinted landscape grows dim and blurred before his eyes, and he knows no more till a pair of impetuous arms are twined about his neck, and Aurora's face is hidden on his shoulder.

It was a paltry hired carriage which Miss Floyd arrived in, and it drove away as soon as she had alighted, and the small amount of luggage she brought had been handed to the eager servants. The banker led his child into the study, where they had held that long conference fourteen months before. A lamp burned upon the library table, and it was to this light that Archibald Floyd led his daughter.

A year had changed the girl to a woman – a woman with great hollow black eyes, and pale haggard cheeks. The course of study at the Parisian finishing school had evidently been too hard for the spoiled heiress.

"Aurora, Aurora," the old man cried piteously, "how ill you look! how altered! how——"

She laid her hand lightly yet imperiously upon his lips.

"Don't speak of me," she said, "I shall recover; but you – you, father – you too are changed."

She was as tall as her father, and, resting her hands upon his shoulders, she looked at him long and earnestly. As she looked, the tears welled slowly up to her eyes which had been dry before, and poured silently down her haggard cheeks.

"My father, my devoted father," she said in a broken voice, "if my heart was made of adamant, I think it might break when I see the change in this beloved face."

The old man checked her with a nervous gesture, a gesture almost of terror.

"Not one word, not one word, Aurora," he said hurriedly; "at least, only one. That person – he is dead?"

"He is."

CHAPTER III.

WHAT BECAME OF THE DIAMOND BRACELET.

AURORA'S relatives were not slow to exclaim upon the change for the worse which a twelvemonth in Paris had made in their young kinswoman. I fear that the Demoiselles Lespard suffered considerably in reputation amongst the circle round Felden Woods from Miss Floyd's impaired good looks. She was out of spirits too, had no appetite, slept badly, was nervous and hysterical, no longer took any interest in her dogs and horses, and was altogether an altered creature. Mrs. Alexander Floyd declared it was perfectly clear that these cruel Frenchwomen had worked poor Aurora to a shadow: the girl was not used to study, she said; she had been accustomed to exercise and open air, and no doubt had pined sadly in the close atmosphere of a school-room.

But Aurora's was one of those impressionable natures which quickly recover from any depressing influence. Early in September Lucy Floyd came to Felden Woods, and found her handsome cousin almost entirely recovered from the drudgery of the Parisian *pension*,[1] but still very loth to talk much of that seminary. She answered Lucy's eager questions very curtly; said that she hated the Demoiselles Lespard and the Rue Saint-Dominique, and that the very memory of Paris was disagreeable to her. Like most young ladies with black eyes and blue-black hair, Miss Floyd was a good hater; so Lucy forbore to ask for more information upon what was so evidently an unpleasant subject to her cousin. Poor Lucy had been mercilessly well educated; she spoke half a dozen languages, knew all about the natural sciences, had read Gibbon, Niebuhr, and Arnold,[2] from the title-page to the printer's name, and looked upon the heiress as a big brilliant dunce; so

---

1   French boarding school for young ladies.
2   Edward Gibbon (1737-94), English historian, author of *The History of the Decline and Fall of the Roman Empire*; Carsten Niebuhr (1733-1815), German traveller who recorded the first scientific expedition to Arabia; Thomas Arnold (1795-1842), educator, famous headmaster of Rugby School, and author of a three-volume history of Rome and five volumes of sermons.

she quietly set down Aurora's dislike to Paris to that young lady's distaste for tuition, and thought little more about it. Any other reasons for Miss Floyd's almost shuddering horror of her Parisian associations lay far beyond Lucy's simple power of penetration.

The fifteenth of September was Aurora's birthday, and Archibald Floyd determined upon this, the nineteenth anniversary of his daughter's first appearance on this mortal scene, to give an entertainment, whereat his county neighbours and town acquaintance might alike behold and admire the beautiful heiress.

Mrs. Alexander came to Felden Woods to superintend the preparations for this birthday ball. She drove Aurora and Lucy into town to order the supper and the band, and to choose dresses and wreaths for the young ladies. The banker's heiress was sadly out of place in a milliner's showroom; but she had that rapid judgment as to colour, and that perfect taste in form, which bespeak the soul of an artist; and while poor mild Lucy was giving endless trouble, and tumbling innumerable boxes of flowers, before she could find any head-dress in harmony with her rosy cheeks and golden hair, Aurora, after one brief glance at the bright *parterres*[1] of painted cambric, pounced upon a crown-shaped garland of vivid scarlet berries, with drooping and tangled leaves of dark shining green, that looked as if they had been just plucked from a running streamlet. She watched Lucy's perplexities with a half-compassionate, half-contemptuous smile.

"Look at that poor bewildered child," she said; "I know that she would like to put pink and yellow against her golden hair. Why, you silly Lucy, don't you know that yours is the beauty which really does *not* want adornment? A few pearls or forget-me-not blossoms, or a crown of water-lilies and a cloud of white areophane, would make you look a sylphide; but I dare say you would like to wear amber satin and cabbage-roses."

From the milliner's they drove to Mr. Gunter's in Berkeley Square,[2] at which world-renowned establishment Mrs. Alexander commanded those preparations of turkeys preserved in jelly, hams cunningly

---

1 Flower beds, here used metaphorically.
2 Gunter's Confectionary Shop, 7–8 Berkeley Square. Richard Gunter ran a catering business from his shop; his firm later caters Aurora's wedding (see 184).

embalmed in rich wines and broths, and other specimens of that sublime art of confectionery which hovers midway between sleight-of-hand and cookery, and in which the Berkeley Square professor is without a rival. When poor Thomas Babington Macaulay's New-Zealander shall come to ponder over the ruins of St. Paul's,[1] perhaps he will visit the remains of this humbler temple in Berkeley Square, and wonder at the ice-pails and jelly-moulds, the refrigerators and stewpans, the hot plates long cold and unheeded, and all the mysterious paraphernalia of the dead art.

From the West End Mrs. Alexander drove to Charing Cross; she had a commission to execute at Dent's,[2] – the purchase of a watch for one of her boys, who was just off to Eton.

Aurora threw herself wearily back in the carriage while Mrs. Alexander and Lucy stopped at the watchmaker's. It was to be observed that, although Miss Floyd had recovered much of her old brilliancy and gaiety of temper, a certain gloomy shade would sometimes steal over her countenance when she was left to herself for a few minutes; a darkly reflective expression quite foreign to her face. This shadow fell upon her beauty now as she looked out of the open window, moodily watching the passers-by. Mrs. Alexander was a long time making her purchase; and Aurora had sat nearly a quarter of an hour blankly staring at the shifting figures in the crowd, when a man hurrying by was attracted by her face at the carriage window, and started, as if at some great surprise. He passed on, however, and walked rapidly towards the Horse Guards; but before he turned the corner, came to a dead stop, stood still for two or three minutes scratching the back of his head reflectively with his big, bare hand, and then walked slowly back towards Mr. Dent's emporium. He was a broad-shouldered, bull-necked, sandy-whiskered fellow, wearing a cut-away coat and a gaudy neckerchief, and smoking a huge cigar, the rank fumes of which struggled with a very powerful odour of rum-and-water

---

1 In his 1840 essay on Leopold Ranke's *History of the Popes of Rome*, Thomas Babington Macaulay envisaged a future day when "some traveller shall, in the midst of a vast solitude, take his stand on a broken arch of London Bridge to sketch the ruins of St. Paul's."

2 Edward John Dent, manufacturer of first-rate clocks and watches, had one of his three London shops at 33 Cockspur Street, Charing Cross.

recently imbibed. This gentleman's standing in society was betrayed by the smooth head of a bull-terrier, whose round eyes peeped out of the pocket of his cut-away coat, and by a Blenheim spaniel carried under his arm. He was the very last person, amongst all the souls between Cockspur Street and the statue of King Charles,[1] who seemed likely to have anything to say to Miss Aurora Floyd; nevertheless he walked deliberately up to the carriage, and, planting his elbows upon the door, nodded to her with friendly familiarity.

"Well," he said, without inconveniencing himself by the removal of the rank cigar, "how do?"

After which brief salutation he relapsed into silence, and rolled his great brown eyes slowly here and there, in contemplative examination of Miss Floyd and the vehicle in which she sat; even carrying his powers of observation so far as to take particular notice of a plethoric morocco-bag lying on the back seat, and to inquire casually whether there was "anythink wallable in the old party's redicule?"

But Aurora did not allow him long for this leisurely employment; for looking at him with her eyes flashing forked lightnings of womanly fury, and her face crimson with indignation, she asked him in a sharp spasmodic tone whether he had anything to say to her.

He had a great deal to say to her; but as he put his head in at the carriage window and made his communication, whatever it might be, in a rum-and-watery whisper, it reached no ears but those of Aurora herself. When he had done whispering, he took a greasy leather-covered account-book, and a short stump of lead-pencil, considerably the worse for chewing, from his breast pocket, and wrote two or three lines upon a leaf, which he tore out and handed to Aurora. "This is the address," he said; "you won't forget to send?"

She shook her head, and looked away from him – looked away with an irrepressible gesture of disgust and loathing.

"You wouldn't like to buy a spannel dawg," said the man, holding the sleek, curly, black-and-tan animal up to the carriage window; "or

---

1   Aurora is waiting opposite Dent's, at 33 Cockspur Street; the equestrian statue of King Charles is at Charing Cross (the junction of the Strand, Whitehall, and Cockspur Street). The dog-fancier is heading along Cockspur Street towards the Horse Guards, a guardhouse and public building located at Whitehall, at the eastern end of St. James's Park.

a French poodle what'll balance a bit of bread on his nose while you count ten? Hay? You should have 'em a bargain – say fifteen pound the two."

"No!"

At this moment Mrs. Alexander emerged from the watchmaker's, just in time to catch a glimpse of the man's broad shoulders as he moved sulkily away from the carriage.

"Has that person been begging of you, Aurora?" she asked, as they drove off.

"No. I once bought a dog of him, and he recognized me."

"And wanted you to buy one to-day?"

"Yes."

Miss Floyd sat gloomily silent during the whole of the homeward drive, looking out of the carriage window, and not deigning to take any notice whatever of her aunt and cousin. I do not know whether it was in submission to that palpable superiority of force and vitality in Aurora's nature which seemed to set her above her fellows, or simply in that inherent spirit of toadyism common to the best of us; but Mrs. Alexander and her fair-haired daughter always paid mute reverence to the banker's heiress, and were silent when it pleased her, or conversed at her royal will. I verily believe that it was Aurora's eyes rather than Archibald Martin Floyd's thousands which overawed all her kinsfolk; and that if she had been a street-sweeper dressed in rags, and begging for halfpence, people would have feared her and made way for her, and bated their breath when she was angry.

The trees in the long avenue of Felden Woods were hung with sparkling coloured lamps, to light the guests who came to Aurora's birthday festival. The long range of windows on the ground-floor was ablaze with light; the crash of the band burst every now and then above the perpetual roll of carriage wheels and the shouted repetition of visitors' names, and pealed across the silent woods: through the long vista of half a dozen rooms opening one into another, the waters of a fountain, sparkling with a hundred hues in the light, glittered amid the dark floral wealth of a conservatory filled with exotics. Great clusters of tropical plants were grouped in the spacious hall; festoons of flowers hung about the vapoury curtains in the arched doorways.

Light and splendour were everywhere around; and amid all, and more splendid than all, in the dark grandeur of her beauty, Aurora Floyd, crowned with scarlet, and robed in white, stood by her father's side.

Amongst the guests who arrive latest at Mr. Floyd's ball are two officers from Windsor, who have driven across country in a mail-phaeton.[1] The elder of these two, and the driver of the vehicle, has been very discontented and disagreeable throughout the journey.

"If I'd had the remotest idea of the distance, Maldon," he said, "I'd have seen you and your Kentish banker very considerably inconvenienced before I would have consented to victimize my horses for the sake of this snobbish party."[2]

"But it won't be a snobbish party," answered the young man impetuously. "Archibald Floyd is the best fellow in Christendom, and as for his daughter——"

"Oh, of course, a divinity, with fifty thousand pounds for her fortune; all of which will no doubt be very tightly settled upon herself if she is ever allowed to marry a penniless scapegrace like Francis Lewis Maldon, of Her Majesty's 11th Hussars. However, I don't want to stand in your way, my boy. Go in and win, and my blessing be upon your virtuous endeavours. I can imagine the young Scotchwoman – red hair (of course you'll call it auburn), large feet, and freckles!"

"Aurora Floyd – red hair and freckles!" The young officer laughed aloud at the stupendous joke. "You'll see her in a quarter of an hour, Bulstrode," he said.

Talbot Bulstrode, Captain of her Majesty's 11th Hussars, had consented to drive his brother-officer from Windsor to Beckenham, and to array himself in his uniform, in order to adorn therewith the festival at Felden Woods, chiefly because, having at two-and-thirty years of age run through all the wealth of life's excitements and amusements, and finding himself a penniless spendthrift in this species of coin, though well enough off for mere sordid riches, he was too tired of himself and the world to care much whither his friends and comrades led him. He was the eldest son of a wealthy Cornish baronet, whose

---

1   A high two-seated carriage drawn by a pair of horses.
2   In the 19th century, a "snob" was someone of a lower rank seeking to emulate or associate with those of superior wealth or rank.

ancestor had received his title straight from the hands of Scottish King James, when baronetcies first came into fashion; the same fortunate ancestor being near akin to a certain noble, erratic, unfortunate, and injured gentleman called Walter Raleigh, and by no means too well used by the same Scottish James. Now of all the pride which ever swelled the breasts of mankind, the pride of Cornishmen is perhaps the strongest; and the Bulstrode family was one of the proudest in Cornwall. Talbot was no alien son of this haughty house; from his very babyhood he had been the proudest of mankind. This pride had been the saving power that had presided over his prosperous career. Other men might have made a downhill road of that smooth pathway which wealth and grandeur made so pleasant; but not Talbot Bulstrode. The vices and follies of the common herd were perhaps retrievable, but vice or folly in a Bulstrode would have left a blot upon a hitherto unblemished escutcheon never to be erased by time or tears. That pride of birth, which was utterly unallied to pride of wealth or station, had a certain noble and chivalrous side, and Talbot Bulstrode was beloved by many a parvenu whom meaner men would have insulted. In the ordinary affairs of life he was as humble as a woman or a child; it was only when Honour was in question that the sleeping dragon of pride which had guarded the golden apples[1] of his youth, purity, probity, and truth, awoke and bade defiance to the enemy. At two-and-thirty he was still a bachelor, not because he had never loved, but because he had never met with a woman whose stainless purity of soul fitted her in his eyes to become the mother of a noble race, and to rear sons who should do honour to the name of Bulstrode. He looked for more than ordinary every-day virtue in the woman of his choice; he demanded those grand and queenly qualities which are rarest in womankind. Fearless truth, a sense of honour keen as his own, loyalty of purpose, unselfishness, a soul untainted by the petty basenesses of daily life, – all these he sought in the being he loved; and at the first warning thrill of emotion caused by a pair of beautiful eyes, he grew critical and captious about their owner, and began to look for infinitesimal stains upon the shining robe of her

---

1   In classical mythology, the golden apples of the Hesperides are guarded by the serpent-dragon Ladon.

virginity. He would have married a beggar's daughter if she had reached his almost impossible standard; he would have rejected the descendant of a race of kings if she had fallen one decimal part of an inch below it. Women feared Talbot Bulstrode; manœuvring mothers shrank abashed from the cold light of those watchful gray eyes; daughters to marry blushed and trembled, and felt their pretty affectations, their ball-room properties, drop away from them under the quiet gaze of the young officer; till from fearing him, the lovely flutterers grew to shun and dislike him, and to leave Bulstrode Castle and the Bulstrode fortune unangled for in the great matrimonial fisheries. So at two-and-thirty Talbot walked serenely safe amid the meshes and pitfalls of Belgravia,[1] secure in the popular belief, that Captain Bulstrode of the 11th Hussars was not a marrying man. This belief was perhaps strengthened by the fact that the Cornishman was by no means the elegant ignoramus whose sole accomplishments consist in parting his hair, waxing his moustaches, and smoking a meerschaum that has been coloured by his valet, and who has become the accepted type of the military man in time of peace.

Talbot Bulstrode was fond of scientific pursuits; he neither smoked, drank, nor gambled. He had only been to the Derby once in his life, and on that one occasion had walked quietly away from the Stand while the great race was being run, and the white faces were turned towards the fatal Corner, and men were sick with terror and anxiety, and frenzied with the madness of suspense. He never hunted, though he rode as well as Mr. Assheton Smith. He was a perfect swordsman, and one of Mr. Angelo's[2] pet pupils; but he had never handled a billiard-cue in his life, nor had he touched a card since the days of his boyhood, when he took a hand at long whist with his father and mother and the parson of the parish, in the south drawing-room at Bulstrode Castle. He had a peculiar aversion to all games of

---

1   The fashionable area around Belgrave Square in London, here used to denote the marriage market of society.

2   Thomas Assheton Smith (1776-1858), sportsman and hunter, was master of the Burton hounds in Lincolnshire from 1806-16 and of the Quorn hounds in Leicestershire from 1816-20. In 1840, he was acclaimed by *Sporting Magazine* as the best fox-hunter of his day. Henry Angelo (1780-1852) was superintendent of sword-exercise to the British army from 1833-52.

chance and skill, contending that it was beneath a gentleman to employ, even for amusement, the implements of the sharper's[1] pitiful trade. His rooms were as neatly kept as those of a woman. Cases of mathematical instruments took the place of cigar-boxes; proof impressions of Raphael adorned the walls ordinarily covered with French prints and water-coloured sporting-sketches from Ackermann's emporium.[2] He was familiar with every turn of expression in Descartes and Condillac, but would have been sorely puzzled to translate the argotic locutions of Monsieur de Kock, *père*.[3] Those who spoke of him summed him up by saying that he wasn't a bit like an officer; but there was a certain cavalry regiment, which he had commanded when a memorable and most desperate charge was made against a bristling wall of Russian cannon,[4] whose ranks told another story of Captain Bulstrode. He had made an exchange into the 11th Hussars on his return from the Crimea, whence, among other distinctions, he had brought a stiff leg, which for a time disqualified him from dancing. It was from pure benevolence, therefore, or from that indifference to all things which is easily mistaken for unselfishness, that Talbot Bulstrode had consented to accept an invitation to the ball at Felden Woods.

The banker's guests were not of that charmed circle familiar to the captain of Hussars; so Talbot, after a brief introduction to his host, fell back among the crowd assembled in one of the doorways, and quietly watched the dancers; not unobserved himself, however, for he was just one of those people who will not pass in a crowd. Tall and broad-chested, with a pale whiskerless face, aquiline nose, clear, cold, gray eyes, thick moustache, and black hair, worn as closely cropped as if he

---

1   Swindler, especially at cards.
2   Rudolph Ackermann, printer and bookseller, located at 96 Strand.
3   Bulstrode's choice of reading is intellectual and philosophical, favouring the French philosophers Réné Descartes and Étienne Condillac over the modern French novelist Paul de Kock, whose rollicking, slangy, and often coarse tales were widely read in England.
4   In the Charge of the Light Brigade (25 October 1854), a mistaken order sent the Light Cavalry Brigade on a heroic but suicidal charge against Russian cannon at Balaclava. Out of 637 officers and men, 247 were wounded or killed. The event was memorialized in Tennyson's "The Charge of the Light Brigade," and was one of the most famous events of the Crimean War.

had lately emerged from Coldbath Fields or Millbank prison,[1] he formed a striking contrast to the yellow-whiskered young cornet who had accompanied him. Even that stiff leg, which in others might have seemed a blemish, added to the distinction of his appearance, and, coupled with the glittering orders on the breast of his uniform, told of deeds of prowess lately done. He took very little delight in the gay assembly revolving before him to one of Charles d'Albert's waltzes.[2] He had heard the same music before, executed by the same band; the faces, though unfamiliar to him, were not new: dark beauties in pink, fair beauties in blue; tall dashing beauties in silks, and laces, and jewels, and splendour; modestly downcast beauties in white crape and rose-buds. They had all been spread for him, those familiar nets of gauze and areophane, and he had escaped them all; and the name of Bulstrode might drop out of the history of Cornish gentry to find no record save upon gravestones, but it would never be tarnished by an unworthy race, or dragged through the mire of a divorce court by a guilty woman.[3] While he lounged against the pillar of a doorway, leaning on his cane, and resting his lame leg, and wondering lazily whether there was anything upon earth that repaid a man for the trouble of living, Cornet Maldon approached him with a woman's gloved hand lying lightly on his arm, and a divinity walking by his side. A divinity! imperiously beautiful in white and scarlet, painfully dazzling to look upon, intoxicatingly brilliant to behold. Captain Bulstrode had served in India, and had once tasted a horrible spirit called *bang*,[4] which made the men who drank it half mad; and he could not help fancying that the beauty of this woman was like the strength of

---

1 Coldbath Fields, erected in 1784, was a notoriously severe prison located on the west side of Clerkenwell. Millbank Prison (in Pimlico) was erected in 1816 in accordance with the views of Jeremy Bentham. Its name was changed from "The Penitentiary" to "Millbank Prison" in 1843.

2 Charles d'Albert (1809-86), a leading composer of dance music.

3 An anachronism: the Divorce Court did not open until January 1858; Aurora's birthday celebration occurs on 15 September 1857. Once the court did open, divorce petitioners had to support their applications with evidence of their spouse's adultery, and, if the petitioner was female, with additional evidence of bigamy, incest, cruelty, etc. Newspaper reporting of such personal details was dreaded and was calculated to be a major deterrent to divorce applications.

4 An infusion of cannabis.

that alcoholic preparation; barbarous, intoxicating, dangerous, and maddening.

His brother-officer presented him to this wonderful creature, and he found that her earthly name was Aurora Floyd, and that she was the heiress of Felden Woods.

Talbot Bulstrode recovered himself in a moment. This imperious creature, this Cleopatra in crinoline, had a low forehead, a nose that deviated from the line of beauty, and a wide mouth. What was she but another trap set in white muslin, and baited with artificial flowers, like the rest? She was to have fifty thousand pounds for her portion, so she didn't want a rich husband; but she was a nobody, so of course she wanted position, and had no doubt read up the Raleigh Bulstrodes in the sublime pages of Burke.[1] The clear gray eyes grew cold as ever, therefore, as Talbot bowed to the heiress. Mr. Maldon found his partner a chair close to the pillar against which Captain Bulstrode had taken his stand, and Mrs. Alexander Floyd swooping down upon the cornet at this very moment, with the dire intent of carrying him off to dance with a lady who executed more of her steps upon the toes of her partner than on the floor of the ball-room, Aurora and Talbot were left to themselves.

Captain Bulstrode glanced downward at the banker's daughter. His gaze lingered upon the graceful head, with its coronal of shining scarlet berries, encircling smooth masses of blue-black hair. He expected to see the modest drooping of the eyelids peculiar to young ladies with long lashes, but he was disappointed; for Aurora Floyd was looking straight before her, neither at him, nor at the lights, nor the flowers, nor the dancers, but far away into vacancy. She was so young, prosperous, admired, and beloved, that it was difficult to account for the dim shadow of trouble that clouded her glorious eyes.

While he was wondering what he should say to her, she lifted her eyes to his face, and asked him the strangest question he had ever heard from girlish lips.

"Do you know if Thunderbolt won the Leger?" she asked.

He was too much confounded to answer for a moment, and she

---

1 Burke's *Peerage*, a dictionary of baronets and peers, first published in 1826 by John Burke.

continued rather impatiently, "They must have heard by six o'clock this evening in London; but I have asked half a dozen people here tonight, and no one seems to know anything about it."

Talbot's close-cropped hair seemed lifted from his head as he listened to this terrible address. Good heavens! what a horrible woman! The hussar's vivid imagination pictured the heir of all the Raleigh Bulstrodes receiving his infantine impressions from such a mother. She would teach him to read out of the 'Racing Calendar;'¹ she would invent a royal alphabet of the turf, and tell him that "D stands for Derby, old England's great race," and "E stands for Epsom, a crack meeting-place," &c. He told Miss Floyd that he had never been to Doncaster in his life, that he had never read a sporting-paper, and that he knew no more of Thunderbolt than of King Cheops.

She looked at him rather contemptuously. "Cheops wasn't much," she said: "he won the Liverpool Autumn Cup in Blink Bonny's year;² but most people said it was a fluke."

Talbot Bulstrode shuddered afresh; but a feeling of pity mingled with his horror. "If I had a sister," he thought, "I would get her to talk to this miserable girl, and bring her to a sense of her iniquity."

Aurora said no more to the captain of Hussars, but relapsed into the old far-away gaze into vacancy, and sat twisting a bracelet round and round upon her finely modelled wrist. It was a diamond bracelet, worth a couple of hundred pounds, which had been given her that day by her father. He would have invested all his fortune in Messrs. Hunt and Roskell's cunning handiwork,³ if Aurora had sighed for gems and gewgaws. Miss Floyd's glance fell upon the glittering ornament, and she looked at it long and earnestly, rather as if she were calculating the value of the stones than admiring the taste of the workmanship.

While Talbot was watching her, full of wondering pity and horror, a young man hurried up to the spot where she was seated, and

---

1   A yearly publication giving particulars of horse-races run or to be run.

2   A chronological error: Blink Bonny won the Derby in 1857, the same year of Aurora's meeting with Bulstrode.

3   One of Victorian England's leading jewellers. Hunt and Roskell's display at the Great Exhibition of 1851 included £100,000 worth of jewellery, including a diamond bouquet of flowers containing nearly 6000 diamonds.

reminded her of an engagement for the quadrille that was forming. She looked at her tablets[1] of ivory, gold, and turquoise, and with a certain disdainful weariness rose and took his arm. Talbot followed her receding form. Taller than most among the throng, her queenly head was not soon lost sight of.

"A Cleopatra with a snub nose two sizes too small for her face, and a taste for horseflesh!" said Talbot Bulstrode, ruminating upon the departed divinity. "She ought to carry a betting-book instead of those ivory tablets. How *distrait*[2] she was all the time she sat here! I dare say she has made a book for the Leger, and was calculating how much she stands to lose. What will this poor old banker do with her? put her into a madhouse, or get her elected a member of the Jockey Club?[3] With her black eyes and fifty thousand pounds, she might lead the sporting world. There has been a female Pope, why should there not be a female 'Napoleon of the Turf'?"[4]

Later, when the rustling leaves of the trees in Beckenham Woods were shivering in that cold gray hour which precedes the advent of the dawn, Talbot Bulstrode drove his friend away from the banker's lighted mansion. He talked of Aurora Floyd during the whole of that long cross-country drive. He was merciless to her follies; he ridiculed, he abused, he sneered at and condemned her questionable tastes. He bade Francis Lewis Maldon marry her at his peril, and wished him joy of *such* a wife. He declared that if he had such a woman for his sister he would shoot her, unless she reformed and burnt her betting-book. He worked himself up into a savage humour about the young lady's delinquencies, and talked of her as if she had done him an unpardonable injury by entertaining a taste for the Turf; till at last the poor meek young cornet plucked up a spirit, and told his superior officer that Aurora Floyd was a very jolly girl, and a good girl, and a perfect

---

1 Dance tablets.
2 Absent-minded; inattentive.
3 Supreme authority in control of horse racing and breeding in Great Britain.
4 The fable of Pope Joan concerns a woman alleged to have been pope in the 9th, 10th, or 11th century. The most widely accepted version claims that Leo IV (d. 855) was succeeded by John Angelicus, who was in fact a woman. According to the fable, Joan's sex was discovered when she gave birth on the road between the Colosseum and St. Clement's. A "Napoleon of the Turf" would resemble Napoleon I in having achieved supremacy in his/her field (here, horse racing) through ruthless ambition.

lady, and that, if she did want to know who won the Leger, it was no business of Captain Bulstrode's, and that he, Bulstrode, needn't make such a howling about it.

While the two men are getting to high words about her, Aurora is seated in her dressing-room, listening to Lucy Floyd's babble about the ball.

"There was never such a delightful party," that young lady said; "and did Aurora see So-and-so, and So-and-so, and So-and-so? and above all, did she observe Captain Bulstrode, who had served all through the Crimean war, and who walked lame, and was the son of Sir John Walter Raleigh Bulstrode, of Bulstrode Castle, near Camelford?"

Aurora shook her head with a weary gesture. No, she hadn't noticed any of these people. Poor Lucy's childish talk was stopped in a moment.

"You are tired, Aurora dear," she said: "how cruel I am to worry you!"

Aurora threw her arms about her cousin's neck, and hid her face upon Lucy's white shoulder.

"I am tired," she said, "very, very tired."

She spoke with such an utterly despairing weariness in her tone, that her gentle cousin was alarmed by her words.

"You are not unhappy, dear Aurora?" she asked anxiously.

"No, no – only tired. There, go, Lucy. Good night, good night."

She gently pushed her cousin from the room, rejected the services of her maid, and dismissed her also. Then, tired as she was, she removed the candle from the dressing-table to a desk on the other side of the room, and seating herself at this desk, unlocked it, and took from one of its inmost recesses the soiled pencil-scrawl which had been given her a week before by the man who tried to sell her a dog in Cockspur Street.

The diamond bracelet, Archibald Floyd's birthday gift to his daughter, lay in its nest of satin and velvet upon Aurora's dressing-table. She took the morocco-case in her hand, looked for a few moments at the jewel, and then shut the lid of the little casket with a sharp metallic snap.

"The tears were in my father's eyes when he clasped the bracelet on my arm," she said, as she reseated herself at the desk. "If he could see me now!"

She wrapped the morocco case in a sheet of foolscap, secured the parcel in several places with red wax and a plain seal, and directed it thus: –

"J.C.,

Care of Mr. Joseph Green,

Bell Inn,

Doncaster."

Early the next morning Miss Floyd drove her aunt and cousin into Croydon, and, leaving them at a Berlin-wool shop, went alone to the post-office, where she registered and posted this valuable parcel.

CHAPTER IV.

AFTER THE BALL.

Two days after Aurora's birthnight festival, Talbot Bulstrode's phaeton dashed once more into the avenue at Felden Woods. Again the captain made a sacrifice on the shrine of friendship, and drove Francis Maldon from Windsor to Beckenham, in order that the young cornet might make those anxious inquiries about the health of the ladies of Mr. Floyd's household, which, by a pleasant social fiction, are supposed to be necessary after an evening of intermittent waltzes and quadrilles.

The junior officer was very grateful for this kindness; for Talbot, though the best of fellows, was not much given to putting himself out of the way for the pleasure of other people. It would have been far pleasanter to the captain to dawdle away the day in his own rooms, lolling over those erudite works which his brother-officers described by the generic title of "heavy reading," or, according to the popular belief of those hare-brained young men, employed in squaring the circle[1] in the solitude of his chamber.

Talbot Bulstrode was altogether an inscrutable personage to his comrades of the 11th Hussars. His black-letter folios, his polished mahogany cases of mathematical instruments, his proof-before-letters engravings,[2] were the fopperies of a young Oxonian rather than an officer who had fought and bled at Inkermann.[3] The young men who breakfasted with him in his rooms trembled as they read the titles of the big books on the shelves, and stared helplessly at the grim saints and angular angels in the pre-Raphaelite

---

1   Attempting to find a square of the same area as a given circle. A famous problem, incapable of geometrical solution.

2   Black-letter folios are those in the Gothic or German type, which was most commonly used in the early days of printing. Proof-before-letters engravings are impressions taken from engraved plates before the printing of the ordinary issue, usually before the inscription is added.

3   One of the major battles of the Crimean War (5 November 1854). British and French forces managed to repulse an unexpected Russian offensive on British positions near Sebastopol. The defensive victory cost more than 2500 British lives.

prints[1] upon the walls. They dared not even propose to smoke in those sacred chambers, and were ashamed of the wet impressions of the rims of the Moselle bottles which they left upon the mahogany cases.

It seemed natural to people to be afraid of Talbot Bulstrode, just as little boys are frightened of a beadle, a policeman, and a schoolmaster, even before they have been told the attributes of these terrible beings. The colonel of the 11th Hussars, a portly gentleman, who rode fifteen stone,[2] and wrote his name high in the Peerage, was frightened of Talbot. That cold gray eye struck a silent awe into the hearts of men and women with its straight penetrating gaze that always seemed to be telling them they were found out. The colonel was afraid to tell his best stories when Talbot was at the mess-table, for he had a dim consciousness that the captain was aware of the discrepancies in those brilliant anecdotes, though that officer had never implied a doubt by either look or gesture. The Irish adjutant forgot to brag about his conquests amongst the fair sex: the younger men dropped their voices when they talked to each other of the side-scenes at Her Majesty's Theatre; and the corks flew faster, and the laughter grew louder, when Talbot left the room.

The captain knew that he was more respected than beloved, and like all proud men who repel the warm feelings of others in utter despite of themselves, he was grieved and wounded because his comrades did not become attached to him.

"Will anybody, out of all the millions upon this wide earth, ever love me?" he thought. "No one ever has as yet. Not even my father and mother. They have been proud of me; but they never loved me. How many a young profligate has brought his parents' gray hairs with sorrow to the grave, and has been beloved with the last heart-beat of those he destroyed, as I have never been in my life! Perhaps my mother would have loved me better, if I had given her more trouble; if I had scattered the name of Bulstrode all over London upon post-obits

---

1   The Pre-Raphaelite Brotherhood, founded in 1848, was inspired by the precision and keenness of fifteenth-century art and devoted to the realistic representation of nature. William Holman Hunt, Dante Gabriel Rossetti and John Everett Millais were among its founding members.

2   A stone is a weight measure equivalent to 14 pounds. Fifteen stone is 210 pounds.

and dishonoured acceptances; if I had been drummed out of my regiment, and had walked down to Cornwall without shoes or stockings, to fall at her feet, and sob out my sins and sorrows in her lap, and ask her to mortgage her jointure for the payment of my debts.[1] But I have never asked anything of her, dear soul, except her love, and that she has been unable to give me. I suppose it is because I do not know how to ask. How often I have sat by her side at Bulstrode, talking of all sorts of indifferent subjects, yet with a vague yearning at my heart to throw myself upon her breast and implore of her to love and bless her son; but held aloof by some icy barrier that I have been powerless all my life to break down! What woman has ever loved me? Not one. They have tried to marry me, because I shall be Sir Talbot Bulstrode of Bulstrode Castle; but how soon they have left off angling for the prize, and shrunk away from me chilled and disheartened! I shudder when I remember that I shall be three-and-thirty next March, and that I have never been beloved. I shall sell out, now the fighting is over, for I am no use amongst the fellows here; and, if any good little thing would fall in love with me, I would marry her and take her down to Bulstrode, to my mother and father, and turn country gentleman."

Talbot Bulstrode made this declaration in all sincerity. He wished that some good and pure creature would fall in love with him, in order that he might marry her. He wanted some spontaneous exhibition of innocent feeling which might justify him in saying, "I am beloved!" He felt little capacity for loving, on his own side; but he thought that he would be grateful to any good woman who would regard him with disinterested affection, and that he would devote his life to making her happy.

"It would be something to feel that if I were smashed in a railway accident, or dropped out of a balloon, some one creature in this world would think it a lonelier place for lack of me. I wonder whether my children would love me? I dare say not. I should freeze their young

---

1 A post-obit bond is issued by an heir to a property, giving the money-lender a lien on the estate after the death of the present owner. An acceptance is a bill of exchange for which one has formally acknowledged liability to pay when due. A jointure is a freehold estate (as in lands or tenements) settled on a widow for her lifetime at least.

affections with the Latin grammar; and they would tremble as they passed the door of my study, and hush their voices into a frightened whisper when papa was within hearing."

Talbot Bulstrode's ideal of woman was some gentle and feminine creature crowned with an aureole of pale auburn hair; some timid soul with downcast eyes, fringed with golden-tinted lashes; some shrinking being, as pale and prim as the mediæval saints in his pre-Raphaelite engravings, spotless as her own white robes, excelling in all womanly graces and accomplishments, but only exhibiting them in the narrow circle of a home.

Perhaps Talbot thought that he had met with his ideal when he entered the long drawing-room at Felden Woods with Cornet Maldon on the seventeenth of September, 1857.

Lucy Floyd was standing by an open piano, with her white dress and pale golden hair bathed in a flood of autumn sunlight. That sunlit figure came back to Talbot's memory long afterwards, after a stormy interval, in which it had been blotted away and forgotten, and the long drawing-room stretched itself out like a picture before his eyes.

Yes, this was his ideal. This graceful girl, with the shimmering light for ever playing upon her hair, and the modest droop in her white eyelids. But undemonstrative as usual, Captain Bulstrode seated himself near the piano, after the brief ceremony of greeting, and contemplated Lucy with grave eyes that betrayed no especial admiration.

He had not taken much notice of Lucy Floyd on the night of the ball; indeed, Lucy was scarcely a candle-light beauty; her hair wanted the sunshine gleaming through it to light up the golden halo about her face, and the delicate pink of her cheeks waxed pale in the glare of the great chandeliers.

While Captain Bulstrode was watching Lucy with that grave contemplative gaze, trying to find out whether she was in any way different from other girls he had known, and whether the purity of her delicate beauty was more than skin deep, the window opposite to him was darkened, and Aurora Floyd stood between him and the sunshine.

The banker's daughter paused on the threshold of the open window, holding the collar of an immense mastiff in both her hands, and looking irresolutely into the room.

Miss Floyd hated morning callers, and she was debating within herself whether she had been seen, or whether it might be possible to steal away unperceived.

But the dog set up a big bark, and settled the question.

"Quiet, Bow-wow," she said; "quiet, quiet, boy."

Yes, the dog was called Bow-wow. He was twelve years old, and Aurora had so christened him in her seventh year, when he was a blundering, big-headed puppy, that sprawled upon the table during the little girl's lessons, upset ink-bottles over her copy-books, and ate whole chapters of Pinnock's abridged histories.[1]

The gentlemen rose at the sound of her voice, and Miss Floyd came into the room and sat down at a little distance from the captain and her cousin, twirling a straw hat in her hand and staring at her dog, who seated himself resolutely by her chair, knocking double-knocks of good temper upon the carpet with his big tail.

Though she said very little, and seated herself in a careless attitude that bespoke complete indifference to her visitors, Aurora's beauty extinguished poor Lucy, as the rising sun extinguishes the stars.

The thick plaits of her black hair made a great diadem upon her low forehead, and crowned her an Eastern empress; an empress with a doubtful nose, it is true, but an empress who reigned by right divine of her eyes and hair. For do not these wonderful black eyes, which perhaps shine upon us only once in a lifetime, in themselves constitute a royalty?

Talbot Bulstrode turned away from his ideal to look at this dark-haired goddess, with a coarse straw hat in her hand and a big mastiff's head lying on her lap. Again he perceived that abstraction in her manner which had puzzled him upon the night of the ball. She listened to her visitors politely, and she answered them when they spoke to her; but it seemed to Talbot as if she constrained herself to attend to them by an effort.

"She wishes me away, I dare say," he thought; "and no doubt considers me a 'slow party,' because I don't talk to her of horses and dogs."

The captain resumed his conversation with Lucy. He found that she talked exactly as he had heard other young ladies talk; that she

---

1   William Pinnock's highly successful abridgements of Goldsmith's histories of England, Greece, and Rome. More than 100 editions were sold before 1858.

knew all they knew, and had been to the places they had visited. The ground they went over was very old indeed, but Lucy traversed it with charming propriety.

"She is a good little thing," Talbot thought; "and would make an admirable wife for a country gentleman. I wish she would fall in love with me."

Lucy told him of some excursion in Switzerland, where she had been during the preceding autumn with her father and mother.

"And your cousin," he asked, "was she with you?"

"No; Aurora was at school in Paris, with the Demoiselles Lespard."

"Lespard, Lespard!" he repeated; "a Protestant pension in the Faubourg Saint-Dominique. Why, a cousin of mine is being educated there, a Miss Trevyllian. She has been there for three or four years. Do you remember Constance Trevyllian at the Demoiselles Lespard, Miss Floyd?" said Talbot, addressing himself to Aurora.

"Constance Trevyllian! Yes, I remember her," answered the banker's daughter.

She said nothing more, and for a few moments there was rather an awkward pause.

"Miss Trevyllian is my cousin," said the captain.

"Indeed!"

"I hope that you were very good friends."

"Oh, yes."

She bent over her dog, caressing his big head, and not even looking up as she spoke of Miss Trevyllian. It seemed as if the subject was utterly indifferent to her, and she disdained even to affect an interest in it.

Talbot Bulstrode bit his lip with offended pride. "I suppose this purse-proud heiress looks down upon the Trevyllians of Tredethlin," he thought, "because they can boast of nothing better than a few hundred acres of barren moorland, some exhausted tin-mines, and a pedigree that dates from the days of King Arthur."

Archibald Floyd came into the drawing-room while the officers were seated there, and bade them welcome to Felden Woods.

"A long drive, gentlemen," he said; "your horses will want a rest. Of course you will dine with us. We shall have a full moon to-night, and you'll have it as light as day for your drive back."

Talbot looked at Francis Lewis Maldon, who was sitting staring at Aurora with vacant, open-mouthed admiration. The young officer knew that the heiress and her fifty thousand pounds were not for him; but it was scarcely the less pleasant to look at her, and wish that like Captain Bulstrode he had been the eldest son of a rich baronet.

The invitation was accepted by Mr. Maldon as cordially as it had been given, and with less than his usual stiffness of manner on the part of Talbot Bulstrode.

The luncheon-bell rang while they were talking, and the little party adjourned to the dining-room, where they found Mrs. Alexander Floyd sitting at the bottom of the table. Talbot sat next to Lucy, with Mr. Maldon opposite to them, while Aurora took her place beside her father.

The old man was attentive to his guests, but the shallowest observer could have scarcely failed to notice his watchfulness of Aurora. It was ever present in his careworn face, that tender, anxious glance which turned to her at every pause in the conversation, and could scarcely withdraw itself from her for the common courtesies of life. If she spoke, he listened, – listened as if every careless, half-disdainful word concealed a deeper meaning which it was his task to discern and unravel. If she was silent, he watched her still more closely, seeking perhaps to penetrate that gloomy veil which sometimes spread itself over her handsome face.

Talbot Bulstrode was not so absorbed by his conversation with Lucy and Mrs. Alexander as to overlook this peculiarity in the father's manner towards his only child. He saw too that when Aurora addressed the banker, it was no longer with that listless indifference, half weariness, half disdain, which seemed natural to her on other occasions. The eager watchfulness of Archibald Floyd was in some measure reflected in his daughter; by fits and starts, it is true, for she generally sank back into that moody abstraction which Captain Bulstrode had observed on the night of the ball; but still it was there, the same feeling as her father's, though less constant and intense. A watchful, anxious, half-sorrowful affection, which could scarcely exist except under abnormal circumstances. Talbot Bulstrode was vexed to find himself wondering about this, and growing every moment less and less attentive to Lucy's simple talk.

"What does it mean?" he thought; "has she fallen in love with some man whom her father has forbidden her to marry, and is the old man trying to atone for his severity? That's scarcely likely. A woman with a head and throat like hers could scarcely fail to be ambitious – ambitious and revengeful, rather than over-susceptible of any tender passion. Did she lose half her fortune upon that race she talked to me about? I'll ask her presently. Perhaps they have taken away her betting-book, or lamed her favourite horse, or shot some pet dog, to cure him of distemper. She is a spoiled child, of course, this heiress, and I dare say her father would try to get a copy of the moon made for her, if she cried for that planet."

After luncheon, the banker took his guests into the gardens that stretched far away upon two sides of the house; the gardens which poor Eliza Floyd had helped to plan nineteen years before.

Talbot Bulstrode walked rather stiffly from his Crimean wound, but Mrs. Alexander and her daughter suited their pace to his, while Aurora walked before them with her father and Mr. Maldon, and with the mastiff close at her side.

"Your cousin is rather proud, is she not?" Talbot asked Lucy, after they had been talking of Aurora.

"Aurora proud! oh, no, indeed: perhaps, if she has any fault at all (for she is the dearest girl that ever lived), it is that she has not sufficient pride; I mean with regard to servants, and that sort of people. She would as soon talk to one of those gardeners as to you or me; and you would see no difference in her manner, except that perhaps it would be a little more cordial to them than to us. The poor people round Felden idolize her."

"Aurora takes after her mother," said Mrs. Alexander; "she is the living image of poor Eliza Floyd."

"Was Mrs. Floyd a countrywoman of her husband's?" Talbot asked. He was wondering how Aurora came to have those great, brilliant, black eyes, and so much of the south in her beauty.

"No; my uncle's wife belonged to a Lancashire family."

A Lancashire family! If Talbot Raleigh Bulstrode could have known that the family name was Prodder; that one member of the haughty house had passed his youth in the pleasing occupations of a cabin-boy, making thick coffee and toasting greasy herrings for the matutinal meal[1] of a surly captain, and receiving more corporal correction from the sturdy toe of his master's boot than sterling copper coin of the realm! If he could have known that the great aunt of this disdainful creature, walking before him in all the majesty of her beauty, had once kept a chandler's shop in an obscure street in Liverpool, and for aught any one but the banker knew, kept it still! But this was a knowledge which had wisely been kept even from Aurora herself, who knew little except that, despite of having been born with that allegorical silver spoon in her mouth, she was poorer than other girls, inasmuch as she was motherless.

Mrs. Alexander, Lucy, and the captain overtook the others upon a rustic bridge, where Talbot stopped to rest. Aurora was leaning over the rough wooden balustrade, looking lazily at the water.

"Did your favourite win the race, Miss Floyd?" he asked, as he watched the effect of her profile against the sunlight; not a very beautiful profile certainly, but for the long black eyelashes, and the radiance under them, which their darkest shadows could never hide.

"Which favourite?" she said.

"The horse you spoke to me about the other night, – Thunderbolt; did he win?"

"No."

"I am very sorry to hear it."

Aurora looked up at him, reddening angrily. "Why so?" she asked.

"Because I thought you were interested in his success."

As Talbot said this, he observed, for the first time, that Archibald Floyd was near enough to overhear their conversation, and, furthermore that he was regarding his daughter with even more than his usual watchfulness.

"Do not talk to me of racing; it annoys papa," Aurora said to the captain, dropping her voice. Talbot bowed. "I was right, then," he thought; "the turf is the skeleton. I dare say Miss Floyd has been doing her best to drag her father's name into the 'Gazette,'[2] and yet he evidently loves her to distraction; while I——" There was something so

1   Breakfast.

2   *The London Gazette*, an official journal issued twice a week, contained lists of government appointments and promotions, names of bankrupts, and other public notices. To "be in the Gazette" meant to be bankrupt.

very pharisaical in the speech, that Captain Bulstrode would not even finish it mentally. He was thinking, "This girl, who, perhaps, has been the cause of nights of sleepless anxiety and days of devouring care, is tenderly beloved by her father; while I, who am a model to all the elder sons of England, have never been loved in my life."

At half-past six the great bell at Felden Woods rang a clamorous peal that went shivering above the trees, to tell the country-side that the family were going to dress for dinner; and another peal at seven, to tell the villagers round Beckenham and West Wickham that Maister Floyd and his household were going to dine; but not altogether an empty or discordant peal, for it told the hungry poor of broken victuals and rich and delicate meats to be had almost for asking in the servants' offices; – shreds of fricandeaux[1] and patches of dainty preparations, quarters of chickens and carcasses of pheasants, which would have gone to fatten the pigs for Christmas, but for Archibald Floyd's strict commands that all should be given to those who chose to come for it.

Mr. Floyd and his visitors did not leave the gardens till after the ladies had retired to dress. The dinner-party was very animated, for Alexander Floyd drove down from the City to join his wife and daughter, bringing with him the noisy boy who was just going to Eton, and who was passionately attached to his cousin Aurora; and whether it was owing to the influence of this young gentleman, or to that fitfulness which seemed a part of her nature, Talbot Bulstrode could not discover, but certain it was that the dark cloud melted away from Miss Floyd's face, and she abandoned herself to the joyousness of the hour with a radiant grace, that reminded her father of the night when Eliza Percival played Lady Teazle[2] for the last time, and took her farewell of the stage in the little Lancashire theatre.

It needed but this change in his daughter to make Archibald Floyd thoroughly happy. Aurora's smiles seemed to shed a revivifying influence upon the whole circle. The ice melted away, for the sun had broken out, and the winter was gone at last. Talbot Bulstrode bewildered his brain by trying to discover why it was that this woman was such a peerless and fascinating creature. Why it was that, argue as he

---

1 Fried or stewed meat, especially veal, served with sauce.
2 The leading female role in Sheridan's *The School for Scandal*.

would against the fact, he was nevertheless allowing himself to be bewitched by this black-eyed siren; freely drinking of that cup of *bang* which she presented to him, and rapidly becoming intoxicated.

"I could almost fall in love with my fair-haired ideal," he thought, "but I cannot help admiring this extraordinary girl. She is like Mrs. Nisbett in her zenith of fame and beauty; she is like Cleopatra sailing down the Cydnus; she is like Nell Gwynne selling oranges; she is like Lola Montes giving battle to the Bavarian students; she is like Charlotte Corday with the knife in her hand, standing behind the friend of the people in his bath;[1] she is like everything that is beautiful, and strange, and wicked and unwomanly, and bewitching; and she is just the sort of creature that many a fool would fall in love with."

He put the length of the room between himself and the enchantress, and took his seat by the grand piano, at which Lucy Floyd was playing slow harmonious symphonies of Beethoven. The drawing-room at Felden Woods was so long, that, seated by this piano, Captain Bulstrode seemed to look back at the merry group about the heiress as he might have looked at a scene on the stage from the back of the boxes. He almost wished for an opera-glass as he watched Aurora's graceful gestures and the play of her sparkling eyes; and then turning to the piano, he listened to the drowsy music, and contemplated Lucy's face, marvellously fair in the light of that full moon of which Archibald Floyd had spoken, the glory of which, streaming in from an open window, put out the dim wax-candles on the piano.

All that Aurora's beauty most lacked was richly possessed by Lucy. Delicacy of outline, perfection of feature, purity of tint, all were there; but while one face dazzled you by its shining splendour, the other

---

1 Talbot associates Aurora with actresses, adventuresses, murderesses, women of extraordinary beauty and heightened sexuality: Louisa Cranstoun Nisbett (1812?-58), an actress of the 1830s and 1840s, noted for her beauty and vivacity; Shakespeare's Cleopatra as she appeared to Mark Antony on her barge on the river Cydnus (*Antony and Cleopatra* II.ii.195-224); Nell Gwynne (1650-1687), the orange girl at Drury Lane who became a leading actress and mistress of Charles II; Lola Montez, pseudonym of Dolores Eliza Rosanna Gilbert (1818-61), Irish dancer and adventuress, whose liaison with King Ludwig I of Bavaria and influence on his policy resulted in mob student opposition and his abdication in 1848; and Charlotte Corday (1768-93), who murdered the French revolutionary Jean-Paul Marat while he was in his bath (a political assassination for which she was immediately arrested and guillotined).

impressed you only with a feeble sense of its charms, slow to come and quick to pass away. There are so many Lucys but so few Auroras; and while you never could be critical with the one, you were merciless in your scrutiny of the other. Talbot Bulstrode was attracted to Lucy by a vague notion that she was just the good and timid creature who was destined to make him happy; but he looked at her as calmly as if she had been a statue, and was as fully aware of her defects as a sculptor who criticises the work of a rival.

But she was exactly the sort of woman to make a good wife. She had been educated to that end by a careful mother. Purity and goodness had watched over her and hemmed her in from her cradle. She had never seen unseemly sights, or heard unseemly sounds. She was as ignorant as a baby of all the vices and horrors of this big world. She was lady-like, accomplished, well informed; and if there were a great many others of precisely the same type of graceful womanhood, it was certainly the highest type, and the holiest, and the best.

Later in the evening, when Captain Bulstrode's phaeton was brought round to the flight of steps in front of the great doors, the little party assembled on the terrace to see the two officers depart, and the banker told his guests how he hoped this visit to Felden would be the beginning of a lasting acquaintance.

"I am going to take Aurora and my niece to Brighton for a month or so," he said, as he shook hands with the captain; "but on our return you must let us see you as often as possible."

Talbot bowed, and stammered his thanks for the banker's cordiality. Aurora and her cousin Percy Floyd, the young Etonian, had gone down the steps, and were admiring Captain Bulstrode's thoroughbred bays, and the captain was not a little distracted by the picture the group made in the moonlight.

He never forgot that picture. Aurora, with her coronet of plaits dead black against the purple air, and her silk dress shimmering in the uncertain light, the delicate head of the bay horse visible above her shoulder, and her ringed white hands caressing the animal's slender ears, while the purblind old mastiff, vaguely jealous, whined complainingly at her side.

How marvellous is the sympathy which exists between some people and the brute creation! I think that horses and dogs understood every word that Aurora said to them, – that they worshipped her from the dim depths of their inarticulate souls, and would have willingly gone to death to do her service. Talbot observed all this with an uneasy sense of bewilderment.

"I wonder whether these creatures are wiser than we?" he thought; "do they recognize some higher attributes in this girl than we can perceive, and worship their sublime presence? If this terrible woman, with her unfeminine tastes and mysterious propensities, were mean, or cowardly, or false, or impure, I do not think that mastiff would love her as he does; I do not think my thorough-breds would let her hands meddle with their bridles: the dog would snarl, and the horses would bite, as such animals used to do in those remote old days when they recognized witchcraft and evil spirits, and were convulsed by the presence of the uncanny. I dare say this Miss Floyd is a good, generous-hearted creature, – the sort of person fast men would call a glorious girl, – but as well read in the 'Racing Calendar' and 'Ruff's Guide' as other ladies in Miss Yonge's novels.[1] I'm really sorry for her."

---

1 While other young ladies (including Lucy) read the pious High-Church novels of Charlotte M. Yonge (1823-1901), Talbot imagines Aurora reading horse-racing guides and periodicals: *Ruff's Guide to the Turf or Pocket Racing Companion* (published from 1842 on) and the *Racing Calendar: Containing an account of the plates, matches, and sweepstakes, run for in Great Britain and Ireland* (established 1776).

CHAPTER V.

JOHN MELLISH.

THE house which the banker hired at Brighton for the month of October was perched high up on the East Cliff, towering loftily above the wind-driven waves; the purple coast of Shoreham was dimly visible from the upper windows in the clear autumn mornings, and the Chain Pier looked like a strip of ribbon below the cliff. A pleasanter situation to my mind than those level terraces towards the west, from the windows of which the sea appears of small extent, and the horizon within half a mile or so of the Parade.

Before Mr. Floyd took his daughter and her cousin to Brighton, he entered into an arrangement which he thought, no doubt, a very great evidence of his wisdom; this was the engagement of a lady, who was to be a compound governess, companion, and chaperon to Aurora, who, as Mrs. Alexander said, was sadly in need of some accomplished and watchful person, whose care it would be to train and prune those exuberant branches of her nature which had been suffered to grow as they would from her infancy. The beautiful shrub was no longer to trail its wild stems along the ground, or shoot upward to the blue skies at its own sweet will; it was to be trimmed and clipped and fastened primly to the stony wall of society with cruel nails and galling strips of cloth. In other words, an advertisement was inserted in the 'Times' newspaper, setting forth that a lady, by birth and education, was required as finishing governess and companion in the household of a gentleman, to whom salary was no object, provided the aforesaid lady was perfect mistress of all the accomplishments under the sun, and was altogether such an exceptional and extraordinary being as could only exist in the advertising columns of a popular journal.

But if the world had been filled with exceptional beings, Mr. Floyd could scarcely have received more answers to his advertisement than came pelting in upon the unhappy little postmaster at Beckenham. The man had serious thoughts of hiring a cart, in which to convey the letters to Felden. If the banker had advertised for a wife, and had stated the amount of his income, he could scarcely have had more answers. It seemed as if the female population of London, with one accord, was seized with the desire to improve the mind and form the manners of the daughter of the gentleman to whom terms were no object. Officers' widows, clergymen's widows, lawyers' and merchants' widows, daughters of gentlemen of high family but reduced means, orphan daughters of all sorts of noble and distinguished people, – declared themselves each and every one to be the person who, out of all living creatures upon this earth, was best adapted for the post. Mrs. Alexander Floyd selected six letters, threw the rest into the waste-paper basket, ordered the banker's carriage, and drove into town to see the six writers thereof. She was a practical and energetic woman, and she put the six applicants through their facings so severely, that when she returned to Mr. Floyd it was to announce that only one of them was good for any thing, and that she was coming down to Felden Woods the next day.

The chosen lady was the widow of an ensign who had died with-in six months of his marriage, and about an hour and a half before he would have succeeded to some enormous property, the particulars of which were never rightly understood by the friends of his unfortu-nate relict. But vague as the story might be, it was quite clear enough to establish Mrs. Walter Powell in life as a disappointed woman. She was a woman with straight light hair, and a lady-like droop of the head. A woman who had left school to marry, and after six months' wedded life had gone back to the same school as instructess of the junior pupils. A woman whose whole existence had been spent in teaching and being taught; who had exercised in her earlier years a species of hand-to-mouth tuition, teaching in the morning that which she learnt over-night; who had never lost an opportunity of improving herself; who had grown mechanically proficient as a musi-cian and an artist, who had a certain parrot-like skill in foreign lan-guages, who had read all the books incumbent upon her to read, and who knew all the things imperative for her to know, and who, beyond all this, and outside the boundary of the schoolroom wall, was igno-rant and soulless and low-minded and vulgar. Aurora swallowed the bitter pill as best she might, and accepted Mrs. Powell as the person chartered for her improvement: – a kind of ballast to be flung into the wandering bark, to steady its erratic course and keep it off rocks and quicksands.

"I must put up with her, Lucy, I suppose," she said; "and I must consent to be improved and formed by the poor faded creature. I wonder whether she will be like Miss Drummond, who used to let me off from my lessons, and read novels while I ran wild in the gardens and stables. I can put up with her, Lucy, as long as I have you with me; but I think I should go mad, if I were to be chained up alone with that grim, pale-faced watch-dog."

Mr. Floyd and his family drove from Felden to Brighton in the banker's roomy travelling-carriage, with Aurora's maid in the rumble, a pile of imperials[1] upon the roof, and Mrs. Powell, with her young charges, in the interior of the vehicle. Mrs. Alexander had gone back to Fulham, having done her duty, as she considered, in securing a protectress for Aurora; but Lucy was to stay with her cousin at Brighton, and to ride with her on the downs. The saddle-horses had gone down the day before with Aurora's groom, a gray-haired and rather surly old fellow who had served Archibald Floyd for thirty years; and the mastiff called Bow-wow travelled in the carriage with his mistress.

About a week after the arrival at Brighton, Aurora and her cousin were walking together on the West Cliff, when a gentleman with a stiff leg rose from a bench upon which he had been seated listening to the band, and slowly advanced to them. Lucy dropped her eyelids with a faint blush; but Aurora held out her hand in answer to Captain Bulstrode's salute.

"I thought I should be sure to meet you down here, Miss Floyd," he said. "I only came this morning, and I was going to call at Folthorpe's for your papa's address. Is he quite well?"

"Quite – yes, that is – pretty well." A shadow stole over her face as she spoke. It was a wonderful face for fitful lights and shades. "But we did not expect to see you at Brighton, Captain Bulstrode; we thought your regiment was still quartered at Windsor."

"Yes, my regiment – that is, the Eleventh is still at Windsor; but I have sold out."[2]

---

1 Luggage trunks adapted for the roof of a coach or carriage.
2 Sold his army commission.

"Sold out!" Both Aurora and her cousin opened their eyes at this intelligence.

"Yes; I was tired of the army. It's dull work now the fighting is all over. I might have exchanged and gone to India, certainly," he added, as if in answer to some argument of his own; "but I'm getting middle-aged, and I am tired of roaming about the world."

"I should like to go to India," said Aurora, looking seaward as she spoke.

"You, Aurora! but why?" exclaimed Lucy.

"Because I hate England."

"I thought it was France you disliked."

"I hate them both. What is the use of this big world, if we are to stop for ever in one place, chained to one set of ideas, fettered to one narrow circle of people, seeing and hearing of the persons we hate for ever and ever, and unable to get away from the odious sound of their names? I should like to turn female missionary, and go to the centre of Africa with Dr. Livingstone and his family;[1] and I would go if it wasn't for papa."

Poor Lucy stared at her cousin in helpless amazement. Talbot Bulstrode found himself falling back into that state of bewilderment in which this girl always threw him. What did she mean, this heiress of nineteen years of age, by her fits of despondency and outbursts of bitterness? Was it not perhaps, after all, only an affectation of singularity?

Aurora looked at him with her brightest smile while he was asking himself this question. "You will come and see papa?" she said.

Captain Bulstrode declared that he desired no greater happiness than to pay his respects to Mr. Floyd, in token whereof he walked with the young ladies towards the East Cliff.

From that morning, the officer became a constant visitor at the banker's. He played chess with Lucy, accompanied her on the piano when she sang, assisted her with valuable hints when she painted in

---

1   David Livingstone (1813-73), African missionary and explorer. Livingstone's wife Mary (daughter of another African missionary) lived in Africa with him from 1844-52 and, together with their children, accompanied him on some of his travels. After his first years of African exploration (1841-56), Livingstone returned to England a national hero. He set off to Africa again in 1858, accompanied by his wife and youngest son. Mary Livingstone died of fever at Shupanga on 27 April 1862.

water-colours, put in lights here and glimpses of sky there, deepened autumnal browns, and intensified horizon purples, and made himself altogether useful to the young lady, who was, as we know, accomplished in all lady-like arts. Mrs. Powell, seated in one of the windows of the pleasant drawing-room, shed the benignant light of her faded countenance and pale-blue eyes upon the two young people, and represented all the proprieties in her own person; Aurora, when the weather prevented her riding, occupied herself more restlessly than profitably by taking up books and tossing them down, pulling Bow-wow's ears, staring out of the windows, drawing caricatures of the promenaders on the cliff, and dragging out a wonderful little watch, with a bunch of dangling inexplicable golden absurdities, to see what o'clock it was.

Talbot Bulstrode, while leaning over Lucy's piano or drawing-board, or pondering about the next move of his queen, had ample leisure to watch the movements of Miss Floyd, and to be shocked at the purposeless manner in which that young lady spent the rainy mornings. Sometimes he saw her poring over 'Bell's Life,'[1] much to the horror of Mrs. Walter Powell, who had a vague idea of the iniquitous proceedings recited in that terrible journal, but who was afraid to stretch her authority so far as to forbid its perusal.

Mrs. Powell looked with silent approbation upon the growing familiarity between gentle Lucy Floyd and the captain. She had feared at first that Talbot was an admirer of Aurora's; but the manner of the two soon dispelled her alarm. Nothing could be more cordial than Miss Floyd's treatment of the officer; but she displayed the same indifference to him that she did to every thing else, except her dog and her father. Was it possible that well-nigh perfect face and those haughty graces had no charm for the banker's daughter? Could it be that she could spend hour after hour in the society of the handsomest and most aristocratic man she had ever met, and yet be as heart-whole as when the acquaintance began? There was one person in the little party who was for ever asking that question, and never able to answer it to her own satisfaction, and that person was Lucy Floyd. Poor Lucy Floyd, who was engaged, night and day, in mentally playing that old

---

1   *Bell's Life in London*, the premier sporting paper of the mid-Victorian period.

German game which Faust and Margaret played together with the full-blown rose in the garden, – "He loves me – loves me not!"[1]

Mrs. Walter Powell's shallow-sighted blue eyes might behold in Lucy Captain Bulstrode's attraction to the East Cliff; but Lucy herself knew better – bitterly, cruelly better.

"Captain Bulstrode's attentions to Miss Lucy Floyd were most evident," Mrs. Powell said one day when the captain left, after a long morning's music and singing and chess. How Lucy hated the prim phrase! None knew so well as she the value of those "attentions." They had been at Brighton six weeks, and for the last five the captain had been with them nearly every morning. He had ridden with them on the downs, and driven with them to the Dyke, and lounged beside them listening to the band, and stood behind them in their box at the pretty little theatre, and crushed with them into the Pavilion to hear Grisi and Mario, and Alboni and poor Bosio.[2] He had attended them through the whole round of Brighton amusements, and had never seemed weary of their companionship. But for all this, Lucy knew what the last leaf upon the rose would tell her, when the many petals should be plucked away, and the poor stem be left bare. She knew how often he forgot to turn over the leaf in the Beethoven sonatas; how often he put streaks of green into an horizon that should have been purple, and touched up the trees in her foreground with rose-pink, and suffered himself to be ignominiously checkmated from sheer inattention, and gave her wandering, random answers when she spoke to him. She knew how restless he was when Aurora read 'Bell's Life,' and how the very crackle of the newspaper made him wince with nervous pain. She knew how tender he was of the purblind mastiff, how eager to be friends with him, how almost sycophantic in his attentions to the big stately animal. Lucy knew, in short, that which

---

1   In the garden scene of Goethe's *Faust* (1808), Margarete pulls the petals off a flower (probably a daisy, not a rose), in order to divine Faust's love for her.

2   The Pavilion at Brighton, Sussex, was built between 1815-21 by John Nash, personal architect of the Prince of Wales, later George IV. Giulia Grisi (1811-69) was a famous Italian soprano and operatic prima donna; Giovanni Mario (1810-83) Grisi's husband and a celebrated operatic tenor; Marietta Alboni (1823-94) an Italian operatic contralto; and Angiolina Bosio (1830-59) a leading soprano, whose brilliant success lasted from 1853 to her early death in 1859.

Talbot as yet did not know himself: she knew that he was fast falling over head and ears in love with her cousin, and she had at the same time a vague idea that he would much rather have fallen in love with herself, and that he was blindly struggling with the growing passion.

It was so; he was falling in love with Aurora. The more he protested against her, the more determinedly he exaggerated her follies, and argued with himself upon the folly of loving her, so much the more surely did he love her. The very battle he was fighting kept her for ever in his mind, until he grew the veriest slave of the lovely vision, which he only evoked in order to endeavour to exorcise.

"How could he take her down to Bulstrode, and introduce her to his father and mother?" he thought; and at the thought she appeared to him illuminating the old Cornish mansion by the radiance of her beauty, fascinating his father, bewitching his mother, riding across the moorland on her thorough-bred mare, and driving all the parish mad with admiration of her.

He felt that his visits to Mr. Floyd's house were fast compromising him in the eyes of its inmates. Sometimes he felt himself bound in honour to make Lucy an offer of his hand; sometimes he argued that no one had any right to consider his attentions more particular to one than to the other of the young ladies. If he had known of that weary game which Lucy was for ever mentally playing with the imaginary rose, I am sure he would not have lost an hour in proposing to her; but Mrs. Alexander's daughter had been far too well educated to betray one emotion of her heart, and she bore her girlish agonies, and concealed her hourly tortures, with the quiet patience common to these simple womanly martyrs. She knew that the last leaf must soon be plucked, and the sweet pain of uncertainty be for ever ended.

Heaven knows how long Talbot Bulstrode might have done battle with his growing passion, had it not been for an event which put an end to his indecision and made him desperate. This event was the appearance of a rival.

He was walking with Aurora and Lucy upon the West Cliff one afternoon in November, when a mail-phaeton and pair suddenly drew up against the railings that separated them from the road, and a big man, with huge masses of Scotch plaid twisted about his waist and shoulders, sprang out of the vehicle, splashing the mud upon his legs, and rushed up to Talbot, taking off his hat as he approached, and bow-ing apologetically to the ladies.

"Why, Bulstrode," he said, "who on earth would have thought of seeing you here? I heard you were in India, man; but what have you done to your leg?"

He was so breathless with hurry and excitement, that he was utterly indifferent to punctuation; and it seemed as much as he could do to keep silence while Talbot introduced him to the ladies as Mr. Mellish, an old friend and school-fellow. The stranger stared with such open-mouthed admiration at Miss Floyd's black eyes, that the captain turned round upon him almost savagely, as he asked what had brought *him* to Brighton.

"The hunting season, my boy. Tired of Yorkshire; know every field, ditch, hedge, pond, sunk fence, and scrap of timber in the three Ridings.[1] I'm staying at the Bedford; I've got my stud with me – give you a mount to-morrow morning if you like. Harriers meet at eleven – Dyke Road. I've a gray that'll suit you to a nicety – carry my weight, and as easy to sit as your arm-chair."

Talbot hated his friend for talking of horses; he felt a jealous terror of him. This, perhaps, was the sort of man whose society would be agreeable to Aurora, – this big, empty-headed Yorkshireman, with his babble about his stud and hunting appointments. But turning sharply round to scrutinize Miss Floyd, he was gratified to find that young lady looking vacantly at the gathering mists upon the sea, and apparently unconscious of the existence of Mr. John Mellish, of Mellish Park, Yorkshire.

This John Mellish was, I have said, a big man, looking even bigger than he was by reason of about eight yards' length of thick shepherd's plaid twisted scientifically about his shoulders. He was a man of thirty years of age at least, but having withal such a boyish exuberance in his manner, such a youthful and innocent joyousness in his face, that he might have been a youngster of eighteen just let loose from some public academy of the muscular Christianity school. I think the Rev. Charles Kingsley[2] would have delighted in this big, hearty, broad-

---

1   The three administrative districts of Yorkshire: the East, West, and North Ridings.

2   Muscular Christianity Schools inculcated the values of Christian manliness represented in, for example, *Tom Brown's Schooldays* (1857), where schoolboy pluck and fair play at games are shown to mature into the adult virtues of moral action, patriotism, and Christian gentlemanliness. The clergyman and novelist Charles Kingsley (1819-75) was an important proponent of Muscular Christianity.

chested young Englishman, with brown hair brushed away from an open forehead, and a thick auburn moustache bordering a mouth for ever ready to expand into a laugh. Such a laugh, too! such a hearty and sonorous peal, that the people on the Parade turned round to look at the owner of those sturdy lungs, and smiled good-naturedly for very sympathy with his honest merriment.

Talbot Bulstrode would have given a hundred pounds to get rid of the noisy Yorkshireman. What business had he at Brighton? Wasn't the biggest county in England big enough to hold him, that he must needs bring his north-country bluster to Sussex, for the annoyance of Talbot's friends?

Captain Bulstrode was not any better pleased when, strolling a little further on, the party met with Archibald Floyd, who had come out to look for his daughter. The old man begged to be introduced to Mr. Mellish, and invited the honest Yorkshireman to dine at the East Cliff that very evening, much to the aggravation of Talbot, who fell sulkily back, and allowed John to make the acquaintance of the ladies. The familiar brute ingratiated himself into their good graces in about ten minutes; and by the time they reached the banker's house was more at his ease with Aurora than was the heir of Bulstrode after two months' acquaintance. He accompanied them to the door-step, shook hands with the ladies and Mr. Floyd, patted the mastiff Bow-wow, gave Talbot a playful sledge-hammer-like slap upon the shoulder, and ran back to the Bedford to dress for dinner. His spirits were so high that he knocked over little boys and tumbled against fashionable young men, who drew themselves up in stiff amazement as the big fellow dashed past them. He sang a scrap of a hunting-song as he ran up the great staircase to his eyrie at the Bedford, and chattered to his valet as he dressed. He seemed a creature especially created to be prosperous; to be the owner and dispenser of wealth, the distributor of good things. People who were strangers to him ran after and served him on speculation, knowing instinctively that they would get ample reward for their trouble. Waiters in a coffee-room deserted other tables to attend upon that at which he was seated. Box-keepers would leave parties of six shivering in the dreary corridors while they found a seat for John Mellish. Mendicants picked him out from the crowd in a busy thoroughfare, and hung about him, and would not be driven away without a dole from the pocket of his roomy waistcoat. He was always spending his money for the convenience of other people. He had an army of old servants at Mellish Park, who adored him and tyrannized over him after the manner of their kind. His stables were crowded with horses that were lame, or wall-eyed, or otherwise disqualified for service, but that lived on his bounty like a set of jolly equine paupers, and consumed as much corn as would have supplied a racing stud. He was perpetually paying for things he neither ordered nor had, and was for ever being cheated by the dear honest creatures about him, who, for all they did their best to ruin him, would have gone through typical fire and water to serve him, and would have clung to him, and worked for him, and supported him out of those very savings for which they had robbed him, when the ruin came. If "Muster John" had a headache, every creature in that disorderly household was unhappy and uneasy till the ailment was cured; every lad in the stables, every servant-maid in the house, was eager that his or her remedy should be tried for his restoration. If you had said at Mellish Park that John's fair face and broad shoulders were not the highest forms of manly beauty and grace, you would have been set down as a creature devoid of all taste or judgement. To the mind of that household, John Mellish in "pink" and pipe-clayed tops was more beautiful than the Apollo Belvidere,[1] whose bronze image in little adorned a niche in the hall. If you had told them that fourteen-stone weight[2] was not indispensable to manly perfection, or that it was possible there were more lofty accomplishments than driving unicorn[3] or shooting forty-seven head of game in a morning, or pulling the bay mare's shoulder into joint that time she got a sprain in the hunting-field, or vanquishing Joe Millings, the East Riding smasher, without so much as losing breath, – those simple-hearted Yorkshire servants would have fairly laughed in your face. Talbot Bulstrode complained that everybody respected him, and nobody loved him. John Mellish might have uttered the reverse of this complaint, had he been so

---

1   "Pink" refers to a scarlet hunting jacket; tops are top-boots, also used for hunting. Pipe-clay is a fine white clay used for cleaning white fabrics. The Apollo Belvedere statue, located in the Vatican Museum, is a restored Roman copy of the Greek original, attributed to Leochares (4th century BC). The Apollo's only garments are his cape, fig leaf, and sandals.
2   Fourteen stone equals 196 lbs.
3   Driving three horses, two abreast and one in front.

minded. Who could help loving the honest, generous squire, whose house and purse were open to all the country-side? Who could feel any chilling amount of respect for the friendly and familiar master who sat upon the table in the big kitchen at Mellish Park, with his dogs and servants round him, and gave them the history of the day's adventures in the hunting-field, till the old blind fox-hound at his feet lifted his big head and set up a feeble music? No; John Mellish was well content to be beloved, and never questioned the quality of the affection bestowed upon him. To him it was all the purest virgin gold; and you might have talked to him for twelve hours at a sitting without convincing him that men and women were vile and mercenary creatures, and that if his servants, and his tenantry, and the poor about his estate, loved him, it was for the sake of the temporal benefits they received of him. He was as unsuspicious as a child, who believes that the fairies in a pantomime are fairies for ever and ever, and that the harlequin is born in patches and a mask. He was as open to flattery as a school-girl who distributes the contents of her hamper among a circle of toadies. When people told him he was a fine fellow, he believed them, and agreed with them, and thought that the world was altogether a hearty, honest place, and that everybody was a fine fellow. Never having an *arrière pensée*[1] himself, he looked for none in the words of other people, but thought that every one blurted out their real opinions, and offended or pleased their fellows, as frankly and blunderingly as himself. If he had been a vicious young man, he would no doubt have gone altogether to the bad, and fallen among thieves. But being blest with a nature that was inherently pure and innocent, his greatest follies were no worse than those of a big school-boy who errs from very exuberance of spirit. He had lost his mother in the first year of his infancy, and his father had died some time before his majority; so there had been none to restrain his actions, and it was something at thirty years of age to be able to look back upon a stainless boyhood and youth, which might have been befouled with the slime of the gutters, and infected with the odour of villanous haunts. Had he not reason to be proud of this?

Is there anything, after all, so grand as a pure and unsullied life – a fair picture, with no ugly shadows lurking in the background – a

---

1   A hidden meaning.

smooth poem, with no crooked, halting line to mar the verse – a noble book, with no unholy page – a simple story, such as our children may read? Can any greatness be greater? can any nobility be more truly noble? When a whole nation mourned with one voice but a few months since; when we drew down our blinds and shut out the dull light of the December day,[1] and listened sadly to the far booming of the guns; when the poorest put aside their work-a-day troubles to weep for a widowed Queen and orphaned children in a desolate palace; when rough omnibus-drivers forgot to blaspheme at each other, and tied decent scraps of crape upon their whips, and went sorrowfully about their common business, thinking of that great sorrow at Windsor, – the words that rose simultaneously to every lip dwelt most upon the spotless character of him who was lost; the tender husband, the watchful father, the kindly master, the liberal patron, the temperate adviser, the stainless gentleman.

It is many years since England mourned for another royal personage who was called a "gentleman." A gentleman who played practical jokes, and held infamous orgies, and persecuted a wretched foreign woman, whose chief sin and misfortune it was to be his wife; a gentleman who cut out his own nether garments, and left the companion of his gayest revels, the genius whose brightness had flung a spurious lustre upon the dreary saturnalia of vice, to die destitute and despairing.[2] Surely there is some hope that we have changed for the better within the last thirty years, inasmuch as we attach a new meaning today to this simple title of "gentleman." I take some pride, therefore, in

---

1   Prince Albert died on 14 December 1861, aged 42.

2   George IV was notorious for his dissolute lifestyle. The "wretched foreign woman" was his estranged wife, Caroline of Brunswick, who returned from Italy a few months after George IV's accession in 1820 to claim her rights as Queen Consort. A bill accusing her of adultery and depriving her of such rights was introduced in the House of Lords and resulted in her humiliating eleven-week "trial". (She died in 1821.) The companion of the Prince Regent's revels was the dandy Beau Brummell, with whom George quarrelled in 1812. Brummell fled to France in 1816 to avoid creditors and lived for fourteen years hopelessly in debt. The reference to "cutting out" garments – and indeed much of this passage – echoes Thackeray's 1845 poem, "Georgius Ultimus," and his 1855 lecture tour, in which he satirized George IV's falsehood, vanity, and excess: "He never acted well by Man or Woman,/ And was as false to his Mistress as to his Wife./ He deserted his Friends and his Principles./ He was so ignorant that he could scarcely Spell;/ But he had some Skill in cutting out Coats. . ." (*Punch*, 11 October 1845).

the two young men of whom I write, for the simple reason that I have no dark patches to gloss over in the history of either of them. I may fail in making you like them; but I can promise that you shall have no cause to be ashamed of them. Talbot Bulstrode may offend you with his sulky pride; John Mellish may simply impress you as a blundering countrified ignoramus; but neither of them shall ever shock you by an ugly word or an unholy thought.

CHAPTER VI.

REJECTED AND ACCEPTED.

THE dinner-party at Mr. Floyd's was a very merry one; and when John Mellish and Talbot Bulstrode left the East Cliff to walk westward, at eleven o'clock at night, the Yorkshireman told his friend that he had never enjoyed himself so much in his life. This declaration must, however, be taken with some reserve; for it was one which John was in the habit of making about three times a week: but he really had been very happy in the society of the banker's family; and, what was more, he was ready to adore Aurora Floyd without any further preparation whatever.

A few bright smiles and sparkling glances, a little animated conversation about the hunting-field and the race-course, combined with half a dozen glasses of those effervescent wines which Archibald Floyd imported from the fair Moselle country, had been quite enough to turn the head of John Mellish, and to cause him to hold wildly forth in the moonlight upon the merits of the beautiful heiress.

"I verily believe I shall die a bachelor, Talbot," he said, "unless I can get that girl to marry me. I've only known her half a dozen hours, and I'm head-over-heels in love with her already. What is it that has knocked me over like this, Bulstrode? I've seen other girls with black eyes and hair, and she knows no more of horses than half the women in Yorkshire; so it isn't that. What is it, then, hey?"

He came to a full stop against a lamp-post, and stared fiercely at his friend as he asked this question.

Talbot gnashed his teeth in silence.

It was no use battling with his fate, then, he thought; the fascination of this woman had the same effect upon others as upon himself; and while he was arguing with, and protesting against, his passion, some brainless fellow, like this Mellish, would step in and win the prize.

He wished his friend good night upon the steps of the Old Ship Hotel, and walked straight to his room, where he sat with his window open to the mild November night, staring out at the moon-lit sea. He determined to propose to Aurora Floyd before twelve o'clock the next day.

Why should he hesitate?

He had asked himself that question a hundred times before, and had always been unable to answer it; and yet he had hesitated. He could not dispossess himself of a vague idea that there was some mystery in this girl's life; some secret known only to herself and her father; some one spot upon the history of the past which cast a shadow on the present. And yet, how could that be? How could that be, he asked himself, when her whole life only amounted to nineteen years, and he had heard the history of those years over and over again? How often he had artfully led Lucy to tell him the simple story of her cousin's girlhood! The governesses and masters that had come and gone at Felden Woods. The ponies and dogs, and puppies and kittens, and petted foals; the little scarlet riding-habit that had been made for the heiress, when she rode after the hounds with her cousin Andrew Floyd. The worst blots that the officer could discover in those early years were a few broken china vases, and a great deal of ink spilt over badly-written French exercises. And after being educated at home until she was nearly eighteen, Aurora had been transferred to a Parisian finishing-school; and that was all. Her life had been the every-day life of other girls of her own position, and she differed from them only in being a great deal more fascinating, and a little more wilful, than the majority.

Talbot laughed at himself for his doubts and hesitations. "What a suspicious brute I must be," he said, "when I imagine I have fallen upon the clue to some mystery simply because there is a mournful tenderness in the old man's voice when he speaks to his only child! If I were sixty-seven years of age, and had such a daughter as Aurora, would there not always be a shuddering terror mingled with my love, – a horrible dread that something would happen to take her away from me? I will propose to Miss Floyd to-morrow."

Had Talbot been thoroughly candid with himself, he would perhaps have added, "Or John Mellish will make her an offer the day after."

Captain Bulstrode presented himself at the house on the East Cliff some time before noon on the next day; but he found Mr. Mellish on the door-step, talking to Miss Floyd's groom and inspecting the horses, which were waiting for the young ladies; for the young ladies were going to ride, and John Mellish was going to ride with them.

"But if you'll join us, Bulstrode," the Yorkshireman said, good-naturedly, "you can ride the gray I spoke of yesterday. Saunders shall go back and fetch him."

Talbot rejected this offer rather sulkily. "I've my own horses here, thank you," he answered. "But if you'll let your groom ride down to the stables and tell my man to bring them up, I shall be obliged to you."

After which condescending request Captain Bulstrode turned his back upon his friend, crossed the road, and folding his arms upon the railings, stared resolutely at the sea. But in five minutes more the ladies appeared upon the door-step, and Talbot, turning at the sound of their voices, was fain to cross the road once more for the chance of taking Aurora's foot in his hand as she sprang into her saddle; but John Mellish was before him again, and Miss Floyd's mare was curveting under the touch of her light hand before the captain could interfere. He allowed the groom to attend to Lucy, and, mounting as quickly as his stiff leg would allow him, he prepared to take his place by Aurora's side. Again he was too late; Miss Floyd had cantered down the hill attended by Mellish, and it was impossible for Talbot to leave poor Lucy, who was a timid horsewoman.

The captain never admired Lucy so little as on horseback. His pale saint with the halo of golden hair seemed to him sadly out of place in a side-saddle. He looked back at the day of his morning visit to Felden, and remembered how he had admired her, and how exactly she corresponded with his ideal, and how determined he was to be bewitched by her rather than by Aurora. "If she had fallen in love with me," he thought, "I would have snapped my fingers at the black-browed heiress, and married this fair-haired angel out of hand. I meant to do that when I sold my commission. It was not for Aurora's sake I left the army, it was not Aurora whom I followed down here. Which did I follow? What did I follow, I wonder? My destiny, I suppose, which is leading me through such a witch's dance as I never thought to tread at the sober age of three-and-thirty. If Lucy had only loved me, it might have been all different."

He was so angry with himself, that he was half inclined to be angry with poor Lucy for not extricating him from the snares of Aurora. If he could have read that innocent heart, as he rode in sulky silence across the stunted turf on the wide downs! If he could have known the slow sick pain in that gentle breast, as the quiet girl by his side lifted her blue eyes every now and then to steal a glance at his hard profile and moody brow! If he could have read her secret later, when, talking of Aurora, he for the first time clearly betrayed the mystery of his own heart! If he could have known how the landscape grew dim before her eyes, and how the brown moorland reeled beneath her horse's hoofs until they seemed going down, down, down into some fathomless depth of sorrow and despair! But he knew nothing of this; and he thought Lucy Floyd a pretty, inanimate girl, who would no doubt be delighted to wear a becoming dress as bridesmaid at her cousin's wedding.

There was to be a dinner-party that evening upon the East Cliff, to which both John Mellish and Talbot were invited; and the captain savagely determined to bring matters to an issue before the night was out.

Talbot Raleigh Bulstrode would have been very angry with you, had you watched him too closely that evening as he fastened the golden solitaire in his narrow cravat before his looking-glass in the bow-window at the Old Ship. He was ashamed of himself for being causelessly savage with his valet, whom he dismissed abruptly before he began to dress; and had not the courage to call the man back again when his own hot hands refused to do their office. He spilt half a bottleful of perfume upon his varnished boots, and smeared his face with a scented waxy compound bought of Monsieur Eugène Rimmel, which promised to *lisser sans graisser* his moustache.[1] He broke one of the crystal-boxes in his dressing-case, and put the bits of broken glass in his waistcoat-pocket from sheer absence of mind. He underwent semi-strangulation with the unbending circular collar in which, as a gentleman, it was his duty to invest himself; and he could have beaten

---

[1] "Smooth (his moustache) without making it greasy." Eugène Rimmel (1820–87) was the author of *The Book of Perfumes* (1865) and the inventor of Rimmel's perfume vaporizer for diffusing fragrances in apartments, ball rooms, etc.

the ivory backs of his brushes upon his head in blind execration of that short, stubborn black hair, which only curled at the *other ends*; and when at last he emerged from his room, it was with a spiteful sensation that every waiter in the place knew his secret, and had a perfect knowledge of every emotion in his breast, and that the very Newfoundland dog lying on the door-step had an inkling of the truth, as he lifted up his big head to look at the captain, and then dropped it again with a contemptuously lazy yawn.

Captain Bulstrode offered a handful of broken glass to the man who drove him to the East Cliff, and then confusedly substituted about fifteen shillings worth of silver coin for that abnormal species of payment. There must have been two or three earthquakes and an eclipse or so going on in some part of the globe, he thought, for this jog-trot planet seemed all tumult and confusion to Talbot Bulstrode. The world was all Brighton, and Brighton was all blue moonlight, and steel-coloured sea, and glancing, dazzling gas-light, and hare-soup and cod and oysters, and Aurora Floyd. Yes, Aurora Floyd, who wore a white silk dress, and a thick circlet of dull gold upon her hair, who looked more like Cleopatra to-night than ever, and who suffered Mr. John Mellish to take her down to dinner. How Talbot hated the Yorkshireman's big fair face, and blue eyes, and white teeth, as he watched the two young people across a phalanx of glass and silver, and flowers and wax-candles, and pickles, and other Fortnum-and-Mason ware![1] Here was a golden opportunity lost, thought the discontented captain, forgetful that he could scarcely have proposed to Miss Floyd at the dinner-table, amidst the jingle of glasses and popping of corks, and with a big powdered footman charging at him with a side-dish or a sauce-tureen while he put the fatal question. The desired moment came a few hours afterwards, and Talbot had no longer any excuse for delay.

The November evening was mild, and the three windows in the drawing-room were open from floor to ceiling. It was pleasant to look out from the hot gas-light upon that wide sweep of moon-lit ocean, with a white sail glimmering here and there against the purple

---

1 High-quality food products from Fortnum and Mason, the exclusive London department store which began as a grocery shop in 1707.

night. Captain Bulstrode sat near one of the open windows, watching that tranquil scene, with, I fear, very little appreciation of its beauty. He was wishing that the people would drop off and leave him alone with Aurora. It was close upon eleven o'clock, and high time they went. John Mellish would of course insist upon waiting for Talbot; this was what a man had to endure on account of some old schoolboy acquaintance. All Rugby[1] might turn up against him in a day or two, and dispute with him for Aurora's smiles. But John Mellish was engaged in a very animated conversation with Archibald Floyd, having contrived with consummate artifice to ingratiate himself in the old man's favour, and the visitors having one by one dropped off, Aurora, with a listless yawn that she took little pains to conceal, strolled out on to the broad iron balcony. Lucy was sitting at a table at the other end of the room, looking at a book of beauty.[2] Oh, my poor Lucy! how much did you see of the Honourable Miss Brownsmith's high forehead and Roman nose? Did not that young lady's handsome face stare up at you dimly through a blinding mist of tears that you were a great deal too well educated to shed? The chance had come at last. If life had been a Haymarket comedy, and the entrances and exits arranged by Mr. Buckstone[3] himself, it could have fallen out no better than this. Talbot Bulstrode followed Aurora on to the balcony; John Mellish went on with his story about the Beverley foxhounds; and Lucy, holding her breath at the other end of the room, knew as well what was going to happen as the captain himself.

Is not life altogether a long comedy, with Fate for the stage-manager, and Passion, Inclination, Love, Hate, Revenge, Ambition, and Avarice by turns in the prompter's box? A tiresome comedy sometimes, with dreary, talkee-talkee front scenes which come to nothing, but only serve to make the audience more impatient as they wait

---

1   Elite public school for boys, which under the headship of Thomas Arnold from 1828-42 became the model British public school for succeeding generations.

2   Annual published between 1833-47, aimed at affluent middle-class women readers. Published by Charles Heath and edited by Lady Blessington, it featured lavish illustrations of fashionable ladies, and was elegantly bound in figured silk, velvet, or gilt morocco.

3   John Baldwin Buckstone (1802-79), Victorian comic actor and dramatist, who managed the Theatre Royal, Haymarket, from 1853-76.

while the stage is set and the great people change their dresses; or a "sensation" comedy,[1] with unlooked-for tableaux and unexpected *dénouements*; but a comedy to the end of the chapter, for the sorrows which seem tragic to us are very funny when seen from the other side of the foot-lights; and our friends in the pit are as much amused with our trumpery griefs as the Haymarket *habitués* when Mr. Box finds his gridiron empty, or Mr. Cox misses his rasher. What can be funnier than other people's anguish? Why do we enjoy Mr. Maddison Morton's farces, and laugh till the tears run down our cheek at the comedian who enacts them? Because there is scarcely a farce upon the British stage which is not, from the rising to the dropping of the curtain, a record of human anguish and undeserved misery. Yes, undeserved and unnecessary torture – there is the special charm of the entertainment. If the man who was weak enough to send his wife to Camberwell *had* crushed a baby behind a chest of drawers, his sufferings wouldn't be half so delightful to an intellectual audience. If the gentleman who became embroiled with his laundress *had* murdered the young lady in the green boots, where would be the fun of that old Adelphi farce in which poor Wright was wont to delight us?[2] And so it is with our friends on the other side of the footlights, who enjoy our troubles all the more because we have not always deserved them, and whose sorrows we shall gloat over by-and-by, when the bell for the next piece begins, and it is their turn to go on and act.

Talbot Bulstrode went out on to the balcony, and the earth stood still for ten minutes or so, and every steel-blue star in the sky glared watchfully down upon the young man in this the supreme crisis of his life.

Aurora was leaning against a slender iron pilaster, looking aslant into the town and across the town to the sea. She was wrapped in an opera cloak; no stiff, embroidered, young-ladyfied garment; but a

---

1 See 52, n.1.

2 See John Maddison Morton, *Box and Cox* (first performed 1 November 1847 at the Lyceum); Joseph Stirling Coyne, *Did you EVER Send Your Wife to Camberwell?* (first performed 16 March 1846 at the Adelphi); and *How to Settle Accounts with your Laundress* (first performed 26 July 1847, also at the Adelphi, starring Edward Wright). Habitués of the Haymarket theatre would have seen performances of *Box and Cox, Married and Settled* in October 1852; *How to Settle Accounts with Your Laundress* in August 1848; and *Did you EVER Send Your Wife to Camberwell?* in July 1848.

voluminous drapery of soft scarlet woollen stuff, such as Semiramide[1] herself might have worn. "She looks like Semiramide," Talbot thought. "How did this Scotch banker and his Lancashire wife come to have an Assyrian for their daughter?"

He began brilliantly, this young man, as lovers generally do.

"I am afraid you must have fatigued yourself this evening, Miss Floyd," he remarked.

Aurora stifled a yawn as she answered him. "I am rather tired," she said.

It wasn't very encouraging. How was he to begin an eloquent speech, when she might fall asleep in the middle of it? But he did; he dashed at once into the heart of his subject, and he told her how he loved her; how he had done battle with this passion, which had been too strong for him; how he loved her as he never thought to love any creature upon this earth; and how he cast himself before her in all humility to take his sentence of life or death from her dear lips.

She was silent for some moments, her profile sharply distinct to him in the moonlight, and those dear lips trembling visibly. Then, with a half-averted face, and in words that seemed to come slowly and painfully from a stifled throat, she gave him his answer.

That answer was a rejection!

Not a young lady's No, which means Yes to-morrow; or which means perhaps that you have not been on your knees in a passion of despair, like Lord Edward Fitz-Morkysh in Miss Oderose's last novel. Nothing of this kind; but a calm negative, carefully and tersely word-ed, as if she feared to mislead him by so much as one syllable that could leave a loophole through which hope might creep into his heart. He was rejected. For a moment it was quite as much as he could do to believe it. He was inclined to imagine that the significa-tion of certain words had suddenly changed, or that he had been in the habit of mistaking them all his life, rather than that those words meant this hard fact; namely, that he, Talbot Raleigh Bulstrode, of

---

1 Semiramide, Queen of Babylon, who murders her husband and is attracted to her own son; the title role of Rossini's opera *Semiramide* (1823).

Bulstrode Castle, and of Saxon extraction,[1] had been rejected by the daughter of a Lombard-Street banker.

He paused – for an hour and a half or so, as it seemed to him – in order to collect himself before he spoke again.

"May I – venture to inquire," he said, – how horribly commonplace the phrase seemed! he could have used no worse had he been inquiring for furnished lodgings, – "may I ask if any prior attachment – to one more worthy——"

"Oh, no, no, no!"

The answer came upon him so suddenly, that it almost startled him as much as her rejection.

"And yet your decision is irrevocable?"

"Quite irrevocable."

"Forgive me if I am intrusive; but – but Mr. Floyd may perhaps have formed some higher views——"

He was interrupted by a stifled sob as she clasped her hands over her averted face.

"Higher views!" she said; "poor dear old man! no, no, indeed."

"It is scarcely strange that I bore you with these questions. It is so hard to think that, meeting you with your affections disengaged, I have yet been utterly unable to win one shadow of regard upon which I might build a hope for the future."

Poor Talbot! Talbot, the splitter of metaphysical straws and chopper of logic, talking of building hopes on shadows, with a lover's delirious stupidity.

"It is so hard to resign every thought of your ever coming to alter your decision of to-night, Aurora," – he lingered on her name for a moment, first because it was so sweet to say it, and secondly, in the hope that she would speak, – "it is so hard to remember the fabric of happiness I had dared to build, and to lay it down here to-night for ever."

---

1 Anglo-Saxons were fashionable in the 1860s, seen as representing sturdy English resistance to Norman-French invaders. This is reflected in Kingsley's *Hereward the Wake* (1866), E.A. Freeman's elegy for Saxon England, *The History of the Norman Conquest* (Vol. 1 published 1867), and William Theed's 1867 statue of Victoria and (the late) Albert in Anglo-Saxon dress.

Talbot quite forgot that, up to the time of the arrival of John Mellish, he had been perpetually arguing against his passion, and had declared to himself over and over again that he would be a consummate fool if he was ever beguiled into making Aurora his wife. He reversed the parable of the fox; for he had been inclined to make faces at the grapes while he fancied them within his reach, and now that they were removed from his grasp, he thought that such delicious fruit had never grown to tempt mankind.

"If – if," he said, "my fate had been happier, I know how proud my father, poor old Sir John, would have been of his eldest son's choice."

How ashamed he felt of the meanness of this speech! The artful sentence had been constructed in order to remind Aurora whom she was refusing. He was trying to bribe her with the baronetcy which was to be his in due time. But she made no answer to the pitiful appeal. Talbot was almost choked with mortification. "I see – I see," he said, "that it is hopeless. Good night, Miss Floyd."

She did not even turn to look at him as he left the balcony; but with her red drapery wrapped tightly round her, stood shivering in the moonlight, with the silent tears slowly stealing down her cheeks.

"Higher views!" she cried bitterly, repeating a phrase that Talbot used, – "higher views! God help him!"

"I must wish you good-night and good-bye at the same time," Captain Bulstrode said, as he shook hands with Lucy.

"Good-bye?"

"Yes; I leave Brighton early to-morrow."

"So suddenly?"

"Why, not exactly suddenly. I always meant to travel this winter. Can I do anything for you – at Cairo?"

He was so pale and cold and wretched-looking, that she almost pitied him – pitied him in spite of the wild joy growing up in her heart. Aurora had refused him – it was perfectly clear – refused *him*! The soft blue eyes filled with tears at the thought that a demigod should have endured such humiliation. Talbot pressed her hand gently in his own clammy palm. He could read pity in that tender look, but possessed no lexicon by which he could translate its deeper meaning.

"You will wish your uncle good-bye for me, Lucy," he said. He called her Lucy for the first time; but what did it matter now? His great affliction set him apart from his fellow-men, and gave him dismal privileges. "Good-night, Lucy; good-night and good-bye. I – I – shall hope to see you again – in a year or two."

The pavement of the East Cliff seemed so much air beneath Talbot Bulstrode's boots as he strode back to the Old Ship; for it is peculiar to us, in our moments of supreme trouble or joy, to lose all consciousness of the earth we tread, and to float upon an atmosphere of sublime egotism.

But the captain did not leave Brighton the next day on the first stage of his Egyptian journey. He stayed at the fashionable watering-place; but he resolutely abjured the neighbourhood of the East Cliff, and, the day being wet, took a pleasant walk to Shoreham through the rain; and Shoreham being such a pretty place, he was no doubt much enlivened by that exercise.

Returning through the fog at about four o'clock, the captain met Mr. John Mellish close against the turnpike outside Cliftonville.

The two men stared aghast at each other.

"Why, where on earth are you going?" asked Talbot.

"Back to Yorkshire by the first train that leaves Brighton."

"But this isn't the way to the station!"

"No; but they're putting the horses in my portmanteau, and my shirts are going by the Leeds cattle-train; and——"

Talbot Bulstrode burst into a loud laugh, a harsh and bitter cachinnation, but affording wondrous relief to that gentleman's overcharged breast.

"John Mellish," he said, "you have been proposing to Aurora Floyd."

The Yorkshireman turned scarlet. "It – it – wasn't honourable of her to tell you," he stammered.

"Miss Floyd has never breathed a word to me upon the subject. I've just come from Shoreham, and you've only lately left the East Cliff. You've proposed, and you've been rejected."

"I have," roared John; "and it's deuced hard when I promised her she should keep a racing stud if she liked, and enter as many colts as she pleased for the Derby, and give her own orders to the trainer, and I'd never interfere; – and – and Mellish Park is one of the finest places in the county; and I'd have won her a bit of blue ribbon to tie up her bonny black hair."

"That old Frenchman was right," muttered Captain Bulstrode: "there *is* a great satisfaction in the misfortune of others.[1] If I go to my dentist, I like to find another wretch in the waiting-room; and I like to have my tooth extracted first, and to see him glare enviously at me as I come out of the torture chamber, knowing that my troubles are over, while his are to come. Good-bye, John Mellish, and God bless you. You're not such a bad fellow after all."

Talbot felt almost cheerful as he walked back to the Ship, and he took a mutton cutlet and tomata sauce, and a pint of Moselle for his dinner: and the food and wine warmed him; and not having slept a wink on the previous night, he fell into a heavy indigestible slumber, with his head hanging over the sofa-cushion, and dreamt that he was at Grand Cairo (or at a place which would have been that city had it not been now and then Bulstrode Castle, and occasionally chambers in the Albany); and that Aurora Floyd was with him, clad in imperial purple, with hieroglyphics on the hem of her robe, and wearing a clown's jacket of white satin and scarlet spots, such as he had once seen foremost in a great race. Captain Bulstrode arose early the next morning, with the full intention of departing from Sussex by the 8.45 express; but suddenly remembering that he had but poorly acknowledged Archibald Floyd's cordiality, he determined on sacrificing his inclinations on the shrine of courtesy, and calling once more at the East Cliff to take leave of the banker. Having once resolved upon this line of action, the captain would fain have hurried that moment to Mr. Floyd's house; but finding that it was only half-past seven, he was compelled to restrain his impatience and await a more seasonable hour. Could he go at nine? Scarcely. At ten? Yes, surely, as he could then leave by the eleven o'clock train. He sent his breakfast away untouched, and sat looking at his watch in a mad hurry for the time to pass, yet growing hot and uncomfortable as the hour drew near.

At a quarter to ten he put on his hat and left the hotel. Mr. Floyd

---

1 François, Duc de la Rochefoucauld (1613-80) in *Maximes Suprimés*: "*Dans l'adversité de nos meilleurs amis, nous trouvons toujours quelque chose qui ne nous déplaît pas.*" (We can always find something in the misfortune of our best friends that is not altogether displeasing.)

was at home, the servant told him – upstairs in the little study, he thought. Talbot waited for no more. "You need not announce me," he said; "I know where to find your master."

The study was on the same floor as the drawing-room; and close against the drawing-room door Talbot paused for a moment. The door was open; the room empty; no, not empty: Aurora Floyd was there, seated with her back towards him, and her head leaning on the cushions of her chair. He stopped for another moment to admire the back view of that small head with its crown of lustrous raven hair, then took a step or two in the direction of the banker's study; then stopped again, then turned back, went into the drawing-room, and shut the door behind him.

She did not stir as he approached her, nor answer when he stammered her name. Her face was as white as the face of a dead woman, and her nerveless hands hung over the cushions of the arm-chair. A newspaper was lying at her feet. She had quietly swooned away sitting there by herself, with no one by to restore her to consciousness.

Talbot flung some flowers from a vase on the table, and dashed the water over Aurora's forehead; then wheeling her chair close to the open window, he set her with her face to the wind. In two or three moments she began to shiver violently, and soon afterwards opened her eyes, and looked at him; as she did so, she put her hands to her head, as if trying to remember something. "Talbot!" she said, "Talbot!"

She called him by his Christian name, she who five-and-thirty hours before had coldly forbidden him to hope.

"Aurora," he cried, "Aurora, I thought I came here to wish your father good-bye; but I deceived myself. I came to ask you once more, and once for all, if your decision of the night before last was irrevocable."

"Heaven knows I thought it was when I uttered it."

"But it was not?"

"Do you wish me to revoke it?"

"Do I wish? do I——"

"Because if you really do, I will revoke it; for you are a brave and honourable man, Captain Bulstrode, and I love you very dearly."

Heaven knows into what rhapsodies he might have fallen, but she put up her hand, as much as to say, "Forbear to-day, if you love me," and hurried from the room. He had accepted the cup of *bang* which the siren had offered, and had drained the very dregs thereof, and was drunken. He dropped into the chair in which Aurora had sat, and, absent-minded in his joyful intoxication, picked up the newspaper that had lain at her feet. He shuddered in spite of himself as he looked at the title of the journal; it was 'Bell's Life.' A dirty copy, crumpled, and beer-stained, and emitting rank odours of inferior tobacco. It was directed to Miss Floyd, in such sprawling penmanship as might have disgraced the potboy of a sporting public-house: –

"MISS FLOID,
fell dun wodes,
kent."

The newspaper had been redirected to Aurora by the housekeeper at Felden. Talbot ran his eye eagerly over the front page; it was almost entirely filled with advertisements (and such advertisements!), but in one column there was an account headed, "FRIGHTFUL ACCIDENT in GERMANY: AN ENGLISH JOCKEY KILLED."

Captain Bulstrode never knew why he read of this accident. It was in no way interesting to him, being an account of a steeple-chase in Prussia, in which a heavy English rider and a crack French horse had been killed. There was a great deal of regret expressed for the loss of the horse, and none for the man who had ridden him, who, the reporter stated, was very little known in sporting circles; but in a paragraph lower down was added this information, evidently procured at the last moment: "The jockey's name was Conyers."

CHAPTER VII.

AURORA'S STRANGE PENSIONER.

ARCHIBALD FLOYD received the news of his daughter's choice with evident pride and satisfaction. It seemed as if some heavy burden had been taken away, as if some cruel shadow had been lifted from the lives of father and daughter.

The banker took his family back to Felden Woods, with Talbot Bulstrode in his train; and the chintz rooms – pretty, cheerful chambers, with bow-windows that looked across the well-kept stable-yard into long glades of oak and beech – were prepared for the ex-hussar, who was to spend his Christmas at Felden.

Mrs. Alexander and her husband were established with her family in the western wing; Mr. and Mrs. Andrew were located at the eastern angle; for it was the hospitable custom of the old banker to summon his kinsfolk about him early in December, and to keep them with him till the bells of picturesque Beckenham church had heralded in the New Year.

Lucy Floyd's cheeks had lost much of their delicate colour when she returned to Felden, and it was pronounced, by all who observed the change, that the air of the East Cliff, and the autumn winds drifting across the bleak downs, had been too much for the young lady's strength.

Aurora seemed to have burst forth into some new and more glorious beauty since the morning upon which she had accepted the hand of Talbot Bulstrode. There was a proud defiance in her manner, which became her better than gentleness becomes far lovelier women. There was a haughty *insouciance* about this young lady which gave new brilliancy to her great black eyes, and new music to her joyous laugh. She was like some beautiful noisy, boisterous waterfall; for ever dancing, rushing, sparkling, scintillating, and utterly defying you to do anything but admire it. Talbot Bulstrode, having once abandoned himself to the spell of the siren, made no further struggle, but fairly fell into the pitfalls of her eyes, and was entangled in the meshy network of her blue-black hair. The greater the tension of the bow-string, the stronger the rebound thereof; and Talbot Bulstrode was as weak to give way at last as he had long been powerful to resist. I must write his story in the commonest words. He could not help it! He loved her; not because he thought her better, or wiser, or lovelier, or more suited to him than many other women, – indeed he had grave doubts upon every one of these points, – but because it was his destiny, and he loved her.

What is that hard word which M. Victor Hugo puts into the mouth of the priest in 'The Hunchback of Notre Dame' as an excuse for the darkness of his sin? 'ANAΓKH![1] It was his fate! So he wrote to his mother, and told her that he had chosen a wife, who was to sit in the halls of Bulstrode, and whose name was to be interwoven with the chronicles of the house; told her, moreover, that Miss Floyd was a banker's daughter, beautiful and fascinating, with big black eyes, and fifty thousand pounds for her dowry. Lady Raleigh Bulstrode answered her son's letter upon a quarter of a quire of note-paper, filled with fearful motherly prayers and suggestions; anxious hopes that he had chosen wisely; questionings as to the opinions and religious principles of the young lady, – much indeed that Talbot would have been sorely puzzled to answer. Enclosed in this was a letter to Aurora, a womanly and tender epistle, in which pride was tempered with love, and which brought big tears welling up to Miss Floyd's eyes, until Lady Bulstrode's firm penmanship grew blotted and blurred beneath the reader's vision.

And whither went poor slaughtered John Mellish? He returned to Mellish Park, carrying with him his dogs, and horses, and grooms, and phaeton, and paraphernalia; but his grief – having unluckily come upon him after the racing season – was too much for him, and he fled away from the roomy old mansion, with its pleasant surroundings of park and woodland; for Aurora Floyd was not for him, and it was all flat, stale, and unprofitable.[2] So he went to Paris, or *Parry*, as he called that imperial city, and established himself in the biggest chambers at Meurice's, and went backwards and forwards between that establishment and Galignani's ten times a day, in quest of the English papers.

---

1   (Greek): force, constraint, necessity, fatality. (See *The Hunchback of Notre-Dame*, Book 6, Chapter 4.)
2   *Hamlet* I.ii.133.

He dined drearily at Véfour's, Philippe's, the Trois Frères, the Maison Dorée, and the Café de Paris. His big voice was heard at every expensive dining place in Paris, ordering "*Toos killyar de mellyour: vous savez;*"[1] but he sent the daintiest dishes away untasted, and would sit for a quarter of an hour counting the toothpicks in the tiny blue vases, and thinking of Aurora. He rode dismally in the Bois de Boulogne, and sat shivering in *cafés chantants*,[2] listening to songs that always seemed set to the same melody. He haunted the circuses, and was wellnigh in love with a fair *manége* rider,[3] who had black eyes, and reminded him of Aurora; till, upon buying the most powerful opera-glass that the Rue de Rivoli could afford, he discovered that the lady's face was an inch deep in a certain white wash called *blanc rosati*,[4] and that the chief glory of her eyes were the rings of Indian ink which surrounded them. He could have dashed that double-barrelled truth-revealer to the ground, and trodden the lenses to powder with his heel, in his passion of despair: better to have been for ever deceived, to have gone on believing that woman to be like Aurora, and to have gone to that circus every night until his hair grew white, but not with age, and until he pined away and died.

The party at Felden Woods was a very joyous one. The voices of children made the house pleasant; noisy lads from Eton and Westminster clambered about the balustrades of the staircases, and played battledore-and-shuttlecock upon the long stone terrace. These young people were all cousins to Aurora Floyd, and loved the banker's daughter with a childish worship, which mild Lucy could never inspire. It was pleasant to Talbot Bulstrode to see that wherever his future wife trod, love and admiration waited upon her footsteps. He was not singular in his passion for this glorious creature, and it could be, after all, no such terrible folly to love one who was beloved by all who knew her. So the proud Cornishman was happy, and gave himself up to his happiness without further protest.

Did Aurora love him? Did she make him due return for the

---

1 "*Tout ce qu'il y a de meilleur, vous savez*" ("Everything of the best, you know!"). The spelling represents Mellish's English accent.
2 Cafés providing musical entertainment.
3 Skilled rider of a trained horse; here, a circus rider.
4 White paint for the face.

passionate devotion, the blind adoration? She admired and esteemed him; she was proud of him – proud of that very pride in his nature which made him so different to herself; and she was too impulsive and truthful a creature to keep this sentiment a secret from her lover. She revealed, too, a constant desire to please her betrothed husband, suppressing at least all outward token of the tastes that were so unpleasant to him. No more copies of 'Bell's Life' littered the ladies' morning-room at Felden; and when Andrew Floyd asked Aurora to ride to meet with him, his cousin refused the offer which would once have been so welcome. Instead of following the Croydon hounds, Miss Floyd was content to drive Talbot and Lucy in a basket-carriage through the frost-bespangled country-side. Lucy was always the companion and confidante of the lovers; it was hard for her to hear their happy talk of the bright future stretching far away before them – stretching down, down the shadowy aisles of Time, to an escutcheoned tomb at Bulstrode, where husband and wife would lie down, full of years and honours, in the days to come. It was hard to have to help them plan a thousand schemes of pleasure, in which – Heaven pity her! – she was to join. But she bore her cross meekly, this pale Elaine[1] of modern days; and she never told Talbot Bulstrode that she had gone mad and loved him, and was fain to die.

Talbot and Aurora were both concerned to see the pale cheeks of their gentle companion; but everybody was ready to ascribe them to a cold, or a cough, or constitutional debility, or some other bodily evil, which was to be cured by drugs and boluses; and no one for a moment imagined that anything could possibly be amiss with a young lady who lived in a luxurious house, went shopping in a carriage and pair, and had more pocket-money than she cared to spend. But the Lily Maid of Astolat lived in a lordly castle, and had doubtless ample pocket-money to buy gorgeous silks for her embroidery, and had little on earth to wish for, and nothing to do; whereby she fell sick for love of Sir Lancelot, and pined and died.

Surely the secret of many sorrows lies in this. How many a grief

---

1 Lucy's love for Talbot is compared to that of Elaine of Astolat for Lancelot in Arthurian legend. Tennyson had recently retold the story of Elaine in *Idylls of the King* (1859).

has been bred of idleness and leisure! How many a Spartan youth has nursed a bosom-devouring fox for very lack of better employment! Do the gentlemen who write the leaders in our daily journals ever die of grief? Do the barristers whose names appear in almost every case reported in those journals go mad for love unrequited? Did the LADY WITH THE LAMP[1] cherish any foolish passion in those days and nights of ceaseless toil, in those long watches of patient devotion far away in the East? Do the curates of over-crowded parishes, the chaplains of gaols and convict-ships, the great medical attendants in the wards of hospitals – do they make for themselves the griefs that kill? Surely not. With the busiest of us there may be some holy moments, some sacred hour snatched from the noise and confusion of the revolving wheel of Life's machinery, and offered up as a sacrifice to sorrow and care; but the interval is brief, and the great wheel rolls on, and we have no time to pine or die.

So Lucy Floyd, having nothing better to do, nursed and made much of her hopeless passion. She set up an altar for the skeleton, and worshipped at the shrine of her grief; and when people told her of her pale face, and the family doctor wondered at the failure of his quinine mixture, perhaps she nourished a vague hope that before the spring-time came back again, bringing with it the wedding-day of Talbot and Aurora, she would have escaped from all this demonstrative love and happiness, and be at rest.

Aurora answered Lady Raleigh Bulstrode's letter with an epistle expressive of such gratitude and humility, such earnest hope of winning the love of Talbot's mother, mingled with a dim fearfulness of never being worthy of that affection, as won the Cornish lady's regard for her future daughter. It was difficult to associate the impetuous girl with that letter, and Lady Bulstrode made an image of the writer that very much differed from the fearless and dashing original. She wrote Aurora a second letter, more affectionately worded than the first, and promised the motherless girl a daughter's welcome at Bulstrode.

"Will she ever let me call her 'mother,' Talbot?" Aurora asked, as

---

1 Florence Nightingale (1820-1910), who superintended the first government-appointed women nurses sent to the British army during the Crimean War (1854-56).

she read Lady Bulstrode's second letter, to her lover. "She is very proud, is she not? – proud of your ancient descent? My father comes from a Glasgow mercantile family, and I do not even know anything about my mother's relations."

Talbot answered her with a grave smile.

"She will accept you for your native worth, dearest Aurora," he said, "and will ask no foolish questions about the pedigree of such a man as Archibald Floyd; a man whom the proudest aristocrat in England might be glad to call his father-in-law. She will reverence my Aurora's transparent soul and candid nature, and will bless me for the choice I have made."

"I shall love her very dearly if she will only let me. Should I have ever cared about horse-racing, and read sporting-papers, if I could have called a good woman 'mother?'"

She seemed to ask this question rather of herself than of Talbot.

Complete as was Archibald Floyd's satisfaction at his daughter's disposal of her heart, the old man could not calmly contemplate a separation from this idolized daughter; so Aurora told Talbot that she could never take up her abode in Cornwall during her father's lifetime; and it was finally arranged that the young couple were to spend half the year in London, and the other half at Felden Woods. What need had the lonely widower of that roomy mansion, with its long picture-gallery and snug suites of apartments, each of them large enough to accommodate a small family? What need had one solitary old man of that retinue of servants, the costly stud in the stables, the new-fangled vehicles in the coach-houses, the hot-house flowers, the pines and grapes and peaches, cultivated by three Scottish gardeners? What need had he of these things? He lived principally in the study in which he had once had a stormy interview with his only child; the study in which hung the crayon portrait of Eliza Floyd; the room which contained an old-fashioned desk he had bought for a guinea in his boyhood, and in which there were certain letters written by a hand that was dead, some tresses of purple-black hair cut from the head of a corpse, and a pasteboard ticket, printed at a little town in Lancashire, calling upon the friends and patrons of Miss Eliza Percival to come to the theatre, for her especial benefit, upon the night of August 20, 1837.

It was decided, therefore, that Felden Woods was to be the country residence of Talbot and Aurora, till such time as the young man should succeed to the baronetcy and Bulstrode Castle, and be required to live upon his estate. In the mean time the ex-hussar was to go into Parliament, if the electors of a certain little borough in Cornwall, which had always sent a Bulstrode to Westminster, should be pleased to return him.

The marriage was to take place early in May, and the honeymoon was to be spent in Switzerland and at Bulstrode Castle. Mrs. Walter Powell thought that her doom was sealed, and that she would have to quit those pleasant pastures after the wedding-day; but Aurora speedily set the mind of the ensign's widow at rest by telling her that as she, Miss Floyd, was utterly ignorant of housekeeping, she would be happy to retain her services after marriage as guide and adviser in such matters.

The poor about Beckenham were not forgotten in Aurora Floyd's morning drives with Lucy and Talbot. Parcels of grocery and bottles of wine often lurked beneath the crimson-lined leopard-skin carriage-rug; and it was no uncommon thing for Talbot to find himself making a footstool of a huge loaf of bread. The poor were very hungry in that bright December weather, and had all manner of complaints, which, however otherwise dissimilar, were all to be benefited by one especial treatment; namely, half-sovereigns, old brown sherry, French brandy, and gunpowder tea.[1] Whether the daughter was dying of consumption, or the father laid up with the rheumatics, or the husband in a raging fever, or the youngest boy recovering from a fall into a copper of boiling water, the above-named remedies seemed alike necessary, and were far more popular than the chicken-broths and cooling fever-drinks prepared by the Felden cook. It pleased Talbot to see his betrothed dispensing good things to the eager recipients of her bounty. It pleased him to think how even his mother must have admired this high-spirited girl, content to sit down in close cottage chambers and talk to rheumatic old women. Lucy distributed little parcels of tracts prepared by Mrs. Alexander, and flannel garments

---

1 An expensive green tea. See 248, where it is described as costing seven shillings a pound.

made by her own white hands; but Aurora gave the half-sovereigns and the old sherry; and I'm afraid these simple cottagers liked the heiress best; although they were wise enough and just enough to know that each lady gave according to her means.

It was in returning from a round of these charitable visits that an adventure befel the little party, which was by no means pleasing to Captain Bulstrode.

Aurora had driven further than usual, and it was striking four as her ponies dashed past Beckenham church and down the hill towards Felden Woods. The afternoon was cold and cheerless; light flakes of snow drifted across the hard road, and hung here and there upon the leafless hedges, and there was that inky blackness in the sky which presages a heavy fall. The woman at the lodge ran out with her apron over her head to open the gates as Miss Floyd's ponies approached, and at the same moment a man rose from a bank by the roadside, and came close up to the little carriage.

He was a broad-shouldered, stout-built fellow, wearing a shabby velveteen cut-away coat, slashed about with abnormal pockets, and white and greasy at the seams and elbows. His chin was muffled in two or three yards of dirty woollen comforter, after the fashion of his kind; and the band of his low-crowned felt hat was ornamented with a short clay pipe, coloured of a respectable blackness. A dingy white dog, with a brass-collar, bow legs, a short nose, blood-shot eyes, one ear, a hanging jaw, and a generally supercilious expression of countenance, rose from the bank at the same moment with his master, and growled ominously at the elegant vehicle and the mastiff Bow-wow trotting by its side.

The stranger was the same individual who had accosted Miss Floyd in Cockspur Street three months before.

I do not know whether Aurora recognized this person; but I know that she touched her ponies' ears with the whip, and that the spirited animals had dashed past the man, and through the gates of Felden, when he sprang forward, caught at their heads, and stopped the light basket-carriage, which rocked under the force of his strong hand.

Talbot Bulstrode leapt from the vehicle, heedless of his stiff leg, and caught the man by the collar.

"Let go that bridle!" he cried, lifting his cane; "how dare you stop this lady's ponies?"

"Because I wanted to speak to her, that's why. Let go o' my coat, will yer?"

The dog made at Talbot's legs, but the young man whirled round his cane and inflicted such chastisement upon the snub nose of that animal as sent him into temporary retirement, howling dismally.

"You are an insolent scoundrel, and I've a good mind to———"

"Yer'd be hinserlent, p'raps, if yer was hungry," answered the man, with a pitiful whine, which was meant to be conciliating. "Such weather as this here's all very well for young swells such as you, as has your dawgs and guns and 'untin'; but the winter's tryin' to a poor man's temper, when he's industrious and willin', and can't get a stroke of honest work to do, or a mouthful of vittals. I only want to speak to the young lady; she knows me well enough."

"Which young lady?"

"Miss Floyd; the heiress."

They were standing a little way from the pony-carriage. Aurora had risen from her seat and flung the reins to Lucy; she was looking towards the two men, pale and breathless, doubtless terrified for the result of the encounter.

Talbot released the man's collar, and went back to Miss Floyd.

"Do you know this person, Aurora?" he asked.

"Yes."

"He is one of your old pensioners, I suppose?"

"He is; do not say anything more to him, Talbot. His manner is rough, but he means no harm. Stop with Lucy while I speak to him."

Rapid and impetuous in all her movements, she sprang from the carriage and joined the man beneath the bare branches of the trees before Talbot could remonstrate.

The dog, which had crawled slowly back to his master's side, fawned upon her as she approached, and was driven away by a fierce growl from Bow-wow, who was little likely to brook any such vulgar rivalry.

The man removed his felt hat, and tugged ceremoniously at a tuft of sandyish hair which ornamented his low forehead.

"You might have spoken to a cove[1] without all this here row, Miss Floyd," he said, in an injured tone.

Aurora looked at him indignantly.

"Why did you stop me here?" she said; "why couldn't you write to me?"

"Because writin's never so much good as speakin', and because such young ladies as you are uncommon difficult to get at. How did I know that your pa mightn't have put his hand upon my letter, and there'd have been a pretty to do? though I dessay, as for that, if I was to go up to the house, and ask the old gent for a trifle, he wouldn't be back'ard in givin' it. I dessay he'd be good for a fi'-pun note; or a tenner, if it came to that."

Aurora's eyes flashed sparks of fire as she turned upon the speaker. "If ever you dare to annoy my father you shall pay dearly for it, Matthew Harrison," she said; "not that I fear anything you can say, but I will not have him annoyed; I will not have him tormented. He has borne enough, and suffered enough, Heaven knows, without that. I will not have him harassed, and his best and tenderest feelings made a market of, by such as you. I will not!"

She stamped her foot upon the frosty ground as she spoke. Talbot Bulstrode saw and wondered at the gesture. He had half a mind to leave the carriage and join Aurora and her petitioner; but the ponies were restless, and he knew that it would not do to abandon the reins to poor timid Lucy.

"You needn't take on so, Miss Floyd," answered the man, whom Aurora had addressed as Matthew Harrison; "I'm sure I want to make things pleasant to all parties. All I ask is that you'll act a little liberal to a cove wot's come down in the world since you see him last. Lord, wot a world it is for ups and downs! If it had been the summer season, I'd have had no needs to worrit you; but what's the good of standin' at the top of Regent Street such weather as this with tarrier-pups and such likes? Old ladies has no eye for dawgs in the winter; and even the gents as cares for rat-catching is gettin' uncommon scarce. There aint nothink doin' on the turf whereby a chap can make a honest penny; nor won't be, come the Craven Meetin'. I'd never have come anigh

---

1 (Slang): chap.

you, miss, if I hadn't been hard up; and I know you'll act liberal."

"Act liberally!" cried Aurora. "Good heavens! if every guinea I have, or ever hope to have, could blot out the business that you trade upon, I'd open my hands and let the money run through them as freely as so much water."

"It was only good-natur'd of me to send you that ere paper, though, miss, eh?" said Mr. Matthew Harrison, plucking a dry twig from the tree nearest him, and chewing it for his delectation.

Aurora and the man had walked slowly onward as they spoke, and were by this time at some distance from the pony-carriage.

Talbot Bulstrode was in a fever of restless impatience.

"Do you know this pensioner of your cousin's, Lucy?" he asked.

"No, I can't remember his face. I don't think he belongs to Beckenham."

"Why, if I hadn't have sent you that ere 'Life,' you wouldn't have know'd; would you now?" said the man.

"No, no, perhaps not," answered Aurora. She had taken her porte-monnaie from her pocket, and Mr. Harrison was furtively regarding the little morocco receptacle with glistening eyes.

"You don't ask me about any of the particklars," he said.

"No. What should I care to know of them?"

"No, certently," answered the man, suppressing a chuckle; "you know enough, if it comes to that; and if you wanted to know any more, I couldn't tell you; for them few lines in the paper is all I could ever get hold of about the business. But I allus said it, and I allus will; if a man as rides up'ards of eleven stone——"

It seemed as if he were in a fair way of rambling on for ever so long, if Aurora had not checked him by an impatient frown. Perhaps he stopped all the more readily as she opened her purse at the same moment, and he caught sight of the glittering sovereigns lurking between leaves of crimson silk. He had no very acute sense of colour; but I am sure that he thought gold and crimson made a pleasing contrast, as he looked at the yellow coin in Miss Floyd's porte-monnaie. She poured the sovereigns into her own gloved palm, and then dropped the golden shower into Mr. Harrison's hands, which were hollowed into a species of horny basin for the reception of her bounty. The great trunk of an oak screened them from the observation of Talbot and Lucy, as Aurora gave the man this money.

"You have no claim on me," she said, stopping him abruptly, as he began a declaration of his gratitude, "and I protest against your making a market of any past events which have come under your knowledge. Remember, once and for ever, that I am not afraid of you; and that if I consent to assist you, it is because I will not have my father annoyed. Let me have the address of some place where a letter may always find you, – you can put it into an envelope and direct it to me here, – and from time to time I promise to send you a moderate remittance; sufficient to enable you to lead an honest life, if you, or any of your set, are capable of doing so; but I repeat, that if I give you this money as a bribe, it is only for my father's sake."

The man uttered some expression of thanks, looking at Aurora earnestly; but there was a stern shadow upon the dark face that forbade any hope of conciliation. She was turning from him, followed by the mastiff, when the bandy-legged dog ran forward, whining and raising himself upon his hind legs to lick her hand.

The expression of her face underwent an immediate change. She shrank from the dog, and he looked at her for a moment with a dim uncertainty in his blood-shot eyes; then, as conviction stole upon the brute mind, he burst into a joyous bark, frisking and capering about Miss Floyd's silk dress, and imprinting dusty impressions of his fore paws upon the rich fabric.

"The pore hanimal knows yer, miss," said the man, deprecatingly; "you was never 'aughty to 'im."

The mastiff Bow-wow made as if he would have torn up every inch of ground in Felden Woods at this juncture; but Aurora quieted him with a look.

"Poor Boxer!" she said; "poor Boxer! so you know me, Boxer."

"Lord, miss, there's no knowin' the faithfulness of them animals."

"Poor Boxer! I think I should like to have you. Would you sell him, Harrison?"

The man shook his head.

"No, miss," he answered, "thank you kindly; there aint much in the way of dawgs as I'd refuse to make a bargain about. If you wanted a mute spannel, or a Russian setter, or a Hile of Skye,[1] I'd get him for you and welcome, and ask nothin' for my trouble; but this here bull-tarrier's father and mother and wife and fambly to me, and there aint money enough in your pa's bank to buy him, miss."

"Well, well," said Aurora, relentingly, "I know how faithful he is. Send me the address, and don't come to Felden again."

She returned to the carriage, and taking the reins from Talbot's hand, gave the restless ponies their head; the vehicle dashed past Mr. Matthew Harrison, who stood hat in hand, with his dog between his legs, until the party had gone by. Miss Floyd stole a glance at her lover's face, and saw that Captain Bulstrode's countenance wore its darkest expression. The officer kept sulky silence till they reached the house, when he handed the two ladies from the carriage and followed them across the hall. Aurora was on the lowest step of the broad stair-case before he spoke.

"Aurora," he said, "one word before you go up-stairs."

She turned and looked at him a little defiantly; she was still very pale, and the fire with which her eyes had flashed upon Mr. Matthew Harrison, dog-fancier and rat-catcher, had not yet died out of the dark orbs. Talbot Bulstrode opened the door of a long chamber under the picture-gallery – half billiard-room, half library, and almost the pleasantest apartment in the house – and stood aside for Aurora to pass him.

The young lady crossed the threshold as proudly as Marie Antoinette going to face her plebeian accusers. The room was empty.

Miss Floyd seated herself in a low easy-chair by one of the two great fireplaces, and looked straight at the blaze.

"I want to ask you about that man, Aurora," Captain Bulstrode said, leaning over a *prie-dieu* chair,[2] and playing nervously with the carved arabesques of the walnut-wood framework.

"About which man?"

This might have been prevarication in some women; from Aurora it was simply defiance, as Talbot knew.

---

1 A Skye terrier.
2 A chair with a tall sloping back used for prayer, or a chair of this form for ordinary use.

"The man who spoke to you in the avenue just now. Who is he, and what was his business with you?" Here Captain Bulstrode fairly broke down. He loved her, reader, he loved her, remember, and he was a coward. A coward under the influence of that most cowardly of all passions, LOVE! – the passion that could leave a stain upon a Nelson's name; the passion which might have made a dastard of the bravest of the three hundred at Thermopylæ, or the six hundred at Balaklava.[1] He loved her, this unhappy young man, and he began to stammer, and hesitate, and apologize, shivering under the angry light in her wonderful eyes. "Believe me, Aurora, that I would not for the world play the spy upon your actions, or dictate to you the objects of your bounty. No, Aurora, not if my right to do so were stronger than it is, and I were twenty times your husband; but that man, that disreputable-looking fellow who spoke to you just now – I don't think he is the sort of person you ought to assist."

"I dare say not," she said; "I have no doubt I assist many people who ought by rights to die in a workhouse or drop on the high-road; but, you see, if I stopped to question their deserts, they might die of starvation while I was making my inquiries; so perhaps it's better to throw away a few shillings upon some unhappy creature who is wicked enough to be hungry, and not good enough to deserve to have anything given him to eat."

There was a recklessness about this speech that jarred upon Talbot, but he could not very well take objection to it; besides, it was leading away from the subject upon which he was so eager to be satisfied.

"But that man, Aurora – who is he?"

"A dog-fancier."

Talbot shuddered.

"I thought he was something horrible," he murmured; "but what, in Heaven's name, could he want of you, Aurora?"

"What most of my petitioners want," she answered; "whether it's

---

1 The stain on Admiral Horatio Nelson's name was his notorious passion for Lady Emma Hamilton, wife of Sir William Hamilton, the British Ambassador in Naples; the three hundred at Thermopylae were the Spartans who defended the Thermopylae pass against the invading Persian army in 480 B.C.; the six hundred at Balaclava were the heroes of the Charge of the Light Brigade during the Crimean War (see 76, n.4).

the curate of a new chapel with mediæval decorations,[1] who wants to rival our Lady of Bons-secours upon one of the hills about Norwood;[2] or a laundress, who has burnt a week's washing, and wants the means to make it good; or a lady of fashion, who is about to inaugurate a home for the children of indigent lucifer-match sellers;[3] or a lecturer upon political economy, or Shelley and Byron, or upon Charles Dickens and the Modern Humorists, who is going to hold forth at Croydon: they all want the same thing; money! If I tell the curate that my principles are evangelical, and that I can't pray sincerely if there are candlesticks on the altar,[4] he is not the less glad of my hundred pounds. If I inform the lady of fashion that I have peculiar opinions about the orphans of lucifer-match sellers, and cherish a theory of my own against the education of the masses, she will shrug her shoulders deprecatingly, but will take care to let me know that any donation Miss Floyd may be pleased to afford will be equally acceptable. If I told them that I had committed half a dozen murders, or that I had a silver statue of the winner of last year's Derby erected on an altar in my dressing-room, and did daily and nightly homage to it, they would take my money and thank me kindly for it, as that man did just now."

"But one word, Aurora: does the man belong to this neighbourhood?"

"No."

"How, then, did you come to know him?"

She looked at him for a moment; steadily, unflinchingly, with a thoughtful expression in that ever-changing countenance; looked as if

---

1 A chapel "with mediæval decorations" would be in Gothic Revival style, which at mid-century was a leading style of church architecture. The church of Notre-Dame-de-Bonsecours in Blosseville, Rouen (built 1840-44) was the first Gothic Revival building to reach completion in France.

2 Norwood is a suburb south of London which was developed from the 1820s on. In 1854 the Crystal Palace was relocated to one of the hills near Norwood.

3 A lucifer match was a wood splint tipped with an inflammable substance, ignitable by friction on a rough surface. In *London Labour and the London Poor* (1851), Henry Mayhew represents lucifer match sellers as amongst the poorest of London's street vendors.

4 The Evangelical party within the Church of England distrusted hallmarks of outward religious ceremony such as candles on the altar.

she were mentally debating some point. Then rising suddenly, she gathered her shawl about her, and walked towards the door. She paused upon the threshold, and said –

"This cross-questioning is scarcely pleasant, Captain Bulstrode. If I choose to give a five-pound note to any person who may ask me for it, I expect full licence to do so; and I will not submit to be called to account for my actions – even by you."

"Aurora!"

The tenderly reproachful tone struck her to the heart.

"You may believe, Talbot," she said, – "you must surely believe that I know too well the value of your love to imperil it by word or deed – you *must* believe this."

CHAPTER VIII.

POOR JOHN MELLISH COMES BACK AGAIN.

JOHN MELLISH grew weary of the great city of Paris. Better love, and contentment, and a crust in a *mansarde*, than stalled oxen or other costly food in the loftiest saloons *au premier*,[1] with the most obsequious waiters to do us homage, repressing so much as a smile at our insular idiom. He grew heartily weary of the Rue de Rivoli, the gilded railings of the Tuileries gardens, and the leafless trees behind them. He was weary of the Place de la Concorde, and the Champs Elysées, and the rattle of the hoofs of the troop about his Imperial Highness's carriage, when Napoleon the Third, or the baby prince, took his airing. The plot was yet a-hatching which was to come so soon to a climax in the Rue Lepelletier.[2] He was tired of the broad Boulevards, and the theatres, and the cafés, and the glove-shops – tired of staring at the jewellers' windows in the Rue de la Paix, picturing to himself the face of Aurora Floyd under the diamond and emerald tiaras displayed therein. He had serious thoughts at times of buying a stove and a basket of charcoal, and asphyxiating himself quietly in the great gilded saloon at Meurice's. What was the use of his money, or his dogs, or his horses, or his broad acres? All these put together would not purchase Aurora Floyd. What was the good of life, if it came to that, since the banker's daughter refused to share it with him? Remember that this big, blue-eyed, curly-haired John Mellish had been from his cradle a spoiled child, – spoiled by poor relations and parasites, servants and toadies, from the first hour to the thirtieth year of his existence, – and it seemed such a very hard thing that this beautiful woman should be denied to him. Had he been an eastern potentate, he would have sent for his vizier, and would have had that official

---

1 A room in the attic (*mansarde*) was cheap; the more elegant rooms were on the floor above street level (*au premier*).

2 The baby prince was Eugène Louis, son of Napoleon III, born in 1856. The plot refers to the attempted assassination of Napoleon III on 14 January 1858. Italian revolutionaries launched a bomb attack as he and the Empress pulled up in their carriage in the Rue Lepelletier. Eight people were killed and 152 wounded.

bow-strung before his eyes, and so made an end of it; but being merely a Yorkshire gentleman and landowner, he had no more to do but to bear his burden quietly. As if he had ever borne anything quietly! He flung half the weight of his grief upon his valet; until that functionary dreaded the sound of Miss Floyd's name, and told a fellow-servant in confidence that his master "made such a howling about that young woman as he offered marriage to at Brighton, that there was no bearing him." The end of it all was, that one night John Mellish gave sudden orders for the striking of his tents, and early the next morning departed for the Great Northern Railway, leaving only the ashes of his fires behind him.

It was only natural to suppose that Mr. Mellish would have gone straight to his country residence, where there was much business to be done by him: foals to be entered for coming races, trainers and stable-boys to be settled with, the planning and laying down of a proposed tan-gallop[1] to be carried out, and a racing stud awaiting the eye of the master. But instead of going from the Dover Railway Station to the Great Northern Hotel, eating his dinner, and starting for Doncaster by the express, Mr. Mellish drove to the Gloucester Coffee-house, and there took up his quarters, for the purpose, as he said, of seeing the Cattle-show.[2] He made a melancholy pretence of driving to Baker Street in a Hansom cab, and roamed hither and thither for a quarter of an hour, staring dismally into the pens, and then fled away precipitately from the Yorkshire gentlemen-farmers, who gave him hearty greeting. He left the Gloucester the next morning in a dog-cart,[3] and drove straight to Beckenham. Archibald Floyd, who knew nothing of this young Yorkshireman's declaration and rejection, had given him a hearty invitation to Felden Woods. Why shouldn't he go there? Only to make a morning call upon the hospitable banker; not to see Aurora; only to take a few long respirations of the air she breathed before he went back to Yorkshire.

---

1 A riding track covered with crushed bark (tan).

2 In the late 1700s, the "Smithfield Club Fat Cattle Show" became an annual Baker Street Christmas event. With greater access to locomotive transportation, the competition outgrew the Agricultural Hall in Baker Street, and similar shows emerged outside London.

3 An open vehicle for ordinary driving with two seats back to back. Originally a sportsman's vehicle, with the hinder seat made to shut up so as to form a box for dogs.

Of course he knew nothing of Talbot Bulstrode's happiness; and it had been one of the chief consolations of his exile to remember that that gentleman had put forth in the same vessel, and had been shipwrecked along with him.

He was ushered into the billiard-room, where he found Aurora Floyd seated at a little table near the fire, making a pencil copy of a proof engraving of one of Rosa Bonheur's pictures,[1] while Talbot Bulstrode sat by her side preparing her pencils.

We feel instinctively that the man who cuts lead-pencils, or holds a skein of silk upon his outstretched hands, or carries lap-dogs, opera-cloaks, camp-stools, or parasols, is "engaged." Even John Mellish had learned enough to know this. He breathed a sigh so loud as to be heard by Lucy and her mother seated by the other fireplace, – a sigh that was on the verge of a groan, – and then held out his hand to Miss Floyd. Not to Talbot Bulstrode. He had vague memories of Roman legends floating in his brain, legends of superhuman generosity and classic self-abnegation; but he could not have shaken hands with that dark-haired young Cornishman, though the tenure of the Mellish estate had hung upon the sacrifice. He could not do it. He seated himself a few paces from Aurora and her lover, twisting his hat about in his hot, nervous hands until the brim was well-nigh limp; and was powerless to utter one sentence, even so much as some poor pitiful remark about the weather.

He was a great spoiled baby of thirty years of age; and I am afraid that, if the stern truth must be told, he saw Aurora Floyd across a mist, that blurred and distorted the bright face before his eyes. Lucy Floyd came to his relief, by carrying him off to introduce him to her mother; and kind-hearted Mrs. Alexander was delighted with his frank, fair English face. He had the good fortune to stand with his back to the light, so that neither of the ladies detected that foolish mist in his blue eyes.

Archibald Floyd would not hear of his visitor's returning to town either that night or the next day.

"You must spend Christmas with us," he said, "and see the New Year in, before you go back to Yorkshire. I have all my children about

---

1 Rosa Bonheur (1822-99), a painter and sculptor famous for her accurate and detailed portrayal of animals.

me at this season, and it is the only time that Felden seems like an old man's home. Your friend Bulstrode stops with us" (Mellish winced as he received this intelligence), "and I sha'n't think it friendly if you refuse to join our party."

What a pitiful coward this John Mellish must have been to accept the banker's invitation, and send the Newport Pagnell[1] back to the Gloucester, and suffer himself to be led away by Mr. Floyd's own man to a pleasant chamber, a few doors from the chintz-rooms occupied by Talbot! But I have said before, that love is a cowardly passion. It is like the toothache; the bravest and strongest succumb to it, and howl aloud under the torture. I don't suppose the Iron Duke[2] would have been ashamed to own that he objected to having his teeth out. I have heard of a great fighting man who could take punishment better than any other of the genii of the ring, but who fainted away at the first grip of the dentist's forceps. John Mellish consented to stay at Felden, and he went between the lights into Talbot's dressing-room, to expostulate with the captain upon his treachery.

Talbot did his best to console his doleful visitant.

"There are more women than one in the world," he said, after John had unbosomed himself of his grief – he didn't think this, the hypocrite, though he said it – "there are more women than one, my dear Mellish; and there are many very charming and estimable girls, who would be glad to win the affections of such a fellow as you."

"I hate estimable girls," said Mr. Mellish; "bother my affections! nobody will ever win my affections; but I love her, I love that beautiful black-eyed creature down-stairs, who looks at you with two flashes of lightning, and rides like young Challoner in a cloth habit;[3] I love her, Bulstrode, and you told me that she'd refused you, and that you were going to leave Brighton by the eight o'clock express, and you didn't; and you sneaked back and made her a second offer, and she accepted you, and, damme, it wasn't fair play."

---

1   His dog-cart, so called after its place of manufacture, Newport Pagnell, Bucks., the hub of the coaching trade.
2   The Duke of Wellington.
3   i.e. Rides like the great jockey Tom Challoner, winner of the St. Leger in 1861, the Oaks and the St. Leger in 1862, and the Derby in 1863, but does so in a woman's restrictive riding habit.

Having said which, Mr. Mellish flung himself upon a chair, which creaked under his weight, and fell to poking the fire furiously.

It was hard for poor Talbot to have to excuse himself for having won Aurora's hand. He could not very well remind John Mellish that if Miss Floyd had accepted him, it was perhaps because she preferred him to the honest Yorkshireman. To John the matter never presented itself in this light. The spoiled child had been cheated out of that toy above all other toys, upon the possession of which he had set his foolish heart. It was as if he had bidden for some crack horse at Tattersall's, in fair and open competition with a friend, who had gone back after the sale to outbid him in some underhand fashion. He could not understand that there had been no dishonesty in Talbot's conduct, and he was highly indignant when that gentleman ventured to hint to him that perhaps, on the whole, it would have been wiser to have kept away from Felden Woods.

Talbot Bulstrode had avoided any further allusion to Mr. Matthew Harrison the dog-fancier; and this, the first dispute between the lovers, had ended in the triumph of Aurora.

Miss Floyd was not a little embarrassed by the presence of John Mellish, who roamed disconsolately about the big rooms, seating himself ever and anon at one of the tables to peer into the lenses of a stereoscope,[1] or to take up some gorgeously-bound volume and drop it on the carpet in gloomy absence of mind, and who sighed heavily when spoken to, and was altogether far from pleasant company. Aurora's warm heart was touched by the piteous spectacle of this rejected lover, and she sought him out once or twice, and talked to him about his racing stud, and asked him how he liked the hunting in Surrey; but John changed from red to white, and from hot to cold, when she spoke to him, and fled away from her with a scared and ghastly aspect, which would have been grotesque had it not been so painfully real.

But by-and-by John found a more pitiful listener to his sorrows than ever Talbot Bulstrode had been; and this gentle and compassionate listener was no other than Lucy Floyd, to whom the big York-

---

1 An instrument developed in the 1830s which produces from two pictures of an object, taken from slightly different points of view, a single image giving the illusion of solidity or relief.

shireman turned in his trouble. Did he know, or did he guess, by some wondrous clairvoyance, that her griefs bore a common likeness to his own, and that she was just the one person, of all others at Felden Woods, to be pitiful to him and patient with him? He was by no means proud, this transparent, boyish, babyish good fellow. Two days after his arrival at Felden, he told all to poor Lucy.

"I suppose you know, Miss Floyd," he said, "that your cousin rejected me. Yes, of course you do; I believe she rejected Bulstrode about the same time; but some men haven't a ha'porth[1] of pride: I must say I think the captain acted like a sneak."

A sneak! Her idol, her adored, her demi-god, her dark-haired and gray-eyed divinity, to be spoken of thus! She turned upon Mr. Mellish with her fair cheeks flushed into a pale glow of anger, and told him that Talbot had a right to do what he had done, and that whatever Talbot did was right.

Like most men whose reflective faculties are entirely undeveloped, John Mellish was blessed with a sufficiently rapid perception; a perception sharpened just then by that peculiar sympathetic prescience, that marvellous clairvoyance of which I have spoken; and in those few indignant words, and that angry flush, he read poor Lucy's secret: she loved Talbot Bulstrode as he loved Aurora – hopelessly.

How he admired this fragile girl, who was frightened of horses and dogs, and who shivered if a breath of the winter air blew across the heated hall, and who yet bore her burden with this quiet, uncomplaining patience! while he, who weighed fourteen stone, and could ride forty miles across country with the bitterest blasts of December blowing in his face, was powerless to endure his affliction. It comforted him to watch Lucy, and to read in those faint signs and tokens, which had escaped even a mother's eye, the sad history of her unrequited affection.

Poor John was too good-natured and unselfish to hold out for ever in the dreary fortress of despair which he had built up for his habitation; and on Christmas-eve, when there were certain rejoicings at Felden, held in especial honour of the younger visitors, he gave way, and joined in their merriment, and was more boyish than the

---

1 A halfpenny worth.

youngest of them, burning his fingers with blazing raisins, suffering his eyes to be bandaged at the will of noisy little players at blindman's-buff, undergoing ignominious penalties in their games of forfeits, performing alternately innkeepers, sheriff's officers, policemen, clergymen, and justices, in the acted charades, lifting the little ones who wanted to see "de top of de Kitmat tee" in his sturdy arms, and making himself otherwise agreeable and useful to young people of from three to fifteen years of age; until at last, under the influence of all this juvenile gaiety, and perhaps two or three glasses of Moselle, he boldly kissed Aurora Floyd beneath the branch of mistletoe, hanging, "for this night only," in the great hall at Felden Woods.

And having done this, Mr. Mellish fairly lost his wits, and was "off his head" for the rest of the evening; making speeches to the little ones at the supper-table, and proposing Mr. Archibald Floyd and the commercial interests of Great Britain, with three times three; leading the chorus of those tiny treble voices with his own sonorous bass; and weeping freely – he never quite knew why – behind his table-napkin. It was through an atmosphere of tears, and sparkling wines, and gas, and hot-house flowers, that he saw Aurora Floyd, looking, ah, how lovely! in those simple robes of white which so much became her, and with a garland of artificial holly round her head. The spiked leaves and the scarlet berries formed themselves into a crown – I think, indeed, that a cheese-plate would have been transformed into a diadem, if Miss Floyd had been pleased to put it on her head – and she looked like the genius of Christmas: something bright and beautiful; too beautiful to come more than once a year.

When the clocks were striking 2 A.M., long after the little ones had been carried away muffled up in opera-cloaks, terribly sleepy, and I'm afraid in some instances under the influence of strong drink, – when the elder guests had all retired to rest, and the lights, with a few exceptions, were fled, the garlands dead, and all but Talbot and John Mellish departed, the two young men walked up and down the long billiard-room, in the red glow of the two declining fires, and talked to each other confidentially. It was the morning of Christmas-day, and it would have been strange to be unfriendly at such a time.

"If you'd fallen in love with the other one, Bulstrode," said John, clasping his old schoolfellow by the hand, and staring at him pathetically, "I could have looked upon you as a brother; she's better suited to you, twenty thousand times better adapted to you, than her cousin, and you ought to have married her – in common courtesy – I mean to say as an honourable – having very much compromised yourself by your attentions – Mrs. Whatshername – the companion – Mrs. Powell – said so – you ought to have married her."

"Married her! Married whom?" cried Talbot rather savagely, shaking off his friend's hot grasp, and allowing Mr. Mellish to sway backward upon the heels of his varnished boots in rather an alarming manner. "Who do you mean?"

"The sweetest girl in Christendom – except one," exclaimed John, clasping his hot hands and elevating his dim blue eyes to the ceiling; "the loveliest girl in Christendom, except one – Lucy Floyd."

"Lucy Floyd!"

"Yes, Lucy; the sweetest girl in——"

"Who says that I ought to marry Lucy Floyd!"

"She says so – no, no, I don't mean that! I mean," said Mr. Mellish, sinking his voice to a solemn whisper, – "I mean that Lucy Floyd loves you! She didn't tell me so – oh, no, bless your soul, – she never uttered a word upon the subject; but she loves you. Yes," continued John, pushing his friend away from him with both hands, and staring at him as if mentally taking his pattern for a suit of clothes, "that girl loves you, and has loved you all along. I am not a fool, and I give you my word and honour that Lucy Floyd loves you."

"Not a fool!" cried Talbot; "you're worse than a fool, John Mellish – you're drunk!"

He turned upon his heel contemptuously, and taking a candle from a table near the door, lighted it, and strode out of the room.

John stood rubbing his hands through his curly hair, and staring helplessly after the captain.

"This is the reward a fellow gets for doing a generous thing," he said, as he thrust his own candle into the burning coals, ignoring any easier mode of lighting it. "It's hard, but I suppose it's human nature."

Talbot Bulstrode went to bed in a very bad humour. Could it be true that Lucy loved him? Could this chattering Yorkshireman have discovered a secret which had escaped the captain's penetration? He remembered how, only a short time before, he had wished that this fair-haired girl might fall in love with him, and now all was trouble and confusion. Guinevere was lady of his heart, and poor Elaine was sadly in the way. Mr. Tennyson's wondrous book had not been given to the world in the year fifty-seven, or no doubt poor Talbot would have compared himself to the knight whose "honour rooted in dishonour stood."[1] Had he been dishonourable? Had he compromised himself by his attentions to Lucy? Had he deceived that fair and gentle creature? The down pillows in the chintz chamber gave no rest to his weary head that night; and when he fell asleep in the late daybreak, it was to dream horrible dreams, and to see in a vision Aurora Floyd standing on the brink of a clear pool of water in a woody recess at Felden, and pointing down through its crystal surface to the corpse of Lucy, lying pale and still amidst lilies and clustering aquatic plants, whose long tendrils entwined themselves with the fair golden hair.[2]

He heard the splash of the water in that terrible dream, and awoke, to find his valet breaking the ice in his bath in the adjoining room. His perplexities about poor Lucy vanished in the broad daylight, and he laughed at a trouble which must have grown out of his own vanity. What was he, that young ladies should fall in love with him? What a weak fool he must have been to have believed for one moment in the drunken babble of John Mellish! So he dismissed the image of Aurora's cousin from his mind, and had eyes, ears, and thought only for Aurora herself, who drove him to Beckenham church in her basket-carriage, and sat by his side in the banker's great square pew.

Alas, I fear he heard very little of the sermon that was preached that day; but, for all that, I declare that he was a good and devout man: a man whom God had blest with the gift of earnest belief; a man who took all blessings from the hand of God reverently, almost fearfully; and as he bowed his head at the end of that Christmas service of rejoicing and thanksgiving, he thanked Heaven for his overflowing cup of gladness, and prayed that he might become worthy of so much happiness.

---

1 A second allusion to Tennyson's *Idylls of the King* (see 126, n.1). The quotation, which describes Lancelot, is from *Elaine*.

2 Although Lucy has just been compared to Elaine of Astolat, who dies of unrequited love for Lancelot, this nightmarish vision recalls Ophelia, especially as represented in John Everett Millais' painting of 1851-2.

He had a vague fear that he was too happy; too much bound up heart and soul in the dark-eyed woman by his side. If she were to die! If she were to be false to him! He turned sick and dizzy at the thought; and even in that sacred temple the Devil whispered to him that there were still pools, loaded pistols, and other certain remedies for such calamities as those, – so wicked as well as cowardly a passion is this terrible fever, Love!

The day was bright and clear, the light snow whitening the ground; every line of hedge-top and tree cut sharply out against the cold blue of the winter sky. The banker proposed that they should send home the carriages, and walk down the hill to Felden; so Talbot Bulstrode offered Aurora his arm, only too glad of the chance of a *tête-à-tête* with his betrothed.

John Mellish walked with Archibald Floyd, with whom the Yorkshireman was an especial favourite; and Lucy was lost amid a group of brothers, sisters, and cousins.

"We were so busy all yesterday with the little people," said Talbot, "that I forgot to tell you, Aurora, that I had had a letter from my mother."

Miss Floyd looked up at him with her brightest glance. She was always pleased to hear anything about Lady Bulstrode.

"Of course there is very little news in the letter," added Talbot, "for there is rarely much to tell at Bulstrode. And yet – yes – there is one piece of news which concerns yourself."

"Which concerns me?"

"Yes. You remember my cousin, Constance Trevyllian?"

"Y-es –"

"She has returned from Paris, her education finished at last, and she, I believe, all-accomplished, and has gone to spend Christmas at Bulstrode. Good heavens, Aurora! what is the matter?"

Nothing very much, apparently. Her face had grown as white as a sheet of letter-paper; but the hand upon his arm did not tremble. Perhaps, had he taken especial notice of it, he would have found it preternaturally still.

"Aurora, what is the matter?"

"Nothing. Why do you ask?"

"Your face is as pale as——"

"It is the cold, I suppose," she said, shivering. "Tell me about your cousin, this Miss Trevyllian; when did she go to Bulstrode Castle?"

"She was to arrive the day before yesterday. My mother was expecting her when she wrote."

"Is she a favourite of Lady Bulstrode's?"

"No very especial favourite. My mother likes her well enough; but Constance is rather a frivolous girl."

"The day before yesterday," said Aurora; "Miss Trevyllian was to arrive the day before yesterday. The letters from Cornwall are delivered at Felden early in the afternoon; are they not?"

"Yes, dear."

"You will have a letter from your mother to-day, Talbot."

"A letter to-day! oh, no, Aurora, she never writes two days running; seldom more than once a week."

Miss Floyd did not make any answer to this, nor did her face regain its natural hue during the whole of the homeward walk. She was very silent, only replying in the briefest manner to Talbot's inquiries.

"I am sure that you are ill, Aurora," he said, as they ascended the terrace steps.

"I am ill."

"But, dearest, what is it? Let me tell Mrs. Alexander, or Mrs. Powell. Let me go back to Beckenham for the doctor."

She looked at him with a mournful earnestness in her eyes.

"My foolish Talbot," she said, "do you remember what Macbeth said to *his* doctor?[1] There are diseases that cannot be ministered to. Let me alone; you will know soon enough – you will know very soon, I dare say."

"But, Aurora, what do you mean by this? What can there be upon your mind?"

"Ah, what indeed! Let me alone, let me alone, Captain Bulstrode."

He had caught her hand; but she broke from him, and ran up the staircase, in the direction of her own apartments.

---

1 "Canst thou not minister to a mind diseas'd" (*Macbeth* V.iii.40).

Talbot hurried to Lucy, with a pale, frightened, face.

"Your cousin is ill, Lucy," he said; "go to her, for Heaven's sake, and see what is wrong."

Lucy obeyed immediately; but she found the door of Miss Floyd's room locked against her; and when she called to Aurora, and implored to be admitted, that young lady cried out, –

"Go away, Lucy Floyd! go away, and leave me to myself, unless you want to drive me mad!"

CHAPTER IX.

HOW TALBOT BULSTRODE SPENT HIS CHRISTMAS.

THERE was no more happiness for Talbot Bulstrode that day. He wandered from room to room, till he was as weary of that exercise as the young lady in Monk Lewis's 'Castle Spectre;'[1] he roamed forlornly hither and thither, hoping to find Aurora, now in the billiard-room, now in the drawing-room. He loitered in the hall, upon the shallow pretence of looking at barometers and thermometers, in order to listen for the opening and shutting of Aurora's door. All the doors at Felden Woods were perpetually opening and shutting that afternoon, as it seemed to Talbot Bulstrode.

He had no excuse for passing the doors of Miss Floyd's apartments, for his own rooms lay at the opposite angle of the house; but he lingered on the broad staircase, looking at the furniture-pictures upon the walls, and not seeing one line in these Wardour-Street productions. He had hoped that Aurora would appear at luncheon; but that dismal meal had been eaten without her; and the merry laughter and pleasant talk of the family assembly had sounded far away to Talbot's ears – far away across some wide ocean of doubt and confusion.

He passed the afternoon in this wretched manner, unobserved by any one but Lucy, who watched him furtively from her distant seat, as he roamed in and out of the drawing-room. Ah, how many a man is watched by loving eyes whose light he never sees! How many a man is cared for by a tender heart whose secret he never learns! A little after dusk, Talbot Bulstrode went to his room to dress. It was some time before the bell would ring; but he would dress early, he thought, so as to make sure of being in the drawing-room when Aurora came down.

He took no light with him, for there were always wax-candles upon the chimney-piece in his room.

---

1   Author Matthew Lewis (1775-1818) was nicknamed "Monk Lewis" after the title of his successful novel, *The Monk* (1796). In his Gothic play, *The Castle Spectre* (1797), Lady Angela enters saying, "I am weary of wandering from room to room; in vain do I change the scene, discontent is everywhere" (I.ii).

It was almost dark in that pleasant chintz chamber, for the fire had been lately replenished, and there was no blaze; but he could just distinguish a white patch upon the green-cloth cover of the writing-table. The white patch was a letter. He stirred the black mass of coal in the grate, and a bright flame went dancing up the chimney, making the room as light as day. He took the letter in one hand, while he lighted one of the candles on the chimney-piece with the other. The letter was from his mother. Aurora Floyd had told him that he would receive such a letter. What did it all mean? The gay flowers and birds upon the papered walls spun round him as he tore open the envelope. I firmly believe that we have a semi-supernatural prescience of the coming of all misfortune; a prophetic instinct, which tells us that such a letter, or such a messenger, carries evil tidings. Talbot Bulstrode had that prescience as he unfolded the paper in his hands. The horrible trouble was before him; a brooding shadow, with a veiled face, ghastly and undefined; but it was *there*.

"MY DEAR TALBOT, – I know that the letter I am about to write will distress and perplex you; but my duty lies not the less plainly before me. I fear that your heart is much involved in your engagement to Miss Floyd." The evil tidings concerned Aurora, then; the brooding shadow was slowly lifting its dark veil, and the face of her he loved best on earth appeared behind it. "But I know," continued that pitiless letter, "that the sense of honour is the strongest part of your nature, and that, however you may have loved this girl" (O God, she spoke of his love in the past!), "you will not suffer yourself to be entrapped into a false position through any weakness of affection. There is some mystery about the life of Aurora Floyd."

This sentence was at the bottom of the first page; and before Talbot Bulstrode's shaking hand could turn the leaf, every doubt, every fear, every presentiment he had ever felt, flashed back upon him with preternatural distinctness.

"Constance Trevyllian came here yesterday; and you may imagine that in the course of the evening you were spoken of, and your engagement discussed."

A curse upon their frivolous women's gossip! Talbot crushed the letter in his hand, and was about to fling it from him; but, no, it *must* be read. The shadow of doubt must be faced, and wrestled with, and vanquished, or there was no more peace upon this earth for him. He went on reading the letter.

"I told Constance that Miss Floyd had been educated in the Rue St.-Dominique, and asked if she remembered her. 'What!' she said, 'is it the Miss Floyd whom there was such a fuss about? the Miss Floyd who ran away from school?' And she told me, Talbot, that a Miss Floyd was brought to the Desmoiselles Lespard by her father last June twelvemonth, and that less than a fortnight after arriving at the school she disappeared; her disappearance of course causing a great sensation and an immense deal of talk among the other pupils, as it was said she had *run away*. The matter was hushed up as much as possible; but you know that girls will talk, and from what Constance tells me, I imagine that very unpleasant things were said about Miss Floyd. Now you say that the banker's daughter only returned to Felden Woods in September last. *Where was she in the interval?*"

He read no more. One glance told him that the rest of the letter consisted of motherly cautions, and admonitions as to how he was to act in this perplexing business.

He thrust the crumpled paper into his bosom, and dropped into a chair by the hearth.

It was so, then! There was a mystery in the life of this woman. The doubts and suspicions, the undefined fears and perplexities, which had held him back at the first, and caused him to wrestle against his love, had not been unfounded. There was good reason for them all, ample reason for them; as there is for every instinct which Providence puts into our hearts. A black wall rose up round about him, and shut him for ever from the woman he loved; this woman whom he loved, so far from wisely, so fearfully well;[1] this woman, for whom he had thanked God in the church only a few hours before. And she was to have been his wife; the mother of his children, perhaps. He clasped his cold hands over his face and sobbed aloud. Do not despise him for those drops of anguish: they were the virgin tears of his manhood. Never since infancy had his eyes been wet before. God forbid that such tears as those should be shed more than once in a lifetime! The agony of that moment was not to be lived through twice. The hoarse sobs rent

---

1 Othello says of himself that he loved "not wisely but too well" (V.ii.344).

and tore his breast as if his flesh had been hacked by a rusty sword; and when he took his wet hands from his face, he wondered that they were not red; for it seemed to him as if he had been weeping blood. What should he do?

Go to Aurora, and ask her the meaning of that letter? Yes; the course was plain enough. A tumult of hope rushed back upon him, and swept away his terror. Why was he so ready to doubt her? What a pitiful coward he was to suspect her – to suspect this girl, whose transparent soul had been so freely unveiled to him; whose every accent was truth! For in his intercourse with Aurora, the quality which he had learned most to reverence in her nature was its sublime candour. He almost laughed at the recollection of his mother's solemn letter. It was so like these simple country people, whose lives had been bounded by the narrow limits of a Cornish village – it was so like them to make mountains out of the veriest mole-hills. What was there so wonderful in that which had occurred? The spoiled child, the wilful heiress, had grown tired of a foreign school, and had run away. Her father, not wishing the girlish escapade to be known, had placed her somewhere else, and had kept her folly a secret. What was there from first to last in the whole affair that was not perfectly natural and probable, the exceptional circumstances of the case duly considered?

He could fancy Aurora, with her cheeks in a flame, and her eyes flashing lightning, flinging a page of blotted exercises into the face of her French master, and running out of the school-room, amid a tumult of ejaculatory babble. The beautiful, impetuous creature! There is nothing a man cannot admire in the woman he loves, and Talbot was half inclined to admire Aurora for having run away from school.

The first dinner-bell had rung during Captain Bulstrode's agony; so the corridors and rooms were deserted when he went to look for Aurora, with his mother's letter in his breast.

She was not in the billiard-room or the drawing-room, but he found her at last in a little inner chamber at the end of the house, with a bay-window looking out over the park. The room was dimly lighted by a shaded lamp, and Miss Floyd was seated in the uncurtained window, with her elbow resting on a cushioned ledge, looking out at the steel-cold wintry sky and the whitened landscape. She was dressed in black; her face, neck, and arms gleaming marble-white against the sombre hue of her dress; and her attitude was as still as that of a statue.

She neither stirred nor looked round when Talbot entered the room.

"My dear Aurora," he said, "I have been looking for you everywhere."

She shivered at the sound of his voice.

"You wanted to see me?"

"Yes, dearest. I want you to explain something to me. A foolish business enough, no doubt, my darling, and, of course, very easily explained; but, as your future husband, I have a right to ask for an explanation; and I know, I know, Aurora, that you will give it in all candour."

She did not speak, although Talbot paused for some moments, awaiting her answer. He could only see her profile, dimly lighted by the wintry sky. He could not see the mute pain, the white anguish, in that youthful face.

"I have had a letter from my mother, and there is something in that letter which I wish you to explain. Shall I read it to you, dearest?"

His voice faltered upon the endearing expression, and he remembered afterwards that it was the last time he had ever addressed her with a lover's tenderness. The day came when she had need of his compassion, and when he gave it freely; but that moment sounded the death-knell of Love. In that moment the gulf yawned, and the cliffs were rent asunder.

"Shall I read you the letter, Aurora?"

"If you please."

He took the crumpled epistle from his bosom, and, bending over the lamp, read it aloud to Aurora. He fully expected at every sentence that she would interrupt him with some eager explanation; but she was silent until he had finished, and even then she did not speak.

"Aurora, Aurora, is this true?"

"Perfectly true."

"But why did you run away from the Rue St.-Dominique?"

"I cannot tell you."

"And where were you between the month of June in the year fifty-six and last September?"

"I cannot tell you, Talbot Bulstrode. This is my secret, which I cannot tell you."

"You cannot tell me! There is upwards of a year missing from your life; and you cannot tell me, your betrothed husband, what you did with that year?"

"I cannot."

"Then, Aurora Floyd, you can never be my wife."

He thought that she would turn upon him, sublime in her indignation and fury, and that the explanation he longed for would burst from her lips in a passionate torrent of angry words; but she rose from her chair, and, tottering towards him, fell upon her knees at his feet. No other action could have struck such terror to his heart. It seemed to him a confession of guilt. But what guilt? what guilt? What was the dark secret of this young creature's brief life?

"Talbot Bulstrode," she said, in a tremulous voice, which cut him to the soul, – "Talbot Bulstrode, Heaven knows how often I have foreseen and dreaded this hour. Had I not been a coward, I should have anticipated this explanation. But I thought – I thought the occasion might never come; or that when it did come you would be generous – and – trust me. If you can trust me, Talbot; if you can believe that this secret is not utterly shameful——"

"Not utterly shameful!" he cried. "O God! Aurora, that I should ever hear you talk like this! Do you think there are any degrees in these things? There must be *no* secret between my wife and me; and the day that a secret, or the shadow of one, arises between us, must see us part for ever. Rise from your knees, Aurora; you are killing me with this shame and humiliation. Rise from your knees; and if we are to part this moment, tell me, tell me, for pity's sake, that I have no need to despise myself for having loved you with an intensity which has scarcely been manly."

She did not obey him, but sank lower in her half-kneeling, half-crouching attitude, her face buried in her hands, and only the coils of her black hair visible to Captain Bulstrode.

"I was motherless from my cradle, Talbot," she said, in a half-stifled voice. "Have pity upon me."

"Pity!" echoed the captain; "*pity!* Why do you not ask me for *justice?* One question, Aurora Floyd; one more question; perhaps the last

I ever may ask of you. Does your father know why you left that school, and where you were during that twelvemonth?"

"He does."

"Thank God, at least, for that! Tell me, Aurora, then – only tell me this, and I will believe your simple word as I would the oath of another woman. Tell me if he approved of your motive in leaving that school; if he approved of the manner in which your life was spent during that twelvemonth. If you can say yes, Aurora, there shall be no more questions between us, and I can make you without fear my loved and honoured wife."

"I cannot," she answered. "I am only nineteen; but within the two last years of my life I have done enough to break my father's heart; to break the heart of the dearest father that ever breathed the breath of life."

"Then all is over between us. God forgive you, Aurora Floyd; but by your own confession you are no fit wife for an honourable man. I shut my mind against all foul suspicions; but the past life of my wife must be a white unblemished page, which all the world may be free to read."

He walked towards the door, and then, returning, assisted the wretched girl to rise, and led her back to her seat by the window, courteously, as if she had been his partner at a ball. Their hands met with as icy a touch as the hands of two corpses. Ah, how much there was of death in that touch! How much had died between those two within the last few hours! – hope, confidence, security, love, happiness; all that makes life worth the holding.

Talbot Bulstrode paused upon the threshold of the little chamber, and spoke once more.

"I shall have left Felden in half an hour, Miss Floyd," he said; "it will be better to allow your father to suppose that the disagreement between us has arisen from something of a trifling nature, and that my dismissal has come from you. I shall write to Mr. Floyd from London, and, if you please, I will so word my letter as to lead him to think this."

"You are very good," she answered. "Yes, I would rather he should think that. It may spare him pain. Heaven knows I have cause to be grateful for anything that will do that."

Talbot bowed and left the room, closing the door behind him. The closing of that door had a dismal sound to his ear. He thought of some frail young creature abandoned by her sister nuns in a living tomb. He thought that he would rather have left Aurora lying rigidly beautiful in her coffin than as he was leaving her to-day.

The jangling, jarring sound of the second dinner-bell clanged out, as he went from the semi-obscurity of the corridor into the glaring gaslight of the billiard-room. He met Lucy Floyd coming towards him in her rustling silk dinner-dress, with fringes and laces and ribbons and jewels fluttering and sparkling about her; and he almost hated her for looking so bright and radiant, remembering, as he did, the ghastly face of the stricken creature he had just left. We are apt to be horribly unjust in the hour of supreme trouble; and I fear that if any one had had the temerity to ask Talbot Bulstrode's opinion of Lucy Floyd just at that moment, the captain would have declared her to be a mass of frivolity and affectation. If you discover the worthlessness of the only woman you love upon earth, you will perhaps be apt to feel maliciously disposed towards the many estimable people about you. You are savagely inclined, when you remember that they for whom you care nothing are so good, while she on whom you set your soul is so wicked. The vessel which you freighted with every hope of your heart has gone down; and you are angry at the very sight of those other ships riding so gallantly before the breeze. Lucy recoiled at the aspect of the young man's face.

"What is it?" she asked; "what has happened, Captain Bulstrode?"

"Nothing – I have received a letter from Cornwall which obliges me to——"

His hollow voice died away into a hoarse whisper before he could finish the sentence.

"Lady Bulstrode – or Sir John – is ill perhaps?" hazarded Lucy.

Talbot pointed to his white lips and shook his head. The gesture might mean anything. He could not speak. The hall was full of visitors and children going into dinner. The little people were to dine with their seniors that day, as an especial treat and privilege of the season. The door of the dining-room was open, and Talbot saw the gray head of Archibald Floyd dimly visible at the end of a long vista of lights and silver and glass and evergreens. The old man had his nephews and nieces and their children grouped about him; but the place at his right hand, the place Aurora was meant to fill, was vacant. Captain Bulstrode turned away from that gaily-lighted scene and ran up the staircase to his room, where he found his servant waiting with his master's clothes laid out, wondering why he had not come to dress.

The man fell back at the sight of Talbot's face, ghastly in the light of the wax-candles on the dressing-table.

"I am going away, Philman," said the captain, speaking very fast, and in a thick indistinct voice. "I am going down to Cornwall by the express to-night, if I can get to Town in time to catch the train. Pack my clothes and come after me. You can join me at the Paddington Station. I shall walk up to Beckenham, and take the first train for Town. Here, give this to the servants for me, will you?"

He took a confused heap of gold and silver from his pocket, and dropped it into the man's hand.

"Nothing wrong at Bulstrode, I hope, sir?" said the servant. "Is Sir John ill?"

"No, no; I've had a letter from my mother – I – you'll find me at the Great Western."

He snatched up his hat, and was hurrying from the room; but the man followed him with his greatcoat.

"You'll catch your death, sir, on such a night as this," the servant said, in a tone of respectful remonstrance.

The banker was standing at the door of the dining-room when Talbot crossed the hall. He was telling a servant to look for his daughter.

"We are all waiting for Miss Floyd," the old man said; "we cannot begin dinner without Miss Floyd."

Unobserved in the confusion, Talbot opened the great door softly, and let himself out into the cold winter's night. The long terrace was all ablaze with the lights in the high narrow windows, as upon the night when he had first come to Felden; and before him lay the park, the trees bare and leafless, the ground white with a thin coating of snow, the sky above gray and starless, – a cold and desolate expanse, in dreary contrast with the warmth and brightness behind. All this was typical of the crisis of his life. He was leaving warm love and hope, for cold resignation or icy despair. He went down the terrace-steps, across the trim garden-walks and out into that wide, mysterious park. The long avenue was ghostly in the gray light, the tracery of the interlacing branches above his head making black shadows, that flickered to and fro upon the whitened ground beneath his feet. He walked for a quarter of a mile before he looked back at the lighted windows behind him. He did not turn, until a bend in the avenue had brought him to a spot from which he could see the dimly lighted bay-window of the room in which he had left Aurora. He stood for some time looking at this feeble glimmer, and thinking – thinking of all he had lost, or all he had perhaps escaped – thinking of what his life was to be henceforth without that woman – thinking that he would rather have been the poorest ploughboy in Beckenham parish than the heir of Bulstrode, if he could have taken the girl he loved to his heart, and believed in her truth.

CHAPTER X.

FIGHTING THE BATTLE.

THE new year began in sadness at Felden Woods, for it found Archibald Floyd watching in the sick-room of his only daughter.

Aurora had taken her place at the long dinner-table upon the night of Talbot's departure; and except for being perhaps a little more vivacious and brilliant than usual, her manner had in no way changed after that terrible interview in the bay-windowed room. She had talked to John Mellish, and had played and sung to her younger cousins; she had stood behind her father, looking over his cards through all the fluctuating fortunes of a rubber of long whist; and the next morning her maid had found her in a raging fever, with burning cheeks and blood-shot eyes, her long purple-black hair all tumbled and tossed about the pillows, and her dry hands scorching to the touch. The telegraph brought two grave London physicians to Felden before noon; and the house was clear of visitors by nightfall, only Mrs. Alexander and Lucy remaining to assist in nursing the invalid. The West-End doctors said very little. This fever was as other fevers to them. The young lady had caught a cold perhaps; she had been imprudent, as these young people will be, and had received some sudden chill. She had very likely over-heated herself with dancing, or had sat in a draught, or eaten an ice. There was no immediate danger to be apprehended. The patient had a superb constitution; there was wonderful vitality in the system; and with careful treatment she would soon come round. Careful treatment meant a two-guinea visit every day from each of these learned gentlemen; though, perhaps, had they given utterance to their inmost thoughts, they would have owned that, for all they could tell to the contrary, Aurora Floyd wanted nothing but to be let alone, and left in a darkened chamber to fight out the battle by herself. But the banker would have had all Saville Row[1] summoned to the sick-bed of his child, if he could by such a measure

---

1   A street then associated with eminent physicians' practices, afterwards supplanted by Harley Street.

have saved her a moment's pain; and he implored the two physicians to come to Felden twice a day if necessary, and to call in other physicians if they had the least fear for their patient. Aurora was delirious; but she revealed very little in that delirium. I do not quite believe that people often make the pretty, sentimental, consecutive confessions under the influence of fever which are so freely attributed to them by the writers of romances. We rave about foolish things in those cruel moments of feverish madness. We are wretched because there is a man with a white hat on in the room; or a black cat upon the counterpane; or spiders crawling about the bed-curtains; or a coal-heaver who *will* put a sack of coals on our chest. Our delirious fancies are like our dreams, and have very little connection with the sorrows or joys which make up the sum of our lives.

So Aurora Floyd talked of horses and dogs, and masters and governesses; of childish troubles that had afflicted her years before, and of girlish pleasures, which, in her normal state of mind, had been utterly forgotten. She seldom recognized Lucy or Mrs. Alexander, mistaking them for all kinds of unlikely people; but she never entirely forgot her father, and, indeed, always seemed to be conscious of his presence, and was perpetually appealing to him, imploring him to forgive her for some act of childish disobedience committed in those departed years of which she talked so much.

John Mellish had taken up his abode at the Grayhound Inn, in Croydon High Street, and drove every day to Felden Woods, leaving his phaeton at the park-gates, and walking up to the house to make his inquiries. The servants took notice of the big Yorkshireman's pale face, and set him down at once as "sweet" upon their young lady. They liked him a great deal better than Captain Bulstrode, who had been too "'igh" and "'aughty" for them. John flung his half-sovereigns right and left when he came to the hushed mansion in which Aurora lay, with loving friends about her. He held the footman who answered the door by the button-hole, and would have gladly paid the man half-a-crown a minute for his time while he asked anxious questions about Miss Floyd's health. Mr. Mellish was warmly sympathized with, therefore, in the servants' hall at Felden. His man had informed the banker's household how he was the best master in England, and how Mellish Park was a species of terrestrial Paradise, maintained for the benefit of trustworthy retainers; and Mr. Floyd's servants expressed a wish that their young lady might get well, and marry the "fair one," as they called John. They came to the conclusion that there had been what they called "a split" between Miss Floyd and the captain, and that he had gone off in a huff; which was like his impudence, seeing that their young lady would have hundreds of thousands of pounds by-and-by, and was good enough for a duke instead of a beggarly officer.

Talbot's letter to Mr. Floyd reached Felden Woods on the 27th of December; but it lay for some time unopened upon the library table. Archibald had scarcely heeded his intended son-in-law's disappearance, in his anxiety about Aurora. When he did open the letter, Captain Bulstrode's words were almost meaningless to him, though he was just able to gather that the engagement had been broken, – by his daughter's wish, as Talbot seemed to infer.

The banker's reply to this communication was very brief; he wrote:

"MY DEAR SIR, – Your letter arrived here some days since, but has only been opened by me this morning. I have laid it aside, to be replied to, D.V.,[1] at a future time. At present I am unable to attend to anything. My daughter is seriously ill.

"Yours obediently,

"ARCHIBALD FLOYD."

"Seriously ill!" Talbot Bulstrode sat for nearly an hour with the banker's letter in his hand, looking at those two words. How much or how little might the sentence mean? At one moment, remembering Archibald Floyd's devotion to his daughter, he thought that this serious illness was doubtless some very trifling business, – some feminine nervous attack, common to young ladies upon any hitch in their love affairs; but five minutes afterwards he fancied that those words had an awful meaning – that Aurora was dying; dying of the shame and anguish of that interview in the little chamber at Felden.

Heaven above! what had he done? Had he murdered this beautiful creature, whom he loved a million times better than himself? Had he killed her with those impalpable weapons, those sharp and cruel

---

1   Abbreviation of *deo volente*: God willing.

words which he had spoken on the 25th of December? He acted the scene over again and again, until the sense of outraged honour, then so strong upon him, seemed to grow dim and confused; and he began almost to wonder why he had quarrelled with Aurora. What if, after all, this secret involved only some school-girl's folly? No; the crouching figure and ghastly face gave the lie to that hope. The secret, whatever it might be, was a matter of life and death to Aurora Floyd. He dared not try to guess what it was. He strove to close his mind against the surmises that would arise to him. In the first days that succeeded that terrible Christmas he determined to leave England. He would try to get some Government appointment that would take him away to the other end of the world, where he could never hear Aurora's name – never be enlightened as to the mystery that had separated them. But now, now that she was ill, – in danger, perhaps, – how could he leave the country? How could he go away to some place where he might one day open the English newspapers and see her name among the list of deaths?

Talbot was a dreary guest at Bulstrode Castle. His mother and his cousin Constance respected his pale face, and held themselves aloof from him in fear and trembling; but his father asked what the deuce was the matter with the boy, that he looked so chapfallen, and why he didn't take his gun and go out on the moors, and get an appetite for his dinner, like a Christian, instead of moping in his own rooms all day long, biting his fingers' ends.

Once, and once only, did Lady Bulstrode allude to Aurora Floyd.

"You asked Miss Floyd for an explanation, I suppose, Talbot?" she said.

"Yes, mother."

"And the result?"

"Was the termination of our engagement. I had rather you would not speak to me of this subject again, if you please, mother."

Talbot took his gun, and went out upon the moors, as his father advised; but it was not to slaughter the last of the pheasants, but to think in peace of Aurora Floyd, that the young man went out. The low-lying clouds upon the moorlands seemed to shut him in like prison-walls. How many miles of desolate country lay between the dark expanse on which he stood and the red-brick mansion at Felden!

– how many leafless hedgerows! – how many frozen streams! It was only a day's journey, certainly, by the Great Western; but there was something cruel in the knowledge that half the length of England lay between the Kentish woods and that far angle of the British Isles upon which Castle Bulstrode reared its weather-beaten walls. The wail of mourning voices might be loud in Kent, and not a whisper of death reach the listening ears in Cornwall. How he envied the lowest servant at Felden, who knew day by day and hour by hour of the progress of the battle between Death and Aurora Floyd! And yet, after all, what was she to him? What did it matter to him if she were well or ill? The grave could never separate them more utterly than they had been separated from the very moment in which he discovered that she was not worthy to be his wife. He had done her no wrong; he had given her a full and fair opportunity of clearing herself from the doubtful shadow on her name; and she had been unable to do so. Nay, more, she had given him every reason to suppose, by her manner, that the shadow was even a darker one than he had feared. Was he to blame, then? Was it his fault if she were ill? Were his days to be misery, and his nights a burden because of her? He struck the stock of his gun violently upon the ground at the thought, and thrust the ramrod down the barrel, and loaded his fowling-piece furiously with nothing; and then, casting himself at full length upon the stunted turf, lay there till the early dusk closed in about him, and the soft evening dew saturated his shooting-coat, and he was in a fair way to be stricken with rheumatic fever.

I might fill chapters with the foolish sufferings of this young man; but I fear he must have become very wearisome to my afflicted readers; to those, at least, who have never suffered from this fever. The sharper the disease, the shorter its continuance; so Talbot will be better by-and-by, and will look back at his old self, and laugh at his old agonies. Surely this inconstancy of ours is the worst of all – this fickleness, by reason of which we cast off our former selves with no more compunction than we feel in flinging away a worn-out garment. Our poor threadbare selves, the shadows of what we were! With what sublime, patronizing pity, with what scornful compassion, we look back upon the helpless dead and gone creatures, and wonder that anything so foolish could have been allowed to cumber the earth! Shall I feel the same contempt ten years hence for myself as I am to-day, as I feel to-day for myself as I was ten years ago? Will the loves and aspirations, the beliefs and desires of to-day, appear as pitiful then as the dead loves and dreams of the bygone decade? Shall I look back in pitying wonder, and think what a fool that young man was, although there was something candid and innocent in his very stupidity, after all? Who can wonder that the last visit to Paris killed Voltaire? Fancy the octogenarian looking round the national theatre, and seeing himself, through an endless vista of dim years, a young man again, paying his court to a "goat-faced cardinal," and being beaten by De Rohan's lackeys in broad daylight.[1]

Have you ever visited some still country town after a lapse of years, and wondered, O fast-living reader! to find the people you knew in your last visit still alive and thriving, with hair unbleached as yet, although you have lived and suffered whole centuries since then? Surely Providence gives us this sublimely egotistical sense of Time as a set-off against the brevity of our lives! I might make this book a companion in bulk to the Catalogue of the British Museum, if I were to tell all that Talbot Bulstrode felt and suffered in the month of January, 1858, – if I were to anatomize the doubts and confusions and self-contradictions, the mental resolutions made one moment to be broken the next. I refrain, therefore, and will set down nothing but the fact, that on a certain Sunday midway in the month, the captain, sitting in the family pew at Bulstrode church, directly facing the monument of Admiral Hartley Bulstrode, who fought and died in the days of Queen Elizabeth, registered a silent oath that, as he was a gentleman and a Christian, he would henceforth abstain from holding any voluntary communication with Aurora Floyd. But for this vow he must have broken down, and yielded to his yearning fear and love, and gone to Felden Woods to throw himself, blind and unquestioning, at the feet of the sick woman.

The tender green of the earliest leaflets was breaking out in bright patches upon the hedgerows round Felden Woods; the ash-buds were

---

1   In 1778, after a thirty-year exile, Voltaire returned from Ferney to Paris. He made a public appearance at the Comédie Française. Here, Braddon imagines Voltaire's thoughts when at the theatre: he recalls paying court to Cardinal Fleury (tutor to Louis IV and powerful chief minister of state) and being beaten in the street by the lackeys of the Chevalier de Rohan-Chabot (on 4 February 1726).

no longer black upon the front of March, and pale violets and prim-roses made exquisite tracery in the shady nooks beneath the oaks and beeches. All nature was rejoicing in the mild April weather, when Aurora lifted her dark eyes to her father's face with something of their old look and familiar light. The battle had been a long and severe one; but it was well-nigh over now, the physicians said. Defeated Death drew back for a while, to wait a better opportunity for making his fatal spring; and the feeble victor was to be carried down-stairs to sit in the drawing-room for the first time since the night of December the 25th.

John Mellish, happening to be at Felden that day, was allowed the supreme privilege of carrying the fragile burden in his strong arms, from the door of the sick chamber to the great sofa by the fire in the drawing-room; attended by a procession of happy people bearing shawls and pillows, vinaigrettes and scent-bottles, and other invalid paraphernalia. Every creature at Felden was devoted to this adored convalescent. Archibald Floyd lived only to minister to her; gentle Lucy waited on her night and day, fearful to trust the service to menial hands; Mrs. Powell, like some pale and quiet shadow, lurked amidst the bed-curtains, soft of foot and watchful of eye, invaluable in the sick-chamber, as the doctors said. Throughout her illness, Aurora had never mentioned the name of Talbot Bulstrode. Not even when the fever was at its worst, and the brain most distraught, had that familiar name escaped her lips. Other names, strange to Lucy, had been repeated by her again and again: the names of places and horses and slangy technicalities of the turf, had interlarded the poor girl's brain-sick babble; but whatever were her feelings with regard to Tal-bot, no word had revealed their depth or sadness. Yet I do not think that my poor dark-eyed heroine was utterly feelingless upon this point. When they first spoke of carrying her down-stairs, Mrs. Powell and Lucy proposed the little bay-windowed chamber, which was small and snug, and had a southern aspect, as the fittest place for the invalid; but Aurora cried out shuddering, that she would never enter that hateful chamber again.

As soon as ever she was strong enough to bear the fatigue of the journey, it was considered advisable to remove her from Felden; and Leamington was suggested by the doctors as the best place for the change. A mild climate and a pretty inland retreat, a hushed and quiet town, peculiarly adapted to invalids, being almost deserted by other visitors after the hunting season.

Shakespeare's birthday had come and gone,[1] and the high festivals at Stratford were over, when Archibald Floyd took his pale daughter to Leamington. A furnished cottage had been engaged for them a mile and a half out of the town; a pretty place, half villa, half farmhouse, with walls of white plaster chequered with beams of black wood, and well-nigh buried in a luxuriant and trimly-kept flowergarden; a pleasant place, forming one of a little cluster of rustic buildings crowded about a gray old church in a nook of the roadway, where two or three green lanes met, and went branching off between overhanging hedges; a most retired spot, yet clamorous with that noise which is of all others cheerful and joyous, – the hubbub of farmyards, the cackle of poultry, the cooing of pigeons, the monotonous lowing of lazy cattle, and the squabbling grunt of quarrelsome pigs. Archibald could not have brought his daughter to a better place. The chequered farmhouse seemed a haven of rest to this poor weary girl of nineteen. It was so pleasant to lie wrapped in shawls, on a chintz-covered sofa, in the open window, listening to the rustic noises in the straw-littered yard upon the other side of the hedge, with her faithful Bow-wow's big fore-paws resting on the cushions at her feet. The sounds in the farmyard were pleasanter to Aurora than the monotonous inflections of Mrs. Powell's voice; but as that lady considered it a part of her duty to read aloud for the invalid's delectation, Miss Floyd was too good-natured to own how tired she was of 'Marmion' and 'Childe Harold,' 'Evangeline,' and 'The Queen of the May,'[2] and how she would have preferred in her present state of mind to listen to a lively dispute between a brood of ducks round the pond in the farmyard, or a trifling discussion in the pigsty, to the sublimest lines ever penned by poet, living or dead. The poor girl had suffered very much, and there was a certain sensuous, lazy pleasure in this slow recovery, this gradual return to strength. Her own nature revived in unison with the bright revival of the genial summer weather. As the trees in the garden

---

1 Shakespeare's birthday is traditionally celebrated on 23 April.

2 Sir Walter Scott's *Marmion* (1808), Lord Byron's *Childe Harolde's Pilgrimage* (1812–18), Henry Wadsworth Longfellow's *Evangeline* (1849), and Alfred, Lord Tennyson's "The May Queen" (1832).

put forth new strength and beauty, so the glorious vitality of her constitution returned with much of its wonted power. The bitter blows had left their scars behind them, but they had not killed her, after all. They had not utterly changed her even, for glimpses of the old Aurora appeared day by day in the pale convalescent; and Archibald Floyd, whose life was at best but a reflected existence, felt his hopes revive as he looked at his daughter. Lucy and her mother had gone back to the villa at Fulham, and to their own family duties; so the Leamington party consisted only of Aurora and her father, and that pale shadow of propriety, the ensign's light-haired widow. But they were not long without a visitor. John Mellish, artfully taking the banker at a disadvantage in some moment of flurry and confusion at Felden Woods, had extorted from him an invitation to Leamington; and a fortnight after their arrival he presented his stalwart form and fair face at the low wooden gates of the chequered cottage. Aurora laughed (for the first time since her illness) as she saw that faithful adorer come, carpet-bag in hand, through the labyrinth of grass and flower-beds towards the open window at which she and her father sat; and Archibald, seeing that first gleam of gaiety in the beloved face, could have hugged John Mellish for being the cause of it. He would have embraced a street tumbler, or the low comedian of a booth at a fair, or a troop of performing dogs and monkeys, or anything upon earth that could win a smile from his sick child. Like the Eastern potentate in the fairy tale, who always offers half his kingdom and his daughter's hand to any one who can cure the princess of her bilious headache, or extract her carious tooth, Archibald would have opened a banking account in Lombard Street, with a fabulous sum to start with, for any one who could give pleasure to this black-eyed girl, now smiling, for the first time in that year, at sight of the big fair-faced Yorkshireman coming to pay his foolish worship at her shrine.

It was not to be supposed that Mr. Floyd had felt no wonder as to the cause of the rupture of his daughter's engagement to Talbot Bulstrode. The anguish and terror endured by him during her long illness had left no room for any other thought; but since the passing away of the danger, he had pondered not a little upon the abrupt rupture between the lovers. He ventured once, in the first week of their stay at Leamington, to speak to her upon the subject, asking why it was she had dismissed the captain. Now if there was one thing more hateful than another to Aurora Floyd, it was a lie. I do not say that she had never told one in the course of her life. There are some acts of folly which carry falsehood and dissimulation at their heels as certainly as the shadows which follow us when we walk towards the evening sun; and we very rarely swerve from the severe boundary-line of right without being dragged ever so much farther than we calculated upon across the border. Alas! my heroine is not faultless. She would take her shoes off to give them to the barefooted poor; she would take the heart from her breast, if she could by so doing heal the wounds she has inflicted upon the loving heart of her father. But a shadow of mad folly has blotted her motherless youth, and she has a terrible harvest to reap from that lightly-sown seed, and a cruel expiation to make for that unforgotten wrong. Yet her natural disposition is all truth and candour; and there are many young ladies, whose lives have been as primly ruled and ordered as the fair pleasure-gardens of a Tyburnian square,[1] who could tell a falsehood with a great deal better grace than Aurora Floyd. So when her father asked her why she had *dismissed* Talbot Bulstrode, she made no answer to that question; but simply told him that the quarrel had been a very painful one, and that she hoped never to hear the captain's name again: although at the same time she assured Mr. Floyd that her lover's conduct had been in nowise unbecoming a gentleman and a man of honour. Archibald implicitly obeyed his daughter in this matter, and the name of Talbot Bulstrode never being spoken, it seemed as if the young man had dropped out of their lives, or as if he had never had any part in the destiny of Aurora Floyd. Heaven knows what Aurora herself felt and suffered in the quiet of her low-roofed, white-curtained little chamber, with the soft May moonlight stealing in at the casement-windows, and creeping in wan radiance about the walls. Heaven only knows the bitterness of the silent battle. Her vitality made her strong to suffer; her vivid imagination intensified every throb of pain. In a dull and torpid soul grief is a slow anguish; but with her it was a fierce and tempestuous emotion, in which past and future seemed rolled

---

1   i.e. The gardens of a square in Tyburnia, a residential district near Tyburn, in London.

together with the present to make a concentrated agony. But, by an all-wise dispensation, the stormy sorrow wears itself out by reason of its very violence, while the dull woe drags its slow length sometimes through weary years, becoming at last engrafted in the very nature of the patient sufferer, as some diseases become part of our constitutions. Aurora was fortunate in being permitted to fight her battle in silence, and to suffer unquestioned. If the dark hollow rings about her eyes told of sleepless nights, Archibald Floyd forbore to torment her with anxious speeches and trite consolations. The clairvoyance of love told him that it was better to let her alone. So the trouble hanging over the little circle was neither seen nor spoken of. Aurora kept her skeleton in some quiet corner, and no one saw the grim skull, or heard the rattle of the dry bones. Archibald Floyd read his newspapers, and wrote his letters; Mrs. Walter Powell tended the convalescent, who reclined during the best part of the day on the sofa in the open window; and John Mellish loitered about the garden and the farmyard, leaned on the low white gate, smoking his cigar, and talking to the men about the place, and was in and out of the house twenty times in an hour. The banker pondered sometimes in serio-comic perplexity as to what was to be done with this big Yorkshireman, who hung upon him like a good-natured monster of six feet two, conjured into existence by the hospitality of a modern Frankenstein. He had invited him to dinner, and, lo, he appeared to be saddled with him for life. He could not tell the friendly, generous, loud-spoken creature to go away. Besides, Mr. Mellish was on the whole very useful, and he did much towards keeping Aurora in apparently good spirits. Yet, on the other hand, was it right to tamper with this great loving heart? Was it just to let the young man linger in the light of those black eyes, and then send him away when the invalid was equal to the effort of giving him his *congé*?[1] Archibald Floyd did not know that John had been rejected by his daughter on a certain autumn morning at Brighton. So he made up his mind to speak frankly, and sound the depths of his visitor's feelings.

Mrs. Powell was making tea at a little table near one of the windows; Aurora had fallen asleep with an open book in her hand; and

---

[1]   Dismissal.

the banker walked with John Mellish up and down an espaliered alley in the golden sunset.

Archibald freely communicated his perplexities to the Yorkshireman. "I need not tell you, my dear Mellish," he said, "how pleasant it is to me to have you here. I never had a son; but if it had pleased God to give me one, I could have wished him to be just such a frank, noble-hearted fellow as yourself. I'm an old man, and have seen a great deal of trouble – the sort of trouble which strikes deeper home to the heart than any sorrows that begin in Lombard Street or on 'Change; but I feel younger in your society, and I find myself clinging to you and leaning on you as a father might upon his son. You may believe, then, that *I* don't wish to get rid of you."

"I do, Mr. Floyd; but do you think that any one else wishes to get rid of me? Do you think I'm a nuisance to Miss Floyd?"

"No, Mellish," answered the banker energetically. "I am sure that Aurora takes pleasure in your society, and seems to treat you almost as if you were her brother; but – but I know your feelings, my dear boy, and what I fear is, that you may perhaps never inspire a warmer feeling in her heart."

"Let me stay and take my chance, Mr. Floyd," cried John, throwing his cigar across the espaliers, and coming to a dead stop upon the gravel-walk in the warmth of his enthusiasm. "Let me stay and take my chance. If there's any disappointment to be borne, I'll bear it like a man; I'll go back to the Park, and you shall never be bothered with me again. Miss Floyd has rejected me once already; but perhaps I was in too great a hurry. I've grown wiser since then, and I've learnt to bide my time. I've one of the finest estates in Yorkshire; I'm not worse looking than the generality of fellows, or worse educated than the generality of fellows. I mayn't have straight hair, and a pale face, and look as if I'd walked out of a three-volume novel, like Talbot Bulstrode. I may be a stone or two over the correct weight for winning a young lady's heart; but I'm sound, wind and limb. I never told a lie, or committed a mean action; and I love your daughter with as true and pure a love as ever man felt for woman. May I try my luck once more?"

"You may, John."

"And have I, – thank you, sir, for calling me John, – have I your good wishes for my success?"

The banker shook Mr. Mellish by the hand as he answered this question.

"You have, my dear John, my best and heartiest wishes."

So there were three battles of the heart being fought in that spring-tide of fifty-eight. Aurora and Talbot, separated from each other by the length and breadth of half England, yet united by an impalpable chain, were struggling day by day to break its links; while poor John Mellish quietly waited in the background, fighting the sturdy fight of the strong heart, which very rarely fails to win the prize it is set upon, however high or far away that prize may seem to be.

CHAPTER XI.

AT THE CHÂTEAU D'ARQUES.

JOHN MELLISH made himself entirely at home in the little Leamington circle after this interview with Mr. Floyd. No one could have been more tender in his manner, more respectful, untiring, and devoted, than was this rough Yorkshireman to the broken old man. Archibald must have been less than human had he not in somewise returned this devotion, and it is therefore scarcely to be wondered that he became very warmly attached to his daughter's adorer. Had John Mellish been the most designing disciple of Macchiavelli, instead of the most transparent and candid of living creatures, I scarcely think he could have adopted a truer means of making for himself a claim upon the gratitude of Aurora Floyd than by the affection he evinced for her father. And this affection was as genuine as all else in that simple nature. How could he do otherwise than love Aurora's father? He *was* her father. He had a sublime claim upon the devotion of the man who loved her; who loved her as John loved, – unreservedly, undoubtingly, childishly; with such blind, unquestioning love as an infant feels for its mother. There may be better women than that mother, perhaps; but who shall make the child believe so?

John Mellish could not argue with himself upon his passion, as Talbot Bulstrode had done. He could not separate himself from his love, and reason with the wild madness. How could he divide himself from that which was himself; more than himself; a diviner self? He asked no questions about the past life of the woman he loved. He never sought to know the secret of Talbot's departure from Felden. He saw her, beautiful, fascinating, perfect; and he accepted her as a great and wonderful fact, like the round midsummer moon shining down on the rustic flower-beds and espaliered garden-walks in the balmy June nights.

So the tranquil days glided slowly and monotonously past that quiet circle. Aurora bore her silent burden; bore her trouble with a grand courage, peculiar to such rich organizations as her own; and none knew whether the serpent had been rooted from her breast, or had made for himself a permanent home in her heart. The banker's most watchful care could not fathom the womanly mystery; but there were times when Archibald Floyd ventured to hope that his daughter was at peace, and Talbot Bulstrode well-nigh forgotten. In any case, it was wise to keep her away from Felden Woods; so Mr. Floyd proposed a tour through Normandy to his daughter and Mrs. Powell. Aurora consented, with a tender smile and gentle pressure of her father's hand. She divined the old man's motive, and recognized the all-watchful love which sought to carry her from the scene of her trouble. John Mellish, who was not invited to join the party, burst forth into such raptures at the proposal, that it would have required considerable hardness of heart to have refused his escort. He knew every inch of Normandy, he said, and promised to be of infinite use to Mr. Floyd and his daughter; which, seeing that his knowledge of Normandy had been acquired in his attendance at the Dieppe steeple-chases, and that his acquaintance with the French language was very limited, seemed rather doubtful. But for all this he contrived to keep his word. He went up to Town and hired an all-accomplished courier, who conducted the little party from town to village, from church to ruin, and who could always find relays of Normandy horses for the banker's roomy travelling-carriage. The little party travelled from place to place until pale gleams of colour returned in transient flushes to Aurora's cheeks. Grief is terribly selfish. I fear that Miss Floyd never took into consideration the havoc that might be going on in the great honest heart of John Mellish. I dare say that if she had ever considered the matter, she would have thought that a broad-shouldered Yorkshireman of six feet two could never suffer seriously from such a passion as love. She grew accustomed to his society; accustomed to have his strong arm handy for her to lean upon when she grew tired; accustomed to his carrying her sketch-book and shawls and camp-stools; accustomed to be waited upon by him all day, and served faithfully by him at every turn; taking his homage as a thing of course, but making him superlatively and dangerously happy by her tacit acceptance of it.

September was half gone when they bent their way homeward, lingering for a few days at Dieppe, where the bathers were splashing about in semi-theatrical costume, and the Etablissement des Bains[1] was all aflame with coloured lanterns, and noisy with nightly concerts.

The early autumnal days were glorious in their balmy beauty. The best part of a year had gone by since Talbot Bulstrode had bade Aurora that adieu which, in one sense at least, was to be eternal. They two, Aurora and Talbot, might meet again, it is true. They might meet, ay, and even be cordial and friendly together, and do each other good service in some dim time to come; but the two lovers who had parted in the little bay-windowed room at Felden Woods could *never* meet again. Between *them* there was death and the grave.

Perhaps some such thoughts as these had their place in the breast of Aurora Floyd as she sat, with John Mellish at her side, looking down upon the varied landscape from the height upon which the ruined walls of the Château d'Arques still rear the proud memorials of a day that is dead. I don't suppose that the banker's daughter troubled herself much about Henry the Fourth,[2] or any other dead-and-gone celebrity who may have left the impress of his name upon that spot. She felt a tranquil sense of the exquisite purity and softness of the air, the deep blue of the cloudless sky, the spreading woods and grassy plains, the orchards, where the trees were rosy with their plenteous burden, the tiny streamlets, the white villa-like cottages and straggling gardens, outspread in a fair panorama beneath her. Carried out of her sorrow by the sensuous rapture we derive from nature, and for the first time discovering in herself a vague sense of happiness, she began to wonder how it was she had outlived her grief by so many months.

She had never during those weary months heard of Talbot Bulstrode. Any change might have come to him without her knowledge.

---

1 "Semi-theatrical costume" probably describes the then very new development of the women's bathing costume, which featured ankle-length trousers, or bloomers, and a long tunic. This radically different mode of dress would not be popular in England until the 1860s. The *Etablissement des Bains* was the building where the baths were located.

2 The Protestant Henri IV became King of France in 1588 but his succession was opposed by the Roman Catholic Holy League. His 1589 victory at Arques, in Normandy, against the Duc de Mayenne was one step in securing his kingdom.

He might have married; might have chosen a prouder and worthier bride to share his lofty name. She might meet him on her return to England with that happier woman leaning upon his arm. Would some good-natured friend tell the bride how Talbot had loved and wooed the banker's daughter? Aurora found herself pitying this happier woman, who would, after all, win but the second love of that proud heart; the pale reflection of a sun that has set; the feeble glow of expiring embers when the great blaze has died out. They had made her a couch with shawls and carriage-rugs, outspread upon a rustic seat, for she was still far from strong; and she lay in the bright September sunshine, looking down at the fair landscape, and listening to the hum of beetles and the chirp of grasshoppers upon the smooth turf.

Her father had walked to some distance with Mrs. Powell, who explored every crevice and cranny of the ruins with the dutiful perseverance peculiar to commonplace people; but faithful John Mellish never stirred from Aurora's side. He was watching her musing face, trying to read its meaning – trying to gather a gleam of hope from some chance expression flitting across it. Neither he nor she knew how long he had watched her thus, when, turning to speak to him about the landscape at her feet, she found him on his knees imploring her to have pity upon him, and to love him, or to let him love her; which was much the same.

"I don't expect you to love *me*, Aurora," he said passionately; "how should you? What is there in a big clumsy fellow like me to win your love? I don't ask that. I only ask you to let me love you, to let me worship you, as the people we see kneeling in the churches here worship their saints. You won't drive me away from you, will you, Aurora, because I presume to forget what you said to me that cruel day at Brighton? You would never have suffered me to stay with you so long, and to be so happy, if you had meant to drive me away at the last! You never could have been so cruel!"

Miss Floyd looked at him with a sudden terror in her face. What was this? What had she done? More wrong, more mischief? Was her life to be one of perpetual wrong-doing? Was she to be for ever bringing sorrow upon good people? Was this John Mellish to be another sufferer by her folly?

"Oh, forgive me!" she cried, "forgive me! I never thought——"

"You never thought that every day spent by your side must make the anguish of parting from you more cruelly bitter. O Aurora, women should think of these things! Send me away from you, and what shall I be for the rest of my life? – a broken man, fit for nothing better than the race-course and the betting-rooms; a reckless man, ready to go to the bad by any road that can take me there; worthless alike to myself and to others. You must have seen such men, Aurora; men whose unblemished youth promised an honourable manhood; but who break up all of a sudden, and go to ruin in a few years of mad dissipation. Nine times out of ten a woman is the cause of that sudden change. I lay my life at your feet, Aurora; I offer you more than my heart – I offer you my destiny. Do with it as you will."

He rose in his agitation, and walked a few paces away from her. The grass-grown battlements sloped away from his feet; an outer and inner moat lay below him, at the bottom of a steep declivity. What a convenient place for suicide, if Aurora should refuse to take pity upon him! The reader must allow that he had availed himself of considerable artifice in addressing Miss Floyd. His appeal had taken the form of an accusation rather than a prayer, and he had duly impressed upon this poor girl the responsibility she would incur in refusing him. And this, I take it, is a meanness of which men are often guilty in their dealings with the weaker sex.

Miss Floyd looked up at her lover with a quiet, half-mournful smile.

"Sit down there, Mr. Mellish," she said, pointing to a camp-stool at her side.

John took the indicated seat, very much with the air of a prisoner in a criminal dock about to answer for his life.

"Shall I tell you a secret?" asked Aurora, looking compassionately at his pale face.

"A secret?"

"Yes; the secret of my parting with Talbot Bulstrode. It was not I who dismissed him from Felden; it was he who refused to fulfil his engagement with me."

She spoke slowly, in a low voice, as if it were painful to her to say the words which told of so much humiliation.

"He did!" cried John Mellish, rising, red and furious, from his seat, eager to run to look for Talbot Bulstrode then and there, in order to inflict chastisement upon him.

"He did, John Mellish, and he was justified in doing so," answered Aurora, gravely. "You would have done the same."

"O Aurora, Aurora!"

"You would. You are as good a man as he, and why should your sense of honour be less strong than his? A barrier arose between Talbot Bulstrode and me, and separated us for ever. That barrier was a secret."

She told him of the missing year in her young life; how Talbot had called upon her for an explanation, and how she had refused to give it. John listened to her with a thoughtful face, which broke out into sunshine as she turned to him and said –

"How would you have acted in such a case, Mr. Mellish?"

"How should I have acted, Aurora? I should have trusted you. But I can give you a better answer to your question, Aurora. I can answer it by a renewal of the prayer I made you five minutes ago. Be my wife."

"In spite of this secret?"

"In spite of a hundred secrets. I could not love you as I do, Aurora, if I did not believe you to be all that is best and purest in woman. I cannot believe this one moment, and doubt you the next. I give my life and honour into your hands. I would not confide them to the woman whom I could insult by a doubt."

His handsome Saxon face was radiant with love and trustfulness as he spoke. All his patient devotion, so long unheeded, or accepted as a thing of course, recurred to Aurora's mind. Did he not deserve some reward, some requital for all this? But there was one who was nearer and dearer to her, dearer than even Talbot Bulstrode had ever been; and that one was the white-haired old man pottering about amongst the ruins on the other side of the grassy platform.

"Does my father know of this, Mr. Mellish?" she asked.

"He does, Aurora. He has promised to accept me as his son; and Heaven knows I will try to deserve that name. Do not let me distress you, dearest. The murder is out now. You know that I still love you; still hope. Let time do the rest."

She held out both her hands to him with a tearful smile. He took those little hands in his own broad palms, and bending down kissed them reverently.

"You are right," she said; "let time do the rest. You are worthy of the love of a better woman than me, John Mellish; but, with the help of Heaven, I will never give you cause to regret having trusted me."

CHAPTER XII.

STEEVE HARGRAVES, THE "SOFTY."

EARLY in October Aurora Floyd returned to Felden Woods, once more "engaged." The county families opened their eyes when the report reached them that the banker's daughter was going to be married, not to Talbot Bulstrode, but to Mr. John Mellish, of Mellish Park, near Doncaster. The unmarried ladies – rather hanging on hand about Beckenham and West Wickham – did not approve of all this chopping and changing. They recognized the taint of the Prodder blood in this fickleness. The spangles and the sawdust were breaking out, and Aurora was, as they had always said, her mother's own daughter. She was a very lucky young woman, they remarked, in being able, after jilting one rich man, to pick up another; but of course a young person whose father could give her fifty thousand pounds on her wedding-day might be permitted to play fast and loose with the male sex, while worthier Marianas moped in their moated granges till gray hairs showed themselves in glistening *bandeaux*,[1] and cruel crow's feet gathered about the corners of bright eyes. It is well to be merry and wise, and honest and true, and to be off with the old love, &c.; but it is better to be Miss Floyd, of the senior branch of Floyd, Floyd, and Floyd, for then you need be none of these things. At least to such effect was the talk about Beckenham when Archibald brought his daughter back to Felden Woods; and a crowd of dressmakers and milliners set to work at the marriage garments as busily as if Miss Floyd had never had any clothes in her life before.

Mrs. Alexander and Lucy came back to Felden to assist in the preparations for the wedding. Lucy had improved very much in appearance since the preceding winter; there was a happier light in her soft blue eyes, and a healthier hue in her cheeks; but she blushed

---

1 Tennyson's "Mariana" (1830) dramatically portrays the frustration of a woman waiting hopelessly for a lover who never comes. *Bandeaux* are narrow fillets or head bands.

crimson when she first met Aurora, and hung back a little from Miss Floyd's caresses.

The wedding was to take place at the end of November. The bride and bridegroom were to spend the winter in Paris, where Archibald Floyd was to join them, and return to England, "in time for the Craven Meeting," as John Mellish said, – for I am sorry to say that, having been so happily successful in his love-affair, this young man's thoughts returned into their accustomed channels; and the creature he held dearest on earth next to Miss Floyd and those belonging to her, was a bay filly called Aurora, and entered for the Oaks and Leger of a future year.

Ought I to apologize for my heroine, because she has forgotten Talbot Bulstrode, and that she entertains a grateful affection for this adoring John Mellish? She ought, no doubt, to have died of shame and sorrow after Talbot's cruel desertion; and Heaven knows that only her youth and vitality carried her through a very severe battle with the grim rider of the pale horse;[1] but having once passed through that dread encounter, she was, however feeble, in a fair way to recover. These passionate griefs, to kill at all, must kill suddenly. The lovers who die for love in our tragedies die in such a vast hurry, that there is generally some mistake or misapprehension about the business, and the tragedy might have been a comedy if the hero or heroine had only waited for a quarter of an hour. If Othello had but lingered a little before smothering his wife, Mistress Emilia might have come in and sworn and protested; and Cassio, with the handkerchief about his leg, might have been in time to set the mind of the valiant Moor at rest, and put the Venetian dog to confusion. How happily Mr. and Mrs. Romeo Montague might have lived and died, thanks to the dear good friar, if the foolish bridegroom had not been in such a hurry to swallow the vile stuff from the apothecary's! and as people are, I hope and believe, a little wiser in real life than they appear to be upon the stage, the worms very rarely get an honest meal off men and women who have died for love. So Aurora walked through the rooms at Felden in which Talbot Bulstrode had so often walked by her side; and if there was any regret at her heart, it was a quiet sorrow, such as we

---

1 A figure of Death (Revelation 6:2).

feel for the dead, – a sorrow not unmingled with pity, for she thought that the proud son of Sir John Raleigh Bulstrode might have been a happier man if he had been as generous and trusting as John Mellish. Perhaps the healthiest sign of the state of her heart was, that she could speak of Talbot freely, cheerfully, and without a blush. She asked Lucy if she had met Captain Bulstrode that year; and the little hypocrite told her cousin, Yes; that he had spoken to them one day in the Park, and that she believed he had gone into Parliament. She *believed!* Why, she knew his maiden speech by heart, though it was on some hopelessly uninteresting bill in which the Cornish mines were in some vague manner involved with the national survey; and she could have repeated it as correctly as her youngest brother could declaim to his "Romans, countrymen, and lovers."[1] Aurora might forget him, and basely marry a fair-haired Yorkshireman; but for Lucy Floyd earth only held this dark knight, with the severe gray eyes and the stiff leg. Poor Lucy, therefore, loved and was grateful to her brilliant cousin for that fickleness which had brought about such a change in the programme of the gay wedding at Felden Woods. The fair young confidante and bridesmaid could assist in the ceremonial now with a good grace. She no longer walked about like a "corpse alive;" but took a hearty womanly interest in the whole affair, and was very much concerned in a discussion as to the merits of pink *versus* blue for the bonnets of the bridesmaids.

The boisterous happiness of John Mellish seemed contagious, and made a genial atmosphere about the great mansion at Felden. Stalwart Andrew Floyd was delighted with his young cousin's choice. No more refusals to join him in the hunting-field; but half the county breakfasting at Felden, and the long terrace and garden luminous with "pink."[2]

Not a ripple disturbed the smooth current of that brief courtship. The Yorkshireman contrived to make himself agreeable to everybody belonging to his dark-eyed divinity. He flattered their weaknesses, he gratified their caprices, he studied their wishes, and paid them all such insidious court, that I'm afraid invidious comparisons were drawn

---

1   *Julius Caesar* III.ii.13.
2   Scarlet hunting jackets.

between John and Talbot, to the disadvantage of the proud young officer.

It was impossible for any quarrel to arise between the lovers, for John followed his mistress about like some big slave, who only lived to do her bidding; and Aurora accepted his devotion with a Sultana-like grace, which became her amazingly. Once more she visited the stables and inspected her father's stud, for the first time since she had left Felden for the Parisian finishing school. Once more she rode across country, wearing a hat which provoked considerable criticism, – a hat which was no other than the now universal turban, or pork-pie, but which was new to the world in the autumn of fifty-eight.[1] Her earlier girlhood appeared to return to her once more. It seemed almost as if the two years and a half in which she had left and returned to her home, and had met and parted with Talbot Bulstrode, had been blotted from her life, leaving her spirits fresh and bright as they were before that stormy interview in her father's study in the June of fifty-six.

The county families came to the wedding at Beckenham church, and were fain to confess that Miss Floyd looked wondrously hand-some in her virginal crown of orange buds and flowers, and her volu-minous Mechlin veil; she had pleaded hard to be married in a bonnet, but had been overruled by a posse of female cousins.[2] Mr. Richard Gunter provided the marriage feast,[3] and sent a man down to Felden to superintend the arrangements, who was more dashing and splendid to look upon than any of the Kentish guests. John Mellish alternately laughed and cried throughout that eventful morning. Heaven knows how many times he shook hands with Archibald Floyd, carrying the banker off into solitary corners, and swearing, with the tears running down his broad cheeks, to be a good husband to the old man's daugh-ter; so that it must have been a relief to the white-haired old Scotch-

1 A small, turban-like crown with a narrow brim, tilted forward to accommodate a high chignon, and sometimes worn with streamers (called "follow-me-lads") hang-ing down behind. These became very fashionable in the 1860s.

2 Bonnets were worn by brides before veils became popular. Veils were commonly worn with orange blossoms; hence Aurora's "virginal crown."

3 Richard Gunter was a fashionable society caterer whose heavily decorated, multi-tiered cakes were a must for society weddings. Mrs. Alexander, Lucy, and Aurora visit his shop in Berkeley Square in preparation for Aurora's 19th birthday (see 69).

man when Aurora descended the staircase, rustling in violet moiré antique, and surrounded by her bridesmaids, to take leave of this dear father before the prancing steeds carried Mr. and Mrs. Mellish to that most prosaic of hymenial stages, the London Bridge Station.

Mrs. Mellish! Yes, she was Mrs. Mellish now. Talbot Bulstrode read of her marriage in that very column of the newspaper in which he had thought perhaps to see her death. How flatly the romance ended! With what a dull cadence the storm died out, and what a common-place gray, every-day sky succeeded the terrors of the lightning! Less than a year since, the globe had seemed to him to collapse, and creation to come to a standstill because of his trouble; and he was now in Parliament, legislating for the Cornish miners, and getting stout, his ill-natured friends said; and she – she who ought, in accordance with all dramatic propriety, to have died out of hand long before this, she had married a Yorkshire landowner, and would no doubt take her place in the county and play My Lady Bountiful in the village, and be chief patroness at the race-balls, and live happily ever afterwards. He crumpled the 'Times' newspaper, and flung it from him in his rage and mortification. "And I once thought that she loved me!" he cried.

And she did love you, Talbot Bulstrode; loved you as she can never love this honest, generous, devoted John Mellish, though she may by-and-by bestow upon him an affection which is a great deal better worth having. She loved you with the girl's romantic fancy and rever-ent admiration; and tried humbly to fashion her very nature anew, that she might be worthy of your sublime excellence. She loved you as women only love in their first youth, and as they rarely love the men they ultimately marry. The tree is perhaps all the stronger when these first frail branches are lopped away to give place to strong and spreading arms, beneath which a husband and children may shelter.

But Talbot could not see all this. He saw nothing but that brief announcement in the 'Times:' "John Mellish, Esq., of Mellish Park, near Doncaster, to Aurora, only daughter of Archibald Floyd, Banker, of Felden Woods, Kent." He was angry with his sometime love, and more angry with himself for feeling that anger; and he plunged furi-ously into blue-books,[1] to prepare himself for the coming session; and

---

1 Parliamentary or Privy Council reports.

again he took his gun and went out upon the "barren, barren moor-land," as he had done in the first violence of his grief, and wandered down to the dreary sea-shore, where he raved about his "Amy, shallow-hearted,"[1] and tried the pitch of his voice against the ides of February should come round, and the bill for the Cornish miners be laid before the Speaker.

Towards the close of January, the servants at Mellish Park prepared for the advent of Master John and his bride. It was a work of love in that disorderly household, for it pleased them that master would have some one to keep him at home, and that the county would be entertained, and festivals held in the roomy rambling mansion. Architects, upholsterers, and decorators had been busy through the short winter days preparing a suite of apartments for Mrs. Mellish; and the western, or as it was called the Gothic, wing of the house had been restored and remodelled for Aurora, until the oak-roofed chambers blazed with rose-colour and gold, like a mediæval chapel. If John could have expended half his fortune in the purchase of a roc's egg to hang in these apartments, he would have gladly done so. He was so proud of his Cleopatra-like bride, his jewel beyond all parallel amid all gems, that he fancied he could not build a shrine rich enough for his treasure. So the house in which honest country squires and their sensible motherly wives had lived contentedly for nearly three centuries was almost pulled to pieces, before John thought it worthy of the banker's daughter. The trainers and grooms and stable-boys shrugged their shoulders superciliously, and spat fragments of straw disdainfully upon the paved stable-yard, as they heard the clatter of the tools of stone-masons and glaziers busy about the façade of the restored apartments. The stable would be *naught* now, they supposed, and Muster Mellish would be always tied to his wife's apron-string. It was a relief to them to hear that Mrs. Mellish was fond of riding and hunting, and would no doubt take to horse-racing in due time, as the legitimate taste of a lady of position and fortune.

---

1   The disappointed lover of Tennyson's "Locksley Hall" (1842) rails about the false love of his cousin Amy. The stanza actually reads: "O my cousin, shallow-hearted! O my Amy, mine no more!/ O the dreary, dreary moorland! O the barren, barren shore!"

The bells of the village church rang loudly and joyously in the clear winter air as the carriage-and-four which had met John and his bride at Doncaster, dashed into the gates of Mellish Park and up the long avenue to the semi-Gothic, semi-barbaric portico of the great door. Hearty Yorkshire voices rang out in loud cheers of welcome as Aurora stepped from the carriage, and passed under the shadow of the porch and into the old oak hall, which had been hung with ever-greens and adorned with floral devices; amongst which figured the legend, "WELCOME TO MELISH!" and other such friendly inscriptions, more conspicuous for their kindly meaning than their strict orthography. The servants were enraptured with their master's choice. She was so brightly handsome, that the simple-hearted creatures accepted her beauty as we accept the sunlight, and felt a genial warmth in that radiant loveliness, which the most classical perfection could never have inspired. Indeed, a Grecian outline might have been thrown away upon the Yorkshire servants, whose uncultivated tastes were a great deal more disposed to recognize splendour of colour than purity of form. They could not choose but admire Aurora's eyes, which they unanimously declared to be "regular shiners;" and the flash of her white teeth, glancing between the full crimson lips; and the bright flush which lighted up her pale olive skin; and the purple lustre of her massive coronal of plaited hair. Her beauty was of that luxuriant and splendid order which has always most effect upon the masses, and the fascination of her manner was almost akin to sorcery in its power over simple people. I lose myself when I try to describe the feminine intoxications, the wonderful fascination exercised by this dark-eyed siren. Surely the secret of her power to charm must have been the wonderful vitality of her nature, by virtue of which she carried life and animal spirits about with her as an atmosphere, till dull people grew merry by reason of her contagious presence; or perhaps the true charm of her manner was that childlike and exquisite uncon-sciousness of self which made her for ever a new creature; for ever impulsive and sympathetic, acutely sensible of all sorrow in others, though of a nature originally joyous in the extreme.

Mrs. Walter Powell had been transferred from Felden Woods to Mellish Park, and was comfortably installed in her prim apartments when the bride and bridegroom arrived. The Yorkshire housekeeper was to abandon the executive power to the ensign's widow, who was to take all trouble of administration off Aurora's hands.

"Heaven help your friends if they ever had to eat a dinner of my ordering, John," Mrs. Mellish said, making free confession of her ignorance; "I am glad, too, that we have no occasion to turn the poor soul out upon the world once more. Those long columns of advertisements in the 'Times' give me a sick pain at my heart when I think of what a governess must have to encounter. I cannot loll back in my carriage and be 'grateful for my advantages,' as Mrs. Alexander says, when I remember the sufferings of others. I am rather inclined to be discontented with my lot, and to think it a poor thing, after all, to be rich and happy in a world where so many must suffer; so I am glad we can give Mrs. Powell something to do at Mellish Park."

The ensign's widow rejoiced very much in that she was to be retained in such comfortable quarters; but she did not thank Aurora for the benefits received from the open hands of the banker's daughter. She did not thank her, because – she hated her. Why did she hate her? She hated her for the very benefits she received, or rather because she, Aurora, had power to bestow such benefits. She hated her as such slow, sluggish, narrow-minded creatures always hate the frank and generous; hated her as envy will for ever hate prosperity; as Haman hated Mordecai from the height of his throne;[1] and as the man of Haman nature would hate, were he supreme in the universe. If Mrs. Walter Powell had been a duchess, and Aurora a crossing-sweeper, she would still have envied her; she would have envied her glorious eyes and flashing teeth, her imperial carriage and generous soul. This pale, whity-brown-haired woman felt herself contemptible in the presence of Aurora, and she resented the bounteous vitality of this nature which made her conscious of the sluggishness of her own. She detested Mrs. Mellish for the possession of attributes which she felt were richer gifts than all the wealth of the house of Floyd, Floyd, and Floyd melted into one mountain of ore. But it is not for a dependent to hate, except in a decorous and gentlewomanly manner – secretly, in the dim recesses of her soul; while she dresses her face with an unvarying smile – a smile which she puts on every morning with her

---

1 Esther 3:5.

clean collar, and takes off at night when she goes to bed.

Now as, by an all-wise dispensation of Providence, it is not possible for one person so to hate another without that other having a vague consciousness of the deadly sentiment, Aurora felt that Mrs. Powell's attachment to her was of no very profound nature. But the reckless girl did not seek to fathom the depth of any inimical feeling which might lurk in her dependent's breast.

"She is not very fond of me, poor soul!" she said; "and I dare say I torment and annoy her with my careless follies. If I were like that dear considerate little Lucy, now—" And with a shrug of her shoulders, and an unfinished sentence such as this, Mrs. Mellish dismissed the insignificant subject from her mind.

You cannot expect these grand, courageous creatures to be frightened of quiet people. And yet, in the great dramas of life, it is the quiet people who do the mischief. Iago was not a noisy person; though, thank Heaven! it is no longer the fashion to represent him as an oily sneak, whom even the most foolish of Moors *could not* have trusted.

Aurora was at peace. The storms that had so nearly shipwrecked her young life had passed away, leaving her upon a fair and fertile shore. Whatever griefs she had inflicted upon her father's devoted heart had not been mortal; and the old banker seemed a very happy man when he came, in the bright April weather, to see the young couple at Mellish Park. Amongst all the hangers-on of that large establishment there was only one person who did not join in the general voice when Mrs. Mellish was spoken of, and that one person was so very insignificant that his fellow-servants scarcely cared to ascertain his opinion. He was a man of about forty, who had been born at Mellish Park, and had pottered about the stables from his babyhood, doing odd jobs for the grooms, and being reckoned, although a little "fond" upon common matters, a very acute judge of horse-flesh. This man was called Stephen, or, more commonly, Steeve Hargraves. He was a squat, broad-shouldered fellow, with a big head, a pale haggard face, – a face whose ghastly pallor seemed almost unnatural, – reddish-brown eyes, and bushy, sandy eyebrows, which formed a species of penthouse over those sinister-looking eyes. He was the sort of man who is generally called *repulsive*, – a man from whom you recoil with a feeling of instinctive dislike, which is, no doubt, both wicked and unjust; for we have no right to take objection to a man because he has an ugly glitter in his eyes, and shaggy tufts of red hair meeting on the bridge of his nose, and big splay feet, which seem made to crush and destroy whatever comes in their way. This was what Aurora Mellish thought when, a few days after her arrival at the Park, she saw Steeve Hargraves for the first time, coming out of the harness-room with a bridle across his arm. She was angry with herself for the involuntary shudder with which she drew back at the sight of this man, who stood at a little distance polishing the brass ornaments upon a set of harness, and furtively regarding Mrs. Mellish as she leaned on her husband's arm, talking to the trainer about the foals at grass in the meadows outside the Park.

Aurora asked who the man was.

"Why, his name is Hargraves, ma'am," answered the trainer; "but we call him Steeve. He's a little bit touched in the upper story, – a little bit 'fond,' as we call it here; but he's useful about the stables when he pleases; that arnt always though, for he's rather a queer temper, and there's none of us has ever been able to get the upper hand of him, as master knows."

John Mellish laughed.

"No," he said; "Steeve has pretty much his own way in the stables, I fancy. He was a favourite groom of my father's twenty years ago; but he got a fall in the hunting-field, which did him some injury about the head, and he's never been quite right since. Of course this, with my poor father's regard for him, gives him a claim upon us, and we put up with his queer ways, don't we, Langley?"

"Well, we do, sir," said the trainer; "though, upon my honour, I'm sometimes half afraid of him, and begin to think he'll get up in the middle of the night and murder some of us."

"Not till some of you have won a hatful of money, Langley. Steeve's a little too fond of the brass[1] to murder any of you for nothing. You shall see his face light up presently, Aurora," said John, beckoning to the stable-man. "Come here, Steeve. Mrs. Mellish wishes you to drink her health."

He dropped a sovereign into the man's broad muscular palm, – the hand of a gladiator, with horny flesh and sinews of iron. Steeve's red

---

1 Slang: too fond of money.

eyes glistened as his fingers closed upon the money.

"Thank you kindly, my lady," he said, touching his cap.

He spoke in a low subdued voice, which contrasted so strangely with the physical power manifest in his appearance that Aurora drew back with a start.

Unhappily for this poor "fond" creature, whose person was in itself repulsive, there was something in this inward, semi-whispering voice which gave rise to an instinctive dislike in those who heard him speak for the first time.

He touched his greasy woollen cap once more, and went slowly back to his work.

"How white his face is!" said Aurora. "Has he been ill?"

"No. He has had that pale face ever since his fall. I was too young when it happened, to remember much about it; but I have heard my father say, that when they brought the poor creature home, his face, which had been florid before, was as white as a sheet of writing-paper, and his voice, until that period strong and gruff, was reduced to the half-whisper in which he now speaks. The doctors did all they could for him, and carried him through an awful attack of brain-fever; but they could never bring back his voice, nor the colour to his cheeks."

"Poor fellow!" said Mrs. Mellish gently; "he is very much to be pitied."

She was reproaching herself, as she said this, for that feeling of repugnance which she could not overcome. It was a repugnance closely allied to terror; she felt as if she could scarcely be happy at Mellish Park while that man was on the premises. She was half inclined to beg her indulgent husband to pension him off, and send him to the other end of the county; but the next moment she was ashamed of her childish folly, and a few hours afterwards had forgotten Steeve Hargraves, the "Softy," as he was politely called in the stables.

Reader, when any creature inspires you with this instinctive unreasoning abhorrence, avoid that creature. He is dangerous. Take warning, as you take warning by the clouds in the sky, and the ominous stillness of the atmosphere when there is a storm coming. Nature cannot lie; and it is nature which has planted that shuddering terror in your breast; an instinct of self-preservation rather than of cowardly fear, which at the first sight of some fellow-creature tells you more plainly than words can speak, "That man is my enemy!"

Had Aurora suffered herself to be guided by this instinct, – had she given way to the impulse which she despised as childish, and caused Stephen Hargraves to be dismissed from Mellish Park, what bitter misery, what cruel anguish, might have been spared to herself and others!

The mastiff Bow-wow had accompanied his mistress to her new home; but Bow-wow's best days were done. A month before Aurora's marriage he had been run over by a pony-carriage in one of the roads about Felden, and had been conveyed, bleeding and disabled, to the veterinary surgeon's, to have one of his hind-legs put into splints, and to be carried through his sufferings by the highest available skill in the science of dog-doctoring. Aurora drove every day to Croydon to see her sick favourite; and at the worst Bow-wow was always well enough to recognize his beloved mistress, and roll his listless, feverish tongue over her white hands, in token of that unchanging brute affection which can only perish with life. So the mastiff was quite lame as well as half blind when he arrived at Mellish Park, with the rest of Aurora's goods and chattels. He was a privileged creature in the roomy mansion; a tiger-skin was spread for him upon the hearth in the drawing-room, and he spent his declining days in luxurious repose, basking in the fire-light or sunning himself in the windows, as it pleased his royal fancy; but, feeble as he was, always able to limp after Mrs. Mellish when she walked on the lawn or in the woody shrubberies which skirted the gardens.

One day, when she had returned from her morning's ride with John and her father, who accompanied them sometimes upon a quiet gray cob, and seemed a younger man for the exercise, she lingered on the lawn in her riding-habit after the horses had been taken back to the stables, and Mr. Mellish and his father-in-law had re-entered the house. The mastiff saw her from the drawing-room window, and crawled out to welcome her. Tempted by the exquisite softness of the atmosphere, she strolled, with her riding-habit gathered under her arm and her whip in her hand, looking for primroses under the clumps of trees upon the lawn. She gathered a cluster of wild-flowers, and was returning to the house, when she remembered some directions respecting a favourite pony that was ill, which she had omitted to give to her groom.

She crossed the stable-yard, followed by Bow-wow, found the groom, gave him her orders, and went back to the gardens. While talking to the man, she had recognized the white face of Steeve Hargraves at one of the windows of the harness-room. He came out while she was giving her directions, and carried a set of harness across to a coach-house on the opposite side of the quadrangle. Aurora was on the threshold of the gates opening from the stables into the gardens, when she was arrested by a howl of pain from the mastiff Bow-wow. Rapid as lightning in every movement, she turned round in time to see the cause of this cry. Steeve Hargraves had sent the animal reeling away from him with a kick from his iron-bound clog. Cruelty to animals was one of the failings of the "Softy." He was not cruel to the Mellish horses, for he had sense enough to know that his daily bread depended upon his attention to them; but Heaven help any outsider that came in his way! Aurora sprang upon him like a beautiful tigress, and catching the collar of his fustian jacket in her slight hands, rooted him to the spot upon which he stood. The grasp of those slender hands, convulsed by passion, was not to be easily shaken off; and Steeve Hargraves, taken completely off his guard, stared aghast at his assailant. Taller than the stable-man by a foot and a half, she towered above him, her cheeks white with rage, her eyes flashing fury, her hat fallen off, and her black hair tumbling about her shoulders, sublime in her passion.

The man crouched beneath the grasp of the imperious creature.

"Let me go!" he gasped, in his inward whisper, which had a hissing sound in his agitation; "let me go, or you'll be sorry; let me go!"

"How dared you!" cried Aurora, – "how dared you hurt him? My poor dog! My poor lame, feeble dog! How dared you to do it? You cowardly dastard! you――"

She disengaged her right hand from his collar and rained a shower of blows upon his clumsy shoulders with her slender whip; a mere toy, with emeralds set in its golden head, but stinging like a rod of flexible steel in that little hand.

"How dared you!" she repeated again and again, her cheeks changing from white to scarlet in the effort to hold the man with one hand.

Her tangled hair had fallen to her waist by this time, and the whip was broken in half a dozen places.

John Mellish, entering the stable-yard by chance at this very moment, turned white with horror at beholding the beautiful fury.

"Aurora! Aurora!" he cried, snatching the man's collar from her grasp, and hurling him half a dozen paces off. "Aurora, what is it?"

She told him in broken gasps the cause of her indignation. He took the splintered whip from her hand, picked up her hat, which she had trodden upon in her rage, and led her across the yard towards the back entrance to the house. It was such bitter shame to him to think that this peerless, this adored creature should do anything to bring disgrace, or even ridicule, upon herself. He would have stripped off his coat and fought with half a dozen coal-heavers, and thought nothing of it; but that she——!

"Go in, go in, my darling girl," he said, with sorrowful tenderness; "the servants are peeping and prying about, I dare say. You should not have done this; you should have told me."

"I should have told you!" she cried impatiently. "How could I stop to tell you when I saw him strike my dog, my poor lame dog?"

"Go in, darling, go in! There, there, calm yourself, and go in."

He spoke as if he had been trying to soothe an agitated child, for he saw by the convulsive heaving of her breast that the violent emotion would terminate in hysteria, as all womanly fury must, sooner or later. He half led, half carried her up a back staircase to her own room, and left her lying on a sofa in her riding-habit. He thrust the broken whip into his pocket, and then, setting his strong white teeth and clenching his fist, went to look for Stephen Hargraves. As he crossed the hall in his way out, he selected a stout leather-thonged hunting-whip from a stand of formidable implements. Steeve, the "Softy," was sitting on a horse-block when John re-entered the stable-yard. He was rubbing his shoulders with a very doleful face, while a couple of grinning stable-boys, who had perhaps witnessed his chastisement, watched him from a respectful distance. They had no inclination to go too near him just then, for the "Softy" had a playful habit of brandishing a big clasp-knife when he felt himself aggrieved; and the bravest lad in the stables had no wish to die from a stab in the abdomen, with the pleasant conviction that his murderer's heaviest punishment might be a fortnight's imprisonment, or an easy fine.

"Now, Mr. Hargraves," said John Mellish, lifting the "Softy" off the horse-block and planting him at a convenient distance for giving full play to the hunting-whip, "it wasn't Mrs. Mellish's business to horsewhip you, but it was her duty to let me do it for her; so take that, you coward."

The leathern thong whistled in the air, and curled about Steeve's shoulders; but John felt there was something despicable in the unequal contest. He threw the whip away, and still holding him by the collar, conducted the "Softy" to the gates of the stable-yard.

"You see that avenue," he said, pointing down a fair glade that stretched before them; "it leads pretty straight out of the Park, and I strongly recommend you, Mr. Stephen Hargraves, to get to the end of it as fast as ever you can, and never to show your ugly white face upon an inch of ground belonging to me again. D'ye hear?"

"E-es, sir."

"Stay! I suppose there's wages or something due to you." He took a handful of money from his waistcoat-pocket and threw it on the ground, sovereigns and half-crowns rolling hither and thither on the gravel-path; then turning on his heel, he left the "Softy" to pick up the scattered treasure. Steeve Hargraves dropped on his knees, and groped about till he had found the last coin; then, as he slowly counted the money from one hand into the other, his white face relapsed into a grin: John Mellish had given him gold and silver amounting to upwards of two years of his ordinary wages.

He walked a few paces down the avenue, and then looking back shook his fist at the house he was leaving behind him.

"You're a fine-spirited madam, Mrs. John Mellish, sure enough," he muttered; "but never you give me a chance of doing you any mischief, or by the Lord, *fond* as I am, I'll do it! They think the 'Softy's' up to naught, perhaps. Wait a bit."

He took his money from his pocket again, and counted it once more, as he walked slowly towards the gates of the Park.

It will be seen, therefore, that Aurora had two enemies, one without and one within her pleasant home: one for ever brooding discontent and hatred within the holy circle of the domestic hearth; the other plotting ruin and vengeance without the walls of the citadel.

CHAPTER XIII.

THE SPRING MEETING.

THE early spring brought Lucy Floyd on a visit to her cousin, a wondering witness of the happiness that reigned at Mellish Park.

Poor Lucy had expected to find Aurora held as something better than the dogs, and a little higher than the horses, in that Yorkshire household; and was considerably surprised to find her dark-eyed cousin a despotic and capricious sovereign, reigning with undisputed sway over every creature, biped or quadruped, upon the estate. She was surprised to see the bright glow in her cheeks, the merry sparkle in her eyes; surprised to hear the light tread of her footstep, the gushing music of her laugh; surprised, in fact, to discover that, instead of weeping over the dry bones of her dead love for Talbot Bulstrode, Aurora had learned to love her husband.

Have I any need to be ashamed of my heroine in that she had forgotten her straight-nosed, gray-eyed Cornish lover, who had set his pride and his pedigree between himself and his affection, and had loved her at best with a reservation, although Heaven only knows how dearly he had loved her? Have I any cause to blush for this poor, impetuous girl, if, turning in the sickness of her sorrowful heart with a sense of relief and gratitude to the honest shelter of John's love, she had quickly learnt to feel for him an affection which repaid him a thousandfold for his long-suffering devotion? Surely it would have been impossible for any true-hearted woman to withhold some such repayment for such a love as that which in every word, and look, and thought, and deed, John Mellish bestowed upon his wife. How could she be for ever his creditor for such a boundless debt? Are hearts like his common amongst our clay? Is it a small thing to be beloved with this loyal and pure affection? Is it laid so often at the feet of any mortal woman that she should spurn and trample upon the holy offering?

He had loved; and more, he had trusted her. He had trusted her, when the man who passionately loved her had left her in an agony of doubt and despair. The cause of this lay in the difference between the two men. John Mellish had as high and stern a sense of honour as

Talbot Bulstrode; but while the proud Cornishman's strength of brain lay in the reflective faculties, the Yorkshireman's acute intellect was strongest in its power of perception. Talbot drove himself half mad with imagining what *might be*; John saw what *was;* and he saw, or fancied he saw, that the woman he loved was worthy of all love; and he gave his peace and honour freely into her keeping.

He had his reward. He had his reward in her frank womanly affection, and in the delight of seeing that she was happy; no cloud upon her face, no shadow on her life, but ever-beaming joy in her eyes, ever-changing smiles upon her lips. She was happy in the calm security of her home, happy in that pleasant stronghold in which she was so fenced about and guarded by love and devotion. I do not know that she ever felt any romantic or enthusiastic love for this big Yorkshireman; but I do know that from the first hour in which she laid her head upon his broad breast she was true to him – true as a wife should be; true in every thought; true in the merest shadow of a thought. A wide gulf yawned around the altar of her home, separating her from every other man in the universe, and leaving her alone with that one man whom she had accepted as her husband. She had accepted him in the truest and purest sense of the word. She had accepted him from the hand of God, as the protector and shelterer of her life; and morning and night, upon her knees, she thanked the gracious Creator who had made this man for her help-meet.

But after duly setting down all this, I have to confess that poor John Mellish was cruelly henpecked. Such big, blustering fellows are created to be the much-enduring subjects of petticoat government; and they carry the rosy garlands until their dying hour with a sublime unconsciousness that those floral chains are not very easy to be broken. Your little man is self-assertive, and for ever on his guard against womanly domination. All tyrannical husbands on record have been little men, from Mr. Daniel Quilp[1] upwards; but who could ever convince a fellow of six foot two in his stockings that he was afraid of his wife? He submits to the pretty tyrant with a quiet smile of resignation. What does it matter? She is so little, so fragile; he could break

---

1   The vicious dwarf in Charles Dickens' *The Old Curiosity Shop* (1841) keeps his mild
     wife in terrified submission.

that tiny wrist with one twist of his big thumb and finger; and in the mean time, till affairs get desperate, and such measures become necessary, it's as well to let her have her own way.

John Mellish did not even debate the point. He loved her, and he laid himself down to be trampled upon by her gracious feet. Whatever she did or said was charming, bewitching, and wonderful to him. If she ridiculed and laughed at him, her laughter was the sweetest harmony in creation; and it pleased him to think that his absurdities could give birth to such music. If she lectured him, she arose to the sublimity of a priestess, and he listened to her and worshipped her as the most noble of living creatures. And with all this, his innate manliness of character preserved him from any taint of that quality our *argot* has christened *spooneyism*.[1] It was only those who knew him well and watched him closely who could fathom the full depths of his tender weakness. The noblest sentiments approach most nearly to the universal, and this love of John's was in a manner universal. It was the love of husband, father, mother, brother, melted into one comprehensive affection. He had a mother's weak pride in Aurora, a mother's foolish vanity in the wonderful creature, the *rara avis*[2] he had won from her nest to be his wife. If Mrs. Mellish was complimented while John stood by, he simpered like a school-girl who blushes at a handsome man's first flatteries. I'm afraid he bored his male acquaintance about "my wife:" her marvellous leap over the bullfinch;[3] the plan she drew for the new stables, "which the architect said was a better plan than he could have drawn himself, sir, by Gad" (a clever man, that Doncaster architect); the surprising way in which she had discovered the fault in the chestnut colt's off fore-leg; the pencil sketch she had made of her dog Bow-wow ("Sir Edwin Landseer[4] might have been proud of such spirit and dash, sir"). All these things did the county gentlemen hear,

---

1   i.e. that our slang calls "spooneyism". Spooneyism is sentimental, foolish amorousness.

2   Rare bird.

3   A quickset hedge (of living plants or shrubbery) with a ditch on one side or the other.

4   Sir Edwin Landseer (1802-73), popular English painter and sculptor, primarily famous as a painter of dogs and other animals, especially in hunting and sporting scenes.

until, perhaps, they grew a shade weary of John's talk of "my wife."
But they were never weary of Aurora herself. She took her place at
once among them; and they bowed down to her and worshipped her,
envying John Mellish the ownership of such a high-bred filly, as I fear
they were but likely, unconsciously, to designate my black-eyed
heroine.

The domain over which Aurora found herself empress was no
inconsiderable one. John Mellish had inherited an estate which
brought him an income of something between sixteen and seventeen
thousand a year. Far-away farms, upon wide Yorkshire wolds and
fenny Lincolnshire flats, owned him master; and the intricate secrets
of his possessions were scarcely known to himself, – known, perhaps,
to none but his land-steward and solicitor, a grave gentleman who
lived in Doncaster, and drove about once a fortnight down to Mellish
Park, much to the horror of its light-hearted master, to whom "business" was a terrible bugbear. Not that I would have the reader for a
moment imagine John Mellish an empty-headed blockhead, with no
comprehension save for his own daily pleasures. He was not a reading
man, nor a business man, nor a politician, nor a student of the natural
sciences. There was an observatory in the Park; but John had fitted it
up as a smoking-room, the revolving openings in the roof being very
convenient for letting out the effluvia of his guests' cheroots and
Havanas; Mr. Mellish caring for the stars very much after the fashion
of that Assyrian monarch who was content to see them shine, and
thank their Maker for their beauty.[1] He was not a spiritualist; and
unless one of the tables at Mellish could have given him "a tip" for the
"Sellinger,"[2] or Great Ebor, he would have cared very little if every
inch of walnut and rosewood in his house had grown oracular. But for
all this he was no fool; he had that brightly clear intellect which very
often accompanies perfect honesty of purpose, and which is the very
intellect of all others most successful in the discomfiture of all knav-

---

1   The Assyrian King Asurbanipal, called Sardanapalus by Greek writers. In Byron's
    play *Sardanapalus* (1821), he is depicted gazing at the stars; "I love them;/ I love to
    watch them in the deep blue vault,/ . . . . but whether they may be/ Gods, as some
    say, or simply lamps of night,/ Worlds, or the lights of worlds, I know nor care not"
    (II.i).
2   Northern dialect for St. Leger.

ery. He was not a creature to despise, for his very weaknesses were manly. Perhaps Aurora felt this, and that it was something to rule over such a man. Sometimes, in an outburst of loving gratitude, she would nestle her handsome head upon his breast, – tall as she was, she was only tall enough to take shelter under his wing, – and tell him that he was the dearest and the best of men, and that, although she might love him to her dying day, she could never, *never* NEVER love him half as much as he deserved. After which, half ashamed of herself for the sentimental declaration, she would alternately ridicule, lecture, and tyrannize over him for the rest of the day.

Lucy beheld this state of things with silent bewilderment. Could the woman who had once been loved by Talbot Bulstrode sink to *this?* The happy wife of a fair-haired Yorkshireman; with her fondest wishes concentred in her namesake the bay filly, which was to run in a weight-for-age race at the York Spring, and was entered for the ensuing Derby; interested in a tan gallop, a new stable; talking of mysterious but evidently all-important creatures, called by such names as Scott and Fobert and Chiffney and Challoner;[1] and to all appearance utterly forgetful of the fact that there existed upon the earth a divinity with fathomless gray eyes, known to mortals as the heir of Bulstrode. Poor Lucy was like to have been driven well-nigh demented by the talk about this bay filly, Aurora, as the Spring Meeting drew near. She was taken to see her every morning by Aurora and John, who, in their anxiety for the improvement of their favourite, looked at the animal upon each visit as if they expected some wonderful physical transformation to have occurred in the stillness of the night.

---

1   "Scott" probably refers to Bill Scott, jockey, four-time Derby winner, nine-time winner of the St. Leger, who famously rode the Derby while drunk in 1846; it may refer to his brother, John Scott, trainer of the Derby winners in 1830s, 40s, and 50s. "Chiffney" is probably the jockey Sam Chifney Jr., who stopped (i.e. rode with deliberate intention not to win) the Derby favourite in 1812 and won the Derby in 1818 and 1820; it may refer to his father, Sam Chifney Sr., the most skilful rider of his day, and the jockey suspected of stopping the Prince of Wales' horse, Escape, in 1781; it could refer to William Chifney, brother of Sam Jr., who trained Derby winners in 1818, 1820, and 1830. John Fobert trained in the Spigot Lodge Stable at Middleham and won the Derby with The Flying Dutchman in 1849. The jockey Tom Challoner won the St. Leger in 1861, the Oaks and the St. Leger in 1862, and the Derby in 1863.

The loose box in which the filly was lodged was watched night and day by an amateur detective force of stable-boys and hangers-on; and John Mellish once went so far as to dip a tumbler into the pail of water provided for the bay filly, Aurora, to ascertain, of his own experience, that the crystal fluid was innocuous; for he grew nervous as the eventful day drew nigh, and was afraid of lurking danger to the filly from dark-minded touts[1] who might have heard of her in London. I fear the touts troubled their heads very little about this graceful two-year old, though she had the blood of Old Melbourne and West Australian in her veins,[2] to say nothing of other aristocracy upon the maternal side. The suspicious gentlemen hanging about York and Doncaster in those early April days were a great deal too much occupied with Lord Glasgow's lot, and John Scott's lot, and Lord Zetland's and Mr. Merry's lot, and other lots of equal distinction, to have much time to prowl about Mellish Park, or peer into that meadow which the young man had caused to be surrounded by an eight-foot fence for the privacy of the Derby winner *in futuro*.[3] Lucy declared the filly to be the loveliest of creatures, and safe to win any number of cups and plates that might be offered for equine competition; but she was always glad, when the daily visit was over, to find herself safely out of reach of those high-bred hind-legs, which seemed to possess a faculty for being in all four corners of the loose box at one and the same moment.

The first day of the Meeting came, and found half the Mellish household established at York: John and his family at an hotel near the betting-rooms; and the trainer, his satellites, and the filly, at a little inn close to the Knavesmire. Archibald Floyd did his best to be interested in the event which was so interesting to his children; but he freely confessed to his grandniece, Lucy, that he heartily wished the Meeting over, and the merits of the bay filly decided. She had stood her trial nobly, John said; not winning with a rush, it is true; in point of fact, being in a manner beaten; but evincing a power to *stay*, which

---

1 Someone who surreptitiously watches the training of racehorses in order to gain information for betting purposes.

2 West Australian, sired by Melbourne, won the Triple Crown in 1853. West Australian was not, in fact, a success at stud.

3 Future Derby winner.

promised better for the future than any two-year-old velocity. When the saddling-bell rang, Aurora, her father, and Lucy were stationed in the balcony, a crowd of friends about them; Mrs. Mellish, with a pencil in her hand, putting down all manner of impossible bets in her excitement, and making such a book as might have been preserved as a curiosity in sporting annals. John was pushing in and out of the ring below; tumbling over small book-men in his agitation; dashing from the ring to the weighing-house; and hanging about the small pale-faced boy who was to ride the filly as anxiously as if the jockey had been a prime minister, and John a family-man with half a dozen sons in need of Government appointments. I tremble to think how many bonuses, in the way of five-pound notes, John promised this pale-faced lad, on condition that the stakes (some small matter amounting to about sixty pounds) were pulled off – pulled off where, I wonder? – by the bay filly Aurora. If the youth had not been of that preternatural order of beings who seem born of an emotionless character to wear silk for the good of their fellow-men, his brain must certainly have been dazed by the variety of conflicting directions which John Mellish gave him within the critical last quarter of an hour; but having received his orders early that morning from the trainer, accompanied with a warning not to suffer himself to be *tewed* (Yorkshire *patois* for worried) by anything Mr. Mellish might say, the sallow-complexioned lad walked about in the calm serenity of innocence, – there are honest jockeys in the world, – and took his seat in the saddle with as even a pulse as if he had been about to ride in an omnibus.

There were some people upon the Stand that morning who thought the face of Aurora Mellish as pleasant a sight as the smooth greensward of the Knavesmire, or the best horse-flesh in the county of York. All forgetful of herself in her excitement, with her natural vivacity multiplied by the animation of the scene before her, she was more than usually lovely; and Archibald Floyd looked at her with a fond emotion, so intermingled with gratitude to Heaven for the happiness of his daughter's destiny as to be almost akin to pain. She was happy; she was thoroughly happy at last, this child of his dead Eliza, this sacred charge left to him by the woman he had loved; she was happy, and she was *safe;* he could go to his grave resignedly to-morrow, if it pleased God, – knowing this. Strange thoughts, perhaps, for a crowded race-course; but our most solemn fancies do not come always in solemn places. Nay, it is often in the midst of crowds and confusion that our souls wing their loftiest flights, and the saddest memories return to us. You see a man sitting at some theatrical entertainment, with a grave, abstracted face, over which no change of those around him has any influence. He may be thinking of his dead wife, dead ten years ago; he may be acting over well-remembered scenes of joy and sorrow; he may be recalling cruel words, never to be atoned for upon earth, angry looks gone to be registered against him in the skies; while his children are laughing at the clown on the stage below him. He may be moodily meditating inevitable bankruptcy or coming ruin, holding imaginary meetings with his creditors, and contemplating prussic acid upon the refusal of his certificate, while his eldest daughter is crying with Pauline Deschappelles.[1] So Archibald Floyd, while the numbers were going up, and the jockeys being weighed, and the book-men clamouring below him, leaned over the broad ledge of the stone balcony, and, looking far away across the grassy amphitheatre, thought of the dead wife who had bequeathed to him this precious daughter.

The bay filly, Aurora, was beaten ignominiously. Mrs. Mellish turned white with despair as she saw the amber jacket, black belt, and blue cap crawling in at the heels of the ruck, the jockey looking pale defiance at the bystanders: as who should say that the filly had never been meant to win, and that the defeat of to-day was but an artfully-concocted *ruse* whereby fortunes were to be made in the future? John Mellish, something used to such disappointments, crept away to hide his discomfiture outside the ring; but Aurora dropped her card and pencil, and, stamping her foot upon the stone flooring of the balcony, told Lucy and the banker that it was a shame, and that the boy must have sold the race, as it was *impossible* the filly could have been fairly beaten. As she turned to say this, her cheeks flushed with passion, and her eyes flashing bright indignation on any one who might stand in the way to receive the angry electric light, she became aware of a pale face and a pair of gray eyes earnestly regarding her from the threshold of an open window two or three paces off; and in another moment

---

1   The heroine of Bulwer Lytton's *The Lady of Lyons, or Love and Pride* (1838).

both she and her father had recognized Talbot Bulstrode.

The young man saw that he was recognized, and approached them, hat in hand, – very, very pale, as Lucy always remembered, – and, with a voice that trembled as he spoke, wished the banker and the two ladies "Good day."

And it was thus that they met, these two who had "parted in silence and tears," more than "half broken-hearted,"[1] to sever, as they thought, for eternity; it was thus – upon this commonplace, prosaic, half-guinea Grand Stand – that Destiny brought them once more face to face.

A year ago, and how often in the spring twilight Aurora Floyd had pictured her possible meeting with Talbot Bulstrode! He would come upon her suddenly, perhaps, in the still moonlight, and she would swoon away and die at his feet of the unendurable emotion. Or they would meet in some crowded assembly; she dancing, laughing with hollow, simulated mirth; and the shock of one glance of those eyes would slay her in her painted glory of jewels and grandeur. How often, ah, how often she had acted the scene and felt the anguish! – only a year ago, less than a year ago, ay, even so lately as on that balmy September day when she had lain on the rustic couch at the Château d'Arques, looking down at the fair Normandy landscape, with faithful John at watch by her side, the tame goats browsing upon the grassy platform behind her, and preternaturally ancient French children teasing the mild, long-suffering animals. And to-day she met him with her thoughts so full of the horse which had just been beaten, that she scarcely knew what she said to her sometime lover. Aurora Floyd was dead and buried, and Aurora Mellish, looking critically at Talbot Bulstrode, wondered how any one could have ever gone near to the gates of death for the love of him.

It was Talbot who grew pale at this unlooked-for encounter; it was Talbot whose voice was shaken in the utterance of those few every-day syllables which common courtesy demanded of him. The captain had not so easily learned to forget. He was older than Aurora, and he had reached the age of two-and-thirty without having ever loved woman, only to be the more desperately attacked by the fatal disease when his time came. He suffered acutely at that sudden meeting.

---

1   A quotation from the first stanza of Byron's "When We Two Parted" (1816).

Wounded in his pride by her serene indifference, dazzled afresh by her beauty, mad with jealous fury at the thought that he had lost her, Captain Bulstrode's feelings were of no very enviable nature; and if Aurora had ever wished to avenge that cruel scene at Felden Woods, her hour of vengeance had most certainly come. But she was too generous a creature to have harboured such a thought. She had submitted in all humility to Talbot's decree; she had accepted his decision, and had believed in its justice; and seeing his agitation to-day, she was sorry for him. She pitied him, with a tender, matronly compassion; such as she, in the safe harbour of a happy home, might be privileged to feel for this poor wanderer, still at sea on life's troubled ocean. Love, and the memory of love, must indeed have died before we can feel like this. The terrible passion must have died that slow and certain death, from the grave of which no haunting ghost ever returns to torment the survivors. It was, and it is not. Aurora might have been shipwrecked and cast on a desert island with Talbot Bulstrode, and might have lived ten years in his company, without ever feeling for ten seconds as she had felt for him once. With these impetuous and impressionable people, who live quickly, a year is sometimes as twenty years; so Aurora looked back at Talbot Bulstrode across a gulf which stretched for weary miles between them, and wondered if they had really ever stood side by side, allied by Hope and Love, in the days that were gone.

While Aurora was thinking of these things, as well as a little of the bay filly, and while Talbot, half choked by a thousand confused emotions, tried to appear preternaturally at his ease, John Mellish, having refreshed his spirits with bottled beer, came suddenly upon the party, and slapped the captain on the back.

He was not jealous, this happy John. Secure in his wife's love and truth, he was ready to face a regiment of her old admirers; indeed, he rather delighted in the idea of avenging Aurora upon this cowardly lover. Talbot glanced involuntarily at the members of the York constabulary on the course below; wondering how they would act if he were to fling John Mellish over the stone balcony, and do a murder then and there. He was thinking this while John was nearly wringing off his hand in cordial salutation, and asking what the deuce had brought him to the York Spring.

Talbot explained rather lamely that, being knocked up by his Parliamentary work, he had come down to spend a few days with an old brother-officer, Captain Hunter, who had a place between York and Leeds.

Mr. Mellish declared that nothing could be more lucky than this. He knew Hunter well; the two men must join them at dinner that day; and Talbot must give them a week at the Park after he left the captain's place.

Talbot murmured some vague protestation of the impossibility of this, to which John paid no attention whatever, hustling his sometime rival away from the ladies in his eagerness to get back to the ring, where he had to complete his book for the next race.

So Captain Bulstrode was gone once more, and throughout the brief interview no one had cared to notice Lucy Floyd, who had been pale and red by turns half a dozen times within the last ten minutes.

John and Talbot returned after the start, with Captain Hunter, who was brought on to the stand to be presented to Aurora, and who immediately entered into a very animated discussion upon the day's racing. How Captain Bulstrode abhorred this idle babble of horse-flesh; this perpetual jargon, alike in every mouth – from Aurora's rosy Cupid's bow to the tobacco-tainted lips of the book-men in the ring! Thank Heaven, this was not *his* wife who knew all the slang of the course, and, with *lorgnette* in hand, was craning her swan-like throat to catch sight of a bend in the Knavesmire and the horse that had a lead of half a mile.

Why had he ever consented to come into this accursed horse-racing county? Why had he deserted the Cornish miners, even for a week? Better to be wearing out his brains over Dryasdust pamphlets and Parliamentary minutes than to be here; desolate amongst this shallow-minded, clamorous multitude, who have nothing to do but to throw up caps and cry huzza for any winner of any race. Talbot, as a bystander, could not but remark this, and draw from this something of a philosophical lesson on life. He saw that there was always the same clamour and the same rejoicing in the crowd, whether the winning jockey wore blue and black belt, yellow and black cap, white with scarlet spots, or any other variety of colour, even to dismal sable; and he could but wonder how this was. Did the unlucky speculators run away and hide themselves while the uplifted voices were rejoicing? When the welkin was rent with the name of Caractacus or Tim Whiffler, where were the men who had backed Buckstone or the Marquis unflinchingly up to the dropping of the flag and the ringing of the bell? When Thormanby came in with a rush, where were the wretched creatures whose fortunes hung on "the Yankee" or Wizard?[1] They were voiceless, these poor unlucky ones, crawling away with sick white faces to gather in groups, and explain to each other, with stable jargon intermingled with oaths, how the victory just over ought not to have been, and never could have been, but for some unlooked-for and preposterous combination of events never before witnessed upon any mortal course. How little is ever seen of the losers in any of the great races run upon this earth! For years and years the name of Louis Napoleon is an empty sound, signifying nothing; when, lo, a few master strokes of policy and *finesse*, a little juggling with those pieces of pasteboard out of which are built the shaky card-palaces men call empires, and creation rings with the same name; the outsider emerges from the ruck, and the purple jacket spotted with golden bees is foremost in the mighty race.[2]

Talbot Bulstrode leaned with folded arms upon the stone balustrade, looking down at the busy life below him, and thinking of these things. Pardon him for his indulgence in dreary platitudes and worn-out sentimentalities. He was a desolate, purposeless man; entered for no race himself; scratched for the matrimonial stakes; embittered by disappointment; soured by doubt and suspicion. He had spent the dull winter months upon the Continent, having no

---

1 Caractacus won the Derby in 1862 at 40:1 odds against the favourites Marquis and Buckstone. Tim Whiffler beat Buckstone by a length in the Doncaster Cup of 1862. Thornanby won the Derby in 1860 against the favourite, Wizard, and the American-bred Umpire (i.e. "the Yankee").

2 Louis Napoleon (1808-73), nephew of Napoleon I, later Napoleon III, spent his childhood and youth in exile and tried unsuccessfully to seize power in 1840. After the revolution of 1848, he returned to Paris and ran for the Constituent Assembly, then for President. He took office as President, and at the end of his four-year term in 1851 carried out a *coup d'état*. He was confirmed emperor in 1852. Louis Napoleon relied heavily on Napoleonic legend to seize power; accordingly, family symbols such as the golden bee (Napoleon I's heraldic badge) were prominent features of his image. The phrase "an empty sound, signifying nothing" adapts *Macbeth* (V.v.26-8).

mind to go down to Bulstrode to encounter his mother's sympathy and his cousin Constance Trevyllian's chatter. He was unjust enough to nourish a secret dislike to that young lady for the good service she had done him by revealing Aurora's flight.

Are we ever really grateful to the people who tell us of the iniquity of those we love? Are we ever really just to the kindly creatures who give us friendly warning of our danger? No, never! We hate them; always involuntarily reverting to them as the first causes of our anguish; always repeating to ourselves that, had they been silent, that anguish need never have been; always ready to burst forth in our wild rage with the mad cry, that "it is better to be much abused than but to know't a little." When the friendly Ancient drops his poisoned hints into poor Othello's ear, it is not Mistress Desdemona, but Iago himself, whom the noble Moor first has a mind to strangle. If poor innocent Constance Trevyllian had been born the veriest cur in the county of Cornwall, she would have had a better chance of winning Talbot's regard than she had now.

Why had he come into Yorkshire? I left that question unanswered just now, for I am ashamed to tell the reasons which actuated this unhappy man. He came, in a paroxysm of curiosity, to learn what kind of life Aurora led with her husband, John Mellish. He had suffered horrible distractions of mind upon this subject; one moment imagining her the most despicable of coquettes, ready to marry any man who had a fair estate and a good position to offer her, and by-and-by depicting her as some white-robed Iphigenia,[1] led a passive victim to the sacrificial shrine. So, when happening to meet his goodnatured brother-officer at the United Service Club, he had consented to run down to Captain Hunter's country place, for a brief respite from Parliamentary minutes and red-tape, the artful hypocrite had never owned to himself that he was burning to hear tidings of his false and fickle love, and that it was some lingering fumes of the old intoxication that carried him down to Yorkshire. But now, now that he met her – met her, the heartless, abominable creature, radiant and happy – mere simulated happiness and feverish mock radiance, no doubt, but

---

1   The daughter of Agamemnon and Clytemnestra. Agamemnon was about to sacrifice Iphigenia to Artemis, but the goddess took pity on the girl and substituted a deer in her place.

too well put on to be quite pleasing to him, – *now he knew her*. He knew her at last, the wicked enchantress, the soulless siren. He knew that she had never loved him; that she was of course powerless to love; good for nothing but to wreath her white arms and flash the dark splendour of her eyes for weak man's destruction; fit for nothing but to float in her beauty above the waves that concealed the bleached bones of her victims. Poor John Mellish! Talbot reproached himself for his hardness of heart in nourishing one spiteful feeling towards a man who was so deeply to be pitied.

When the race was done, Captain Bulstrode turned, and beheld the black-eyed sorceress in the midst of a group gathered about a grave Patriarch with gray hair and the look of one accustomed to command.

This grave Patriarch was John Pastern.

I write his name with respect, even as it was reverentially whispered there, till, travelling from lip to lip, every one present knew that a great man was amongst them. A very quiet, unassuming veteran, sitting with his womankind about him, – his wife and daughter, as I think, – self-possessed and grave, while men were busy with his name in the crowd below, and while tens of thousands were staked in trusting dependence on his acumen. What golden syllables might have fallen from those oracular lips, had the veteran been so pleased! What hundreds would have been freely bidden for a word, a look, a nod, a wink, a mere significant pursing-up of the lips from that great man! What is the fable of the young lady who discoursed pearls and diamonds to a truth such as this? Pearls and diamonds must be of large size which would be worth the secrets of those Richmond stables, the secrets which Mr. Pastern might tell if he chose. Perhaps it is the knowledge of this which gives him a calm, almost clerical, gravity of manner. People come to him and fawn upon him, and tell him that such and such a horse from his stable has won, or looks safe to win; and he nods pleasantly, thanking them for the kind information; while perhaps his thoughts are far away on Epsom Downs or Newmarket Heath, winning future Derbys and Two Thousands with colts that are as yet unfoaled.

John Mellish is on intimate terms with the great man, to whom he presents Aurora, and of whom he asks advice upon a matter that has been troubling him for some time. His trainer's health is failing him, and he wants assistance in the stables; a younger man, honest and clever. Does Mr. Pastern know such a one?

The veteran tells him, after due consideration, that he does know of a young man; honest, he believes, as times go, who was once employed in the Richmond stables, and who had written to him only a few days before, asking for his influence in getting him a situation. "But the lad's name has slipped my memory," added Mr. Pastern; "he was but a lad when he was with me; but, bless my soul, that's ten years ago! I'll look up his letter, when I go home, and write to you about him. I know he's clever, and I believe he's honest; and I shall be only too happy," concluded the old gentleman, gallantly, "to do anything to oblige Mrs. Mellish."

ﾠﾠﾠﾠﾠﾠﾠﾠﾠﾠﾠﾠﾠﾠEND OF VOL. I.

VOLUME II

CHAPTER XIV.

"LOVE TOOK UP THE GLASS OF TIME, AND TURNED IT IN HIS GLOWING HANDS."[1]

TALBOT BULSTRODE yielded at last to John's repeated invitations, and consented to pass a couple of days at Mellish Park.

He despised and hated himself for the absurd concession. In what a pitiful farce had the tragedy ended! A visitor in the house of his rival. A calm spectator of Aurora's every-day, commonplace happiness. For the space of two days he had consented to occupy this most preposterous position. Two days only; then back to the Cornish miners, and the desolate bachelor's lodgings in Queen's Square, Westminster; back to his tent in life's Great Sahara. He could not for the very soul of him resist the temptation of beholding the inner life of that Yorkshire mansion. He wanted to know for certain – what was it to him, I wonder? – whether she was really happy, and had utterly forgotten him. They all returned to the Park together, Aurora, John, Archibald Floyd, Lucy, Talbot Bulstrode, and Captain Hunter. The last-named officer was a jovial gentleman, with a hook nose and auburn whiskers; a gentleman whose intellectual attainments were of no very oppressive order, but a hearty, pleasant guest in an honest country mansion, where there is cheer and welcome for all.

Talbot could but inwardly confess that Aurora became her new position. How everybody loved her! What an atmosphere of happiness she created about her wherever she went! How joyously the dogs barked and leapt at sight of her, straining their chains in the desperate effort to approach her! How fearlessly the thorough-bred mares and foals ran to the paddock-gates to bid her welcome, bending down their velvet nostrils to nestle upon her shoulder, responsive to the touch of her caressing hand! Seeing all this, how could Talbot refrain from remembering that this same sunlight might have shone upon

---

1   Another quotation from Tennyson's "Locksley Hall" (1842) (see also 186). Like the "shallow-hearted" Amy of the poem, Talbot transfers his affections away from his first love; in contrast to the embittered speaker of "Locksley Hall," however, Braddon is optimistic concerning the second loves of Aurora and Talbot.

that dreary castle far away by the surging western sea? She might have been his, this beautiful creature; but at what price? At the price of honour; at the price of every principle of his mind, which had set up for himself a holy and perfect standard – a pure and spotless ideal for the wife of his choice. Forbid it, manhood! He might have weakly yielded; he might have been happy, with the blind happiness of a lotus-eater,[1] but not the reasonable bliss of a Christian. Thank Heaven for the strength which had been given to him to escape from the silken net! Thank Heaven for the power which had been granted to him to fight the battle!

Standing by Aurora's side in one of the wide windows of Mellish Park, looking far out over the belted lawn to the glades in which the deer lay basking drowsily in the April sunlight, he could not repress the thought uppermost in his mind.

"I am – very glad – to see you so happy, Mrs. Mellish."

She looked at him with frank, truthful eyes, in whose brightness there was not one latent shadow.

"Yes," she said, "I am very, very happy. My husband is very good to me. He loves – and trusts me."

She could not resist that one little stab – the only vengeance she ever took upon him; but a stroke that pierced him to the heart.

"Aurora! Aurora! Aurora!" he cried.

That half-stifled cry revealed the secret of wounds that were not yet healed. Mrs. Mellish turned pale at the traitorous sound. This man must be cured. The happy wife, secure in her own stronghold of love and confidence, could not bear to see this poor fellow still adrift.

She by no means despaired of his cure, for experience had taught her, that although love's passionate fever takes several forms, there are very few of them incurable. Had she not passed safely through the ordeal herself, without one scar to bear witness of the old wounds?

She left Captain Bulstrode staring moodily out of the window, and went away to plan the saving of this poor shipwrecked soul.

She ran in the first place to tell Mr. John Mellish of her discovery, as it was her custom to carry to him every scrap of intelligence great and small.

---

1 In the *Odyssey*, the weary veterans of the Trojan War are tempted to abandon their homeward voyage when they eat the sweet fruit of the lotus. Tennyson's poem "The Lotos-Eaters" was published in 1832.

"My dearest old Jack," she said — it was another of her customs to address him by every species of exaggeratedly endearing appellation; it may be that she did this for the quieting of her own conscience, being well aware that she tyrannized over him — "my darling boy, I have made a discovery."

"About the filly?"

"About Talbot Bulstrode."

John's blue eyes twinkled maliciously. He was evidently half prepared for what was coming.

"What is it, Lolly?"

Lolly was a corruption of Aurora, devised by John Mellish.

"Why, I'm really afraid, my precious darling, that he hasn't quite got over——"

"My taking you away from him!" roared John. "I thought as much. Poor devil — poor Talbot! I could see that he would have liked to fight me on the stand at York. Upon my word, I pity him!" and in token of his compassion Mr. Mellish burst into that old joyous, boisterous, but musical laugh, which Talbot might almost have heard at the other end of the house.

This was a favourite delusion of John's. He firmly believed that he had won Aurora's affection in fair competition with Captain Bulstrode; pleasantly ignoring that the captain had resigned all pretensions to Miss Floyd's hand nine or ten months before his own offer had been accepted.

The genial, sanguine creature had a habit of deceiving himself in this manner. He saw all things in the universe just as he wished to see them; all men and women good and honest; life one long, pleasant voyage in a well-fitted ship, with only first-class passengers on board. He was one of those men who are likely to cut their throats or take prussic acid upon the day they first encounter the black visage of Care.

"And what are we to do with this poor fellow, Lolly?"

"Marry him!" exclaimed Mrs. Mellish.

"Both of us?" said John simply.

"My dearest pet, what an obtuse old darling you are! No; marry him to Lucy Floyd, my first cousin once removed, and keep the Bulstrode estate in the family."

"Marry him to Lucy!"

"Yes; why not? She has studied enough, and learnt history, and geography, and astronomy, and botany, and geology, and conchology, and entomology enough; and she has covered I don't know how many China jars with impossible birds and flowers; and she has illuminated missals, and read High-Church novels.[1] So the next best thing she can do is to marry Talbot Bulstrode."

John had his own reasons for agreeing with Aurora in this matter. He remembered that secret of poor Lucy's, which he had discovered more than a year before at Felden Woods: the secret which had been revealed to him by some mysterious sympathetic power belonging to hopeless love. So Mr. Mellish declared his hearty concurrence in Aurora's scheme, and the two amateur match-makers set to work to devise a complicated man-trap, in the which Talbot was to be entangled; never for a moment imagining that, while they were racking their brains in the endeavour to bring this piece of machinery to perfection, the intended victim was quietly strolling across the sunlit lawn towards the very fate they desired for him.

Yes, Talbot Bulstrode lounged with languid step to meet his Destiny, in a wood upon the borders of the Park; a part of the Park, indeed, inasmuch as it was within the boundary-fence of John's domain. The wood-anemones trembled in the spring breezes, deep in those shadowy arcades; pale primroses showed their mild faces amid their sheltering leaves; and in shady nooks, beneath low-spreading boughs of elm and beech, oak and ash, the violets hid their purple beauty from the vulgar eye. A lovely spot, soothing by its harmonious influence; a very forest sanctuary, without whose dim arcades man cast his burden down, to enter in a child. Captain Bulstrode had felt in no very pleasant humour as he walked across the lawn; but some softening influence stole upon him, on the threshold of that sylvan shelter, which made him feel a better man. He began to question himself as to how he was playing his part in the great drama of life.

---

1   Such novels promulgated the High-Church Anglican views associated with the Oxford movement, which favoured ceremony and ecclesiastical organization, and generally made the Anglican Church more like the Catholic. The best-known High-Church novelists were Elizabeth Missing Sewell (1815-1906) and Charlotte M. Yonge (1823-1901).

"Good heavens!" he thought, "what a shameful coward, what a negative wretch, I have become by this one grief of my manhood! An indifferent son, a careless brother, a useless, purposeless creature, content to dawdle away my life in feeble pottering with political economy. Shall I ever be in earnest again? Is this dreary doubt of every living creature to go with me to my grave? Less than two years ago my heart sickened at the thought that I had lived to two-and-thirty years of age, and had never been loved. Since then – since then – since then I had lived through life's brief fever; I have fought manhood's worst and sharpest battle, and find myself – where? Exactly where I was before; still companionless upon the dreary journey; only a little nearer to the end."

He walked slowly onward into the woodland aisle, other aisles branching away from him right and left into deep glades and darkening shadow. A month or so later, and the mossy ground beneath his feet would be one purple carpet of hyacinths, the very air thick with a fatal-scented vapour from the perfumed bulbs.

"I asked too much," said Talbot, in that voiceless argument we are perpetually carrying on with ourselves; "I asked too much; I yielded to the spell of the siren, and was angry because I missed the white wings of the angel. I was bewitched by the fascinations of a beautiful woman, when I should have sought for a noble-minded wife."

He went deeper and deeper into the wood, going to his fate, as another man was to do before the coming summer was over; but to what a different fate! The long arcades of beech and elm had reminded him from the first of the solemn aisles of a cathedral. The saint was only needed. And coming suddenly to a spot where a new arcade branched off abruptly on his right hand, he saw, in one of the sylvan niches, as fair a saint as had ever been modelled by the hand of artist and believer, – the same golden-haired angel he had seen in the long drawing-room at Felden Woods, – Lucy Floyd, with the pale aureola about her head, her large straw-hat in her lap filled with anemones and violets, and the third volume of a novel in her hand.

How much in life often hangs, or seems to us to hang, upon what is called by playwrights, "a situation!" But for this sudden encounter, but for thus coming upon this pretty picture, Talbot Bulstrode might have dropped into his grave ignorant to the last of Lucy's love for him. But, given a sunshiny April morning (April's fairest bloom, remember, when the capricious nymph is mending her manners, aware that her lovelier sister May is at hand, and anxious to make a good impression before she drops her farewell curtsy, and weeps her last brief shower of farewell tears) – given a balmy spring morning, solitude, a wood, wild-flowers, golden hair and blue eyes, and is the result difficult to arrive at?

Talbot Bulstrode, leaning against the broad trunk of a beech, looked down at the fair face, which crimsoned under his eyes; and the first glimmering hint of Lucy's secret began to dawn upon him. At that moment he had no thought of profiting by the discovery, no thought of what he was afterwards led on to say. His mind was filled with the storm of emotion that had burst from him in that wild cry to Aurora. Rage and jealousy, regret, despair, envy, love, and hate, – all the conflicting feelings that had struggled like so many demons in his soul at sight of Aurora's happiness, were still striving for mastery in his breast; and the first words he spoke revealed the thoughts that were uppermost.

"Your cousin is very happy in her new life, Miss Floyd?" he said.

Lucy looked up at him with surprise. It was the first time he had spoken to her of Aurora.

"Yes," she answered quietly, "I think she is happy."

Captain Bulstrode whisked the end of his cane across a group of anemones, and decapitated the tremulous blossoms. He was thinking, rather savagely, what a shame it was that this glorious Aurora could be happy with big, broad-shouldered, jovial-tempered John Mellish. He could not understand the strange anomaly; he could not discover the clue to the secret; he could not comprehend that the devoted love of this sturdy Yorkshireman was in itself strong enough to conquer all difficulties, to outweigh all differences.

Little by little, he and Lucy began to talk of Aurora, until Miss Floyd told her companion all about that dreary time at Felden Woods, during which the life of the heiress was well-nigh despaired of. So she had loved him truly, then, after all; she had loved, and had suffered, and had lived down her trouble, and had forgotten him, and was happy. The story was all told in that one sentence. He looked blankly back at the irrecoverable past, and was angry with the pride of the Bulstrodes, which had stood between himself and his happiness.

He told sympathizing Lucy something of his sorrow; told her that misapprehension – mistaken pride – had parted him from Aurora. She tried, in her gentle, innocent fashion, to comfort the strong man in his weakness, and in trying revealed – ah, how simply and transparently! – the old secret, which had so long been hidden from him.

Heaven help the man whose heart is caught at the rebound by a fair-haired divinity, with dove-like eyes, and a low tremulous voice softly attuned to his grief. Talbot Bulstrode saw that he was beloved; and, in very gratitude, made a dismal offer of the ashes of that fire which had burnt so fiercely at Aurora's shrine. Do not despise this poor Lucy if she accepted her cousin's forgotten lover with humble thankfulness; nay, with a tumult of wild delight, and with joyful fear and trembling. She loved him so well, and had loved him so long. Forgive and pity her, for she was one of those pure and innocent creatures whose whole being resolves itself into *affection;* to whom passion, anger, and pride are unknown; who live only to love, and who love until death. Talbot Bulstrode told Lucy Floyd that he had loved Aurora with the whole strength of his soul, but that, now the battle was over, he, the stricken warrior, needed a consoler for his declining days: would she, could she, give her hand to one who would strive to the uttermost to fulfil a husband's duty, and to make her happy? Happy! She would have been happy if he had asked her to be his slave; happy if she could have been a scullery-maid at Bulstrode Castle, so that she might have seen the dark face she loved once or twice a day through the obscure panes of some kitchen window.

But she was the most undemonstrative of women, and, except by her blushes, and her drooping eyelids, and the tear-drop trembling upon the soft auburn lashes, she made no reply to the captain's appeal, until at last, taking her hand in his, he won from her a low-consenting murmur which meant Yes.

Good heavens! how hard it is upon such women as these that they feel so much and yet display so little feeling! The dark-eyed, impetuous creatures, who speak out fearlessly, and tell you that they love or hate you – flinging their arms round your neck or throwing the carving-knife at you, as the case may be – get full value for all their emotion; but these gentle creatures love, and make no sign. They sit, like Patience on a monument,smiling at grief; and no one reads the mournful meaning of that sad smile. Concealment, like the worm i' the bud, feeds on their damask cheeks;[1] and compassionate relatives tell them that they are bilious, and recommend some homely remedy for their pallid complexions. They are always at a disadvantage. Their inner life may be a tragedy, all blood and tears, while their outer existence is some dull domestic drama of every-day life. The only outward sign Lucy Floyd gave of the condition of her heart was that one tremulous, half-whispered affirmative; and yet what a tempest of emotion was going forward within! The muslin folds of her dress rose and fell with the surging billows; but, for the very life of her, she could have uttered no better response to Talbot's pleading.

It was only by-and-by, after she and Captain Bulstrode had wandered slowly back to the house, that her emotion betrayed itself. Aurora met her cousin in the corridor out of which their rooms opened, and, drawing Lucy into her own dressing-room, asked the truant where she had been.

"Where have you been, you runaway girl? John and I have wanted you half a dozen times."

Miss Lucy Floyd explained that she had been in the wood with the last new novel, – a High-Church novel, in which the heroine rejected the clerical hero because he did not perform the service according to the Rubric.[2] Now Miss Lucy Floyd made this admission with so much confusion and so many blushes, that it would have appeared as if there were some lurking criminality in the fact of spending an April morning in a wood; and being further examined as to why she had stayed so long, and whether she had been alone all the time, poor Lucy fell into a pitiful state of embarrassment, declaring that she had been alone; that is to say, part of the time – or at least most of the time; but that Captain Bulstrode——

But in trying to pronounce his name, – this beloved, this sacred name, – Lucy Floyd's utterance failed her; she fairly broke down, and burst into tears.

Aurora laid her cousin's face upon her breast, and looked down,

---

1   *Twelfth Night* II.iv.111-15.
2   Directions for the conduct of the divine service inserted in liturgical books.

with a womanly, matronly glance, into those tearful blue eyes.

"Lucy, my darling," she said, "is it really and truly as I think – as I wish: – Talbot loves you?"

"He has asked me to marry him," Lucy whispered.

"And you – you have consented – you love him?"

Lucy Floyd only answered by a new burst of tears.

"Why, my darling, how this surprises me! How long has it been so, Lucy? How long have you loved him?"

"From the hour I first saw him," murmured Lucy; "from the day he first came to Felden. O Aurora! I know how foolish and weak it was; I hate myself for the folly; but he is so good, so noble, so——"

"My silly darling; and because he is good and noble, and has asked you to be his wife, you shed as many tears as if you had been asked to go to his funeral. My loving, tender Lucy, you loved him all the time, then; and you were so gentle and good to me – to me, who was selfish enough never to guess——My dearest, you are a hundred times better suited to him than ever I was, and you will be as happy – as happy as I am with that ridiculous old John."

Aurora's eyes filled with tears as she spoke. She was truly and sincerely glad that Talbot was in a fair way to find consolation, still more glad that her sentimental cousin was to be made happy.

Talbot Bulstrode lingered on a few days at Mellish Park; – happy ah! too happy days for Lucy Floyd – and then departed, after receiving the congratulations of John and Aurora.

He was to go straight to Alexander Floyd's villa at Fulham, and plead his cause with Lucy's father. There was little fear of his meeting other than a favourable reception; for Talbot Bulstrode of Bulstrode Castle was a very great match for a daughter of the junior branch of Floyd, Floyd, and Floyd, a young lady whose expectations were considerably qualified by half a dozen brothers and sisters.

So Captain Bulstrode went back to London as the betrothed lover of Lucy Floyd; went back with a subdued gladness in his heart, all unlike the stormy joys of the past. He was happy in the choice he had made calmly and dispassionately. He had loved Aurora for her beauty and her fascination; he was going to marry Lucy because he had seen much of her, had observed her closely, and believed her to be all that a woman should be. Perhaps, if stern truth must be told, Lucy's chief charm in the captain's eyes lay in that reverence for himself which she so *naïvely* betrayed. He accepted her worship with a quiet, unconscious serenity, and thought her the most sensible of women.

Mrs. Alexander was utterly bewildered when Aurora's sometime lover pleaded for her daughter's hand. She was too busy a mother amongst her little flock to be the most penetrating of observers, and she had never suspected the state of Lucy's heart. She was glad, therefore, to find that her daughter did justice to her excellent education, and had too much good sense to refuse so advantageous an offer as that of Captain Bulstrode; and she joined with her husband in perfect approval of Talbot's suit. So, there being no let or hindrance, and as the lovers had long known and esteemed each other, it was decided, at the captain's request, that the wedding should take place early in June, and that the honeymoon should be spent at Bulstrode Castle.

At the end of May, Mr. and Mrs. Mellish went to Felden, on purpose to attend Lucy's wedding, which took place with great style at Fulham, Archibald Floyd presenting his grand-niece with a cheque for five thousand pounds after the return from church.

Once during that marriage ceremony Talbot Bulstrode was nigh upon rubbing his eyes, thinking that the pageant must be a dream. A dream surely; for here was a pale, fair-haired girl by his side, while the woman he had chosen two years before stood amidst a group behind him, and looked on at the ceremony, a pleased spectator. But when he felt the little gloved hand trembling upon his arm, as the bride and bridegroom left the altar, he remembered that it was no dream, and that life held new and solemn duties for him from that hour.

Now my two heroines being married, the reader versed in the physiology of novel writing may conclude that my story is done, that the green curtain is ready to fall upon the last act of the play, and that I have nothing more to do than to entreat indulgence for the shortcomings of the performance and the performers. Yet, after all, does the business of the real life-drama always end upon the altar-steps? Must the play needs be over when the hero and heroine have signed their names in the register? Does man cease to be, to do, and to suffer when he gets married? And is it necessary that the novelist, after devoting three volumes to the description of a courtship of six weeks' duration, should reserve for himself only half a page in which to tell us the events of two-thirds of a lifetime? Aurora is married, and settled, and happy; sheltered, as one would imagine, from all dangers, safe under the wing of her stalwart adorer; but it does not therefore follow that the story of her life is done. She has escaped shipwreck for a while, and has safely landed on a pleasant shore; but the storm may still lower darkly upon the horizon, while the hoarse thunder grumbles threateningly in the distance.

CHAPTER XV.

MR. PASTERN'S LETTER.

MR. JOHN MELLISH reserved to himself one room upon the ground-floor of his house: a cheerful, airy apartment, with French windows opening upon the lawn; windows that were sheltered from the sun by a verandah overhung with jessamine and roses. It was altogether a pleasant room for the summer season, the floor being covered with an India matting instead of a carpet, and many of the chairs being made of light basket-work. Over the chimney-piece hung a portrait of John's father, and opposite to this work of art there was the likeness of the deceased gentleman's favourite hunter, surmounted by a pair of brightly polished spurs, the glistening rowels of which had often pierced the sides of that faithful steed. In this chamber Mr. Mellish kept his whips, canes, foils, single-sticks, boxing-gloves, spurs, guns, pistols, powder and shot flasks, fishing-tackle, boots, and tops; and many happy mornings were spent by the master of Mellish Park in the pleasing occupation of polishing, repairing, inspecting, and otherwise setting in order, these possessions. He had as many pairs of hunting-boots as would have supplied half Leicestershire – with tops to match. He had whips enough for all the Melton Hunt.[1] Surrounded by these treasures, as it were in a temple sacred to the deities of the race-course and the hunting-field, Mr. John Mellish used to hold solemn audiences with his trainer and his head-groom upon the business of the stable.

It was Aurora's custom to peep into this chamber perpetually, very much to the delight and distraction of her adoring husband, who found the black eyes of his divinity a terrible hindrance to business; except, indeed, when he could induce Mrs. Mellish to join in the discussion upon hand, and lend the assistance of her powerful intellect to the little conclave. I believe that John thought she could have handicapped the horses for the Chester Cup as well as Mr. Topham himself. She was such a brilliant creature, that every little smattering of knowl-

---

1   Melton Mowbray, in Leicestershire, was the hunting capital of England.

poor in the neighbourhood of the Yorkshire mansion had
ason to bless the coming of the banker's daughter. Aurora
othing better than to ride from cottage to cottage, chatting
e simple villagers, and finding out their wants. She never
he worthy creatures very remiss in stating their necessities, and
sekeeper at Mellish Park had enough to do in distributing
s bounties amongst the cottagers who came to the servants'
h pencil orders from Mrs. Mellish. Mrs. Walter Powell some-
entured to take Aurora to task on the folly and sinfulness of
e called indiscriminate almsgiving; but Mrs. Mellish would
ch a flood of eloquence upon her antagonist, that the ensign's
was always glad to retire from the unequal contest. Nobody
r been able to argue with Archibald Floyd's daughter. Impul-
l impetuous, she had always taken her own course, whether for
woe, and nobody had been strong enough to hinder her.
urning on this lovely June morning from one of these charita-
editions, Mrs. Mellish dismounted from her horse at a little
e leading into the wood, and ordered the groom to take the
home.
ave a fancy for walking through the wood, Joseph," she said;
ch a lovely morning. Take care of Mazeppa;[1] and if you see Mr.
n, tell him that I shall be home directly."
e man touched his hat, and rode off, leading Aurora's horse.
s. Mellish gathered up the folds of her habit, and strolled slowly
he wood, under whose shadow Talbot Bulstrode and Lucy had
ered on that eventful April day which sealed the young lady's

w Aurora had chosen to ramble homewards through this wood
se, being thoroughly happy, the warm gladness of the summer
er filled her with a sense of delight which she was loth to cur-
he drowsy hum of the insects, the rich colouring of the woods,
ent of wild-flowers, the ripple of water, – all blended into one
ous whole, and made the earth lovely.

rora's horse is named for Byron's poem *Mazeppa* (1819). The poem's hero,
azeppa, is bound naked on the back of a wild horse, which is lashed into mad-
s.

edge she possessed appeared to such good account as to make her
seem an adept in any subject of which she spoke; and the simple Yorkshireman believed in her as the wisest as well as the noblest and fairest
of women.

Mr. and Mrs. Mellish returned to Yorkshire immediately after
Lucy's wedding. Poor John was uneasy about his stables; for his trainer
was a victim to chronic rheumatism, and Mr. Pastern had not as yet
made any communication respecting the young man of whom he had
spoken on the Stand at York.

"I shall keep Langley," John said to Aurora, speaking of his old
trainer; "for he's an honest fellow, and his judgment will always be of
use to me. He and his wife can still occupy the rooms over the stables;
and the new man, whoever he may be, can live in the lodge on the
north side of the Park. Nobody ever goes in at that gate; so the lodge-
keeper's post is a sinecure, and the cottage has been shut up for the last
year or two. I wish John Pastern would write."

"And I wish whatever you wish, my dearest life," Aurora said duti-
fully to her happy slave.

Very little had been heard of Steeve Hargraves, the "Softy," since
the day upon which John Mellish had turned him neck and crop out
of his service. One of the grooms had seen him in a little village close
to the Park, and Stephen had informed the man that he was getting
his living by doing odd jobs for the doctor of the parish, and looking
after that gentleman's horse and gig; but the "Softy" had seemed
inclined to be sulky, and had said very little about himself or his sentiments. He made very particular inquiries, though, about Mrs. Mellish,
and asked so many questions as to what Aurora did and said, where
she went, whom she saw, and how she agreed with her husband, that
at last the groom, although only a simple country lad, refused to
answer any more interrogatories about his mistress.

Steeve Hargraves rubbed his coarse, sinewy hands, and chuckled as
he spoke of Aurora.

"She's a rare proud one, – a regular high-spirited lady," he said, in
that whispering voice that always sounded strange. "She laid it on to
me with that riding-whip of hers; but I bear no malice – I bear no
malice. She's a beautiful creature, and I wish Mr. Mellish joy of his
bargain."

The groom scarcely knew how to take this, not being fully aware if it was intended as a compliment or an impertinence. So he nodded to the "Softy," and strode off, leaving him still rubbing his hands and whispering about Aurora Mellish, who had long ago forgotten her encounter with Mr. Stephen Hargraves.

How was it likely that she should remember him, or take heed of him? How was it likely that she should take alarm because the pale-faced widow, Mrs. Walter Powell, sat by her hearth and hated her? Strong in her youth and beauty, rich in her happiness, sheltered and defended by her husband's love, how should she think of danger? How should she dread misfortune? She thanked God every day that the troubles of her youth were past, and that her path in life led henceforth through smooth and pleasant places, where no perils could come.

Lucy was at Bulstrode Castle, winning upon the affections of her husband's mother, who patronized her daughter-in-law with lofty kindness, and took the blushing timorous creature under her sheltering wing. Lady Bulstrode was very well satisfied with her son's choice. He might have done better, certainly, as to position and fortune, the lady hinted to Talbot; and in her maternal anxiety, she would have preferred his marrying any one rather than the cousin of *that* Miss Floyd who ran away from school, and caused such a scandal at the Parisian seminary. But Lady Bulstrode's heart warmed to Lucy, who was so gentle and humble, and who always spoke of Talbot as if he had been a being far "too bright and good," &c., much to the gratification of her ladyship's maternal vanity.

"She has a very proper affection for you, Talbot," Lady Bulstrode said, "and, for so young a creature, promises to make an excellent wife; far better suited to you, I am sure, than her cousin could ever have been."

Talbot turned fiercely upon his mother, very much to the lady's surprise.

"Why will you be for ever bringing Aurora's name into the question, mother?" he cried. "Why cannot you let her memory rest? You parted us for ever, – you and Constance, – and is not that enough? She is married, and she and her husband are a very happy couple. A man might have a worse wife than Mrs. Mellish, I can tell you; and

John seems to appreciate her value

"You need not be so violent, T offended dignity. "I am very glad t since her school-days, and I hope th wife," she added, with an emphasis very great hopes of the continuance

"My poor mother is offended w Bulstrode swept out of the room. "I and that nobody will ever truly love tle Lucy loves me after her fashion; l if she and I belonged to different or flying woman must have loved my think. But, after all, perhaps my mot wife is better suited to me than Auro

So we dismiss Talbot Bulstrode for yet not quite satisfied. What mortal world? It is a part of our earthly na wanting, always to have a vague, dull, i be appeased. Sometimes, indeed, we happiness we are still unsatisfied, for it were too full, and we grow cold with because of its fulness, it may possibly b mistake this life would be, what a v unfinished and imperfect story, if it we better! Taken by itself, it is all trouble future as the keynote of the present, ho whole becomes! How little does it sig complete, our wishes not fulfilled, if th ment are to come hereafter!

Little more than a week after Lucy's horse immediately after breakfast, upoi and, accompanied by the old groom wh father, went out on an excursion among Park, as it was her habit to do once or tw

---

1   See Robert Paltock's romance, *The Life and Adv* (1751), in which the adventurer-hero Peter W woman who has fallen.

There is something satisfactory, too, in the sense of possession; and Aurora felt, as she looked down the long avenues, and away through distant loopholes in the wood to the wide expanse of park and lawn, and the picturesque, irregular pile of building beyond, half Gothic, half Elizabethan, and so lost in a rich tangle of ivy and bright foliage as to be beautiful at every point, – she felt, I say, that all the fair picture was her own, or her husband's, which was the same thing. She had never for one moment regretted her marriage with John Mellish. She had never, as I have said already, been inconstant to him by one thought.

In one part of the wood the ground rose considerably; so that the house, which lay low, was distinctly visible whenever there was a break in the trees. This rising ground was considered the prettiest spot in the wood, and here a summer-house had been erected: a fragile, wooden building, which had fallen into decay of late years, but which was still a pleasant resting-place upon a summer's day, being furnished with a wooden table and a broad bench, and sheltered from the sun and wind by the lower branches of a magnificent beech. A few paces away from this summer-house there was a pool of water, the surface of which was so covered with lilies and tangled weeds as to have beguiled a short-sighted traveller into forgetfulness of the danger beneath. Aurora's way led her past this spot, and she started with a momentary sensation of terror on seeing a man lying asleep by the side of the pool. She quickly recovered herself, remembering that John allowed the public to use the footpath through the wood; but she started again when the man, who must have been a bad sleeper to be aroused by her light footstep, lifted his head, and displayed the white face of the "Softy."

He rose slowly from the ground upon seeing Mrs. Mellish, and crawled away, looking at her as he went, but not making any acknowledgment of her presence.

Aurora could not repress a brief terrified shudder; it seemed as if her footfall had startled some viperish creature, some loathsome member of the reptile race, and scared it from its lurking-place.

Steeve Hargraves disappeared amongst the trees as Mrs. Mellish walked on, her head proudly erect, but her cheek a shade paler than before this unexpected encounter with the "Softy."

Her joyous gladness in the bright summer's day had forsaken her as suddenly as she had met Stephen Hargraves; that bright smile, which was even brighter than the morning sunshine, faded out, and left her face unnaturally grave.

"Good heavens!" she exclaimed, "how foolish I am! I am actually afraid of that man, – afraid of that pitiful coward who could hurt my feeble old dog. As if such a creature as that could do one any mischief!"

Of course this was very wisely argued, as no coward ever by any chance worked any mischief upon this earth since the Saxon prince was stabbed in the back while drinking at his kinswoman's gate, or since brave King John and his creature plotted together what they should do with the little boy Arthur.[1]

Aurora walked slowly across the lawn towards that end of the house at which the apartment sacred to Mr. Mellish was situated. She entered softly at the open window, and laid her hand upon John's shoulder, as he sat at a table covered with a litter of account-books, racing-lists, and disorderly papers.

He started at the touch of the familiar hand.

"My darling, I'm so glad you've come in. How long you've been!"

She looked at her little jewelled watch. Poor John had loaded her with trinkets and gewgaws. His chief grief was that she was a wealthy heiress, and that he could give her nothing but the adoration of his simple, honest heart.

"Only half-past one, you silly old John," she said. "What made you think me late?"

"Because I wanted to consult you about something, and to tell you something. Such good news!"

"About what?"

"About the trainer."

She shrugged her shoulders, and pursed up her red lips with a bewitching little gesture of indifference.

---

1   On 18 March 978, King Edward the Martyr was murdered at Corfe in Dorset when visiting his half-brother Ethelred and his stepmother Elfthryth. His brother's retainers came out to meet him with signs of respect, but stabbed him before he had dismounted. King John and Hubert plan the death of Arthur in Shakespeare's *King John* (III.iii.65-68).

"Is that all?" she said.

"Yes; but aint you glad we've got the man at last – the very man to suit us, I think? Where's John Pastern's letter?"

Mr. Mellish searched amongst the litter of papers upon the table, while Aurora, leaning against the framework of the open window, watched him, and laughed at his embarrassment.

She had recovered her spirits, and looked the very picture of careless gladness as she leaned in one of those graceful and unstudied attitudes peculiar to her, supported by the framework of the window, and with the trailing jessamine waving round her in the soft summer breeze. She lifted her ungloved hand, and gathered the roses above her head as she talked to her husband.

"You most disorderly and unmethodical of men," she said, laughing; "I wouldn't mind betting five to one you won't find it."

I'm afraid that Mr. Mellish muttered an oath as he tossed about the heterogeneous mass of papers in his search for the missing document.

"I had it five minutes before you came in, Aurora," he said, "and now there's not a sign of it——Oh, here it is!"

Mr. Mellish unfolded the letter, and, smoothing it out upon the table before him, cleared his throat preparatory to reading the epistle. Aurora still leaned against the window-frame, half in and half out of the room, singing a snatch of a popular song, and trying to gather an obstinate half-blown rose which grew provokingly out of reach.

"You're attending, Aurora?"

"Yes, dearest and best."

"But do come in. You can't hear a word there."

Aurora shrugged her shoulders, as who should say, "I submit to the command of a tyrant," and advanced a couple of paces from the window; then looking at John with an enchantingly insolent toss of her head, she folded her hands behind her, and told him she would "be good." She was a careless, impetuous creature, dreadfully forgetful of what Mrs. Walter Powell called her "responsibilities;" every mortal thing by turns, and never any one thing for two minutes together; happy, generous, affectionate; taking life as a glorious summer's holiday, and thanking God for the bounty which made it so pleasant to her.

Mr. John Pastern began his letter with an apology for having so long deferred writing. He had lost the address of the person he had wished to recommend, and had waited until the man wrote to him a second time.

"I think he will suit you very well," the letter went on to say, "as he is well up in his business, having had plenty of experience, as groom, jockey, and trainer. He is only thirty years of age, but met with an accident some time since, which lamed him for life. He was half killed in a steeple-chase in Prussia, and was for upwards of a year in a hospital at Berlin. His name is James Conyers, and he can have a character from———"

The letter dropped out of John Mellish's hand as he looked up at his wife. It was not a scream which she had uttered. It was a gasping cry, more terrible to hear than the shrillest scream that ever came from the throat of woman in all the long history of womanly distress.

"Aurora! Aurora!"

He looked at her, and his own face changed and whitened at the sight of hers. So terrible a transformation had come over her during the reading of that letter, that the shock could not have been greater had he looked up and seen another person in her place.

"It's wrong; it's wrong!" she cried hoarsely; "you've read the name wrong. It can't be that!"

"What name?"

"What name?" she echoed fiercely, her face flaming up with a wild fury, – "that name! I tell you, it *can't* be. Give me the letter."

He obeyed her mechanically, picking up the paper and handing it to her, but never removing his eyes from her face.

She snatched it from him; looked at it for a few moments, with her eyes dilated and her lips apart; then, reeling back two or three paces, her knees bent under her, and she fell heavily to the ground.

edge she possessed appeared to such good account as to make her seem an adept in any subject of which she spoke; and the simple York-shireman believed in her as the wisest as well as the noblest and fairest of women.

Mr. and Mrs. Mellish returned to Yorkshire immediately after Lucy's wedding. Poor John was uneasy about his stables; for his trainer was a victim to chronic rheumatism, and Mr. Pastern had not as yet made any communication respecting the young man of whom he had spoken on the Stand at York.

"I shall keep Langley," John said to Aurora, speaking of his old trainer; "for he's an honest fellow, and his judgment will always be of use to me. He and his wife can still occupy the rooms over the stables; and the new man, whoever he may be, can live in the lodge on the north side of the Park. Nobody ever goes in at that gate; so the lodge-keeper's post is a sinecure, and the cottage has been shut up for the last year or two. I wish John Pastern would write."

"And I wish whatever you wish, my dearest life," Aurora said duti-fully to her happy slave.

Very little had been heard of Steeve Hargraves, the "Softy," since the day upon which John Mellish had turned him neck and crop out of his service. One of the grooms had seen him in a little village close to the Park, and Stephen had informed the man that he was getting his living by doing odd jobs for the doctor of the parish, and looking after that gentleman's horse and gig; but the "Softy" had seemed inclined to be sulky, and had said very little about himself or his senti-ments. He made very particular inquiries, though, about Mrs. Mellish, and asked so many questions as to what Aurora did and said, where she went, whom she saw, and how she agreed with her husband, that at last the groom, although only a simple country lad, refused to answer any more interrogatories about his mistress.

Steeve Hargraves rubbed his coarse, sinewy hands, and chuckled as he spoke of Aurora.

"She's a rare proud one, – a regular high-spirited lady," he said, in that whispering voice that always sounded strange. "She laid it on to me with that riding-whip of hers; but I bear no malice – I bear no malice. She's a beautiful creature, and I wish Mr. Mellish joy of his bargain."

The groom scarcely knew how to take this, not being fully aware if it was intended as a compliment or an impertinence. So he nodded to the "Softy," and strode off, leaving him still rubbing his hands and whispering about Aurora Mellish, who had long ago forgotten her encounter with Mr. Stephen Hargraves.

How was it likely that she should remember him, or take heed of him? How was it likely that she should take alarm because the pale-faced widow, Mrs. Walter Powell, sat by her hearth and hated her? Strong in her youth and beauty, rich in her happiness, sheltered and defended by her husband's love, how should she think of danger? How should she dread misfortune? She thanked God every day that the troubles of her youth were past, and that her path in life led henceforth through smooth and pleasant places, where no perils could come.

Lucy was at Bulstrode Castle, winning upon the affections of her husband's mother, who patronized her daughter-in-law with lofty kindness, and took the blushing timorous creature under her sheltering wing. Lady Bulstrode was very well satisfied with her son's choice. He might have done better, certainly, as to position and fortune, the lady hinted to Talbot; and in her maternal anxiety, she would have preferred his marrying any one rather than the cousin of *that* Miss Floyd who ran away from school, and caused such a scandal at the Parisian seminary. But Lady Bulstrode's heart warmed to Lucy, who was so gentle and humble, and who always spoke of Talbot as if he had been a being far "too bright and good," &c., much to the gratification of her ladyship's maternal vanity.

"She has a very proper affection for you, Talbot," Lady Bulstrode said, "and, for so young a creature, promises to make an excellent wife; far better suited to you, I am sure, than her cousin could ever have been."

Talbot turned fiercely upon his mother, very much to the lady's surprise.

"Why will you be for ever bringing Aurora's name into the question, mother?" he cried. "Why cannot you let her memory rest? You parted us for ever, – you and Constance, – and is not that enough? She is married, and she and her husband are a very happy couple. A man might have a worse wife than Mrs. Mellish, I can tell you; and

John seems to appreciate her value in his rough way."

"You need not be so violent, Talbot," Lady Bulstrode said, with offended dignity. "I am very glad to hear that Miss Floyd has altered since her school-days, and I hope that she may continue to be a good wife," she added, with an emphasis which insinuated that she had no very great hopes of the continuance of Mr. Mellish's happiness.

"My poor mother is offended with me," Talbot thought, as Lady Bulstrode swept out of the room. "I know I am an abominable bear, and that nobody will ever truly love me so long as I live. My poor little Lucy loves me after her fashion; loves me in fear and trembling, as if she and I belonged to different orders of beings; very much as the flying woman must have loved my countryman, Peter Wilkins,[1] I think. But, after all, perhaps my mother is right, and my gentle little wife is better suited to me than Aurora would have been."

So we dismiss Talbot Bulstrode for a while, moderately happy, and yet not quite satisfied. What mortal ever was *quite* satisfied in this world? It is a part of our earthly nature always to find something wanting, always to have a vague, dull, ignorant yearning which cannot be appeased. Sometimes, indeed, we are happy; but in our wildest happiness we are still unsatisfied, for it seems then as if the cup of joy were too full, and we grow cold with terror at the thought that, even because of its fulness, it may possibly be dashed to the ground. What a mistake this life would be, what a wild feverish dream, what an unfinished and imperfect story, if it were not a prelude to something better! Taken by itself, it is all trouble and confusion; but taking the future as the keynote of the present, how wondrously harmonious the whole becomes! How little does it signify that our joys here are not complete, our wishes not fulfilled, if the completion and the fulfilment are to come hereafter!

Little more than a week after Lucy's wedding, Aurora ordered her horse immediately after breakfast, upon a sunny summer morning, and, accompanied by the old groom who had ridden behind John's father, went out on an excursion amongst the villages round Mellish Park, as it was her habit to do once or twice a week.

---

1   See Robert Paltock's romance, *The Life and Adventures of Peter Wilkins, a Cornishman* (1751), in which the adventurer-hero Peter Wilkins rescues and marries a flying woman who has fallen.

The poor in the neighbourhood of the Yorkshire mansion had good reason to bless the coming of the banker's daughter. Aurora loved nothing better than to ride from cottage to cottage, chatting with the simple villagers, and finding out their wants. She never found the worthy creatures very remiss in stating their necessities, and the housekeeper at Mellish Park had enough to do in distributing Aurora's bounties amongst the cottagers who came to the servants' hall with pencil orders from Mrs. Mellish. Mrs. Walter Powell sometimes ventured to take Aurora to task on the folly and sinfulness of what she called indiscriminate almsgiving; but Mrs. Mellish would pour such a flood of eloquence upon her antagonist, that the ensign's widow was always glad to retire from the unequal contest. Nobody had ever been able to argue with Archibald Floyd's daughter. Impulsive and impetuous, she had always taken her own course, whether for weal or woe, and nobody had been strong enough to hinder her.

Returning on this lovely June morning from one of these charitable expeditions, Mrs. Mellish dismounted from her horse at a little turnstile leading into the wood, and ordered the groom to take the animal home.

"I have a fancy for walking through the wood, Joseph," she said; "it's such a lovely morning. Take care of Mazeppa;[1] and if you see Mr. Mellish, tell him that I shall be home directly."

The man touched his hat, and rode off, leading Aurora's horse.

Mrs. Mellish gathered up the folds of her habit, and strolled slowly into the wood, under whose shadow Talbot Bulstrode and Lucy had wandered on that eventful April day which sealed the young lady's fate.

Now Aurora had chosen to ramble homewards through this wood because, being thoroughly happy, the warm gladness of the summer weather filled her with a sense of delight which she was loth to curtail. The drowsy hum of the insects, the rich colouring of the woods, the scent of wild-flowers, the ripple of water, – all blended into one delicious whole, and made the earth lovely.

---

1 Aurora's horse is named for Byron's poem *Mazeppa* (1819). The poem's hero, Mazeppa, is bound naked on the back of a wild horse, which is lashed into madness.

There is something satisfactory, too, in the sense of possession; and Aurora felt, as she looked down the long avenues, and away through distant loopholes in the wood to the wide expanse of park and lawn, and the picturesque, irregular pile of building beyond, half Gothic, half Elizabethan, and so lost in a rich tangle of ivy and bright foliage as to be beautiful at every point, – she felt, I say, that all the fair picture was her own, or her husband's, which was the same thing. She had never for one moment regretted her marriage with John Mellish. She had never, as I have said already, been inconstant to him by one thought.

In one part of the wood the ground rose considerably; so that the house, which lay low, was distinctly visible whenever there was a break in the trees. This rising ground was considered the prettiest spot in the wood, and here a summer-house had been erected: a fragile, wooden building, which had fallen into decay of late years, but which was still a pleasant resting-place upon a summer's day, being furnished with a wooden table and a broad bench, and sheltered from the sun and wind by the lower branches of a magnificent beech. A few paces away from this summer-house there was a pool of water, the surface of which was so covered with lilies and tangled weeds as to have beguiled a short-sighted traveller into forgetfulness of the danger beneath. Aurora's way led her past this spot, and she started with a momentary sensation of terror on seeing a man lying asleep by the side of the pool. She quickly recovered herself, remembering that John allowed the public to use the footpath through the wood; but she started again when the man, who must have been a bad sleeper to be aroused by her light footstep, lifted his head, and displayed the white face of the "Softy."

He rose slowly from the ground upon seeing Mrs. Mellish, and crawled away, looking at her as he went, but not making any acknowledgment of her presence.

Aurora could not repress a brief terrified shudder; it seemed as if her footfall had startled some viperish creature, some loathsome member of the reptile race, and scared it from its lurking-place.

Steeve Hargraves disappeared amongst the trees as Mrs. Mellish walked on, her head proudly erect, but her cheek a shade paler than before this unexpected encounter with the "Softy."

Her joyous gladness in the bright summer's day had forsaken her as suddenly as she had met Stephen Hargraves; that bright smile, which was even brighter than the morning sunshine, faded out, and left her face unnaturally grave.

"Good heavens!" she exclaimed, "how foolish I am! I am actually afraid of that man, – afraid of that pitiful coward who could hurt my feeble old dog. As if such a creature as that could do one any mischief!"

Of course this was very wisely argued, as no coward ever by any chance worked any mischief upon this earth since the Saxon prince was stabbed in the back while drinking at his kinswoman's gate, or since brave King John and his creature plotted together what they should do with the little boy Arthur.[1]

Aurora walked slowly across the lawn towards that end of the house at which the apartment sacred to Mr. Mellish was situated. She entered softly at the open window, and laid her hand upon John's shoulder, as he sat at a table covered with a litter of account-books, racing-lists, and disorderly papers.

He started at the touch of the familiar hand.

"My darling, I'm so glad you've come in. How long you've been!"

She looked at her little jewelled watch. Poor John had loaded her with trinkets and gewgaws. His chief grief was that she was a wealthy heiress, and that he could give her nothing but the adoration of his simple, honest heart.

"Only half-past one, you silly old John," she said. "What made you think me late?"

"Because I wanted to consult you about something, and to tell you something. Such good news!"

"About what?"

"About the trainer."

She shrugged her shoulders, and pursed up her red lips with a bewitching little gesture of indifference.

---

1   On 18 March 978, King Edward the Martyr was murdered at Corfe in Dorset when visiting his half-brother Ethelred and his stepmother Elfthryth. His brother's retainers came out to meet him with signs of respect, but stabbed him before he had dismounted. King John and Hubert plan the death of Arthur in Shakespeare's *King John* (III.iii.65-68).

"Is that all?" she said.

"Yes; but aint you glad we've got the man at last – the very man to suit us, I think? Where's John Pastern's letter?"

Mr. Mellish searched amongst the litter of papers upon the table, while Aurora, leaning against the framework of the open window, watched him, and laughed at his embarrassment.

She had recovered her spirits, and looked the very picture of careless gladness as she leaned in one of those graceful and unstudied attitudes peculiar to her, supported by the framework of the window, and with the trailing jessamine waving round her in the soft summer breeze. She lifted her ungloved hand, and gathered the roses above her head as she talked to her husband.

"You most disorderly and unmethodical of men," she said, laughing; "I wouldn't mind betting five to one you won't find it."

I'm afraid that Mr. Mellish muttered an oath as he tossed about the heterogeneous mass of papers in his search for the missing document.

"I had it five minutes before you came in, Aurora," he said, "and now there's not a sign of it——Oh, here it is!"

Mr. Mellish unfolded the letter, and, smoothing it out upon the table before him, cleared his throat preparatory to reading the epistle. Aurora still leaned against the window-frame, half in and half out of the room, singing a snatch of a popular song, and trying to gather an obstinate half-blown rose which grew provokingly out of reach.

"You're attending, Aurora?"

"Yes, dearest and best."

"But do come in. You can't hear a word there."

Aurora shrugged her shoulders, as who should say, "I submit to the command of a tyrant," and advanced a couple of paces from the window; then looking at John with an enchantingly insolent toss of her head, she folded her hands behind her, and told him she would "be good." She was a careless, impetuous creature, dreadfully forgetful of what Mrs. Walter Powell called her "responsibilities;" every mortal thing by turns, and never any one thing for two minutes together; happy, generous, affectionate; taking life as a glorious summer's holiday, and thanking God for the bounty which made it so pleasant to her.

Mr. John Pastern began his letter with an apology for having so long deferred writing. He had lost the address of the person he had wished to recommend, and had waited until the man wrote to him a second time.

"I think he will suit you very well," the letter went on to say, "as he is well up in his business, having had plenty of experience, as groom, jockey, and trainer. He is only thirty years of age, but met with an accident some time since, which lamed him for life. He was half killed in a steeple-chase in Prussia, and was for upwards of a year in a hospital at Berlin. His name is James Conyers, and he can have a character from——"

The letter dropped out of John Mellish's hand as he looked up at his wife. It was not a scream which she had uttered. It was a gasping cry, more terrible to hear than the shrillest scream that ever came from the throat of woman in all the long history of womanly distress.

"Aurora! Aurora!"

He looked at her, and his own face changed and whitened at the sight of hers. So terrible a transformation had come over her during the reading of that letter, that the shock could not have been greater had he looked up and seen another person in her place.

"It's wrong; it's wrong!" she cried hoarsely; "you've read the name wrong. It can't be that!"

"What name?"

"What name?" she echoed fiercely, her face flaming up with a wild fury, – "that name! I tell you, it *can't* be. Give me the letter."

He obeyed her mechanically, picking up the paper and handing it to her, but never removing his eyes from her face.

She snatched it from him; looked at it for a few moments, with her eyes dilated and her lips apart; then, reeling back two or three paces, her knees bent under her, and she fell heavily to the ground.

CHAPTER XVI.

MR. JAMES CONYERS.

THE first week in July brought James Conyers, the new trainer, to Mellish Park. John had made no particular inquiries as to the man's character of any of his former employers, as a word from Mr. Pastern was all-sufficient.

Mr. Mellish had endeavoured to discover the cause of Aurora's agitation at the reading of John Pastern's letter. She had fallen like a dead creature at his feet; she had been hysterical throughout the remainder of the day, and delirious in the ensuing night, but she had not uttered one word calculated to throw any light upon the secret of her strange manifestation of emotion.

Her husband sat by her bedside upon the day after that on which she had fallen into the death-like swoon; watching her with a grave, anxious face, and earnest eyes that never wandered from her own.

He was suffering very much the same agony that Talbot Bulstrode had endured at Felden on the receipt of his mother's letter. The dark wall was slowly rising and separating him from the woman he loved. He was now to discover the tortures known only to the husband whose wife is parted from him by that which has more power to sever than any width of land or wide extent of ocean – *a secret*.

He watched the pale face lying on the pillow; the large, black, haggard eyes, wide open, and looking blankly out at the far-away purple tree-tops in the horizon; but there was no clue to the mystery in any line of that beloved countenance; there was little more than an expression of weariness, as if the soul, looking out of that white face, was so utterly enfeebled as to have lost all power to feel anything but a vague yearning for rest.

The wide casement windows were open, but the day was hot and oppressive – oppressively still and sunny; the landscape sweltering under a yellow haze, as if the very atmosphere had been opaque with molten gold. Even the roses in the garden seemed to feel the influence of the blazing summer sky, dropping their heavy heads like human sufferers from headache. The mastiff Bow-wow, lying under an acacia upon the lawn, was as peevish as any captious elderly gentle-man, and snapped spitefully at a frivolous butterfly that wheeled, and spun, and threw somersaults about the dog's head. Beautiful as was this summer's day, it was one on which people are apt to lose their tem-pers, and quarrel with each other, by reason of the heat; every man feeling a secret conviction that his neighbour is in some way to blame for the sultriness of the atmosphere, and that it would be cooler if he were out of the way. It was one of those days on which invalids are especially fractious, and hospital nurses murmur at their vocation; a day on which third-class passengers travelling long distances by excur-sion train are savagely clamorous for beer at every station, and hate each other for the narrowness and hardness of the carriage seats, and for the inadequate means of ventilation provided by the railway com-pany; a day on which stern business men revolt against the ceaseless grinding of the wheel, and, suddenly reckless of consequences, rush wildly to the Crown and Sceptre, to cool their overheated systems with water souchy and still hock;[1] an abnormal day, upon which the machinery of every-day life gets out of order, and runs riot through-out twelve suffocating hours.

John Mellish, sitting patiently by his wife's side, thought very little of the summer weather. I doubt if he knew whether the month was January or June. For him earth only held one creature, and she was ill and in distress − distress from which he was powerless to save her − distress the very nature of which he was ignorant.

His voice trembled when he spoke to her.

"My darling, you have been very ill," he said.

She looked at him with a smile so unlike her own that it was more painful to him to see than the loudest agony of tears, and stretched out her hand. He took the burning hand in his, and held it while he talked to her.

"Yes, dearest, you have been ill; but Morton says the attack was merely hysterical, and that you will be yourself again to-morrow, so there's no occasion for anxiety on that score. What grieves me, dar-ling, is to see that there is something on your mind; something which

---

1   Water souchy is fish (properly perch), boiled and served in its own liquor. Still hock
    is non-sparkling German white wine.

has been the real cause of your illness."

She turned her face upon the pillow, and tried to snatch her hand from his in her impatience, but he held it tightly in both his own.

"Does my speaking of yesterday distress you, Aurora?" he asked gravely.

"Distress me? Oh, no!"

"Then tell me, darling, why the mention of that man, the trainer's name, had such a terrible effect upon you."

"The doctor told you that the attack was hysterical," she said coldly; "I suppose I was hysterical and nervous yesterday."

"But the name, Aurora, the name. This James Conyers – who is he?" He felt the hand he held tighten convulsively upon his own, as he mentioned the trainer's name.

"Who is this man? – Tell me, Aurora. For God's sake, tell me the truth."

She turned her face towards him once more, as he said this.

"If you only want the truth from me, John, you must ask me nothing. Remember what I said to you at the Château d'Arques. It was a secret that parted me from Talbot Bulstrode. You trusted me then, John, – you must trust me to the end; if you cannot trust me——" she stopped suddenly, and the tears welled slowly up to her large, mournful eyes, as she looked at her husband.

"What, dearest?"

"We must part; as Talbot and I parted."

"Part!" he cried; "my love, my love! Do you think there is anything upon this earth strong enough to part us, except death? Do you think that any combination of circumstances, however strange, however inexplicable, would ever cause me to doubt your honour; or to tremble for my own? Could I be here if I doubted you? could I sit by your side, asking you these questions, if I feared the issue? Nothing shall shake my confidence; nothing can. – But have pity on me; think how bitter a grief it is to sit here, with your hand in mine, and to know that there is a secret between us. Aurora, tell me, – this man, this Conyers, – what is he, and who is he?"

"You know that as well as I do. A groom once; afterwards a jockey; and now a trainer."

"But you know him?"

"I have seen him."

"When?"

"Some years ago, when he was in my father's service."

John Mellish breathed more freely for a moment. The man had been a groom at Felden Woods, that was all. This accounted for the fact of Aurora's recognizing his name; but not for her agitation. He was no nearer the clue to the mystery than before.

"James Conyers was in your father's service," he said thoughtfully; "but why should the mention of his name yesterday have caused you such emotion?"

"I cannot tell you."

"It is another secret, then, Aurora," he said reproachfully; "or has this man anything to do with the old secret of which you told me at the Château d'Arques?"

She did not answer him.

"Ah, I see; I understand, Aurora," he added, after a pause. – "This man was a servant at Felden Woods; a spy, perhaps; and he discovered the secret, and traded upon it, as servants often have done before. This caused your agitation at hearing his name. You were afraid that he would come here and annoy you, making use of this secret to extort money, and keeping you in perpetual terror of him. I think I can understand it all. I am right; am I not?"

She looked at him with something of the expression of a hunted animal that finds itself at bay.

"Yes, John."

"This man – this groom – knows something of – of the secret."

"He does."

John Mellish turned away his head, and buried his face in his hands. What cruel anguish! what bitter degradation! This man, a groom, a servant, was in the confidence of his wife; and had such power to harass and alarm her, that the very mention of his name was enough to cast her to the earth, as if stricken by sudden death. What, in the name of heaven, could this secret be, which was in the keeping of a servant, and yet could not be told to him? He bit his lip till his strong teeth met upon the quivering flesh, in the silent agony of that thought. What could it be? He had sworn, only a minute before, to trust in her blindly to the end; and yet, and yet—— His massive frame shook from head to heel in that noiseless struggle; doubt and despair rose like twin-demons in his soul; but he wrestled with them, and overcame them; and, turning with a white face to his wife, said quietly –

"I will press these painful questions no further, Aurora. I will write to Pastern, and tell him that the man will not suit us; and——"

He was rising to leave her bedside, when she laid her hand upon his arm.

"Don't write to Mr. Pastern, John," she said; "the man will suit you very well, I dare say. I had rather he came."

"You wish him to come here?"

"Yes."

"But he will annoy you; he will try to extort money from you."

"He would do that in any case, since he is alive. I thought that he was dead."

"Then you really wish him to come here?"

"I do."

John Mellish left his wife's room inexpressibly relieved. – The secret could not be so very terrible after all, since she was willing that the man who knew it should come to Mellish Park; where there was at least a remote chance of his revealing it to her husband. Perhaps, after all, this mystery involved others rather than herself, – her father's commercial integrity – her mother? He had heard very little of that mother's history; perhaps she——Pshaw! why weary himself with speculative surmises? He had promised to trust her, and the hour had come in which he was called upon to keep his promise. He wrote to Mr. Pastern, accepting his recommendation of James Conyers, and waited rather impatiently to see what kind of man the trainer was.

He received a letter from Conyers, very well written and worded, to the effect that he would arrive at Mellish Park upon the 3rd of July.

Aurora had recovered from her brief hysterical attack when this letter arrived; but as she was still weak and out of spirits, her medical man recommended change of air; so Mr. and Mrs. Mellish drove off to Harrogate upon the 28th of June, leaving Mrs. Powell behind them at the Park.

The ensign's widow had been scrupulously kept out of Aurora's room during her short illness; being held at bay by John, who coolly shut the door in the lady's sympathetic face, telling her that he'd wait upon his wife himself, and that when he wanted female assistance he would ring for Mrs. Mellish's maid.

Now Mrs. Walter Powell, being afflicted with that ravenous curiosity common to people who live in other people's houses, felt herself deeply injured by this line of conduct. There were mysteries and secrets afloat, and she was not to be allowed to discover them; there was a skeleton in the house, and she was not to anatomize the bony horror. She scented trouble and sorrow as carnivorous animals scent their prey; and yet she who hated Aurora was not to be allowed to riot at the unnatural feast.

Why is it that the dependents in a household are so feverishly inquisitive about the doings and sayings, the manners and customs, the joys and sorrows, of those who employ them? Is it that, having abnegated for themselves all active share in life, they take an unhealthy interest in those who are in the thick of the strife? Is it because, being cut off in a great measure by the nature of their employment from family ties and family pleasures, they feel a malicious delight in all family trials and vexations, and the ever-recurring breezes which disturb the domestic atmosphere? Remember this, husbands and wives, fathers and sons, mothers and daughters, brothers and sisters, when you quarrel. *Your servants enjoy the fun.* Surely that recollection ought to be enough to keep you for ever peaceful and friendly. Your servants listen at your doors, and repeat your spiteful speeches in the kitchen, and watch you while they wait at table, and understand every sarcasm, every innuendo, every look, as well as those at whom the cruel glances and the stinging words are aimed. They understand your sulky silence, your studied and over-acted politeness. The most polished form your hate and anger can take is as transparent to those household spies as if you threw knives at each other, or pelted your enemy with the side-dishes and vegetables, after the fashion of disputants in a pantomime. Nothing that is done in the parlour is lost upon these quiet, well-behaved watchers from the kitchen. They laugh at you; nay worse, they pity you. They discuss your affairs, and make out your income, and settle what you can afford to do and what you can't afford to do; they prearrange the disposal of your wife's fortune, and look prophetically forward to the day when you will avail yourself of the advantages of the new Bankruptcy Act.[1] They know why you live on bad terms with your eldest daughter, and why your favourite son was turned out of doors; and they take a morbid interest in every dismal secret of your life. You don't allow them followers; you look blacker than thunder if you see Mary's sister or John's poor old mother sitting meekly in your hall; you are surprised if the postman brings them letters, and attribute the fact to the pernicious system of over-educating the masses; you shut them from their homes and their kindred, their lovers and their friends; you deny them books, you grudge them a peep at your newspaper; and then you lift up your eyes and wonder at them because they are inquisitive, and because the staple of their talk is scandal and gossip.

Mrs. Walter Powell, having been treated by most of her employers, as a species of upper servant, had acquired all the instincts of a servant; and she determined to leave no means untried in order to discover the cause of Aurora's illness, which the doctor had darkly hinted to her had more to do with the mind than the body.

John Mellish had ordered a carpenter to repair the lodge at the north gate, for the accommodation of James Conyers; and John's old trainer, Langley, was to receive his colleague and introduce him to the stables.

The new trainer made his appearance at the lodge-gates in the glowing July sunset; he was accompanied by no less a person than Steeve Hargraves the "Softy," who had been lurking about the station upon the look out for a job, and who had been engaged by Mr. Conyers to carry his portmanteau.

To the surprise of the trainer, Stephen Hargraves set down his burden at the park gates.

"You'll have to find some one else to carry it th' rest 't' ro-ad," he said, touching his greasy cap, and extending his broad palm to receive the expected payment.

Mr. James Conyers was rather a dashing fellow, with no small amount of that quality which is generally termed "swagger," so he

---

1 The Bankruptcy Act of 1861 established that all insolvents could, by surrendering their property for distribution to creditors, absolve themselves of liability and earn the right to reestablish themselves.

turned sharply round upon the "Softy" and asked him what the devil he meant.

"I mean that I mayn't go inside yon geates," muttered Stephen Hargraves; "I mean that I've been toorned oot of yon pleace that I've lived in, man and boy, for forty year, – toorned oot like a dog, neck and crop."

Mr. Conyers threw away the stump of his cigar and stared superciliously at the "Softy."

"What does the man mean?" he asked of the woman who had opened the gates.

"Why, poor fellow, he's a bit fond, sir, and him and Mrs. Mellish didn't get on very well: she has a rare spirit, and I *have* heard that she horsewhipped him for beating her favourite dog. Any ways, master turned him out of his service."

"Because my lady had horsewhipped him. Servants'-hall justice all the world over," said the trainer, laughing, and lighting a second cigar from a metal fusee-box in his waistcoat pocket.

"Yes, that's joostice, aint it?" the "Softy" said eagerly. "You wouldn't like to be toorned oot of a pleace as you'd lived in forty year, would you? But Mrs. Mellish has a rare spirit, bless her pretty feace!"

The blessing enunciated by Mr. Stephen Hargraves had such a very ominous sound, that the new trainer, who was evidently a shrewd, observant fellow, took his cigar from his mouth on purpose to stare at him. The white face, lighted up by a pair of red eyes with a dim glimmer in them, was by no means the most agreeable of countenances; but Mr. Conyers looked at the man for some moments, holding him by the collar of his coat in order to do so with more deliberation: then pushing the "Softy" away with an affably contemptuous gesture, he said, laughing –

"You're a character, my friend, it strikes me; and not too safe a character either. I'm dashed if I should like to offend you. There's a shilling for your trouble, my man," he added tossing the money into Steeve's extended palm with careless dexterity.

"I suppose I can leave my portmanteau here till to-morrow, ma'am?" he said, turning to the woman at the lodge. "I'd carry it down to the house myself if I wasn't lame."

He was such a handsome fellow, and had such an easy, careless manner, that the simple Yorkshire woman was quite subdued by his fascinations.

"Leave it here, sir, and welcome," she said, curtsying, "and my master shall take it to the house for you as soon as he comes in. Begging your pardon, sir, but I suppose you're the new gentleman that's expected in the stables?"

"Precisely."

"Then I was to tell you, sir, that they've fitted up the north lodge for you: but you was to please go straight to the house, and the house-keeper was to make you comfortable and give you a bed for to-night."

Mr. Conyers nodded, thanked her, wished her good night, and limped slowly away, through the shadows of the evening, and under the shelter of the over-arching trees. He stepped aside from the broad carriage-drive on to the dewy turf that bordered it, choosing the soft-est, mossiest places with a sybarite's instinct. Look at him as he takes his slow way under those glorious branches, in the holy stillness of the summer sunset, his face sometimes lighted by the low, lessening rays, sometimes darkened by the shadows of the leaves above his head. He is wonderfully handsome – wonderfully and perfectly handsome – the very perfection of physical beauty; faultless in proportion, as if each line in his face and form had been measured by the sculptor's rule, and carved by the sculptor's chisel. He is a man about whose beauty there can be no dispute, whose perfection servant-maids and duchesses must alike confess – albeit they are not bound to admire; yet it is rather a sensual type of beauty, this splendour of form and colour, unallied to any special charm of expression. Look at him now, as he stops to rest, leaning against the trunk of a tree, and smoking his big cigar with easy enjoyment. He is thinking. His dark-blue eyes, deeper in colour by reason of the thick black lashes which fringe them, are half closed, and have a dreamy, semi-sentimental expression, which might lead you to suppose the man was musing upon the beauty of the summer sunset. He is thinking of his losses on the Chester Cup, the wages he is to get from John Mellish, and the perquisites likely to appertain to the situation. You give him credit for thoughts to match with his dark, violet-hued eyes, and the exquisite modelling of his mouth and chin; you give him a mind as æsthetically perfect as his face and figure, and you recoil on discovering what a vulgar, every-day sword may lurk under that beautiful scabbard. Mr. James Conyers is, perhaps, no worse than other men of his station; but he is decidedly no better. He is only very much handsomer; and you have no right to be angry with him because his opinions and sentiments are exactly what they would have been if he had had red hair and a pug nose. With what wonderful wisdom has George Eliot told us that people are not any better because they have long eyelashes![1] Yet it must be that there is something anomalous in this outward beauty and inward ugliness; for, in spite of all experience, we revolt against it, and are incredulous to the last, believing that the palace which is outwardly so splendid can scarcely be ill furnished within. Heaven help the woman who sells her heart for a handsome face, and awakes when the bargain has been struck, to discover the foolishness of such an exchange!

It took Mr. Conyers a long while to walk from the lodge to the house. I do not know how, technically, to describe his lameness. He had fallen, with his horse, in the Prussian steeple-chase, which had so nearly cost him his life, and his left leg had been terribly injured. The bones had been set by wonderful German surgeons, who put the shattered leg together as if it had been a Chinese puzzle, but who, with all their skill, could not prevent the contraction of the sinews, which had left the jockey lamed for life, and no longer fit to ride in any race whatever. He was of the middle height, and weighed something over eleven stone, and had never ridden except in Continental steeple-chases.

Mr. James Conyers paused a few paces from the house, and gravely contemplated the irregular pile of buildings before him.

"A snug crib," he muttered; "plenty of tin hereabouts, I should think, from the look of the place."

Being ignorant of the geography of the neighbourhood, and

---

1   In Chapter 15 of *Adam Bede* (1859), Hetty Sorrel's beauty (including that of her eyelashes) misleads Arthur Donnithorne and Adam Bede about her true shallowness of character. The narrator points out that there is "no direct correlation between eyelashes and morals."

being, moreover, by no means afflicted by an excess of modesty, Mr. Conyers went straight to the principal door, and rang the bell sacred to visitors and the family.

He was admitted by a grave old man-servant, who, after deliberately inspecting his brown shooting-coat, coloured shirt-front, and felt hat, asked him, with considerable asperity, what he was pleased to want.

Mr. Conyers explained that he was the new trainer, and that he wished to see the housekeeper; but he had hardly finished doing so, when a door in an angle of the hall was softly opened, and Mrs. Walter Powell peeped out of the snug little apartment sacred to her hours of privacy.

"Perhaps the young man will be so good as to step in here," she said, addressing herself apparently to space, but indirectly to James Conyers.

The young man took off his hat, uncovering a mass of luxuriant brown curls, and limped across the hall in obedience to Mrs. Powell's invitation.

"I dare say I shall be able to give you any information you require."

James Conyers smiled, wondering whether the bilious-looking party, as he mentally designated Mrs. Powell, could give him any information about the York Summer Meeting; but he bowed politely, and said he merely wanted to know where he was to hang out – he stopped and apologized – where he was to sleep that night, and whether there were any letters for him. But Mrs. Powell was by no means inclined to let him off so cheaply. She set to work to pump him, and laboured so assiduously that she soon exhausted that very small amount of intelligence which he was disposed to afford her, being perfectly aware of the process to which he was subjected, and more than equal to the lady in dexterity. The ensign's widow, therefore, ascertained little more than that Mr. Conyers was a perfect stranger to John Mellish and his wife, neither of whom he had ever seen.

Having failed to gain much by this interview, Mrs. Powell was anxious to bring it to a speedy termination.

"Perhaps you would like a glass of wine after your walk?" she said;

"I'll ring for some, and I can inquire at the same time about your letters. I dare say you are anxious to hear from the relatives you have left at home."

Mr. Conyers smiled for the second time. He had neither had a home nor any relatives to speak of, since the most infantine period of his existence; but had been thrown upon the world a sharp-witted adventurer at seven or eight years old. The "relatives" for whose communication he was looking out so eagerly were members of the humbler class of book-men with whom he did business.

The servant despatched by Mrs. Powell returned with a decanter of sherry and about half a dozen letters for Mr. Conyers.

"You'd better bring the lamp, William," said Mrs. Powell, as the man left the room; "for I'm sure you'll never be able to read your letters by this light," she added politely to Mr. Conyers.

The fact was, that Mrs. Powell, afflicted by that diseased curiosity of which I have spoken, wanted to know what kind of correspondents these were whose letters the trainer was so anxious to receive, and sent for the lamp in order that she might get the full benefit of any scraps of information to be got at by rapid glances and dexterously stolen peeps.

The servant brought a brilliant camphine-lamp,[1] and Mr. Conyers, not at all abashed by Mrs. Powell's condescension, drew his chair close to the table, and after tossing off a glass of sherry, settled himself to the perusal of his letters.

The ensign's widow, with some needlework in her hand, sat directly opposite to him at the small round table, with nothing but the pedestal of the lamp between them.

James Conyers took up the first letter, examined the superscription and seal, tore open the envelope, read the brief communication upon half a sheet of note-paper, and thrust it into his waistcoat-pocket. Mrs. Powell, using her eyes to the utmost, saw nothing but a few lines in a scratchy plebeian handwriting, and a signature which, seen at a disadvantage upside-down, didn't look unlike "Johnson." The second envelope contained only a tissue-paper betting-list; the third held a dirty scrap of paper with a few words scrawled in pencil; but at sight of the

---

1   Camphine is an illuminating oil obtained by distillation from turpentine.

uppermost envelope of the remaining three Mr. James Conyers started as if he had been shot. Mrs. Powell looked from the face of the trainer to the superscription of the letter, and was scarcely less surprised than Mr. Conyers. The superscription was in the handwriting of Aurora Mellish.

It was a peculiar hand; a hand about which there could be no mistake; not an elegant Italian hand, sloping, slender, and feminine, but large and bold, with ponderous up-strokes and down-strokes, easy to recognize at a greater distance than that which separated Mrs. Powell from the trainer. There was no room for any doubt. Mrs. Mellish had written to her husband's servant, and the man was evidently familiar with her hand, yet surprised at receiving her letter.

He tore open the envelope, and read the contents eagerly twice over, frowning darkly as he read.

Mrs. Powell suddenly remembered that she had left part of her needlework upon a cheffonier behind the young man's chair, and rose quietly to fetch it. He was so much engrossed by the letter in his hand that he was not aware of the pale face which peered for one brief moment over his shoulder, as the faded, hungry eyes stole a glance at the writing on the page.

The letter was written on the first side of a sheet of note-paper, with only a few words carried over to the second page. It was this second page which Mrs. Powell saw. The words written at the top of the leaf were these: – "Above all, *express no surprise.* – A."

There was no ordinary conclusion to the letter; no other signature than this big capital A.[1]

---

1 Aurora's signature links her to the adulterous Hester Prynne in Nathaniel Hawthorne's *The Scarlet Letter* (1850).

CHAPTER XVII.

THE TRAINER'S MESSENGER.

MR. JAMES CONYERS made himself very much at home at Mellish Park. Poor Langley, the invalid trainer, who was a Yorkshireman, felt himself almost bewildered by the easy insolence of his town-bred successor. Mr. Conyers looked so much too handsome and dashing for his office, that the grooms and stable-boys bowed down to him, and paid court to him as they had never done to simple Langley, who had been very often obliged to enforce his commands with a horsewhip or a serviceable leather strap. James Conyers's handsome face was a capital with which that gentleman knew very well how to trade, and he took the full amount of interest that was to be got for it without compunction. I am sorry to be obliged to confess that this man, who had sat in the artists' studios and the life academies for Apollo and Antinous,[1] was selfish to the backbone; and so long as he was well fed and clothed and housed and provided for, cared very little whence the food and clothing came, or who kept the house that sheltered him, or filled the purse which he jingled in his trousers-pocket. Heaven forbid that I should be called upon for his biography. I only know that he sprang from the mire of the streets, like some male Aphrodite rising from the mud;[2] that he was a blackleg in the gutter at four years of age, and a "welsher" in the matter of marbles and hardbake before his fifth birthday.[3] Even then he was for ever reaping the advantage of a handsome face; for tender-hearted matrons, who would have been deaf to the cries of a snub-nosed urchin, petted and compassionated the pretty boy.

In his earliest childhood he learned therefore to trade upon his beauty, and to get the most that he could for that merchandise; and he

---

1 Apollo (god of the sun, prophecy, divination, the arts, and music) and Antinous (favourite of the Emperor Hadrian), both famous for their beauty, are frequently represented in painting and sculpture.
2 Conyers shares the goddess Aphrodite's physical beauty, but originates from the lower-class streets of London while she is born from the sea.
3 A blackleg is a turf swindler; hardbake is almond toffee.

grew up utterly unprincipled, and carried his handsome face out into the world to help him on to fortune. He was extravagant, lazy, luxurious, and selfish; but he had that easy indifferent grace of manner which passes with shallow observers for good-nature. He would not have gone three paces out of his way to serve his best friend; but he smiled and showed his handsome white teeth with equal liberality to all his acquaintance; and took credit for being a frank, generous-hearted fellow on the strength of that smile. He was skilled in the uses of that gilt gingerbread of generosity which so often passes current for sterling gold. He was dexterous in the handling of those cogged dice[1] which have all the rattle of the honest ivories. A slap on the back, a hearty shake of the hand, often went as far from him as the loan of a sovereign from another man, and Jim Conyers was firmly believed in by the doubtful gentlemen with whom he associated, as a good-natured fellow who was nobody's enemy but his own. He had that superficial Cockney cleverness which is generally called knowledge of the world; knowledge of the worst side of the world, and utter ignorance of all that is noble upon earth, it might perhaps be more justly called. He had matriculated in the streets of London, and graduated on the race-course; he had never read any higher literature than the Sunday papers and the 'Racing Calendar,' but he contrived to make a very little learning go a long way, and was generally spoken of by his employers as a superior young man, considerably above his station.

Mr. Conyers expressed himself very well contented with the rustic lodge which had been chosen for his dwelling-house. He condescendingly looked on while the stable-lads carried the furniture, selected for him by the housekeeper from the spare servants' rooms, from the house to the lodge, and assisted in the arrangement of the tiny rustic chambers, limping about in his shirt-sleeves, and showing himself wonderfully handy with a hammer and a pocketful of nails. He sat upon a table and drank beer with such charming affability, that the stable-lads were as grateful to him as if he had treated them to that beverage. Indeed, seeing the frank cordiality with which James Conyers smote the lads upon the back, and prayed them to be active with the can, it was almost difficult to remember that he was not the giver

---

1   Loaded dice, used for cheating.

of the feast, and that it was Mr. John Mellish who would have to pay the brewer's bill. What, amongst all the virtues, which adorn this earth, can be more charming than the generosity of upper servants? With what hearty hospitality they pass the bottle! how liberally they throw the seven-shilling gunpowder[1] into the teapot! how unsparingly they spread the twenty-penny fresh butter on the toast! and what a glorious welcome they give to the droppers-in of the servants' hall! It is scarcely wonderful that the recipients of their bounty forget that it is the master of the household who will be called upon for the expenses of the banquet, and who will look ruefully at the total of the quarter's housekeeping.

It was not to be supposed that so dashing a fellow as Mr. James Conyers could, in the lodginghouse-keepers' *patois*, "do for" himself. He required a humble drudge to black his boots, make his bed, boil his kettle, cook his dinner, and keep the two little chambers at the lodge in decent order. Casting about in a reflective mood for a fitting person for this office, his recreant fancy hit upon Steeve Hargraves the "Softy." He was sitting upon the sill of an open window in the little parlour of the lodge, smoking a cigar and drinking out of a can of beer, when this idea came into his head. He was so tickled by the notion, that he took his cigar from his mouth in order to laugh at his ease.

"The man's a character," he said, still laughing, "and I'll have him to wait upon me. He's been forbid the place, has he? Turned out neck and crop because my Lady Highropes horsewhipped him. Never mind that; *I'll* give him leave to come back, if it's only for the fun of the thing."

He limped out upon the high-road half an hour after this, and went into the village to find Steeve Hargraves. He had little difficulty in doing this, as everybody knew the "Softy," and a chorus of boys volunteered to fetch him from the house of the doctor, in whose service he did odd jobs, and brought him to Mr. Conyers five minutes afterwards, looking very hot and dirty, but as pale of complexion as usual.

Stephen Hargraves agreed very readily to abandon his present occupation and to wait upon the trainer, in consideration of five

---

1   See 129, n.1.

shillings a week and his board and lodging; but his countenance fell when he discovered that Mr. Conyers was in the service of John Mellish, and lived on the outskirts of the park.

"You're afraid of setting foot upon his estate, are you?" said the trainer, laughing. "Never mind, Steeve, *I* give you leave to come, and I should like to see the man or woman in that house who'll interfere with any whim of mine. *I* give you leave. You understand."

The "Softy" touched his cap and tried to look as if he understood; but it was very evident that he did not understand, and it was some time before Mr. Conyers could persuade him that his life would be safe within the gates of Mellish Park. But he was ultimately induced to trust himself at the north lodge, and promised to present himself there in the course of the evening.

Now Mr. James Conyers had exerted himself as much in order to overcome the cowardly objections of this rustic clown as he could have done if Steeve Hargraves had been the most accomplished body servant in the three Ridings.[1] Perhaps there was some deeper motive than any regard for the man himself in this special preference for the "Softy;" some lurking malice, some petty spite, the key to which was hidden in his own breast. If, while standing smoking in the village street, *chaffing* the "Softy" for the edification of the lookers-on, and taking so much trouble to secure such an ignorant and brutish esquire, – if one shadow of the future, so very near at hand, could have fallen across his path, surely he would have instinctively recoiled from the striking of that ill-omened bargain.

But James Conyers had no superstition; indeed, he was so pleasantly free from that weakness as to be a disbeliever in all things in heaven and on earth, except himself and his own merits; so he hired the "Softy," for the fun of the thing, as he called it, and walked slowly back to the park gates to watch for the return of Mr. and Mrs. Mellish, who were expected that afternoon.

The woman at the lodge brought him out a chair, and begged him to rest himself under the portico. He thanked her with a pleasant smile, and sitting down amongst the roses and honeysuckles, lighted another cigar.

"You'll find the north lodge dull, I'm thinking, sir," the woman said, from the open window, where she had reseated herself with her needlework.

"Well, it isn't very lively, ma'am, certainly," answered Mr. Conyers, "but it serves my purpose well enough. The place is lonely enough for a man to be murdered there and nobody be any the wiser; but as I have nothing to lose, it will answer well enough for me."

He might perhaps have said a good deal more about the place, but at this moment the sound of wheels upon the high-road announced the return of the travellers, and two or three minutes afterwards the carriage dashed through the gate, and past Mr. James Conyers.

Whatever power this man might have over Aurora, whatever knowledge of a compromising secret he might have obtained and traded upon, the fearlessness of her nature showed itself now as always, and she never flinched at the sight of him. If he had placed himself in her way on purpose to watch the effect of his presence, he must surely have been disappointed; for except that a cold shadow of disdain passed over her face as the carriage drove by him, he might have imagined himself unseen. She looked pale and careworn, and her eyes seemed to have grown larger, since her illness; but she held her head as erect as ever, and had still the air of imperial grandeur which constituted one of her chief charms.

"So that is Mr. Mellish," said Conyers, as the carriage disappeared. "He seems very fond of his wife."

"Ay, sure; and he is too. Fond of her! Why they say there isn't another such couple in all Yorkshire. And she's fond of him, too, bless her handsome face! But who wouldn't be fond of Master John?"

Mr. Conyers shrugged his shoulders; these patriarchal habits and domestic virtues had no particular charm for him.

"She had plenty of money, hadn't she?" he asked, by way of bringing the conversation into a more rational channel.

"Plenty of money! I should think so. They say her pa gave her fifty thousand pounds down on her wedding-day; not that our master wants money; he's got enough and to spare."

"Ah, to be sure," answered Mr. Conyers; "that's always the way of it. The banker gave her fifty thousand, did he? If Miss Floyd had married a poor devil, now, I don't suppose her father would have given her fifty sixpences."

"Well, no; if she'd gone against his wishes, I don't suppose he would. He was here in the spring, – a nice, white-haired old gentleman; but failing fast."

"Failing fast. And Mrs. Mellish will come into a quarter of a million at his death, I suppose. Good afternoon, ma'am. It's a queer world." Mr. Conyers took up his stick, and limped away under the trees, repeating this ejaculation as he went. It was a habit with this gentleman to attribute the good fortune of other people to some eccentricity in the machinery of life, by which he, the only really deserving person in the world, had been deprived of his natural rights. He went through the wood into a meadow where some of the horses under his charge were at grass, and spent upwards of an hour lounging about the hedgerows, sitting on gates, smoking his pipe, and staring at the animals, which seemed about the hardest work he had to do in his capacity of trainer. "It isn't a very hard life, when all's said and done," he thought, as he looked at a group of mares and foals, who, in their eccentric diversions, were performing a species of Sir Roger de Coverley[1] up and down the meadow. "It isn't a very hard life; for as long as a fellow swears hard and fast at the lads, and gets rid of plenty of oats, he's right enough. These country gentlemen always judge a man's merits by the quantity of corn they have to pay for. Feed their horses as fat as pigs, and never enter 'em except among such a set of screws as an active pig could beat; and they'll swear by you. They'd think more of having a horse win the Margate Plate, or the Hampstead Heath Sweepstakes, than if he ran a good fourth in the Derby. Bless their innocent hearts! I should think fellows with plenty of money and no brains must have been invented for the good of fellows with plenty of brains and no money; and that's how we contrive to keep our equilibrium in the universal see-saw."

Mr. James Conyers, puffing lazy clouds of transparent blue smoke from his lips, and pondering thus, looked as sentimental as if he had been ruminating upon the last three pages of the 'Bride of Abydos,' or the death of Paul Dombey.[2] He had that romantic style of beauty

---

1   A popular country dance and the traditional wind-up at the end of a ball.
2   At the end of Byron's *Bride of Abydos* (1813), the heroine Zuleika dies of grief after her lover, Selim, is killed by her father. Paul Dombey, the child hero of Dickens' *Dombey and Son* (1847-48), dies in chapter 16 of the novel.

peculiar to dark-blue eyes and long black lashes; and he could not wonder what he should have for dinner without a dreamy pensiveness in the purple shadows of those deep-blue orbs. He had found the sentimentality of his beauty almost of greater use to him than the beauty itself. It was this sentimentality which always put him at an advantage with his employers. He looked like an exiled prince doing menial service in bitterness of spirit and a turned-down collar. He looked like Lara[1] returned to his own domains to train the horses of a usurper. He looked, in short, like anything but what he was, – a selfish, good-for-nothing, lazy scoundrel, who was well up in the useful art of doing the minimum of work, and getting the maximum of wages.

He strolled slowly back to his rustic habitation, where he found the "Softy" waiting for him; the kettle boiling upon a handful of bright fire, and some tea-things laid out upon the little round table. Mr. Conyers looked rather contemptuously at the humble preparations.

"I've mashed the tea for 'ee," said the "Softy;" "I thought you'd like a coop."

The trainer shrugged his shoulders.

"I can't say I'm particular attached to the cat-lap," he said, laughing; "I've had rather too much of it when I've been in training, – half-and-half, warm tea and cold-drawn castor-oil. I'll send you into Doncaster for some spirits to-morrow, my man: or to-night, perhaps," he added reflectively, resting his elbow upon the table and his chin in the hollow of his hand.

He sat for some time in this thoughtful attitude, his retainer Steeve Hargraves watching him intently all the while, with that half-wondering, half-admiring stare with which a very ugly creature – a creature so ugly as to know it is ugly – looks at a very handsome one.

At the close of his reverie, Mr. Conyers took out a clumsy silver watch, and sat for a few minutes staring vacantly at the dial.

"Close upon six," he muttered at last. "What time do they dine at the house, Steeve?"

---

1   The hero of Byron's *Lara* (1814) returns to his usurped domains in Spain after the pirating adventures described in *The Corsair*. Lara (whose real name is Conrad) does not train horses, but the narrator endows Conyers with his general demeanour of romantic aloofness and intrinsic gentility.

"Seven o'clock," answered the "Softy."

"Seven o'clock. Then you'd have time to run there with a message, or a letter, and catch 'em just as they're going in to dinner."

The "Softy" stared aghast at his new master.

"A message or a letter," he repeated; "for Mr. Mellish?"

"No; for Mrs. Mellish."

"But I daren't," exclaimed Stephen Hargraves; "I daren't go nigh the house; least of all to speak to her. I don't forget the day she horse-whipped me. I've never seen her since, and I don't want to see her. You think I am a coward, don't 'ee?" he said, stopping suddenly, and looking at the trainer, whose handsome lips were curved into a contemptuous smile. "You think I'm a coward, don't 'ee, now?" he repeated.

"Well, I don't think you are over-valiant," answered Mr. Conyers, "to be afraid of a woman, though she was the veriest devil that ever played fast and loose with a man."

"Shall I tell you what it is I am afraid of?" said Steeve Hargraves, hissing the words through his closed teeth in that unpleasant whisper peculiar to him. "It isn't Mrs. Mellish. It's myself. It's *this*," – he grasped something in the loose pocket of his trousers as he spoke, – "it's *this*. I'm afraid to trust myself a-nigh her, for fear I should spring upon her, and cut her thro-at from ear to ear. I've seen her in my dreams sometimes, with her beautiful white thro-at laid open, and streaming oceans of blood; but, for all that, she's always had the broken whip in her hand, and she's always laughed at me. I've had many a dream about her; but I've never seen her dead or quiet; and I've never seen her without the whip."

The contemptuous smile died away from the trainer's lips as Steeve Hargraves made this revelation of his sentiments, and gave place to a darkly thoughtful expression, which overshadowed the whole of his face.

"I've no such wonderful love for Mrs. Mellish myself," he said; "but she might live to be as old as Methuselah, for aught I care, if she'd——" He muttered something between his teeth, and walked up the little staircase to his bedroom, whistling a popular tune as he went.

He came down again with a dirty-looking leather desk in his hand; which he flung carelessly on to the table. It was stuffed with crumpled untidy-looking letters and papers, from among which he had considerable difficulty in selecting a tolerably clean sheet of note-paper.

"You'll take a letter to Mrs. Mellish, my friend," he said to Stephen, stooping over the table and writing as he spoke; "and you'll please to deliver it safe into her own hands. The windows will all be open this sultry weather, and you can watch till you see her in the drawing-room; and when you do, contrive to beckon her out, and give her this."

He had folded the sheet of paper by this time, and had sealed it carefully in an adhesive envelope.

"There's no need of any address," he said, as he handed the letter to Steeve Hargraves; "you know who it's for, and you won't give it to anybody else. There, get along with you. She'll say nothing to *you*, man, when she sees who the letter comes from."

The "Softy" looked darkly at his new employer; but Mr. James Conyers rather piqued himself upon a quality which he called deter-mination, but which his traducers designated obstinacy, and he made up his mind that no one but Steeve Hargraves should carry the letter.

"Come," he said, "no nonsense, Mr. Stephen! Remember this: if I choose to employ you, and if I choose to send you on any errand whatsoever, there's no one in that house will dare to question my right to do it. Get along with you!"

He pointed, as he spoke, with the stem of his pipe, to the Gothic roof and ivied chimneys of the old house gleaming amongst a mass of foliage. "Get along with you, Mr. Stephen, and bring me an answer to that letter," he added, lighting his pipe and seating himself in his favourite attitude upon the window-sill, – an attitude which, like everything about him, was a half-careless, half-defiant protest of his superiority to his position. "You needn't wait for a written answer. Yes or No will be quite enough, you may tell Mrs. Mellish."

The "Softy" whispered something, half inaudible, between his teeth; but he took the letter, and pulling his shabby rabbit-skin cap over his eyes, walked slowly off in the direction to which Mr. Conyers had pointed, with a half-contemptuous action, a few moments before.

"A queer fish," muttered the trainer, lazily watching the awkward figure of his attendant; "a queer fish; but it's rather hard if I can't manage *him*. I've twisted his betters round my little finger before to-day."

Mr. Conyers forgot that there are some natures which, although inferior in everything else, are strong by reason of their stubbornness, and not to be twisted out of their natural crookedness by any trick of management or skilfulness of handling.

The evening was sunless but sultry; there was a lowering darkness in the leaden sky, and an unnatural stillness in the atmosphere that prophesied the coming of a storm. The elements were taking breath for the struggle, and lying silently in wait against the breaking of their fury. It would come by-and-by, the signal for the outburst, in a long, crackling peal of thunder that would shake the distant hills and flutter every leaf in the wood.

The trainer looked with an indifferent eye at the ominous aspect of the heavens. "I must go down to the stables, and send some of the boys to get the horses under cover," he said; "there'll be a storm before long." He took his stick and limped out of the cottage, still smoking; indeed, there were very few hours in the day, and not many during the night, in which Mr. Conyers was unprovided with his pipe or cigar.

Steeve Hargraves walked very slowly along the narrow pathway which led across the park to the flower-garden and lawn before the house. This north side of the park was wilder and less well kept than the rest; but the thick undergrowth swarmed with game, and the young hares flew backwards and forwards across the pathway, startled by the "Softy's" shambling tread, while every now and then the partridges rose in pairs from the tangled grass, and skimmed away under the low roof of foliage.

"If I was to meet Mr. Mellish's keeper here, he'd look at me black enough, I dare say," muttered the "Softy," "though I aint after the game. Lookin' at a pheasant's high treason in his mind, curse him!"

He put his hands low down in his pockets, as if scarcely able to resist the temptation to wring the neck of a splendid cock-pheasant that was strutting through the high grass, with a proud serenity of manner that implied a knowledge of the game-laws. The trees on the north side of the Park formed a species of leafy wall which screened the lawn, so that, coming from this northern side, the "Softy" emerged at once from the shelter into the smooth grass bordering this lawn, which was separated from the Park by an invisible fence.

As Steeve Hargraves, still sheltered from observation by the trees, approached the place, he saw that his errand was shortened, for Mrs. Mellish was leaning upon a low iron gate, with the dog Bow-wow, the dog that he had beaten, at her side.

He had left the narrow pathway and struck in amongst the undergrowth, in order to make a shorter cut to the flower-garden, and as he came from under the shelter of the low branches which made a leafy cave about him, he left a long track of parted grass behind him, like the track of the footstep of a tiger, or the trail of a slow, ponderous serpent creeping towards its prey.[1]

Aurora looked up at the sound of the shambling footstep, and, for the second time since she had beaten him, she encountered the gaze of the "Softy." She was very pale, almost as pale as her white dress, which was unenlivened by any scrap of colour, and which hung about her in loose folds that gave a statuesque grace to her figure. She was dressed with such evident carelessness that every fold of muslin seemed to tell how far away her thoughts had been when that hasty toilette was made. Her black brows contracted as she looked at the "Softy."

"I thought Mr. Mellish had dismissed you," she said, "and that you had been forbidden to come here?"

"Yes, ma'am, Muster Mellish did turn me out of the house I'd lived in, man and boy, nigh upon forty year; but I've got a new pleace now, and my new master sent me to you with a letter."

Watching the effect of his words, the "Softy" saw a leaden change come over the pale face of his listener.

"What new master?" she asked.

Steeve Hargraves lifted his hand and pointed across his shoulder. She watched the slow motion of that clumsy hand, and her eyes seemed to grow larger as she saw the direction to which it pointed.

"Your new master is the trainer, James Conyers, – the man who lives at the north lodge?" she said.

"Yes, ma'am."

---

1 Hargraves is represented as the serpent in Aurora's Eden. See Milton's *Paradise Lost*, Book 9.

"What does he want with you?" she asked.

"I keep his place in order for him, ma'am, and run errands for him; and I've brought a letter."

"A letter? Ah, yes, give it me."

The "Softy" handed her the envelope. She took it slowly, without removing her eyes from his face, but watching him with a fixed and earnest look that seemed as if it would have fathomed something beneath the dull red eyes which met hers. A look that betrayed some doubtful terror hidden in her own breast, and a vague desire to penetrate the secrets of his.

She did not look at the letter, but held it half crushed in the hand hanging by her side.

"You can go," she said.

"I was to wait for an answer."

The black brows contracted again, and this time a bright gleam of fury kindled in the great black eyes.

"There is no answer," she said, thrusting the letter into the bosom of her dress, and turning to leave the gate; "there is no answer, and there shall be none till I choose. Tell your master that."

"It wasn't to be a written answer," persisted the "Softy;" "it was to be Yes or No, that's all; but I was to be sure and wait for it."

The half-witted creature saw some feeling of hate and fury in her face beyond her contemptuous hatred of himself, and took a savage pleasure in tormenting her. She struck her foot impatiently upon the grass, and plucking the letter from her breast, tore open the envelope, and read the few lines it contained. Few as they were, she stood for nearly five minutes with the open letter in her hand, separated from the "Softy" by the iron fence, and lost in thought. The silence was only broken during this pause by an occasional growl from the mastiff, who lifted his heavy lip, and showed his feeble teeth for the edification of his old enemy.

She tore the letter into a hundred morsels, and flung it from her before she spoke. "Yes," she said at last; "tell your master that."

Steeve Hargraves touched his cap and went back through the grassy trail he had left, to carry this message to the trainer.

"She hates me bad enough," he muttered, as he stopped once to look back at the quiet white figure on the lawn, "but she hates t'oother chap worse."

CHAPTER XVIII.

OUT IN THE RAIN.

THE second dinner-bell rang five minutes after the "Softy" had left Aurora, and Mr. John Mellish came out upon the lawn to look for his wife. He came whistling across the grass, and whisking the roses with his pocket-handkerchief in very gaiety of heart. He had quite forgotten the anguish of that miserable morning after the receipt of Mr. Pastern's letter. He had forgotten all but that his Aurora was the loveliest and dearest of women, and that he trusted her with the boundless faith of his big, honest heart. "Why should I doubt such a noble, impetuous creature?" he thought; "doesn't every feeling and every sentiment write itself upon her lovely, expressive face in characters the veriest fool could read? If I please her, what bright smiles light up in her black eyes! If I vex her, – as I do, poor awkward idiot that I am, a hundred times a day, – how the two black arches contract over her pretty impertinent nose, while the red lips pout defiance and disdain! Shall I doubt her because she keeps one secret from me, and freely tells me I must for ever remain ignorant of it; when an artful woman would try to set my mind at rest with some shallow fiction invented to deceive me? Heaven bless her! no doubt of her shall ever darken my life again, come what may."

It was easy for Mr. Mellish to make this mental vow, believing fully that the storm was past, and that lasting fair weather had set in.

"Lolly darling," he said, winding his great arm round his wife's waist, "I thought I had lost you."

She looked up at him with a sad smile.

"Would it grieve you much, John," she said in a low voice, "if you were really to lose me?"

He started as if he had been struck, and looked anxiously at her pale face.

"Would it grieve me, Lolly!" he repeated; "not for long; for the people who came to your funeral would come to mine. But, my darling, my darling, what can have made you ask this question? Are you ill, dearest? You have been looking pale and tired for the last few days, and I have thought nothing of it. What a careless wretch I am!"

"No, no, John," she said; "I don't mean that. I know you would grieve, dear, if I were to die. But suppose something were to happen which would separate us for ever, – something which would compel me to leave this place never to return to it, – what then?"

"What then, Lolly?" answered her husband gravely. "I would rather see your coffin laid in the empty niche beside my mother's in the vault yonder," – he pointed in the direction of the parish church, which was close to the gates of the park, – "than I would part with you thus. I would rather know you to be dead and happy than I would endure any doubt about your fate. Oh, my darling, why do you speak of these things? I couldn't part with you – I couldn't! I would rather take you in my arms and plunge with you into the pond in the wood; I would rather send a bullet into your heart, and see you lying murdered at my feet."

"John, John, my dearest and truest!" she said, her face lighting up with a new brightness, like the sudden breaking of the sun through a leaden cloud, "not another word, dear: we will never part. Why should we? There is very little upon this wide earth that money cannot buy; and it shall help to buy our happiness. We will never part, darling; never."

She broke into a joyous laugh as she watched his anxious, half-wondering face.

"Why, you foolish John, how frightened you look!" she said. "Haven't you discovered yet that I like to torment you now and then with such questions as these, just to see your big blue eyes open to their widest extent? Come, dear; Mrs. Powell will look white thunder at us when we go in, and make some meek conventional reply to our apologies for this delay, to the effect that she doesn't care in the least how long she waits for dinner, and that on the whole she would rather never have any dinner at all. Isn't it strange, John, how that woman hates me?"

"Hates *you*, dear, when you're so kind to her!"

"But she hates me for being kind to her, John. If I were to give her my diamond-necklace, she'd hate me for having it to give. She hates us because we're rich and young and handsome," said Aurora, laughing; "and the very opposite of her namby-pamby, pale-faced self."

It was strange that from this moment Aurora seemed to regain her natural gaiety of spirits, and to be what she had been before the receipt of Mr. Pastern's letter. Whatever dark cloud had hovered over her head, since the day upon which that simple epistle had caused such a terrible effect, seemed to have been suddenly removed. Mrs. Walter Powell was not slow to perceive this change. The eyes of love, clear-sighted though they may be, are dull indeed beside the eyes of hate. *Those* are never deceived. Aurora had wandered out of the drawing-room, listless and dispirited, to stroll wearily upon the lawn; – Mrs. Powell, seated in one of the windows, had watched her every movement, and had seen her in the distance speaking to some one (she had been unable to distinguish the "Softy" from her post of observation); – and this same Aurora returned to the house almost another creature. There was a look of determination about the beautiful mouth (which female critics called too wide), a look not usual to the rosy lips, and a resolute brightness in the eyes, which had some significance surely, Mrs. Powell thought, if she could only have found the key to that hidden meaning. Ever since Aurora's brief illness, the poor woman had been groping for this key – groping in mazy darknesses which baffled her utmost powers of penetration. Who and what was this groom, that Aurora should write to him, as she most decidedly had written? Why was he to express no surprise, and what cause could there be for his expressing any surprise in the simple economy of Mellish Park? The mazy darknesses were more impenetrable than the blackest night, and Mrs. Powell wellnigh gave up all hope of ever finding any clue to the mystery. And now behold a new complication had arisen in Aurora's altered spirits. John Mellish was delighted with this alteration. He talked and laughed until the glasses near him vibrated with his noisy mirth. He drank so much sparkling Moselle that his butler Jarvis (who had grown gray in the service of the old squire, and had poured out Master John's first glass of champagne) refused at last to furnish him with any more of that beverage; offering him in its stead some very expensive hock, the name of which was in fourteen unpronounceable syllables, and which John tried to like, but didn't.

"We'll fill the house with visitors for the shooting season, Lolly, darling," said Mr. Mellish. "If they come on the 1st of September, they'll all be comfortably settled for the Leger. The dear old Dad will come of course, and trot about on his white pony like the best of men and bankers in Christendom. Captain and Mrs. Bulstrode will come too; and we shall see how our little Lucy looks, and whether solemn Talbot beats her in the silence of the matrimonial chamber. Then there's Hunter, and a host of fellows; and you must write me a list of any nice people you'd like to ask down here; and we'll have a glorious autumn; won't we, Lolly?"

"I hope so, dear," said Mrs. Mellish, after a little pause, and a repetition of John's eager question. She had not been listening very attentively to John's plans for the future, and she startled him rather by asking him a question very wide from the subject upon which he had been speaking.

"How long do the fastest vessels take going to Australia, John?" she asked quietly.

Mr. Mellish stopped with his glass in his hand to stare at his wife as she asked this question.

"How long do the fastest vessels take to go to Australia?" he repeated. "Good gracious me, Lolly, how should I know? Three weeks or a month – no, I mean three months; but, in mercy's name, Aurora, why do you want to know?"

"The average length of the voyage is, I believe, about three months; but some fast-sailing packets do it in seventy, or even in sixty-eight days," interposed Mrs. Powell, looking sharply at Aurora's abstracted face from under cover of her white eyelashes.

"But why, in goodness name, do you want to know, Lolly?" repeated John Mellish. "You don't want to go to Australia, and you don't know anybody who's going to Australia."

"Perhaps Mrs. Mellish is interested in the Female Emigration movement,"[1] suggested Mrs. Powell: "it is a most delightful work."

Aurora replied neither to the direct nor the indirect question. The cloth had been removed[2] (for no modern customs had ever disturbed

---

1   In the 1850s and 1860s, prompted by a large number of "redundant" women in England and a shortage of women in the colonies, feminists promoted emigration for middle-class women unemployable in England. The Female Middle Class Emigration Society was formed in 1862.

2   The tablecloth was traditionally removed after the main courses and before dessert.

the conservative economy of Mellish Park), and Mrs. Mellish sat, with a cluster of pale cherries in her hand, looking at the reflection of her own face in the depths of the shining mahogany.

"Lolly!" exclaimed John Mellish, after watching his wife for some minutes, "you are as grave as a judge. What can you be thinking of?"

She looked up at him with a bright smile, and rose to leave the dining-room.

"I'll tell you one of these days, John," she said. "Are you coming with us, or are you going out upon the lawn to smoke?"

"If you'll come with me, dear," he answered, returning her smile with the frank glance of unchangeable affection which always beamed in his eyes when they rested on his wife. "I'll go out and smoke a cigar, if you'll come with me, Lolly."

"You foolish old Yorkshireman," said Mrs. Mellish, laughing, "I verily believe you'd like me to smoke one of your choice cigars, by way of keeping you company."

"No, darling, I'd never wish to see you do anything that didn't square – that wasn't compatible," interposed Mr. Mellish, gravely, "with the manners of the noblest lady, and the duties of the truest wife in England. If I love to see you ride across country with a red feather in your hat, it is because I think that the good old sport of English gentlemen was meant to be shared by their wives, rather than by people whom I would not like to name;[1] and because there is a fair chance that the sight of your Spanish hat and scarlet plume at the meet may go some way towards keeping Miss Wilhelmina de Lancy (who was born plain Scroggins, and christened Sarah) out of the field. I think our British wives and mothers might have the battle in their own hands, and win the victory for themselves and their daughters, if they were a little braver in standing to their ground; if they were not quite so tenderly indulgent to the sins of eligible young noblemen, and, in their estimate of a man's qualifications for the marriage state,

---

1   i.e. Prostitutes. In the 1850s and 60s, women entered the traditionally masculine sport of hunting in increasing numbers. Their supporters, like John Mellish, argued that ladies' presence would refine the manners of the hunting field. The morality of the hunt became widely debated during the Skittles affair of 1860-61, when the well-known courtesan Catherine Walters ("Skittles") was banned from the field by the Quorn Master.

were not so entirely guided by the figures in his banker's book. It's a sad world, Lolly; but John Mellish, of Mellish Park, was never meant to set it right."[1]

Mr. Mellish stood on the threshold of a glass-door which opened on to a flight of steps leading to the lawn, as he delivered himself of this homily, the gravity of which was quite at variance with the usual tenour of his discourse. He had a cigar in his hand, and was going to light it, when Aurora stopped him.

"John, dear," she said, "my most unbusiness-like of darlings, have you forgotten that poor Langley is so anxious to see you, that he may give you up the old accounts before the new trainer takes the stable business into his hands? He was here half an hour before dinner, and begged that you would see him to-night."

Mr. Mellish shrugged his shoulders.

"Langley's as honest a fellow as ever breathed," he said. "I don't want to look into his accounts. I know what the stable costs me yearly on an average, and that's enough."

"But for his satisfaction, dear."

"Well, well, Lolly, to-morrow morning, then."

"No, dear, I want you to ride out with me to-morrow."

"To-morrow evening."

"You 'meet the Captains at the Citadel,'" said Aurora, laughing; "that is to say, you dine at Holmbush with Colonel Pevensey. Come, darling, I insist on your being business-like for once in a way; come to your sanctum sanctorum, and we'll send for Langley, and look into the accounts."

The pretty tyrant linked her arm in his, and led him to the other end of the house, and into that very room in which she had swooned away at the hearing of Mr. Pastern's letter. She looked thoughtfully out at the dull evening sky as she closed the windows. The storm had not yet come, but the ominous clouds still brooded low over the earth, and the sultry atmosphere was heavy and airless. Mrs. Mellish made a wonderful show of her business habits, and appeared to be very much interested in the mass of cornchandlers', veterinary surgeons', saddlers', and harness-makers' accounts with which the old

---

1   *Hamlet* I.v.188-9.

trainer respectfully bewildered his master. But about ten minutes after John had settled himself to his weary labour, Aurora threw down the pencil with which she had been working a calculation (by a process of so wildly original a nature, as to utterly revolutionize Cocker,[1] and annihilate the hackneyed notion that twice two are four), and floated lightly out of the room, with some vague promise of coming back presently, leaving Mr. Mellish to arithmetic and despair.

Mrs. Walter Powell was seated in the drawing-room reading, when Aurora entered that apartment with a large black-lace shawl wrapped about her head and shoulders. Mrs. Mellish had evidently expected to find the room empty; for she started and drew back at the sight of the pale-faced widow, who was seated in a distant window, making the most of the last faint rays of summer twilight. Aurora paused for a moment a few paces within the door, and then walked deliberately across the room towards the furthest window from that at which Mrs. Powell was seated.

"Are you going out in the garden this dull evening, Mrs. Mellish?" asked the ensign's widow.

Aurora stopped half-way between the window and the door to answer her.

"Yes," she said coldly.

"Allow me to advise you not to go far. We are going to have a storm."

"I don't think so."

"What, my dear Mrs. Mellish, not with that thunder-cloud yonder?"

"I will take my chance of being caught in it, then. The weather has been threatening all the afternoon. The house is insupportable to-night."

"But you will surely not go far?"

Mrs. Mellish did not appear to hear this last remonstrance. She hurried through the open window, and out upon the lawn, striking northwards towards that little iron gate across which she had talked to the "Softy."

---

1   Edward Cocker (1631-75), arithmetician and author of a very popular arithmetic text that is speculated to have appeared in over 100 editions.

The arch of the leaden sky seemed to contract above the tree-tops in the park, shutting in the earth as if with a roof of hot iron, after the fashion of those cunningly-contrived metal torture-chambers which we read of; but the rain had not yet come.

"What can take her into the garden on such an evening as this?" thought Mrs. Powell, as she watched the white dress receding in the dusky twilight. "It will be dark in ten minutes, and she is not usually so fond of going out alone."

The ensign's widow laid down the book in which she had appeared so deeply interested, and went to her own room, where she selected a comfortable gray cloak from a heap of primly folded garments in her capacious wardrobe. She muffled herself in this cloak, hurried down stairs with a soft but rapid step, and went out into the garden through a little lobby near John Mellish's room. The blinds in the squire's sanctum were not drawn down, and Mrs. Powell could see the master of the house bending over his paper under the light of a reading lamp, with the rheumatic trainer seated by his side. It was by this time quite dark, but Aurora's white dress was faintly visible upon the other side of the lawn.

Mrs. Mellish was standing beside the little iron gate when the ensign's widow emerged from the house. The white dress was motionless for some time, and the pale watcher, lurking under the shade of a long verandah, began to think that her trouble was wasted, and that perhaps, after all, Aurora had no special purpose in this evening ramble.

Mrs. Walter Powell felt cruelly disappointed. Always on the watch for some clue to the secret whose existence she had discovered, she had fondly hoped that even this unseasonable ramble might be some link in the mysterious chain she was so anxious to fit together. But it appeared that she was mistaken. The unseasonable ramble was very likely nothing more than one of Aurora's caprices – a womanly foolishness signifying nothing.

No! The white dress was no longer motionless, and in the unnatural stillness of the hot night Mrs. Powell heard the distant scrooping noise of a hinge revolving slowly, as if guided by a cautious hand. Mrs. Mellish had opened the iron gate, and had passed to the other side of the invisible barrier which separated the gardens from the Park. In another moment she had disappeared under the shadow of the trees which made a belt about the lawn.

Mrs. Powell paused, almost terrified by her unlooked-for discovery.

What, in the name of all that was darkly mysterious, could Mrs. Mellish have to do between nine and ten o'clock on the north side of the Park – the wildly kept, deserted north side, in which, from year's end to year's end, no one but the keepers ever walked?

The blood rushed hotly up to Mrs. Powell's pale face, as she suddenly remembered that the disused, dilapidated lodge upon this north side had been given to the new trainer as a residence. Remembering this was nothing, but remembering this in connection with that mysterious letter signed "A." was enough to send a thrill of savage, horrible joy through the dull veins of the dependent. What should she do? Follow Mrs. Mellish, and discover where she was going? How far would this be a safe thing to attempt?

She turned back and looked once more through the window of John's room. He was still bending over the papers, still in as apparently hopeless confusion of mind. There seemed little chance of his business being finished very quickly. The starless night and her dark dress alike sheltered the spy from observation.

"If I were close behind her, she would never see me," she thought.

She struck across the lawn to the iron gate and passed into the Park. The brambles and the tangled undergrowth caught at her dress as she paused for a moment looking about her in the summer night.

There was no trace of Aurora's white figure among the leafy alleys stretching in wild disorder before her.

"I'll not attempt to find the path she took," thought Mrs. Powell; "I know where to find her."

She groped her way into the narrow footpath leading to the lodge. She was not sufficiently familiar with the place to take the short cut which the "Softy" had made for himself through the grass that afternoon, and she was some time walking from the iron gate to the lodge.

The front windows of this rustic lodge faced a road that led to the stables; the back of the building looked towards the path down which Mrs. Powell went, and the two small windows in this back wall were both dark.

The ensign's widow crept softly round to the front, looked about her cautiously, and listened. There was no sound but the occasional rustle of a leaf, tremulous even in the still atmosphere, as if by some internal prescience of the coming storm. With a slow, careful footstep, she stole towards the little rustic window and looked into the room within.

She had not been mistaken when she had said that she knew where to find Aurora.

Mrs. Mellish was standing with her back to the window. Exactly opposite to her sat James Conyers the trainer, in an easy attitude, and with his pipe in his mouth. The little table was between them, and the one candle which lighted the room was drawn close to Mr. Conyers's elbow, and had evidently been used by him for the lighting of his pipe. Aurora was speaking. The eager listener could hear her voice, but not her words; and she could see by the trainer's face that he was listening intently. He was listening intently, but a dark frown contracted his handsome eyebrows, and it was very evident that he was not too well satisfied with the bent of the conversation.

He looked up when Aurora ceased speaking, shrugged his shoulders, and took his pipe out of his mouth. Mrs. Powell, with her pale face close against the window-pane, watched him intently.

He pointed with a careless gesture to an empty chair near Aurora, but she shook her head contemptuously, and suddenly turned towards the window; so suddenly, that Mrs. Powell had scarcely time to recoil into the darkness before Aurora had unfastened the iron latch and flung the narrow casement open.

"I cannot endure this intolerable heat," she exclaimed, impatiently; "I have said all I have to say, and need only wait for your answer."

"You don't give me much time for consideration," he said, with an insolent coolness which was in strange contrast to the restless vehemence of her manner. "What sort of answer do you want?"

"Yes or No."

"Nothing more?"

"No, nothing more. You know my conditions; they are all written here," she added, putting her hand upon an open paper which lay upon the table; "they are all written clearly enough for a child to understand. Will you accept them? Yes or No?"

"That depends upon circumstances," he answered, filling his pipe, and looking admiringly at the nail of his little finger, as he pressed the tobacco into the bowl.

"Upon what circumstances?"

"Upon the inducement which you offer, my dear Mrs. Mellish."

"You mean the price?"

"That's a low expression," he said, laughing; "but I suppose we both mean the same thing. The inducement must be a strong one which will make me do all that," – he pointed to the written paper, – "and it must take the form of solid cash. How much is it to be?"

"That is for you to say. Remember what I have told you. Decline to-night and I telegraph to my father to-morrow morning, telling him to alter his will."

"Suppose the old gentleman should be carried off in the interim, and leave that pleasant sheet of parchment standing as it is. I hear that he's old and feeble; it might be worth while calculating the odds upon such an event. I've risked my money on a worse chance before to-night."

She turned upon him with so dark a frown as he said this, that the insolently heartless words died upon his lips and left him looking at her gravely.

"Egad," he said, "you're as great a devil as ever you were. I doubt if that isn't a good offer after all. Give me two thousand down, and I'll take it."

"Two thousand pounds!"

"I ought to have said twenty, but I've always stood in my own light."

Mrs. Powell, crouching down beneath the open casement, had heard every word of this brief dialogue; but at this juncture, half-forgetful of all danger in her eagerness to listen, she raised her head until it was nearly on a level with the window-sill. As she did so, she recoiled with a sudden thrill of terror. She felt a puff of hot breath upon her cheek, and the garments of a man rustling against her own.

She was not the only listener.

The second spy was Stephen Hargraves the "Softy."

"Hush!" he whispered, grasping Mrs. Powell by the wrist, and pinning her in her crouching attitude by the muscular force of his horny hand; "it's only me; Steeve the 'Softy,' you know; the stable-helper that *she*" (he hissed out the personal pronoun with such a furious impetus that it seemed to whistle sharply through the stillness), – "the fondy that she horsewhipped. I know you, and I know you're here to listen. He sent me into Doncaster to fetch this" (he pointed to a bottle under his arm); "he thought it would take me four or five hours to go and get back; but I ran all the way, for I knew there was soomat oop."

He wiped his streaming face with the ends of his coarse necker-chief as he finished speaking. His breath came in panting gasps, and Mrs. Powell could hear the laborious beating of his heart in the stillness.

"I won't tell o' you," he said, "and you won't tell o' me. I've got the stripes upon my shoulder where she cut me with the whip to this day. I look at 'em sometimes, and they help to keep me in mind. She's a fine madam, aint she, and a great lady too? Ay, sure she is; but she comes to meet her husband's servant on the sly, after dark, for all that. Maybe the day isn't far off when *she'll* be turned from these gates, and warned off this ground; and the merciful Lord send that I live to see it. Hush!"

With her wrist still pinioned in his strong grasp, he motioned her to be silent, and bent his pale face forward; every feature rigid, in the listening expectancy of his hungry gaze.

"Listen," he whispered; "listen! Every fresh word damns her deeper than the last."

The trainer was the first to speak after this pause in the dialogue within the cottage. He had quietly smoked out his pipe, and had emptied the ashes of his tobacco upon the table before he took up the thread of the conversation at the point at which he had dropped it.

"Two thousand pounds," he said, "that is the offer, and I think it ought to be taken freely. Two thousand down, in Bank-of-England notes (fives and tens, higher figures might be awkward), or sterling coin of the realm. You understand; two thousand down. That's *my* alternative; or I leave this place to-morrow morning – with all belonging to me."

"By which course you would get nothing," said Mrs. John Mellish, quietly.

"Shouldn't I? What does the chap in the play get for his trouble when the blackamoor smothers his wife?[1] I should get nothing – but my revenge upon a tiger-cat, whose claws have left a mark upon me that I shall carry to my grave." He lifted his hair with a careless gesture of his hand, and pointed to a scar upon his forehead, a white mark, barely visible in the dim light of the tallow-candle. "I'm a good-natured, easy-going fellow, Mrs. John Mellish, but I don't forget. Is it to be the two thousand pounds, or war to the knife?"

Mrs. Powell waited eagerly for Aurora's answer; but before it came, a round heavy rain-drop pattered upon the light hair of the ensign's widow. The hood of her cloak had fallen back, leaving her head uncovered. This one large drop was the warning of the coming storm. The signal peal of thunder rumbled slowly and hoarsely in the distance, and a pale flash of lightning trembled on the white faces of the two listeners.

"Let me go," whispered Mrs. Powell, "let me go; I must get back to the house before the rain begins."

The "Softy" slowly relaxed his iron grip upon her wrist. He had held it unconsciously, in his utter abstraction to all things except the two speakers in the cottage.

Mrs. Powell rose from her knees, and crept noiselessly away from the lodge. She remembered the vital necessity of getting back to the house before Aurora, and of avoiding the shower. Her wet garments would betray her if she did not succeed in escaping the coming storm. She was of a spare, wizen figure, encumbered with no superfluous flesh, and she ran rapidly along the narrow sheltered pathway leading to the iron gate through which she had followed Aurora.

The heavy rain-drops fell at long intervals upon the leaves. A second and a third peal of thunder rattled along the earth, like the horrible roar of some hungry animal creeping nearer and nearer to its prey. Blue flashes of faint lightning lit up the tangled intricacies of the wood, but the fullest fury of the storm had not yet burst forth.

The rain-drops came at shorter intervals as Mrs. Powell passed out of the wood, through the little iron gate; faster still as she hurried across the lawn; faster yet as she reached the lobby-door, which she

---

1   From Othello's murder of Desdemona, Iago gets nothing but psychological satisfaction.

had left ajar an hour before, and sat down panting upon a little bench within, to recover her breath before she went any further. She was still sitting on this bench, when the fourth peal of thunder shook the low roof above her head, and the rain dropped from the starless sky with such a rushing impetus, that it seemed as if a huge trap-door had been opened in the heavens, and a celestial ocean let down to flood the earth.

"I think my lady will be nicely caught," muttered Mrs. Walter Powell.

She threw her cloak aside upon the lobby bench, and went through a passage leading to the hall. One of the servants was shutting the hall-door.

"Have you shut the drawing-room windows, Wilson?" she asked.

"No, ma'am; I am afraid Mrs. Mellish is out in the rain. Jarvis is getting ready to go and look for her, with a lantern and the gig-umbrella."

"Then Jarvis can stop where he is; Mrs. Mellish came in half an hour ago. You may shut all the windows, and close the house for the night."

"Yes, ma'am."

"By-the-by, what o'clock is it, Wilson? My watch is slow."

"A quarter past ten, ma'am, by the dining-room clock."

The man locked the hall-door, put up an immense iron bar, which worked with some rather complicated machinery, and had a bell hanging at one end of it, for the frustration of all burglarious and designing ruffians.

From the hall the man went to the drawing-room, where he carefully fastened the long range of windows; from the drawing-room to the lobby; and from the lobby to the dining-room, where he locked the half-glass door opening into the garden. This being done, all communication between the house and the garden was securely shut off.

"He shall know of her goings-on, at any rate," thought Mrs. Powell, as she dogged the footsteps of the servant to see that he did his work. The Mellish household did not take very kindly to this deputy mistress; and when the footman went back to the servants' hall, he informed his colleagues that SHE was pryin' and pokin' about sharper than hever, and watchin' of a feller like a old 'ouse-cat. Mr. Wilson was a cockney, and had been newly-imported into the establishment.

When the ensign's widow had seen the last bolt driven home to its socket, and the last key turned in its lock, she went back to the drawing-room and seated herself at the lamp-lit table, with some delicate morsel of old-maidish fancy-work, which seemed to be the converse of Penelope's embroidery, as it appeared to advance at night, and retrograde by day.[1] She had hastily smoothed her hair and rearranged her dress, and she looked as uncomfortably neat as when she came down to breakfast in the fresh primness of her matutinal toilette.

She had been sitting at her work for about ten minutes when John Mellish entered the room, emerging weary but triumphant from his struggle with the simple rules of multiplication and subtraction. Mr. Mellish had evidently suffered severely in the contest. His thick brown hair was tumbled into a rough mass that stood nearly upright upon his head, his cravat was untied, and his shirt-collar thrown open for the relief of his capacious throat; and these and many other marks of the struggle he bore upon him when he entered the drawing-room.

"I've broken loose from school at last, Mrs. Powell," he said, flinging his big frame upon one of the sofas, to the imminent peril of the German-spring cushions; "I've broken away before the flag dropped, for Langley would have liked to keep me there till midnight. He followed me to the door of this room with fourteen bushels of oats that was down in the cornchandler's account and was not down in the book he keeps to check the cornchandler. Why the deuce don't he put it down in his book and make it right, then, I ask, instead of bothering me? What's the good of his keeping an account to check the cornchandler if he don't make his account the same as the cornchandler's? But it's all over!" he added, with a great sigh of relief, "it's all over! and all I can say is, I hope the new trainer isn't honest."

"Do you know much of the new trainer, Mr. Mellish?" asked Mrs. Powell, blandly; rather as if she wished to amuse her employer by the exertion of her conversational powers than for the gratification of any mundane curiosity.

---

1 Penelope, Odysseus' faithful wife in the *Odyssey*, puts off unwelcome suitors by pretending she cannot remarry until she has finished weaving a shroud for Laertes, Odysseus' father. She weaves by day, but unravels her work at night.

"Deuced little," returned John, indifferently. "I haven't even seen the fellow yet; but John Pastern recommended him, and he's sure to be all right; besides, Aurora knows the man: he was in her father's service once."

"Oh, indeed!" said Mrs. Powell, giving the two insignificant words a significant little jerk; "oh, indeed! Mrs. Mellish knows him, does she? Then of course he's a trustworthy person. He's a remarkably handsome young man."

"Remarkably handsome, is he?" said Mr. Mellish, with a careless laugh. "Then I suppose all the maids will be falling in love with him, and neglecting their work to look out of the windows that open on to the stable-yard, hey? That's the sort of thing when a man has a handsome groom, aint it? Susan and Sarah, and all the rest of 'em, take to cleaning the windows, and wearing new ribbons in their caps?"

"I really don't know anything about that, Mr. Mellish," answered the ensign's widow, simpering over her work as if the question they were discussing was so very far away that it was impossible for her to be serious about it; "but my experience has thrown me into a very large number of families." (She said this with perfect truth, as she had occupied so many situations that her enemies had come to declare she was unable to remain in any one household above a twelvemonth, by reason of her employers' discovery of her real nature.) "I have occupied positions of trust and confidence," continued Mrs. Powell, "and I regret to say that I have seen much domestic misery arise from the employment of handsome servants, whose appearance and manners are superior to their station. Mr. Conyers is not at all the sort of person I should like to see in a household in which I had the charge of young ladies."

A sick, half-shuddering faintness crept through John's herculean frame as Mrs. Powell expressed herself thus; so vague a feeling that he scarcely knew whether it was mental or physical, any better than he knew what it was that he disliked in this speech of the ensign's widow. The feeling was as transient as it was vague. John's honest blue eyes looked wonderingly round the room.

"Where's Aurora?" he said; "gone to bed?"

"I believe Mrs. Mellish has retired to rest," Mrs. Powell answered.

"Then I shall go too. The place is as dull as a dungeon without her," said Mr. Mellish, with agreeable candour. "Perhaps you'll be good enough to make me a glass of brandy-and-water before I go, Mrs. Powell, for I've got the cold shivers after those accounts."

He rose to ring the bell; but before he had gone three paces from the sofa, an impatient knocking at the closed outer shutters of one of the windows arrested his footsteps.

"Who, in mercy's name, is that?" he exclaimed, staring at the direction from which the noise came, but not attempting to respond to the summons.

Mrs. Powell looked up to listen, with a face expressive of nothing but innocent wonder.

The knocking was repeated more loudly and impatiently than before.

"It must be one of the servants," muttered John; "but why doesn't he go round to the back of the house? I can't keep the poor devil out upon such a night as this, though," he added good-naturedly, unfastening the window as he spoke. The sashes opened inwards, the Venetian shutters outwards. He pushed these shutters open, and looked out into the darkness and the rain.

Aurora, shivering in her drenched garments, stood a few paces from him, with the rain beating down straight and heavily upon her head.

Even in that obscurity her husband recognized her.

"My darling," he cried, "is it you? You out at such a time, and on such a night! Come in, for mercy's sake; you must be drenched to the skin."

She came into the room; the wet hanging in her muslin dress streamed out upon the carpet on which she trod, and the folds of her lace shawl clung tightly about her figure.

"Why did you let them shut the windows?" she said, turning to Mrs. Powell, who had risen, and was looking the picture of ladylike uneasiness and sympathy. "You knew that I was in the garden."

"Yes, but I thought you had returned, my dear Mrs. Mellish," said the ensign's widow, busying herself with Aurora's wet shawl, which she attempted to remove, but which Mrs. Mellish plucked impatiently away from her. "I saw you go out, certainly; and I saw you leave the lawn in the direction of the north lodge; but I thought you had returned some time since."

The colour faded out of John Mellish's face.

"The north lodge!" he said. "Have you been to the north lodge?"

"I have been in the *direction of the north lodge*," Aurora answered, with a sneering emphasis upon the words. "Your information is perfectly correct, Mrs. Powell, though I did not know you had done me the honour of watching my actions."

Mr. Mellish did not appear to hear this. He looked from his wife to his wife's companion with a half-bewildered expression – an expression of newly-awakened doubt, of dim, struggling perplexity – that was very painful to see.

"The north lodge!" he repeated; "what were you doing at the north lodge, Aurora?"

"Do you wish me to stand here in my wet clothes while I tell you?" asked Mrs. Mellish, her great black eyes blazing up with indignant pride. "If you want an explanation for Mrs. Powell's satisfaction, I can give it here; if only for your own, it will do as well upstairs."

She swept towards the door, trailing her wet shawl after her, but not less queenly, even in her dripping garments; Semiramide and Cleopatra may have been out in wet weather. On the threshold of the door she paused and looked back at her husband.

"I shall want you to take me to London to-morrow, Mr. Mellish," she said. Then with one haughty toss of her beautiful head, and one bright flash of her glorious eyes, which seemed to say, "Slave, obey and tremble!" she disappeared, leaving Mr. Mellish to follow her, meekly, wonderingly, fearfully; with terrible doubts and anxieties creeping, like venomous living creatures, stealthily into his heart.

CHAPTER XIX.

MONEY MATTERS.

ARCHIBALD FLOYD was very lonely at Felden Woods without his daughter. He took no pleasure in the long drawing-room, or the billiard-room and library, or the pleasant galleries, in which there were all manner of easy corners, with abutting bay-windows, damask cushioned oaken benches, china vases as high as tables, all enlivened by the alternately sternly masculine and simperingly feminine faces of those ancestors whose painted representations the banker had bought in Wardour Street.[1] (Indeed, I fear those Scottish warriors, those bewigged worthies of the Northern Circuit, those taper-waisted ladies with pointed stomachers, tucked-up petticoats, pannier-hoops, and blue-ribbon bedizened crooks, had been painted to order, and that there were such items in the account of the Wardour Street *rococo* merchant as, "To one knight banneret, killed at Bosworth 25*l*. 5*s*." The old banker, I say, grew sadly weary of his gorgeous mansion, which was of little avail to him without Aurora.

People are not so very much happier for living in handsome houses, though it is generally considered such a delightful thing to occupy a mansion which would be large enough for a hospital, and take your simple meal at the end of a table long enough to accommodate a board of railway directors. Archibald Floyd could not sit beside both the fireplaces in his long drawing-room, and he felt strangely lonely looking from the easy-chair on one hearth-rug, through a vista of velvet-pile and satin-damask, walnut-wood, buhl, malachite, china, parian, crystal, and ormolu,[2] at that solitary second hearth-rug and those empty easy-chairs. He shivered in his dreary grandeur. His five-and-forty by thirty feet of velvet-pile might have been a patch of

---

1 Street in London known for antique dealers. By the 19th century, the shops there had a dubious reputation, and the term "Wardour Street" was used to designate fakes.

2 Buhl is brass or tortoise-shell inlay; malachite a bright green mineral used for ornament; parian fine white porcelain; and ormolu a gold-coloured alloy of copper, zinc, and tin.

yellow sand in the Great Sahara for any pleasure he derived from its occupation. The billiard-room, perhaps, was worse; for the cues and balls were every one made precious by Aurora's touch; and there was a great fine-drawn seam upon the green cloth, which marked the spot where Miss Floyd had ripped it open that time she made her first juvenile essay at a cannon.[1]

The banker locked the doors of both these splendid apartments, and gave the keys to his housekeeper.

"Keep the rooms in order, Mrs. Richardson," he said, "and keep them thoroughly aired; but I shall only use them when Mr. and Mrs. Mellish come to me."

And having shut up these haunted chambers, Mr. Floyd retired to that snug little study in which he kept his few relics of the sorrowful past.

It may be said that the Scottish banker was a very stupid old man, and that he might have invited the county families to his gorgeous mansion; that he might have summoned his nephews and their wives, with all grand nephews and nieces appertaining, and might thus have made the place merry with the sound of fresh young voices, and the long corridors noisy with the patter of restless little feet. He might have lured literary and artistic celebrities to his lonely hearth-rug, and paraded the lions of the London season upon his velvet-pile. He might have entered the political arena, and have had himself nominated for Beckenham, Croydon, or West Wickham. He might have done almost anything; for he had very nearly as much money as Aladdin, and could have carried dishes of uncut diamonds to the father of any princess whom he might take it into his head to marry. He might have done almost anything, this ridiculous old banker; yet he did nothing but sit brooding over his lonely hearth – for he was old and feeble, and he sat by the fire even in the bright summer weather – thinking of the daughter who was far away.

He thanked God for her happy home, for her devoted husband, for her secure and honourable position; and he would have given the last drop of his blood to obtain for her these advantages; but he was, after all, only mortal, and he would rather have had her by his side.

---

1 In billiards, a "cannon" refers to the player's ball hitting two balls successively.

Why did he not surround himself with society, as brisk Mrs. Alexander urged, when she found him looking pale and care-worn? Why? Because society was not Aurora. Because all the brightest *bon-mots* of all the literary celebrities who have ever walked this earth seemed dull to him when compared with his daughter's idlest babble. Literary lions! Political notabilities! Out upon them! When Sir Edward Bulwer Lytton and Mr. Charles Dickens should call in Mr. Makepeace Thackeray and Mr. Wilkie Collins,[1] to assist them in writing a work, in fifteen volumes or so, about Aurora, the banker would be ready to offer them a handsome sum for the copyright. Until then, he cared very little for the best book in Mr. Mudie's collection.[2] When the members of the legislature should bring their political knowledge to bear upon Aurora, Mr. Archibald Floyd would be happy to listen to them. In the interim, he would have yawned in Lord Palmerston's face or turned his back upon Earl Russell.[3]

The banker had been a kind uncle, a good master, a warm friend, and a generous patron; but he had never loved any creature except his wife Eliza and the daughter she had left to his care. Life is not long enough to hold many such attachments as these; and the people who love very intensely are apt to concentrate the full force of their affection upon one object. For twenty years this black-eyed girl had been the idol before which the old man had knelt; and now that the divinity is taken away from him, he falls prostrate and desolate before the empty shrine. Heaven knows how bitterly this beloved child had made him suffer, how deeply she had plunged the reckless dagger to the very core of his loving heart, and how freely, gladly, tearfully, and hopefully he had forgiven her. But she had never atoned for the past. It is poor consolation which Lady Macbeth gives to her remorseful husband when she tells him that "what's done cannot be undone;"[4] but it is painfully and terribly true. Aurora could not restore the year

---

1 Prominent Victorian novelists.
2 Mudie's Circulating Library, in New Oxford Street, was the largest of the Victorian circulating libraries. The standard format for a novel at the time was three volumes.
3 Henry John Temple (1784-1865), third Viscount Palmerston, was Prime Minister from 1855-58 and from 1859 until his death in 1865; Lord John Russell, first Earl Russell (1792-1878), was Prime Minister from 1846-52 and from 1865-66.
4 *Macbeth* V.ii.68.

which she had taken out of her father's life, and which his anguish and despair had multiplied by ten. She could not restore the equal balance of the mind which had once experienced a shock so dreadful as to shatter its serenity, as we shatter the mechanism of a watch when we let it fall violently to the ground. The watchmaker patches up the damage, and gives us a new wheel here, and a spring there, and sets the hands going again; but they never go so smoothly as when the watch was fresh from the hands of the maker, and they are apt to stop suddenly with no shadow of warning. Aurora could not atone. Whatever the nature of that girlish error which made the mystery of her life, it was not to be undone. She could more easily have baled the ocean dry with a soup-ladle, – and I dare say she would gladly have gone to work to spoon out the salt water, if by so doing she could have undone that bygone mischief. But she could not; she could not! Her tears, her penitence, her affection, her respect, her devotion, could do much; but they could not do this.

The old banker invited Talbot Bulstrode and his young wife to make themselves at home at Felden, and drive down to the Woods as freely as if the place had been some country mansion of their own. They came sometimes, and Talbot entertained his great uncle-in-law with the troubles of the Cornish miners, while Lucy sat listening to her husband's talk with unmitigated reverence and delight. Archibald Floyd made his guests very welcome upon these occasions, and gave orders that the oldest and costliest wines in the cellar should be brought out for the captain's entertainment; but sometimes in the very middle of Talbot's discourses upon political economy the old man would sigh wearily, and look with a dimly yearning gaze far away over the tree-tops in a northward direction, towards that distant Yorkshire household in which his daughter was the queen.

Perhaps Mr. Floyd had never quite forgiven Talbot Bulstrode for the breaking off of the match between him and Aurora. The banker had certainly of the two suitors preferred John Mellish; but he would have considered it only correct if Captain Bulstrode had retired from the world upon the occasion of Aurora's marriage, and broken his heart in foreign exile, rather than advertising his indifference by a union with poor little Lucy. Archibald looked wonderingly at his fair-haired niece, as she sat before him in the deep bay-window, with the sunshine upon her amber tresses and the crisp folds of her peach-coloured dress, looking for all the world like one of the painted heroines so dear to the pre-Raphaelite brotherhood,[1] and marvelled how it was that Talbot could have come to admire her. She was very pretty, certainly, with pink cheeks, a white nose, and rose-coloured nostrils, and a species of beauty which consists in very careful finishing off and picking out of the features; but, oh, how tame, how cold, how weak, beside that Egyptian goddess, that Assyrian queen with the flashing eyes and the serpentine coils of purple-black hair!

Talbot Bulstrode was very calm, very quiet, but apparently sufficiently happy. I use that word "sufficiently" advisedly. It is a dangerous thing to be too happy. Your high-pressure happiness, your sixty-miles-an-hour enjoyment, is apt to burst up and come to a bad end. Better the quietest parliamentary train,[2] which starts very early in the morning and carries its passengers safe into the terminus when the shades of night come down, than that rabid, rushing express, which does the journey in a quarter of the time, but occasionally topples over a bank, or rides pickaback upon a luggage train, in its fiery impetuosity.

Talbot Bulstrode was substantially happier with Lucy than he ever could have been with Aurora. His fair young wife's undemonstrative worship of him soothed and flattered him. Her gentle obedience, her entire concurrence in his every thought and whim, set his pride at rest. She was not eccentric, she was not impetuous. If he left her alone all day in the snug little house in Halfmoon Street which he had furnished before his marriage, he had no fear of her calling for her horse and scampering away into Rotten Row,[3] with not so much as a groom to attend upon her. She was not strong-minded. She could be

---

1   See 84, n.1. In *Lady Audley's Secret*, the heroine is painted by a Pre-Raphaelite painter, whose exaggerated style reveals her as a beautiful fiend. Lucy's association with the Pre-Raphaelites seems to have no such negative connotations.

2   Sixty mph was a very fast speed for Victorian trains; it was the speed limit for the South Eastern Railway until after 1900. "Parliamentary" trains were so called because parliament required every railroad to run at least one train per day along its entire route, making all stops and charging no more than a penny a mile. Although slow, such trains were cheap – cheaper than the regular third-class fare.

3   Famous equestrian track in the south part of Hyde Park, strongly associated with the demi-monde of high-class prostitutes on horseback.

happy without the society of Newfoundlands and Skye terriers. She did not prefer Landseer's dog-pictures above all other examples of modern art. She might have walked down Regent Street a hundred times without being once tempted to loiter upon the curb-stone and bargain with suspicious-looking merchants for a "noice leetle dawg." She was altogether gentle and womanly, and Talbot had no fear to trust her to her own sweet will, and no need to impress upon her the necessity of lending her feeble little hands to the mighty task of sustaining the dignity of the Raleigh Bulstrodes.

She would cling to him sometimes half lovingly, half timidly, and, looking up with a pretty deprecating smile into his coldly handsome face, ask him, falteringly, if he was *really* REALLY happy.

"Yes, my darling girl," the Cornish captain would answer, being very well accustomed to the question, "decidedly, very happy."

His calm business-like tone would rather disappoint poor Lucy, and she would vaguely wish that her husband had been a little more like the heroes in the High-Church novels, and a little less devoted to Adam Smith, McCulloch,[1] and the Cornish mines.

"But you don't love me as you loved Aurora, Talbot?" (There were profane people who corrupted the captain's Christian name into "Tal;" but Mrs. Bulstrode was not more likely to avail herself of that disrespectful abbreviation than she was to address her gracious Sovereign as "Vic.") "But you don't love me as you loved Aurora, Talbot dear?" the pleading voice would urge, so tenderly anxious to be contradicted.

"Not *as* I loved Aurora, perhaps, darling."

"Not as much?"

"As much and better, my pet; with a more enduring and a wiser love."

If this was a little bit of a fib when the captain first said it, is he to be utterly condemned for the falsehood? How could he resist the loving blue eyes so ready to fill with tears if he had answered coldly; the softly pensive voice, tremulous with emotion; the earnest face; the caressing hand laid so lightly upon his coat-collar? He must have been

---

1   Adam Smith (1723-90), political economist and author of *The Wealth of Nations* (1776); John Ramsay McCulloch (1789-1864), political economist and statistician.

more than mortal had he given any but loving answers to those loving questions. The day soon came when his answers were no longer tinged with so much as the shadow of falsehood. His little wife crept stealthily, almost imperceptibly, into his heart; and if he remembered the fever-dream of the past, it was only to rejoice in the tranquil security of the present.

Talbot Bulstrode and his wife were staying at Felden Woods for a few days during the burning July weather, and sat down to dinner with Mr. Floyd upon the day succeeding the night of the storm. They were disturbed in the very midst of that dinner by the unexpected arrival of Mr. and Mrs. Mellish, who rattled up to the door in a hired vehicle just as the second course was being placed upon the table.

Archibald Floyd recognized the first murmur of his daughter's voice, and ran out into the hall to welcome her.

She showed no eagerness to throw herself into her father's arms, but stood looking at John Mellish with a weary, absent expression, while the stalwart Yorkshireman allowed himself to be gradually disencumbered of a chaotic load of travelling-bags, sun-umbrellas, shawls, magazines, newspapers, and over-coats.

"My darling, my darling!" exclaimed the banker, "what a happy surprise, what an unexpected pleasure!"

She did not answer him, but, with her arms about his neck, looked mournfully into his face.

"She would come," said John Mellish, addressing himself generally; "she would come. The deuce knows why! But she said she must come, and what could I do but bring her? If she asked me to take her to the moon, what could I do but take her? But she wouldn't bring any luggage to speak of, because we're going back to-morrow."

"Going back to-morrow!" repeated Mr. Floyd; "impossible!"

"Bless your heart!" cried John, "what's impossible to Lolly? If she wanted to go to the moon, she'd go, don't I tell you? She'd have a special engine, or a special balloon, or a special something or other, and she'd go. When we were in Paris she wanted to see the big fountains play; and she told me to write to the Emperor and ask him to have them set going for her. She did, by Jove!"

Lucy Bulstrode came forward to bid her cousin welcome; but I fear that a sharp jealous pang thrilled through that innocent heart at the thought that those fatal black eyes were again brought to bear upon Talbot's life.

Mrs. Mellish put her arms about her cousin as tenderly as if she had been embracing a child.

"You here, dearest Lucy!" she said. "I am so very glad!"

"He loves me," whispered little Mrs. Bulstrode, "and I never, never can tell you how good he is."

"Of course not, my darling," answered Aurora, drawing her cousin aside while Mr. Mellish shook hands with his father-in-law and Talbot Bulstrode. "He is the most glorious of princes, the most perfect of saints, is he not? and you worship him all day; you sing silent hymns in his praise, and perform high mass in his honour, and go about telling his virtues upon an imaginary rosary. Ah, Lucy, how many kinds of love there are! and who shall say which is the best or highest? I see plain, blundering John Mellish yonder, with unprejudiced eyes; I know his every fault, I laugh at his every awkwardness. Yes, I laugh now, for he is dropping those things faster than the servants can pick them up."

She stopped to point to poor John's chaotic burden.

"I see all this as plainly as I see the deficiencies of the servant who stands behind my chair; and yet I love him with all my heart and soul, and I would not have one fault corrected, or one virtue exaggerated, for fear it should make him different to what he is."

Lucy Bulstrode gave a little half-resigned sigh.

"What a blessing that my poor cousin is happy!" she thought; "and yet how can she be otherwise than miserable with that absurd John Mellish?"

What Lucy meant, perhaps, was this: – How could Aurora be otherwise than wretched in the companionship of a gentleman who had neither a straight nose nor dark hair. Some women never outlive that school-girl infatuation for straight noses and dark hair? Some girls would have rejected Napoleon the Great because he wasn't "tall," or would have turned up their noses at the author of 'Childe Harold' if they had happened to see him in a stand-up collar. If Lord Byron had never turned down his collars, would his poetry have been as popular as it was? If Mr. Alfred Tennyson were to cut his hair, would that operation modify our opinion of 'The

Queen of the May'?[1] Where does that marvellous power of association begin and end? Perhaps there may have been a reason for Aurora's contentment with her commonplace, prosaic husband. Perhaps she had learned at a very early period of her life that there are qualities even more valuable than exquisitely-modelled features or clustering locks. Perhaps, having begun to be foolish very early, she had outstripped her contemporaries in the race, and had earlier learned to be wise.

Archibald Floyd led his daughter and her husband into the dining-room, and the dinner-party sat down again with the two unexpected guests, and the luke-warm salmon brought in again for Mr. and Mrs. Mellish.

Aurora sat in her old place on her father's right hand. In the old girlish days Miss Floyd had never occupied the bottom of the table, but had loved best to sit close to that foolishly-doting parent, pouring out his wine for him in defiance of the servants, and doing other loving offices which were deliciously inconvenient to the old man.

To-day Aurora seemed especially affectionate. That fondly-clinging manner had all its ancient charm to the banker. He put down his glass with a tremulous hand to gaze at his darling child, and was dazzled with her beauty, and drunken with the happiness of having her near him.

"But, my darling," he said, by-and-by, "what do you mean by talking about going back to Yorkshire to-morrow?"

"Nothing, papa, except that I *must* go," answered Mrs. Mellish, determinedly.

"But why come, dear, if you could only stop one night?"

"Because I wanted to see you, dearest father, and talk to you about – about money matters."

"That's it," exclaimed John Mellish, with his mouth half full of salmon and lobster-sauce. "That's it! Money matters! That's all I can

---

1   Napoleon's height was 5 foot, 2 inches; Byron habitually wore his shirt collars turned down, not tied with a cravat; and numerous contemporary accounts testify to the length and abundance of Tennyson's hair. On meeting Tennyson in 1857, Nathaniel Hawthorne wrote: "He had on a black wide awake hat, with round crown and wide irregular brim, beneath which came down his long black hair, looking terribly tangled." The poem referred to is "The May Queen"; Braddon is remembering the refrain, "I'm to be Queen o' the May."

get out of her. She goes out late last night, and roams about the garden, and comes in wet through and through, and says she must come
to London about money matters. What should she want with money
matters? If she wants money, she can have as much as she wants. She
shall write the figures, and I'll sign the cheque; or she shall have a
dozen blank cheques to fill in just as she pleases. What is there upon
this earth that I'd refuse her? If she dipped a little too deep, and put
more money than she could afford upon the bay filly, why doesn't she
come to me instead of bothering you about money matters? You
know I said so in the train, Aurora, ever so many times. Why bother
your poor papa about it?"

The poor papa looked wonderingly from his daughter to his
daughter's husband. What did it all mean? Trouble, vexation, weariness
of spirit, humiliation, disgrace?

Ah, Heaven help that enfeebled mind whose strength has been
shattered by one great shock! Archibald Floyd dreaded the token of a
coming storm in every chance cloud on the summer's sky.

"Perhaps I may prefer to spend my *own* money, Mr. John Mellish,"
answered Aurora, "and pay any foolish bets I have chosen to make out
of my *own* purse, without being under an obligation to any one."

Mr. Mellish returned to his salmon in silence.

"There is no occasion for a great mystery, papa," resumed Aurora;
"I want some money for a particular purpose, and I have come to
consult with you about my affairs. There is nothing very extraordinary in that, I suppose?"

Mrs. John Mellish tossed her head, and flung this sentence at the
assembly, as if it had been a challenge. Her manner was so defiant, that
even Talbot and Lucy felt called upon to respond with a gentle dis-
senting murmur.

"No, no, of course not; nothing more natural," muttered the captain; but he was thinking all the time, – "Thank God I married the
other one."

After dinner the little party strolled out of the drawing-room windows on to the lawn, and away towards that iron bridge upon which
Aurora had stood, with her dog by her side, less than two years ago, on
the occasion of Talbot Bulstrode's second visit to Felden Woods. Lingering upon that bridge on this tranquil summer's evening, what

could the captain do but think of that September day, barely two years agone? Barely two years! not two years! And how much had been done and thought and suffered since! How contemptible was the narrow space of time! yet what terrible eternities of anguish, what centuries of heart-break, had been compressed into that pitiful sum of days and weeks! When the fraudulent partner in some house of business puts the money which is not his own upon a Derby favourite, and goes home at night a loser, it is strangely difficult for that wretched defaulter to believe that it is not twelve hours since he travelled the road to Epsom confident of success, and calculating how he should invest his winnings. Talbot Bulstrode was very silent, thinking of the influence which this family of Felden Woods had had upon his destiny. His little Lucy saw that silence and thoughtfulness, and, stealing softly to her husband, linked her arm in his. She had a right to do it now. Yes, to pass her little soft white hand under his coat-sleeve, and even look up, almost boldly, in his face.

"Do you remember when you first came to Felden, and we stood upon this very bridge?" she asked: for she too had been thinking of that far-away time in the bright September of '57. "Do you remember, Talbot dear?"

She had drawn him away from the banker and his children, in order to ask this all-important question.

"Yes, perfectly, darling. As well as I remember your graceful figure seated at the piano in the long drawing-room, with the sunshine on your hair."

"You remember that! – you remember *me!*" exclaimed Lucy, rapturously.

"Very well, indeed."

"But I thought – that is, I know – that you were in love with Aurora then."

"I think not."

"You only think not?"

"How can I tell!" cried Talbot. "I freely confess that my first recollection connected with this place is of a gorgeous black-eyed creature, with scarlet in her hair; and I can no more disassociate her image from Felden Woods than I can, with my bare right hand, pluck up the trees which give the place its name. But if you entertain one distrustful thought of that pale shadow of the past, you do yourself and me a grievous wrong. I made a mistake, Lucy; but, thank Heaven! I saw it in time."

It is to be observed that Captain Bulstrode was always peculiarly demonstrative in his gratitude to Providence for his escape from the bonds which were to have united him to Aurora. He also made a great point of the benign compassion in which he held John Mellish. But in despite of this, he was apt to be rather captious and quarrelsomely disposed towards the Yorkshireman; and I doubt if John's little stupidities and weakness were, on the whole, very displeasing to him. There are some wounds which never quite heal. The jagged flesh may reunite; cooling medicines may subdue the inflammation; even the scar left by the dagger-thrust may wear away, until it disappears in that gradual transformation which every atom of us is supposed by physiologists to undergo; but the wound *has been*, and to the last hour of our lives there are unfavourable winds which can make us wince with the old pain.

Aurora treated her cousin's husband with the calm cordiality which she might have felt for a brother. She bore no grudge against him for the old desertion; for she was happy with her husband. She was happy with the man who loved and believed in her, with a strength of confidence which had survived every trial of his simple faith. Mrs. Mellish and Lucy wandered away among the flower-beds by the water-side, leaving the gentlemen on the bridge.

"So you are very, very happy, my Lucy?" said Aurora.

"Oh, yes, yes, dear. How could I be otherwise? Talbot is so good to me. I know, of course, that he loved you first, and that he doesn't love me quite − in the same way, you know − perhaps, in fact − not as much." Lucy Bulstrode was never tired of harping on this unfortunate minor string. "But I am very happy. You must come and see us, Aurora dear. Our house is so pretty!"

Mrs. Bulstrode hereupon entered into a detailed description of the furniture and decorations in Halfmoon Street, which is perhaps scarcely worthy of record. Aurora listened rather absently to the long catalogue of upholstery, and yawned several times before her cousin had finished.

"It's a very pretty house, I dare say, Lucy," she said at last, "and John and I will be very glad to come and see you some day. I wonder, Lucy, if I were to come in any trouble or disgrace to your door, whether you would turn me away?"

"Trouble! disgrace!" repeated Lucy looking frightened.

"You wouldn't turn me away, Lucy, would you? No; I know you better than that. You'd let me in secretly, and hide me away in one of the servants' bedrooms, and bring me food by stealth, for fear the captain should discover the forbidden guest beneath his roof. You'd serve two masters, Lucy, in fear and trembling."

Before Mrs. Bulstrode could make any answer to this extraordinary speech the approach of the gentlemen interrupted the feminine conference.

It was scarcely a lively evening, this July sunset at Felden Woods. Archibald Floyd's gladness in his daughter's presence was something damped by the peculiarity of her visit; John Mellish had some shadowy remnants of the previous night's disquietude hanging about him; Talbot Bulstrode was thoughtful and moody; and poor little Lucy was tortured by vague fears of her brilliant cousin's influence. I don't suppose that any member of that "attenuated" assembly felt very much regret when the great clock in the stable-yard struck eleven, and the jingling bedroom candlesticks were brought into the room.

Talbot and his wife were the first to say good-night. Aurora lingered at her father's side, and John Mellish looked doubtfully at his dashing white sergeant, waiting to receive the word of command.

"You may go, John," she said; "I want to speak to papa."

"But I can wait, Lolly."

"On no account," answered Mrs. Mellish sharply. "I am going into papa's study to have a quiet confabulation with him. What end would be gained by your waiting? You've been yawning in our faces all the evening. You're tired to death, I know, John; so go at once, my precious pet, and leave papa and me to discuss our money matters." She pouted her rosy lips, and stood upon tiptoe, while the big Yorkshireman kissed her.

"How you do henpeck me, Lolly!" he said rather sheepishly.

"Good-night, sir. God bless you! Take care of my darling."

He shook hands with Mr. Floyd, parting from him with that half-affectionate, half-reverent manner which he always displayed to Aurora's father. Mrs. Mellish stood for some moments silent and motionless, looking after her husband; while her father, watching her looks, tried to read their meaning.

How quiet are the tragedies of real life! That dreadful scene between the Moor and his Ancient[1] takes place in the open street of Cyprus, according to modern usage. I can scarcely fancy Othello and Iago debating about poor Desdemona's honesty in St. Paul's Church-yard, or even in the marketplace of a country town; but perhaps the Cyprus street was a dull one, a *cul-de-sac*, it may be, or at least a desert-ed thoroughfare, something like that in which Monsieur Melnotte falls upon the shoulder of General Damas and sobs out his lamenta-tions.[2] But our modern tragedies seem to occur indoors, and in places where we should least look for scenes of horror. Who can forget that tempestuous scene of jealous fury and mad violence which took place in a second floor in Northumberland Street, while the broad daylight was streaming in through the dusty windows, and the common Lon-don cries ascending from the pavement below?[3]

Any chance traveller driving from Beckenham to West Wickham would have looked, perhaps enviously, at the Felden mansion, and sighed to be lord of that fair expanse of park and garden; yet I doubt if in the county of Kent there was any creature more disturbed in mind

---

1   *Othello* III.iii.

2   In Bulwer Lytton's play *The Lady of Lyons* (1838), Claude Melnotte, believing him-self betrayed by his wife Pauline, bursts into grief in a Lyons street, and is consoled by General Damas. Elsewhere, Aurora compares Conyers to a false Claude Melnotte (see 349, n.1).

3   At 11:45 a.m. on 12 July 1861, at Number 16 Northumberland Street, Strand, workmen witnessed a terribly wounded man (Major Murray) crying "murder" and trying to escape from a window. They went upstairs and found, in a dusty solicitor's office, a hideous spectacle. Another severely wounded man (Mr. Roberts) was crouched on the floor, surrounded by evidence of a terrible fight: pools of blood, broken wine bottles, pistols, and overturned furniture. Roberts died of his wounds; Murray survived, and related his side of the story. He had been lured into the rooms on false pretences; Roberts had tried to kill him; and he had fought for his life. He had no idea why he had been attacked, but police established that Roberts had become obsessed with Murray's mistress, and had planned to kill him out of jealousy.

than Archibald Floyd the banker. Those few moments during which Aurora stood in thoughtful silence were as so many hours to his anxious mind. At last she spoke.

"Will you come to the study, papa?" she said; "this room is so big, and so dimly lighted. I always fancy there are listeners in the corners."

She did not wait for an answer; but led the way to a room upon the other side of the hall, – the room in which she and her father had been so long closeted together upon the night before her departure for Paris. The crayon portrait of Eliza Floyd looked down upon Archibald and his daughter. The face wore so bright and genial a smile that it was difficult to believe that it was the face of the dead.

The banker was the first to speak.

"My darling girl," he said, "what is it you want with me?"

"Money, papa. Two thousand pounds."

She checked his gesture of surprise, and resumed before he could interrupt her.

"The money you settled upon me on my marriage with John Mellish is invested in our own bank, I know. I know, too, that I can draw upon my account when and how I please; but I thought that if I wrote a cheque for two thousand pounds the unusual amount might attract attention, – and it might possibly fall into your hands. Had this occurred you would perhaps have been alarmed, at any rate astonished. I thought it best, therefore, to come to you myself and ask you for the money, especially as I must have it in notes."

Archibald Floyd grew very pale. He had been standing while Aurora spoke; but as she finished he dropped into a chair near his little office table, and resting his elbow upon an open desk leaned his head on his hand.

"What do you want money for, my dear?" he asked gravely.

"Never mind that, papa. It is my money, is it not; and I may spend it as I please?"

"Certainly, my dear, certainly," he answered, with some slight hesitation. "You shall spend whatever you please. I am rich enough to indulge any whim of yours, however foolish, however extravagant. But your marriage settlement was rather intended for the benefit of your children – than – than for – anything of this kind; and I scarcely know if you are justified in touching it without your husband's permission;[1] especially as your pin-money is really large enough to enable you to gratify any reasonable wish."

The old man pushed his gray hair away from his forehead with a weary action and a tremulous hand. Heaven knows that even in that desperate moment Aurora took notice of the feeble hand and the whitening hair.

"*Give* me the money, then, papa," she said. "Give it me from your own purse. You are rich enough to do that."

"Rich enough! Yes, if it were twenty times the sum," answered the banker slowly. Then, with a sudden burst of passion, he exclaimed, "O Aurora, Aurora! why do you treat me so badly? Have I been so cruel a father that you can't confide in me? Aurora, why do you want this money?"

She clasped her hands tightly together, and stood looking at him for a few moments irresolutely.

"I cannot tell you," she said, with grave determination. "If I were to tell you – what – what I think of doing, you might thwart me in my purpose. Father! father!" she cried, with a sudden change in her voice and manner, "I am hemmed in on every side by difficulty and danger; and there is only one way of escape – except death. Unless I take that one way, I must die. I am very young, – too young and happy, perhaps, to die willingly. Give me the means of escape."

"You mean this sum of money?"

"Yes."

"You have been pestered by some connection – some old associate of – his?"

"No!"

"What then?"

"I cannot tell you."

They were silent for some moments. Archibald Floyd looked imploringly at his child, but she did not answer that earnest gaze. She stood before him with a proudly downcast look: the eyelids drooping

---

1   Under common law, a married woman could not own property. In practice, how-ever, a separate estate could be held on her behalf by a trustee. Such a trust was negotiated before marriage, under a marriage settlement. Aurora's settlement comes from her father, and is presumably managed by him. Technically, she can call upon it without her husband's consent; Archibald Floyd's objections are moral, not legal.

over the dark eyes, not in shame, not in humiliation; only in the stern determination to avoid being subdued by the sight of her father's distress.

"Aurora," he said at last, "why not take the wisest and the safest step? Why not tell John Mellish the truth? The danger would disappear; the difficulty would be overcome. If you are persecuted by this low rabble, who so fit as he to act for you? Tell him, Aurora – tell him all!"

"No, no, no!"

She lifted her hands and clasped them upon her pale face.

"No, no; not for all this wide world!" she cried.

"Aurora," said Archibald Floyd, with a gathering sternness upon his face, which overspread the old man's benevolent countenance like some dark cloud, – "Aurora, – God forgive me for saying such words to my own child, – but I must insist upon your telling me that this is no new infatuation, no new madness, which leads you to——" He was unable to finish his sentence.

Mrs. Mellish dropped her hands from before her face, and looked at him with her eyes flashing fire, and her cheeks in a crimson blaze.

"Father," she cried, "how dare you ask me such a question? New infatuation! New madness! Have I suffered so little, do you think, from the folly of my youth? Have I paid so small a price for the mistake of my girlhood, that you should have cause to say these words to me to-night? Do I come of so bad a race," she said, pointing indignantly to her mother's portrait, "that you should think so vilely of me? Do I——"

Her tragical appeal was rising to its climax, when she dropped suddenly at her father's feet, and burst into a tempest of sobs.

"Papa, papa, pity me!" she cried; "pity me!"

He raised her in his arms, and drew her to him, and comforted her, as he had comforted her for the loss of a Scotch terrier-pup twelve years before, when she was small enough to sit on his knee, and nestle her head in his waistcoat.

"Pity you, my dear!" he said. "What is there I would not do for you to save you one moment's sorrow? If my worthless life could help you; if——"

"You will give me the money, papa?" she asked, looking up at him half coaxingly through her tears.

"Yes, my darling; to-morrow morning."

"In bank-notes?"

"In any manner you please. But, Aurora, why see these people? Why listen to their disgraceful demands? Why not tell the truth?"

"Ah, why, indeed!" she said thoughtfully. "Ask me no questions, dear papa; but let me have the money to-morrow, and I promise you that this shall be the very last you hear of my old troubles."

She made this promise with such perfect confidence that her father was inspired with a faint ray of hope.

"Come, darling papa," she said; "your room is near mine; let us go up-stairs together."

She entwined her arm in his, and led him up the broad staircase; only parting from him at the door of his room.

Mr. Floyd summoned his daughter into the study early the next morning, while Talbot Bulstrode was opening his letters, and Lucy strolling up and down the terrace with John Mellish.

"I have telegraphed for the money, my darling," the banker said. "One of the clerks will be here with it by the time we have finished breakfast."

Mr. Floyd was right. A card inscribed with the name of a Mr. George Martin was brought to him during breakfast.

"Mr. Martin will be good enough to wait in my study," he said.

Aurora and her father found the clerk seated at the open window, looking admiringly through festoons of foliage, which clustered round the frame of the lattice, into the richly-cultivated garden. Felden Woods was a sacred spot in the eyes of the junior clerks in Lombard Street, and a drive to Beckenham in a Hansom cab on a fine summer's morning, to say nothing of such chance refreshment as pound-cake and old Madeira, or cold fowl and Scotch ale, was considered no small treat.

Mr. George Martin, who was labouring under the temporary affliction of being only nineteen years of age, rose in a confused flutter of respect and surprise, and blushed very violently at sight of Mrs. Mellish.

Aurora responded to his reverential salute with such a pleasant nod as she might have bestowed upon the younger dogs in the stable-yard, and seated herself opposite to him at the little table by the window. It was such an excruciatingly narrow table that the crisp ribbons about Aurora's muslin dress rustled against the drab trousers of the junior clerk as Mrs. Mellish sat down.

The young man unlocked a little morocco pouch which he wore suspended from a strap across his shoulder, and produced a roll of crisp notes; so crisp, so white and new, that, in their unsullied freshness, they looked more like notes on the Bank of Elegance than the circulating medium of this busy, money-making nation.

"I have brought the cash for which you telegraphed, sir," said the clerk.

"Very good, Mr. Martin," answered the banker. "Here is my cheque ready written for you. The notes are——?"

"Twenty fifties, twenty-five twenties, fifty tens," the clerk said glibly.

Mr. Floyd took the little bundle of tissue-paper, and counted the notes with the professional rapidity which he still retained.

"Quite correct," he said, ringing the bell, which was speedily answered by a simpering footman. "Give this gentleman some lunch. You will find the Madeira very good," he added kindly, turning to the blushing junior; "it's a wine that is dying out; and by the time you're my age, Mr. Martin, you won't be able to get such a glass as I can offer you to-day. Good morning."

Mr. George Martin clutched his hat nervously from the empty chair on which he had placed it, knocked down a heap of papers with his elbow, bowed, blushed, and stumbled out of the room, under convoy of the simpering footman, who nourished a profound contempt for the young men from the "hoffice."

"Now, my darling," said Mr. Floyd, "here is the money. Though, mind, I protest against——"

"No, no, papa, not a word," she interrupted; "I thought that was all settled last night."

He sighed with the same weary sigh as on the night before, and seating himself at his desk, dipped a pen into the ink.

"What are you going to do, papa?"

"I'm only going to take the numbers of the notes."

"There is no occasion."

"There is always occasion to be business-like," said the old man firmly, as he checked the numbers of the notes one by one upon a sheet of paper with rapid precision.

Aurora paced up and down the room impatiently while this operation was going forward.

"How difficult it has been to me to get this money!" she exclaimed. "If I had been the wife and daughter of two of the poorest men in Christendom, I could scarcely have had more trouble about this two thousand pounds. And now you keep me here while you number the notes, not one of which is likely to be exchanged in this country."

"I learnt to be business-like when I was very young, Aurora," answered Mr. Floyd, "and I have never been able to forget my old habits."

He completed his task in defiance of his daughter's impatience, and handed her the packet of notes when he had done.

"I will keep the list of numbers, my dear," he said. "If I were to give it to you, you would most likely lose it."

He folded the sheet of paper and put it in a drawer of his desk.

"Twenty years hence, Aurora," he said, "should I live so long, I should be able to produce this paper, if it were wanted."

"Which it never will be, you dear methodical papa," answered Aurora. "My troubles are ended now. Yes," she added, in a graver tone, "I pray God that my troubles may be ended now."

She encircled her arms about her father's neck, and kissed him tenderly.

"I must leave you, dearest, to-day," she said; "you must not ask me why, – you must ask me nothing! You must only love and trust me, – as my poor John trusts me, – faithfully, hopefully, through everything."

CHAPTER XX.

CAPTAIN PRODDER.

WHILE the Doncaster express was carrying Mr. and Mrs. Mellish northwards, another express journeyed from Liverpool to London with its load of passengers.

Amongst these passengers there was a certain broad-shouldered and rather bull-necked individual, who attracted considerable attention during the journey, and was an object of some interest to his fellow-travellers and the railway officials at the two or three stations where the train stopped.

He was a man of about fifty years of age, but his years were worn very lightly, and only recorded by some wandering streaks and patches of gray amongst his thick blue-black stubble of hair. His complexion, naturally dark, had become of such a bronzed and coppery tint by perpetual exposure to meridian suns, tropical hot winds, the fiery breath of the simoom,[1] and the many other trifling inconveniences attendant upon an out-door life, as to cause him to be frequently mistaken for the inhabitant of some one of those countries in which the complexion of the natives fluctuates between burnt sienna, Indian red, and Vandyke brown. But it was rarely long before he took an opportunity to rectify this mistake, and to express that hearty contempt and aversion for all *furriners* which is natural to the unspoiled and unsophisticated Briton.

Upon this particular occasion he had not been half an hour in the society of his fellow-passengers before he had informed them that he was a native of Liverpool, and the captain of a merchant vessel trading, in a manner of speaking, he said, everywhere; that he had run away from his father and his home at a very early period of his life; and had shifted for himself in different parts of the globe ever since; that his Christian name was Samuel and his surname Prodder, and that his father had been, like himself, a captain in the merchant's service. He chewed so much tobacco and drank so much fiery Jamaica

---

1   Hot, dry, dust-laden wind.

rum from a pocket-pistol in the intervals of his conversation, that the first-class compartment in which he sat was odorous with the compound perfume. But he was such a hearty, loud-spoken fellow, and there was such a pleasant twinkle in his black eyes, that the passengers (with the exception of one crusty old lady) treated him with great good-humour, and listened very patiently to his talk.

"Chewin' aint smokin', you know, is it?" he said, with a great guffaw, as he cut himself a terrible block of Cavendish; "and railway companies aint got any laws against that. They can put a fellow's pipe out, but he can chew his quid in their faces; though I won't say which is wust for their carpets, neither."

I am sorry to be compelled to confess that this brown-visaged merchant-captain, who said *wust*, and chewed Cavendish tobacco, was uncle to Mrs. John Mellish of Mellish Park; and that the motive for this very journey was neither more nor less than his desire to become acquainted with his niece.

He imparted this fact – as well as much other information relating to himself, his tastes, habits, adventures, opinions, and sentiments – to his travelling companions in the course of the journey.

"Do you know for why I'm going to London by this identical train?" he asked generally, as the passengers settled themselves into their places after taking refreshment at Rugby.

The gentlemen looked over their newspapers at the talkative sailor, and a young lady looked up from her book; but nobody volunteered to speculate an opinion upon the mainspring of Mr. Prodder's actions.

"I'll tell you for why," resumed the merchant captain, addressing the assembly, as if in answer to their eager questioning. "I'm going to see my niece, which I have never seen before. When I ran away from father's ship, the *Ventur'some*, nigh upon forty year ago, and went aboard the craft of a captain by the name of Mobley, which was a good master to me for many a day, I had a little sister as I had left behind at Liverpool, which was dearer to me than my life." He paused to refresh himself with rather a demonstrative sip from the pocket-pistol. – "But if *you*," he continued generally, "if *you* had a father that'd fetch you a clout of the head as soon as look at you, *you'd* run away perhaps; and so did I. I took the opportunity to be missin' one night as father was settin' sail from Yarmouth Harbour; and not settin' that wonderful store by me which some folks do by their only sons, he shipped his anchor without stoppin' to ask many questions, and left me hidin' in one of the little alleys which cut the Town of Yarmouth through and across, like they cut the cakes they make there. There was many in Yarmouth that knew me, and there wasn't one that didn't say, 'Sarve him right,' when they heard how I'd given father the slip; and the next day Cap'en Mobley gave me a berth as cabin-boy aboard the *Mariar Anne.*"

Mr. Prodder again paused to partake of refreshment from his portable spirit-store, and this time politely handed the pocket-pistol to the company.

"Now perhaps you'll not believe me," he resumed, after his friendly offer had been refused, and the wicker-covered vessel replaced in his capacious pocket, – "you won't perhaps believe me when I tell you, as I tell you candid, that up to last Saturday week I never could find the time nor the opportunity to go back to Liverpool, and ask after the little sister that I'd left no higher than the kitchen table, and that had cried fit to break her poor little heart when I went away. But whether you believe it or whether you don't, it's as true as gospel," cried the sailor, thumping his ponderous fist upon the padded elbow of the compartment in which he sat; "it's as true as gospel. I've coasted America, North and South; I've carried West-Indian goods to the East Indies, and East-Indian goods to the West Indies; I've traded in Norwegian goods between Norway and Hull; I've carried Sheffield goods from Hull to South America; I've traded between all manner of countries and all manner of docks; but somehow or other I've never had the time to spare to go on shore at Liverpool, and find out the narrow little street in which I left my sister Eliza, no higher than the table, more than forty years ago, until last Saturday was a week. Last Saturday was a week I touched at Liverpool with a cargo of furs and poll-parrots, – what you may call fancy goods; and I said to my mate, I said, 'I'll tell you what I'll do, Jack; I'll go ashore, and see my little sister Eliza.'"

He paused once more, and a softening change came over the brightness of his black eyes. This time he did not apply himself to the pocket-pistol. This time he brushed the back of his brown hand across his eye-lashes, and brought it away with a drop or two of moisture glittering upon the bronzed skin. Even his voice was changed when he continued, and had mellowed to a richer and more mournful depth, until it very much resembled the melodious utterance which twenty-one years before had assisted to render Miss Eliza Percival the popular tragedian of the Preston and Bradford circuit.

"God forgive me," continued the sailor, in that altered voice; "but throughout my voyages I'd never thought of my sister Eliza but in two ways; sometimes one, sometimes t'other. One way of thinking of her, and expecting to see her, was as the little sister that I'd left, not altered by so much as one lock of her hair being changed from the identical curl into which it was twisted the morning she cried and clung about me on board the *Ventur'some*, having come aboard to wish father and me good-bye. – Perhaps I oftenest thought of her in this way. Anyhow, it was in this way, and no other, that I always saw her in my dreams. The other way of thinking of her, and expectin' to see her, was as a handsome, full-grown, buxom, married woman, with a troop of saucy children hanging on to her apron-string, and every one of 'em askin' what Uncle Samuel had brought 'em from foreign parts. Of course this fancy was the most rational of the two; but the other fancy, of the little child with the long black curly hair, would come to me very often, especially at night when all was quiet aboard, and when I took the wheel in a spell while the helmsman turned in. Lord bless you, ladies and gentlemen! many a time of a starlight night, when we've been in them latitudes where the stars are brighter than common, I've seen the floating mists upon the water take the very shape of that light figure of a little girl in a white pinafore, and come skipping towards me across the waves. I don't mean that I've seen a ghost, you know; but I mean that I could have seen one if I'd had the mind, and that I've seen as much of a one as folks ever do see upon this earth: the ghosts of their own memories and their own sorrows, mixed up with the mists of the sea or the shadows of the trees wavin' back'ards and for'ards in the moonlight, or a white curtain agen a window, or something of that sort. Well, I was such a precious old fool with these fancies and fantigs," – Mr. Samuel Prodder seemed rather to pride himself upon the latter word, as something out of the common, – "that when I went ashore at Liverpool, last Saturday was a week, I couldn't keep my eyes off the little girls in white pinafores as passed me by in the streets, thinkin' to see my Eliza skippin' along, with her black curls flyin' in the wind, and a bit of chalk, to play hop-scotch with, in her hand; so I was obliged to say to myself, quite serious, 'Now, Samuel Prodder, the little girl you're a lookin' for must be fifty years of age, if she's a day, and it's more than likely that she's left off playin' hop-scotch and wearin' white pinafores by this time.' If I hadn't kept repeatin' this, internally like, all the way I went, I should have stopped half the little girls in Liverpool to ask 'em if their name was Eliza, and if they'd ever had a brother as ran away and was lost. I had only one thought of how to set about findin' her, and that was to walk straight to the back street in which I remembered leavin' her forty years before. I'd no thought that those forty years could make any more change than to change her from a girl to a woman, and it seemed almost strange to me that they could make as much change as that. There was one thing I never thought of; and if my heart beat loud and quick when I knocked at the little front-door of the very identical house in which we'd lodged, it was with nothing but hope and joy. The forty years that had sent railways spinning all over England hadn't made much difference in the old house; it was forty years dirtier, perhaps, and forty years shabbier, and it stood in the very heart of the town instead of on the edge of the open country; but, exceptin' that, it was pretty much the same; and I expected to see the same landlady come to open the door, with the same dirty artificial flowers in her cap, and the same old slippers down at heel scrapin' after her along the bit of oilcloth. It gave me a kind of a turn when I didn't see this identical landlady, though she'd have been turned a hundred years old if she'd been alive; and I might have prepared myself for the disappointment if I'd thought of that, but I hadn't; and when the door was opened by a young woman with sandy hair, brushed backwards as if she'd been a Chinese, and no eyebrows to speak of, I did feel disappointed. The young woman had a baby in her arms, a black-eyed baby, with its eyes opened so wide that it seemed as if it had been very much surprised with the look of things on first comin' into the world, and hadn't quite recovered itself yet; so I thought to myself, as soon as I clapped eyes on the little one, why, as sure as a gun, that's my sister Eliza's baby; and my sister Eliza's married, and lives here still. But the young woman had never heard the name of Prodder, and didn't think there was anybody in the neighbourhood as ever had. I felt my heart, which had been beatin' louder and quicker every minute, stop all of a sudden when she said this, and seemed to drop down like a dead weight; but I thanked her for her civil answers to my questions, and went on to the next house to inquire there. I might have saved myself the trouble, for I made the same inquiries at every house on each side of the street, going straight from door to door, till the people thought I was a sea-farin' tax-gatherer; but nobody had never heard the name of Prodder, and the oldest inhabitant in the street hadn't lived there ten years. I was quite disheartened when I left the neighbourhood, which had once been so familiar, and which seemed so strange and small and mean and shabby now. I'd had so little thought of failing to find Eliza in the very house in which I'd left her, that I'd made no plans beyond. So I was brought to a dead stop; and I went back to the tavern where I'd left my carpet-bag, and I had a chop brought me for my dinner, and I sat with my knife and fork before me thinkin' what I was to do next. When Eliza and I had parted forty years before, I remembered father leavin' her in charge of a sister of my mother's (my poor mother had been dead a year), and I thought to myself, the only chance there is left for me now is to find Aunt Sarah."

By the time Mr. Prodder arrived at this stage of his narrative his listeners had dropped off gradually, the gentlemen returning to their newspapers, and the young lady to her book, until the merchant-captain found himself reduced to communicate his adventures to one goodnatured-looking young fellow, who seemed interested in the brown-faced sailor, and encouraged him every now and then with an assenting nod or a friendly "Ay, ay, to be sure."

"'The only chance I can see,' ses I," continued Mr. Prodder, "'is to find aunt Sarah.' I found aunt Sarah. She'd been keepin' a shop in the general line when I went away forty year ago, and she was keepin' the same shop in the general line when I came back last Saturday week; and there was the same flyblown handbills of ships that was to sail immediate, and that had sailed two year ago, accordin' to the date upon the bills; and the same wooden sugar-loaves wrapped up in white paper; and the same lattice-work gate, with a bell that rang as loud as if it was meant to give the alarm to all Liverpool as well as to my aunt Sarah in the parlour behind the shop. The poor old soul was standing behind the counter, serving two ounces of tea to a customer, when I went in. Forty years had made so much change in her, that I shouldn't have known her if I hadn't known the shop. She wore black curls upon her forehead, and a brooch like a brass butterfly in the middle of the curls, where the parting ought to have been, and she wore a beard; and the curls were false, but the beard wasn't; and her voice was very deep, and rather manly, and she seemed to me to have grown manly altogether in the forty years that I'd been away. She tied up the two ounces of tea, and then asked me what I pleased to want. I told her that I was little Sam, and that I wanted my sister Eliza."

The merchant-captain paused, and looked out of the window for upwards of five minutes before he resumed his story. When he did resume it, he spoke in a very low voice, and in short detached sentences, as if he couldn't trust himself with long ones for fear he should break down in the middle of them.

"Eliza had been dead one-and-twenty years. Aunt Sarah told me all about it. She'd tried the artificial flower-makin'; and she hadn't liked it. And she'd turned play-actress. And when she was nine-and-twenty, she'd married; she'd married a gentleman that had no end of money; and she'd gone to live at a fine place somewheres in Kent. I've got the name of it wrote down in my memorandum-book. But she'd been a good and generous friend to aunt Sarah; and aunt Sarah was to have gone to Kent to see her, and to stop all the summer with her. But while aunt was getting ready to go for that very visit, my sister Eliza died, leaving a daughter behind her, which is the niece that I'm goin' to see. I sat down upon the three-legged wooden stool against the counter, and hid my face in my hands; and I thought of the little girl that I'd seen playin' at hop-scotch forty years before, until I thought my heart would burst; but I didn't shed a tear. Aunt Sarah took a big brooch out of her collar, and showed me a ring of black hair behind a bit of glass, with a gold frame round it. – 'Mr. Floyd had this brooch made a purpose for me,' she said; 'he has always been a liberal gentleman to me, and he comes down to Liverpool once in two or three years, and takes tea with me in yon back parlour; and I've no call to keep a shop, for he allows me a handsome income; but I should die of the mopes if it wasn't for the business.' There was Eliza's name and the date of her death engraved upon the back of the brooch. I tried to remember where I'd been and what I'd been doing that year. But I couldn't, sir. All the life that I looked back upon seemed muddled and mixed up, like a dream; and I could only think of the little sister I'd said good-bye to, aboard the *Ventur'some* forty years before. I got round by little and little, and I was able half an hour afterwards to listen to aunt Sarah's talk. She was nigh upon seventy, poor old soul, and she'd always been a good one to talk. She asked me if it wasn't a great thing for the family that Eliza had made such a match; and if I wasn't proud to think that my niece was a young heiress, that spoke all manner of languages, and rode in her own carriage? and if that oughtn't to be a consolation to me? But I told her that I'd rather have found my sister married to the poorest man in Liverpool, and alive and well, to bid me welcome back to my native town. Aunt Sarah said if those were my religious opinions, she didn't know what to say to me. And she showed me a picture of Eliza's tomb in Beckenham churchyard, that had been painted expressly for her by Mr. Floyd's orders. Floyd was the name of Eliza's husband. And then she showed me a picture of Miss Floyd, the heiress, at the age of ten, which was the image of Eliza all but the pinafore; and it's that very Miss Floyd that I'm going to see."

"And I dare say," said the kind listener, "that Miss Floyd will be very much pleased to see her sailor uncle."

"Well, sir, I think she will," answered the captain. "I don't say it from any pride I take in myself, Lord knows; for I know I'm a rough and ready sort of a chap, that 'u'd be no great ornament in a young lady's drawing-room; but if Eliza's daughter's anything like Eliza, I know what she'll say and what she'll do, as well as if I see her saying and doing it. She'll clap her pretty little hands together, and she'll clasp her arms round my neck, and she'll say, 'Lor, uncle, I am *so* glad to see you!' And when I tell her that I was her mother's only brother, and that me and her mother was very fond of one another, she'll burst out a cryin', and she'll hide her pretty face upon my shoulder, and she'll sob as if her dear little heart was going to break for love of the mother that she never saw. That's what she'll do," said Captain Prodder, "and I don't think the truest born lady that ever was could do any better."

The goodnatured traveller heard a great deal more from the captain of his plans for going to Beckenham to claim his niece's affections, in spite of all the fathers in the world.

"Mr. Floyd's a good man, I dare say, sir," he said; "but he's kept his daughter apart from her aunt Sarah, and it is but likely he'll try to keep her from me. But if he does he'll find he's got a toughish customer to deal with in Captain Samuel Prodder."

The merchant-captain reached Beckenham as the evening shadows were deepening amongst the Felden oaks and beeches, and the long rays of red sunshine fading slowly out in the low sky. He drove up to the old red-brick mansion in a hired fly, and presented himself at the hall-door just as Mr. Floyd was leaving the dining-room to finish the evening in his lonely study.

The banker paused, to glance with some slight surprise at the loosely-clad, weather-beaten looking figure of the sailor, and mechanically put his hand amongst the gold and silver in his pocket. He thought the seafaring man had come to present some petition for himself and his comrades. A life-boat was wanted somewhere on the Kentish coast, perhaps: and this pleasant-looking bronze-coloured man had come to collect funds for the charitable work.

He was thinking this, when, in reply to the town-bred footman's question, the sailor uttered the name of Prodder; and in the one moment of its utterance his thoughts flew back over one-and-twenty years, and he was madly in love with a beautiful actress, who owned blushingly to that plebeian cognomen. The banker's voice was faint and husky as he turned to the captain, and bade him welcome to Felden Woods.

"Step this way, Mr. Prodder," he said, pointing to the open door of the study. "I am very glad to see you. I – I – have often heard of you. You are my dead wife's runaway brother."

Even amidst his sorrowful recollection of that brief happiness of the past, some natural alloy of pride had its part, and he closed the study-door carefully before he said this.

"God bless you, sir," he said, holding out his hand to the sailor. "I see I am right. Your eyes are like Eliza's. You and yours will always be welcome beneath my roof. Yes, Samuel Prodder, – you see I know your Christian name; – and when I die you will find you have not been forgotten."

The captain thanked his brother-in-law heartily, and told him that he neither asked or wished for anything except permission to see his niece, Aurora Floyd.

As he made this request, he looked towards the door of the little room, evidently expecting that the heiress might enter at any moment. He looked terribly disappointed when the banker told him that Aurora was married, and lived near Doncaster; but that if he had happened to come ten hours earlier he would have found her at Felden Woods.

Ah! who has not heard those common words? Who has not been told that, if they had come sooner, or gone earlier, or hurried their pace, or slackened it, or done something that they have not done, the whole course of life would have been otherwise? Who has not looked back regretfully at the past, which, differently fashioned, would have made the present other than it is? We think it hard that we cannot take the fabric of our life to pieces, as a mantua-maker[1] unpicks her work, and make up the stuff another way. How much waste we might save in the cloth, how much better a shape we might make the garment, if we only had the right to use our scissors and needle again, and re-fashion the past by the experience of the present!

"To think, now, that I should have been comin' yesterday!" exclaimed the captain; "but put off my journey because it was a Friday! If I'd only knowed!"

Of course, Captain Prodder, if you had only known what it was not given you to know, you would no doubt have acted more prudently; and so would many other people. If Mr. William Palmer had known that detection was to dog the footsteps of crime, and the gallows to follow at the heels of detection, he would most likely have hesitated long before he mixed the strychnine-pills for the friend whom, with cordial voice, he was entreating to be of good cheer.[2] We spend the best part of our lives in making mistakes, and the poor remainder in reflecting how very easily we might have avoided them.

---

1 Dressmaker.

2 William Palmer, doctor and mass murderer, was tried and executed for the 1855 murder of his friend and gambling companion whom he poisoned while they were drinking together in celebration of a win. Palmer was also suspected of murdering his uncle, wife, four children, several illegitimate children, his mother-in-law, and several creditors.

Mr. Floyd explained, rather lamely, perhaps, how it was that the Liverpool spinster had never been informed of her grand-niece's marriage with Mr. John Mellish; and the merchant-captain announced his intention of starting for Doncaster early the next morning.

"Don't think that I want to intrude upon your daughter, sir," he said, as if perfectly acquainted with the banker's nervous dread of such a visit. "I know her station's high above me, though she's my own sister's only child; and I make no doubt that those about her would be ready enough to turn up their noses at a poor old salt that has been tossed and tumbled about in every variety of weather for this forty year. I only want to see her once in a way, and to hear her say, perhaps, 'Lor, uncle, what a rum old chap you are!' There!" exclaimed Samuel Prodder, suddenly, "I think if I could only once hear her call me uncle, I could go back to sea, and die happy, though I never came ashore again."

CHAPTER XXI.

"HE ONLY SAID, I AM A-WEARY."[1]

MR. JAMES CONYERS found the long summer's days hang rather heavily upon his hands at Mellish Park, in the society of the rheumatic ex-trainer, the stable-boys, and Steeve Hargraves the "Softy," and with no literary resources except the last Saturday's 'Bell's Life,' and sundry flimsy sheets of shiny, slippery tissue-paper, forwarded him by post from King Charles's Croft, in the busy town of Leeds.

He might have found plenty of work to do in the stables, perhaps, if he had had a mind to do it; but after the night of the storm there was a perceptible change in his manner; and the showy pretence of being very busy, which he had made on his first arrival at the Park, was now exchanged for a listless and undisguised dawdling and an unconcerned indifference, which caused the old trainer to shake his gray head, and mutter to his hangers-on that the new chap warn't up to mooch, and was evidently too grand for his business.

Mr. James cared very little for the opinion of these simple York-shiremen; and he yawned in their faces, and stifled them with his cigar smoke, with a dashing indifference that harmonized well with the gorgeous tints of his complexion and the lustrous splendour of his lazy eyes. He had taken the trouble to make himself very agreeable on the day succeeding his arrival, and had distributed his hearty slaps on the shoulder and friendly digs in the ribs, right and left, until he slapped and dug himself into considerable popularity amongst the friendly rustics, who were ready to be bewitched by his handsome face and flashy manner. But after his interview with Mrs. Mellish in the cottage by the north gates, he seemed to abandon all desire to please, and to grow suddenly restless and discontented: so restless and so discontented that he felt inclined even to quarrel with the unhappy "Softy," and led his red-haired retainer a sufficiently uncomfortable life with his whims and vagaries.

---

1   The refrain of Tennyson's "Mariana" (1830), altered from "She said, 'I am aweary.'"

Stephen Hargraves bore this change in his new master's manner with wonderful patience. Rather too patiently, perhaps; with that slow, dogged, uncomplaining patience of those who keep something in reserve as a set-off against present forbearance, and who invite rather than avoid injury, rejoicing in anything which swells the great account, to be squared in future storm and fury. The "Softy" was a man who could hoard his hatred and vengeance, hiding the bad passions away in the dark corners of his poor shattered mind, and bringing them out in the dead of the night to "kiss and talk to," as the Moor's wife kissed and conversed with the strawberry-embroidered cambric.[1] There must surely have been very little "society" at Cyprus, or Mrs. Othello could scarcely have been reduced to such insipid company.

However it might be, Steeve bore Mr. Conyers's careless insolence so very meekly that the trainer laughed at his attendant for a poor-spirited hound, whom a pair of flashing black eyes and a lady's toy riding-whip could frighten out of the poor remnant of wit left in his muddled brain. He said something to this effect when Steeve displeased him once, in the course of the long, temper-trying summer's day; and the "Softy" turned away with something very like a chuckle of savage pleasure in acknowledgement of the compliment. He was more obsequious than ever after it, and was humbly thankful for the ends of cigars which the trainer liberally bestowed upon him, and went into Doncaster for more spirits and more cigars in the course of the day, and fetched and carried as submissively as that craven-spirited hound to which his employer had politely compared him.

Mr. Conyers did not even make a pretence of going to look at the horses on this blazing 5th of July, but lolled on the window-sill, with his lame leg upon a chair, and his back against the framework of the little casement, smoking, drinking, and reading his price-lists all through the sunny day. The cold brandy-and-water which he poured, without half an hour's intermission, down his handsome throat, seemed to have far less influence upon him than the same amount of liquid would have had upon a horse. It would have put the horse out of condition, perhaps; but it had no effect whatever upon the trainer.

---

1 *Othello* III.iii.291–6.

Mrs. Powell, walking for the benefit of her health in the north shrubberies, and incurring imminent danger of a sun-stroke for the same praiseworthy reason, contrived to pass the lodge, and to see Mr. Conyers lounging, dark and splendid, on the window-sill, exhibiting a kit-cat[1] of his handsome person framed in the clustering foliage which hung about the cottage walls. She was rather embarrassed by the presence of the "Softy," who was sweeping the door-step, and who gave her a glance of recognition as she passed, – a glance which might perhaps have said, "We know his secrets, you and I, handsome and insolent as he is; we know the paltry price at which he can be bought and sold. But we keep our counsel; we keep our counsel till time ripens the bitter fruit upon the tree, though our fingers itch to pluck it while it is still green."

Mrs. Powell stopped to give the trainer good day, expressing as much surprise at seeing him at the north lodge as if she had been given to understand that he was travelling in Kamschatka; but Mr. Conyers cut her civilities short with a yawn, and told her with easy familiarity that she would be conferring a favour upon him by sending him that morning's 'Times' as soon as the daily papers arrived at the Park. The ensign's widow was too much under the influence of the graceful impertinence of his manner to resist it as she might have done, and returned to the house, bewildered and wondering, to comply with his request. So through the oppressive heat of the summer's day the trainer smoked, drank, and took his ease, while his dependent and follower watched him with a puzzled face, revolving vaguely and confusedly in his dull, muddled brain the events of the previous night.

But Mr. James Conyers grew weary at last even of his own ease; and that inherent restlessness which caused Rasselas to tire of his happy valley,[2] and sicken for the free breezes on the hill-tops and the clamour of the distant cities, arose in the bosom of the trainer, and grew so strong that he began to chafe at the rural quiet of the north

---

1   A portrait, less than half length, but including the hands, so named after the Kit-Cat Club of Whig politicians formed in the early eighteenth century. The club's dining room was too low to accommodate full half-size portraits.

2   In Samuel Johnson's *The History of Rasselas, Prince of Abyssinia* (1759), the hero grows weary of the security, delight, and repose of the happy valley where his people dwell.

lodge, and to shuffle his poor lame leg wearily from one position to another in sheer discontent of mind, which, by one of those many subtle links between spirit and matter that tell us we are mortal, communicated itself to his body, and gave him that chronic disorder which is popularly called "the fidgets." An unquiet fever, generated amidst the fibres of the brain, and finding its way by that physiological telegraph, the spinal marrow, to the remotest stations on the human railway.

Mr. James suffered from this common complaint to such a degree, that as the solemn strokes of the church-clock vibrated in sonorous music above the tree-tops of Mellish Park in the sunny evening atmosphere, he threw down his pipe with an impatient shrug of the shoulders, and called to the "Softy" to bring him his hat and walking-stick.

"Seven o'clock," he muttered, "only seven o'clock. I think there must have been twenty-four hours in this blessed summer's day."

He stood looking from the little casement-window with a discontented frown contracting his handsome eyebrows, and a peevish expression distorting his full, classically-moulded lips, as he said this. He glanced through the little casement, made smaller by its clustering frame of roses and clematis, jessamine and myrtle, and looking like the port-hole of a ship that sailed upon a sea of summer verdure. He glanced through the circular opening left by that scented framework of leaves and blossoms, into the long glades, where the low sunlight was flickering upon waving fringes of fern. He followed with his listless glance the wandering intricacies of the underwood, until they led his weary eyes away to distant patches of blue water, slowly changing to opal and rose-colour in the declining light. He saw all these things with a lazy apathy, which had no power to recognize their beauty, or to inspire one latent thrill of gratitude to Him who had made them. He had better have been blind; surely he had better have been blind.

He turned his back upon the evening sunshine, and looked at the white face of Steeve Hargraves, the "Softy," with every whit as much pleasure as he had felt in looking at nature in her loveliest aspect.

"A long day," he said, – "an infernally tedious, wearisome day. Thank God, it's over."

Strange that, as he uttered this impious thanksgiving, no subtle influence of the future crept through his veins to chill the slackening pulses of his heart, and freeze the idle words upon his lips. If he had known what was so soon to come; if he had known, as he thanked God for the death of one beautiful summer's day, never to be born again, with its twelve hours of opportunity for good or evil, – surely he would have grovelled on the earth, stricken with a sudden terror, and wept aloud for the shameful history of the life which lay behind him.

He had never shed tears but once since his childhood, and then those tears were scalding drops of baffled rage and vengeful fury at the utter defeat of the greatest scheme of his life.

"I shall go into Doncaster to-night, Steeve," he said to the "Softy," who stood deferentially awaiting his master's pleasure, and watching him, as he had watched him all day, furtively but incessantly; "I shall spend the evening in Doncaster, and – and – see if I can pick up a few wrinkles about the September meeting; not that there's anything worth entering amongst this set of screws, Lord knows," he added, with undisguised contempt for poor John's beloved stable. "Is there a dog-cart, or a trap of any kind, I can drive over in?" he asked of the "Softy."

Mr. Hargraves said that there was a Newport Pagnell, which was sacred to Mr. John Mellish, and a gig that was at the disposal of any of the upper servants when they had occasion to go into Doncaster, as well as a covered van, which some of the lads drove into the town every day for the groceries and other matters required at the house.

"Very good," said Mr. Conyers; "you may run down to the stables, and tell one of the boys to put the fastest pony of the lot into the Newport Pagnell, and to bring it up here, and to look sharp."

"But nobody but Muster Mellish rides in the Newport Pagnell," suggested the "Softy," with an accent of alarm.

"What of that, you cowardly hound?" cried the trainer contemptuously. "I'm going to drive it to-night, don't you hear? D – n his Yorkshire insolence! Am I to be put down by *him?* It's his handsome wife that he takes such pride in, is it? Lord help him! Whose money bought the dog-cart, I wonder? Aurora Floyd's, perhaps. And I'm not to ride in it, I suppose, because it's my lord's pleasure to drive his black-eyed lady in the sacred vehicle. Look you here, you brainless idiot, and understand me, if you can!" cried Mr. James Conyers in a sudden rage, which crimsoned his handsome face, and lit up his lazy eyes with a new fire, – "look you here, Stephen Hargraves! if it wasn't that I'm tied hand and foot, and have been plotted against and thwarted by a woman's cunning, at every turn, I could smoke my pipe in yonder house, or in a better house, this day."

He pointed with his finger to the pinnacled roof, and the reddened windows glittering in the evening sun, visible far away amongst the trees.

"Mr. John Mellish!" he said. "If his wife wasn't such a she-devil as to be too many guns for the cleverest man in Christendom, I'd soon make *him* sing small. Fetch the Newport Pagnell!" he cried suddenly, with an abrupt change of tone; "fetch it, and be quick! I'm not safe to myself when I talk of this. I'm not safe when I think how near I was to half a million of money," he muttered under his breath.

He limped out into the open air, fanning himself with the wide brim of his felt hat, and wiping the perspiration from his forehead.

"Be quick!" he cried impatiently to his deliberate attendant, who had listened eagerly to every word of his master's passionate talk, and who now stood watching him even more intently than before, – "be quick, man, can't you? I don't pay you five shillings a week to stare at me. Fetch the trap! I've worked myself into a fever, and nothing but a rattling drive will set me right again."

The "Softy" shuffled off as rapidly as it was within the range of his ability to walk. He had never been seen to run in his life; but had a slow, side-long gait, which had some faint resemblance to that of the lower reptiles, but very little in common with the motions of his fellow-men.

Mr. James Conyers limped up and down the little grassy lawn in front of the north lodge. The excitement which had crimsoned his face gradually subsided, as he vented his disquietude in occasional impatient exclamations. "Two thousand pounds!" he muttered; "a pitiful, paltry two thousand! Not a twelvemonth's interest on the money I ought to have had – the money I should have had, if——"

He stopped abruptly, and growled something like an oath between his set teeth, as he struck his stick with angry violence into the soft grass. It is especially hard when we are reviling our bad fortune, and quarrelling with our fate, to find at last, on wandering backwards to the source of our ill-luck, that the primary cause of all has been our own evil-doing. It was this that made Mr. Conyers stop abruptly in his reflections upon his misfortunes, and break off with a smothered oath, and listen impatiently for the wheels of the Newport Pagnell.

The "Softy" appeared presently, leading the horse by the bridle. He had not presumed to seat himself in the sacred vehicle, and he stared wonderingly at James Conyers as the trainer tumbled about the chocolate-cloth cushions, arranging them afresh for his own ease and comfort. Neither the bright varnish of the dark-brown panels, nor the crimson crest, nor the glittering steel ornaments on the neat harness, nor any of the exquisitely-finished appointments of the light vehicle, provoked one word of criticism from Mr. Conyers. He mounted as easily as his lame leg would allow him, and taking the reins from the "Softy," lighted his cigar preparatory to starting.

"You needn't sit up for me to-night," he said, as he drove into the dusty high road: "I shall be late."

Mr. Hargraves shut the iron gates with a loud clanking noise upon his new master.

"But I shall, though," he muttered, looking askant through the bars at the fast disappearing Newport Pagnell, which was now little more than a black spot in a white cloud of dust; "but I shall sit up, though. You'll come home drunk, I lay." (Yorkshire is so pre-eminently a horse-racing and betting county, that even simple country folk who have never wagered a sixpence in the quiet course of their lives say "I lay" where a Londoner would say "I dare say.") "You'll come home drunk, I lay; folks generally do from Doncaster; and I shall hear some more of your wild talk. Yes, yes," he said in a slow, reflective tone; "it's very wild talk, and I can't make top nor tail of it yet – not yet; but it seems to me somehow as if I knew what it all meant, only I can't put it together – I can't put it together. There's something missin', and the want of that something hinders me putting it together."

He rubbed his stubble of coarse red hair with his two strong, awkward hands, as if he would fain have rubbed some wanting intelligence into his head.

"Two thousand pound!" he said, walking slowly back to the cottage. "Two thousand pound! It's a power of money! Why it's two thousand pound that the winner gets by the great race at Newmarket, and there's all the gentlefolks ready to give their ears for it. There's great lords fighting and struggling against each other for it; so it's no wonder a poor fond chap like me thinks summat about it."

He sat down upon the step of the lodge-door to smoke the cigar-ends which his benefactor had thrown him in the course of the day; but he still ruminated upon this subject, and he still stopped some-times, between the extinction of one cheroot-stump and the illumi-nating of another, to mutter, "Two thousand pound! Twenty hundred pound! Forty times fifty pound!" with an unctuous chuckle after the enunciation of each figure, as if it was some privilege even to be able to talk of such vast sums of money. So might some doating lover, in the absence of his idol, murmur the beloved name to the summer breeze.

The last crimson lights upon the patches of blue water died out beneath the gathering darkness; but the "Softy" sat, still smoking, and still ruminating, till the stars were high in the purple vault above his head. A little after ten o'clock he heard the rattling of wheels and the tramp of horses' hoofs upon the high road, and going to the gate he looked out through the iron bars. As the vehicle dashed by the north gates he saw that it was one of the Mellish-Park carriages which had been sent to the station to meet John and his wife.

"A short visit to Loon'on," he muttered. "I lay she's been to fetch t' brass."

The greedy eyes of the half-witted groom peered through the iron bars at the passing carriage, as if he would have fain looked through its opaque panels in search of that which he had denominated "the brass." He had a vague idea that two thousand pounds would be a great bulk of money, and that Aurora would carry it in a chest or a bundle that might be perceptible through the carriage-window.

"I'll lay she's been to fetch t' brass," he repeated, as he crept back to the lodge-door.

He resumed his seat upon the door-step, his cigar-ends, and his reverie, rubbing his head very often, sometimes with one hand, some-times with both, but always as if he were trying to rub some wanting sense or power of perception into his wretched brains. Sometimes he gave a short restless sigh, as if he had been trying all this time to guess some difficult enigma, and was on the point of giving it up.

It was long after midnight when Mr. James Conyers returned, very much the worse for brandy-and-water and dust. He tumbled over the "Softy," still sitting on the step of the open door, and then cursed Mr. Hargraves for being in the way.

"B't s'nc' y' h'v' ch's'n t' s't 'p," said the trainer, speaking a language entirely composed of consonants, "y' m'y dr'v' tr'p b'ck t' st'bl's."

By which rather obscure speech he gave the "Softy" to understand that he was to take the dog-cart back to Mr. Mellish's stable-yard.

Steeve Hargraves did his drunken master's bidding, and leading the horse homewards through the quiet night, found a cross boy with a lantern in his hand waiting at the gate of the stable-yard, and by no means disposed for conversation, except, indeed, to the extent of the one remark that he, the cross boy, hoped the new trainer wasn't going to be up to this game every night, and hoped the mare, which had been bred for a racer, hadn't been ill used.

All John Mellish's horses seemed to have been bred for racers, and to have dropped gradually from prospective winners of the Derby, Oaks, Chester Cup, Great Ebor, Yorkshire Stakes, Leger, and Doncaster Cup, – to say nothing of minor victories in the way of Northumberland Plates, Liverpool Autumn Cups, and Curragh Handicaps, through every variety of failure and defeat, – into the every-day ignominy of harness. Even the van which carried groceries was drawn by a slim-legged, narrow-chested, high-shouldered animal called the "Yorkshire Childers," and bought, in its sunny colt-hood, at a great price by poor John.

Mr. Conyers was snoring aloud in his little bedroom when Steeve Hargraves returned to the lodge. The "Softy" stared wonderingly at the handsome face brutalized by drink, and the classical head flung back upon the crumpled pillow in one of those wretched positions which intoxication always chooses for its repose. Steeve Hargraves rubbed his head harder even than before, as he looked at the perfect profile, the red, half-parted lips, the dark fringe of lashes on the faintly crimson-tinted cheeks.

"Perhaps I might have been good for summat if I had been like *you*," he said, with a half-savage melancholy. "I shouldn't have been ashamed of myself then. I shouldn't have crept into dark corners to hide myself, and think why I wasn't like other people, and what a bitter, cruel shame it was that I wasn't like 'em. *You've* no call to hide yourself from other folks; nobody tells you to get out of the way for an ugly hound, as you told me this morning, hang you! The world's smooth enough for you."

So may Caliban have looked at Prospero with envy and hate in his heart before going to his obnoxious tasks of dish-washing and trencher-scraping.[1]

He shook his fist at the unconscious sleeper as he finished speaking, and then stooped to pick up the trainer's dusty clothes, which were scattered upon the floor.

"I suppose I'm to brush these before I go to bed," he muttered, "that my lord may have 'em ready when he wakes in th' morning."

He took the clothes on his arm and the light in his hand, and went down to the lower room, where he found a brush and set to work sturdily, enveloping himself in a cloud of dust, like some ugly Arabian genii who was going to transform himself into a handsome prince.

He stopped suddenly in his brushing, by-and-by, and crumpled the waistcoat in his hand.

"There's some paper!" he exclaimed. "A paper sewed up between stuff and linin'."

He omitted the definite article before each of the substantives, as is a common habit with his countrymen when at all excited.

"A bit o' paper," he repeated, "between stuff and linin'! I'll rip t' waistcoat open and see what 'tis."

He took his clasp-knife from his pocket, carefully unripped a part of one of the seams in the waistcoat, and extracted a piece of paper folded double, – a decent-sized square of rather thick paper, partly printed, partly written.

He leaned over the light with his elbows on the table and read the contents of this paper, slowly and laboriously, following every word with his thick forefinger, sometimes stopping a long time upon one syllable, sometimes trying back half a line or so, but always plodding patiently with his ugly forefinger.

---

1   *The Tempest* II.ii.184-9.

When he came to the last word, he burst suddenly into a loud chuckle, as if he had just succeeded in guessing that difficult enigma which had puzzled him all the evening.

" I know it all now," he said. "I can put it all together now. His words; and hers; and the money. I can put it all together, and make out the meaning of it. She's going to give him the two thousand pound to go away from here and say nothing about this."

He refolded the paper, replaced it carefully in its hiding-place between the stuff and lining of the waistcoat, then searched in his capacious pocket for a fat leathern book, in which, amongst all sorts of odds and ends, there were some needles and a tangled skein of black thread. Then, stooping over the light, he slowly sewed up the seam which he had ripped open, – dexterously and neatly enough, in spite of the clumsiness of his big fingers.

CHAPTER XXII.

STILL CONSTANT.

MR. JAMES CONYERS took his breakfast in his own apartment upon the morning after his visit to Doncaster, and Stephen Hargraves waited upon him; carrying him a basin of muddy coffee, and enduring his ill-humour with the long-suffering which seemed peculiar to this hump-backed, low-voiced stable-helper.

The trainer rejected the coffee, and called for a pipe, and lay smoking half the summer morning, with the scent of the roses and honeysuckle floating into his close chamber, and the July sunshine glorifying the sham roses and blue lilies that twisted themselves in floricultural monstrosity about the cheap paper on the walls.

The "Softy" cleaned his master's boots, set them in the sunshine to air, washed the breakfast-things, swept the door-step, and then seated himself upon it to ruminate, with his elbows on his knees and his hands twisted in his coarse red hair. The silence of the summer atmosphere was only broken by the drowsy hum of the insects in the wood, and the occasional dropping of some early-blighted leaf.

Mr. Conyers's temper had been in no manner improved by his night's dissipation in the town of Doncaster. Heaven knows what entertainment he had found in those lonely streets, that grass-grown market-place and tenantless stalls, or that dreary and hermetically-sealed building, which looks like a prison on three sides and a chapel on the fourth, and which, during the September meeting, bursts suddenly into life and light with huge posters flaring against its gaunt walls, and a bright blue-ink announcement of Mr. and Mrs. Charles Mathews, or Mr. and Mrs. Charles Kean,[1] for five nights only. Normal amusement in the town of Doncaster between

---

1   Charles Mathews (1803-78), leading actor and dramatist, manager of Covent Garden (1839-42) and of the Lyceum (1847-55). The Mrs. Mathews referred to here is his second wife, the American actress Lizzie Davenport, whom he married in 1857. Charles Kean (1811?-68) was a prominent Shakespearian actor and his wife, Ellen Tree (1806-80), a popular leading lady.

these two oases in the year's dreary circle, the spring and autumn meetings, there is none. But of abnormal and special entertainment there may be much; only known to such men as Mr. James Conyers, to whom the most sinuous alley is a pleasant road, so long as it leads, directly or indirectly, to the betting-man's god – Money.

However this might be, Mr. Conyers bore upon him all the symptoms of having, as the popular phrase has it, made a night of it. His eyes were dim and glassy; his tongue hot and furred, and uncomfortably large for his parched mouth; his hand so shaky that the operation which he performed with a razor before his looking-glass was a toss-up between suicide and shaving. His heavy head seemed to have been transformed into a leaden box full of buzzing noises; and after getting half through his toilet he gave it up for a bad job, and threw himself upon the bed he had just left, a victim to that biliary derangement which inevitably follows an injudicious admixture of alcoholic and malt liquors.

"A tumbler of Hochheimer," he muttered, "or even the third-rate Chablis they give one at a *table-d'hôte*, would freshen me up a little; but there's nothing to be had in this abominable place except brandy-and-water."

He called to the "Softy," and ordered him to mix a tumbler of the last-named beverage, cold and weak.

Mr. Conyers drained the cool and lucid draught, and flung himself back upon the pillow with a sigh of relief. He knew that he would be thirsty again in five or ten minutes, and that the respite was a brief one; but still it was a respite.

"Have they come home?" he asked.

"Who?"

"Mr. and Mrs. Mellish, you idiot!" answered the trainer fiercely. "Who else should I bother my head about? Did they come home last night while I was away?"

The "Softy" told his master that he had seen one of the carriages drive past the north gates at a little after ten o'clock on the preceding night, and that he supposed it contained Mr. and Mrs. Mellish.

"Then you'd better go up to the house and make sure," said Mr. Conyers; "I want to know."

"Go up to th' house?"

"Yes, coward! – yes, sneak! Do you suppose that Mrs. Mellish will eat you?"

"I don't suppose nought o' t' sort," answered the "Softy" sulkily; "but I'd rather not go."

"But I tell you I want to know," said Mr. Conyers; "I want to know if Mrs. Mellish is at home, and what she's up to, and whether there are any visitors at the house, and all about her. Do you understand?"

"Yes, it's easy enough to understand, but it's rare and difficult to do," replied Steeve Hargraves. "How am I to find out? Who's to tell me?"

"How do I know?" cried the trainer, impatiently; for Stephen Hargraves's slow, dogged stupidity was throwing the dashing James Conyers into a fever of vexation. "How do I know? Don't you see that I'm too ill to stir from this bed? I'd go myself if I wasn't. And can't you go and do what I tell you without standing arguing there until you drive me mad?"

Steeve Hargraves muttered some sulky apology, and shuffled out of the room. Mr. Conyers's handsome eyes followed him with a dark frown. It is not a pleasant state of health which succeeds a drunken debauch; and the trainer was angry with himself for the weakness which had taken him to Doncaster upon the preceding evening, and thereby inclined to vent his anger upon other people.

There is a great deal of vicarious penance done in this world. Lady's-maids are apt to suffer for the follies of their mistresses, and Lady Clara Vere de Vere's French Abigail is extremely likely to have to atone for young Laurence's death by patient endurance of my lady's ill-temper and much unpicking and remaking of bodices, which would have fitted her ladyship well enough in any other state of mind than the remorseful misery which is engendered of an evil conscience. The ugly gash across young Laurence's throat, to say nothing of the cruel slanders circulated after the inquest, may make life almost unendurable to the poor meek nursery-governess who educates Lady Clara's younger sisters; and the younger sisters themselves, and mamma and papa, and my lady's youthful confidantes, and even her haughtiest adorers, all have their share in the expiation of her ladyship's wickedness.[1] For she will not – or she *cannot* – meekly own that she has been guilty, and shut herself away from the world, to make her own atonement and work her own redemption. So she thrusts the burden of her sins upon other people's shoulders, and travels the first stage to captious and disappointed old-maidism.

The commercial gentlemen who make awkward mistakes in the City, the devotees of the turf whose misfortunes keep them away from Mr. Tattersall's premises on a settling-day,[2] can make innocent women and children carry the weight of their sins, and suffer the penalties of their foolishness. Papa still smokes his Cabanas at fourpence-halfpenny apiece, or his mild Turkish at nine shillings a pound, and still dines at the Crown and Sceptre in the drowsy summer weather, when the bees are asleep in the flowers at Morden College, and the fragrant hay newly stacked in the meadows beyond Blackheath. But mamma must wear her faded silk, or have it dyed, as the case may be; and the children must forego the promised happiness, the wild delight, of sunny rambles on a shingly beach, bordered by yellow sands that stretch away to hug an ever changeful and yet ever constant ocean in their tawny arms. And not only mamma and the little ones, but other mothers and other little ones, must help in the heavy sum of penance for the defaulter's iniquities. The baker may have calculated upon receiving that long-standing account, and may have planned a new gown for his wife, and a summer treat for his little ones, to be paid for by the expected money; and the honest tradesman, soured by the disappointment of having to disappoint those he loves, is likely to be cross to them into the bargain; and even to grudge her Sunday out to the household drudge who waits at his little table. The influence of the strong man's evil deed slowly percolates through insidious channels of which he never knows or dreams. The deed of folly or of guilt does its fatal work when the sinner who committed it has forgotten

---

1   In Tennyson's "Lady Clara Vere de Vere" (1832), the insolent aristocrat Lady Clara encourages and then spurns her suitor, Laurence. When he slits his throat, she languishes as an old maid. The suffering French Abigail and nursery-governess are Braddon's inventions.

2   At Tattersall's, located at Hyde Park Corner, bets were taken all week and settled each Monday.

his wickedness. Who shall say where or when the results of one man's evil doing shall cease? The seed of sin engenders no common root, shooting straight upwards through the earth, and bearing a given crop. It is the germ of a foul running weed, whose straggling suckers travel underground beyond the ken of mortal eye, beyond the power of mortal calculation. If Louis XV. had been a conscientious man, terror and murder, misery and confusion, might never have reigned upon the darkened face of beautiful France. If Eve had rejected the fatal fruit we might all have been in Eden to-day.

Mr. James Conyers, then, after the manner of mankind, vented his spleen upon the only person who came in his way, and was glad to be able to despatch the "Softy" upon an unpleasant errand, and make his attendant as uncomfortable as he was himself.

"My head rocks as if I was on board a steam-packet," he muttered, as he lay alone in his little bedroom, "and my hand shakes so that I can't hold my pipe steady while I fill it. I'm in a nice state to have to talk to *her*. As if it wasn't as much as I can do at the best of times to be a match for her."

He flung aside his pipe half filled, and turned his head wearily upon the pillow. The hot sun and the buzz of the insects tormented him. There was a big bluebottle fly blundering and wheeling about amongst the folds of the dimity bed-curtains; a fly which seemed the very genius of delirium tremens; but the trainer was too ill to do more than swear at his purple-winged tormentor.

He was awakened from a half-doze by the treble voice of a small stable-boy in the room below. He called out angrily for the lad to come up and state his business. His business was a message from Mr. John Mellish, who wished to see the trainer immediately.

"*Mr.* Mellish," muttered James Conyers to himself. "Tell your master I'm too ill to stir, but that I'll wait upon him in the evening," he said to the boy. "You can see I'm ill, if you've got any eyes, and you can say that you found me in bed."

The lad departed with these instructions, and Mr. Conyers returned to his own thoughts, which appeared to be by no means agreeable to him.

To drink spirituous liquors and play all-fours[1] in the sanded

---

1   A card game associated with raffish characters.

taproom of a sporting public is no doubt a very delicious occupation, and would be altogether Elysian and unobjectionable if one could always be drinking spirits and playing all-fours. But as the finest picture ever painted by Raphael or Rubens is but a dead blank of canvas upon the reverse, so there is generally a disagreeable *other* side to all the pleasures of earth, and a certain reaction after card-playing and brandy-drinking which is more than equivalent in misery to the pleasures which have preceded it. Mr. Conyers, tossing his hot head from side to side upon a pillow which seemed even hotter, took a very different view of life to that which he had expounded to his boon companions only the night before in the tap-room of the Lion and Lamb, Doncaster.

"I should liked to have stopped over the Leger," he muttered, "for I meant to make a hatful of money out of the Conjuror; for if what they say at Richmond is anything like truth, he's safe to win. But there's no going against my lady when her mind's made up. It's take it or leave it – yes or no – and be quick about it."

Mr. Conyers garnished his speech with two or three expletives common enough amongst the men with whom he had lived, but not to be recorded here; and, closing his eyes, fell into a doze; a half-waking, half-sleeping torpidity; in which he felt as if his head had become a ton-weight of iron, and was dragging him backwards through the pillow into a bottomless abyss.

While the trainer lay in this comfortless semi-slumber Stephen Hargraves walked slowly and sulkily through the wood on his way to the invisible fence, from which point he meant to reconnoitre the premises.

The irregular façade of the old house fronted him across the smooth breadth of lawn, dotted and broken by particoloured flower-beds; by rustic clumps of gnarled oak supporting mighty clusters of vivid scarlet geraniums, all aflame in the sunshine; by trellised arches laden with trailing roses of every varying shade, from palest blush to deepest crimson; by groups of evergreens, whose every leaf was rich in beauty and luxuriance, whose every tangled garland would have made a worthy chaplet for a king.

The "Softy," in the semi-darkness of his soul, had some glimmer of that light which was altogether wanting in Mr. James Conyers. He felt that these things were beautiful. The broken lines of the ivy-covered house-front, Gothic here, Elizabethan there, were in some manner pleasant to him. The scattered rose-leaves on the lawn; the flickering shadows of the evergreens upon the grass; the song of a skylark too lazy to soar, and content to warble among the bushes; the rippling sound of a tiny waterfall far away in the wood, – made a language of which he only understood a few straggling syllables here and there, but which was not altogether a meaningless jargon to him, as it was to the trainer; to whose mind Holborn Hill would have conveyed as much of the sublime as the untrodden pathways of the Jungfrau.[1] The "Softy" dimly perceived that Mellish Park was beautiful, and he felt a fiercer hatred against the person whose influence had ejected him from his old home.

The house fronted the south, and the Venetian shutters were all closed upon this hot summer's day. Stephen Hargraves looked for his old enemy Bow-wow, who was likely enough to be lying on the broad stone steps before the hall-door; but there was no sign of the dog's presence anywhere about. The hall-door was closed, and the Venetian shutters, under the rose and clematis shadowed verandah which sheltered John Mellish's room, were also closed. The "Softy" walked round by the fence which encircled the lawn to another iron gate which opened close to John's room, and which was so completely overshadowed by a clump of beeches as to form a safe point of observation. This gate had been left ajar by Mr. Mellish himself, most likely, for that gentleman had a happy knack of forgetting to shut the doors and gates which he opened; and the "Softy," taking courage from the stillness round and about the house, ventured into the garden, and crept stealthily towards the closed shutters before the windows of Mr. Mellish's apartment, with much of the manner which might distinguish some wretched mongrel cur who trusts himself within ear-shot of a mastiff's kennel.

The mastiff was out of the way on this occasion, for one of the shutters was ajar; and when Stephen Hargraves peeped cautiously into

---

1   Holborn Hill was the section of the main London thoroughfare, Holburn, extending from Fetter Lane to Farringdon Street; the Jungfrau region of the Swiss Alps is famous for its forbidding mountains, green pastures, and sublime scenery.

the room, he was relieved to find it empty. John's elbow-chair was pushed a little way from the table, which was laden with open pistol-cases and breech-loading revolvers. These, with two or three silk handkerchiefs, a piece of chamois-leather, and a bottle of oil, bore witness that Mr. Mellish had been beguiling the morning in the pleasing occupation of inspecting and cleaning the fire-arms, which formed the chief ornament of his study.

It was his habit to begin this operation with great preparation, and altogether upon a gigantic scale; to reject all assistance with scorn; to put himself in a violent perspiration at the end of half an hour, and to send one of the servants to finish the business, and restore the room to its old order.

The "Softy" looked with a covetous eye at the noble array of guns and pistols. He had that innate love of these things which seems to be implanted in every breast, whatever its owner's state or station. He had hoarded his money once to buy himself a gun; but when he had saved the five-and-thirty shillings demanded by a certain pawnbroker of Doncaster for an old-fashioned musket, which was almost as heavy as a small cannon, his courage failed him, and he could not bring himself to part with the precious coins, whose very touch could send a shrill of rapture through the slow current of his blood. No, he could not surrender such a sum of money to the Doncaster pawnbroker even for the possession of his heart's desire; and as the stern money-lender refused to take payment in weekly instalments of sixpences, Stephen was fain to go without the gun, and to hope that some day or other Mr. John Mellish would reward his services by the gift of some disused fowling-piece by Forsythe or Manton. But there was no hope of such happiness now. A new dynasty reigned at Mellish, and a black-eyed queen, who hated him, had forbidden him to sully her domain with the traces of his shambling foot. He felt that he was in momentary peril upon the threshold of that sacred chamber, which, during his long service at Mellish Park, he had always regarded as a very temple of the beautiful; but the sight of fire-arms upon the table had a magnetic attraction for him, and he drew the Venetian shutter a little way further ajar, and slid himself in through the open window. Then, flushed and trembling with excitement, he dropped into John's chair, and began to handle the precious implements of warfare upon pheasants and partridges, and to turn them about in his big, clumsy hands.

Delicious as the guns were, and delightful though it was to draw one of the revolvers up to his shoulder, and take aim at an imaginary pheasant, the pistols were even still more attractive; for with them he could not refrain from taking imaginary aim at his enemies. Sometimes at James Conyers, who had snubbed and abused him, and had made the bread of dependence bitter to him; very often at Aurora; once or twice at poor John Mellish; but always with a darkness upon his pallid face which would have promised little mercy, had the pistol been loaded and the enemy near at hand.

There was one pistol, a small one, and an odd one apparently, for he could not find its fellow, which took a peculiar hold upon his fancy. It was as pretty as a lady's toy, and small enough to be carried in a lady's pocket, but the hammer snapped upon the nipple, when the "Softy" pulled the trigger, with a sound that evidently meant mischief.

"To think that such a little thing as this could kill a big man like you," muttered Mr. Hargraves, with a jerk of his head in the direction of the north lodge.

He had this pistol still in his hand when the door was suddenly opened, and Aurora Mellish stood upon the threshold.

She spoke as she opened the door, almost before she was in the room.

"John, dear," she said, "Mrs. Powell wants to know whether Colonel Maddison dines here to-day with the Lofthouses."

She drew back with a shudder that shook her from head to foot, as her eyes met the "Softy's" hated face instead of John's familiar glance.

In spite of the fatigue and agitation which she had endured within the last few days, she was not looking ill. Her eyes were unnaturally bright, and a feverish colour burned in her cheeks. Her manner, always impetuous, was restless and impatient to-day, as if her nature had been charged with a terrible amount of electricity, till she were likely at any moment to explode in some tempest of anger or woe.

"*You* here!" she exclaimed.

The "Softy" in his embarrassment was at a loss for an excuse for his presence. He pulled his shabby hair-skin cap off, and twisted it round and round in his great hands; but he made no other recognition of his late master's wife.

"Who sent you to this room?" asked Mrs. Mellish; "I thought you had been forbidden this place. The house at least," she added, her face crimsoning indignantly as she spoke, "although Mr. Conyers may choose to bring you to the north lodge. Who sent you here?"

"Him," answered Mr. Hargraves, doggedly, with another jerk of his head towards the trainer's abode.

"James Conyers?"

"Yes."

"What does he want here, then?"

"He told me to come down t' th' house, and see if you and master'd come back."

"Then you can go and tell him that we have come back," she said contemptuously; "and that if he'd waited a little longer he would have had no occasion to send his spies after me."

The "Softy" crept towards the window, feeling that his dismissal was contained in these words, and looking rather suspiciously at the array of driving and hunting whips over the mantel-piece. Mrs. Mellish might have a fancy for laying one of these about his shoulders, if he happened to offend her.

"Stop!" she said impetuously, as he had his hand upon the shutter to push it open; "since you are here, you can take a message, or a scrap of writing," she said contemptuously, as if she could not bring herself to call any communication between herself and Mr. Conyers a note, or a letter. "Yes; you can take a few lines to your master. Stop there while I write."

She waved her hand with a gesture which expressed plainly, "Come no nearer; you are too obnoxious to be endured except at a distance," and seated herself at John's writing-table.

She scratched two lines with a quill-pen upon a slip of paper, which she folded while the ink was still wet. She looked for an envelope amongst her husband's littered paraphernalia of account-books, bills, receipts, and price-lists, and finding one after some little trouble, put the folded paper into it, fastened the gummed flap with her lips, and handed the missive to Mr. Hargraves, who had watched her with hungry eyes, eager to fathom this new stage in the mystery.

Was the two thousand pounds in that envelope? he thought. No;

surely, such a sum of money must be a huge pile of gold and silver, – a mountain of glittering coin. He had seen cheques sometimes, and bank-notes, in the hands of Langley the trainer, and he had wondered how it was that money could be represented by those pitiful bits of paper.

"I'd rayther hav't i' goold," he thought: "if 'twas mine, I'd have it all i' goold and silver."

He was very glad when he found himself safely clear of the whips and Mrs. John Mellish, and as soon as he reached the shelter of the thick foliage upon the northern side of the Park, he set to work to examine the packet which had been intrusted to him.

Mrs. Mellish had liberally moistened the adhesive flap of the envelope, as people are apt to do when they are in a hurry; the consequence of which carelessness was that the gum was still so wet that Stephen Hargraves found no difficulty in opening the envelope without tearing it. He looked cautiously about him, convinced himself that he was unobserved, and then drew out the slip of paper. It contained very little to reward him for his trouble, only these few words, scrawled in Aurora's most careless hand: –

"Be on the southern side of the wood, near the turnstile, between half-past eight and nine."

The "Softy" grinned as he slowly made himself master of this communication.

"It's oncommon hard wroitin', t' make out th' shapes o' th' letters," he said, as he finished his task. "Whoy can't gentlefolks wroit like Ned Tiller, oop at th' Red Lion, – printin' loike? It's easier to read, and a deal prettier to look at."

He refastened the envelope, pressing it down with his dirty thumb to make it adhere once more, and not much improving its appearance thereby.

"He's one of your rare careless chaps," he muttered as he surveyed the letter; "*he* won't stop t' examine if it's been opened before. What's insoide were hardly worth th' trouble of openin' it; but perhaps it's as well to know it too."

Immediately after Stephen Hargraves had disappeared through the open window Aurora turned to leave the room by the door, intending to go in search of her husband.

Russ Van Atta Gets 4 Hits, Pitches Shutout in MLB Debut

Cieradkowski, Gary. "98. Russ Van Atta: The Babe, Oil and One Dead Finger." *Infinitecardset.blogspot.com*, 2011.

Drebinger, John. "Fists Fly as Yanks rout Senators, 16–0." *New York Times,* April 26, 1933.

Linthurst, Randolph. "A Most Spectacular Debut." *Baseball Research Journal*, Society for American Baseball Research, 1975.

Alex Rodriguez's 4 Clutch Hits in the 2009 Postseason

Postgame press conferences following Game 2 of 2009 ALDS, Game 2 of ALCS, Game 3, and Game 4 of World Series, ASAPSports.com.

Alex Rodriguez press conference, February 17, 2009.

Alex Rodriguez Gets Hit No. 3000, a HR

Coffey, Sean; Madden, Bill; Thompson, Teri; Slattery, Dennis. "Alex Rodriguez Gets 3,000[th] Hit Baseball Back as Yankees Donate $150,000 to Fan's Charity." *New York Daily News*, July 3, 2015.

She was arrested on the threshold by Mrs. Powell, who was standing at the door, with the submissive and deferential patience of paid companionship depicted in her insipid face.

"*Does* Colonel Maddison dine here, my dear Mrs. Mellish?" she asked meekly; yet with a pensive earnestness which suggested that her life, or at any rate her peace of mind, depended upon the answer. "I am *so* anxious to know, for of course it will make a difference with the fish, – and perhaps we ought to have some mulligatawny; or at any rate a dish of curry amongst the *entrées*; for these elderly East-Indian officers are so——"

"I don't know," answered Aurora, curtly. "Were you standing at the door long before I came out, Mrs. Powell?"

"Oh, no," answered the ensign's widow, "not long. Did you not hear me knock?"

Mrs. Powell would not have allowed herself to be betrayed into anything so vulgar as an abbreviation by the torments of the rack; and would have neatly rounded her periods while the awful wheel was stretching every muscle of her agonized frame, and the executioner waiting to give the *coup de grâce*.[1]

"Did you not hear me knock?" she asked.

"No," said Aurora; "you didn't knock! Did you?"

Mrs. Mellish made an alarming pause between the two sentences.

"Oh, yes, too-wice," answered Mrs. Powell, with as much emphasis as was consistent with gentility upon the elongated word; "I knocked too-wice; but you seemed so very much preoccupied that——"

"I didn't hear you," interrupted Aurora; "you should knock rather louder when you *want* people to hear, Mrs. Powell. I – I came here to look for John, and I shall stop and put away his guns. Careless fellow! – he always leaves them lying about."

"Shall I assist you, dear Mrs. Mellish?"

"Oh, no, thank you."

"But pray allow me – guns are *so* interesting. Indeed, there is very little either in art or nature which, properly considered, is not——"

"You had better find Mr. Mellish, and ascertain if the colonel *does* dine here, I think, Mrs. Powell," interrupted Aurora, shutting the lids

---

1 A blow used to finish off a person condemned to death.

of the pistol-cases, and replacing them upon their accustomed shelves.

"Oh, if you wish to be alone, certainly," said the ensign's widow, looking furtively at Aurora's face bending over the breech-loading revolvers, and then walking genteelly and noiselessly out of the room.

"Who was she talking to?" thought Mrs. Powell. "I could hear her voice, but not the other person's. I suppose it was Mr. Mellish; and yet he is not generally so quiet."

She stopped to look out of a window in the corridor, and found the solution of her doubts in the shambling figure of the "Softy," making his way northwards, creeping stealthily under shadow of the plantation that bordered the lawn. Mrs. Powell's faculties were all cultivated to a state of unpleasant perfection, and she was able, actually as well as figuratively, to see a great deal farther than most people.

John Mellish was not to be found in the house, and on making inquiries of some of the servants, Mrs. Powell learnt that he had strolled up to the north lodge to see the trainer, who was confined to his bed.

"Indeed!" said the ensign's widow; "then I think, as we really ought to know about the colonel and the mulligatawny, I will walk to the north lodge myself, and see Mr. Mellish."

She took a sun-umbrella from the stand in the hall, and crossed the lawn northwards at a smart pace, in spite of the heat of the July noontide. "If I can get there before Hargraves," she thought, "I may be able to find out why he came to the house."

The ensign's widow did reach the lodge before Stephen Hargraves, who stopped, as we know, under shelter of the foliage in the loneliest pathway of the wood, to decipher Aurora's scrawl. She found John Mellish seated with the trainer, in the little parlour of the lodge, discussing the stable arrangement; the master talking with considerable animation, the servant listening with a listless *nonchalance* which had a certain air of depreciation, not to say contempt, for poor John's racing stud. Mr. Conyers had risen from his bed at the sound of his employer's voice in the little room below, and had put on a dusty shooting-coat and a pair of shabby slippers, in order to come down and hear what Mr. Mellish had to say.

"I'm sorry to hear you're ill, Conyers," John said heartily, with a freshness in his strong voice which seemed to carry health and strength in its very tone. "As you weren't well enough to look in at the house, I thought I'd come over here and talk to you about business. I want to know whether we ought to take Monte Christo out of his York engagement, and if you think it would be wise to let Northern Dutchman take his chance for the Great Ebor. Hey?"

Mr. Mellish's query resounded through the small room, and made the languid trainer shudder. Mr. Conyers had all the peevish susceptibility to discomfort or inconvenience which go to make a man above his station. Is it a merit to be above one's station, I wonder, that people make such a boast of their unfitness for honest employments, and sturdy but progressive labour? The flowers in the fables, that want to be trees, always get the worst of it, I remember. Perhaps that is because they can do nothing but complain. There is no objection to their growing into trees, if they can, I suppose; but a great objection to their being noisy and disagreeable because they can't. With the son of the simple Corsican advocate who made himself Emperor of France the world had every sympathy; but with poor Louis Philippe, who ran away from a throne at the first shock that disturbed its equilibrium,[220] I fear, very little. Is it quite right to be angry with the world because it worships success? for is not success, in some manner, the stamp of divinity? Self-assertion may deceive the ignorant for a time; but when the noise dies away, we cut open the drum, and find that it was emptiness that made the music. Mr. Conyers contented himself with declaring that he walked on a road which was unworthy of his footsteps; but as he never contrived to get an inch farther upon the great highway of life, there is some reason to suppose that he had his opinion entirely to himself. Mr. Mellish and his trainer were still discussing stable matters when Mrs. Powell reached the north lodge. She stopped for a few minutes in the rustic doorway, waiting for a pause in the conversation. She was too well bred to interrupt Mr. Mellish in his talk, and there was a chance that she might hear something by lingering. No contrast could be stronger than that presented by the two men. John, broad-shouldered and stalwart; his short crisp chestnut hair brushed

---

1   The son of the Corsican advocate was Napoleon I. Louis-Philippe (1773-1850), the "citizen-king" of France, abdicated in 1848 when faced with an insurrectionary movement and died in exile in England two years later.

away from his square forehead; his bright open blue eyes beaming honest sunshine upon all they looked at; his loose gray clothes neat and well made; his shirt in the first freshness of the morning's toilet; everything about him made beautiful by the easy grace which is the peculiar property of the man who has been born a gentleman, and which neither all the cheap finery which Mr. Moses can sell, nor all the expensive absurdities which Mr. Tittlebat Titmouse can buy,[1] will ever bestow upon the *parvenu* or the vulgarian. The trainer, handsomer than his master by as much as Antinous[2] in Grecian marble is handsomer than the substantially-shod and loose-coated young squires in Mr. Millais' designs;[3] as handsome as it is possible for this human clay to be, with every feature moulded to the highest type of positive beauty, and yet, every inch of him, a boor. His shirt soiled and crumpled, his hair rough and uncombed; his unshaven chin, dark with the blue bristles of his budding beard, and smeared with the traces of last night's liquor; his dingy hands, supporting this dingy chin, and his elbows bursting half out of the frayed sleeves of his shabby shooting-jacket, leaning on the table in an attitude of indifferent insolence. His countenance expressive of nothing but dissatisfaction with his own lot, and contempt for the opinions of other people. All the homilies that could be preached upon the time-worn theme of beauty and its worthlessness, could never argue so strongly as this mute evidence presented by Mr. Conyers himself in his slouching posture and his unkempt hair. Is beauty, then, so little, one asks, on looking at the trainer and his employer? Is it better to be clean, and well dressed, and gentlemanly, than to have a classical profile and a thrice-worn shirt?

Finding very little to interest her in John's stable-talk, Mrs. Powell made her presence known, and once more asked the all-important question about Colonel Maddison.

1　By mid-century, the firm of E. (Elias) Moses and Son was a leader in cut-price, ready-to-wear clothing. In Samuel Warren's comic novel, *Ten Thousand A Year* (1841), Mr. Tittlebat Titmouse, a draper's assistant, falsely inherits a fortune and an estate. He lives in high style, contracting a fashionable marriage and buying a seat in parliament before he is unmasked.

2　See 246, n.1.

3　John Everett Millais (1829-96), Pre-Raphaelite painter and one of the foremost illustrators of Victorian books and periodicals, including the Moxon *Tennyson*, Trollope's *Framley Parsonage*, and *Orley Farm*.

"Yes," John answered; "the old boy is sure to come. Let's have plenty of chutnee, and boiled rice, and preserved ginger, and all the rest of the unpleasant things that Indian officers live upon. Have you seen Lolly?"

Mr. Mellish put on his hat, gave a last instruction to the trainer, and left the cottage.

"Have you seen Lolly?" he asked again.

"Ye-es," replied Mrs. Powell; "I have only lately left Mrs. Mellish in your room; she had been speaking to that half-witted person – Hargraves, I think he is called."

"Speaking to *him?*" cried John; "speaking to him in my room? Why, the fellow is forbidden to cross the threshold of the house, and Mrs. Mellish abominates the sight of him. Don't you remember the day he flogged her dog, you know, and Lolly horse – had hysterics?" added Mr. Mellish, choking himself with one word and substituting another.

"Oh, yes, I remember that little – ahem! – unfortunate occurrence perfectly," replied Mrs. Powell, in a tone which, in spite of its amiability, implied that Aurora's escapade was not a thing to be easily forgotten.

"Then it's not likely, you know, that Lolly would talk to the man. You must be mistaken, Mrs. Powell."

The ensign's widow simpered and lifted her eyebrows, gently shaking her head, with a gesture that seemed to say, "Did you ever find *me* mistaken?"

"No, no, my dear Mr. Mellish," she said, with a half-playful air of conviction, "there was no mistake on my part. Mrs. Mellish was talking to the half-witted person; but you know the person is a sort of servant to Mr. Conyers, and Mrs. Mellish may have had a message for Mr. Conyers."

"A message for *him!*" roared John, stopping suddenly and planting his stick upon the ground in a movement of unconcealed passion; "what messages should she have for *him? Why* should she want people fetching and carrying between her and him?"

Mrs. Powell's pale eyes lit up with a faint yellow flame in their greenish pupils as John broke out thus. "It is coming – it is coming –

it is coming!" her envious heart cried, and she felt that a faint flush of triumph was gathering in her sickly cheeks.

But in another moment John Mellish recovered his self-command. He was angry with himself for that transient passion. "Am I going to doubt her again?" he thought. "Do I know so little of the nobility of her generous soul that I am ready to listen to every whisper, and terrify myself with every look?"

They had walked about a hundred yards away from the lodge by this time. John turned irresolutely, as if half inclined to go back.

"A message for Conyers," he said to Mrs. Powell; – "ay, ay, to be sure. It's likely enough she might want to send him a message, for she's cleverer at all the stable business than I am. It was she who told me not to enter Cherry-stone for the Chester Cup, and, egad! I was obstinate, and I was licked; as I deserved to be, for not listening to my dear girl."

Mrs. Powell would fain have boxed John's ear, had she been tall enough to reach that organ. Infatuated fool! would he never open his dull eyes and see the ruin that was preparing for him?

"You *are* a good husband, Mr. Mellish," she said with a gentle melancholy. "Your wife *ought* to be happy!" she added, with a sigh which plainly hinted that Mrs. Mellish was miserable.

"A good husband!" cried John, "not half good enough for her. What can I do to prove that I love her? What can I do? Nothing, except to let her have her own way; and what a little that seems! Why, if she wanted to set that house on fire, for the pleasure of making a bonfire," he added, pointing to the rambling mansion in which his blue eyes had first seen the light, "I'd let her do it, and look on with her at the blaze."

"Are you going back to the lodge?" Mrs. Powell asked quietly, not taking any notice of this outbreak of marital enthusiasm.

They had retraced their steps, and were within a few paces of the little garden before the north lodge.

Going back?" said John; "no – yes."

Between his utterance of the negative and the affirmative he had looked up, and seen Stephen Hargraves entering the little garden-gate. The "Softy" had come by the short cut through the wood. John Mellish quickened his pace, and followed Steeve Hargraves across the little garden to the threshold of the door. At the threshold he paused.

The rustic porch was thickly screened by the spreading branches of the roses and honeysuckle, and John was unseen by those within. He did not himself deliberately listen; he only waited for a few moments, wondering what to do next. In those few moments of indecision he heard the trainer speak to his attendant.

"Did you see her?" he asked.

"Ay, sure, I see her."

"And she gave you a message?"

"No, she gave me this here."

"A letter?" cried the trainer's eager voice; "give it me."

John Mellish heard the tearing of the envelope and the crackling of the crisp paper; and knew that his wife had been writing to his servant. He clenched his strong right hand until the nails dug into the muscular palm; then turning to Mrs. Powell, who stood close behind him, simpering meekly, as she would have simpered at an earthquake, or a revolution, or any other national calamity not peculiarly affecting herself, he said quietly –

"Whatever directions Mrs. Mellish has given are sure to be right; I won't interfere with them." He walked away from the north lodge as he spoke, looking straight before him, homewards; as if the unchanging lode-star of his honest heart were beckoning to him across the dreary Slough of Despond,[1] and bidding him take comfort.

"Mrs. Powell," he said, turning rather sharply upon the ensign's widow, "I should be very sorry to say anything likely to offend you, in your character of – of a guest beneath my roof; but I shall take it as a favour to myself if you will be so good as to remember, that I require no information respecting my wife's movements from you, or from any one. Whatever Mrs. Mellish does, she does with my full consent, my perfect approbation. Cæsar's wife must not be suspected,[2] and by Jove, ma'am! – you'll pardon the expression, – John Mellish's wife must not be watched."

"Watched! – information!" exclaimed Mrs. Powell, lifting her pale eyebrows to the extreme limits allowed by nature. "My dear Mr. Mell-

---

1   In John Bunyan's allegory, *The Pilgrim's Progress* (1678), the Slough of Despond is the first obstacle encountered by the pilgrim, Christian.

2   Traditional, based on Plutarch's *Life of Julius Caesar*.

ish, when I really only casually remarked, in reply to a question of your own, that I believed Mrs. Mellish had——"

"Oh, yes," answered John, "I understand. There are several ways by which you can go to Doncaster from this house. You can go across the fields, or round by Harper's Common, an out-of-the-way, roundabout route, but you get there all the same, you know, ma'am. *I* generally prefer the high road. It mayn't be the shortest way, perhaps; but it's certainly the straightest."

The corners of Mrs. Powell's thin lower lip dropped, perhaps the eighth of an inch, as John made these observations; but she very quickly recovered her habitually genteel simper, and told Mr. Mellish that he really had such a droll way of expressing himself as to make his meaning scarcely so clear as could be wished.

But John had said all that he wanted to say, and walked steadily onwards; looking always towards that quarter in which the pole-star might be supposed to shine, guiding him back to his home.

That home so soon to be desolate! – with such ruin brooding above it as in his darkest doubts, his wildest fears, he had never shadowed forth!

CHAPTER XXIII.

ON THE THRESHOLD OF DARKER MISERIES.

JOHN went straight to his own apartment to look for his wife; but he found the guns put back in their usual places, and the room empty. Aurora's maid, a smartly dressed girl, came tripping out of the servants' hall, where the rattling of knives and forks announced that a very substantial dinner was being done substantial justice to, to answer John's eager inquiries. She told him that Mrs. Mellish had complained of a headache, and had gone to her room to lie down. John went upstairs, and crept cautiously along the carpeted corridor, fearful of every footfall which might break the repose of his wife. The door of her dressing-room was ajar: he pushed it softly open, and went in. Aurora was lying upon the sofa, wrapped in a loose white dressing-gown, her masses of ebon hair uncoiled and falling about her shoulders in serpentine tresses, that looked like shining blue-black snakes released from poor Medusa's head to make their escape amid the folds of her garments. Heaven knows what a stranger sleep may have been for many a night to Mrs. Mellish's pillow; but she had fallen into a heavy slumber on this hot summer's day. Her cheeks were flushed with a feverish crimson, and one small hand lay under her head twisted in the tangled masses of her glorious hair.

John bent over her with a tender smile.

"Poor girl!" he thought; "thank God that she can sleep, in spite of the miserable secrets which have come between us. Talbot Bulstrode left her because he could not bear the agony that I am suffering now. What cause had he to doubt her? What cause compared to that which I have had a fortnight ago – the other night – this morning? And yet – and yet I trust her, and will trust her, please God, to the very end."

He seated himself in a low easy-chair close beside the sofa upon which his sleeping wife lay, and resting his head upon his arm, watched her, thought of her, perhaps prayed for her; and after a little while fell asleep himself, snoring in bass harmony with Aurora's regular breathing. He slept and snored, this horrible man, in the hour of his trouble, and behaved himself altogether in a manner most unbecoming in a hero. But then he is not a hero. He is stout and strongly built, with a fine broad chest, and unromantically robust health. There is more chance of his dying of apoplexy than of fading gracefully in a decline, or breaking a blood-vessel in a moment of intense emotion. He sleeps calmly, with the warm July air floating in upon him from the open window, and comforting him with its balmy breath, and he fully enjoys that rest of body and mind. Yet even in his tranquil slumber there is a vague something, some lingering shadow of the bitter memories which sleep has put away from him, that fills his breast with a dull pain, an oppressive heaviness, which cannot be shaken off. He slept until half a dozen different clocks in the rambling old house had come to one conclusion, and declared it to be five in the afternoon; and he awoke with a start to find his wife watching him, Heaven knows how intently, with her black eyes filled with solemn thought, and a strange earnestness in her face.

"My poor John!" she said, bending her beautiful head and resting her burning forehead upon his hand; "how tired you must have been, to sleep so soundly in the middle of the day! I have been awake for nearly an hour, watching you – "

"Watching me, Lolly! – why?"

"And thinking how good you are to me. Oh, John, John! what can I ever do – what can I ever do to atone to you for all——"

"Be happy, Aurora," he said huskily, "be happy, and – and send that man away."

"I will, John; he shall go soon, dear, – to-night!"

"What! – then that letter was to dismiss him?" asked Mr. Mellish.

"You know that I wrote to him?"

"Yes, darling, it was to dismiss him, – say that it was so, Aurora. Pay him what money you like to keep the secret that he discovered, but send him away, Lolly, send him away. The sight of him is hateful to me. Dismiss him, Aurora, or I must do so myself."

He rose in his passionate excitement, but Aurora laid her hand softly upon his arm.

"Leave all to me," she said quietly. "Believe me that I will act for the best. For the best, at least, if you couldn't bear to lose me; and you couldn't bear that, could you, John?"

"Lose you! My God, Aurora! why do you say such things to me? I *wouldn't* lose you. Do you hear, Lolly? I *wouldn't*. I'd follow you to the farthest end of the universe, and Heaven take pity upon those that came between us!"

His set teeth, the fierce light in his eyes, and the iron rigidity of his mouth, gave an emphasis to his words which my pen could never give if I used every epithet in the English language.

Aurora rose from her sofa, and twisting her hair into a thickly-rolled mass at the back of her head, seated herself near the window, and pushed back the Venetian shutter.

"These people dine here to-day, John?" she asked listlessly.

"The Lofthouses and Colonel Maddison? Yes, my darling; and it's ever so much past five. Shall I ring for your afternoon cup of tea?"

"Yes, dear; and take some with me, if you will."

I'm afraid that in his inmost heart Mr. Mellish did not cherish any very great affection for the decoctions of bohea and gunpowder[1] with which his wife dosed him; but he would have dined upon cod-liver oil had she served the banquet; and he strung his nerves to their extreme tension at her supreme pleasure, and affected to highly relish the post-meridian[2] dishes of tea which his wife poured out for him in the sacred seclusion of her dressing-room.

Mrs. Powell heard the comfortable sound of the chinking of the thin egg-shell china and the rattling of the spoons, as she passed the half-open door on her way to her own apartment, and was mutely furious as she thought that love and harmony reigned within the chamber where the husband and wife sat at tea.

Aurora went down to the drawing-room an hour after this, gorgeous in maize-coloured silk and voluminous flouncings of black lace, with her hair plaited in a diadem upon her head, and fastened with three diamond stars which John had bought for her in the Rue de la Paix, and which were cunningly fixed upon wire springs, which caused them to vibrate with every chance movement of her beautiful head. You will say, perhaps, that she was arrayed too gaudily for the reception of an old Indian officer and a country clergyman and his wife; but if she loved handsome dresses better than simpler attire, it

---

1   Bohea is black tea; on gunpowder tea see 129, n.1.
2   Afternoon.

was from no taste for display, but rather from an innate love of splendour and expenditure, which was a part of her expansive nature. She had always been taught to think of herself as Miss Floyd, the banker's daughter, and she had been taught also to spend money as a duty which she owed to society.

Mrs. Lofthouse was a pretty little woman, with a pale face and hazel eyes. She was the youngest daughter of Colonel Maddison, and was, "By birth, you know, my dear, far superior to poor Mrs. Mellish, who, in spite of her wealth, is only," &c. &c. &c., as Margaret Lofthouse remarked to her female acquaintance. She could not very easily forget that her father was the younger brother of a baronet, and had distinguished himself in some terrific manner by bloodthirsty demolition of Sikhs,[1] far away in the untractable East; and she thought it rather hard that Aurora should possess such cruel advantages through some pettifogging commercial genius on the part of her Glasgow ancestors.

But as it was impossible for honest people to know Aurora without loving her, Mrs. Lofthouse heartily forgave her her fifty thousand pounds, and declared her to be the dearest darling in the wide world; while Mrs. Mellish freely returned her friendliness, and caressed the little woman as she had caressed Lucy Bulstrode, with a superb yet affectionate condescension, such as Cleopatra may have had for her handmaidens.

The dinner went off pleasantly enough. Colonel Maddison attacked the side-dishes specially provided for him, and praised the Mellish-Park cook. Mr. Lofthouse explained to Aurora the plan of a new schoolhouse which she intended to build for the improvement of John's native parish. She listened patiently to the rather wearisome details, in which a bakehouse and a washhouse and a Tudor chimney seemed the leading features. She had heard so much of this before; for there was scarcely a church, or a hospital, or a model lodging-house, or a refuge for any misery or destitution whatever, that had been lately elevated to adorn this earth, for which the banker's daughter had

---

1 Presumably during the Sikh Wars of 1845-46 and 1848-49, campaigns fought between the Sikhs and the British which resulted in the British annexation of the Punjab.

not helped to pay. But her heart was wide enough for them all, and she was always glad to hear of the bakehouse and washhouse and the Tudor chimney all over again. If she was a little less interested upon this occasion than usual, Mr. Lofthouse did not observe her inattention, for in the simple earnestness of his own mind, he thought it scarcely possible that the schoolhouse topic could fail to be interesting. Nothing is so difficult as to make people understand that you don't care for what they themselves especially affect. John Mellish could not believe that the entries for the Great Ebor were not interesting to Mr. Lofthouse, and the country clergyman was fully convinced that the details of his philanthropic schemes for the regeneration of his parish could not be otherwise than delightful to his host. But the master of Mellish Park was very silent, and sat with his glass in his hand, looking across the dinner-table and Mrs. Lofthouse's head, at the sunlit tree-tops between the lawn and the north lodge. Aurora, from her end of the table, saw that gloomy glance, and a resolute shadow darkened her face, expressive of the strengthening of some rooted purpose deep hidden in her heart. She sat so long at dessert, with her eyes fixed upon an apricot in her plate, and the shadow upon her face deepening every moment, that poor Mrs. Lofthouse was in utter despair of getting the significant look which was to release her from the bondage of hearing her father's stories of tiger-shooting and pig-sticking for the two or three hundredth time. Perhaps she never would have got that feminine signal,[1] had not Mrs. Powell, with a significant "hem!" made some observation about the sinking sun.

The ensign's widow was one of those people who declare that there is a perceptible difference in the length of the days upon the twenty-third or twenty-fourth of June, and who go on announcing the same fact until the long winter evenings come with the twenty-first of December, and it is time for them to declare the converse of their late proposition. It was some remark of this kind that aroused Mrs. Mellish from her reverie, and caused her to start up suddenly, quite forgetful of the conventional simpering beck to her guest.

---

1   The signal for the ladies to proceed to the drawing room for coffee or tea, leaving the gentlemen to smoke and drink port (or, in this case, claret).

"Past eight!" she said; "no, it's surely not so late?"

"Yes, it is, Lolly," John Mellish answered, looking at his watch; "a quarter past."

"Indeed! I beg your pardon, Mrs. Lofthouse; shall we go into the drawing-room?"

"Yes, dear, do," said the clergyman's wife, "and let's have a nice chat. Papa will drink too much claret if he tells the pig-sticking stories," she added in a confidential whisper. "Ask your dear, kind husband not to let him have too much claret; because he's sure to suffer with his liver to-morrow, and say that Lofthouse ought to have restrained him. He always says that it's poor Reginald's fault for not restraining him."

John looked anxiously after his wife, as he stood with the door in his hand, while the three ladies crossed the hall. He bit his lip as he noticed Mrs. Powell's unpleasantly-precise figure close to Aurora's shoulder.

"I think I spoke pretty plainly, though, this morning," he thought, as he closed the door and returned to his friends.

A quarter-past eight; twenty minutes past; five-and-twenty minutes past. Mrs. Lofthouse was rather a brilliant pianist, and was never happier than when interpreting Thalberg and Benedict upon her friends' Collard-and-Collards. There were old-fashioned people round Doncaster who believed in Collard and Collard, and were thankful for the melody to be got out of a good honest grand, in a solid rosewood case, unadorned with carved glorification, or ormolu fret-work.[1] At seven-and-twenty minutes past eight Mrs. Lofthouse was seated at Aurora's piano, in the first agonies of a prelude in six flats; a prelude which demanded such extraordinary uses of the left hand across the right, and the right over the left, and such exercise of

---

1 Sigismond Thalberg (1812-71), Austrian pianist and composer; Sir Julius Benedict (1804-85), German-born conductor, pianist, and composer of piano music. Collard-and-Collard were popular London piano manufacturers, second in production only to Broadwood in 1850. The passage refers to several changes in piano manufacture at mid-century. By 1860, the grand was becoming old fashioned, having been largely replaced by the upright. Moreover, there was a vogue for heavily decorated pianos: the jury for musical instruments at the 1853 Crystal Palace Exhibition in New York commented on the "tawdry decorations" on some pianos, and was especially critical of "gingerbread radiating in hideous splendours."

the thumbs in all sorts of positions, – in which, according to all ortho-
dox theories of the pre-Thalberg-ite school,[1] no pianist's thumbs
should ever be used, – that Mrs. Mellish felt that her friend's attention
was not very likely to wander from the keys.

Within the long, low-roofed drawing-room at Mellish Park there
was a snug little apartment, hung with innocent rosebud-sprinkled
chintzes, and furnished with maple-wood chairs and tables. Mrs. Lofthouse had not been seated at the piano more than five minutes when
Aurora strolled from the drawing-room to this inner chamber, leaving
her guest with no audience but Mrs. Powell. She lingered for a
moment on the threshold to look back at the ensign's widow, who sat
near the piano in an attitude of rapt attention.

"She is watching me," thought Aurora, "though her pink eyelids
are drooping over her eyes, and she seems to be looking at the border
of her pocket-handkerchief. She sees me with her chin or her nose,
perhaps. How do I know? She is all eyes! Bah! am I going to be afraid
of *her*, when I was never afraid of *him?* What should I fear except" –
(her head changed from its defiant attitude to a drooping posture, and
a sad smile curved her crimson lips) – "except to make you unhappy,
my dear, my *husband*. Yes," with a sudden lifting of her head, and re-
assumption of its proud defiance, "my own true husband! the husband
who has kept his marriage-vow as unpolluted as when first it issued
from his lips!"

I am writing what she thought, remember, not what she said; for
she was not in the habit of thinking aloud, nor did I ever know anybody who was.

Aurora took up a shawl that she had flung upon the sofa, and
threw it lightly over her head, veiling herself with a cloud of black
lace, through which the restless, shivering diamonds shone out like
stars in a midnight sky. She looked like Hecate,[2] as she stood on the
threshold of the French window lingering for a moment with a deep-

---

1 Sigismond Thalberg's virtuoso piano technique involved dividing the melody
   between the two hands so that a bass could be played with the left hand and an
   accompaniment with the right, thus producing the effect of three different hands.
2 Queen of the moon and the night; a mysterious sinister goddess having to do with
   ghosts and witchcraft. Hecate is one of the hags to whom Macbeth goes after the
   appearance of Banquo at his feast.

laid purpose in her heart, and a resolute light in her eyes. The clock in the steeple of the village-church struck the three-quarters after eight while she lingered for those few moments. As the last chime died away in the summer air, she looked up darkly at the evening sky, and walked with a rapid footstep out upon the lawn towards the southern end of the wood that bordered the Park.

CHAPTER XXIV.

CAPTAIN PRODDER CARRIES BAD NEWS TO HIS NIECE'S HOUSE.

WHILE AURORA stood upon the threshold of the open window, a man was lingering upon the broad stone steps before the door of the entrance hall, remonstrating with one of John Mellish's servants, who held supercilious parley with the intruder, and kept him at arm's length with the contemptuous indifference of a well-bred servant.

This stranger was Captain Samuel Prodder, who had arrived at Doncaster late in the afternoon, had dined at the Reindeer, and had come over to Mellish Park in a gig driven by a hanger-on of that establishment. The gig and the hanger-on were both in waiting at the bottom of the steps; and if there had been anything wanting to turn the balance of the footman's contempt for Captain Prodder's blue coat, loose shirt-collar, and silver watch chain, the gig from the Reindeer would have done it.

"Yes, Mrs. Mellish is at home," the gentleman in plush replied, after surveying the sea-captain with a leisurely and critical air, which was rather provoking to poor Samuel; "but she's engaged."

"But perhaps she'll put off her engagements for a bit when she hears who it is as wants to see her," answered the captain, diving into his capacious pocket. "She'll tell a different story, I dare say, when you take her that bit of pasteboard."

He handed the man a card, or rather let me say a stiff square of thick pasteboard, inscribed with his name, so disguised by the flourishing caprices of the engraver as to be not very easily deciphered by unaccustomed eyes. The card bore Captain Prodder's address as well as his name, and informed his acquaintances that he was part-owner of the *Nancy Jane*, and that all consignments of goods were to be made to him at &c. &c.

The footman took the document between his thumb and finger, and examined it as minutely as if it had been some relic of the middle ages. A new light dawned upon him as he deciphered the information about the *Nancy Jane*, and he looked at the captain for the first time with some approach to human interest in his countenance.

"Is it cigars you want to dispose hof?" he asked, "or bandannas? If it's cigars, you might come round to our 'all, and show us the harticle."

"Cigars!" roared Samuel Prodder. "Do you take me for a smuggler, you——?" Here followed one of those hearty seafaring epithets with which polite Mr. Chucks was apt to finish his speeches. "I'm your missus's own uncle; leastways, I – I knew her mother when she was a little gal," he added, in considerable confusion; for he remembered how far away his sea-captainship thrust him from Mrs. Mellish and her well-born husband; "so just take her my card, and look sharp about it, will you?"

"We've a dinner-party," the footman said, coldly, "and I don't know if the ladies have returned to the drawing-room; but if you're anyways related to missis – I'll go and see."

The man strolled leisurely away, leaving poor Samuel biting his nails in mute vexation at having let slip that ugly fact of her relationship.

"That swab in the same cut coat as Lord Nelson wore aboard the *Victory*, will look down upon her now he knows she's niece to a old sea-captain that carries dry goods on commission, and can't keep his tongue between his teeth," he thought.

The footman came back while Samuel Prodder was upbraiding himself for his folly, and informed him that Mrs. Mellish was not to be found in the house.

"Who's that playin' upon the pianer, then?" asked Mr. Prodder, with sceptical bluntness.

"Oh, that's the clugyman's wife," answered the man, contemptuously; "a *ciddyvong*[1] guvness, I should think, for she plays too well for a real lady. Missus don't play – leastways only pawlkers, and that sort of think. Good night."

He closed the two half-glass doors upon Captain Prodder without further ceremony, and shut Samuel out of his niece's house.

"To think that I played hopscotch and swopped marbles for hard-bake with this gal's mother," thought the captain, "and that her servant turns up his nose at me and shuts the door in my face!"

---

1   *Ci-devant* (former), pronounced with English accent.

It was in sorrow rather than in anger that the disappointed sailor thought this. He had scarcely hoped for anything better. It was only natural that those about his niece should flout at and contemptuously treat him. Let him get to *her* – let him come only for a moment face to face with Eliza's child, and he did not fear the issue.

"I'll walk through the Park," he said to the man who had driven him from Doncaster; "it's a nice evenin', and there's pleasant walks under the trees to win'ard. You can drive back into the high road, and wait for me agen that 'ere turnstile I took notice of as we come along."

The driver nodded, smacked his whip, and drove his elderly gray pony towards the Park-gates. Captain Samuel Prodder went, slowly and deliberately enough, – the way that it was appointed for him to go. The Park was a strange territory to him; but while driving past the outer boundaries he had looked admiringly at chance openings in the wood, revealing grassy amphitheatres enriched by spreading oaks, whose branches made a shadowy tracery upon the sunlit turf. He had looked with a seaman's wonder at the inland beauties of the quiet domain, and had pondered whether it might not be a pleasant thing for an old sailor to end his days amid such monotonous woodland tranquillity, far away from the sound of wreck and tempest, and the mighty voices of the dreadful deep; and, in his disappointment at not seeing Aurora, it was some consolation to the captain to walk across the dewy grass in the evening shadows in the direction where, with a sailor's unerring topographical instinct, he knew the turnstile must be situated.

Perhaps he had some hope of meeting his niece in the pathway across the Park. The man had told him that she was out. She could not be far away, as there was a dinner-party at the house; and she was scarcely likely to leave her guests. She was wandering about the Park, most likely, with some of them.

The shadows of the trees grew darker upon the grass as Captain Prodder drew nearer to the wood; but it was that sweet summer-time in which there is scarcely one positively dark hour amongst the twenty-four; and though the village-clock chimed the half-hour after nine as the sailor entered the wood, he was able to distinguish the outlines of two figures advancing towards him from the other end of the long arcade, that led in a slanting direction to the turnstile.

The figures were those of a man and woman; the woman wearing some light-coloured dress, which shimmered in the dusk; the man leaning on a stick, and obviously very lame.

"Is it my niece and one of her visitors?" thought the captain; "maybe it is. I'll lay by to port of 'em, and let 'em pass me."

Samuel Prodder stepped aside under the shadow of the trees to the left of the grassy avenue through which the two figures were approaching, and waited patiently until they drew near enough for him to distinguish the woman's face. The woman was Mrs. Mellish, and she was walking on the left of the man, and was therefore nearest to the captain. Her head was turned away from her companion, as if in utter scorn and defiance of him, although she was talking to him at that moment. Her face, proud, pale, and disdainful, was visible to the seaman in the chill, shadowy light of the newly-risen moon. A low line of crimson behind the black trunks of a distant group of trees marked where the sun had left its last track, in a vivid streak that looked like blood.

Captain Prodder gazed in loving wonder at the beautiful face turned towards him. He saw the dark eyes, with their sombre depth, dark in anger and scorn, and the luminous shimmer of the jewels that shone through the black veil upon her haughty head. He saw her, and his heart grew chill at the sight of her pale beauty in the mysterious moonlight.

"It might be my sister's ghost," he thought, "coming upon me in this quiet place; it's a'most difficult to believe as it's flesh and blood."

He would have advanced, perhaps, and addressed his niece, had he not been held back by the words which she was speaking as she passed him – words that jarred painfully upon his heart, telling, as they did, of anger and bitterness, discord and misery.

"Yes, hate you!" she said in a clear voice, which seemed to vibrate sharply in the dusk,—— "hate you! hate you! hate you!" She repeated the hard phrase, as if there were some pleasure and delight in uttering it, which in her ungovernable anger she could not deny herself. "What other words do you expect from me?" she cried, with a low mocking laugh, which had a tone of deeper misery, and more utter hopelessness than any outbreak of womanly weeping. "Would you have me love you? or respect you? or tolerate you?" Her voice rose with each rapid question, merging into an hysterical sob, but never melting into tears. "Would you have me tell you anything else than what I tell you to-night? I hate and abhor you! I look upon you as the primary cause of every sorrow I have ever known, of every tear I have ever shed, of every humiliation I have endured; every sleepless night, every weary day, every despairing hour, I have ever passed. More than this, – yes, a thousand, thousand times more, – I look upon *you* as the first cause of my father's wretchedness. Yes, even before my own mad folly in believing in you, and thinking you – what? – Claude Melnotte, perhaps!¹ – a curse upon the man who wrote the play, and the player who acted in it, if it helped to make me what I was when I met you! I say again, I hate you! your presence poisons my home, your abhorred shadow haunts my sleep – no, not my sleep, for how should I ever sleep knowing that you are near?"

Mr. Conyers, being apparently weary of walking, leaned against the trunk of a tree to listen to the end of this outbreak, looking insolent defiance at the speaker. But Aurora's passion had reached that point in which all consciousness of external things passes away in the complete egoism of anger and hate. She did not see his superciliously indifferent look; her dilated eyes stared straight before her into the dark recess from which Captain Prodder watched his sister's only child. Her restless hands rent the fragile border of her shawl in the strong agony of her passion. Have you ever seen this kind of woman in a passion? Impulsive, nervous, sensitive, sanguine; with such a one passion is a madness – brief, thank Heaven! and expending itself in sharply cruel words, and convulsive rendings of lace and ribbon, or coroner's juries might have to sit even oftener than they do. It is fortunate for mankind that speaking daggers is often quite as great a satisfaction to us as using them, and that we can threaten very cruel things without meaning to carry them out. Like the little children who say, "Won't I just tell your mother!" and the terrible editors who write, "Won't I

---

1 Claude Melnotte, a self-educated gardener's son, is the hero of Bulwer Lytton's *The Lady of Lyons* (1838). Claude marries the rich Pauline Deschappelles when disguised as a foreign prince, but he earns her love through the courageous service and meteoric rise in the army which prove him a princely (though commonly born) man.

give you a castigation in the Market-Deeping 'Spirit of the Times,' or the 'Walton-on-the-Naze Athenæum!'"[1]

"If you are going to give us much more of this sort of thing," said Mr. Conyers, with aggravating stolidity, "perhaps you won't object to my lighting a cigar?"

Aurora took no notice of his quiet insolence; but Captain Prodder, involuntarily clenching his fist, bounded a step forward in his retreat, and shook the leaves of the underwood about his legs.

"What's that?" exclaimed the trainer.

"My dog, perhaps," answered Aurora; "he's about here with me."

"Curse the purblind cur!" muttered Mr. Conyers, with an unlighted cigar in his mouth. He struck a lucifer-match against the back of a tree, and the vivid sulphurous light shone full upon his handsome face.

"A rascal!" thought Captain Prodder; – "a good-looking, heartless scoundrel! What's this between my niece and him? He isn't her husband, surely, for he don't look like a gentleman. But if he aint her husband, who is he?"

The sailor scratched his head in his bewilderment. His senses had been almost stupefied by Aurora's passionate talk, and he had only a confused feeling that there was trouble and wretchedness of some kind or other around and about his niece.

"If I thought he'd done anything to injure her," he muttered, "I'd pound him into such a jelly that his friends would never know his handsome face again as long as there was life in his carcass."

Mr. Conyers threw away the burning match, and puffed at his newly-lighted cigar. He did not trouble himself to take it from his lips as he addressed Aurora, but spoke between his teeth, and smoked in the pauses of his discourse.

"Perhaps, if you've – calmed yourself down – a bit," he said, "you'll be so good as – to come to business. What do you want me to do?"

"You know as well as I do," answered Aurora.

"You want me to leave this place?"

---

1   A comic threat. These tiny towns do exist (Market Deeping is in Lincolnshire and Walton-on-the-Naze is in Essex), but the editorial views of their (imaginary) literary journals would carry little weight!

"Yes; for ever."

"And to take what you give me – and be satisfied."

"Yes."

"What if I refuse?"

She turned sharply upon him as he asked this question, and looked at him for a few moments in silence.

"What if I refuse?" he repeated, still smoking.

"Look to yourself!" she cried, between her set teeth; "that's all. Look to yourself!"

"What! you'd kill me, I suppose?"

"No," answered Aurora; "but I'd tell all; and get the release which I ought to have sought for two years ago."[1]

"Oh, ah, to be sure!" said Mr. Conyers; "a pleasant thing for Mr. Mellish, and our poor papa, and a nice bit of gossip for the newspapers! I've a good mind to put you to the test, and see if you've pluck enough to do it, my lady."

She stamped her foot upon the turf, and tore the lace in her hands, throwing the fragments away from her; but she did not answer him.

"You'd like to stab me, or shoot me, or strangle me, as I stand here; wouldn't you, now?" asked the trainer, mockingly.

"Yes," cried Aurora, "I would!" She flung her head back with a gesture of disdain as she spoke.

"Why do I waste my time in talking to you?" she said. "My worst words can inflict no wound upon such a nature as yours. My scorn is no more painful to you than it would be to any of the loathsome creatures that creep about the margin of yonder pool."

The trainer took his cigar from his mouth, and struck the ashes away with his little finger.

"No," he said with a contemptuous laugh; "I'm not very thin-skinned; and I'm pretty well used to this sort of thing, into the bargain. But suppose, as I remarked just now, we drop this style of

---

1   An anachronism. This discussion takes place in July 1859; the Divorce Court did not open until January 1858, so Aurora could not have sought any release from her marriage "two years ago" (i.e. in the summer of 1857). Once the court did open, cases were reported in the *Times* and other newspapers, revealing intimate details of matrimonial conflict, infidelity, cruelty, etc. This dreaded publicity was calculated as a major deterrent to divorce.

conversation, and come to business. We don't seem to be getting on very fast this way."

At this juncture, Captain Prodder, who, in his extreme desire to strangle his niece's companion, had advanced very close upon the two speakers, knocked off his hat against the lower branches of the tree which sheltered him.

There was no mistake this time about the rustling of the leaves. The trainer started, and limped towards Captain Prodder's hiding-place.

"There's some one listening to us," he said. "I'm sure of it this time; – that fellow Hargraves, perhaps. I fancy he's a sneak."

Mr. Conyers supported himself against the very tree behind which the sailor stood, and beat amongst the undergrowth with his stick, but did not succeed in encountering the legs of the listener.

"If that soft-headed fool *is* playing the spy upon me," cried the trainer, savagely, "he'd better not let me catch him, for I'll make him remember it, if I do."

"Don't I tell you that my dog followed me here?" exclaimed Aurora contemptuously.

A low rustling of the grass on the other side of the avenue, and at some distance from the seaman's place of concealment, was heard as Mrs. Mellish spoke.

"*That's* your dog, if you like," said the trainer; "the other was a man. Come on a little way further, and let's make a finish of this business; it's past ten o'clock."

Mr. Conyers was right. The church clock had struck ten five minutes before, but the solemn chimes had fallen unheeded upon Aurora's ear, lost amid the angry voices raging in her breast. She started as she looked around her at the summer darkness in the woods, and the flaming yellow moon, which brooded low upon the earth, and shed no light upon the mysterious pathways and the water-pools in the wood.

The trainer limped away, Aurora walking by his side, yet holding herself as far aloof from him as the grassy pathway would allow. They were out of hearing, and almost out of sight, before the sea-captain could emerge from a state of utter stupefaction so far as to be able to look at the business in its right bearings.

"I ought to ha' knocked him down," he muttered at last, "whether he's her husband or whether he isn't. I ought to have knocked him down, and I would have done it, too," added the captain resolutely, "if it hadn't been that my niece seemed to have a good fiery spirit of her own, and to be able to fire a jolly good broadside in the way of hard words. I'll find my skull-thatcher if I can," said Captain Prodder, groping for his hat amongst the brambles, and the long grass, "and then I'll just run up to the turnstile and tell my mate to lay at anchor a bit longer with the horse and shay.[1] He'll be wonderin' what I'm up to; but I won't go back just yet, I'll keep in the way of my niece and that swab with the game leg."

The captain found his hat, and walked down to the turnstile, where he found the young man from the Reindeer fast asleep, with the reins loose in his hands, and his head upon his knees. The horse, with his head in an empty nose-bag, seemed as fast asleep as the driver.

The young man woke at the sound of the turnstile creaking upon its axis, and the step of the sailor in the road.

"I aint going to get aboard just yet," said Captain Prodder; "I'll take another turn in the wood as the evenin's so pleasant. I come to tell you I wouldn't keep you much longer, for I thought you'd think I was dead."

"I did a'most," answered the charioteer candidly. "My word! – aint you been a time!"

"I met Mr. and Mrs. Mellish in the wood," said the captain, "and I stopped to have a look at 'em. She's a bit of a spitfire, aint she?" asked Samuel, with affected carelessness.

The young man from the Reindeer shook his head dubiously.

"I doan't know about that," he said; "she's a rare favourite hereabouts, with poor folks and gentry too. They do say as she horsewhipped a poor fond chap as they'd got in the stables, for ill-usin' her dog; and serve him right too," added the young man decisively. "Them Softies is allus vicious."

Captain Prodder pondered rather doubtfully upon this piece of information. He was not particularly elated by the image of his sister's

---

1 Dialect: Chaise.

child laying a horsewhip upon the shoulders of her half-witted servant. This trifling incident didn't exactly harmonize with his idea of the beautiful young heiress, playing upon all manner of instruments, and speaking half a dozen languages.

"Yes," repeated the driver, "they *do* say as she gave t' fondy a good whopping; and damme if I don't admire her for it."

"Ay, ay!" answered Captain Prodder thoughtfully. "Mr. Mellish walks lame, don't he?" he asked, after a pause.

"Lame!" cried the driver; "Lord bless your heart! not a bit of it. John Mellish is as fine a young man as you'll meet in this Riding. Ay, and finer too. I ought to know. I've seen him walk into our house often enough, in the race week."

The captain's heart sank strangely at this information. The man with whom he had heard his niece quarrelling was not her husband, then. The squabble had seemed natural enough to the uninitiated sailor while he looked at it in a matrimonial light; but seen from another aspect it struck sudden terror to his sturdy heart, and blanched the ruddy hues in his brown face. "Who was he, then?" he thought; "who was it as my niece was talking to – after dark, – alone, – a mile off her own home – eh?"

Before he could seek for a solution to the unuttered question which agitated and alarmed him, the report of a pistol rang sharply through the wood, and found an echo under a distant hill.

The horse pricked up his ears, and jibbed a few paces; the driver gave a low whistle.

"I thought so," he said. "Poachers! This side of the wood's chock full of game; and though Squire Mellish is allus threatenin' to prosecute 'em, folks know pretty well as he'll never do it."

The broad-shouldered, strong-limbed sailor leaned against the turnstile, trembling in every limb.

What was that which his niece said a quarter of an hour before, when the man had asked her whether she would like to shoot him?

"Leave your horse," he said, in a gasping voice; "tie him to the stile, and come with me. If – if – it's poachers, we'll – we'll catch 'em."

The young man looped the reins across the turnstile. He had no very great terror of any inclination for flight latent in the gray horse from the Reindeer. The two men ran in the wood; the captain running in the direction in which his sharp ears told him the shot had been fired.

The moon was slowly rising in the tranquil heavens, but there was very little light yet in the wood.

The captain stopped near a rustic summer-house falling into decay, and half buried amidst the tangled foliage that clustered about the mouldering thatch and the dilapidated woodwork.

"It was hereabout the shot was fired," muttered the captain; "about a hundred yards due nor'ard of the stile. I could take my oath as it weren't far from this spot I'm standin' on."

He looked about him in the dim light. He could see no one; but an army might have hidden amongst the trees that encircled the open patch of turf on which the summer-house had been built. He listened; with his hat off, and his big hand pressed tightly on his heart, as if to still its tumultuous beating. He listened, as eagerly as he had often listened, far out on a glassy sea, for the first faint breath of a rising wind; but he could hear nothing except the occasional croaking of the frogs in the pond near the summer-house.

"I could have sworn it was about here the shot was fired," he repeated. "God grant as it *was* poachers, after all! but it's given me a turn that's made me feel like some cockney lubber aboard a steamer betwixt Bristol and Cork. Lord, what a blessed old fool I am!" muttered the captain, after walking slowly round the summer-house to convince himself that there was no one hidden in it. "One 'ud think I'd never heerd the sound of a ha'p'orth of powder before to-night."

He put on his hat, and walked a few paces forward, still looking about cautiously, and still listening; but much easier in his mind than when first he had re-entered the wood.

He stopped suddenly, arrested by a sound which has of itself, without any reference to its power of association, a mysterious and chilling influence upon the human heart. This sound was the howling of a dog, – the prolonged, monotonous howling of a dog. A cold sweat broke out upon the sailor's forehead. That sound, always one of terror to his superstitious nature, was doubly terrible to-night.

"It means death!" he muttered, with a groan. "No dog ever howled like that except for death."

He turned back, and looked about him. The moonlight glimmered faintly upon the broad patch of stagnant water near the summer-house, and upon its brink the captain saw two figures, black against the summer atmosphere: a prostrate figure, lying close to the edge of the water; and a large dog, with his head uplifted to the sky, howling piteously.

It was the bounden duty of poor John Mellish, in his capacity of host, to sit at the head of his table, pass the claret-jug, and listen to Colonel Maddison's stories of the pig-sticking and the tiger-hunting, as long as the Indian officer chose to talk for the amusement of his friend and his son-in-law. It was perhaps lucky that patient Mr. Lofthouse was well up in all the stories, and knew exactly which departments of each narrative were to be laughed at, and which were to be listened to with silent and awe-stricken attention; for John Mellish made a very bad audience upon this occasion. He pushed the filberts towards the colonel at the very moment when "the tigress was crouching for a spring, upon the rising ground exactly above us, sir, and when, by Jove! Charley Maddison felt himself at pretty close quarters with the enemy, sir, and never thought to stretch his legs under this mahogany, or any other man's, sir;" and he spoiled the officer's best joke by asking him for the claret in the middle of it.

The tigers and the pigs were confusion and weariness of spirit to Mr. Mellish. He was yearning for the moment when, with any show of decency, he might make for the drawing-room, and find out what Aurora was doing in the still summer twilight. When the door was opened and fresh wine brought in, he heard the rattling of the keys under Mrs. Lofthouse's manipulation, and rejoiced to think that his wife was seated quietly, perhaps, listening to those sonatas in C flat, which the rector's wife delighted to interpret.

The lamps were brought in before Colonel Maddison's stories were finished; and when John's butler came to ask if the gentleman would like coffee, the worthy Indian officer said, "Yes, by all means, and a cheroot with it. No smoking in the drawing-room, eh, Mellish? Petticoat government and window-curtains, I dare say. Clara doesn't like my smoke at the Rectory, and poor Lofthouse writes his sermons in the summer-house; for he can't write without a weed, you know, and a volume of Tillotson, or some of these fellows, to prig from[1] – eh, George?" said the facetious gentleman, digging his son-in-law in the ribs with his fat old fingers, and knocking over two or three wine-glasses in his ponderous jocosity.

How dreary it all seemed to John Mellish to-night! He wondered how people felt who had no social mystery brooding upon their hearth; no domestic skeleton cowering in their homely cupboard. He looked at the rector's placid face with a pang of envy. There was no secret kept from *him*. There was no perpetual struggle rending *his* heart; no dreadful doubts and fears that would not be quite lulled to rest; no vague terror incessant and unreasoning; no mute argument for ever going forward, with plaintiff's counsel and defendant's counsel continually pleading the same cause, and arriving at the same result. Heaven take pity upon those who have to suffer such silent misery, such secret despair! We look at our neighbours' smiling faces, and say, in bitterness of spirit, that A is a lucky fellow, and that B can't be as much in debt as his friends say he is; that C and his pretty wife are the happiest couple we know; and to-morrow B is in the 'Gazette,'[2] and C is weeping over a dishonoured home, and a group of motherless children, who wonder what mamma has done that papa should be so sorry. The battles are very quiet, but they are for ever being fought. We keep the fox hidden under our cloak, but the teeth of the animal are none the less sharp, nor the pain less terrible to bear; a little more terrible, perhaps, for being endured silently. John Mellish gave a long sigh of relief when the Indian officer finished his third cheroot, and pronounced himself ready to join the ladies. The lamps in the drawing-room were lighted, and the curtains drawn before the open windows, when the three gentlemen entered. Mrs. Lofthouse was asleep upon one of the sofas, with a Book of Beauty[3] lying open at her feet, and Mrs. Powell, pale and sleepless, – sleepless as trouble and sorrow, as jealousy and hate, as anything that is ravenous and unappeasable, – sat

---

1   John Tillotson (1630-94), Archbishop of Canterbury, famous for his sermons, which went through numerous editions and translations. To "prig" means to plunder or steal.

2   See 94, n.2.

3   See 114, n.2.

at her embroidery, working laborious monstrosities upon delicate cambric muslin.

The colonel dropped heavily into a luxurious easy-chair, and quietly abandoned himself to repose. Mr. Lofthouse awoke his wife, and consulted her about the propriety of ordering the carriage. John Mellish looked eagerly round the room. To him it was empty. The rector and his wife, the Indian officer, and the ensign's widow, were only so many "phosphorescent spectralities," "phantasm captains;"[1] in short, they were not Aurora.

"Where's Lolly?" he asked, looking from Mrs. Lofthouse to Mrs. Powell; "where's my wife?"

"I really do not know," answered Mrs. Powell, with icy deliberation. "I've not been watching Mrs. Mellish."

The poisoned darts glanced away from John's preoccupied breast. There was no room in his wounded heart for such a petty sting as this.

"Where's my wife?" he cried passionately; "you *must* know where she is. She's not here. Is she up-stairs? Is she out of doors?"

"To the best of my belief," replied the ensign's widow, with more than usual precision, "Mrs. Mellish is in some part of the grounds; she has been out of doors ever since we left the dining-room."

The French clock upon the mantelpiece chimed the three-quarters after ten as she finished speaking: as if to give emphasis to her words and to remind Mr. Mellish how long his wife had been absent. He bit his lip fiercely, and strode towards one of the windows. He was going to look for his wife; but he stopped as he flung aside the window-curtain, arrested by Mrs. Powell's uplifted hand.

"Hark!" she said, "there is something the matter, I fear. Did you hear that violent ringing at the hall-door?"

Mr. Mellish let fall the curtain, and re-entered the room.

"It's Aurora, no doubt," he said; "they've shut her out again, I suppose. I beg, Mrs. Powell, that you will prevent this in future. Really,

1 This imagery is drawn from phantasmagoria entertainments, popular in the early 19th century, in which audiences saw images of ghosts, spectres, skeletons, etc. apparently hanging in mid-air (this effect was produced by images projected from a magic lantern onto a semi-transparent screen). "Phantasm Captains" is a quotation from Thomas Carlyle's *Latter-day Pamphlets*, No. 1: "The Present Time" (1850).

ma'am, it is hard that my wife should be shut out of her own house."

He might have said much more, but he stopped, pale and breathless, at the sound of a hubbub in the hall, and rushed to the room-door. He opened it and looked out, with Mrs. Powell and Mr. and Mrs. Lofthouse crowding behind him, and looking over his shoulder.

Half a dozen servants were clustered round a roughly-dressed, sea-faring-looking man, who, with his hat off and his disordered hair falling about his white face, was telling in broken sentences, scarcely intelligible for the speaker's agitation, that a murder had been done in the wood.

CHAPTER XXV.

THE DEED THAT HAD BEEN DONE IN THE WOOD.

THE bare-headed seafaring man who stood in the centre of the hall was Captain Samuel Prodder. The scared faces of the servants gathered round him told more plainly than his own words, which came hoarsely from his parched white lips, the nature of the tidings that he brought.

John Mellish strode across the hall, with an awful calmness on his white face; and parting the hustled group of servants with his strong arms, as a mighty wind rends asunder the storm-beaten waters, he placed himself face to face with Captain Prodder.

"Who are you?" he asked sternly: "and what has brought you here?"

The Indian officer had been aroused by the clamour, and had emerged, red and bristling with self-importance, to take his part in the business in hand.

There are some pies in the making of which everybody yearns to have a finger. It is a great privilege, after some social convulsion has taken place, to be able to say, "I was there at the time the scene occurred, sir;" or, "I was standing as close to him when the blow was struck, ma'am, as I am to you at this moment." People are apt to take pride out of strange things. An elderly gentleman at Doncaster, showing me his comfortably-furnished apartments, informed me, with evident satisfaction, that Mr. William Palmer[1] had lodged in those very rooms.

Colonel Maddison pushed aside his daughter and her husband, and struggled out into the hall.

"Come, my man," he said, echoing John's interrogatory, "let us hear what has brought you here at such a remarkably unseasonable hour."

The sailor gave no direct answer to the question. He pointed with his thumb across his shoulder towards that dismal spot in the lonely wood, which was as present to his mental vision now as it had been to his bodily eyes a quarter of an hour before.

---

1 See 305, n.2.

"A man!" he gasped; "a man – lyin' close agen' the water's edge, – shot through the heart!"

"Dead?" asked some one, in an awful tone. The voices and the questions came from whom they would, in the awe-stricken terror of those first moments of overwhelming horror and surprise. No one knew who spoke except the speakers; perhaps even they were scarcely aware that they had spoken.

"Dead?" asked one of those eager listeners.

"Stone dead."

"A man – shot dead in the wood!" cried John Mellish; "what man?"

"I beg your pardon, sir," said the grave old butler, laying his hand gently upon his master's shoulder: "I think, from what this person says, that the man who has been shot is – the new trainer, Mr. – Mr.——"

"Conyers!" exclaimed John. "Conyers! who – who should shoot him?" The question was asked in a hoarse whisper. It was impossible for the speaker's face to grow whiter than it had been, from the moment in which he had opened the drawing-room door, and looked out into the hall; but some terrible change not to be translated into words came over it at the mention of the trainer's name.

He stood motionless and silent, pushing his hair from his forehead, and staring wildly about him.

The grave butler laid his warning hand for a second time upon his master's shoulder.

"Sir – Mr. Mellish," he said, eager to arouse the young man from the dull, stupid quiet into which he had fallen, – "excuse me, sir; but if my mistress should come in suddenly, and hear of this, she might be upset, perhaps. Wouldn't it be better to——"

"Yes, yes!" cried John Mellish, lifting his head suddenly, as if aroused into immediate action by the mere suggestion of his wife's name, – "yes! clear out of the hall, every one of you," he said, addressing the eager group of pale-faced servants. "And you, sir," he added to Captain Prodder, "come with me."

He walked towards the dining-room door. The sailor followed him, still bare-headed, still with a semi-bewildered expression in his dusky face.

"It aint the first time I've seen a man shot," he thought; "but it's the first time I've felt like this."

Before Mr. Mellish could reach the dining-room, before the servants could disperse and return to their proper quarters, one of the half-glass doors, which had been left ajar, was pushed open by the light touch of a woman's hand, and Aurora Mellish entered the hall.

"Ah, ha!" thought the ensign's widow, who looked on at the scene, snugly sheltered by Mr. and Mrs. Lofthouse; "my lady is caught a second time in her evening rambles. What will he say to her goings-on to-night, I wonder?"

Aurora's manner presented a singular contrast to the terror and agitation of the assembly in the hall. A vivid crimson flush glowed in her cheeks and lit up her shining eyes. She carried her head high, in that queenly defiance which was her peculiar grace. She walked with a light step; she moved with easy, careless gestures. It seemed as if some burden which she had long carried had been suddenly removed from her. But at sight of the crowd in the hall she drew back with a look of alarm.

"What has happened, John?" she cried; "what is wrong?"

He lifted his hand with a warning gesture, – a gesture that plainly said: Whatever trouble or sorrow there may be, let her be spared the knowledge of it; let her be sheltered from the pain.

"Yes, my darling," he answered quietly, taking her hand and leading her into the drawing-room; "there is something wrong. An accident has happened – in the wood yonder; but it concerns no one whom you care for. Go, dear; I will tell you all, by-and-by. Mrs. Lofthouse, you will take care of my wife. Lofthouse, come with me. Allow me to shut the door, Mrs. Powell, if you please," he added to the ensign's widow, who did not seem inclined to leave her post upon the threshold of the drawing-room. "Any curiosity which you may have about the business shall be satisfied in due time. For the present, you will oblige me by remaining with my wife and Mrs. Lofthouse."

He paused, with his hand upon the drawing-room door, and looked at Aurora.

She was standing with her shawl upon her arm, watching her husband; and she advanced eagerly to him as she met his glance.

"John," she exclaimed, "for mercy's sake, tell me the truth! *What* is this accident?"

He was silent for a moment, gazing at her eager face, – that face whose exquisite mobility expressed every thought; then, looking at her with a strange solemnity, he said gravely, "You were in the wood just now, Aurora?"

"I was," she answered; "I have only just left the grounds. A man passed me, running violently, about a quarter of an hour ago. I thought he was a poacher. Was it to him the accident happened?"

"No. There was a shot fired in the wood some time since. Did you hear it?"

"I did," replied Mrs. Mellish, looking at him with sudden terror and surprise. "I knew there were often poachers about near the road, and I was not alarmed by it. Was there anything wrong in that shot? Was any one hurt?"

Her eyes were fixed upon his face, dilated with that look of wondering terror.

"Yes; a – a man was hurt."

Aurora looked at him in silence, – looked at him with a stony face, whose only expression was an utter bewilderment. Every other feeling seemed blotted away in that one sense of wonder.

John Mellish led her to a chair near Mrs. Lofthouse, who had been seated, with Mrs. Powell, at the other end of the room, close to the piano, and too far from the door to overhear the conversation which had just taken place between John and his wife. People do not talk very loudly in moments of intense agitation. They are liable to be deprived of some portion of their vocal power in the fearful crisis of terror or despair. A numbness seizes the organ of speech; a partial paralysis disables the ready tongue; the trembling lips refuse to do their duty. The soft pedal of the human instrument is down, and the tones are feeble and muffled, wandering into weak minor shrillness, or sinking to husky basses, beyond the ordinary compass of the speaker's voice. The stentorian accents in which Claude Melnotte bids adieu to Mademoiselle Deschappelle mingle very effectively with the brazen clamour of the Marseillaise Hymn;[1] the sonorous tones in

---

1   At the end of Act IV of *The Lady of Lyons* (see Chapter XXIV), the commoner and hero Claude Melnotte leaves the rich Pauline Deschappelles (whom he has married under false pretences) to join the army and prove himself "a better man than a prince." The play's setting is Lyons, 1795; the "Marseillaise" the national song of the French Republic, composed in 1792.

which Mistress Julia appeals to her Hunchback guardian are pretty sure to bring down the approving thunder of the eighteenpenny gallery; but I doubt if the noisy energy of stage-grief is true to nature, however wise in art. I'm afraid that an actor who would play Claude Melnotte with a pre-Raphaelite fidelity to nature would be an insufferable bore, and utterly inaudible beyond the third row in the pit.[1] The artist must draw his own line between nature and art, and map out the extent of his own territory. If he finds that cream-coloured marble is more artistically beautiful than a rigid presentment of actual flesh and blood, let him stain his marble of that delicate hue until the end of time. If he can represent five acts of agony and despair without once turning his back to his audience or sitting down, let him do it. If he is conscientiously true to his *art*, let him choose for himself how true he shall be to nature.

John Mellish took his wife's hand in his own, and grasped it with a convulsive pressure that almost crushed the delicate fingers.

"Stay here, my dear, till I come back to you," he said. "Now, Lofthouse!"

Mr. Lofthouse followed his friend into the hall, where Colonel Maddison had been making the best use of his time by questioning the merchant-captain.

"Come, gentlemen," said John, leading the way to the dining-room; "come, colonel, and you too, Lofthouse; and you, sir," he added to the sailor, "step this way."

The *débris* of the dessert still covered the table, but the men did not advance far into the room. John stood aside as the others went in, and entering the last, closed the door behind him, and stood with his back against it.

"Now," he said, turning sharply upon Samuel Prodder, "what is this business?"

---

1   In James Sheridan Knowles' *The Hunchback* (1832), Mistress Julia gets carried away by London society, abandons her fiancé Sir Thomas Clifford, and gets engaged to the Earl of Rochdale. As the marriage approaches, her love for Clifford revives, and she pleads with her guardian to break off the engagement with the earl. Because Victorian theatres were large, acting was necessarily stylized, and stage-grief "noisy." As Braddon (who acted herself) observes, realistic acting styles would have been "utterly inaudible." On the Pre-Raphaelite Brotherhood, see Chapter IV.

"I'm afraid it's sooicide – or – or murder," answered the sailor gravely. "I've told this good gentleman all about it."

This good gentleman was Colonel Maddison, who seemed delighted to plunge into the conversation.

"Yes, my dear Mellish," he said eagerly; "our friend, who describes himself as a sailor, and who had come down to see Mrs. Mellish, whose mother he knew when he was a boy, has told me all about this shocking affair. Of course the body must be removed immediately, and the sooner your servants go out with lanterns for that purpose the better. Decision, my dear Mellish, decision and prompt action are indispensable in these sad catastrophes."

"The body removed!" repeated John Mellish; "the man is dead, then."

"Quite dead," answered the sailor; "he was dead when I found him, though it wasn't above seven minutes after the shot was fired. I left a man with him – a young man as drove me from Doncaster – and a dog, – some big dog that watched beside him, – howling awful, and wouldn't leave him."

"Did you – see – the man's face?"

"Yes."

"You are a stranger here," said John Mellish; "it is useless, therefore, to ask you if you know who the man is."

"No, sir," answered the sailor, "I didn't know him; but the young man from the Reindeer——"

"He recognized him?"

"Yes; he said he'd seen the man in Doncaster only the night before; and that he was your – trainer, I think he called him."

"Yes, yes."

"A lame chap."

"Come, gentlemen," said John, turning to his friends, "what are we to do?"

"Send the servants into the wood," replied Colonel Maddison, "and have the body carried——"

"Not here," cried John Mellish, interrupting him, – "not here; it would kill my wife."

"Where did the man live?" asked the colonel.

"In the north lodge. A cottage against the northern gates, which are never used now."

"Then let the body be taken there," answered the Indian soldier; "let one of your people run for the parish constable; and you'd better send for the nearest surgeon immediately, though, from what our friend here says, a hundred of 'em couldn't do any good. It's an awful business! Some poaching fray, I suppose."

"Yes, yes," answered John quickly; "no doubt."

"Was the man disliked in the neighbourhood?" asked Colonel Maddison; "had he made himself in any manner obnoxious?"

"I should scarcely think it likely. He had only been with me about a week."

The servants, who had dispersed at John's command, had not gone very far. They had lingered in corridors and lobbies, ready at a moment's notice to rush out into the hall again, and act their minor parts in the tragedy. They preferred doing anything to returning quietly to their own quarters.

They came out eagerly at Mr. Mellish's summons. He gave his orders briefly, selecting two of the men, and sending the others about their business.

"Bring a couple of lanterns," he said; "and follow us across the Park towards the pond in the wood."

Colonel Maddison, Mr. Lofthouse, Captain Prodder, and John Mellish, left the house together. The moon, still slowly rising in the broad, cloudless heavens, silvered the quiet lawn, and shimmered upon the tree-tops in the distance. The three gentlemen walked at a rapid pace, led by Samuel Prodder, who kept a little way in advance, and followed by a couple of grooms, who carried darkened stable-lanterns.

As they entered the wood, they stopped involuntarily, arrested by that solemn sound which had first drawn the sailor's attention to the dreadful deed that had been done – the howling of the dog. It sounded in the distance like a low, feeble wail: a long monotonous death-cry.

They followed that dismal indication of the spot to which they were to go. They made their way through the shadowy avenue, and emerged upon the silvery patch of turf and fern, where the rotting summer-house stood in its solitary decay. The two figures – the prostrate figure on the brink of the water, and the figure of the dog with uplifted head – still remained exactly as the sailor had left them three-quarters of an hour before. The young man from the Reindeer stood aloof from these two figures, and advanced to meet the newcomers as they drew near.

Colonel Maddison took a lantern from one of the men, and ran forward to the water's edge. The dog rose as he approached, and walked slowly round the prostrate form, sniffing at it, and whining piteously. John Mellish called the animal away.

"This man was in a sitting posture when he was shot," said Colonel Maddison, decisively. "He was sitting upon this bench."

He pointed to a dilapidated rustic seat close to the margin of the stagnant water.

"He was sitting upon this bench," repeated the colonel; "for he's fallen close against it, as you see. Unless I'm very much mistaken, he was shot from behind."

"You don't think he shot himself, then?" asked John Mellish.

"Shot himself!" cried the colonel; "not a bit of it. But we'll soon settle that. If he shot himself, the pistol must be close against him. Here, bring a loose plank from that summer-house, and lay the body upon it," added the Indian officer, speaking to the servants.

Captain Prodder and the two grooms selected the broadest plank they could find. It was moss-grown and rotten, and straggling wreaths of wild clematis were entwined about it; but it served the purpose for which it was wanted. They laid it upon the grass, and lifted the body of James Conyers on to it, with his handsome face – ghastly and horrible in the fixed agony of sudden death – turned upward to the moonlit sky. It was wonderful how mechanically and quietly they went to work, promptly and silently obeying the colonel's orders.

John Mellish and Mr. Lofthouse searched the slippery grass upon the bank, and groped amongst the fringe of fern, without result. There was no weapon to be found anywhere within a considerable radius of the body.

While they were searching in every direction for this missing link in the mystery of the man's death, the parish-constable arrived with the servant who had been sent to summon him.

He had very little to say for himself, except that he supposed it was poachers as had done it; and that he also supposed all particklars would come out at the inquest. He was a simple rural functionary, accustomed to petty dealings with refractory tramps, contumacious poachers, and impounded cattle, and was scarcely master of the situation in any great emergency.

Mr. Prodder and the servants lifted the plank upon which the body lay, and struck into the long avenue leading northward, walking a little ahead of the three gentlemen and the constable. The young man from the Reindeer returned to look after his horse, and to drive round to the north lodge, where he was to meet Mr. Prodder. All had been done so quietly that the knowledge of the catastrophe had not passed beyond the domains of Mellish Park. In the summer evening stillness James Conyers was carried back to the chamber from whose narrow window he had looked out upon the beautiful world, weary of its beauty, only a few hours before.

The purposeless life was suddenly closed. The careless wanderer's journey had come to an unthought-of end. What a melancholy record, what a meaningless and unfinished page! Nature, blindly bountiful to the children whom she has yet to know, had bestowed her richest gifts upon this man. She had created a splendid image, and had chosen a soul at random, ignorantly enshrining it in her most perfectly fashioned clay. Of all who read the story of this man's death in the following Sunday's newspapers, there was not one who shed a tear for him; there was not one who could say, "That man once stepped out of his way to do me a kindness; and may the Lord have mercy upon his soul!"

Shall I be sentimental, then, because he is dead, and regret that he was not spared a little longer, and allowed a day of grace in which he might repent? Had he lived for ever, I do not think he would have lived long enough to become that which it was not in his nature to be. May God, in His infinite compassion, have pity upon the souls which He has Himself created; and where He has withheld the light, may He excuse the darkness! The phrenologists who examined the head of William Palmer[1] declared that he was so utterly deficient in

---

1   On phrenology, see 62, n.1; on Palmer see 305, n.2.

moral perception, so entirely devoid of conscientious restraint, that he could not help being what he was. Heaven keep us from too much credence in that horrible fatalism! Is a man's destiny here and hereafter to depend upon bulbous projections scarcely perceptible to uneducated fingers, and good and evil propensities which can be measured by the compass or weighed in the scale?

The dismal *cortège* slowly made its way under the silver moonlight, the trembling leaves making a murmuring music in the faint summer air, the pale glowworms shining here and there amid the tangled verdure. The bearers of the dead walked with a slow but steady tramp in advance of the rest. All walked in silence. What should they say? In the presence of death's awful mystery, life made a pause. There was a brief interval in the hard business of existence; a hushed and solemn break in the working of life's machinery.

"There'll be an inquest," thought Mr. Prodder, "and I shall have to give evidence. I wonder what questions they'll ask me?"

He did not think this once, but perpetually; dwelling with a half-stupid persistence upon the thought of that inquisition which must most infallibly be made, and those questions that might be asked. The honest sailor's simple mind was cast astray in the utter bewilderment of this night's mysterious horror. The story of life was changed. He had come to play his humble part in some sweet domestic drama of love and confidence, and he found himself involved in a tragedy; a horrible mystery of hatred, secrecy, and murder; a dreadful maze, from whose obscurity he saw no hope of issue.

A beacon-light glimmered in the lower window of the cottage by the north gates, – a feeble ray, that glittered like a gem from out a bower of honeysuckle and clematis. The little garden-gate was closed, but it only fastened with a latch.

The bearers of the body paused before entering the garden, and the constable stepped aside to speak to Mr. Mellish.

"Is there anybody lives in the cottage?" he asked.

"Yes," answered John; "the trainer employed an old hanger-on of my own, – a half-witted fellow called Hargraves."

"It's him as burns the light in there, most likely, then," said the constable. "I'll go in and speak to him first. Do you wait here till I come out again," he added, turning to the men who carried the body.

The lodge-door was on the latch. The constable opened it softly, and went in. A rushlight was burning upon the table, the candlestick placed in a basin of water. A bottle half filled with brandy, and a tumbler, stood near the light; but the room was empty. The constable took his shoes off, and crept up the little staircase. The upper floor of the lodge consisted of two rooms, – one, sufficiently large and comfortable, looking towards the stable-gates; the other, smaller and darker, looked out upon a patch of kitchen-garden and on the fence which separated Mr. Mellish's estate from the high road. The larger chamber was empty; but the door of the smaller was ajar; and the constable, pausing to listen at that half-open door, heard the regular breathing of a heavy sleeper.

He knocked sharply upon the panel.

"Who's there?" asked the person within, starting up from a truckle bedstead. "Is't thou, Muster Conyers?"

"No," answered the constable. "It's me, William Dork, of Little Meslingham. Come down-stairs; I want to speak to you."

"Is there aught wrong?"

"Yes."

"Poachers?"

"That's as may be," answered Mr. Dork. "Come down-stairs, will you?"

Mr. Hargraves muttered something to the effect that he would make his appearance as soon as he could find sundry portions of his rather fragmentary toilet. The constable looked into the room, and watched the "Softy" groping for his garments in the moonlight. Three minutes afterwards Stephen Hargraves slowly shambled down the angular wooden stairs, which wound in a corkscrew fashion, affected by the builders of small dwellings, from the upper to the lower floor.

"Now," said Mr. Dork, planting the "Softy" opposite to him, with the feeble rays of the rushlight upon his sickly face, – "now then, I want you to answer me a question. At what time did your master leave the house?"

"At half-past seven o'clock," answered the "Softy," in his whispering voice; "she was stroikin the half-hour as he went out."

He pointed to a small Dutch clock in a corner of the room. His countrymen always speak of a clock as "she."

"Oh, he went out at half-past seven o'clock, did he?" said the constable; "and you haven't seen him since, I suppose?"

"No. He told me he should be late, and I wasn't to sit oop for him. He swore at me last night for sitting oop for him. But is there aught wrong?" asked the "Softy."

Mr. Dork did not condescend to reply to this question. He walked straight to the door, opened it, and beckoned to those who stood without in the summer moonlight, patiently waiting for his summons. "You may bring him in," he said.

They carried their ghastly burden into the pleasant rustic chamber – the chamber in which Mr. James Conyers had sat smoking and drinking a few hours before. Mr. Morton, the surgeon from Meslingham, the village nearest to the Park-gates, arrived as the body was being carried in, and ordered a temporary couch of mattresses to be spread upon a couple of tables placed together, in the lower room, for the reception of the trainer's corpse.

John Mellish, Samuel Prodder, and Mr. Lofthouse remained outside the cottage. Colonel Maddison, the servants, the constable, and the doctor, were all clustered round the corpse.

"He has been dead about an hour and a quarter," said the doctor, after a brief inspection of the body. "He has been shot in the back; the bullet has not penetrated the heart, for in that case there would have been no hæmorrhage. He has respired after receiving the shot; but death must have been almost instantaneous."

Before making his examination, the surgeon had assisted Mr. Dork, the constable, to draw off the coat and waistcoat of the deceased. The bosom of the waistcoat was saturated with the blood that had flowed from the parted lips of the dead man.

It was Mr. Dork's business to examine these garments, in the hope of finding some shred of evidence which might become a clue to the secret of the trainer's death. He turned out the pockets of the shooting coat, and of the waistcoat; one of these pockets contained a handful of halfpence, a couple of shillings, a fourpenny-piece, and a rusty watch-key; another held a little parcel of tobacco wrapped in an old betting-list, and a broken meerschaum pipe, black and greasy with the essential oil of bygone shag and bird's-eye. In one of the waistcoat pockets Mr. Dork found the dead man's silver watch, with a blood-stained ribbon and a worthless gilt seal. Amongst all these things there was nothing calculated to throw any light upon the mystery. Colonel Maddison shrugged his shoulders as the constable emptied the paltry contents of the trainer's pockets on to a little dresser at one end of the room.

"There's nothing here that makes the business any clearer," he said; "but to my mind it's plain enough. The man was new here, and he brought new ways with him from his last situation. The poachers and vagabonds have been used to have it all their own way about Mellish Park, and they didn't like this poor fellow's interference. He wanted to play the tyrant, I dare say, and made himself obnoxious to some of the worst of the lot; and he's caught it hot, poor chap! – that's all I've got to say."

Colonel Maddison, with the recollection of a refractory Punjaub[1] strong upon him, had no very great reverence for the mysterious spark that lights the human temple. If a man made himself obnoxious to other men, other men were very likely to kill him. This was the soldier's simple theory; and, having delivered himself of his opinion respecting the trainer's death, he emerged from the cottage, and was ready to go home with John Mellish, and drink another bottle of that celebrated tawny port which had been laid in by his host's father twenty years before.

The constable stood close against a candle, that had been hastily lighted and thrust unceremoniously into a disused blacking-bottle, with the waistcoat still in his hands. He was turning the blood-stained garment inside out; for while emptying the pockets he had felt a thick substance that seemed like a folded paper, but the whereabouts of which he had not been able to discover. He uttered a suppressed exclamation of surprise presently; for he found the solution of this difficulty. The paper was sewn between the inner lining and the outer material of the waistcoat. He discovered this by examining the seam, a part of which was sewn with coarse stitches and a thread of a different colour to the rest. He ripped open this part of the seam, and drew out the paper, which was so much bloodstained as to be undecipherable to Mr. Dork's rather obtuse vision. "I'll say naught about it, and keep

---

1   See 340, n.1.

it to show to th' coroner," he thought; "I'll lay he'll make something out of it." The constable folded the document and secured it in a leathern pocket-book, a bulky receptacle, the very aspect of which was wont to strike terror to rustic defaulters. "I'll show it to th' coroner," he thought; "and if aught particklar comes out, I may get something for my trouble."

The village surgeon having done his duty, prepared to leave the crowded little room, where the gaping servants still lingered, as if loth to tear themselves away from the ghastly figure of the dead man, over which Mr. Morton had spread a patchwork coverlet, taken from the bed in the chamber above. The "Softy" had looked on quietly enough at the dismal scene, watching the faces of the small assembly, and glancing furtively from one to another beneath the shadow of his bushy red eyebrows. His haggard face, always of a sickly white, seemed to-night no more colourless than usual. His slow whispering tones were not more suppressed than they always were. If he had a hang-dog manner and a furtive glance, the manner and the glance were both common to him. No one looked at him; no one heeded him. After the first question as to the hour at which the trainer left the lodge had been asked and answered, no one spoke to him. If he got in anybody's way, he was pushed aside; if he said anything, nobody listened to him. The dead man was the sole monarch of that dismal scene. It was to him they looked with awe-stricken glances; it was of him they spoke in subdued whispers. All their questions, their suggestions, their conjectures, were about him, and him alone. There is this to be observed in the physiology of every murder, – that before the coroner's inquest the sole object of public curiosity is the murdered man; while immediately after that judicial investigation the tide of feeling turns; the dead man is buried and forgotten, and the suspected murderer becomes the hero of men's morbid imaginations.

John Mellish looked in at the door of the cottage to ask a few questions.

"Have you found anything, Dork?" he asked.

"Nothing particklar, sir."

"Nothing that throws any light upon this business?"

"No, sir."

"You are going home, then, I suppose?"

"Yes, sir, I must be going back now; if you'll leave some one here to watch——"

"Yes, yes," said John; "one of the servants shall stay."

"Very well, then, sir; I'll just take the names of the witnesses that'll be examined at the inquest, and I'll go over and see the coroner early to-morrow morning."

"The witnesses; ah, to be sure. Who will you want?"

Mr. Dork hesitated for a moment, rubbing the bristles upon his chin.

"Well, there's this man here, Hargraves, I think you called him," he said presently; "we shall want him; for it seems he was the last that saw the deceased alive, leastways as I can hear on yet; then we shall want the gentleman as found the body, and the young man as was with him when he heard the shot: the gentleman as found the body is the most particklar of all, and I'll speak to him at once."

John Mellish turned round, fully expecting to see Mr. Prodder at his elbow, where he had been some time before. John had a perfect recollection of seeing the loosely-clad seafaring figure standing behind him in the moonlight; but, in the terrible confusion of his mind, he could not remember exactly *when* it was that he had last seen the sailor. It might have been only five minutes before; it might have been a quarter of an hour. John's ideas of time were annihilated by the horror of the catastrophe which had marked this night with the red brand of murder. It seemed to him as if he had been standing for hours in the little cottage-garden, with Reginald Lofthouse by his side, listening to the low hum of the voices in the crowded room, and waiting to see the end of the dreary business.

Mr. Dork looked about him in the moonlight, entirely bewildered by the disappearance of Samuel Prodder.

"Why, where on earth has he gone?" exclaimed the constable. "We *must* have him before the coroner. What'll Mr. Hayward say to me for letting him slip through my fingers?"

"The man was here a quarter of an hour ago, so he can't be very far off," suggested Mr. Lofthouse. "Does anybody know who he is?"

No; nobody knew anything about him. He had appeared as mysteriously as if he had risen from the earth, to bring terror and confusion upon it with the evil tidings which he bore. Stay; some one suddenly remembered that he had been accompanied by Bill Jarvis, the young man from the Reindeer, and that he had ordered the young man to drive his trap to the north gates, and wait for him there.

The constable ran to the gates upon receiving this information; but there was no vestige of the horse and gig, or of the young man. Samuel Prodder had evidently taken advantage of the confusion, and had driven off in the gig under cover of the general bewilderment.

"I'll tell you what I'll do, sir," said William Dork, addressing Mr. Mellish. "If you'll lend me a horse and trap, I'll drive into Doncaster, and see if this man's to be found at the Reindeer. We *must* have him for a witness."

John Mellish assented to this arrangement. He left one of the grooms to keep watch in the death chamber, in company with Stephen Hargraves the "Softy;" and, after bidding the surgeon good night, walked slowly homewards with his friends. The church clock was striking twelve as the three gentlemen left the wood, and passed through the little iron gateway on to the lawn.

"We had better not tell the ladies more than we are obliged to tell them about this business," said John Mellish, as they approached the house, where the lights were still burning in the hall and drawing-room; "we shall only agitate them by letting them know the worst."

"To be sure, to be sure, my boy," answered the colonel. "My poor little Maggie always cries if she hears of anything of this kind; and Lofthouse is almost as big a baby," added the soldier, glancing rather contemptuously at his son-in-law, who had not spoken once during that slow homeward walk.

John Mellish thought very little of the strange disappearance of Captain Prodder. The man had objected to be summoned as a witness, perhaps, and had gone. It was only natural. He did not even know his name; he only knew him as the mouthpiece of evil tidings, which had shaken him to the very soul. That this man Conyers – this man of all others, this man towards whom he had conceived a deeply-rooted aversion, an unspoken horror – should have perished mysteriously by an unknown hand, was an event so strange and appalling as to deprive him for a time of all power of thought, all capability of reasoning. Who had killed this man, – this penniless good-for-nothing trainer? Who could have had any motive for such a deed? Who——?

The cold sweat broke out upon his brow in the anguish of the thought.

Who had done this deed?

It was not the work of any poacher. No. It was very well for Colonel Maddison, in his ignorance of antecedent facts, to account for it in that manner; but John Mellish knew that he was wrong. James Conyers had only been at the Park a week. He had neither time nor opportunity for making himself obnoxious; and, beyond that, he was not the man to make himself obnoxious. He was a selfish, indolent rascal, who only loved his own ease, and who would have allowed the young partridges to be wired under his very nose. Who, then, had done this deed?

There was only one person who had any motive for wishing to be rid of this man. One person who, made desperate by some great despair, enmeshed perhaps by some net hellishly contrived by a villain, hopeless of any means of extrication, in a moment of madness, might have – No! In the face of every evidence that earth could offer, – against reason, against hearing, eyesight, judgement, and memory, – he would say, as he said now, *No!* She was innocent! She was innocent! She had looked in her husband's face, the clear light had shone from her luminous eyes, a stream of electric radiance penetrating straight to his heart, – and he had trusted her.

"I'll trust her at the worst," he thought. "If all living creatures upon this wide earth joined their voices in one great cry of upbraiding, I'd stand by her to the very end, and defy them."

Aurora and Mrs. Lofthouse had fallen asleep upon opposite sofas; Mrs. Powell was walking softly up and down the long drawing-room, waiting and watching, – waiting for a fuller knowledge of this ruin which had come upon her employer's household.

Mrs. Mellish sprang up suddenly at the sound of her husband's step as he entered the drawing-room.

"Oh, John!" she cried, running to him and laying her hands upon his broad shoulders, "thank Heaven you are come back! Now tell me all! Tell me all, John! I am prepared to hear anything, no matter what. This is no ordinary accident. The man who was hurt——"

Her eyes dilated as she looked at him, with a glance of intelligence that plainly said, "I can guess what has happened."

"The man was very seriously hurt, Lolly," her husband answered quietly.

"What man?"

"The trainer recommended to me by John Pastern."

She looked at him for a few moments in silence.

"Is he dead?" she asked, after that brief pause.

"He is."

Her head sank forward upon her breast, and she walked away, quietly returning to the sofa from which she had arisen.

"I am very sorry for him," she said; "he was not a good man. I am sorry he was not allowed time to repent of his wickedness."

"You knew him, then?" asked Mrs. Lofthouse, who had expressed unbounded consternation at the trainer's death.

"Yes; he was in my father's service some years ago."

Mr. Lofthouse's carriage had been waiting ever since eleven o'clock, and the rector's wife was only too glad to bid her friends good-night, and to drive away from Mellish Park and its fatal associations; so, though Colonel Maddison would have preferred stopping to smoke another cheroot while he discussed the business with John Mellish, he was fain to submit to feminine authority, and take his seat by his daughter's side in the comfortable landau, which was an open or a close carriage as the convenience of its proprietor dictated. The vehicle rolled away upon the smooth carriage-drive; the servants closed the hall-doors, and lingered about, whispering to each other, in little groups in the corridors and on the staircases, waiting until their master and mistress should have retired for the night. It was difficult to think that the business of life was to go on just the same though a murder had been done upon the outskirts of the Park, and even the housekeeper, a severe matron at ordinary times, yielded to the common influence, and forgot to drive the maids to their dormitories in the gabled roof.

All was very quiet in the drawing-room where the visitors had left their host and hostess to hug those ugly skeletons which are put away in the presence of company. John Mellish walked slowly up and down the room. Aurora sat staring vacantly at the guttering wax candles in the old-fashioned silver branches; and Mrs. Powell, with her embroidery in full working order, threaded her needles and snipped away the fragments of her delicate cotton as carefully as if there had been no such thing as crime or trouble in the world, and no higher purpose in life than the achievement of elaborate devices upon French cambric.

She paused now and then to utter some polite commonplace. She regretted such an unpleasant catastrophe; she lamented the disagreeable circumstances of the trainer's death; indeed, she in a manner inferred that Mr. Conyers had shown himself wanting in good taste and respect for his employer by the mode of his death; but the point to which she recurred most frequently was the fact of Aurora's presence in the grounds at the time of the murder.

"I so much regret that you should have been out of doors at the time, my dear Mrs. Mellish," she said; "and, as I should imagine from the direction which you took on leaving the house, actually near the place where the unfortunate person met his death. It will be so unpleasant for you to have to appear at the inquest."

"Appear at the inquest!" cried John Mellish, stopping suddenly, and turning fiercely upon the placid speaker. "Who says that my wife will have to appear at the inquest?"

"I merely imagined it probable that——"

"Then you'd no business to imagine it, ma'am," retorted Mr. Mellish, with no very great show of politeness. "My wife will not appear. Who should ask her to do so? Who should wish her to do so? What has she to do with to-night's business? or what does she know of it more than you or I, or any one else in this house?"

Mrs. Powell shrugged her shoulders.

"I thought that, from Mrs. Mellish's previous knowledge of this unfortunate person, she might be able to throw some light upon his habits and associations," she suggested mildly.

"Previous knowledge!" roared John. "What knowledge should Mrs. Mellish have of her father's grooms? What interest should she take in their habits or associations?"

"Stop," said Aurora, rising and laying her hand lightly on her husband's shoulder. "My dear, impetuous John, why do you put yourself into a passion about this business? If they choose to call me as a witness, I will tell all I know about this man's death; which is nothing but that I heard a shot fired while I was in the grounds."

She was very pale; but she spoke with a quiet determination, a calm resolute defiance of the worst that fate could reserve for her.

"I will tell anything that is necessary to tell," she said; "I care very little what."

With her hand still upon her husband's shoulder, she rested her head on his breast, like some weary child nestling in its only safe shelter.

Mrs. Powell rose, and gathered together her embroidery in a pretty, lady-like receptacle of fragile wicker-work. She glided to the door, selected her candlestick, and then paused on the threshold to bid Mr. and Mrs. Mellish good night.

"I am sure you must need rest after this terrible affair," she simpered; "so I will take the initiative. It is nearly one o'clock. *Good night.*"

If she had lived in the Thane of Cawdor's family, she would have wished Macbeth and his wife a good night's rest after Duncan's murder; and would have hoped they would sleep well; she would have curtsied and simpered amidst the tolling of alarm-bells, the clashing of vengeful swords, and the blood-bedabbled visages of the drunken grooms. It must have been the Scottish queen's *companion* who watched with the truckling physician, and played the spy upon her mistress's remorseful wanderings, and told how it was the conscience-stricken lady's habit to do thus and thus; no one but a genteel mercenary would have been so sleepless in the dead hours of the night, lying in wait for the revelation of horrible secrets, the muttered clues to deadly mysteries.

"Thank God, she's gone at last!" cried John Mellish, as the door closed very softly and very slowly upon Mrs. Powell. "I hate that woman, Lolly."

Heaven knows I have never called John Mellish a hero; I have never set him up as a model of manly perfection or infallible virtue; and if he is not faultless, if he has those flaws and blemishes which seem a constituent part of our imperfect clay, I make no apology for him; but trust him to the tender mercies of those who, not being *quite* perfect themselves, will, I am sure, be merciful to him. He hated those who hated his wife, or did her any wrong, however small. He loved those who loved her. In the great power of his wide affection, all self-esteem was annihilated. To love her was to love him; to serve her was to do him treble service; to praise her was to make him vainer than the vainest school-girl. He freely took upon his shoulders every debt that she owed, whether of love or of hate; and he was ready to pay either species of account to the uttermost farthing, and with no mean interest upon the sum total. "I hate that woman, Lolly," he repeated; "and I sha'n't be able to stand her much longer."

Aurora did not answer him. She was silent for some moments, and when she did speak, it was evident that Mrs. Powell was very far away from her thoughts.

"My poor John!" she said, in a low soft voice, whose melancholy tenderness went straight to her husband's heart; "my dear, how happy we were together for a little time! How very happy we were, my poor boy!"

"Always, Lolly," he answered, – "always, my darling."

"No, no, no!" said Aurora suddenly; "only for a little while. What a horrible fatality has pursued us! what a frightful curse has clung to me! The curse of disobedience, John; the curse of Heaven upon my disobedience.[1] To think that this man should have been sent here, and that he——"

She stopped, shivering violently, and clinging to the faithful breast that sheltered her.

John Mellish quietly led her to her dressing-room, and placed her in the care of her maid.

"Your mistress has been very much agitated by this night's business," he said to the girl; "keep her as quiet as you possibly can."

Mrs. Mellish's bedroom, a comfortable and roomy apartment, with a low ceiling and deep bay windows, opened into a morning-room, in which it was John's habit to read the newspapers and sporting periodicals, while his wife wrote letters, drew pencil sketches of dogs and horses, or played with her favourite Bow-wow. They had been very childish and idle and happy in this pretty chintz-hung chamber; and going into it to-night in utter desolation of heart, Mr. Mellish felt his sorrows all the more bitterly for the remembrance of those bygone joys. The shaded lamp was lighted on the morocco-covered writing-table, and glimmered softly on the picture-frames, caressing the pretty modern paintings, the simple, domestic-story pictures which adorned

---

1   i.e. Disobedience to her father. See *Paradise Lost* (Book 1, Line 1). This reinforces the previous comparison of Aurora to Eve (see 256, n.1). By implication, John is Adam: he too will lose his Eden.

the subdued gray walls. This wing of the old house had been refurnished for Aurora, and there was not a chair or a table in the room that had not been chosen by John Mellish with a special view to the comfort and the pleasure of his wife. The upholsterer had found him a liberal employer, the painter and the sculptor a noble patron. He had walked about the Royal Academy with a catalogue and a pencil in his hand, choosing all the "pretty" pictures for the ornamentation of his wife's rooms. A lady in a scarlet riding-habit and three-cornered beaver hat, a white pony, and a pack of greyhounds, a bit of stone terrace and sloping turf, a flower-bed, and a fountain, made poor John's idea of a pretty picture; and he had half a dozen variations of such familiar subjects in his spacious mansion. He sat down to-night, and looked hopelessly round the pleasant chamber, wondering whether Aurora and he would ever be happy again: wondering if this dark, mysterious, storm-threatening cloud would ever pass from the horizon of his life, and leave the future bright and clear.

"I have not been good enough," he thought; "I have intoxicated myself with my happiness, and have made no return for it. What am I that I should have won the woman I love for my wife, while other men are laying down the best desires of their hearts a willing sacrifice, and going out to fight the battle for their fellow-men?[1] What an indolent good-for-nothing wretch I have been! – How blind, how ungrateful, how undeserving!"

John Mellish buried his face in his broad hands, and repented of the carelessly happy life which he had led for one-and-thirty thoughtless years. He had been awakened from his unthinking bliss by a thunder-clap, that had shattered the fairy castle of his happiness, and laid it level with the ground; and in his simple faith he looked into his own life for the cause of the ruin which had overtaken him. Yes, it must be so; he had not deserved his happiness, he had not earned his good fortune. Have you ever thought of this, ye simple country squires, who give blankets and beef to your poor neighbours in the cruel winter-time, who are good and gentle masters, faithful husbands, and tender fathers, and who lounge away your easy lives in the pleasant places of this beautiful earth? Have you ever thought that,

---

1   Probably a reference to the Indian Mutiny (1857-59), which was contemporaneous with the novel's plot.

when all our good deeds have been gathered together, and set in the balance, the sum of them will be very small when set against the benefits you have received? It will be a very small percentage which you will yield your Master for the ten talents intrusted to your care. Remember John Howard, fever-stricken and dying; Mrs. Fry labouring in criminal prisons; Florence Nightingale in the bare hospital chambers, in the close and noxious atmosphere, amongst the dead and the dying. These are the people who return cent. per cent. for the gifts intrusted to them.[1] These are the saints whose good deeds shine amongst the stars for ever and ever; these are the indefatigable workers who, when the toil and turmoil of the day is done, hear the Master's voice in the still even-time; welcoming them to His rest.

John Mellish, looking back at his life, humbly acknowledged that it had been a comparatively useless one. He had distributed happiness to the people who had come into his way; but he had never gone out of his way to make people happy. I dare say that Dives was a liberal master to his own servants, although he did not trouble himself to look after the beggar who sat at his gates. The Israelite who sought instruction from the lips of inspiration was willing to do his duty to his neighbour, but had yet to learn the broad signification of that familiar epithet; and poor John, like the rich young man, was ready to serve his Master faithfully, but had yet to learn the manner of his service.[2]

"If I could save *her* from the shadow of sorrow or disgrace, I would start to-morrow barefoot on a pilgrimage to Jerusalem," he thought. "What is there that I would not do for her? what sacrifice would seem too great? what burden too heavy to bear?"

END OF VOL. II

---

1   On the parable of the talents, see Matthew 25:14-30. Braddon refers to three great social reformers of the 18th and 19th centuries: John Howard (1726-90), English philanthropist and reformer in public health and prisons, who died of camp fever in Kherson, Ukraine; Elizabeth Fry (1780-1845), Quaker philanthropist who crusaded to alleviate conditions for criminals and the insane; and Florence Nightingale (1820-1910), founder of modern nursing and heroine of the Crimean War.

2   A plethora of biblical references: for the story of Dives, see Luke 16:19-31; on the Israelite who seeks instruction from Jesus on duty to his neighbour, see especially Luke 10:25-37, but also Matthew 22:34-40 and Mark 12:28-31. For the parable of the rich man, see Mark 10:17-23, Matthew 19:16-22, and Luke 18:18-23.

VOLUME III

CHAPTER XXVI.

AT THE GOLDEN LION.

MR. WILLIAM DORK, the constable, reached Doncaster at about a quarter-past one o'clock upon the morning after the murder, and drove straight to the Reindeer. That hotel had been closed for a couple of hours, and it was only by the exercise of his authority that Mr. Dork obtained access, and a hearing from the sleepy landlord. The young man who had driven Mr. Prodder was found after considerable difficulty, and came stumbling down the servants' staircase in a semi-somnolent state to answer the constable's inquiries. He had driven the seafaring gentleman, whose name he did not know, direct to the Doncaster station, in time to catch the mail-train, which started at 12.50. He had parted with the gentleman at the door of the station three minutes before the train started.

This was all the information that Mr. Dork could obtain. If he had been a sharp London detective, he might have made his arrangements for laying hands upon the fugitive sailor at the first station at which the train stopped; but being merely a simple rural functionary, he scratched his stubbled head, and stared at the landlord of the Reindeer in utter mental bewilderment.

"He was in a devil of a hurry, this chap," he muttered rather sulkily. "What did he want to coot away for?"

The young man who had acted as charioteer could not answer this question. He only knew that the seafaring gentleman had promised him half a sovereign if he caught the mail-train, and that he had earned his reward.

"Well, I suppose it aint so very particklar," said Mr. Dork, sipping a glass of rum, which he had ordered for his refreshment. "You'll have to appear to-morrow, and you can tell nigh as much as t'other chap," he added, turning to the young man. "You was with him when the shot were fired, and you warn't far when he found the body. You'll have to appear and give evidence whenever the inquest's held. I doubt if it'll be to-morrow; for there won't be much time to give notice to the coroner."

Mr. Dork wrote the young man's name in his pocket-book, and the landlord vouched for his being forthcoming when called upon. Having done thus much, the constable left the inn, after drinking another glass of rum, and refreshing John Mellish's horse with a handful of oats and a drink of water. He drove at a brisk pace back to the Park stables, delivered the horse and gig to the lad who had waited for his coming, and returned to his comfortable dwelling in the village of Meslingham, about a mile from the Park gates.

I scarcely know how to describe that long, quiet, miserable day which succeeded the night of the murder. Aurora Mellish lay in a dull stupor, not able to lift her head from the pillows upon which it rested, scarcely caring to raise her eyelids from the aching eyes they sheltered. She was not ill, nor did she affect to be ill. She lay upon the sofa in her dressing-room, attended by her maid, and visited at intervals by John, who roamed hither and thither about the house and grounds, talking to innumerable people, and always coming to the same conclusion, namely, that the whole affair was a horrible mystery, and that he heartily wished the inquest well over. He had visitors from twenty miles round his house, – for the evil news had spread far and wide before noon, – visitors who came to condole and to sympathize, and wonder, and speculate, and ask questions, until they fairly drove him mad. But he bore all very patiently. He could tell them nothing except that the business was as dark a mystery to him as it could be to them, and that he had no hope of finding any solution to the ghastly enigma. They one and all asked him the same question: "Had any one a motive for killing this man?"

How could he answer them? He might have told them that if twenty persons had had a powerful motive for killing James Conyers, it was possible that a one-and-twentieth person who had no motive might have done the deed. That species of argument which builds up any hypothesis out of a series of probabilities may, after all, lead very often to false conclusions.

Mr. Mellish did not attempt to argue the question. He was too weary and sick at heart, too anxious for the inquest to be over, and be free to carry Aurora away with him, and turn his back upon the familiar place, which had been hateful to him ever since the trainer had crossed its threshold.

"Yes, my darling," he said to his wife, as he bent over her pillow, "I shall take you away to the south of France directly this business is settled. You shall leave the scene of all past associations, all bygone annoyances. We will begin the world afresh."

"God grant that we may be able to do so," Aurora answered gravely. "Ah, my dear, I cannot tell you that I am sorry for this man's death. If he had died nearly two years ago, when I thought he did, how much misery he would have saved me!"

Once in the course of that long summer's afternoon Mr. Mellish walked across the park to the cottage at the north gates. He could not repress a morbid desire to look upon the lifeless clay of the man whose presence had caused him such vague disquietude, such instinctive terror. He found the "Softy" leaning on the gate of the little garden, and one of the grooms standing at the door of the death-chamber.

"The inquest is to be held at the Golden Lion, at ten o'clock tomorrow morning," Mr. Mellish said to the men. "You, Hargraves, will be wanted as a witness."

He walked into the darkened chamber. The groom understood what he came for, and silently withdrew the white drapery that covered the trainer's dead face.

Accustomed hands had done their awful duty. The strong limbs had been straightened. The lower jaw, which had dropped in the agony of sudden death, was supported by a linen bandage; the eyelids were closed over the dark-violet eyes; and the face, which had been beautiful in life, was even yet more beautiful in the still solemnity of death. The clay which in life had lacked so much, in its lack of a beautiful soul to light it from within, found its level in death. The worthless soul was gone, and the physical perfection that remained had lost its only blemish. The harmony of proportion, the exquisitely-modelled features, the charms of detail, – all were left; and the face which James Conyers carried to the grave was handsomer than that which had smiled insolent defiance upon the world in the trainer's lifetime.

John Mellish stood for some minutes looking gravely at that marble face.

"Poor fellow!" thought the generous-hearted young squire; "it was a hard thing to die so young. I wish he had never come here. I wish

Lolly had confided in me, and let me made a bargain with this man to stop away and keep her secret. Her secret! her father's secret more likely. What secret could she have had, that a groom was likely to discover? It may have been some mercantile business, some commercial transaction of Archibald Floyd's, by which the old man fell into his servant's power. It would be only like my glorious Aurora, to take the burden upon her own shoulders, and to bear it bravely through every trial."

It was thus that John Mellish had often reasoned upon the mystery which divided him from his wife. He could not bear to impute even the shadow of evil to her. He could not endure to think of her as a poor helpless woman entrapped into the power of a mean-spirited hireling, who was only too willing to make his market out of her secrets. He could not tolerate such an idea as this; and he sacrificed poor Archibald Floyd's commercial integrity for the preservation of Aurora's womanly dignity. Ah, how weak and imperfect a passion is this boundless love! How ready to sacrifice others for that one loved object, which *must* be kept spotless in our imaginations, though a hecatomb of her fellow-creatures are to be blackened and befouled for her justification! If Othello could have established Desdemona's purity by the sacrifice of the reputation of every lady in Cyprus, do you think he would have spared the fair inhabitants of the friendly isle? No; he would have branded every one of them with infamy, if he could by so doing have rehabilitated the wife he loved. John Mellish *would* not think ill of his wife. He resolutely shut his eyes to all damning evidence. He clung with a desperate tenacity to his belief in her purity, and only clung the more tenaciously as the proofs against her became more numerous.

The inquest was held at a road-side inn, within a quarter of a mile of the north gates – a quiet little place, only frequented on market-days by the country people going backwards and forwards between Doncaster and the villages beyond Meslingham. The coroner and his jury sat in a long bare room, in which the frequenters of the Golden Lion were wont to play bowls in wet weather. The surgeon, Steeve Hargraves, Jarvis, the young man from the Reindeer, William Dork the constable, and Mr. Mellish, were the only witnesses called: but Colonel Maddison and Mr. Lofthouse were both present during the brief proceedings.

The inquiry into the circumstances of the trainer's death occupied a very short time. Nothing was elicited by the brief examination of the witnesses which in any way led to the elucidation of the mystery. John Mellish was the last person interrogated, and he answered the questions put to him with prompt decision. There was one inquiry, however, which he was unable to answer, although it was a very simple one. Mr. Hayward, the coroner, anxious to discover so much of the history of the dead man as might lead eventually to the discovery of his murderer, asked Mr. Mellish if his trainer had been a bachelor or a married man.

"I really cannot answer that question," said John; "I should imagine that he was a single man, as neither he nor Mr. Pastern told me anything to the contrary. Had he been married, he would have brought his wife with him, I should suppose. My trainer, Langley, was married when he entered my service, and his wife and children have occupied the premises over my stables for some years."

"You infer, then, that James Conyers was unmarried?"

"Most decidedly."

"And it is your opinion that he had made no enemies in the neighbourhood?"

"It is next to impossible that he could have done so."

"To what cause, then, do you attribute his death?"

"To an unhappy accident. I can account for it in no other way. The path through the wood is used as a public thoroughfare, and the whole of the plantation is known to be infested with poachers. It was past ten o'clock at night when the shot was heard. I should imagine that it was fired by a poacher whose eyes deceived him in the shadowy light."

The coroner shook his head. "You forget, Mr. Mellish," he said, "that the cause of death was not an ordinary gun-shot wound. The shot heard was the report of a pistol, and the deceased was killed by a pistol-bullet."

John Mellish was silent. He had spoken in good faith as to his impression respecting the cause of the trainer's death. In the press and hurry, the horror and confusion of the two last days, the smaller details of the awful event had escaped his memory.

"Do you know any one amongst your servants, Mr. Mellish," asked the coroner, "whom you would consider likely to commit an act of violence of this kind? Have you any one of an especially vindictive character in your household?"

"No," answered John, decisively; "I can answer for my servants as I would for myself. They were all strangers to this man. What motive could they possibly have had to seek his death?"

Mr. Hayward rubbed his chin, and shook his head reflectively.

"There was this superannuated trainer whom you spoke of just now, Mr. Mellish," he said. "I am well aware that the post of trainer in your stables is rather a good thing. A man may save a good deal of money out of his wages and perquisites with such a master as you. This former trainer may not have liked being superseded by the deceased. He may have felt some animus towards his successor."

"Langley!" cried John Mellish; "he is as good a fellow as ever breathed. He was not superseded; he resigned the active part of his work at his own wish, and he retained his full wages by mine. The poor fellow has been confined to his bed for the last week."

"Humph," muttered the coroner. "Then you can throw no light upon this business, Mr. Mellish?"

"None whatever. I have written to Mr. Pastern, in whose stables the deceased was employed, telling him of the circumstances of the trainer's death, and begging him to forward the information to any relative of the murdered man. I expect an answer by to-morrow's post; and I shall be happy to submit that answer to you."

Prior to the examination of the witnesses, the jurymen had been conducted to the north lodge, where they had beheld the mortal remains of James Conyers. Mr. Morton had accompanied them, and had endeavoured to explain to them the direction which the bullet had taken, and the manner in which, according to his own idea, the shot must have been fired. The jurymen who had been empannelled to decide upon this awful question were simple agriculturists and petty tradesmen, who grudged the day's lost labour, and who were ready to accept any solution of the mystery which might be suggested to them by the coroner. They hurried back to the Golden Lion, listened deferentially to the evidence and to Mr. Hayward's address, retired to an adjoining apartment, where they remained in consultation for the space of about five minutes, and whence they emerged with a very rambling form of decision, which Mr. Hayward reduced into a verdict of wilful murder against some person or persons unknown.

Very little had been said about the disappearance of the seafaring man who had carried the tidings of the murder to Mr. Mellish's house. Nobody for a moment imagined that the evidence of this missing witness might have thrown some ray of light upon the mystery of the trainer's death. The seafaring man had been engaged in conversation with the young man from the Reindeer at the time when the shot was fired; he was therefore not the actual murderer; and strangely significant as his hurried flight might have been to the acute intelligence of a well-trained metropolitan police-officer, no one amongst the rustic officials present at the inquest attached any importance to the circumstance. Nor had Aurora's name been once mentioned during the brief proceedings. Nothing had transpired which in any way revealed her previous acquaintance with James Conyers; and John Mellish drew a deep breath, a long sigh of relief, as he left the Golden Lion and walked homewards. Colonel Maddison, Mr. Lofthouse, and two or three other gentlemen lingered on the threshold of the little inn, talking to Mr. Hayward, the coroner.

The inquest was terminated; the business was settled; and the mortal remains of James Conyers could be carried to the grave at the pleasure of his late employer. All was over. The mystery of death and the secrets of life would be buried peacefully in the grave of the murdered man; and John Mellish was free to carry his wife away with him whithersoever he would. Free, have I said? No; for ever and for ever the shadow of that bygone mystery would hang like a funeral pall between himself and the woman he loved. For ever and for ever the recollection of that ghastly undiscovered problem would haunt him in sleeping and in waking, in the sunlight and in the darkness. His nobler nature, triumphing again and again over the subtle influences of damning suggestions and doubtful facts, was again and again shaken, although never quite defeated. He fought the battle bravely, though it was a very hard one, and it was to endure perhaps to the end of time. That voiceless argument was for ever to be argued; the spirits of Faith and Infidelity were for ever to be warring with each other in that tortured breast, until the end of life; until he died, perhaps, with his head lying upon his wife's bosom, with his cheek fanned by her warm breath; but ignorant to the very last of the real nature of that dark something, that nameless and formless horror with which he had wrestled so patiently and so long.

"I'll take her away with me," he thought; "and when we are divided by a thousand miles of blue water from the scene of her secret, I will fall on my knees before her, and beseech her to confide in me."

He passed by the north lodge with a shudder, and walked straight along the high road towards the principal entrance of the Park. He was close to the gates when he heard a voice, a strange suppressed voice, calling feebly to him to stop. He turned round and saw the "Softy" making his way towards him with a slow, shambling run. Of all human beings, except perhaps that one who now lay cold and motionless in the darkened chamber at the north lodge, this Steeve Hargraves was the last whom Mr. Mellish cared to see. He turned with an angry frown upon the "Softy," who was wiping the perspiration from his pale face with the ragged end of his neck-handkerchief, and panting hoarsely.

"What is the matter?" asked John. "What do you want with me?"

"It's th' coroner," gasped Stephen Hargraves, – "th' coroner and Mr. Lofthouse, th' parson. They want to speak to ye, sir, oop at the Loion."

"What about?"

Steeve Hargraves gave a ghastly grin.

"I doan't know, sir," he whispered. "It's hardly loikely they'd tell me. There's summat oop, though, I'll lay; for Mr. Lofthouse was as whoite as ashes, and seemed strangely oopset about summat. Would you be pleased to step oop and speak to 'un directly, sir? – that was my message."

"Yes, yes; I'll go," answered John absently.

He had taken his hat off, and was passing his hand over his hot forehead in a half-bewildered manner. He turned his back upon the "Softy," and walked rapidly away, retracing his steps in the direction of the roadside inn.

Stephen Hargraves stood staring after him until he was out of sight, and then turned and walked on slowly towards the turnstile leading into the wood.

"*I* know what they've found," he muttered; "and *I* know what they want with him. He'll be some time oop there; so I'll slip across the wood and tell her. Yes," – he paused, rubbing his hands, and laughing a slow voiceless laugh, which distorted his ugly face, and made him horrible to look upon, – "yes, it will be nuts[1] for me to tell her."

---

1   (Slang): A source of pleasure or delight.

CHAPTER XXVII.

"MY WIFE! MY WIFE! WHAT WIFE?
I HAVE NO WIFE."

THE Golden Lion had reassumed its accustomed air of rustic tranquillity when John Mellish returned to it. The jurymen had gone
back to their different avocations, glad to have finished the business so
easily; the villagers, who had hung about the inn to hear what they
could of the proceedings, were all dispersed; and the landlord was eating his dinner, with his wife and family, in the comfortable little bar-
parlour. He put down his knife and fork as John entered the sanded
bar, and left his meal to receive such a distinguished visitor.

"Mr. Hayward and Mr. Lofthouse are in the coffee-room, sir," he
said. "Will you please to step this way?"

He opened the door of a carpeted room, furnished with shining
mahogany tables, and adorned by half a dozen gaudily-coloured
prints of the Doncaster meetings, the great match between Voltigeur
and Flying Dutchman, and other events which had won celebrity for
the northern race-course. The coroner was sitting at the bottom of
one of the long tables, with Mr. Lofthouse standing near him. William
Dork, the Meslingham constable, stood near the door, with his hat in
his hand, and with rather an alarmed expression dimly visible in his
ruddy face. Mr. Hayward and Mr. Lofthouse were both very pale.

One rapid glance was enough to show all this to John Mellish, –
enough to show him this, and something more: a basin of blood-
stained water before the coroner, and an oblong piece of wet paper,
which lay under Mr. Hayward's clenched hand.

"What is the matter? Why did you send for me?" John asked.

Bewildered and alarmed as he had been by the message which had
summoned him hurriedly back to the inn, he was still more so by the
confusion evident in the coroner's manner as he answered this question.

"Pray sit down, Mr. Mellish," he said. "I – I – sent for you – at –
the – the advice of Mr. Lofthouse, who – who, as a clergyman and a
family man, thought it incumbent upon me——"

Reginald Lofthouse laid his hand upon the coroner's arm with a warning gesture. Mr. Hayward stopped for a moment, cleared his throat, and then continued speaking, but in an altered tone.

"I have had occasion to reprehend William Dork for a breach of duty, which, though I am aware it may have been, as he says, purely unintentional and accidental——"

"It was indeed, sir," muttered the constable submissively. "If I'd ha' know'd——"

"The fact is, Mr. Mellish, that on the night of the murder, Dork, in examining the clothes of the deceased, discovered a paper, which had been concealed by the unhappy man between the outer material and the lining of his waistcoat. This paper was so stained by the blood in which the breast of the waistcoat was absolutely saturated, that Dork was unable to decipher a word of its contents. He therefore was quite unaware of the importance of the paper; and, in the hurry and confusion consequent on the very hard duty he has done for the last two days, he forgot to produce it at the inquest. He had occasion to make some memorandum in his pocket-book almost immediately after the verdict had been given, and this circumstance recalled to his mind the existence of the paper. He came immediately to me, and consulted me upon this very awkward business. I examined the document, washed away a considerable portion of the stains which had rendered it illegible, and have contrived to decipher the greater part of it."

"The document is of some importance, then?" John asked.

He sat at a little distance from the table, with his head bent and his fingers rattling nervously against the side of his chair. He chafed horribly at the coroner's pompous slowness. He suffered an agony of fear and bewilderment. Why had they called him back? What was this paper? How *could* it concern him?

"Yes," Mr. Hayward answered; "the document is certainly an important one. I have shown it to Mr. Lofthouse, for the purpose of taking his advice upon the subject. I have not shown it to Dork; but I detained Dork in order that you may hear from him how and where the paper was found, and why it was not produced at the inquest."

"Why should I ask any questions upon the subject?" cried John, lifting his head suddenly, and looking from the coroner to the clergyman. "How should this paper concern me?"

"I regret to say that it does concern you very materially, Mr. Mellish," the rector answered gently.

John's angry spirit revolted against that gentleness. What right had they to speak to him like this? Why did they look at him with those grave, pitying faces? Why did they drop their voices to that horrible tone in which the bearers of evil tidings pave their way to the announcement of some overwhelming calamity?

"Let me see this paper, then, if it concerns me," John said very carelessly. "Oh, my God!" he thought, "what is this misery that is coming upon me? What is this hideous avalanche of trouble which is slowly descending to crush me?"

"You do not wish to hear anything from Dork?" asked the coroner.

"No, no!" cried John savagely. "I only want to see that paper." He pointed as he spoke to the wet and blood-stained document under Mr. Hayward's hand.

"You may go, then, Dork," the coroner said quietly; "and be sure you do not mention this business to any one. It is a matter of purely private interest, and has no reference to the murder. You will remember?"

"Yes, sir."

The constable bowed respectfully to the three gentlemen and left the room. He was very glad to be so well out of the business.

"They needn't have *called* me," he thought. (To *call*, in the northern *patois*, is to scold, to abuse.) "They needn't have said it was repri – what's its name – to keep the paper. I might have burnt it, if I'd liked, and said naught about it."

"Now," said John, rising and walking to the table as the door closed upon the constable, "now then, Mr. Hayward, let me see this paper. If it concerns me, or any one connected with me, I have a right to see it."

"A right which I will not dispute," the coroner answered gravely, as he handed the blood-stained document to Mr. Mellish. "I only beg you to believe in my heartfelt sympathy with you in this——"

"Let me alone!" cried John, waving the speaker away from him as he snatched the paper from his hand; "let me alone! Can't you see that I'm nearly mad?"

He walked to the window, and with his back to the coroner and Mr. Lofthouse, examined the blotched and blotted document in his hands. He stared for a long time at those blurred and half-illegible lines before he became aware of their full meaning. But at last the signification of that miserable paper grew clear to him, and with a loud cry of anguish he dropped into the chair from which he had risen, and covered his face with his strong right hand. He held the paper in the left, crumpled and crushed by the convulsive pressure of his grasp.

"My God!" he ejaculated, after that first cry of anguish, – "my God! I never thought of this. I never could have imagined this."

Neither the coroner nor the clergyman spoke. What could they say to him? Sympathetic words could have no power to lessen such a grief as this; they would only fret and harass the strong man in his agony; it was better to obey him; it was far better to let him alone.

He rose at last, after a silence that seemed long to the spectators of his grief.

"Gentlemen," he said, in a loud, resolute voice that resounded through the little room, "I give you my solemn word of honour that when Archibald Floyd's daughter married me, she believed this man, James Conyers, to be dead."

He struck his clenched fist upon the table, and looked with proud defiance at the two men. Then, with his left hand, the hand that grasped the blood-stained paper, thrust into his breast, he walked out of the room. He walked out of the room and out of the house, but not homewards. A grassy lane, opposite the Golden Lion, led away to a great waste of brown turf, called Harper's Common. John Mellish walked slowly along this lane, and out upon this quiet common-land, lonely even in the broad summer daylight. As he closed the five-barred gate at the end of the lane, and emerged upon the open waste, he seemed to shut the door of the world that lay behind him, and to stand alone with his great grief, under the low, sunless, summer sky. The dreary scene before him, and the gray atmosphere above his head, seemed in strange harmony with his grief. The reedy water-pools, unbroken by a ripple; the barren verdure, burnt a dull grayish brown by the summer sun; the bloomless heather, and the flowerless rushes, – all things upon which he looked took a dismal colouring from his own desolation, and seemed to make him the more desolate.

The spoiled child of fortune, – the popular young squire, who had never been contradicted in nearly two-and-thirty years, – the happy husband, whose pride in his wife had touched upon that narrow boundary-line which separates the sublime from the ridiculous, – ah! whither had they fled, all these shadows of the happy days that were gone? They had vanished away; they had fallen into the black gulf of the cruel past. The monster who devours his children had taken back these happy ones, and a desolate man was left in their stead. A desolate man, who looked at a broad ditch and a rushy bank, a few paces from where he stood, and thought, "Was it I who leapt that dike a month ago to gather forget-me-nots for my wife?"

He asked himself that question, reader, which we must all ask ourselves sometimes. Was he really that creature of the irrecoverable past? Even as I write this, I can see that common-land of which I write. The low sky, the sunburnt grass, the reedy water-pools, the flat landscape stretching far away on every side to regions that are strange to me. I can recall every object in that simple scene, – the atmosphere of the sunless day, the sounds in the soft summer air, the voices of the people near me; I can recall everything except – *myself.* This miserable *ego* is the one thing that I cannot bring back; the one thing that seems strange to me; the one thing that I can scarcely believe in. If I went back to that northern common-land to-morrow, I should recognize every hillock, every scrap of furze, or patch of heather. The few years that have gone by since I saw it will have made a scarcely perceptible difference in the features of the familiar place. The slow changes of nature, immutable in her harmonious law, will have done their work according to that unalterable law; but this wretched me has undergone so complete a change, that if you could bring me back that *alter ego* of the past, I should be unable to recognize the strange creature; and yet it is by no volcanic shocks, no rending asunder of rocky masses, no great convulsions, or terrific agonies of nature, that the change has come about; it is rather by a slow, monotonous wearing away of salient points; an imperceptible adulteration of this or that constituent part; an addition here, and a subtraction there, that the transformation takes place. It is hard to make a man believe in the physiologists, who declare that the hand which uses his pen to-day is not the same hand that guided the quill with which he wrote seven years ago. He finds it very difficult to believe this; but let him take out of some forgotten writing-desk, thrust into a corner of his lumber-room, those letters which he wrote seven years ago, and which were afterwards returned to him by the lady to whom they were addressed, and the question which he will ask himself, as he reads the faded lines, will most surely be, "Was it I who wrote this bosh? Was it I who called a lady with white eyelashes 'the guiding star of a lonely life'? Was it I who was 'inexpressibly miserable' with one *s*, and looked 'forward with unutterable anxiety to the party in Onslow Square, at which I once more should look into those soft blue eyes?' What party in Onslow Square? *Non mi recordo.*[1] 'Those soft blue eyes' were garnished with white lashes, and the lady to whom the letters were written, jilted me, to marry a rich soap-boiler." Even the law takes cognizance of this wonderful transformation. The debt which Smith contracts in 1850 is null and void in 1857.[2] The Smith of '50 may have been an extravagant rogue; the Smith of '57 may be a conscientious man, who would not cheat his creditors of a farthing. Shall Smith the second be called upon to pay the debts of Smith the first? I leave that question to Smith's conscience and the metaphysicians. Surely the same law should hold good in breach of promise of marriage.[3] Smith the first may have adored Miss Brown; Smith the second may detest her. Shall Smith of 1857 be called upon to perform the contract entered into by that other Smith of 1850? The French criminal law goes still further. The murderer whose crime remains unsuspected for ten years can laugh at the police-officers who discover his guilt in the eleventh. Surely this must be because the real murderer is no longer amenable to justice; because the hand that struck the blow, and the brain that plotted the deed, are alike vanished.

---

1   "I do not remember": stock answer used by an Italian servant of Queen Caroline during her "trial" for adultery in the House of Lords in 1820. The phrase passed into English idiom as a means of not expressing facts which it is convenient to forget.

2   This refers to the six-year limitation period concerning legal actions for debt. See 21 Jac.I.C.16 s.3 (AD 1623-4).

3   The unilateral breaking of an engagement to marry. In theory, the injured party could bring a case for damages for breach of promise; in practice, this legal solution was rare and frowned upon.

Poor John Mellish, with the world of the past crumbled at his feet, looked out at the blank future, and mourned for the people who were dead and gone.

He flung himself at full length upon the stunted grass, and taking the crumpled paper from his breast, unfolded it and smoothed it out before him.

It was a certificate of marriage. The certificate of a marriage which had been solemnized at the parish church of Dover, upon the 2nd of July, 1856, between James Conyers, bachelor, rough-rider, of London, son of Joseph Conyers, stage-coachman, and Susan, his wife, and Aurora Floyd, spinster, daughter of Archibald Floyd, banker, of Felden Woods, Kent.

CHAPTER XXVIII.

AURORA'S FLIGHT.

MRS. MELLISH sat in her husband's room on the morning of the inquest, amongst the guns and fishing-rods, the riding-boots and hunting-whips, and all the paraphernalia of sportsmanship. She sat in a capacious wicker-work arm-chair, close to the open window, with her head lying back upon the chintz-covered cushions, and her eyes wandering far away across the lawn and flower-beds towards the winding pathway by which it was likely John Mellish would return from the inquest at the Golden Lion.

She had openly defied Mrs. Powell, and had locked the door of this quiet chamber upon that lady's stereotyped civilities and sympathetic simperings. She had locked the door upon the outer world, and she sat alone in the pleasant window, the full-blown roses showering their scented petals upon her lap with every breath of the summer breeze, and the butterflies hovering about her. The old mastiff sat by her side, with his heavy head lying on her lap, and his big dim eyes lifted to her face. She sat alone, I have said; but Heaven knows she was not companionless. Black care and corroding anxiety kept her faithful company, and would not budge from her side. What companions are so adhesive as trouble and sorrow? what associates so tenacious, what friends so watchful and untiring? This wretched girl stood alone in the centre of a sea of troubles, fearful to stretch out her hands to those who loved her, lest she should drag them into that ocean which was rising to overwhelm her.

"Oh, if I could suffer alone!" she thought; "if I could suffer all this misery alone, I think I would go through it to the last without complaining; but the shame, the degradation, the anguish, will come upon others more heavily than upon me. What will they not suffer? what will they not endure, if the wicked madness of my youth should become known to the world?"

Those others, of whose possible grief and shame she thought with such cruel torture, were her father and John Mellish. Her love for her husband had not lessened by one iota her love for that indulgent father, on whom the folly of her girlhood had brought such bitter suffering. Her generous heart was wide enough for both. She had acknowledged no "divided duty,"[1] and would have repudiated any encroachment of the new affection upon the old. The great river of her love widened into an ocean, and embraced a new shore with its mighty tide; but that far-away source of childhood, from which affection first sprang in its soft infantine purity, still gushed in crystal beauty from its unsullied spring. She would perhaps scarcely have recognized the coldly-measured affection of mad Lear's youngest daughter – the affection which could divide itself with mathematical precision between father and husband.[2] Surely love is too pure a sentiment to be so weighed in the balance. Must we subtract something from the original sum when we are called upon to meet a new demand? or has not affection rather some magic power by which it can double its capital at any moment when there is a run upon the bank? When Mrs. John Anderson becomes the mother of six children, she does not say to her husband, "My dear John, I shall be compelled to rob you of six-tenths of my affection in order to provide for the little ones." No; the generous heart of the wife grows larger to meet the claims upon the mother, as the girl's heart expanded with the new affection of the wife. Every pang of grief which Aurora felt for her husband's misery was doubled by the image of her father's sorrow. She could not divide these two in her own mind. She loved them, and was sorry for them, with an equal measure of love and sorrow.

"If – if the truth should be discovered at this inquest," she thought, "I can never see my husband again; I can never look in his face any more. I will run away to the end of the world, and hide myself from him for ever."

She had tried to capitulate with her fate; she had endeavoured to escape the full measure of retribution, and she had failed. She had done evil that good might come of it, in the face of that command which says that all such evil-doing shall be wasted sin, useless iniquity.

---

1 In *Othello* I.iii.181, Desdemona acknowledges her duty divided between husband and father.

2 When King Lear asks his daughters how much they love him, Cordelia answers that, when she marries, her husband "shall carry/Half my love with him, half my care and duty" (I.i.101-3).

She had deceived John Mellish in the hope that the veil of deception might never be rent in twain, that the truth might be undiscovered to the end, and the man she loved spared from cruel shame and grief. But the fruits of that foolish seed, sown long ago in the day of her disobedience,[1] had grown up around her and hedged her in upon every side, and she had been powerless to cut a pathway for herself through the noxious weeds that her own hands had planted.

She sat with her watch in her hand, and her eyes wandered every now and then from the gardens before her to the figures on the dial. John Mellish had left the house at a little after nine o'clock, and it was now nearly two. He had told her that the inquest would be over in a couple of hours, and that he would hurry home directly it was finished, to tell her the result. What would be the result of that inquest? What inquiries might be made? what evidence might, by some unhappy accident, be produced to compromise or to betray her? She sat in a dull stupor, waiting to receive her sentence. What would it be? Condemnation or release? *If* her secret should escape detection, if James Conyers should be allowed to carry the story of his brief married life to the grave, what relief, what release for the wretched girl, whose worst sin had been to mistake a bad man for a good one; the ignorant trustfulness of a child who is ready to accept any shabby pilgrim for an exiled nobleman or a prince in disguise!

It was half-past two, when she was startled by the sound of a shambling footstep upon the gravelled pathway underneath the verandah. The footstep slowly shuffled on for a few paces; then paused, then shuffled on again; and at last a face that she hated made itself visible at the angle of the window, opposite to that against which she sat. It was the white face of the "Softy," which was poked cautiously forward a few inches within the window-frame. The mastiff sprang up with a growl, and made as if he would have flown at that ugly leering face, which looked like one of the hideous decorations of a Gothic building; but Aurora caught the animal's collar with both her hands, and dragged him back.

"Be quiet, Bow-wow," she said; "quiet, boy, – quiet."

---

1   See *Paradise Lost* (Book 1, Line 1). The third reference comparing Aurora to Eve. See also 256, n.1 and 380, n.1.

She still held him with one firm hand, soothing him with the other. "What do you want?" she asked, turning upon the "Softy" with a cold icy grandeur of disdain, which made her look like Nero's wife defying her false accusers.[1] "What do you want with me? Your master is dead, and you have no longer an excuse for coming here. You have been forbidden the house and the grounds. If you forget this another time, I shall request Mr. Mellish to remind you."

She lifted her disengaged hand and laid it upon the window-sash; she was going to draw it down, when Stephen Hargraves stopped her.

"Don't be in such a hoory," he said; "I want to speak to you. I've coom straight from th' inquest. I thought you might want to know all about it. I coom out o' friendliness, though you did pay into me with th' horsewhip."

Aurora's heart beat tempestuously against her aching breast. Ah! what hard duty that poor heart had done lately! what icy burdens it had borne, what horrible oppression of secrecy and terror had weighed upon it, crushing out all hope and peace! An agony of suspense and dread convulsed that tortured heart as the "Softy" tempted her, tempted her to ask him the issue of the inquest, that she might receive from his lips the sentence of life or death. She little knew how much of her secret this man had discovered; but she knew that he hated her, and that he suspected enough to know his power of torturing her.

She lifted her proud head and looked at him with a steady glance of defiance. "I have told you that your presence is disagreeable," she said. "Stand aside, and let me shut the window."

The "Softy" grinned insolently, and holding the window-frame with one of his broad hands, put his head into the room. Aurora rose to leave the window; but he laid the other hand upon her wrist, which shrunk instinctively from contact with his hard horny palm.

"I tell you I've got summat particklar to say to you," he whispered. "You shall hear all about it. I was one of th' witnesses at th' inquest, and I've been hanging about ever since, and I know everything."

---

1 Octavia, first wife of Nero, was falsely accused by Nero of adultery with a slave and banished to Campania. She was later (again falsely) accused of conspiracy against Nero and ordered to kill herself.

Aurora flung her head back disdainfully, and tried to wrench her wrist from that strong grasp.

"Let me go!" she said. "You shall suffer for this insolence when Mr. Mellish returns."

"But he won't be back just yet awhile," said the "Softy," grinning. "He's gone back to the Golden Lion. Th' coroner and Mr. Lofthouse, th' parson, sent for him to tell him summat – *summat about you!*" hissed Mr. Stephen Hargraves, with his dry white lips close to Aurora's ear.

"What do you mean?" cried Mrs. Mellish, still writhing in the "Softy's" grasp, still restraining her dog from flying at him with her disengaged hand; "what do you mean?"

"I mean what I say," answered Steeve Hargraves; "I mean that it's all found out. They know everything; and they've sent for Mr. Mellish to tell him. They've sent for him to tell him what you was to him that's dead."

A low wail broke from Aurora's lips. She had expected to hear this, perhaps; she had, at any rate, dreaded it; she had only fought against receiving the tidings from this man; but he had conquered her; he had conquered her as the dogged obstinate nature, however base, however mean, will always conquer the generous and impulsive soul. He had secured his revenge, and had contrived to be the witness of her agony. He released her wrist as he finished speaking, and looked at her – looked at her with an insolently triumphant leer in his small eyes.

She drew herself up, proudly still, proudly and bravely in spite of all, but with her face changed – changed from its former expression of restless pain to the dull blankness of despair.

"They found th' certificate," said the "Softy." "He'd carried it about with him, sewed up in's waistco-at."

The certificate! Heaven have pity upon her girlish ignorance! She had never thought of that; she had never remembered that miserable scrap of paper which was the legal evidence of her folly. She had dreaded the presence of that husband who had arisen, as if from the grave, to pursue and torment her; but she had forgotten that other evidence of the parish register, which might also arise against her at any moment. She had feared the finding of something – some letter – some picture – some accidental record amongst the possessions of the murdered man; but she had never thought of this most conclusive evidence, this most incontrovertible proof. She put her hand to her head, trying to realize the full horror of her position. The certificate of her marriage with her father's groom was in the hands of John Mellish.

"What will he think of me?" she thought. "How would he ever believe me if I were to tell him that I had received what I thought positive evidence of James Conyers's death a year before my second marriage? How *could* he believe in me? I have deceived him too cruelly to dare to ask his confidence."

She looked about, trying to collect herself, trying to decide upon what she ought to do, and in her bewilderment and agony forgot for a moment the greedy eyes which were gloating upon her misery. But she remembered herself presently, and turning sternly upon Stephen Hargraves, spoke to him with a voice which was singularly clear and steady.

"You have told me all that you have to tell," she said; "be so good as to get out of the way while I shut the window."

The "Softy" drew back and allowed her to close the sashes; she bolted the window, and drew down the Venetian blind, effectually shutting out her spy, who crept away slowly and reluctantly towards the shrubbery, through which he could make his way safely out of the grounds.

"I've paid her out," he muttered, as he shambled off under the shelter of the young trees; "I've paid her out pretty tidy. It's almost better than money," he said, laughing silently – "it's almost better than money to pay off them kind of debts."

Aurora seated herself at John Mellish's desk, and wrote a few hurried lines upon a sheet of paper that lay uppermost amongst letters and bills.

"MY DEAR LOVE," – she wrote, – "I cannot remain here to see you after the discovery which has been made to-day. I am a miserable coward; and I cannot meet your altered looks, I cannot hear your altered voice. I have no hope that you can have any other feeling for me than contempt and loathing. But on some future day, when I am far away from you, and the bewilderment of my present misery has grown less, I will write and explain everything. Think of me mercifully, if you can; and if you can believe that, in the wicked concealments of the last few weeks, the mainspring of my conduct has been my love for you, you will only believe the truth. God bless you, my best and truest. The pain of leaving you for ever is less than the pain of knowing that you had ceased to love me. Good-bye."

She lighted a taper, and sealed the envelope which contained this letter.

"The spies who hate and watch me shall not read this," she thought, as she wrote John's name upon the envelope.

She left the letter upon the desk, and, rising from her seat, looked round the room, – looked with a long lingering gaze, that dwelt on each familiar object. How happy she had been amongst all that masculine litter! how happy with the man she had believed to be her husband! how innocently happy before the coming down of that horrible storm-cloud which had overwhelmed them both! She turned away with a shudder.

"I have brought disgrace and misery upon all who have loved me," she thought. "If I had been less cowardly, – if I had told the truth, – all this might have been avoided, if I had confessed the truth to Talbot Bulstrode."

She paused at the mention of that name.

"I will go to Talbot," she thought. "He is a good man. I will go to him; I shall have no shame now in telling him all. He will advise me what to do; he will break this discovery to my poor father."

Aurora had dimly foreseen this misery when she had spoken to Lucy Bulstrode at Felden; she had dimly foreseen a day in which all would be discovered, and she would fly to Lucy to ask for a shelter.

She looked at her watch.

"A quarter past three," she said. "There is an express that leaves Doncaster at five. I could walk the distance in the time."

She unlocked the door, and ran up-stairs to her own rooms. There was no one in the dressing-room; but her maid was in the bedroom, arranging some dresses in a huge wardrobe.

Aurora selected her plainest bonnet and a large gray cloak, and quietly put them on before the cheval glass in one of the pretty French windows. The maid, busy with her own work, did not take any particular notice of her mistress's actions; for Mrs. Mellish was accustomed to wait upon herself, and disliked any officious attention.

"How pretty the rooms look!" Aurora thought, with a weary sigh; "how simple and countrified! It was for *me* that the new furniture was chosen, – for me that the bath-room and conservatory were built."

She looked through the vista of brightly-carpeted rooms.

Would they ever seem as cheerful as they had once done to their master? Would he still occupy them, or would he lock the doors, and turn his back upon the old house in which he had lived such an untroubled life for nearly two-and-thirty years?

"My poor boy, my poor boy!" she thought. "Why was I ever born to bring such sorrow upon him?"

There was no egotism in her sorrow for his grief. She knew that he had loved her, and she knew that this parting would be the bitterest agony of his life; but in the depth of mortification which her own womanly pride had undergone, she could not look beyond the present shame of the discovery made that day, to a future of happiness and release.

"He will believe that I never loved him," she thought. "He will believe that he was the dupe of a designing woman, who wished to regain the position she had lost. What will he not think of me that is base and horrible?"

The face which she saw in the glass was very pale and rigid; the large dark eyes dry and lustrous, the lips drawn tightly down over the white teeth.

"I look like a woman who could cut her throat in such a crisis as this," she thought. "How often I have wondered at the desperate deeds done by women! I shall never wonder again."

She unlocked her dressing-case, and took a couple of bank-notes and some loose gold from one of the drawers. She put these in her purse, gathered her cloak about her, and walked towards the door.

She paused on the threshold to speak to her maid, who was still busy in the inner room.

"I am going into the garden, Parsons," she said; "tell Mr. Mellish that there is a letter for him in his study."

The room in which John kept his boots and racing accounts was called a "study" by the respectful household.

The dog Bow-wow lifted himself lazily from his tiger-skin rug as Aurora crossed the hall, and came sniffing about her, and endeavoured to follow her out of the house. But she ordered him back to his rug, and the submissive animal obeyed her, as he had often done in his youth, when his young mistress used to throw her doll into the water at Felden, and send the faithful mastiff to rescue that fair-haired waxen favourite. He obeyed her now, but a little reluctantly; and he watched her suspiciously as she descended the flight of steps before the door.

She walked at a rapid pace across the lawn, and into the shrubbery, going steadily southwards, though by that means she made her journey longer; for the north lodge lay towards Doncaster. In her way through the shrubbery she met two people, who walked closely side by side, engrossed in a whispering conversation, and who both started and changed countenance at seeing her. These two people were the "Softy" and Mrs. Powell.

"So," she thought, as she passed this strangely-matched pair, "my two enemies are laying their heads together to plot my misery. It is time that I left Mellish Park."

She went out of a little gate, leading into some meadows. Beyond these meadows there was a long shady lane that led behind the house to Doncaster. It was a path rarely chosen by any of the household at the Park, as it was the longest way to the town.

Aurora stopped at about a mile from the house which had been her own, and looked back at the picturesque pile of building, half hidden under the luxuriant growth of a couple of centuries.

"Good-bye, dear home, in which I was an impostor and a cheat," she said; "good-bye, for ever and for ever, my own dear love."

While Aurora uttered these few words of passionate farewell, John Mellish lay upon the sun-burnt grass, staring absently at the still water-pools under the gray sky, – pitying her, praying for her, and forgiving her from the depth of his honest heart.

CHAPTER XXIX.

JOHN MELLISH FINDS HIS HOME DESOLATE.

THE sun was low in the western sky, and distant village-clocks had struck seven, when John Mellish walked slowly away from that lonely waste of stunted grass called Harper's Common, and strolled homewards in the peaceful evening.

The Yorkshire squire was still very pale. He walked with his head bent forward upon his breast, and the hand that grasped the crumpled paper thrust into the bosom of his waistcoat; but a hopeful light shone in his eyes, and the rigid lines of his mouth had relaxed into a tender smile – a smile of love and forgiveness. Yes, he had prayed for her and forgiven her, and he was at peace. He had pleaded her cause a hundred times in the dull quiet of that summer's afternoon, and had excused her and forgiven her. Not lightly, Heaven is a witness; not without a sharp and cruel struggle, that had rent his heart with tortures undreamed of before.

This revelation of the past was such bitter shame to him; such horrible degradation; such irrevocable infamy. His love, his idol, his empress, his goddess – it was of her he thought. By what hellish witchcraft had she been ensnared into the degrading alliance, recorded in this miserable scrap of paper? The pride of five unsullied centuries arose, fierce and ungovernable, in the breast of the country gentleman, to resent this outrage upon the woman he loved. O God! had all his glorification of her been the vain-boasting of a fool who had not known what he talked about? He was answerable to the world for the past as well as for the present. He had made an altar for his idol, and had cried aloud to all who came near her, to kneel down and perform their worship at her shrine; and he was answerable to these people for the purity of their divinity. He could not think of her as less than the idol which his love had made her – perfect, unsullied, unassailable. Disgrace, where she was concerned, knew in his mind no degrees.

It was not his own humiliation he thought of when his face grew hot as he imagined the talk there would be in the country if this fatal indiscretion of Aurora's youth ever became generally known; it was the thought of her shame that stung him to the heart. He never once disturbed himself with any prevision of the ridicule which was likely to fall upon himself.

It was here that John Mellish and Talbot Bulstrode were so widely different in their manner of loving and suffering. Talbot had sought a wife who should reflect honour upon himself, and had fallen away from Aurora at the first trial of his faith, shaken with horrible apprehensions of his own danger. But John Mellish had submerged his very identity into that of the woman he loved. She was his faith and his worship, and it was for her departed glory that he wept in this cruel day of shame. The wrong which he found so hard to forgive was not her wrong against him; but that other and more fatal wrong against herself. I have said that his affection was universal, and partook of all the highest attributes of that sublime self-abnegation which we call Love. The agony which he felt to-day was the agony which Archibald Floyd had suffered years before. It was vicarious torture, endured for Aurora, and not for himself; and in his struggle against that sorrowful anger which he felt for her folly, every one of her perfections took up arms upon the side of indignation, and fought against their own mistress. Had she been less beautiful, less queenly, less generous, great and noble, he might have forgiven her that self-inflicted shame more easily. But she was so perfect; and how could she, how could she?

He unfolded the wretched paper half a dozen times, and read and re-read every word of that commonplace legal document, before he could convince himself that it was not some vile forgery, concocted by James Conyers for purposes of extortion. But he prayed for her, and forgave her. He pitied her with more than a mother's tender pity, with more than a sorrowful father's anguish.

"My poor dear!" he said, "my poor dear! she was only a school-girl when this certificate was first written: an innocent child; ready to believe in any lies told her by a villain."

A dark frown obscured the Yorkshireman's brow as he thought this; a frown that would have promised no good to Mr. James Conyers, had not the trainer passed out of the reach of all earthly good and evil.

"Will God have mercy upon a wretch like that?" thought John Mellish; "will that man be forgiven for having brought disgrace and misery upon a trusting girl?"

It will perhaps be wondered at, that John Mellish, who suffered his servants to rule in his household, and allowed his butler to dictate to him what wines he should drink; who talked freely to his grooms, and bade his trainer sit in his presence, – it will be wondered at, perhaps, that this frank, free-spoken, simple-mannered young man should have felt so bitterly the shame of Aurora's unequal marriage. It was a common saying in Doncaster, that Squire Mellish of the Park had no pride; that he would clap poor folks on the shoulder and give them good-day as he lounged in the quiet street; that he would sit upon the cornchandler's counter, slashing his hunting-whip upon those popular tops, about which a legend was current, to the effect that they were always cleaned with champagne, – and discussing the prospects of the September Meeting; and that there was not within the three Ridings, a better landlord or a nobler-hearted gentleman. And all this was perfectly true. John Mellish was entirely without personal pride; but there was another pride, which was wholly inseparable from his education and position, and this was the pride of caste. He was strictly conservative; and although he was ready to talk to his good friend the saddler, or his trusted retainer the groom, as freely as he would have held converse with his equals, he would have opposed all the strength of his authority against the saddler had that honest tradesman attempted to stand for his native town,[1] and would have annihilated the groom with one angry flash of his bright blue eyes had the servant infringed by so much as an inch upon the broad extent of territory that separated him from his master.

The struggle was finished before John Mellish arose from the brown turf and turned towards the home which he had left early that morning, ignorant of the great trouble that was to fall upon him, and only dimly conscious of some dark foreboding of the coming of an unknown horror. The struggle was over, and there was now only hope in his heart – the hope of clasping his wife to his breast, and comforting her for all the past. However bitterly he might feel the humiliation of this madness of her ignorant girlhood, it was not for him to remind her of it; his duty was to confront the world's slander or the world's

---

1   In 1858 the property qualifications for members of the House of Commons were
      formally abolished.

ridicule, and oppose his own breast to the storm, while she was shielded by the great shelter of his love. His heart yearned for some peaceful foreign land, in which his idol would be far away from all who could tell her secret, and where she might reign once more glorious and unapproachable. He was ready to impose any cheat upon the world, in his greediness of praise and worship for her – for her. How tenderly he thought of her, walking slowly homewards in that tranquil evening! He thought of her waiting to hear from him the issue of the inquest, and he reproached himself for his neglect when he remembered how long he had been absent.

"But my darling will scarcely be uneasy," he thought; "she will hear all about the inquest from some one or other, and she will think that I have gone into Doncaster on business. She will know nothing of the finding of this detestable certificate. No one need know of it. Lofthouse and Hayward are honourable men, and they will keep my poor girl's secret; they will keep the secret of her foolish youth, – my poor, poor girl!"

He longed for that moment which he fancied so near; the moment in which he should fold her in his arms and say, "My dearest one, be at peace; there is no longer any secret between us. Henceforth your sorrows are my sorrows, and it is hard if I cannot help you to carry the load lightly. We are one, my dear. For the first time since our wedding-day, we are truly united."

He expected to find Aurora in his own room, for she had declared her intention of sitting there all day; and he ran across the broad lawn to the rose-shadowed verandah that sheltered his favourite retreat. The blind was drawn down and the window bolted, as Aurora had bolted it in her wish to exclude Mr. Stephen Hargraves. He knocked at the window, but there was no answer.

"Lolly has grown tired of waiting," he thought.

The second dinner-bell rang in the hall while Mr. Mellish lingered outside this darkened window. The commonplace sound reminded him of his social duties.

"I must wait till dinner is over, I suppose, before I talk to my darling," he thought. "I must go through all the usual business, for the edification of Mrs. Powell and the servants, before I can take my darling to my breast, and set her mind at ease for ever."

John Mellish submitted himself to the indisputable force of those ceremonial laws which we have made our masters, and he was prepared to eat a dinner for which he had no appetite, and wait two hours for that moment for whose coming his soul yearned, rather than provoke Mrs. Powell's curiosity by any deviation from the common course of events.

The windows of the drawing-room were open, and he saw the glimmer of a pale muslin dress at one of them. It belonged to Mrs. Powell, who was sitting in a contemplative attitude, gazing at the evening sky.

She was not thinking of that western glory of pale crimson and shining gold. She was thinking that if John Mellish cast off the wife who had deceived him, and who had never legally been his wife, the Yorkshire mansion would be a fine place to live in; a fine place for a housekeeper who knew how to obtain influence over her master, and who had the secret of his married life and his wife's disgrace to help her on to power.

"He's such a blind, besotted fool about her," thought the ensign's widow, "that if he breaks with her to-morrow, he'll go on loving her just the same, and he'll do anything to keep her secret. Let it work which way it will, they're in my power – they're both in my power; and I'm no longer a poor dependent, to be sent away, at a quarter's notice, when it pleases them to be tired of me."

The bread of dependence is not a pleasant diet; but there are many ways of eating the same food. Mrs. Powell's habit was to receive all favours grudgingly, as she would have given, had it been her lot to give instead of to receive. She measured others by her own narrow gauge, and was powerless to comprehend or believe in the frank impulses of a generous nature. She knew that she was a useless member of poor John's household, and that the young squire could have easily dispensed with her presence. She knew, in short, that she was retained by reason of Aurora's pity for her friendlessness; and having neither gratitude nor kindly feelings to give in return for her comfortable shelter, she resented her own poverty of nature, and hated her entertainers for their generosity. It is a property of these narrow natures so to resent the attributes they can envy, but cannot even understand; and Mrs. Powell had been far more at ease in households in which she had been treated as a lady-like drudge than she had ever been at Mellish Park, where she was received as an equal and a guest. She had eaten the bitter bread upon which she had lived so long in a bitter spirit; and her whole nature had turned to gall from the influence of that disagreeable diet. A moderately-generous person can bestow a favour, and bestow it well; but to receive a boon with perfect grace requires a far nobler and more generous nature.

John Mellish approached the open window at which the ensign's widow was seated, and looked into the room. Aurora was not there. The long saloon seemed empty and desolate. The decorations of the temple looked cold and dreary, for the deity was absent.

"No one here!" exclaimed Mr. Mellish, disconsolately.

"No one here but me," murmured Mrs. Powell, with an accent of mild deprecation.

"But where is my wife, ma'am?"

He said those two small words, "my wife," with such a tone of resolute defiance, that Mrs. Powell looked up at him as he spoke, and thought, "He has seen the certificate."

"Where is Aurora?" repeated John.

"I believe that Mrs. Mellish has gone out."

"Gone out! where?"

"You forget, sir," said the ensign's widow reproachfully, – "you appear to forget your special request that I should abstain from all supervision of Mrs. Mellish's arrangements. Prior to that request, which I may venture to suggest was unnecessarily emphatic, I had certainly considered myself, as the humble individual chosen by Miss Floyd's aunt, and invested by her with a species of authority over the young lady's actions, in some manner responsible for——"

John Mellish chafed horribly under the merciless stream of long words, which Mrs. Powell poured upon his head.

"Talk about that another time, for Heaven's sake, ma'am," he said impatiently. "I only want to know where my wife is. Two words will tell me that, I suppose?"

"I am sorry to say that I am unable to afford you any information upon that subject," answered Mrs. Powell; "Mrs. Mellish quitted the house at half-past three o'clock, dressed for walking. I have not seen her since."

Heaven forgive Aurora for the trouble it had been her lot to bring upon those who best loved her! John's heart grew sick with terror at this first failure of his hope. He had pictured her waiting to receive him, ready to fall upon his breast in answer to his passionate cry, "Aurora, come! come, dear love! the secret has been discovered, and is forgiven."

"Somebody knows where my wife has gone, I suppose, Mrs. Powell?" he said fiercely, turning upon the ensign's widow in his wrathful sense of disappointment and alarm. He was only a big child, after all, with a child's alternate hopefulness and despair; with a child's passionate devotion for those he loved, and ignorant terror of danger to those beloved ones.

"Mrs. Mellish may have made a confidante of Parsons," replied the ensign's widow; "but she certainly did not enlighten *me* as to her intended movements. Shall I ring the bell for Parsons?"

"If you please."

John Mellish stood upon the threshold of the French window, not caring to enter the handsome chamber of which he was the master. Why should he go into the house? It was no home for him without the woman who had made it so dear and sacred; dear, even in the darkest hour of sorrow and anxiety; sacred, even in despite of the trouble his love had brought upon him.

The maid Parsons appeared in answer to a message sent by Mrs. Powell; and John strode into the room and interrogated her sharply as to the departure of her mistress.

The girl could tell very little, except that Mrs. Mellish had said that she was going into the garden, and that she had left a letter in the study for the master of the house. Perhaps Mrs. Powell was even better aware of the existence of this letter than the Abigail herself. She had crept stealthily into John's room after her interview with the "Softy" and her chance encounter of Aurora. She had found the letter lying on the table, sealed with a crest and monogram that were engraved upon a blood-stone worn by Mrs. Mellish amongst the trinkets on her watch-chain. It was not possible therefore to manipulate this letter with any safety, and Mrs. Powell had contented herself by guessing darkly at its contents. The "Softy" had told her of the fatal discovery of the morning, and she instinctively comprehended the meaning of that sealed letter. It was a letter of explanation and farewell, perhaps; perhaps only of farewell.

John strode along the corridor that led to his favourite room. The chamber was dimly lighted by the yellow evening sunlight which streamed from between the Venetian blinds, and drew golden bars upon the matted floor. But even in that dusky and uncertain light he saw the white patch upon the table, and sprang with tigerish haste upon the letter his wife had left for him.

He drew up the Venetian blind, and stood in the embrasure of the window, with the evening sunlight upon his face, reading Aurora's letter. There was neither anger nor alarm visible in his face as he read; only supreme love and supreme compassion.

"My poor darling! my poor girl! How could she think that there could ever be such a word as good-bye between us! Does she think so lightly of my love as to believe that it could fail her now, when she wants it most? Why, if that man had lived," he thought, his face darkening with the memory of that unburied clay which yet lay in the still chamber at the north lodge, – "if that man had lived, and had claimed her, and carried her from me by the right of the paper in my breast, I would have clung to her still; I would have followed wherever he went, and would have lived near him, that she might have known where to look for a defender from every wrong: I would have been his servant, the willing servant and contented hanger-on of a boor, if I could have served her by enduring his insolence. So, my dear, my dear," murmured the young squire, with a tender smile, "it was worse than foolish to write this letter to me, and even more useless than it was cruel to run away from the man who would follow you to the farthest end of this wide world."

He put the letter into his pocket, and took his hat from the table. He was ready to start – he scarcely knew for what destination; for the end of the world, perhaps – in his search for the woman he loved. But he was going to Felden Woods before beginning the longer journey, as he fully believed that Aurora would fly to her father in her foolish terror.

"To think that anything could ever happen to change or lessen my love for her," he said; "foolish girl! foolish girl!"

He rang for his servant, and ordered the hasty packing of his smallest portmanteau. He was going to town for a day or two, and he was going alone. He looked at his watch; it was only a quarter after eight, and the mail left Doncaster at half-past twelve. There was plenty of time, therefore; a great deal too much time for the feverish impatience of Mr. Mellish, who would have chartered a special engine to convey him, had the railway officials been willing. There were four long hours during which he must wait, wearing out his heart in his anxiety to follow the woman he loved, to take her to his breast and comfort and shelter her, to tell her that true love knows neither decrease nor change. He ordered the dog-cart to be got ready for him at eleven o'clock. There was a slow train that left Doncaster at ten; but as it reached London only ten minutes before the mail, it was scarcely desirable as a conveyance. Yet after the hour had passed for its starting, Mr. Mellish reproached himself bitterly for that lost ten minutes, and was tormented by a fancy that, through the loss of those very ten minutes, he should miss the chance of an immediate meeting with Aurora.

It was nine o'clock before he remembered the necessity of making some pretence of sitting down to dinner. He took his place at the end of the long table, and sent for Mrs. Powell, who appeared in answer to his summons, and seated herself with a well-bred affectation of not knowing that the dinner had been put off for an hour and a half.

"I'm sorry I've kept you so long, Mrs. Powell," he said, as he sent the ensign's widow a ladleful of clear soup, that was of the temperature of lemonade. "The truth is, that I – I – find I shall be compelled to run up to town by the mail."

"Upon no unpleasant business, I hope?"

"Oh, dear no, not at all. Mrs. Mellish has gone up to her father's place, and – and – has requested me to follow her," added John, telling a lie with considerable awkwardness, but with no very great remorse. He did not speak again during dinner. He ate anything that his servants put before him, and took a good deal of wine; but he ate and drank alike unconsciously, and when the cloth had been removed, and he was left alone with Mrs. Powell, he sat staring at the reflection of the wax-candles in the depths of the mahogany. It was only when the lady gave a little ceremonial cough, and rose with the intention of simpering out of the room, that he roused himself from his long reverie, and looked up suddenly.

"Don't go just this moment, if you please, Mrs. Powell," he said. "If you'll sit down again for a few minutes, I shall be glad. I wished to say a word or two to you before I leave Mellish Park."

He rose as he spoke, and pointed to a chair. Mrs. Powell seated herself, and looked at him earnestly; with an eager, viperish earnestness, and a nervous movement of her thin lips.

"When you came here, Mrs. Powell," said John, gravely, "you came as my wife's guest, and as my wife's friend. I need scarcely say that you could have had no better claim upon my friendship and hospitality. If you had brought a regiment of dragoons with you, as the condition of your visit, they would have been welcome; for I believed that your coming would give pleasure to my poor girl. If my wife had been indebted to you for any word of kindness, for any look of affection, I would have repaid that debt a thousand-fold, had it lain in my power to do so by any service, however difficult. You would have lost nothing by your love for my poor motherless girl, if any devotion of mine could have recompensed you for that tenderness. It was only reasonable that I should look to you as the natural friend and counsellor of my darling; and I did so, honestly and confidently. Forgive me if I tell you that I very soon discovered how much I had been mistaken in entertaining such a hope. I soon saw that you were no friend to my wife."

"Mr. Mellish!"

"Oh, my dear madam, you think because I keep hunting-boots and guns in the room I call my study, and because I remember no more of the Latin that my tutor crammed into my head than the first line of the Eton Syntax, – you think, because I'm not clever, that I must needs be a fool. That's your mistake, Mrs. Powell; I'm not clever enough to be a fool, and I've just sufficient perception to see any danger that assails those I love. You don't like my wife; you grudge her her youth and her beauty, and my foolish love for her; and you've watched, and listened, and plotted – in a lady-like way of course – to do her some evil. Forgive me if I speak plainly. Where Aurora is concerned, I feel very strongly. To hurt her little finger is to torture my whole body. To stab her once is to stab me a hundred times. I have no wish to be discourteous to a lady; I am only sorry that you have been unable to love a poor girl who has rarely failed to win friends amongst those who have known her. Let us part without animosity, but let us understand each other for the first time. You do not like us, and it is better that we should part before you learn to hate us."

The ensign's widow waited in utter stupefaction until Mr. Mellish stopped, from want of breath, perhaps, rather than from want of words.

All her viperish nature rose in white defiance of him as he walked up and down the room, chafing himself into a fury with his recollection of the wrong she had done him in not loving his wife.

"You are perhaps aware, Mr. Mellish," she said, after an awful pause, "that under such circumstances the annual stipend due to me for my services cannot be expected to cease at your caprice; and that, although you may turn me out of doors," – Mrs. Powell descended to this very commonplace locution, and stooped to the vernacular in her desire to be spiteful, – "you must understand that you will be liable for my salary until the expiration of——"

"Oh, pray do not imagine that I shall repudiate any claim you may make upon me, Mrs. Powell," said John, eagerly; "Heaven knows it has been no pleasure to me to speak as plainly as I have spoken to-night. I will write a cheque for any amount you may consider proper as compensation for this change in our arrangements. I might have been more polite, perhaps; I might have told you that my wife and I think of travelling on the Continent, and that we are, therefore, breaking up our household. I have preferred telling you the plain truth. Forgive me if I have wounded you."

Mrs. Powell rose, pale, menacing, terrible; terrible in the intensity of her feeble wrath, and in the consciousness that she had power to stab the heart of the man who had affronted her.

"You have merely anticipated my own intention, Mr. Mellish," she said. "I could not possibly have remained a member of your household after the very unpleasant circumstances that have lately transpired. My worst wish is, that you may find yourself involved in no greater trouble through your connection with Mr. Floyd's daughter. Let me add one word of warning before I have the honour of wishing you good evening. Malicious people might be tempted to smile at your enthusiastic mention of your 'wife;' remembering that the person to whom you allude is Aurora Conyers, the widow of your groom, and that she has never possessed any legal claim to the title you bestow upon her."

If Mrs. Powell had been a man, she would have found her head in contact with the Turkey carpet of John's dining-room before she could have concluded this speech; as she was a woman, John Mellish stood looking her full in the face, waiting till she had finished speaking. But he bore the stab she inflicted without flinching under its cruel pain, and he robbed her of the gratification she had hoped for. He did not let her see his anguish.

"If Lofthouse has told her the secret," he cried, when the door had closed upon Mrs. Powell, "I'll horsewhip him in the church."

CHAPTER XXX.

AN UNEXPECTED VISITOR.

AURORA found a civil railway official at the Doncaster station, who was ready to take a ticket for her, and find her a comfortable seat in an empty carriage; but before the train started, a couple of sturdy farmers took their seats upon the spring cushions opposite Mrs. Mellish. They were wealthy gentlemen, who farmed their own land, and travelled express; but they brought a powerful odour of the stable-yard into the carriage, and they talked with that honest northern twang which always has a friendly sound to the writer of this story. Aurora, with her veil drawn over her pale face, attracted very little of their attention. They talked of farming-stock and horse-racing, and looked out of the window every now and then to shrug their shoulders at somebody else's agriculture.

I believe they were acquainted with the capabilities of every acre of land between Doncaster and Harrow, and knew how it might have been made "worth ten shillin' an acre more than it was, too, sir," as they perpetually informed each other.

How wearisome their talk must have seemed to the poor lonely creature who was running away from the man she loved, – from the man who loved her, and would love to the end of time!

"I didn't mean what I wrote," she thought. "My poor boy would never love me less. His great heart is made up of unselfish love and generous devotion. But he would be so sorry for me; he would be so sorry! He could never be proud of me again; he could never boast of me any more. He would be always resenting some insult, or imagining some slight. It would be too painful for him. He would see his wife pointed at as the woman who had married her groom. He would be embroiled in a hundred quarrels, a hundred miseries. I will make the only return that I can ever make to him for his goodness to me: I will give him up, and go away and hide myself from him for ever." She tried to imagine what John's life would be without her. She tried to think of him in some future time, when he should have worn out his grief, and reconciled himself to her loss. But she could not, she could not! She could not endure any image of *him* in which he was separated from his love for her.

"How should I ever think of him without thinking of his love for me?" she thought. "He loved me from the first moment in which he saw me. I have never known him except as a lover; generous, pure, and true."

And in this mind Aurora watched the smaller stations, which looked like mere streaks of whitened woodwork as the express tore past them; though every one of them was a milestone upon the long road which was separating her from the man she loved.

Ah, careless wives, who think it a small thing, perhaps, that your husbands are honest and generous, constant and true, and who are apt to grumble because your next-door neighbours have started a carriage, while you are fain to be content with eighteenpenny airings in vehicles procured at the nearest cab-stand, – stop and think of this wretched girl, who in this hour of desolation recalled a thousand little wrongs she had done to her husband, and would have laid herself under his feet to be walked over by him could she have thus atoned for her petty tyrannies, her pretty caprices! Think of her in her loneliness, with her heart yearning to go back to the man she loved, and with her love arrayed against herself and pleading for him. She changed her mind a hundred times during that four hours' journey; sometimes thinking that she would go back by the next train, and then again remembering that her first impulse had been, perhaps, after all, only too correct, and that John Mellish's heart had turned against her in the cruel humiliation of that morning's discovery.

Have you ever tried to imagine the anger of a person whom you have never seen angry? Have you ever called up the image of a face that has never looked on you except in love and gentleness, and invested that familiar countenance with the blank sternness of estrangement? Aurora did this. She acted over and over again in her weary brain the scene that might have taken place between her husband and herself. She remembered that scene in the hackneyed stage-play, which everybody affects to ridicule and secretly weeps at. She remembered Mrs. Haller and the Stranger, the children, the Countess, the cottage, the jewels, the parchments, and all the old familiar properties of that well-known fifth act in the simple, social tragedy; and she pictured to herself John Mellish retiring into some distant country with his rheumatic trainer Langley, and becoming a misanthropical hermit, after the manner of the injured German.[1]

What was her life to be henceforth? She shut her eyes upon that blank future.

"I will go back to my father," she thought; "I will go back to him again, as I went before. But this time there shall be no falsehoods, no equivocations; and this time nothing shall tempt me to leave him again."

Amid all her perplexities, she clung to the thought that Lucy and Talbot would help her. She would appeal to passionless Talbot Bulstrode in behalf of her poor heart-broken John. "Talbot will tell me what is right and honourable to be done," she thought. "I will hold by what he says. He shall be the arbiter of my future."

I do not believe that Aurora had ever entertained any very passionate devotion for the handsome Cornishman; but it is very certain that she had always respected him. It may be that any love she had felt for him had grown out of that very respect, and that her reverence for his character was made all the greater by the contrast between him and the base-born schemer for whom her youth had been sacrificed. She had submitted to the decree which had separated her from her affianced lover, for she had believed in its justice; and she was ready now to submit to any decision pronounced by the man, in whose sense of honour she had unbounded confidence.

She thought of all these things again and again and again, while the farmers talked of sheep and turnips, of Thorley's food, swedes, and beans, and corn, and clover, and of mysterious diseases, which they discussed gravely, under such terms as "red gum," "finger and toe," &c. They alternated this talk with a dash of turf scandal; and even in the all-absorbing perplexities of her domestic sorrows, Mrs. Mellish could have turned fiercely upon these innocent farmers when they pooh-

---

1   Mrs. Haller, the heroine of August Von Kotzebue's *The Stranger* (produced at Drury Lane in 1798), commits adultery, betraying her worthy husband. She repents and retires to the country; meanwhile, her husband ("The Stranger," also the "injured German"), lives as a hermit with his servant Francis. Act V reunites them; the "parchment" is Adelaide's confession of adultery, offered to her husband so that he might obtain a divorce.

poohed John's stable, and made light of the reputation of her name-sake the bay filly, and declared that no horse that came out of the squire's stables was ever anything better than a plater or a screw.[1]

The journey came to an end, only too quickly, it seemed to Aurora: too quickly, for every mile widened the gulf she had set between herself and the home she loved; every moment only brought the realization of her loss more fully home to her mind.

"I will abide by Talbot Bulstrode's advice," she kept saying to herself; indeed, this thought was the only reed to which she clung in her trouble. She was not a strong-minded woman. She had the generous, impulsive nature which naturally turns to others for help and comfort. Secretiveness had no part in her organization, and the one concealment of her life had been a perpetual pain and grief to her.

It was past eight o'clock when she found herself alone amidst the bustle and confusion of the King's Cross terminus. She sent a porter for a cab, and ordered the man to drive to Halfmoon Street. It was only a few days since she had met Lucy and Talbot at Felden Woods, and she knew that Mr. Bulstrode and his wife were detained in town, waiting for the prorogation of the House.

It was Saturday evening, and therefore a holiday for the young advocate of the Cornish miners and their rights; but Talbot spent his leisure amongst Blue-books and Parliamentary Minutes, and poor Lucy, who might have been shining, a pale star, at some crowded *conversazione*,[2] was compelled to forego the pleasure of struggling upon the staircase of one of those wise individuals who insist upon inviting their acquaintances to pack themselves into the smallest given space consistent with the preservation of life, and trample upon each other's lace flounces and varnished boots with smiling equanimity. Perhaps, in the universal fitness of things, even these fashionable evenings have a certain solemn purpose, deeply hidden under considerable surface-frivolity. It may be that they serve as moral gymnasia, in which the thews and sinews of social amenity are racked and tortured, with a view to their increased power of endurance. It is good for a man to

---

1 A plater is an inferior race horse. On screw, see 63, n.1.

2 An "At Home," or private assembly for conversation, social recreation, and amusement.

have his favourite corn trodden upon, and yet be compelled to smile under the torture; and a woman may learn her first great lesson in fortitude from the destruction of fifty guineas' worth of Mechlin,[1] and the necessity of assuring the destroyer that she is rather gratified than otherwise by the sacrifice. *Noblesse oblige.*[2] It is good to "suffer and be strong."[3] Cold coffee and tepid ice-cream may not be the most strengthening or delightful of food; but there may be a moral diet provided at these social gatherings which is not without its usefulness.

Lucy willingly abandoned her own delights; for she had that lady-like appreciation of society which had been a part of her education. Her placid nature knew no abnormal tendencies. She liked the amusements that other girls of her position liked. She had none of the eccentric predilections which had been so fatal to her cousin. She was not like that lovely and illustrious Spanish lady[4] who is said to love the cirque better than the opera, and to have a more intense appreciation of a series of flying plunges through tissue-paper-covered hoops than of the most elaborate *fioriture* of tenor or soprano. She gave up something, therefore, in resigning the stereotyped gaieties of the London season. But Heaven knows, it was very pleasant to her to make the sacrifice. Her inclinations were fatted lambs, which she offered willingly upon the altar of her idol. She was never happier than when sitting by her husband's side, making extracts from the Blue-books to be quoted in some pamphlet that he was writing; or if she was ever happier, it was only when she sat in the ladies' gallery, straining her eyes athwart the floriated iron fretwork,[5] which screened her from any wandering glances of distracted members, in her vain efforts to see her husband in his place on the Government benches, and very rarely seeing more than the crown of Mr. Bulstrode's hat.

She sat by Talbot's side upon this evening, busy with some pretty

---

1 Lace produced at Mechlin, Brussels.

2 Noble birth entails the duty to live up to one's rank.

3 An ironic allusion to Henry Wadsworth Longfellow's 1839 poem "The Light of Stars," in which the speaker enjoins the reader to be "resolute and calm" as hopes depart: "Know how sublime a thing it is/ To suffer and be strong."

4 Probably Isabella II of Spain, who was caricatured as a circus performer in contemporary political cartoons.

5 From 1778 to 1834 women were banned from the galleries of the House of Commons. After 1834 part of the Strangers' gallery was screened by trellis work and set aside for women.

needlework, and listening with patient attention to her husband's perusal of the proof-sheets of his last pamphlet. It was a noble specimen of the stately and ponderous style of writing, and it abounded in crushing arguments and magnificent climaxes, which utterly annihilated somebody (Lucy didn't exactly make out who), and most incontrovertibly established something, though Mrs. Bulstrode couldn't quite understand what. It was enough for her that he had written that wonderful composition, and that it was his rich baritone voice that rolled out the studied Johnsonese.[1] If he had pleased to read Greek to her, she would have thought it pleasant to listen. Indeed there were pet passages of Homer which Mr. Bulstrode now and then loved to recite to his wife, and which the little hypocrite pretended to admire. No cloud had darkened the calm heaven of Lucy's married life. She loved, and was beloved. It was a part of her nature to love in a reverential attitude, and she had no wish to approach nearer to her idol. To sit at her sultan's feet and replenish his chibouque; to watch him while he slept, and wave the punkah[2] above his seraphic head; to love and admire and pray for him, – made up the sum of her heart's desire.

It was close upon nine o'clock, when Mr. Bulstrode was interrupted in the very crowning sentence of his peroration by a double knock at the street-door. The houses in Halfmoon Street are small, and Talbot flung down his proof-sheet with a gesture expressive of considerable irritation. Lucy looked up, half sympathizingly, half apologetically, at her lord and master. She held herself in a manner responsible for his ease and comfort.

"Who can it be, dear?" she murmured; "at such a time, too!"

"Some annoyance or other, I dare say, my dear," answered Talbot. "But whoever it is, I won't see them to-night. I suppose, Lucy, I've given you a pretty fair idea of the effect of this upon my honourable friend the member for――"

Before Mr. Bulstrode could name the borough of which his honourable friend was the representative, a servant announced that Mrs.

---

1 In the style of Dr. Samuel Johnson (1709-84) – that is, abounding in words derived or made up from Latin.
2 A chibouque is a long Turkish tobacco pipe; a punkah is a large swinging fan attached to the ceiling and worked by ropes, usually by native Indian servants ("punkah-wallahs").

Mellish was waiting below to see the master of the house.

"Aurora!" exclaimed Lucy, starting from her seat and dropping the fairy implements of her work in a little shower upon the carpet; "Aurora! It can't be, surely? Why, Talbot, she only went back to Yorkshire a few days ago."

"Mr. and Mrs. Mellish are both below, I suppose?" Mr. Bulstrode said to the servant.

"No, sir; Mrs. Mellish came alone in a cab from the station, I believe. Mrs. Mellish is in the library, sir. I asked her to walk upstairs; but she requested to see you alone, sir, if you please."

"I'll come directly," answered Talbot. "Tell Mrs. Mellish I will be with her immediately."

The door closed upon the servant, and Lucy ran towards it, eager to hurry to her cousin.

"Poor Aurora!" she said; "there must be something wrong, surely. Uncle Archibald has been taken ill, perhaps; he was not looking well when we left Felden. I'll go to her, Talbot; I'm sure she'd like to see me first."

"No, Lucy; no," answered Mr. Bulstrode, laying his hand upon the door, and standing between it and his wife; "I had rather you didn't see your cousin until I have seen her. It will be better for me to see her first." His face was very grave, and his manner almost stern as he said this. Lucy shrank from him as if he had wounded her. She understood him, very vaguely, it is true; but she understood that he had some doubt or suspicion of her cousin, and for the first time in his life Mr. Bulstrode saw an angry light kindled in his wife's blue eyes.

"Why should you prevent my seeing Aurora?" Lucy asked; "she is the best and dearest girl in the world. Why shouldn't I see her?"

Talbot Bulstrode stared in blank amazement at his mutinous wife.

"Be reasonable, my dear Lucy," he answered very mildly; "I hope always to be able to respect your cousin – as much as I respect you. But if Mrs. Mellish leaves her husband in Yorkshire, and comes to London without his permission, – for he would never permit her to come alone, – she must explain to me why she does so before I can suffer my wife to receive her."

Poor Lucy's fair head drooped under this reproof.

She remembered her last conversation with her cousin; that conversation in which Aurora had spoken of some far-off day of trouble, that might bring her to ask for comfort and shelter in Halfmoon Street. Had the day of trouble come already?

"Is it wrong of Aurora to come alone, Talbot, dear?" Lucy asked meekly.

"Is it wrong?" repeated Mr. Bulstrode, fiercely. "Would it be wrong for you to go tearing from here to Cornwall, child?"

He was irritated by the mere imagination of such an outrage, and he looked at Lucy as if he half suspected her of some such intention.

"But Aurora may have had some very particular reason, dear?" pleaded his wife.

"I cannot imagine any reason powerful enough to justify such a proceeding," answered Talbot; "but I shall be better able to judge of that when I've heard what Mrs. Mellish has to say. Stay here, Lucy, till I send for you."

"Yes, Talbot."

She obeyed as submissively as a child; but she lingered near the door after her husband had closed it upon her, with a mournful yearning in her heart. She wanted to go to her cousin, and comfort her, if she had need of comfort. She dreaded the effect of her husband's cold and passionless manner upon Aurora's impressionable nature.

Mr. Bulstrode went down to the library to receive his kinswoman. It would have been strange if he had failed to remember that Christmas evening, nearly two years before, upon which he had gone down to the shadowy room at Felden, with every hope of his heart crushed, to ask for comfort from the woman he loved. It would have been strange if, in the brief interval that elapsed between his leaving the drawing-room and entering the library, his mind had not flown back to that day of desolation. If there was an infidelity to Lucy in that sharp thrill of pain that pierced his heart as the old memory came back, the sin was as short-lived as the agony which it brought with it. He was able now to say, in all singleness of heart, "I made a wise choice, and I shall never repent having made it."

The library was a small apartment at the back of the dining-room.

It was dimly lighted, for Aurora had lowered the lamp. She did not want Mr. Bulstrode to see her face.

"My dear Mrs. Mellish," said Talbot gravely, "I am so surprised at this visit, that I scarcely know how to say I am glad to see you. I fear something must have happened to cause your travelling alone. John is ill, perhaps, or——"

He might have said much more if Aurora had not interrupted him by casting herself upon her knees before him, and looking up at him with a pale, agonized face, that seemed almost ghastly in the dim lamp-light.

It was impossible to describe the look of horror that came over Talbot Bulstrode's face as she did this. It was the Felden scene over again. He came to her in the hope that she would justify herself, and she tacitly acknowledged her humiliation.

She was a guilty woman, then; a guilty creature, whom it would be his painful duty to cast out of that pure household. She was a poor, lost, polluted wretch, who must not be admitted into the holy atmosphere of a Christian gentleman's home.

"Mrs. Mellish! Mrs. Mellish!" he cried, "what is the meaning of this? Why do you give me this horrible pain again? Why do you insist upon humiliating yourself and me by such a scene as this?"

"Oh, Talbot, Talbot!" answered Aurora, "I come to you because you are good and honourable. I am a desolate, wretched woman, and I want your help – I want your advice. I will abide by it; I will, Talbot Bulstrode; so help me, Heaven."

Her voice was broken by her sobs. In her passionate grief and confusion she forgot that it was just possible such an appeal as this might be rather bewildering in its effect upon Talbot. But perhaps, even amid his bewilderment, the young Cornishman saw, or fancied he saw, something in Aurora's manner which had no fellowship with guilt; or with such guilt as he had at first dreaded. I imagine that it must have been so; for his voice was softer and his manner kinder when he next addressed her.

"Aurora," he said, "for pity's sake, be calm. Why have you left Mellish Park? What is the business in which I can help or advise you? Be calm, my dear girl, and I will try and understand you. God knows how much I wish to be a friend to you, for I stand in a brother's place, you know, my dear, and demand a brother's right to question your actions. I am sorry you came up to town alone, because such a step was calculated to compromise you; but if you will be calm and tell me why you came, I may be able to understand your motives. Come, Aurora, try and be calm."

She was still on her knees, sobbing hysterically. Talbot would have summoned his wife to her assistance, but he could not bear to see the two women associated until he had discovered the cause of Aurora's agitation.

He poured some water into a glass, and gave it her. He placed her in an easy-chair near the open window, and then walked up and down the room until she had recovered herself. "Talbot Bulstrode," she said quietly, after a long pause, "I want you to help me in the crisis of my life. I must be candid with you, therefore, and tell you that which I would have died rather than tell you two years ago. You remember the night upon which you left Felden?"

"Remember it? Yes, yes."

"The secret which separated us then, Talbot, was the one secret of my life, – the secret of my disobedience, the secret of my father's sorrow. You asked me to give you an account of that one year which was missing out of the history of my life. I could not do so, Talbot; *I would not!* My pride revolted against the horrible humiliation. If you had discovered the secret yourself, and had accused me of the disgraceful truth, I would have attempted no denial; but with my own lips to utter the hateful story – no, no, I could have borne anything better than that. But now that my secret is common property, in the keeping of police-officers and stable-boys, I can afford to tell you all. When I left the school in the Rue Saint-Dominique, I ran away to marry my father's groom!"

"Aurora!"

Talbot Bulstrode dropped into the chair nearest him, and sat blankly staring at his wife's cousin. Was this the secret humiliation which had prostrated her at his feet in the chamber at Felden Woods?

"Oh, Talbot, how could I have told you this? How can I tell you now why I did this mad and wicked thing, blighting the happiness of my youth by my own act, and bringing shame and grief upon my father? I had no romantic, overwhelming love for this man. I cannot plead the excuses which some women urge for their madness. I had only a school-girl's sentimental fancy for his dashing manner, only a school-girl's frivolous admiration of his handsome face. I married him because he had dark-blue eyes, and long eyelashes, and white teeth, and brown hair. He had insinuated himself into a kind of intimacy with me, by bringing me all the empty gossip of the race-course, by extra attention to my favourite horses, by pampering my pets. All these things brought about association between us; he was always my companion in my rides; and he contrived, before long, to tell me his story. Bah! why should I weary you with it?" cried Aurora scornfully. "He was a prince in disguise, of course; he was a gentleman's son; his father had kept his hunters; he was at war with fortune; he had been ill-used and trampled down in the battle of life. His talk was something to this effect, and I believed him. Why should I disbelieve him? I had lived all my life in an atmosphere of truth. My governess and I talked perpetually of the groom's romantic story. She was a silly woman, and encouraged my folly; out of mere stupidity, I believe, and with no suspicion of the mischief she was doing. We criticised the groom's handsome face, his white hands, his aristocratic manners. I mistook insolence for good breeding; Heaven help me! And as we saw scarcely any society at that time, I compared my father's groom with the few guests who came to Felden; and the town-bred impostor profited by comparison with rustic gentlemen. Why should I stay to account to you for my folly, Talbot Bulstrode? I could never succeed in doing so, though I talked for a week; I cannot account to myself for my madness. I can only look back to that horrible time, and wonder why I was mad."

"My poor Aurora! my poor Aurora!"

He spoke in the pitying tone with which he might have comforted her had she been a child. He was thinking of her in her childish ignorance, exposed to the insidious advances of an unscrupulous schemer, and his heart bled for the motherless girl.

"My father found some letters written by this man, and discovered that his daughter had affianced herself to his groom. He made this discovery while I was out riding with James Conyers, – the groom's name was Conyers, – and when I came home there was a fearful scene between us. I was mad enough and wicked enough to defend my conduct, and to reproach my father with the illiberality of his sentiments. I went even further: I reminded him that the house of Floyd and Floyd had had a very humble origin. He took me to Paris upon the following day. I thought myself cruelly treated. I revolted against the ceremonial monotony of the *pension;* I hated the studies, which were ten times more difficult than anything I had ever experienced with my governess; I suffered terribly from the conventual seclusion, for I had been used to perfect freedom amongst the country roads round Felden: and amidst all this, the groom pursued me with letters and messages; for he had followed me to Paris, and spent his money recklessly in bribing the servants and hangers-on of the school. He was playing for a high stake, and he played so desperately that he won. I ran away from school, and married him at Dover, within eight or nine hours of my escape from the Rue Saint-Dominique."

She buried her face in her hands, and was silent for some time.

"Heaven have pity upon my wretched ignorance!" she said at last; "the illusion under which I had married this man ended in about a week. At the end of that time I discovered that I was the victim of a mercenary wretch, who meant to use me to the uttermost as a means of wringing money from my father. For some time I submitted, and my father paid, and paid dearly, for his daughter's folly; but he refused to receive the man I had married, or to see me until I separated myself from that man. He offered the groom an income, on the condition of his going to Australia, and resigning all association with me for ever. But the man had a higher game to play. He wanted to bring about a reconciliation with my father; and he thought that in due time that tender father's resolution would have yielded to the force of his love. It was little better than a year after our marriage that I made a discovery that transformed me in one moment from a girl into a woman; a revengeful woman, perhaps, Mr. Bulstrode. I discovered that I had been wronged, deceived, and outraged by a wretch who laughed at my ignorant confidence in him. I had learned to hate the man long before this occurred: I had learned to despise his shallow trickeries, his insolent pretensions; but I do not think I felt his deeper infamy the less keenly for that. We were travelling in the south of France, my husband playing the great gentleman upon my father's money, when this discovery was made by me – or not by me; for it was forced upon me by a woman who knew my story and pitied me. Within half an hour of obtaining this knowledge, I acted upon it. I wrote to James Conyers, telling him I had discovered that which gave me the right to call upon the law to release me from him;[1] and if I refrained from doing so, it was for my father's sake, and not for his. I told him that so long as he left me unmolested and kept my secret, I would remit him money from time to time. I told him that I left him to the associations he had chosen for himself; and that my only prayer was, that God, in His mercy, might grant me complete forgetfulness of him. I left this letter for him with the *concierge*, and quitted the hotel in such a manner as to prevent his obtaining any trace of the way I had gone. I stopped in Paris for a few days, waiting for a reply to a letter I had written to my father, telling him that James Conyers was dead. Perhaps that was the worst sin of my life, Talbot. I deceived my father; but I believed that I was doing a wise and merciful thing in setting his mind at rest. He would have never been happy so long as he had believed the man lived. You understand all now, Talbot," she said mournfully. "You remember the morning at Brighton?"

"Yes, yes; and the newspaper with the marked paragraph – the report of the jockey's death."

"That report was false, Talbot Bulstrode," cried Aurora. "James Conyers was not killed."

Talbot's face grew suddenly pale. He began to understand something of the nature of that trouble which had brought Aurora to him.

"What, he was still living, then?" he said anxiously.

"Yes; until the night before last."

"But where – where has he been all this time?"

"During the last ten days – at Mellish Park."

She told him the terrible story of the murder. The trainer's death

---

1 An anachronism. The Divorce Court did not open until January 1858; Aurora left Conyers in the summer of 1857. Also an error of fact: even after the court opened, under the notorious double standard of the Divorce Act, a husband's adultery alone did not entitle his wife to a divorce. The stereotyped edition goes some way to correcting the latter error. The passage is changed as follows: "I had discovered that *which, coupled with his brutality to me on more than one occasion*, gave me the right to call upon the law" (emphasis added). Conyers' adultery, compounded with brutality, might well have entitled Aurora to a divorce; this change does not, however, deal with the anachronism noted above.

had not yet been reported in the London papers. She told him the dreadful story; and then, looking up at him with an earnest, imploring face, as she might have done had he been indeed her brother, she entreated him to help and counsel her in this terrible hour of need.

"Teach me how to do what is best for my dear love," she said. "Don't think of me or my happiness, Talbot; think only of him. I will make any sacrifice; I will submit to anything. I want to atone to my poor dear for all the misery I have brought upon him."

Talbot Bulstrode did not make any reply to this earnest appeal. The administrative powers of his mind were at work; he was busy summing up facts and setting them before him, in order to grapple with them fairly; and he had no attention to waste upon sentiment or emotion. He was walking up and down the room, with his eyebrows knitted sternly over his cold gray eyes, and his head bent.

"How many people know this secret, Aurora?" he asked presently.

"I can't tell you that; but I fear it must be very generally known," answered Mrs. Mellish, with a shuddering recollection of the "Softy's" insolence. "I heard of the discovery that had been made from a hanger-on of the stables, a man who hates me, – a man whom I – had a misunderstanding with."

"Have you any idea who it was that shot this Conyers?"

"No, not the least idea."

"You do not even guess at any one?"

"No."

Talbot took a few more turns up and down the small apartment, in evident trouble and perplexity of mind. He left the room presently, and called at the foot of the staircase: "Lucy, my dear, come down to your cousin."

I'm afraid Mrs. Bulstrode must have been lurking somewhere about the outside of the drawing-room door, for she flew down the stairs at the sound of the strong voice, and was by her husband's side two or three seconds after he had spoken.

"O Talbot!" she said, "how long you have been! I thought you would never send for me. What has been the matter with my poor darling?"

"Go in to her, and comfort her, my dear," Mr. Bulstrode answered, gravely: "she has had enough trouble, Heaven knows, poor girl. Don't ask her any questions, Lucy; but make her as comfortable as you can, and give her the best room you can find for her. She will stay with us as long as she remains in town."

"Dear, dear Talbot," murmured the young Cornishman's grateful worshipper, "how kind you are!"

"Kind!" cried Mr. Bulstrode; "she has need of friends, Lucy; and, God knows, I will act a brother's part towards her, faithfully and bravely. Yes, bravely!" he added, raising his head with an almost defiant gesture as he slowly ascended the stairs.

What was the dark cloud which he saw brooding so fatally over the far horizon? He dared not think of what it was, – he dared not even acknowledge its presence; but there was a sense of trouble and horror in his breast that told him the shadow was there.

Lucy Bulstrode ran into the library, and flung herself upon her cousin's breast, and wept with her. She did not ask the nature of the sorrow which had brought Aurora an unexpected and uninvited guest to that modest little dwelling-house. She only knew that her cousin was in trouble, and that it was her happy privilege to offer her shelter and consolation. She would have fought a sturdy battle in defence of this privilege; but she adored her husband for the generosity which had granted it to her without a struggle. For the first time in her life, poor gentle Lucy took a new position with her cousin. It was her turn to protect Aurora; it was her turn to display a pretty motherly tenderness for the desolate creature whose aching head rested on her bosom.

The West-End clocks were striking three, in the dead middle of the night, when Mrs. Mellish fell into a feverish slumber, even in her sleep, even in her sleep repeating again and again: "My poor John! my poor dear love! what will become of him? my own faithful darling!"

CHAPTER XXXI.

TALBOT BULSTRODE'S ADVICE.

TALBOT BULSTRODE went out early upon the quiet Sunday morning after Aurora's arrival, and walked down to the Telegraph Company's Office at Charing Cross, whence he despatched a message to Mr. John Mellish. It was a very brief message, only telling Mr. Mellish to come to town without delay, and that he would find Aurora in Half-moon Street. Mr. Bulstrode walked quietly homewards in the morning sunshine, after having performed this duty. Even the London streets were bright and dewy in that early sunlight, for it was only a little after seven o'clock, and the fresh morning breezes came sweeping over the house-tops, bringing health and purity from Shooter's Hill and Highgate, Streatham and Barnsbury, Richmond and Hampstead. The white morning mists were slowly melting from the worn grass in the Green Park; and weary creatures, who had had no better shelter than the quiet sky, were creeping away to find such wretched resting-places as they might, in that free city, in which, to sit for an unreasonable time upon a doorstep, or to ask a rich citizen for the price of a loaf, is to commit an indictable offence.

Surely it was impossible for any young legislator not quite worn out by a life-long struggle with the time which was never meant to be set right, – surely it was impossible for any fresh-hearted prosperous young Liberal to walk through those quiet streets without thinking of these things. Talbot Bulstrode thought very earnestly and very mournfully. To what end were his labours, after all? He was fighting for a handful of Cornish miners; doing battle with the rampant spirit of circumlocution for the sake of a few benighted wretches, buried in the darkness of a black abyss of ignorance a hundred times deeper and darker than the material obscurities in which they laboured. He was working his hardest and his best that these men might be taught, in some easy, unambitious manner, the simplest elements of Christian love and Christian duty. He was working for these poor far-away creatures, in their forgotten corner of the earth; and here, around and about him, was ignorance more terrible, because, hand-in-hand with ignorance of all good, there was the fatal experience of all evil. The simple Cornish miner who uses his pickaxe in the region of his friend's skull, when he wishes to enforce an argument, does so because he knows no other species of emphasis. But in the London universities of crime, knavery and vice and violence and sin matriculate and graduate day by day; to take their degrees in the felon's dock or on the scaffold. How could he be otherwise than sorrowful, thinking of these things? Were the Cities of the Plain[1] worse than this city; in which there were yet so many good and earnest men labouring patiently day by day, and taking little rest? Was the great accumulation of evil so heavy that it rolled for ever back upon the untiring Sisyphus?[2] Or did they make some imperceptible advance towards the mountain-top, despite of all discouragement?

With this weary question debating itself in his brain, Mr. Bulstrode walked along Piccadilly towards the comfortable bachelor's quarters, whose most commonplace attributes Lucy had turned to favour and to prettiness; but at the door of the Gloucester Coffee-house Talbot paused to stare absently at a nervous-looking chestnut mare, who insisted upon going through several lively performances upon her hind-legs, very much to the annoyance of an unshaven ostler, and not particularly to the advantage of a smart little dog-cart to which she was harnessed.

"You needn't pull her mouth to pieces, my man," cried a voice from the doorway of the hotel; "use her gently, and she'll soon quiet herself. Steady, my girl; steady!" added the owner of this voice, walking to the dog-cart as he spoke.

Talbot had good reason to stop short, for this gentleman was Mr. John Mellish, whose pale face, and loose, disordered hair betokened a sleepless night.

He was going to spring into the dog-cart, when his old friend tapped him on the shoulder.

"This is rather a lucky accident, John; for you're the very person I want to see," said Mr. Bulstrode. "I've just telegraphed to you."

---

1   Sodom and Gomorrah, destroyed by God in Genesis 19.
2   For his defiance of the gods, Sisyphus was punished by being forced for eternity to roll a huge stone up a hill. Every time he got it nearly to the top, it always rolled back to the bottom and he had to start again.

John Mellish stared with a blank face.

"Don't hinder me, please," he said; "I'll talk to you by-and-by. I'll call upon you in a day or two. I'm just off to Felden. I've only been in town an hour and a half, and should have gone down before, if I had not been afraid of knocking up the family."

He made another attempt to get into the vehicle, but Talbot caught him by the arm.

"You needn't go to Felden," he said; "your wife's much nearer."

"Eh?"

"She's at my house. Come and have some breakfast."

There was no shadow upon Talbot Bulstrode's mind as his old schoolfellow caught him by the hand, and nearly dislocated his wrist in a paroxysm of joy and gratitude. It was impossible for him to look beyond that sudden burst of sunshine upon John's face. If Mr. Mellish had been separated from his wife for ten years, and had just returned from the Antipodes for the sole purpose of seeing her again, he could scarcely have appeared more delighted at the prospect of a speedy meeting.

"Aurora here!" he said; "at your house? My dear old fellow, you can't mean it! But of course I ought to have known she'd come to you. She couldn't have done anything better or wiser, after having been so foolish as to doubt me."

"She came to me for advice, John. She wanted me to advise her how to act for your happiness, – yours, you great Yorkshireman, and not her own."

"Bless her noble heart!" cried Mr. Mellish, huskily. "And you told her——"

"I told her nothing, my dear fellow; but I tell you to take your lawyer down to Doctor's Commons with you to-morrow morning, get a new licence and marry your wife for the second time, in some quiet, little, out-of-the-way church in the City."

Aurora had risen very early upon that peaceful Sunday morning. The few hours of feverish and fitful sleep had brought very little comfort to her. She stood with her weary head leaning against the window-frame, and looked hopelessly out into the empty London street. She looked out into the desolate beginning of a new life, the blank uncertainty of an unknown future. All the minor miseries peculiar to a toilet in a strange room were doubly miserable to her. Lucy had brought the poor luggageless traveller all the paraphernalia of the toilet-table, and had arranged everything with her own busy hands. But the most insignificant trifle that Aurora touched in her cousin's chamber brought back the memory of some costly toy chosen for her by her husband. She had travelled in her white morning-dress, and the soft lace and muslin were none the fresher for her journey; but as two of Lucy's dresses joined together scarcely fitted her stately cousin, Mrs. Mellish was fain to be content with her limp muslin. What did it matter? The loving eyes which noted every shred of ribbon, every morsel of lace, every fold of her garments, were, perhaps, never to look upon her again. She twisted her hair into a careless mass at the back of her head, and had completed her toilet, when Lucy came to the door, tenderly anxious to know how she had slept.

"I will abide by Talbot's decision," she repeated to herself again and again. "If he says it is best for my dear that we should part, I will go away for ever. I will ask my father to take me far away, and my poor darling shall not even know where I have gone. I will be true in what I do, and will do it thoroughly."

She looked to Talbot Bulstrode as a wise judge, to whose sentence she would be willing to submit. Perhaps she did this because her own heart kept for ever repeating, "Go back to the man who loves you. Go back, go back! There is no wrong you can do him so bitter as to desert him. There is no unhappiness you can bring upon him equal to the unhappiness of losing you. Let *me* be your guide. Go back, go back!"

But this selfish monitor must not be listened to. How bitterly this poor girl, so old in experience of sorrow, remembered the selfish sin of her mad marriage! She had refused to sacrifice a school-girl's foolish delusion; she had disobeyed the father who had given her seventeen years of patient love and devotion; and she looked at all the misery of her youth as the fatal growth of this evil seed, so rebelliously sown. Surely such a lesson was not to be altogether unheeded! Surely it was powerful enough to teach her the duty of sacrifice! It was this thought that steeled her against the pleadings of her own affection. It was for this that she looked to Talbot Bulstrode as the arbiter of her future. Had she been a Roman Catholic, she would have gone to her confessor, and appealed to a priest – who, having no social ties of his own, must, of course, be the best judge of all the duties involved in domestic relations – for comfort and succour; but being of another faith, she went to the man whom she most respected, and who, being a husband himself, might, as she thought, be able to comprehend the duty that was due to her husband.

She went down-stairs with Lucy into a little inner room upon the drawing-room floor; a snug apartment, opening into a mite of a conservatory. It was Mr. and Mrs. Bulstrode's habit to breakfast in this cosy little chamber, rather than in that awful temple of slippery morocco, funereal bronze, and ghastly mahogany, which upholsterers insist upon as the only legitimate place in which an Englishman may take his meals. Lucy loved to sit opposite her husband at the small round table, and minister to his morning appetite from her pretty breakfast equipage of silver and china. She knew – to the smallest weight employed at Apothecaries' Hall, I think – how much sugar Mr. Bulstrode liked in his tea. She poured the cream into his cup as carefully as if she had been making up a prescription. He took the simple beverage in a great shallow breakfast-cup of fragile turquoise Sèvres, that had cost seven guineas; and had been made for Madame du Barry, the *rococo* merchant had told Talbot.[1] (Had his customer been a lady, I fear Marie Antoinette would have been described as the original possessor of this porcelain.) Mrs. Bulstrode loved to minister to her husband. She picked the bloated livers of martyred geese out of the Strasburg pies for his delectation; she spread the butter upon his dry toast; and pampered and waited on him, serving him as only such women serve their idols. But this morning she had her cousin's sorrows to comfort; and she established Aurora in a capacious chintz-covered easy-chair on the threshold of the conservatory, and seated herself at her feet.

"My poor pale darling!" she said, tenderly, "what can I do to bring the roses back to your cheeks?"

---

1 Sèvres is costly porcelain made at Sèvres, France. Madame du Barry (1743-93) was mistress of Louis XV after the death of Madame de Pompadour. She was executed during the Terror. A *rococo* merchant deals in antiques in the often ornate style of Louis XIV or Louis XV.

"Love me and pity me, dear," Aurora answered, gravely; "but don't ask me any questions."

The two women sat thus for some time, Aurora's handsome head bent over Lucy's fair face, and her hands clasped in both Lucy's hands. They talked very little, and only spoke then of indifferent matters, or of Lucy's happiness and Talbot's parliamentary career. The little clock over the chimney-piece struck the quarter before eight – they were very early, these unfashionable people – and a minute afterwards Mrs. Bulstrode heard her husband's step upon the stairs, returning from his ante-breakfast walk. It was his habit to take a constitutional stroll in the Green Park, now and then, so Lucy had thought nothing of this early excursion.

"Talbot has let himself in with his latch-key," said Mrs. Bulstrode; "and I may pour out the tea, Aurora. But listen, dear; I think there's some one with him."

There was no need to bid Aurora listen; she had started from her low seat, and stood erect and motionless, breathing in a quick, agitated manner, and looking towards the door. Besides Talbot Bulstrode's step there was another, quicker and heavier; a step she knew so well.

The door was opened, and Talbot entered the room, followed by a visitor, who pushed aside his host with very little attention to the laws of civilized society, and, indeed, nearly drove Mr. Bulstrode backwards into a gilded basket of flowers. But this stalwart John Mellish had no intention of being unmannerly or brutal. He pushed aside his friend only as he would have pushed, or tried to push, aside a regiment of soldiers with fixed bayonets, or a Lancaster gun, or a raging ocean, or any other impediment that had come between him and Aurora. He had her in his arms before she could even cry his name aloud, in her glad surprise; and in another moment she was sobbing on his breast.

"My darling! my pet! my own!" he cried, smoothing her dark hair with his broad hand, and blessing her and weeping over her, – "my own love! How could you do this? how could you wrong me so much? My own precious darling! had you learnt to know me no better than *this*, in all our happy married life?"

"I came to ask Talbot's advice, John," she said, earnestly; "and I mean to abide by it, however cruel it may seem."

Mr. Bulstrode smiled gravely, as he watched these two foolish people. He was very much pleased with his part in the little domestic drama; and he contemplated them with a sublime consciousness of being the author of all this happiness. For they were happy. The poet has said, there are some moments – very rare, very precious, very brief – which stand by themselves, and have their perfect fulness of joy within their own fleeting span, taking nothing from the past, demanding nothing of the future. Had John and Aurora known that they were to be separated by the breadth of Europe for the remainder of their several lives, they would not the less have wept joyful tears at the pure blissfulness of this meeting.

"You asked me for my advice, Aurora," said Talbot, "and I bring it you. Let the past die with the man who died the other night. The future is not yours to dispose of; it belongs to your husband, John Mellish."

Having delivered himself of these oracular sentences, Mr. Bulstrode seated himself at the breakfast-table, and looked into the mysterious and cavernous interior of a raised pie, with such an intent gaze, that it seemed as if he never meant to look out of it. He devoted so many minutes to this serious contemplation, that by the time he looked up again, Aurora had become quite calm, while Mr. Mellish affected an unnatural gaiety, and exhibited no stronger sign of past emotion than a certain inflamed appearance in the region of his eyelids.

But this stalwart, devoted, impressionable Yorkshireman ate a most extraordinary repast in honour of this reunion. He spread mustard on his muffins. He poured Worcester sauce into his coffee, and cream over his devilled cutlets. He showed his gratitude to Lucy by loading her plate with comestibles she didn't want. He talked perpetually, and devoured incongruous viands in utter absence of mind. He shook hands with Talbot so many times across the breakfast-table, that he exposed the lives or limbs of the whole party to imminent peril from the boiling water in the urn. He threw himself into a paroxysm of coughing, and made himself scarlet in the face, by an injudicious use of cayenne pepper; and he exhibited himself altogether in such an imbecile light that Talbot Bulstrode was compelled to have recourse to all sorts of expedients to keep the servants out of the room during the progress of that rather noisy and bewildering repast.

The Sunday papers were brought to the master of the house

before breakfast was over; and while John talked, ate, and gesticulated, Mr. Bulstrode hid himself behind the open leaves of the latest edition of the 'Weekly Dispatch,' reading a paragraph that appeared in that journal.

This paragraph gave a brief account of the murder and the inquest at Mellish; and wound up by that rather stereotyped sentence, in which the public are informed that "the local police are giving unremitting attention to the affair, and we think we may venture to affirm that they have obtained a clue which will most probably lead to the early discovery of the guilty party."

Talbot Bulstrode, with the newspaper still before his face, sat for some little time frowning darkly at the page upon which this paragraph appeared. The horrible shadow, whose nature he would not acknowledge even to himself, once more lowered upon the horizon which had just seemed so bright and clear.

"I would give a thousand pounds," he thought, "if I could find the murderer of this man."

CHAPTER XXXII.

ON THE WATCH.

VERY soon after breakfast, upon that happy Sabbath of reunion and contentment, John Mellish drove Aurora to Felden Woods. It was necessary that Archibald Floyd should hear the story of the trainer's death, from the lips of his own children, before newspaper paragraphs terrified him with some imperfect outline of the truth.

The dashing phaeton in which Mr. Bulstrode was in the habit of driving his wife was brought to the door as the church-bells were calling devout citizens to their morning duties; and at that unseemly hour John Mellish smacked his whip, and dashed off in the direction of Westminster Bridge.

Talbot Bulstrode's horses soon left London behind them, and before long the phaeton was driving upon trim park-like roads, overshadowed by luxuriant foliage, and bordered here and there by exquisitely-ordered gardens and rustic villas, that glittered whitely in the sunshine. The holy peace of the quiet Sabbath was upon every object that they passed, even upon the leaves and flowers, as it seemed to Aurora. The birds sang subdued and murmuring harmonies; the light summer breeze scarcely stirred the deep grass, on which the lazy cattle stood to watch the phaeton dash by.

Ah, how happy Aurora was, seated by the side of the man whose love had outlasted every trial! How happy now that the dark wall that had divided them was shattered, and they were indeed united! John Mellish was as tender and pitying towards her, as a mother to her forgiven child. He asked no explanations; he sought to know nothing of the past. He was content to believe that she had been foolish and mistaken; and that the mistake and folly of her life would be buried in the grave of the murdered trainer.

The lodge-keeper at Felden Woods exclaimed as he opened the gates to his master's daughter. He was an old man, and he had opened the same gates more than twenty years before, when the banker's dark-eyed bride had first entered her husband's mansion.

Archibald Floyd welcomed his children heartily. How could he ever be otherwise than unutterably happy in the presence of his darling, however often she might come, with whatever eccentricity she might time her visits?

Mrs. Mellish led her father into his study.

"I must speak to you alone, papa," she said; "but John knows all I have to say. There are no secrets between us now. There never will be again."

Aurora had a painful story to tell her father, for she had to confess to him that she had deceived him upon the occasion of her return to Felden Woods after her parting with James Conyers.

"I told you a story, father," she said, "when I told you that my husband was dead. But Heaven knows, I believed that I should be forgiven the sin of that falsehood, for I thought that it would spare you grief and trouble of mind; and surely anything would have been justifiable that could have done that. I suppose good never can come out of evil, for I have been bitterly punished for my sin. I received a newspaper within a few months of my return, in which there was a paragraph describing the death of James Conyers. The paragraph was not correct, for the man had escaped with his life; and when I married John Mellish, my first husband was alive."

Archibald Floyd uttered a cry of despair, and half rose from his easy-chair; but Aurora knelt upon the ground by his side, with her arms about him, soothing and comforting him.

"It is all over now, dear father," she said; "it is all over. The man is dead. I will tell you how he died by-and-by. It is all over. John knows all; and I am to marry him again. Talbot Bulstrode says that it is necessary, as our marriage was not legal. My own dear father, there is to be no more secrecy, no more unhappiness, – only love, and peace, and union for all of us."

She told the old man the story of the trainer's death, dwelling very little upon the particulars, and telling nothing of her own doings that night, except that she had been in the wood at the time of the murder, and that she had heard the pistol fired.

It was not a pleasant story, this story of murder and violence and treachery within the boundary of his daughter's home. Even amid Aurora's assurances that all sorrow was past, that doubt and uncertainty were to vanish away before security and peace, Archibald Floyd could not control this feeling. He was restless and uneasy in spite of himself. He took John Mellish out upon the terrace in the afternoon sunshine, while Aurora lay asleep upon one of the sofas in the long drawing-room, and talked to him of the trainer's death as they walked up and down. There was nothing to be elicited from the young squire that threw any light upon the catastrophe, and Archibald Floyd tried in vain to find any issue out of the darkness of the mystery.

"Can you imagine any one having any motive for getting rid of this man?" the banker asked.

John shrugged his shoulders. He had been asked this question so often before, and had been always obliged to give the same reply.

No; he knew of no motive which any one about Mellish could be likely to have.

"Had the man any money about him?" asked Mr. Floyd.

"Goodness knows whether he had or not," John answered carelessly; "but I should think it wasn't likely he had much. He had been out of a situation, I believe, for some time before he came to me, and he had spent a good many months in a Prussian hospital. I don't suppose he was worth robbing."

The banker remembered the two thousand pounds which he had given to his daughter. What had Aurora done with that money? Had she known of the trainer's existence when she asked for it? and had she wanted it for him? She had not explained this in her hurried story of the murder, and how could he press her upon so painful a subject? Why should he not accept her own assurance that all was over, and that nothing remained but peace?

Archibald Floyd and his children spent a tranquil day together; not talking much, for Aurora was completely worn out by the fatigue and excitement she had undergone. What had her life been but agitation and terror since the day upon which Mr. John Pastern's letter had come to Mellish to tell her of the existence of her first husband? She slept through the best part of the day, lying upon a sofa, and with John Mellish sitting by her side keeping watch over her. She slept while the bells of Beckenham church summoned the parishioners to afternoon service, and while her father went to assist in those quiet devotions, and to kneel on his hassock in the old square pew, and pray for the peace of his beloved child. Heaven knows how earnestly the old man prayed for his daughter's happiness, and how she filled his thoughts; not distracting him from more sacred thoughts, but blending her image with his worship in alternate prayer and thanksgiving! Those who watched him as he sat, with the sunshine on his gray head, listening reverentially to the sermon, little knew how much trouble had been mingled with the great prosperity of his life. They pointed him out respectfully to strangers, as a man whose signature across a slip of paper could make that oblong morsel of beaten rag into an incalculable sum of money; a man who stood upon a golden pinnacle with the Rothschilds and Montefiores and Couttses;[1] who could afford to pay the National Debt any morning that the whim seized him; and who was yet a plain man, and simple as a child, as anybody might see, the admiring parishioners would add, as the banker came out of church shaking hands right and left, and nodding to the charity children.

I'm afraid the children dropped lower curtsies in the pathway of Mr. Floyd than even before the Vicar of Beckenham; for they had learned to associate the image of the banker with buns and tea, with sixpences and oranges, gambols on the smooth lawn at Felden Woods, and jovial feasts in monster tents to the music of clashing brazen bands, and with even greater treats in the way of excursions to a Crystal Palace on a hill,[2] an enchanted fairyland of wonders, from which it was delicious to return in the dewy evening, singing hymns of rejoicing that shook the vans in which they travelled.

The banker had distributed happiness right and left; but the money which might have paid the National Debt had been impotent to save the life of the dark-eyed woman he had loved so tenderly, or to spare him one pang of uneasiness about his idolized child. Had not that allpowerful wealth been rather the primary cause of his daughter's

---

1   The Rothschild family, most famous of all European banking dynasties, had by the 1820s bank branches in Frankfurt, London, Vienna, Paris, and Naples. Sir Moses Montefiore (1784-1885), Jewish philanthropist, accumulated a huge fortune on the London stock exchange. Thomas Coutts (1735-1822) founded the banking house of Coutts & Co. in the Strand.
2   Erected in Hyde Park for the Great Exhibition in 1851, the Crystal Palace was reconstructed in 1854 on Sydenham Hill. Visitors flocked there, brought by the Crystal Palace and West End Railway Line, built in 1856.

trouble, since it had cast her, young, inexperienced, and trusting, a prey into the mercenary hands of a bad man, who would not have cared to persecute her but for the money that had made her such a golden prize for any adventurer who might please to essay the hazard of winning her?

With the memory of these things always in his mind, it was scarcely strange that Archibald Floyd should bear the burden of his riches meekly and fearfully, knowing that, whatever he might be in the Stock Exchange, he was in the sight of Heaven only a feeble old man, very assailable by suffering, very liable to sorrow, and humbly dependent on the mercy of the Hand that is alone powerful to spare or to afflict, as seemeth good to Him who guides it.

Aurora awoke out of her long sleep while her father was at church. She awoke to find her husband watching her; the Sunday papers lying forgotten on his knee, and his honest eyes fixed on the face he loved.

"My own dear John," she said, as she lifted her head from the pillows, supporting herself upon her elbow, and stretching out one hand to Mr. Mellish, "my own dear boy, how happy we are together now! Will anything ever come to break our happiness again, my dear? Can Heaven be so cruel as to afflict us any more?"

The banker's daughter, in the sovereign vitality of her nature, had rebelled against sorrow as a strange and unnatural part of her life. She had demanded happiness almost as a right; she had wondered at her afflictions, and been unable to understand why she should be thus afflicted. There are natures which accept suffering with patient meekness, and acknowledge the justice by which they suffer; but Aurora had never done this. Her joyous soul had revolted against sorrow, and she arose now in the intense relief which she felt in her release from the bonds that had been so hateful to her, and challenged Providence with her claim to be happy for evermore.

John Mellish thought very seriously upon this matter. He could not forget the night of the murder, – the night upon which he had sat alone in his wife's chamber pondering upon his unworthiness.

"Do you think we deserve to be happy, Lolly?" he said presently. "Don't mistake me, my darling. I know that you're the best and brightest of living creatures, – tender-hearted, loving, generous, and true. But do you think we take life quite seriously enough, Lolly dear?

I'm sometimes afraid that we're too much like the careless children in the pretty childish allegory, who played about amongst the flowers on the smooth grass in the beautiful garden, until it was too late to set out upon the long journey on the dark road which would have led them to Paradise. What shall we do, my darling, to deserve the blessings God has given us so freely; the blessings of youth and strength, and love and wealth? What shall we do, dear? I don't want to turn Mellish into a Philanstery[1] exactly, nor to give up my racing-stud, if I can help it," John said reflectively; "but I want to do something, Lolly, to prove that I am grateful to Providence. Shall we build a lot of schools, or a church, or alms-houses, or something of that sort? Lofthouse would like me to put up a painted window in Mellish church, and a new pulpit with a patent sounding-board; but I can't see that painted windows and sounding-boards do much good in a general way. I want to do something, Aurora, to prove my gratitude to the Providence that has given me the loveliest and best of women for my true-hearted wife."

The banker's daughter smiled almost mournfully upon her devoted husband.

"Have I been such a blessing to you, John," she said, "that you should be grateful for me? Have I not brought you far more sorrow than happiness, my poor dear?"

"No," shouted Mr. Mellish emphatically. "The sorrow you have brought me has been nothing to the joy I have felt in your love. My own dearest girl, to be sitting here by your side to-day, and to hear you tell me that you love me, is enough happiness to set against all the trouble of mind that I have endured since the man that is dead came to Mellish."

I hope my poor John Mellish will be forgiven if he talked a great deal of nonsense to the wife he loved. He had been her lover from the first moment in which he had seen her, darkly beautiful, upon the gusty Brighton Parade; and he was her lover still. No shadow of contempt had ever grown out of his familiarity with her. And indeed I am disposed to take objection to that old proverb;[2] or at least to

---

1   A phalanstery [sic] is an association of people who live cooperatively according to the philosophies of Fourier.

2   i.e. Familiarity breeds contempt.

believe that contempt is only engendered of familiarity with things which are in themselves base and spurious. The priest, who is familiar with the altar, learns no contempt for its sacred images; but it is rather the ignorant neophyte who sneers and sniggers at things which he cannot understand. The artist becomes only more reverent as toil and study make him more familiar with his art; its eternal sublimity grows upon him, and he worships the far-away Goddess of Perfection as humbly when he drops his brush or his chisel after a life of patient labour, as he did when first he ground colour or pointed rough blocks of marble for his master. And I cannot believe that a good man's respect for the woman he loves can be lessened by that sweet and every-day familiarity in which a hundred household virtues and gentle beauties – never dreamed of in the ball-rooms where he first danced with an unknown idol in gauzy robes and glimmering jewels – grow upon him, until he confesses that the wife of ten years' standing is even ten times dearer than the bride of a week's honeymoon.

Archibald Floyd came back from church, and found his two children sitting side by side in one of the broad windows, watching for his arrival, and whispering together like lovers, as I have said they were.

They dined pleasantly together later in the evening; and a little after dark the phaeton was brought round to the terrace-steps, and Aurora kissed her father as she wished him good night.

"You will come up to town, and be present at the marriage, sir, I know," John whispered, as he took his father-in-law's hand. "Talbot Bulstrode will arrange all about it. It is to take place at some out-of-the-way little church in the City. Nobody will be any the wiser, and Aurora and I will go back to Mellish as quietly as possible. There's only Lofthouse and Hayward know the secret of the certificate, and they——"

John Mellish stopped suddenly. He remembered Mrs. Powell's parting sting. *She* knew the secret. But how could she have come by that knowledge? It was impossible that either Lofthouse or Hayward could have told her. They were both honourable men, and they had pledged themselves to be silent.

Archibald Floyd did not observe his son-in-law's embarrassment; and the phaeton drove away, leaving the old man standing on the terrace-steps looking after his daughter.

"I must shut up this place," he thought, "and go to Mellish to finish my days. I cannot endure these separations; I cannot bear this suspense. It is a pitiful sham, my keeping house, and living in all this dreary grandeur. I'll shut up the place, and ask my daughter to give me a quiet corner in her Yorkshire home, and a grave in the parish churchyard."

The lodge-keeper turned out of his comfortable Gothic habitation to open the clanking iron gates for the phaeton; but John drew up his horses before they dashed into the road, for he saw that the man wanted to speak to him.

"What is it, Forbes?" he asked.

"Oh, it's nothing particular, sir," the man said, "and perhaps I oughtn't to trouble you about it; but did you expect any one down to-day, sir?"

"Expect any one here? – no!" exclaimed John.

"There's been a person inquirin', sir, this afternoon, – two persons, I may say, in a shay-cart, but one of 'em asked particular if you was here, sir, and if Mrs. Mellish was here; and when I said yes, you was, the gent says it wasn't worth troublin' you about – the business as he'd come upon – and as he'd call another time. And he asked me what time you'd be likely to be leavin' the Woods; and I said I made no doubt you'd stay to dinner up at the house. So he says, 'All right,' and drives off."

"He left no message, then?"

"No, sir. He said nothin' more than what I've told you."

"Then his business could have been of no great importance, Forbes," answered John, laughing. "So we needn't worry our heads about him. Good-night."

Mr. Mellish dropped a five-shilling piece into the lodge-keeper's hand, gave Talbot's horses their heads, and the phaeton rolled off London-wards over the crisp gravel of the well-kept Beckenham roads.

"Who could the man have been?" Aurora asked, as they left the gates.

"Goodness knows, my dear," John answered carelessly. "Somebody on racing business, perhaps."

Racing business seems to be in itself such a mysterious business that it is no strange thing for mysterious people to be always turning up in relation to it. Aurora, therefore, was content to accept this explanation; but not without some degree of wonderment.

"I can't understand the man coming to Felden after you, John," she said. "How could he know that you were to be there to-day?"

"Ah, how indeed, Lolly!" returned Mr. Mellish. "He chanced it, I suppose. A sharp customer, no doubt; wants to sell a horse, I dare say, and heard I didn't mind giving a good price for a good thing."

Mr. Mellish might have gone even further than this, for there were many *horsey* gentlemen in his neighbourhood, past masters in the art they practised, who were wont to say that the young squire, judiciously manipulated, might be induced to give a remarkably good price for a very bad thing; and there were many broken-down, slim-legged horses in the Mellish stables that bore witness to the same fact. Those needy *chevaliers d'esprit*[1] who think that Burke's landed gentry[2] were created by Providence and endowed with the goods of this world for their especial benefit, just as pigeons are made plump and nice-eating for the delectation of hawks, drove a wholesale trade upon the young man's frank simplicity and hearty belief in his fellow-creatures. I think it is Eliza Cook who says, "It is better to trust and be deceived, than own the mean, poor spirit that betrays;"[3] and if there is any happiness in being "done," poor John enjoyed that fleeting delight pretty frequently.

There was a turn in the road between Beckenham and Norwood; and as the phaeton swept round, a chaise or dog-cart, a shabby vehicle enough, with a rakish-looking horse, drove close up, and the man who was driving asked the squire to put him in the nearest way to London. The vehicle had been behind them all the way from Felden, but had kept at a very respectful distance until now.

"Do you want to get to the City or the West End?" John asked.

"The West End."

"Then you can't do better than follow us," answered Mr. Mellish;

---

1 Gentlemen who live on their wits.

2 In John Burke's *Dictionary to the Landed Gentry*, originally published between 1833–38 as *A Genealogical and Heraldic History of the Commoners of Great Britain and Ireland*.

3 The reference is to the poem "Love On," by Eliza Cook (1818–89), a Victorian poet whose domestic sentiments appealed to popular taste: "Who would not rather trust and be deceived,/ Than own the mean, cold spirit that betrays?"

"the road's clean enough, and your horse seems a good one to go. You can keep us in sight, I suppose?"

"Yes, sir, and thank ye."

"All right, then."

Talbot Bulstrode's thorough-breds dashed off, but the rakish-looking horse kept his ground behind them. He had something of the insolent, off-hand assurance of a butcher's horse, accustomed to whirl a bare-headed blue-coated master through the sharp morning air.

"I was right, Lolly," Mr. Mellish said, as he left the dog-cart behind.

"How do you mean, dear?" asked Aurora.

"The man who spoke to us just now is the man who has been inquiring for me at Felden. He's a Yorkshireman."

"A Yorkshireman!"

"Yes; didn't you hear the north-country twang?"

No: she had not listened to the man, nor heeded him. How should she think of anything but her new-born happiness – the new-born confidence between herself and the husband she loved?

Do not think her hard-hearted or cruel if she forgot that it was the death of a fellow-creature, a sinful man stricken down in the prime of youth and health, that had given her this welcome release. She had suffered so much, that the release could not be otherwise than welcome, let it come how it might.

Her nature, frank and open as the day, had been dwarfed and crippled by the secret that had blighted her life. Can it be wondered, then, that she rejoiced now that all need of secrecy was over, and this generous spirit might expand as it pleased?

It was past ten when the phaeton turned into Halfmoon Street. The men in the dog-cart had followed John's directions to the letter; for it was only in Piccadilly that Mr. Mellish had lost sight of them amongst other vehicles travelling backwards and forwards on the lamp-lit thoroughfare.

Talbot and Lucy received their visitors in one of the pretty little drawing-rooms. The young husband and wife had spent a quiet day together; going to church in the morning and afternoon, dining alone, and sitting in the twilight, talking happily and confidentially. Mr. Bulstrode was no Sabbath-breaker; and John Mellish had reason to consider himself a peculiarly privileged person, inasmuch as the thorough-breds had been permitted to leave their stables for his service; to say nothing of the groom, who had been absent from his hard seat in the servants' pew at a fashionable chapel, in order that he might accompany John and Aurora to Felden.

The little party sat up rather late, Aurora and Lucy talking affectionately together, side by side, upon a sofa in the shadow of the room, while the two men lounged in the open window. John told his host the history of the day, and in doing so casually mentioned the man who had asked him the way to London.

Strange to say, Talbot Bulstrode seemed especially interested in this part of the story. He asked several questions about the men. He asked what they were like; what was said by either of them; and made many other inquiries, which seemed equally trivial.

"Then they followed you into town, John?" he said finally.

"Yes; I only lost sight of them in Piccadilly, five minutes before I turned the corner of the street."

"Do you think they had any motive in following you?" asked Talbot.

"Well, I fancy so; they're on the look-out for information, I expect. The man who spoke to me looked something like a tout. I've heard that Lord Stamford's rather anxious about my West-Australian colt, the Pork Butcher. Perhaps his people have set these men to work to find out if I'm going to run him in the Leger."

Talbot Bulstrode smiled bitterly, almost mournfully, at the vanity of horse-flesh. It was painful to see this light-hearted young squire looking in such ignorant hopefulness towards an horizon upon which graver and more thoughtful men could see a dreadful shadow lowering. Mr. Bulstrode was standing close to the balcony; he stepped out amongst the china boxes of mignonette,[1] and looked down into the quiet street. A man was leaning against a lamp-post, some few paces from Talbot's house, smoking a cigar, and with his face turned towards the balcony. He finished his cigar deliberately, threw the end into the road, and walked away while Talbot kept watch; but Mr. Bulstrode did not leave his post of observation, and about a quarter of an hour afterwards he saw the same man lounging slowly along the pavement

---

1 Plant (*reseda odorata*) cultivated for the fragrance of its blossoms.

upon the other side of the street. John, who sat within the shadow of the window-curtains, lolling against them, and creasing their delicate folds with the heavy pressure of his broad back, was utterly unconscious of all this.

Early the next morning Mr. Bulstrode and Mr. Mellish took a Hansom cab, and rattled down to Doctors' Commons,[1] where, for the second time in his life, John gave himself up to be fought for by white-aproned ecclesiastical touts, and eventually obtained the Archbishop of Canterbury's gracious sanction of his marriage with Aurora, widow of James Conyers, only daughter of Archibald Floyd, banker. From Doctors' Commons the two gentlemen drove to a certain quiet, out-of-the-way church within the sound of Bow bells,[2] but so completely hidden amongst piles of warehouses, top-heavy chimneys, sloping roofs, and other eccentricities of masonry, that any unhappy bridegroom, who had appointed to be married there, was likely enough to spend the whole of the wedding-day in futile endeavours to find the church-door. Here John discovered a mouldy clerk, who was fetched from some habitation in the neighbourhood with considerable difficulty, by a boy, who volunteered to accomplish anything under heaven for a certain copper consideration; and to this clerk Mr. Mellish gave notice of a marriage which was to take place upon the following day, by special licence.

"I'll take my second marriage-certificate back with me," John said, as he left the church; "and then I should like to see who'll dare to look me in the face, and tell me that my darling is not my own lawfully-wedded wife."

He was thinking of Mrs. Powell as he said this. He was thinking of the pale, spiteful eyes that had looked at him, and of the woman's tongue that had stabbed him with all a little nature's great capacity for hate. He would be able to defy her now; he would be able to defy every creature in the world who dared to breathe a syllable against his beloved wife.

---

1 The College of Advocates and Doctors of Law, located near St. Paul's Cathedral, housing the Ecclesiastical and Admiralty Courts and the advocates practising there. After the Matrimonial Causes Act (1857), the Court of Probate Act (1857), and the High Court of Admiralty Act (1859), the Colleges ceased to function. They were demolished in 1867.

2 The church bells of St. Mary-le-Bow, Cheapside.

Early the next morning the marriage took place. Archibald Floyd, Talbot Bulstrode, and Lucy were the only witnesses; that is to say, the only witnesses with the exception of the clerk and the pew-opener, and a couple of men who lounged into the church when the ceremony was half over, and slouched about one of the side aisles, looking at the monuments, and talking to each other in whispers, until the parson took off his surplice, and John came out of the vestry with his wife upon his arm.

Mr. and Mrs. Mellish did not return to Halfmoon Street; they drove straight to the Great Northern Station, whence they started by the afternoon express for Doncaster. John was anxious to return; for remember that he had left his household under very peculiar circumstances, and strange reports might have arisen in his absence.

The young squire would perhaps have scarcely thought of this, had not the idea been suggested to him by Talbot Bulstrode, who particularly urged upon him the expediency of returning immediately.

"Go back, John," said Mr. Bulstrode, "without an hour's unnecessary delay. If by any chance there should be some further disturbance about this murder, it will be much better for you, and Aurora too, to be on the spot. I will come down to Mellish myself in a day or two, and will bring Lucy with me, if you will allow me."

"Allow you, my dear Talbot!"

"I *will* come, then. Good-bye, and God bless you! Take care of your wife."

CHAPTER XXXIII.

CAPTAIN PRODDER GOES BACK TO DONCASTER.

MR. SAMUEL PRODDER, returning to London after having played his insignificant part in the tragedy at Mellish Park, found that city singularly dull and gloomy. He put up at some dismal boarding-house, situated amid a mazy labyrinth of brick and mortar between the Tower and Wapping, and having relations with another boarding-house in Liverpool. He took up his abode at this place, in which he was known and respected. He drank rum-and-water, and played cribbage with other seamen, made after the same pattern as himself. He even went to an East-End theatre upon the Saturday night after the murder, and sat out the representation of a nautical drama,[1] which he would have been glad to have believed in, had it not promulgated such wild theories in the science of navigation, and exhibited such extraordinary experiments in the manoeuvring of the man-of-war, upon which the action of the play took place, as to cause the captain's hair to stand on end in the intensity of his wonder. The things people did upon that ship curdled Samuel Prodder's blood, as he sat in the lonely grandeur of the eighteenpenny boxes. It was quite a common thing for them to walk unhesitatingly through the bulwarks and disappear in what ought to have been the sea. The extent of browbeating and humiliation borne by the captain of that noble vessel; the amount of authority exercised by a sailor with loose legs; the agonies of sea-sickness, represented by a comic countryman, who had no particular business on board the gallant bark; the proportion of hornpipe-dancing and nautical ballad-singing gone through, as compared to the work that was done, – all combined to impress poor Samuel with such a novel view of her Majesty's naval service, that he was very glad when the captain who had been browbeaten suddenly repented of all his sins, – not without a sharp reminder from the prompter, who informed the

---

[1] Nautical melodramas, featuring elaborate marine spectacle and starring the heroic English tar, were popular throughout the 19th century. The Surrey Theatre, the headquarters of nautical melodrama, drew much of its audience from patrons of Prodder's type: sailors, watermen, dock workers, etc.

dramatis personæ in a confidential voice that it was *parst* twelve, and they'd better cut it short, – joined the hands of the contumacious sailor and a young lady in white muslin, and begged them to be 'appy.

It was in vain that the captain sought distraction from the one idea upon which he had perpetually brooded since the night of his visit to Mellish Park. He would be wanted in Yorkshire to tell what he knew of the dark history of that fatal night. He would be called upon to declare at what hour he had entered the wood, whom he had met there, what he had seen and heard there. They would extort from him that which he would have died rather than tell. They would cross-examine, and bewilder, and torment him, until he told them every-thing, – until he repeated, syllable by syllable, the passionate words that had been said, – until he told them how, within a quarter of an hour of the firing of the pistol, he had been the witness of a desperate scene between his niece and the murdered man, – a scene in which concentrated hate, vengeful fury, illimitable disdain and detestation had been expressed by her – by her alone: – the man had been calm and moderate enough. It was she who had been angry; it was she who had given loud utterance to her hate.

Now, by reason of one of those strange inconsistencies common to weak human nature, the captain, though possessed night and day by a blind terror of being suddenly pounced upon by the minions of the law, and compelled to betray his niece's secret, could not rest in his safe retreat amid the labyrinths of Wapping,[1] but must needs pine to return to the scene of the murder. He wanted to know the result of the inquest. The Sunday papers gave a very meagre account, only hinting darkly at suspected parties. He wanted to ascertain for himself what had happened at the inquest, and whether his absence had given rise to suspicion. He wanted to see his niece again, – to see her in the daylight, undisturbed by passion. He wanted to see this beautiful tigress in her calmer moods, if she ever had any calmer moods. Heav-en knows the simple merchant-captain was well-nigh distracted as he thought of his sister Eliza's child, and the awful circumstances of his first and only meeting with her.

---

1   A hamlet in the parish of Whitechapel, chiefly inhabited by seafaring men and tradesmen supplying shipping and seamen.

Was she – that which he feared people might be led to think her, if they heard the story of that scene in the wood? No, no, no!

She was his sister's child, – the child of that merry, impetuous little girl, who had worn a pinafore and played hop-scotch. He remembered his sister flying into a rage with one Tommy Barnes for unfair practices in that very game, and upbraiding him almost as passionately as Aurora had upbraided the dead man. But if Tommy Barnes had been found strangled by a skipping-rope or shot dead from a pea-shooter in the next street a quarter of an hour afterwards, would Eliza's brother have thought that she must needs be guilty of the boy's murder? The captain had gone so far as to reason thus, in his trouble of mind. His sister Eliza's child would be likely to be passionate and impetuous; but his sister Eliza's child would be a generous, warm-hearted creature, incapable of any cruelty in either thought or deed. He remembered his sister Eliza boxing his ears on the occasion of his gouging out the eyes of her wax-doll; but he remembered the same dark-eyed child sobbing piteously at the spectacle of a lamb that a heartless butcher was dragging to the slaughter-house.

But the more seriously Captain Prodder revolved this question in his mind, the more decidedly his inclination pointed to Doncaster; and early upon that very morning on which the quiet marriage had taken place in the obscure City church, he repaired to a magnificent Israelitish temple of fashion in the Minories,[1] and there ordered a suit of such clothes as were most affected by elegant landsmen. The Israelitish salesman recommended something light and lively in the fancy-check line; and Mr. Prodder, submitting to that authority as beyond all question, invested himself in a suit which he had contemplated solemnly athwart a vast expanse of plate-glass, before entering the temple of the Graces. It was "Our aristocratic tourist,"[2] at seventy-seven shillings and sixpence, and was made of a fleecy and rather powdery-looking cloth; in which the hues of baked and unbaked bricks predominated over a more delicate hearthstone tint, – which

---

1   A London street between Aldgate and the Tower; a place of general trade.

2   Ironically, this name is itself a mark of vulgarity. In 1863 Disraeli observed that "aristocratic" had become a "favoured and hackneyed epithet" among tradesmen trying to market something as stylish.

latter the shopman declared to be a colour that West-End tailors had vainly striven to emulate.

The captain, dressed in "Our aristocratic tourist," which suit was of the ultra cut-away and peg-toppy[1] order, and with his sleeves and trousers inflated by any chance summer's breeze, had perhaps more of the appearance of a tombola than is quite in accordance with a strictly artistic view of the human figure. In his desire to make himself utterly irrecognizable as the seafaring man who had carried the tidings of the murder to Mellish Park, the captain had tortured himself by substituting a tight circular collar and a wisp of purple ribbon for the honest half-yard of snowy linen which it had been his habit to wear turned over the loose collar of his blue coat. He suffered acute agonies from this modern device, but he bore them bravely; and he went straight from the tailor's to the Great Northern Railway Station, where he took his ticket for Doncaster. He meant to visit that town as an aristocratic tourist; he would keep himself aloof from the neighbourhood of Mellish Park, but he would be sure to hear the result of the inquest, and he would be able to ascertain for himself whether any trouble had come upon his sister's child.

The sea-captain did not travel by that express which carried Mr. and Mrs. Mellish to Doncaster, but by an earlier and a slower train, which lumbered quietly along the road, conveying inferior persons, to whom time was not measured by a golden standard,[2] and who smoked, and slept, and ate, and drank resignedly enough, through the eight or nine hours' journey.

It was dusk when Samuel Prodder reached the quiet racing-town from which he had fled away in the dead of the night so short a time before. He left the station, and made his way to the market-place, and from the market-place he struck into a narrow lane that led him to an obscure street upon the outskirts of the town. He had a great terror of being led by some unhappy accident into the neighbourhood of the Reindeer, lest he should be recognized by some hanger-on of that hotel.

---

1 Peg-top trousers (wide at the hips and narrow at the ankles) were in fashion *circa* 1858-65.
2 i.e. Those who do not equate time with money.

Half-way between the beginning of the straggling street and the point at which it dwindled and shrank away into a country lane, the captain found a little public-house called the Crooked Rabbit, – such an obscure and out-of-the-way place of entertainment that poor Samuel thought himself safe in seeking for rest and refreshment within its dingy walls. There was a framed-and-glazed legend of "good beds" hanging behind an opaque window-pane, – beds for which the landlord of the Crooked Rabbit was in the habit of asking and receiving almost fabulous prices during the great Leger week. But there seemed little enough doing at the humble tavern just now, and Captain Prodder walked boldly in, ordered a steak and a pint of ale, with a glass of rum-and-water, hot, to follow, at the bar, and engaged one of the good beds for his accommodation. The landlord, who was a fat man, lounged with his back against the bar reading the sporting news in the 'Manchester Guardian;' and it was the landlady who took Mr. Prodder's orders and showed him the way into an awkwardly-shaped parlour, which was much below the rest of the house, and into which the uninitiated visitor was apt to precipitate himself head foremost, as into a well or pit. There were several small mahogany tables in this room, all adorned with sticky arabesques, formed by the wet impressions of the bottom rims of pewter pots; there were so many spittoons that it was almost impossible to walk from one end of the room to the other without taking unintentional foot-baths of sawdust; there was an old bagatelle-table, the cloth of which had changed from green to dingy yellow, and was frayed and tattered like a poor man's coat; and there was a low window, the sill of which was almost on a level with the pavement of the street.

The merchant-captain threw off his hat, loosened the slip of ribbon and the torturing circular collar supplied him by the Israelitish outfitter, and cast himself into a shining mahogany arm-chair close to this window. The lower panes were shrouded by a crimson curtain, and he lifted this very cautiously and peered for a few moments into the street. It was lonely enough and quiet enough in the dusky summer's evening. Here and there lights twinkled in a shop window, and upon one threshold a man stood talking to his neighbour. With one thought always paramount in his mind, it is scarcely strange that Samuel Prodder should fancy these people must necessarily be talking of the murder.

The landlady brought the captain the steak he had ordered, and the tired traveller seated himself at one of the tables and discussed his simple meal. He had eaten nothing since seven o'clock that morning, and he made very short work of the three-quarters of a pound of meat that had been cooked for him. He finished his beer, drank his rum-and-water, smoked a pipe, and then, as he had the room still to himself, he made an impromptu couch of Windsor chairs arranged in a row, and, in his own *parlance*, turned-in upon this rough hammock to take a brief stretch.

He might have set his mind at rest, perhaps, before this, had he chosen. He could have questioned the landlady about the murder at Mellish Park; she was likely to know as much as any one else he might meet at the Crooked Rabbit. But he had refrained from doing this because he did not wish to draw attention to himself in any way, as a person in the smallest degree interested in the murder. How did he know what inquiries had possibly been made for the missing witness? There was perhaps some enormous reward offered for his apprehension, and a word or a look might betray him to the greedy eyes of those upon the watch to obtain it.

Remember that this broad-shouldered seafaring man was as ignorant as a child of all things beyond the deck of his own vessel, and the watery highroads he had been wont to navigate. Life along shore was a solemn mystery to him, – the law of the British dominions a complication of inscrutable enigmas, only to be spoken of and thought of in a spirit of reverence and wonder. If anybody had told him that he was likely to be seized upon as an accessory before the fact,[1] and hung out of hand for his passive part in the Mellish Park catastrophe, he would have believed them implicitly. How did he know how many Acts of Parliament his conduct in leaving Doncaster without giving his evidence might come under? It might be high treason, lesemajesty,[2] – anything in the world that is unpronounceable and awful, – for aught this simple sailor knew to the contrary. But in all this it was not his own safety that Captain Prodder thought of. That was of very little moment to this light-hearted, easy-going sailor. He had

---

1   One who helps to plan or is privy to a crime before the fact.
2   Offence against sovereign authority.

perilled his life too often on the high seas to set any exaggerated value upon it ashore. If they chose to hang an innocent man, they must do their worst; it would be their mistake, not his; and he had a simple seaman-like faith, rather vague, perhaps, and not very reduceable to anything like thirty-nine articles,[1] which told him there were sweet little cherubs sitting up aloft who would take good care that any such sublunary mistake should be rectified in a certain supernal log-book,[2] upon whose pages Samuel Prodder hoped to find himself set down as an honest and active sailor, always humbly obedient to the signals of his Commander.

It was for his niece's sake, then, that the sailor dreaded any discovery of his whereabouts; and it was for her sake that he resolved upon exercising the greatest degree of caution of which his simple nature was capable.

"I won't ask a single question," he thought; "there's sure to be a pack of lubbers dropping in here, by-and-by, and I shall hear 'em talking about the business as likely as not. These country folks would have nothing to talk about if they didn't overhaul the ship's books of their betters."

The captain slept soundly for upwards of an hour, and was awakened at the end of that time by the sound of voices in the room, and the fumes of tobacco. The gas was flaring high in the low-roofed parlour when he opened his eyes, and at first he could scarcely distinguish the occupants of the room for the blinding glare of light.

"I won't get up," he thought; "I'll sham asleep for a bit, and see whether they happen to talk about the business."

There were only three men in the room. One of them was the landlord, whom Samuel Prodder had seen reading in the bar; and the other two were shabby-looking men, with by no means too respectable a stamp either upon their persons or their manners. One of them wore a velveteen cut-away coat with big brass buttons, knee-breeches, blue stockings, and highlows. The other was a pale-faced man, with mutton-chop whiskers, and dressed in a shabby-genteel

---

1 Articles of religion in the Book of Common Prayer defining the Church of England's position in matters of dogma.

2 i.e. That any such earthly mistake would be corrected in God's divine record.

costume, that gave indication of general vagabondage rather than of any particular occupation.

They were talking of horses when Captain Prodder awoke, and the sailor lay for some time listening to a jargon that was utterly unintelligible to him. The men talked of Lord Zetland's lot, of Lord Glasgow's lot, and the Leger and the Cup, and made offers to bet with each other, and quarrelled about the terms, and never came to an agreement, in a manner that was utterly bewildering to poor Samuel; but he waited patiently, still feigning to be asleep, and not in any way disturbed by the men, who did not condescend to take any notice of him.

"They'll talk of the other business presently," he thought; "they're safe to talk of it."

Mr. Prodder was right.

After discussing the conflicting merits of half the horses in the racing calendar, the three men abandoned the fascinating subject; and the landlord re-entering the room after having left it to fetch a fresh supply of beer for his guests, asked if either of them had heard if anything new had turned up about that business at Mellish Park.

"There's a letter in to-day's 'Guardian,'" he added, before receiving any reply to his question, "and a pretty strong one. It tries to fix the murder upon some one in the house, but it don't exactly name the party. It wouldn't be safe to do that yet awhile, I suppose."

Upon the request of the two men, the landlord of the Crooked Rabbit read the letter in the Manchester daily paper. It was a very clever letter, and a spirited one, giving a synopsis of the proceedings at the inquest, and commenting very severely upon the manner in which that investigation had been conducted. Mr. Prodder quailed until the Windsor chairs trembled beneath him as the landlord read one passage, in which it was remarked that the stranger who carried the news of the murder to the house of the victim's employer, the man who had heard the report of the pistol, and had been chiefly instrumental in the finding of the body, had not been forthcoming at the inquest.

"He had disappeared mysteriously and abruptly, and no efforts were made to find him," wrote the correspondent of the 'Guardian.' "What assurance can be given for the safety of any man's life when such a crime as the Mellish Park murder is investigated in this loose and indifferent manner? The catastrophe occurred within the boundary of the Park fence. Let it be discovered whether any person in the Mellish household had a motive for the destruction of James Conyers. The man was a stranger to the neighbourhood. He was not likely, therefore, to have made enemies outside the boundary of his employer's estate, but he may have had some secret foe within that limit. Who was he? where did he come from? what were his antecedents and associations? Let each one of these questions be fully sifted, let a cordon be drawn round the house, and every creature living in it be held under the surveillance of the law until patient investigation has done its work, and such evidence has been collected as must lead to the detection of the guilty person."

To this effect was the letter which the landlord read in a loud and didactic manner, that was very imposing, though not without a few stumbles over some hard words, and a good deal of slap-dash jumping at others.

Samuel Prodder could make very little of the composition, except that it was perfectly clear he had been missed at the inquest, and his absence commented upon. The landlord and the shabby-genteel man talked long and discursively upon the matter; the man in the velveteen coat, who was evidently a thorough-bred cockney and only newly arrived in Doncaster, required to be told the whole story before he was upon a footing with the other two. He was very quiet, and generally spoke between his teeth, rarely taking the unnecessary trouble of removing his short clay-pipe from his mouth, except when it required refilling. He listened to the story of the murder very intently, keeping one eye upon the speaker and the other on his pipe, and nodding approvingly now and then in the course of the narrative.

He took his pipe from his mouth when the story was finished, and filled it from an india-rubber pouch, which had to be turned inside-out in some mysterious manner before the tobacco could be extricated from it. While he was packing the loose fragments of shag or bird's-eye neatly into the bowl of the pipe with his stumpy little finger, he said, with supreme carelessness –

"I know'd Jim Conyers."

"Did you now?" exclaimed the landlord, opening his eyes very wide.

"I know'd him," repeated the man, "as intimate as I know'd my own mother; and when I read of the murder in the newspaper last Sunday, you might have knocked me down with a feather. 'Jim's got it at last,' I said; for he was one of them coves that goes through the world cock-a-doodling over other people to sich a extent, that when they *do* drop in for it, there's not many particular sorry for 'em. He was one of your selfish chaps, this here; and when a chap goes through this life makin' it his leadin' principle to care about nobody, he must- n't be surprised if it ends by nobody carin' for him. Yes, I know'd Jim Conyers," added the man, slowly and thoughtfully, "and I know'd him under rather pecooliar circumstances."

The landlord and the other man pricked up their ears at this point of the conversation.

The trainer at Mellish Park had, as we know, risen to popularity from the hour in which he had fallen upon the dewy turf in the wood, shot through the heart.

"If there wasn't any particklar objections," the landlord of the Crooked Rabbit said, presently, "I should oncommonly like to hear anything you've got to tell about the poor chap. There's a deal of interest took about the matter in Doncaster, and my customers have scarcely talked of anything else since the inquest."

The man in the velveteen coat rubbed his chin and smoked his pipe reflectively. He was evidently not a very communicative man; but it was also evident that he was rather gratified by the distinction of his position in the little public-house parlour.

This was no other than Mr. Matthew Harrison, the dog-fancier; Aurora's pensioner, the man who had traded upon her secret, and made himself the last link between her and the low-born husband she had abandoned.

Samuel Prodder lifted himself from the Windsor chairs at this juncture. He was too much interested in the conversation to be able to simulate sleep any longer. He got up, stretched his legs and arms, made elaborate show of having just awakened from a profound and refreshing slumber, and asked the landlord of the Crooked Rabbit to mix him another glass of that pineapple-rum grog.

The captain lighted his pipe while his host departed upon this errand. The seaman glanced rather inquisitively at Mr. Harrison; but he was fain to wait until the conversation took its own course, and offered him a safe opportunity of asking a few questions.

"The pecooliar circumstances under which I know'd James Cony-ers," pursued the dog-fancier, after having taken his own time and smoked out half a pipeful of tobacco, to the acute aggravation of his auditory, "was a woman, – and a stunner she was, too; one of your regular spitfires, that'll knock you into the middle of next week if you so much as asks her how she does in a manner she don't approve of. She was a woman, she was, and a handsome one, too; but she was more than a match for James, with all his brass. Why, I've seen her great black eyes flash fire upon him," said Mr. Harrison, looking dreamily before him, as if he could even at that moment see the flash-ing eyes of which he spoke; "I've seen her look at him, as if she'd wither him up from off the ground he trod upon, with that contempt she felt for him."

Samuel Prodder grew strangely uneasy as he listened to this man's talk of flashing black eyes and angry looks directed at James Conyers. Had he not seen his niece's shining orbs flame fire upon the dead man only a quarter of an hour before he received his death-wound? Only so long – Heaven help that wretched girl! – only so long before the man for whom she had expressed unmitigated hate had fallen by the hand of an unknown murderer.

"She must have been a tartar, this young woman of yours," the landlord observed to Mr. Harrison.

"She was a tartar," answered the dog-fancier: "but she was the right sort, too, for all that; and what's more, she was a kind friend to me. There's never a quarter-day goes by that I don't have cause to say so."

He poured out a fresh glass of beer as he spoke, and tossed the liquor down his capacious throat with the muttered sentiment, "Here's towards her."

Another man had entered the room while Mr. Prodder had sat smoking his pipe and drinking his rum-and-water, a hump-backed, white-faced man, who sneaked into the public-house parlour as if he had no right to be there, and seated himself noiselessly at one of the tables.

Samuel Prodder remembered this man. He had seen him through the window in the lighted parlour of the north lodge when the body of James Conyers had been carried into the cottage. It was not likely, however, that the man had seen the captain.

"Why, if it isn't Steeve Hargraves from the Park!" exclaimed the landlord, as he looked round and recognized the "Softy"; "he'll be able to tell plenty, I dare say. We've been talking of the murder, Steeve," he added, in a conciliatory manner.

Mr. Hargraves rubbed his clumsy hands about his head, and looked furtively, yet searchingly, at each member of the little assembly.

"Ay, sure," he said; "folks don't seem to me to talk about owght else. It was bad enoogh oop at the Park; but it seems worse in Doncaster."

"Are you stayin' up town, Steeve?" asked the landlord, who seemed to be upon pretty intimate terms with the late hanger-on of Mellish Park.

"Yes, I'm stayin' oop town for a bit; I've been out of place since the business oop there; you know how I was turned out of the house that had sheltered me ever since I was a boy, and you know who did it. Never mind that; I'm out o' place now, but you may draw me a mug of ale; I've money enough for that."

Samuel Prodder looked at the "Softy" with considerable interest. He had played a small part in the great catastrophe, yet it was scarcely likely that he should be able to throw any light upon the mystery. What was he but a poor half-witted hanger-on of the murdered man, who had lost all by his patron's untimely death?

The "Softy" drank his beer, and sat, silent, ungainly, and disagreeable to look upon, amongst the other men.

"There's a reg'lar stir in the Manchester papers about this murder, Steeve," the landlord said, by way of opening a conversation; "it don't seem to me as if the business was goin' to be let drop over-quietly. There'll be a second inquest, I reckon, or a examination, or a memorial to the Secretary of State, or summat o' that sort, before long."

The "Softy's" face, expressionless almost always, expressed nothing now but stolid indifference; the stupid indifference of a half-witted ignoramus, to whose impenetrable intellect even the murder of his own master was a far-away and obscure event, not powerful enough to awaken any effort of attention.

"Yes; I'll lay there'll be a stir about it before long," the landlord continued. "The papers put it down very strong that the murder must have been done by some one in the house; by some one as had more knowledge of the man, and more reason to be angry against him, than strangers could have. Now you, Hargraves, were living at the place; you must have seen and heard things that other people haven't had the opportunity to hear. What do *you* think about it?"

Mr. Hargraves scratched his head reflectively.

"The papers are cleverer nor me," he said at last; "it wouldn't do for a poor fond chap like me to go agen such as them. I think what they think. I think it was some one about the pleace did it; some one that had good reason to be spiteful again him that's dead."

An imperceptible shudder passed over the "Softy's" frame as he alluded to the murdered man. It was strange with what gusto the other three men discussed the ghastly subject; returning to it persistently in spite of every interruption, and in a manner licking their lips over its gloomiest details. It was surely more strange that they should do this, than that Stephen Hargraves should exhibit some reluctance to talk freely upon the dismal topic.

"And who do you think had cause to be spiteful agen him, Steeve?" asked the landlord. "Had him and Mr. Mellish fell out about the management of the stable?"

"Him and *Mr.* Mellish had never had an angry word pass between 'em, as I've heerd of," answered the "Softy."

He laid such a singular emphasis upon the word *Mr.* that the three men looked at him wonderingly, and Captain Prodder took his pipe from his mouth and grasped the back of a neighbouring chair as firmly as if he had entertained serious thoughts of flinging that trifle of furniture at the "Softy's" head.

"Who else could it have been, then, as had a spite against the man?" asked some one.

Samuel Prodder scarcely knew who it was who spoke, for his attention was concentrated upon Stephen Hargraves; and he never once removed his gaze from the white face, and dull, blinking eyes.

"Who was it that went to meet him late at night in the north lodge?" whispered the "Softy." "Who was it that couldn't find words that was bad enough for him, or looks that was angry enough for him? Who was it that wrote him a letter, – I've got it, and I mean to keep it too, – askin' of him to be in the wood at such-and-such a time upon the very night of the murder? Who was it that met him there in the dark, – as others could tell as well as me? Who was it that did this?"

No one answered. The men looked at each other and at the "Softy" with open mouths, but said nothing. Samuel Prodder grasped the top-most bar of the wooden chair still more tightly, and his broad bosom rose and fell beneath his tourist waistcoat like a raging sea; but he sat in the shadow of the queerly-shaped room, and no one noticed him.

"Who was it that ran away from her own home and hid herself, after the inquest?" whispered the "Softy." "Who was it that was afraid to stop in her own house, but must run away to London without leaving word where she was gone for anybody? Who was it that was seen upon the mornin' before the murder, meddlin' with her husband's guns and pistols, and was seen by more than me, as them that saw her will testify when the time comes? Who was this?"

Again there was no answer. The raging sea laboured still more heavily under Captain Prodder's waistcoat, and his grasp tightened, if it could tighten, on the rail of the chair; but he uttered no word. There was more to come, perhaps, yet; and he might want every chair in the room as instruments with which to appease his vengeance.

"You was talkin', when I just came in, a while ago, of a young woman in connection with Mr. James Conyers, sir," said the "Softy," turning to Matthew Harrison; "a black-eyed woman, you said; might she have been his wife?"

The dog-fancier started, and deliberated for a few moments before he answered.

"Well, in a manner of speaking, she was his wife," he said at last, rather reluctantly.

"She was a bit above him, loike – wasn't she?" asked the "Softy." "She had more money than she knew what to do with – eh?"

The dog-fancier stared at the questioner.

"You know who she was, I suppose?" he said suspiciously.

"I think I do," whispered Stephen Hargraves. "She was the daughter of Mr. Floyd, the rich banker oop in London; and she married our squire while her first husband was alive; and she wrote a letter to him that's dead, askin' of him to meet her upon the night of the murder."

Captain Prodder flung aside the chair. It was too poor a weapon with which to wreak his wrath; and with one bound he sprang upon the "Softy," seizing the astonished wretch by the throat, and overturning a table, with a heap of crashing glasses and pewter pots, that rolled away into the corners of the room.

"It's a lie!" roared the sailor; "you foul-mouthed hound! you know that it's a lie! Give me something," cried Captain Prodder; "give me something, somebody, and give it quick, that I may pound this man into a mash as soft as a soaked ship's biscuit; for if I use my fists to him I shall murder him, as sure as I stand here. It's my sister Eliza's child you want to slander, is it? You'd better have kept your mouth shut while you was in her own uncle's company. I meant to have kep' quiet here," cried the captain, with a vague recollection that he had betrayed himself and his purpose; "but was I to keep quiet and hear lies told of my own niece? Take care," he added, shaking the "Softy," till Mr. Hargraves's teeth chattered in his head, "or I'll knock those crooked teeth of yours down your ugly throat, to hinder you from telling any more lies of my dead sister's only child."

"They weren't lies," gasped the "Softy," doggedly; "I said I've got the letter, and I have got it. Let me go, and I'll show it to you."

The sailor released the dirty wisp of cotton neckerchief by which he had held Stephen Hargraves; but he still retained a grasp upon his coat-collar.

"Shall I show you the letter?" asked the "Softy."

"Yes."

Mr. Hargraves fumbled in his pockets for some minutes, and ultimately produced a dirty scrap of crumpled paper.

It was the brief scrawl which Aurora had written to James Conyers, telling him to meet her in the wood. The murdered man had thrown it carelessly aside after reading it, and it had been picked up by Stephen Hargraves.

He would not trust the precious document out of his own clumsy hands, but held it before Captain Prodder for inspection.

The sailor stared at it, anxious, bewildered, fearful; he scarcely knew how to estimate the importance of the wretched scrap of circumstantial evidence. There were the words, certainly, written in a bold, scarcely feminine, hand. But these words in themselves proved nothing until it could be proved that his niece had written them.

"How do I know as my sister Eliza's child wrote that?" he asked.

"Ay, sure; but she did though," answered the "Softy." "But, coom, let me go now, will you?" he added, with cringing civility; "I didn't know you was her uncle. How was I to know owght about it? I don't want to make any mischief agen Mrs. Mellish, though she's been no friend to me. I didn't say anything at the inquest, did I? though I might have said as much as I've said to-night, if it comes to that, and have told no lies. But when folks bother *me* about him that's dead, and ask this and that and t'oother, and go on as if I had a right to know all about it, I'm free to tell my thoughts, I suppose? surely I'm free to tell my thoughts?"

"I'll go straight to Mr. Mellish, and tell him what you've said, you scoundrel!" cried the captain.

"Ay, do," whispered Stephen Hargraves maliciously; "there's some of it that'll be stale news to him, anyhow."

CHAPTER XXXIV.

THE DISCOVERY OF THE WEAPON WITH WHICH JAMES CONYERS HAD BEEN SLAIN.

MR. AND MRS. MELLISH returned to the house in which they had been so happy; but it is not to be supposed that the pleasant country mansion could be again, all in a moment, the home that it had been before the advent of James Conyers the trainer, and the acting of the tragedy that had so abruptly concluded his brief service.

No; every pang that Aurora had felt, every agony that John had endured, had left a certain impress upon the scene in which it had been suffered. The subtle influences of association hung heavily about the familiar place. We are the slaves of such associations, and we are powerless to stand against their silent force. Scraps of colour and patches of gilding upon the walls will bear upon them, as plainly as if they were covered with hieroglyphical inscriptions, the shadows of the thoughts of those who have looked upon them. Transient and chance effects of light or shade will recall the same effects, seen and observed – as Fagin observed the broken spike upon the guarded dock[1] – in some horrible crisis of misery and despair. The commonest household goods and chattels will bear mute witness of your agonies: an easy-chair will say to you, "It was upon me you cast yourself in that paroxysm of rage and grief;" the pattern of a dinner-service may recall to you that fatal day on which you pushed your food untasted from you, and turned your face, like grief-stricken King David, to the wall.[2] The bed you lay upon, the curtains that sheltered you, the pattern of the paper on the walls, the common every-day sounds of the

---

1   In Charles Dickens' *Oliver Twist* (1837-8), while Fagin waits for the jury to deliver his death sentence, his mind dwells obsessively upon small details: "he fell to counting the iron spikes before him, and wondering how the head of one had been broken off" (Chapter 52).

2   In 2 Samuel 12:15 David grieves for his dying child by fasting and lying on the ground; in 2 Samuel 18:33 he goes to his chamber and weeps; in 2 Samuel 19:4 he covers his face as he weeps for Absalom. It is Hezekiah who turns his face to the wall when he is told by Isaiah that he will die: "Then Hezekiah turned his face to the wall and prayed to the Lord" (2 Kings 20:2).

household, coming muffled and far-away to that lonely room in which you hid yourself, – all these bear record of your sorrow, and of that hideous double action of the mind which impresses these things most vividly upon you at the very time when it would seem they should be most indifferent.

But every sorrow, every pang of wounded love, or doubt, or jealousy, or despair, is a fact – a fact once, and a fact for ever; to be outlived, but very rarely to be forgotten; leaving such an impress upon our lives as no future joys can quite wear out. The murder has been done, and the hands are red.[1] The sorrow has been suffered; and however beautiful Happiness may be to us, she can never be the bright virginal creature she once was; for she has passed through the valley of the shadow of death,[2] and we have discovered that she is not immortal.

It is not to be expected, then, that John Mellish and his wife Aurora could feel quite the same in the pretty chambers of the Yorkshire mansion as they had felt before the first shipwreck of their happiness. They had been saved from peril and destruction, and landed, by the mercy of Providence, high and dry upon the shore that seemed to promise them pleasure and security henceforth. But the memory of the tempest was yet new to them; and upon the sands that were so smooth to-day they had seen yesterday the breakers beating with furious menace, and hurrying onward to destroy them.

The funeral of the trainer had not yet taken place, and it was scarcely a pleasant thing for Mr. Mellish to remember that the body of the murdered man still lay, stark and awful, in the oak coffin that stood upon trestles in the rustic chamber at the north lodge.

"I'll pull that place down, Lolly," John said, as he turned away from an open window, through which he could see the Gothic chimneys of the trainer's late habitation glimmering redly above the trees. "I'll pull the place down, my pet. The gates are never used, except by the stable-boys; I'll knock them down, and the lodge too, and build some loose boxes for the brood-mares with the materials. And we'll go

---

1 In the sleepwalking scene in *Macbeth* Lady Macbeth tries to wash her hands of imaginary blood: "What, will these hands ne'er be clean?" (V.ii.43).
2 Psalm 23.

away to the south of France, darling, and run across to Italy, if you like, and forget all about this horrid business."

"The funeral will take place to-morrow, John, will it not?" Aurora asked.

"To-morrow, dear! – to-morrow is Wednesday, you know. It was upon Thursday night that——"

"Yes, yes," she answered, interrupting him. "I know; I know."

She shuddered as she spoke, remembering the ghastly circumstances of the night to which he alluded; remembering how the dead man had stood before her, strong in health and vitality, and had insolently defied her hatred. Away from Mellish Park, she had only remembered that the burden of her life had been removed from her, and that she was free. But here – here upon the scene of the hideous story – she recollected the manner of her release; and that memory oppressed her even more terribly than her old secret, her only sorrow.

She had never seen or known in this man, who had been murdered, one redeeming quality, one generous thought. She had known him as a liar, a schemer, a low and paltry swindler, a selfish spendthrift, extravagant to wantonness upon himself, but meaner than words could tell towards others; a profligate, a traitor, a glutton, a drunkard. This is what she had found behind her school-girl's fancy for a handsome face, for violet-tinted eyes, and soft-brown curling hair. Do not call her hard, then, if sorrow had no part in the shuddering horror she felt as she conjured up the image of him in his death-hour, and saw the glazing eyes turned angrily upon her. She was little more than twenty; and it had been her fate always to take the wrong step, always to be misled by the vague finger-posts upon life's high-road, and to choose the longest, and crookedest, and hardest way towards the goal she sought to reach.

Had she, upon the discovery of her first husband's infidelity, called the law to her aid, – she was rich enough to command its utmost help, though Sir Cresswell Cresswell did not then keep the turnpike upon such a royal road to divorce as he does now, – she might have freed herself from the hateful chains so foolishly linked together,[1] and

---

1 This passage states explicitly that Aurora's separation in the summer of 1857 predates the Divorce Court (which opened in January 1858 with Sir Cresswell Cresswell as judge). (See 434, n.1 for a related anachronism.) Braddon is wrong in stating that Aurora could have obtained a divorce before the court opened: in 186 years of

might have defied this dead man to torment or assail her.

But she had chosen to follow the counsel of expediency, and it had led her upon the crooked way through which I have striven to follow her. I feel that there is much need of apology for her. Her own hands had sown the dragon's teeth,[1] from whose evil seed had sprung up armed men, strong enough to rend and devour her. But then, if she had been faultless, she could not have been the heroine of this story; for I think some wise man of old remarked, that the perfect women were those who left no histories behind them,[2] but went through life upon such a tranquil course of quiet well-doing as left no footprints on the sands of time; only mute records hidden here and there, deep in the grateful hearts of those who had been blest by them.

The presence of the dead man within the boundary of Mellish Park made itself felt throughout the household that had once been such a jovial one. The excitement of the catastrophe had passed away, and only the dull gloom remained – a sense of oppression not to be cast aside. It was felt in the servants' hall, as well as in Aurora's luxurious apartments. It was felt by the butler as well as by the master. No worse deed of violence than the slaughter of an unhappy stag, who had rushed for a last refuge to the Mellish Park flower-garden, and had been run down by furious hounds upon the velvet lawn, had ever before been done within the boundary of the young squire's home. The house was an old one, and had stood, gray and ivy-shrouded, through the perilous days of civil war. There were secret passages, in which loyal squires of Mellish Park had hidden from ferocious

---

divorce by Act of Parliament, only four women obtained divorces, and in all cases adultery was compounded by incest or bigamy. The Stereotyped edition smoothed over this error by deleting the statement that Sir Cresswell Cresswell's "turnpike" was not yet open, and by adding references to Conyers' "brutality" in Chapters XXX and XXXVI, thus giving Aurora grounds for divorce under the new Act. Attentive readers, however, would still be aware that Aurora's separation in the summer of 1857 predates the Divorce Court by about six months. Braddon is, however, correct about the cost of Parliamentary divorce: about £1000, more if hotly contested.

1   In classical mythology, Cadmus is instructed by Athena to sow dragon's teeth in the ground. When he does so, armed men rise from the earth and immediately start fighting one another.

2   The "wise man of old" is possibly Thucydides: "Great . . . is her of whom there is the least talk among men whether in praise or blame" (*The History of the Peloponnesian War*, Book 2, Section 6.46).

Roundheads bent upon riot and plunder. There were broad hearth-stones, upon which sturdy blows had been given and exchanged by strong men in leathern jerkins and clumsy iron-heeled boots; but the Royalist Mellish had always ultimately escaped, – up a chimney, or down a cellar, or behind a curtain of tapestry; and the wicked Praise-the-Lord Thompsons, and Smiter-of-the-Philistines Joneses, had departed after plundering the plate-chest and emptying the wine-bar-rels.[1] There had never before been set upon the place in which John Mellish had first seen the light, the red hand of MURDER.

It was not strange, then, that the servants sat long over their meals, and talked in solemn whispers of the events of the past week. There was more than the murder to talk about. There was the flight of Mrs. Mellish from beneath her husband's roof upon the very day of the inquest. It was all very well for John to give out that his wife had gone up to town upon a visit to her cousin, Mrs. Bulstrode. Such ladies as Mrs. Mellish do not go upon visits without escort, without a word of notice, without the poorest pretence of bag and baggage. No; the mis-tress of Mellish Park had fled away from her home under the infl-uence of some sudden panic. Had not Mrs. Powell said as much, or hinted as much? for when did that lady-like creature ever vulgarize her opinions by stating them plainly? The matter was obvious. Mr. Mellish had taken, no doubt, the wisest course: he had pursued his wife and had brought her back, and had done his best to hush up the matter; but Aurora's departure had been a flight, – a sudden and unpremeditated flight.

The lady's-maid, – ah, how many handsome dresses, given to her by a generous mistress, lay neatly folded in the girl's boxes on the sec-ond story! – told how Aurora had come to her room, pale and wild-looking, and had dressed herself unassisted for that hurried journey, upon the day of the inquest. The girl liked her mistress, loved her, per-haps; for Aurora had a wondrous and almost dangerous faculty for winning the love of those who came near her; but it was so pleasant to have something to say about this all-absorbing topic, and to be able

---

1   The "loyal" squires of Mellish were Royalists, supporters of the monarchy during the Civil War. Their attackers would have been members of the Parliamentary party (called "Roundheads" because they cut their hair short). "Praise-the-Lord Thomp-son" and "Smiter-of-the-Philistines Jones" are parodies of Puritan names.

to make oneself a feature in the solemn conclave. At first they had talked only of the murdered man, speculating upon his life and history, and building up a dozen theoretical views of the murder. But the tide had turned now, and they talked of their mistress; not connecting her in any positive or openly expressed manner with the murder, but commenting upon the strangeness of her conduct, and dwelling much upon those singular coincidences by which she had happened to be roaming in the park upon the night of the catastrophe, and to run away from her home on the day of the inquest.

"It *was* odd, you know," the cook said; "and them black-eyed women are generally regular spirity ones. *I* shouldn't like to offend Master John's wife. Do you remember how she paid into t' 'Softy'?"

"But there was naught o' sort between her and the trainer, was there?" asked some one.

"I don't know about that. But 'Softy' said she hated him like poison, and that there was no love lost between 'em."

But why should Aurora have hated the dead man? The ensign's widow had left the sting of her venom behind her, and had suggested to these servants, by hints and innuendos, something so far more base and hideous than the truth, that I will not sully these pages by recording it. But Mrs. Powell had of course done this foul thing without the utterance of one ugly word that could have told against her gentility, had it been repeated aloud in a crowded drawing-room. She had only shrugged her shoulders, and lifted her straw-coloured eyebrows, and sighed half regretfully, half deprecatingly; but she had blasted the character of the woman she hated as shamefully as if she had uttered a libel too gross for Holywell Street.[1] She had done a wrong that could only be undone by the exhibition of the blood-stained certificate in John's keeping, and the revelation of the whole story connected with that fatal scrap of paper. She had done this before packing her boxes; and she had gone away from the house that had sheltered her, well-pleased at having done this wrong; and comforting herself yet further by the intention of doing more mischief through the medium of the penny post.

It is not to be supposed that the Manchester paper, which had

---

1   Area in London known for the sale of pornography.

caused so serious a discussion in the humble parlour of the Crooked Rabbit, had been overlooked in the servants' hall at Mellish Park. The Manchester journals were regularly forwarded to the young squire from that metropolis of cotton-spinning and horse-racing; and the mysterious letter in the 'Guardian' had been read and commented upon. Every creature in that household, from the fat housekeeper, who had kept the keys of the store-room through nearly three generations, to the rheumatic trainer, Langley, had a certain interest in the awful question. A nervous footman turned pale as that passage was read which declared that the murder had been committed by some member of the household; but I think there were some younger and more adventurous spirits – especially a pretty housemaid, who had seen the thrilling drama of 'Susan Hopley'[1] performed at the Doncaster theatre during the spring meeting – who would have rather liked to be accused of the crime, and to emerge spotless and triumphant from the judicial ordeal, through the evidence of an idiot, or a magpie, or a ghost, or some other witness common and popular in criminal courts.

Did Aurora know anything of all this? No; she only knew that a dull and heavy sense of oppression in her own breast made the very summer atmosphere floating in at the open windows seem stifling and poisonous; that the house, which had once been so dear to her, was as painfully and perpetually haunted by the ghastly presence of the murdered man, as if the dead trainer had stalked palpably about the corridors wrapped in a blood-stained winding-sheet.

She dined with her husband alone in the great dining-room. They were very silent at dinner, for the presence of the servants sealed their lips upon the topic that was uppermost in their minds. John looked anxiously at his wife every now and then, for he saw that her face had grown paler since her arrival at Mellish; but he waited until they were alone before he spoke.

"My darling," he said, as the door closed behind the butler and his

---

1 In George Dibdin Pitt's melodrama *Susan Hopley, or, the Vicissitudes of a Servant Girl* (1841), Susan's master is murdered and her brother (Andrew) vanishes. Andrew is suspected, but Susan solves the case aided by several visions, including one in which she sees two men murdering Andrew and her master, and concealing Andrew's body behind a panel.

subordinate, "I am sure you are ill. This business has been too much for you."

"It is the air of this house that seems to oppress me, John," answered Aurora. "I had forgotten all about this dreadful business while I was away. Now that I have come back, and find that the time which has been so long to me – so long in misery and anxiety, and so long in joy, my own dear love, through you – is in reality only a few days, and that the murdered man still lies near us, I – ; I shall be better when – when the funeral is over, John."

"My poor darling, I was a fool to bring you back. I should never have done so, but for Talbot's advice. He urged me so strongly to come back directly. He said that if there should be any disturbance about the murder, we ought to be upon the spot."

"Disturbance! What disturbance?" cried Aurora.

Her face blanched as she spoke, and her heart sank within her. What further disturbance could there be? Was the ghastly business as yet unfinished, then? She knew – alas! only too well – that there could be no investigation of this matter which would not bring her name before the world linked with the name of the dead man. How much she had endured in order to keep that shameful secret from the world! How much she had sacrificed in the hope of saving her father from humiliation! And now, at the last, when she had thought that the dark chapter of her life was finished, the hateful page blotted out, – now, at the very last, there was a probability of some new disturbance which would bring her name and her history into every newspaper in England.

"Oh, John, John!" she cried, bursting into a passion of hysterical sobs, and covering her face with her clasped hands; "am I never to hear the last of this? Am I never, never, never to be released from the consequences of my miserable folly?"

The butler entered the room as she said this; she rose hurriedly, and walked to one of the windows, in order to conceal her face from the man.

"I beg your pardon, sir," the old servant said; "but they've found something in the park, and I thought perhaps you might like to know——"

"They've found something! What?" exclaimed John, utterly bewildered between his agitation at the sight of his wife's grief and his endeavour to understand the man.

"A pistol, sir. One of the stable-lads found it just now. He went to the wood with another boy to look at the place where – the – the man was shot; and he's brought back a pistol he found there. It was close against the water, but hid away among the weeds and rushes. Whoever threw it there, thought, no doubt, to throw it in the pond; but Jim, that's one of the boys, fancied he saw something glitter, and sure enough it was the barrel of a pistol; and I think must be the one that the trainer was shot with, Mr. John."

"A pistol!" cried Mr. Mellish; "let me see it."

His servant handed him the weapon. It was small enough for a toy, but none the less deadly in a skilful hand. It was a rich man's fancy, deftly carried out by some cunning gunsmith, and enriched by elaborate inlaid work of purple steel and tarnished silver. It was rusty, from exposure to rain and dew; but Mr. Mellish knew the pistol well, for it was his own.

It was his own; one of his pet playthings; and it had been kept in the room which was only entered by privileged persons, – the room in which his wife had busied herself with the rearrangement of his guns upon the day of the murder.

CHAPTER XXXV.

UNDER A CLOUD.

TALBOT BULSTRODE and his wife came to Mellish Park a few days after the return of John and Aurora. Lucy was pleased to come to her cousin; pleased to be allowed to love her without reservation; grateful to her husband for his gracious goodness in setting no barrier between her and the friend she loved.

And Talbot, – who shall tell the thoughts that were busy in his mind, as he sat in a corner of the first-class carriage, to all outward appearance engrossed in the perusal of a 'Times' leader?

I wonder how much of the Thunderer's noble Saxon English Mr. Bulstrode comprehended that morning! The broad white paper on which the 'Times' is printed serves as a convenient screen for a man's face. Heaven knows what agonies have been sometimes endured behind that printed mask! A woman, married, and a happy mother, glances carelessly enough at the Births and Marriages and Deaths, and reads perhaps that the man she loved, and parted with, and broke her heart for, fifteen or twenty years before, has fallen, shot through the heart, far away upon an Indian battle-field. She holds the paper firmly enough before her face; and her husband goes on with his breakfast, and stirs his coffee, or breaks his egg, while she suffers her agony, – while the comfortable breakfast-table darkens and goes away from her, and the long-ago day comes back upon which the cruel ship left Southampton, and the hard voices of well-meaning friends held forth monotonously upon the folly of improvident marriages. Would it not be better, by-the-by, for wives to make a practice of telling their husbands all the sentimental little stories connected with the pre-matrimonial era? Would it not be wiser to gossip freely about Charles's dark eyes and moustache, and to hope that the poor fellow is getting on well in the Indian service, than to keep a skeleton, in the shape of a phantom ensign in the 87th, hidden away in some dark chamber of the feminine memory?

But other than womanly agonies are suffered behind the 'Times.' The husband reads bad news of the railway company in whose shares he has so rashly invested that money which his wife believes safely lodged in the jog-trot, three-percent.-yielding Consols. The dashing son, with Newmarket tendencies, reads evil tidings of the horse he has backed so boldly, perhaps at the advice of a Manchester prophet, who warranted putting his friends in the way of winning a hatful of money for the small consideration of three-and-sixpence in postage-stamps. Visions of a book that it will not be very easy to square; of a black list of play or pay engagements; of a crowd of angry book-men clamorous for their dues, and not slow to hint at handy horse-ponds, and possible tar and feathers, for defaulting swells and sneaking "welshers"; all these things flit across the disorganized brain of the young man, while his sisters are entreating to be told whether the 'Crown Diamonds' is to be performed that night, and if "dear Miss Pyne" will warble Rode's air before the curtain falls. The friendly screen hides his face; and by the time he has looked for the Covent Garden advertisements, and given the required information, he is able to set the paper down and proceed calmly with his breakfast, pondering ways and means as he does so.

Lucy Bulstrode read a High-Church novel, while her husband sat with the 'Times' before his face, thinking of all that had happened to him since he had first met the banker's daughter. How far away that old love-story seemed to have receded since the quiet domestic happiness of his life had begun in his marriage with Lucy! He had never been false, in the remotest shadow of a thought, to his second love; but now that he knew the secret of Aurora's life, he could but look back and wonder how he should have borne that cruel revelation if John's fate had been his; if he had trusted the woman he loved in spite of the world, in spite of her own strange words, which had so terribly strengthened his worst fears, so cruelly redoubled his darkest doubts.

"Poor girl!" he thought; "it was scarcely strange that she should shrink from telling that humiliating story. I was not tender enough. I confronted her in my obstinate and pitiless pride. I thought of myself rather than of her, and of her sorrow. I was barbarous and ungentlemanly; and then I wondered that she refused to confide in me."

Talbot Bulstrode, reasoning after the fact, saw the weak points of his conduct with a preternatural clearness of vision, and could not repress a sharp pang of regret that he had not acted more generously.

There was no infidelity to Lucy in this thought. He would not have exchanged his devoted little wife for the black-browed divinity of the past, though an all-powerful fairy had stood at his side ready to cancel his nuptials and tie a fresh knot between him and Aurora. But he was a gentleman, and he felt that he had grievously wronged, insulted and humiliated a woman whose worst fault had been the trusting folly of an innocent girl.

"I left her on the ground in that room at Felden," he thought, – "kneeling on the ground, with her beautiful head bowed down before me. O my God, can I ever forget the agony of that moment! Can I ever forget what it cost me to do that which I thought was right!"

The cold perspiration broke out upon his forehead as he remembered that bygone pain, as it may do with a cowardly person who recalls too vividly the taking out of a three-pronged double-tooth, or the cutting off of a limb.

"John Mellish was ten times wiser than I," thought Mr. Bulstrode; "he trusted to his instinct, and recognized a true woman when he met her. I used to despise him at Rugby because he couldn't construe Cicero. I never thought he'd live to be wiser than me."

Talbot Bulstrode folded the 'Times' newspaper, and laid it down in the empty seat by his side. Lucy shut the third volume of her novel. How should she care to read when it pleased her husband to desist from reading?

"Lucy," said Mr. Bulstrode, taking his wife's hand (they had the carriage to themselves – a piece of good fortune which often happens to travellers who give the guard half-a-crown), – "Lucy, I once did your cousin a great wrong; I want to atone for it now. If any trouble, which no one yet foresees, should come upon her, I want to be her friend. Do you think I am right in wishing this, dear?"

"Right, Talbot!"

Mrs. Bulstrode could only repeat the word in unmitigated surprise. When did she ever think him anything but the truest and wisest and most perfect of created beings?

Everything seemed very quiet at Mellish when the visitors arrived. There was no one in the drawing-room, nor in the smaller room within the drawing-room; the venetians were closed, for the day was close and sultry; there were vases of fresh flowers upon the tables; but there were no open books, no litter of frivolous needlework or drawing-materials, to indicate Aurora's presence.

"Mr. and Mrs. Mellish expected you by the later train, I believe, sir," the servant said, as he ushered Talbot and his wife into the drawing-room.

"Shall I go and look for Aurora?" Lucy said to her husband. "She is in the morning-room, I dare say."

Talbot suggested that it would be better, perhaps, to wait till Mrs. Mellish came to them. So Lucy was fain to remain where she was. She went to one of the open windows, and pushed the shutters apart. The blazing sunshine burst into the room, and drowned it in light. The smooth lawn was aflame with scarlet geraniums and standard roses, and all manner of gaudily-coloured blossoms; but Mrs. Bulstrode looked beyond this vividly-tinted *parterre*[1] to the thick woods, that loomed darkly purple against the glowing sky.

It was in that very wood that her husband had declared his love for her; the same wood that had since been outraged by violence and murder.

"The – the man is buried, I suppose, Talbot?" she said to her husband.

"I believe so, my dear."

"I should never care to live in this place again, if I were Aurora."

The door opened before Mrs. Bulstrode had finished speaking, and the mistress of the house came towards them. She welcomed them affectionately and kindly, taking Lucy in her arms, and greeting her very tenderly; but Talbot saw that she had changed terribly within the few days that had passed since her return to Yorkshire, and his heart sank as he observed her pale face and the dark circles about her hollow eyes.

Could she have heard——? Could anybody have given her reason to suppose——?

"You are not well, Mrs. Mellish," he said, as he took her hand.

"No, not very well. This oppressive weather makes my head ache."

"I am sorry to see you looking ill. Where shall I find John?" asked Mr. Bulstrode.

---

1 Flower bed.

Aurora's pale face flushed suddenly.

"I – I – don't know," she stammered. "He is not in the house; he has gone out – to the stables – or to the farm, I think. I'll send for him."

"No, no," Talbot said, intercepting her hand on its way to the bell. "I'll go and look for him. Lucy will be glad of a chat with you, I dare say, Aurora, and will not be sorry to get rid of me."

Lucy, with her arm about her cousin's waist, assented to this arrangement. She was grieved to see the change in Aurora's looks, the unnatural constraint of her manner.

Mr. Bulstrode walked away, hugging himself upon having done a very wise thing.

"Lucy is a great deal more likely to find out what is the matter than I am," he thought. "There is a sort of freemasonry between women, an electric affinity, which a man's presence always destroys. How deathly pale Aurora looks! Can it be possible that the trouble I expected has come so soon?"

He went to the stables, but not so much to look for John Mellish as in the hope of finding somebody intelligent enough to furnish him with a better account of the murder than any he had yet heard.

"Some one else, as well as Aurora, must have had a reason for wishing to get rid of this man," he thought. "There must have been some motive: revenge, – gain, – something which no one has yet fathomed."

He went into the stable-yard; but he had no opportunity of making his investigation, for John Mellish was standing in a listless attitude before a small forge, watching the shoeing of one of his horses. The young squire looked up with a start as he recognized Talbot, and gave him his hand, with a few straggling words of welcome. Even in that moment Mr. Bulstrode saw that there was perhaps a greater change in John's appearance than in that of Aurora. The Yorkshireman's blue eyes had lost their brightness, his step its elasticity; his face seemed sunken and haggard, and he evidently avoided meeting Talbot's eye. He lounged listlessly away from the forge, walking at his guest's side in the direction of the stable-gates; but he had the air of a man who neither knows nor cares whither he is going.

"Shall we go to the house?" he said. "You must want some

luncheon after your journey." He looked at his watch as he said this. It was half-past three, an hour after the usual time for luncheon at Mellish.

"I've been in the stables all the morning," he said. "We're busy making our preparations for the York Summer."

"What horses do you run?" Mr. Bulstrode asked, politely affecting to be interested in a subject that was utterly indifferent to him, in the hope that stable-talk might rouse John from his listless apathy.

"What horses!" repeated Mr. Mellish vaguely. "I – I hardly know. Langley manages all that for me, you know; and – I – I forget the names of the horses he proposed, and———"

Talbot Bulstrode turned suddenly upon his friend, and looked him full in the face. They had left the stables by this time, and were in a shady pathway that led through a shrubbery towards the house.

"John Mellish," he said, "this is not fair towards an old friend. You have something on your mind, and you are trying to hide it from me."

The squire turned away his head.

"I have something on my mind, Talbot," he said quietly. "If you could help me, I'd ask your help more than any man's. But you can't – you can't!"

"But suppose I think I *can* help you?" cried Mr. Bulstrode. "Suppose I mean to try and do so, whether you will or no? I think I can guess what your trouble is, John; but I thought you were a braver man than to give way under it; I thought you were just the sort of man to struggle through it nobly and bravely, and to get the better of it by your own strength of will."

"What do you mean!" exclaimed John Mellish. "You can guess – you know   you thought! Have you no mercy upon me, Talbot Bulstrode? Can't you see that I'm almost mad, and that this is no time for you to force your sympathy upon me? Do you want me to betray myself? Do you want me to betray———"

He stopped suddenly, as if the words had choked him, and, passionately stamping his foot upon the ground, walked on hurriedly, with his friend still by his side.

The dining-room looked dreary enough when the two men entered it, although the table gave promise of a very substantial luncheon; but there was no one to welcome them, or to officiate at the banquet.

John seated himself wearily in a chair at the bottom of the table.

"You had better go and see if Mrs. Bulstrode and your mistress are coming to luncheon," he said to a servant, who left the room with his master's message, and returned three minutes afterwards to say that the ladies were not coming.

The ladies were seated side by side upon a low sofa in Aurora's morning-room. Mrs. Mellish sat with her head upon her cousin's shoulder. She had never had a sister, remember; and gentle Lucy stood in place of that near and tender comforter. Talbot was perfectly right; Lucy had accomplished that which he would have failed to bring about. She had found the key to her cousin's unhappiness.

"Ceased to love you, dear!" exclaimed Mrs. Bulstrode, echoing the words that Aurora had last spoken. "Impossible!"

"It is true, Lucy," answered Mrs. Mellish, despairingly. "He has ceased to love me. There is a black cloud between us now, now that all secrets are done away with. It is very bitter for me to bear, Lucy; for I thought we should be so happy and united. But – but it is only natural. He feels the degradation so much. How can he look at me without remembering who and what I am? The widow of his groom! Can I wonder that he avoids me?"

"Avoids you, dear?"

"Yes, avoids me. We have scarcely spoken a dozen words to each other since the night of our return. He was so good to me, so tender and devoted during the journey home, telling me again and again that this discovery had not lessened his love, that all the trial and horror of the past few days had only shown him the great strength of his affection; but on the night of our return, Lucy, he changed – changed suddenly and inexplicably; and now I feel that there is a gulf between us that can never be passed again. He is alienated from me for ever!"

"Aurora, all this is impossible," remonstrated Lucy. "It is your own morbid fancy, darling."

"My fancy!" cried Aurora bitterly. "Ah, Lucy, you cannot know how much I love my husband, if you think that I could be deceived in one look or tone of his. Is it my fancy that he averts his eyes when he speaks to me? Is it my fancy that his voice changes when he pronounces my name? Is it my fancy that he roams about the house like a ghost, and paces up and down his room half the night through? If these things are my fancy, Heaven have mercy upon me, Lucy; for I must be going mad."

Mrs. Bulstrode started as she looked at her cousin. Could it be possible that all the trouble and confusion of the past week or two had indeed unsettled this poor girl's intellect?

"My poor Aurora!" she murmured, smoothing the heavy hair away from her cousin's tearful eyes: "my poor darling! how is it possible that John should change towards you? He loved you so dearly, so devotedly; surely nothing could alienate him from you."

"I used to think so, Lucy," Aurora murmured in a low, heart-broken voice; "I used to think nothing could ever come to part us. He said he would follow me to the uttermost end of the world; he said that no obstacle on earth should ever separate us; and now——"

She could not finish the sentence, for she broke into convulsive sobs, and hid her face upon her cousin's shoulder, staining Mrs. Bulstrode's pretty silk dress with her hot tears.

"Oh, my love, my love!" she cried piteously, "why didn't I run away and hide myself from you? why didn't I trust to my first instinct, and run away from you for ever? Any suffering would be better than this! any suffering would be better than this!"

Her passionate grief merged into a fit of hysterical weeping, in which she was no longer mistress of herself. She had suffered for the past few days more bitterly than she had ever suffered yet. Lucy understood all that. She was one of those people whose tenderness instinctively comprehends the griefs of others. She knew how to treat her cousin; and in less than an hour after this emotional outbreak Aurora was lying on her bed, pale and exhausted, but sleeping peacefully. She had carried the burden of her sorrow in silence during the past few days, and had spent sleepless nights in brooding over her trouble. Her conversation with Lucy had unconsciously relieved her, and she slumbered calmly after the storm. Lucy sat by the bed watching the sleeper for some time, and then stole on tiptoe from the room.

She went, of course, to tell her husband all that had passed, and to take counsel from his sublime wisdom.

She found Talbot in the drawing-room alone; he had eaten a

dreary luncheon in John's company, and had been hastily left by his host immediately after the meal. There had been no sound of carriage-wheels upon the gravelled drive all that morning; there had been no callers at Mellish Park since John's return; for a horrible scandal had spread itself throughout the length and breadth of the county, and those who spoke of the young squire and his wife talked in solemn under-tones, and gravely demanded of each other whether some serious step should not be taken about the business which was uppermost in every body's mind.

Lucy told Talbot all that Aurora had said to her. This was no breach of confidence in the young wife's code of morality; for were not she and her husband immutably one, and how *could* she have any secret from him?

"I thought so!" Mr. Bulstrode said, when Lucy had finished her story.

"You thought what, dear?"

"That the breach between John and Aurora was a serious one. Don't look so sorrowful, my darling. It must be our business to reunite these divided lovers. You shall comfort Aurora, Lucy; and I'll look after John."

Talbot Bulstrode kissed his little wife, and went straight away upon his friendly errand. He found John Mellish in his own room, – the room in which Aurora had written to him upon the day of her flight; the room from which the murderous weapon had been stolen by some unknown hand. John had hidden the rusty pistol in one of the locked drawers of his Davenport; but it was not to be supposed that the fact of its discovery could be locked up or hidden away. *That* had been fully discussed in the servants' hall; and who shall doubt that it had travelled further, percolating through some of those sinuous channels which lead away from every household?

"I want you to come for a walk with me, Mr. John Mellish," said Talbot, imperatively; "so put on your hat, and come into the park. You are the most agreeable gentleman I ever had the honour to visit, and the attention you pay your guests is really something remarkable."

Mr. Mellish made no reply to this speech. He stood before his friend, pale, silent, and sullen. He was no more like the hearty Yorkshire squire whom we have known, than he was like Viscount

Palmerston or Lord Clyde.[1] He was transformed out of himself by some great trouble that was preying upon his mind; and being of a transparent and childishly truthful disposition, was unable to disguise his anguish.

"John, John!" cried Talbot, "we were little boys together at Rugby, and have backed each other in a dozen childish fights. Is it kind of you to withhold your friendship from me now, when I have come here on purpose to be a friend to you – to you and to Aurora?"

John Mellish turned away his head as his friend mentioned that familiar name; and the gesture was not lost upon Mr. Bulstrode.

"John, why do you refuse to trust me?"

"I don't refuse. I——Why did you come to this accursed house?" cried John Mellish, passionately; "why did you come here, Talbot Bulstrode? You don't know the blight that is upon this place, and those who live in it, or you would have no more come here than you would willingly go to a plague-stricken city. Do you know that since I came back from London not a creature has called at this house? Do you know that when I and – and – my wife – went to church on Sunday, the people we knew sneaked away from our path as if we had just recovered from typhus fever? Do you know that the cursed gaping rabble come from Doncaster to stare over the park-palings, and that this house is a show to half the West Riding? Why do you come here? You will be stared at, and grinned at, and scandalized, – you, who—— Go back to London to-night, Talbot, if you don't want to drive me mad."

"Not till you trust me with your troubles, John," answered Mr. Bulstrode firmly. "Put on your hat, and come out with me. I want you to show me the spot where the murder was done."

"You may get some one else to show it you," muttered John, sullenly; "I'll not go there!"

"John Mellish!" cried Talbot suddenly, "am I to think you a coward and a fool? By the heaven that's above me, I shall think so if you persist in this nonsense. Come out into the park with me; I have the

---

1 On Palmerston, see 278, n.3. Lord Clyde was Sir Colin Campbell, Baron Clyde (1792-1863), great 19th-century general, famous for his service in the Crimea, who was sent to India by Palmerston as commander-in-chief in the wake of the Indian Mutiny, where his successes earned him national acclaim in England.

claim of past friendship upon you, and I'll not have that claim set aside by any folly of yours."

The two men went out upon the lawn, John complying moodily enough with his friend's request, and walked silently across the park towards that portion of the wood in which James Conyers had met his death. They had reached one of the loneliest and shadiest avenues in this wood, and were, in fact, close against the spot from which Samuel Prodder had watched his niece and her companion on the night of the murder, when Talbot stopped suddenly, and laid his hand on the squire's shoulder.

"John," he said, in a determined tone, "before we go to look at the place where this bad man died, you must tell me your trouble."

Mr. Mellish drew himself up proudly, and looked at the speaker with gloomy defiance lowering upon his face.

"I will tell no man that which I do not choose to tell," he said firmly; and then with a sudden change that was terrible to see, he cried impetuously, "Why do you torment me, Talbot? I tell you that I can't trust you − I can't trust any one upon earth. If − if I told you − the horrible thought that − if I told you, it would be your duty to − I − Talbot, Talbot, have pity upon me − let me alone − go away from me − I——"

Stamping furiously, as if he would have trampled down the cowardly despair for which he despised himself, and beating his forehead with his clenched fists, John Mellish turned away from his friend, and, leaning against the gnarled branch of a great oak, wept aloud. Talbot Bulstrode waited till the paroxysm had passed away before he spoke again; but when his friend had grown calmer, he linked his arm about him, and drew him away almost as tenderly as if the big Yorkshireman had been some sorrowing woman, sorely in need of manly help and comfort.

"John, John," he said gravely, "thank God for this; thank God for anything that breaks the ice between us. I know what your trouble is, poor old friend, and I know that you have no cause for it. Hold up your head, man, and look straightforward to a happy future. I know the black thought that has been gnawing at your poor foolish manly heart: *you think that Aurora murdered the groom!*"

John Mellish, started, shuddering convulsively.

"No, no," he gasped; "who said so – who said——?"

"You think this, John," continued Talbot Bulstrode; "and you do her the most grievous wrong that ever yet was done to woman; a more shameful wrong than I committed when I thought that Aurora Floyd had been guilty of some base intrigue."

"You don't know——" stammered John.

"I don't know! I know all, and foresaw trouble for you, before *you* saw the cloud that was in the sky. But I never dreamt of this. I thought the foolish country people would suspect your wife, as it always pleases people to try and fix a crime upon the person in whom that crime would be more particularly atrocious. I was prepared for this; but to think that you – you, John, who should have learned to know your wife by this time – to think that you should suspect the woman you have loved of a foul and treacherous murder!"

"How do we know that the – that the man was murdered?" cried John vehemently. "Who says that the deed was treacherously done? He may have goaded her beyond endurance, insulted her generous pride, stung her to the very quick, and in the madness of her passion – having that wretched pistol in her possession – she may——"

"Stop!" interrupted Talbot. "What pistol? you told me the weapon had not been found."

"It was found upon the night of our return."

"Yes; but why do you associate this weapon with Aurora? What do you mean by saying that the pistol was in her possession?"

"Because – O my God! Talbot, why do you wring these things from me?"

"For your own good, and for the justification of an innocent woman; so help me, Heaven!" answered Mr. Bulstrode. "Do not be afraid to be candid with me, John. Nothing would ever make me believe Aurora Mellish guilty of this crime."

The Yorkshireman turned suddenly towards his friend, and leaning upon Talbot Bulstrode's shoulder, wept for the second time during that woodland ramble.

"May God in heaven bless you for this, Talbot!" he cried passionately. "Ah, my love, my dear, what a wretch I have been to you! but Heaven is my witness that, even in my worst agony of doubt and horror, my love has never lessened. It never could! – it never could!"

"John, old fellow," said Mr. Bulstrode, cheerfully, "perhaps, instead of talking this nonsense, which leaves me entirely in the dark as to everything that has happened since you left London, you will do me the favour to enlighten me as to the cause of these foolish suspicions."

They had reached the ruined summer-house and the pool of stagnant water, on the margin of which James Conyers had met with his death. Mr. Bulstrode seated himself upon a pile of broken timber, while John Mellish paced up and down the smooth patch of turf between the summer-house and the water, and told, disjointedly enough, the story of the finding of the pistol, which had been taken out of his room.

"I saw that pistol upon the day of the murder," he said. "I took particular notice of it; for I was cleaning my guns that morning, and I left them all in confusion while I went down to the lodge to see the trainer. When I came back – I——"

"Well, what then?"

"Aurora had been setting my guns in order."

"You argue, therefore, that your wife took the pistol?"

John looked piteously at his friend; but Talbot's grave smile reassured him.

"No one else had permission to go into the room," he answered. "I keep my papers and accounts there, you know; and it's an understood thing that none of the servants are allowed to go there, except when they clean the room."

"To be sure! But the room is not locked, I suppose?"

"Locked! of course not!"

"And the windows – which open to the ground – are sometimes left open, I dare say?"

"Almost always in such weather as this."

"Then, my dear John, it may be just possible that some one who had not permission to enter the room did, nevertheless, enter it, for the purpose of abstracting this pistol. Have you asked Aurora why she took upon herself to rearrange your guns? – she had never done such a thing before, I suppose?"

"Oh, yes, very often. I'm rather in the habit of leaving them about after cleaning them; and my darling understands all about them as well as I do. She has often put them away for me."

"Then there was nothing particular in her doing so upon the day of the murder. Have you asked her how long she was in your room, and whether she can remember seeing this particular pistol, among others?"

"Ask her!" exclaimed John; "how could I ask her, when——"

"When you have been mad enough to suspect her. No, my poor old friend; you made the same mistake that I committed at Felden. You presupposed the guilt of the woman you loved; and you were too great a coward to investigate the evidence upon which your suspicions were built. Had I been wise enough, instead of blindly questioning this poor bewildered girl, to tell her plainly what it was that I suspected, the incontrovertible truth would have flashed out of her angry eyes, and one indignant denial would have told me how basely I had wronged her. You shall not make the mistake that I made, John. You must go frankly and fearlessly to the wife you love, tell her of the suspicion that over-clouds her fame, and implore her to help you to the uttermost of her power in unravelling the mystery of this man's death. The assassin *must* be found, John; for so long as he remains undiscovered, you and your wife will be the victims of every penny-a-liner[1] who finds himself at a loss for a paragraph."

"Yes," Mr. Mellish answered bitterly, "the papers have been hard at it already; and there's been a fellow hanging about the place for the last few days whom I've had a very strong inclination to thrash. Some reporter, I suppose, come to pick up information."

"I suppose so," Talbot answered thoughtfully; "what sort of a man was he?"

"A decent-looking fellow enough; but a Londoner, I fancy, and – stay!" exclaimed John suddenly, "there's a man coming towards us from the turnstile, and unless I'm considerably mistaken, it's the very fellow."

Mr. Mellish was right.

The wood was free to any foot-passenger who pleased to avail himself of the pleasant shelter of spreading beeches, and the smooth carpet of mossy turf, rather than tramp wearily upon the dusty highway.

---

1 A hack journalist, paid by the line.

The stranger advancing from the turnstile was a decent-looking person, dressed in dark tight-fitting clothes, and making no unnecessary or ostentatious display of linen, for his coat was buttoned tightly to the chin. He looked at Talbot and John as he passed them, – not insolently, or even inquisitively, but with one brightly rapid and searching glance, which seemed to take in the most minute details in the appearance of both gentlemen. Then, walking on a few paces, he stopped and looked thoughtfully at the pond, and the bank above it.

"This is the place, I think, gentlemen?" he said, in a frank and rather free-and-easy manner.

Talbot returned his look with interest.

"If you mean the place where the murder was committed, it is," he said.

"Ah, I understood so," answered the stranger, by no means abashed.

He looked at the bank, regarding it, now from one point, now from another, like some skilful upholsterer taking the measure of a piece of furniture. Then walking slowly round the pond, he seemed to plumb the depth of the stagnant water with his small gray eyes.

Talbot Bulstrode watched the man as he took this mental photograph of the place. There was a business-like composure in his manner, which was entirely different to the eager curiosity of a scandalmonger and a busybody.

Mr. Bulstrode rose as the man walked away, and went slowly after him.

"Stop where you are, John," he said, as he left his companion; "I'll find out who this fellow is."

He walked on, and overtook the stranger at about a hundred yards from the pond.

"I want to have a few words with you before you leave the Park, my friend," he said quietly; "unless I'm very much mistaken, you are a member of the detective police, and come here with credentials from Scotland Yard."

The man shook his head, with a quiet smile.

"I'm not obliged to tell everybody my business," he answered coolly; "this footpath is a public thoroughfare, I believe?"

"Listen to me, my good fellow," said Mr. Bulstrode. "It may serve your purpose to beat about the bush; but I have no reason to do so, and therefore may as well come to the point at once. If you are sent here for the purpose of discovering the murderer of James Conyers, you can be more welcome to no one than to the master of that house."

He pointed to the Gothic chimneys as he spoke.

"If those who employ you have promised you a liberal reward, Mr. Mellish will willingly treble the amount they may have offered you. He would not give you cause to complain of his liberality, should you succeed in accomplishing the purpose of your errand. If you think you will gain anything by underhand measures, and by keeping yourself dark, you are very much mistaken; for no one can be better able or more willing to give you assistance in this than Mr. and Mrs. Mellish."

The detective – for he had tacitly admitted the fact of his profession – looked doubtfully at Talbot Bulstrode.

"You're a lawyer, I suppose?" he said.

"I am Mr. Talbot Bulstrode, member of Penruthy, and the husband of Mrs. Mellish's first cousin."

The detective bowed.

"My name is Joseph Grimstone, of Scotland Yard and Ball's Pond,"[1] he said; "and I certainly see no objection to our working together. If Mr. Mellish is prepared to act on the square, I'm prepared to act with him, and to accept any reward his generosity may offer. But if he or any friend of his wants to hoodwink Joseph Grimstone, he'd better think twice about the game before he tries it on; that's all."

Mr. Bulstrode took no notice of this threat, but looked at his watch before replying to the detective.

"It's a quarter-past six," he said. "Mr. Mellish dines at seven. Can you call at the house, say at nine, this evening? You shall then have all the assistance it is in our power to give you."

"Certainly, sir. At nine this evening."

"We shall be prepared to receive you. Good afternoon."

Mr. Grimstone touched his hat, and strolled quietly away under the shadow of the beeches, while Talbot Bulstrode walked back to rejoin his friend.

---

1   An area in Islington.

It may be as well to take this opportunity of stating the reason of the detective's early appearance at Mellish Park. Upon the day of the inquest, and consequently the next day but one after the murder, two anonymous letters, worded in the same manner, and written by the same hand, were received respectively by the head of the Doncaster constabulary and by the chief of the Scotland-Yard detective confederacy.

These anonymous communications – written in a hand which, in spite of all attempt at disguise, still retained the spidery peculiarities of feminine caligraphy – pointed, by a sinuous and inductive process of reasoning, at Aurora Mellish as the murderess of James Conyers. I need scarcely say that the writer was no other than Mrs. Powell. She has disappeared for ever from my story, and I have no wish to blacken a character which can ill afford to be slandered. The ensign's widow actually believed in the guilt of her beautiful patroness. It is so easy for an envious woman to believe horrible things of the more prosperous sister whom she hates.

CHAPTER XXXVI.

REUNION.

"WE are on the verge of a precipice," Talbot Bulstrode thought, as he prepared for dinner in the comfortable dressing-room allotted to him at Mellish, – "we are on the verge of a precipice, and nothing but a bold grapple with the worst can save us. Any reticence, any attempt at keeping back suspicious facts, or hushing up awkward coincidences would be fatal to us. If John had made away with this pistol with which the deed was done, he would have inevitably fixed a most fearful suspicion upon his wife. Thank God I came here to-day! We must look matters straight in the face, and our first step must be to secure Aurora's help. So long as she is silent as to her share in the events of that day and night, there is a link missing in the chain, and we are all at sea. John must speak to her to-night; or perhaps it will be better for me to speak."

Mr. Bulstrode went down to the drawing-room, where he found his friend pacing up and down, solitary and wretched.

"The ladies are going to dine up-stairs," said Mr. Mellish, as Talbot joined him. "I have just had a message to say so. Why does she avoid me, Talbot? why does my wife avoid me like this? We have scarcely spoken to each other for days."

"Shall I tell you why, you foolish John?" answered Mr. Bulstrode. "Your wife avoids you because you have chosen to alienate yourself from her, and because she thinks, poor girl, that she has lost your affection. She fancies that the discovery of her first marriage has caused a revulsion of feeling, and that you no longer love her."

"No longer love her!" cried John. "O my God! she ought to know that, if I could give my life for her fifty times over, I would do it, to save her one pang. I would do it, so help me, Heaven, though she were the guiltiest wretch that had ever crawled the earth!"

"But no one asks you to do anything of the kind," said Mr. Bulstrode. "You are only requested to be reasonable and patient, to put a proper trust in Providence, and to be guided by people who are rather less impetuous than your ungovernable self."

"I will do what you like, Talbot; I will do what you like."

Mr. Mellish pressed his friend's hand. Had he ever thought, when he had seen Talbot an accepted lover at Felden, and had hated him with a savage and wild Indian-like fury, that he would come to be thus humbly grateful to him; thus pitifully dependent upon his superior wisdom? He wrung the young politician's hand, and promised to be as submissive as a child beneath his guidance.

In compliance, therefore, with Talbot's commands, he ate a few morsels of fish, and drank a couple of glasses of sherry; and having thus gone through a show of dining, he went with Mr. Bulstrode to seek Aurora.

She was sitting with her cousin in the morning-room, looking terribly pale in the dim dusk of the August evening, – pale and shadowy in her loose white muslin dress. She had only lately risen after a long feverish slumber, and had pretended to dine out of courtesy to her guest. Lucy had tried in vain to comfort her cousin. This passionate, impetuous, spoiled child of fortune and affection refused all consolation, crying out again and again that she had lost her husband's love, and that there was nothing left for her upon earth.

But in the very midst of one of these despondent speeches, she sprang up from her seat, erect and trembling, with her parted lips quivering and her dark eyes dilated, startled by the sound of a familiar step, which within the last few days had been seldom heard in the corridor outside her room. She tried to speak, but her voice failed her; and in another moment the door had been dashed open by a strong hand, and her husband stood in the room, holding out his arms and calling to her.

"Aurora! Aurora! my own dear love, my own poor darling!"

She was folded to his breast before she knew that Talbot Bulstrode stood close behind him.

"My own darling," John said, "my own dearest, you cannot tell how cruelly I have wronged you. But, oh, my love, the wrong has brought unendurable torture with it. My poor guiltless girl! how could I – how could I——But I was mad, and it was only when Talbot——"

Aurora lifted her head from her husband's breast and looked wonderingly into his face, utterly unable to guess the meaning of these broken sentences.

Talbot laid his hand upon his friend's shoulder. "You will frighten your wife if you go on in this manner, John," he said quietly. "You mustn't take any notice of his agitation, my dear Mrs. Mellish. There is no cause, believe me, for all this outcry. Will you sit down by Lucy and compose yourself? It is eight o'clock, and between this and nine we have some serious business to settle."

"Serious business!" repeated Aurora vaguely. She was intoxicated by her sudden happiness. She had no wish to ask any explanation of the mystery of the past few days. It was all over, and her faithful husband loved her as devotedly and tenderly as ever. How could she wish to know more than this?

She seated herself at Lucy's side, in obedience to Talbot; but she still held her husband's hand, she still looked in his face, for the moment most supremely unconscious that the scheme of creation included anything beyond this stalwart Yorkshireman.

Talbot Bulstrode lighted the lamp upon Aurora's writing-table, – a shaded lamp, which only dimly illuminated the twilight room, – and then, taking his seat near it, said gravely –

"My dear Mrs. Mellish, I shall be compelled to say something which I fear may inflict a terrible shock upon you. But this is no time for reservation; scarcely a time for ordinary delicacy. Will you trust in the love and friendship of those who are around you, and promise to bear this new trial bravely? I believe and hope that it will be a very brief one."

Aurora looked wonderingly at her husband, not at Talbot.

"A new trial?" she said inquiringly.

"You know that the murderer of James Conyers has not yet been discovered?" said Mr. Bulstrode.

"Yes, yes; but what of that?"

"My dear Mrs. Mellish, my dear Aurora! the world is apt to take a morbid delight in horrible ideas. There are some people who think that you are guilty of this crime!"

"*I!*"

She rose suddenly from her low seat, and turned her face towards the lamplight, with a look of such blank amazement, such utter wonder and bewilderment, that had Talbot Bulstrode until that moment believed her guilty, he must thenceforth and for ever have been firmly convinced of her innocence.

"*I!*" she repeated.

Then turning to her husband, with a sudden alteration in her face, that blank amazement changing to a look of sorrow, mingled with reproachful wonder, she said in a low voice –

"*You* thought this of me, John; *you* thought this!"

John Mellish bowed his head before her. "I did, my dear," he murmured – "God forgive me for my wicked folly – I did think this, Aurora. But I pitied you, and was sorry for you, my own dear love; and when I thought it most, I would have died to save you from shame or sorrow. My love has never changed, Aurora; my love has never changed."

She gave him her hand, and once more resumed her seat. She sat for some moments in silence, as if trying to collect her thoughts, and to understand the meaning of this strange scene.

"Who suspects me of this crime?" she said presently. "Has any one else suspected me? Any one besides – my husband?"

"I can scarcely tell you, my dear Mrs. Mellish," answered Talbot; "when an event of this kind takes place, it is very difficult to say who may or may not be suspected. Different persons set up different theories: one man writes to a newspaper to declare that, in his opinion, the crime was committed by some person within the house; another man writes as positively to another paper, asserting that the murderer was undoubtedly a stranger. Each man brings forward a mass of suppositious evidence in favour of his own argument, and each thinks a great deal more of proving his own cleverness than of furthering the ends of justice. No shadow of slander must rest upon this house, or upon those who live in it. It is necessary, therefore, imperatively necessary, that the real murderer should be found. A London detective is already at work. These men are very clever; some insignificant circumstance, forgotten by those most interested in discovering the truth, would often be enough to set a detective on the right track. This man is coming here at nine o'clock; and we are to give him all the assistance we can. Will you help us, Aurora?"

"Help you! How?"

"By telling us all you know of the night of the murder. Why were you in the wood that night?"

"I was there to meet the dead man."

"For what purpose?"

Aurora was silent for some moments, and then looking up with a bold, half-defiant glance, she said suddenly –

"Talbot Bulstrode, before you blame or despise me, remember how the tie that bound me to this man had been broken. The law would have set me free from him, if I had been brave enough to appeal to the law; and was I to suffer all my life because of the mistake I had made in not demanding a release from the man whose gross infidelity entitled me to be divorced from him?[1] Heaven knows I had borne with him patiently enough. I had endured his vulgarity, his insolence, his presumption; I had gone penniless while he spent my father's money in a gambling-booth on a race-course, and dinnerless while he drank champagne with cheats and reprobates. Remember this, when you blame me most. I went into the wood that night to meet him for the last time upon this earth. He had promised me that he would emigrate to Australia upon the payment of a certain sum of money."

"And you went that night to pay it to him?" cried Talbot eagerly.

"I did. He was insolent, as he always was; for he hated me for having discovered that which shut him out from all claim upon my fortune. He hated himself for his folly in not having played his cards better. Angry words passed between us; but it ended in his declaring his intention of starting for Liverpool early the next morning, and – "

"You gave him the money?"

"Yes."

"But tell me, – tell me, Aurora," cried Talbot, almost too eager to find words, "how long had you left him when you heard the report of the pistol?"

"Not more than ten minutes."

"John Mellish," exclaimed Mr. Bulstrode, "was there any money found upon the person of the murdered man?"

"No – yes; I believe there was a little silver," Mr. Mellish answered vaguely.

"A little silver!" cried Talbot contemptuously. "Aurora, what was the sum you gave James Conyers upon the night of his death?"

"Two thousand pounds."

---

1   See 434, n.1.

"In a cheque?"

"No; in notes."

"And that money has never been heard of since?"

No; John Mellish declared that he had never heard of it.

"Thank God!" exclaimed Mr. Bulstrode; "we shall find the murderer."

"What do you mean?" asked John.

"Whoever killed James Conyers, killed him in order to rob him of the money that he had upon him at the time of his death."

"But who could have known of the money?" asked Aurora.

"Anybody; the pathway through the wood is a public thoroughfare. Your conversation with the murdered man may have been overheard. You talked about the money, I suppose?"

"Yes."

"Thank God, thank God! Ask your wife's pardon for the cruel wrong you have done her, John, and then come downstairs with me. It's past nine, and I dare say Mr. Grimstone is waiting for us. But stay, – one word, Aurora. The pistol with which this man was killed was taken from this house, from John's room. Did you know that?"

"No; how should I know it?" Mrs. Mellish asked naïvely.

"That fact is against the theory of the murder having been committed by a stranger. Is there any one of the servants whom you could suspect of such a crime, John?"

"No," answered Mr. Mellish decisively; "not one."

"And yet the person who committed the murder must have been the person who stole your pistol. You, John, declare that very pistol to have been in your possession upon the morning before the murder."

"Most certainly."

"You put John's guns back into their places upon that morning, Aurora," said Mr. Bulstrode; "do you remember seeing that particular pistol?"

"No," Mrs. Mellish answered; "I should not have known it from the others."

"You did not find any of the servants in the room that morning?"

"Oh, no," Aurora answered immediately; "Mrs. Powell came into the room while I was there. She was always following me about; and I suppose she had heard me talking to——"

"Talking to whom?"

"To James Conyers's hanger-on and messenger, Stephen Hargraves – the 'Softy,' as they call him."

"You were talking to him? Then this Stephen Hargraves was in the room that morning?"

"Yes; he brought me a message from the murdered man, and took back my answer."

"Was he alone in the room?"

"Yes; I found him there when I went in, expecting to find John. I dislike the man, – unjustly, perhaps; for he is a poor, half-witted creature, who I dare say scarcely knows right from wrong; and I was angry at seeing him. He must have come in through the window."

A servant entered the room at this moment. He came to say that Mr. Grimstone had been waiting below for some time, and was anxious to see Mr. Bulstrode.

Talbot and John went down-stairs together. They found Mr. Joseph Grimstone sitting at a table in a comfortable room that had lately been sacred to Mrs. Powell, with the shaded lamp drawn close to his elbow, and a greasy little memorandum-book open before him. He was thoughtfully employed making notes in this memorandum-book with a stumpy morsel of lead-pencil – when do these sort of people begin their pencils, and how is it that they always seem to have arrived at the stump? – when the two gentlemen entered.

John Mellish leaned against the mantel-piece, and covered his face with his hand. For any practical purpose, he might as well have been in his own room. He knew nothing of Talbot's reason for this interview with the detective officer. He had no shadowy idea, no growing suspicion shaping itself slowly out of the confusion and obscurity, of the identity of the murderer. He only knew that his Aurora was innocent; that she had indignantly refuted his base suspicion; and that he had seen the truth, radiant as the light of inspiration, shining out of her beautiful face.

Mr. Bulstrode rang, and ordered a bottle of sherry for the delectation of the detective; and then, in a careful and business-like manner, he recited all that he had been able to discover upon the subject of the murder. Joseph Grimstone listened very quietly, following Talbot Bulstrode with a shining track of lead-pencil hieroglyphics over the greasy paper, just as Tom Thumb strewed crumbs of bread in the forest-pathway, with a view to his homeward guidance. The detective only looked up now and then to drink a glass of sherry, and smack his lips with the quiet approval of a connoisseur. When Talbot had told all that he had to tell, Mr. Grimstone thrust the memorandum-book into a very tight breast-pocket, and taking his hat from under the chair upon which he had been seated, prepared to depart.

"If this information about the money is quite correct, sir," he said, "I think I can see my way through the affair; that is, if we can have the numbers of the notes. I can't stir a peg without the numbers of the notes."

Talbot's countenance fell. Here was a death-blow. Was it likely that Aurora, that impetuous and unbusiness-like girl, had taken the numbers of the notes, which, in utter scorn and loathing, she had flung as a last bribe to the man she hated?

"I'll go and make inquiries of Mrs. Mellish," he said; "but I fear it is scarcely likely I shall get the information you want."

He left the room; but five minutes afterwards returned triumphant.

"Mrs. Mellish had the notes from her father," he said. "Mr. Floyd took a list of the numbers before he gave his daughter the money."

"Then if you'll be so good as to drop Mr. Floyd a line, asking for that list by return of post, I shall know how to act," replied the detective. "I haven't been idle this afternoon, gentlemen, any more than you. I went back after I parted with you, Mr. Bulstrode, and had another look at the pond. I found something to pay me for my trouble."

He took from his waistcoat-pocket a small object, which he held between his finger and thumb.

Talbot and John looked intently at this dingy object, but could make nothing out of it. It seemed to be a mere disc of rusty metal.

"It's neither more nor less than a brass button," the detective said, with a smile of quiet superiority; "maker's name, Crosby, Birmingham. There's marks upon it which seem uncommon like blood; and unless I'm very much mistaken, it'll be found to fit pretty correct into the barrel of your pistol, Mr. Mellish. So what we've got to do is to find a gentleman wearin', or havin' in his possession, a waistcoat with buttons by Crosby, Birmingham, and one button missin'; and if we happen to find the same gentleman changin' one of the notes that Mr. Floyd took the numbers of, I don't think we shall be *very* far off layin' our hands on the man we want."

With which oracular speech Mr. Grimstone departed, charged with a commission to proceed forthwith to Doncaster, to order the immediate printing and circulating of a hundred bills,[1] offering a reward of 200*l.* for such information as would lead to the apprehension of the murderer of James Conyers. This reward to be given by Mr. Mellish, and to be over and above any reward offered by the Government.

---

1 Posters.

CHAPTER XXXVII.

THE BRASS BUTTON BY CROSBY, BIRMINGHAM.

MR. MATTHEW HARRISON and Captain Prodder were both accommodated with suitable entertainment at the sign of the Crooked Rabbit; but while the dog-fancier appeared to have ample employment in the neighbourhood, – employment of a mysterious nature, which kept him on the tramp all day, and sent him home at sunset, tired and hungry, to his hostelry, – the sailor, having nothing whatever to do, and a great burden of care upon his mind, found the time hang very heavily upon his hands; although, being naturally of a social and genial temper, he made himself very much at home in his strange quarters. From Mr. Harrison the captain obtained much information respecting the secret of all the sorrow that had befallen his niece. The dog-fancier had known James Conyers from his boyhood; had known his father, the "swell" coachman of a Brighton Highflyer, or Sky-rocket, or Electric, and the associate of the noblemen and gentlemen of that princely era, in which it was the right thing for the youthful aristocracy to imitate the manners of Mr. Samuel Weller,[1] senior. Matthew Harrison had known the trainer in his brief and stormy married life, and had accompanied Aurora's first husband as a humble dependent and hanger-on in that foreign travel which had been paid for out of Archibald Floyd's cheque-book. The honest captain's blood boiled as he heard that shameful story of treachery and extortion practised upon an ignorant school-girl. Oh, that he had been by to avenge those outrages upon the child of the dark-eyed sister he had loved! His rage against the undiscovered murderer of the dead man was redoubled when he remembered how comfortably James Conyers had escaped from his vengeance.

---

1 A "swell" is someone stylishly dressed. In the early 19th century coachmen became fashionable figures, to the extent that the aristocracy imitated them, driving their own private carriages, and mimicking their manners and duties (even pretending to deliver parcels). Mr. Samuel Weller Senior was the coachman father of Sam Weller, the irrepressible Cockney valet to Mr. Pickwick in Charles Dickens' *The Pickwick Papers* (1836-7).

Mr. Stephen Hargraves, the "Softy," took good care to keep out of the way of the Crooked Rabbit, having no wish to encounter Captain Prodder a second time; but he still hung about the town of Doncaster, where he had a lodging up a wretched alley, hidden away behind one of the back streets, – a species of lair common to every large town, only to be found by the inhabitants of the locality.

The "Softy" had been born and bred, and had lived his life, in such a narrow radius, that the uprooting of one of the oaks in Mellish Park could scarcely be a slower or more painful operation than the severing of those ties of custom which held the boorish hanger-on to the neighbourhood of the household in which he had so long been an inmate. But now that his occupation at Mellish Park was for ever gone, and his patron, the trainer, dead, he was alone in the world, and had need to look out for a fresh situation.

But he seemed rather slow to do this. He was not a very prepossessing person, it must be remembered, and there were not very many services for which he was fitted. Although upwards of forty years of age, he was generally rather loosely described as a young man who understood all about horses; and this qualification was usually sufficient to procure for any individual whatever some kind of employment in the neighbourhood of Doncaster. The "Softy" seemed, however, rather to keep aloof from the people who knew and could have recommended him; and when asked why he did not seek a situation, gave evasive answers, and muttered something to the effect that he had saved a little bit of money at Mellish Park, and had no need to come upon the parish if he was out of work for a week or two.

John Mellish was so well known as a generous paymaster, that this was a matter of surprise to no one. Steeve Hargraves had no doubt had pretty pickings in that liberal household. So the "Softy" went his way unquestioned, hanging about the town in a lounging, uncomfortable manner, sitting in some public-house taproom half the day and night, drinking his meagre liquor in a sullen and unsocial style peculiar to himself, and consorting with no one.

He made his appearance at the railway station one day, and groped helplessly through all the time-tables pasted against the walls: but he could make nothing of them unaided, and was at last compelled to appeal to a good-tempered-looking official who was busy on the platform.

"I want th' Liverpool trayuns," he said, "and I can find naught about 'em here."

The official knew Mr. Hargraves, and looked at him with a stare of open wonder.

"My word, Steeve," he said laughing, "what takes you to Liverpool? I thought you'd never been further than York in your life?"

"Maybe I haven't," the "Softy" answered sulkily; "but that's no reason I shouldn't go now. I've heard of a situation at Liverpool as I think'll suit me."

"Not better than the place you had with Mr. Mellish."

"Perhaps not," muttered Mr. Hargraves, with a frown darkening over his ugly face; "but Mellish Park be no pleace for me now, and arnt been for a long time past."

The railway official laughed.

The story of Aurora's chastisement of the half-witted groom was pretty well known amongst the townspeople of Doncaster; and I am sorry to say there were very few members of that sporting community who did not admire the mistress of Mellish Park something more by reason of this little incident in her history.

Mr. Hargraves received the desired information about the railway route between Doncaster and Liverpool, and then left the station.

A shabby-looking little man, who had also been making some inquiries of the same official who had talked to the "Softy," and had consequently heard the above brief dialogue, followed Stephen Hargraves from the station into the town. Indeed, had it not been that the "Softy" was unusually slow of perception, he might have discovered that upon this particular day the same shabby-looking little man generally happened to be hanging about any and every place to which he, Mr. Hargraves, betook himself. But the cast-off retainer of Mellish Park did not trouble himself with any such misgivings. His narrow intellect, never wide enough to take in many subjects at a time, was fully absorbed by other considerations; and he loitered about with a gloomy and preoccupied expression in his face, that by no means enhanced his personal attractions.

It is not to be supposed that Mr. Joseph Grimstone let the grass grow under his feet after his interview with John Mellish and Talbot Bulstrode. He had heard enough to make his course pretty clear to him, and he went to work quietly and sagaciously to win the reward offered to him.

There was not a tailor's shop in Doncaster or its vicinity into which the detective did not make his way. There was not a garment *confectionnée*[1] by any of the civil purveyors upon whom he intruded that Mr. Grimstone did not examine; not a drawer of odds and ends which he did not ransack, in his search for buttons by "Crosby, maker, Birmingham." But for a long time he made his inquisition in vain. Before the day succeeding that of Talbot's arrival at Mellish Park was over, the detective had visited every tailor or clothier in the neighbourhood of the racing metropolis of the north, but no traces of "Crosby, maker, Birmingham," had he been able to find. Brass waistcoat-buttons are not particularly affected by the leaders of the fashion in the present day, and Mr. Grimstone found almost every variety of fastening upon the waistcoats he examined, except that one special style of button, a specimen of which, out of shape and blood-stained, he carried deep in his trousers-pocket.

He was returning to the inn at which he had taken up his abode, and where he was supposed to be a traveller in the Glenfield starch and sugar-plum line, tired and worn out with a day's useless work, when he was attracted by the appearance of some ready-made garments gracefully festooned about the door of a Doncaster pawnbroker, who exhibited silver teaspoons, oil-paintings, boots and shoes, dropsical watches, doubtful rings, and remnants of silk and satin, in his artistically-arranged window.

Mr. Grimstone stopped short before the money-lender's portal.

"I won't be beaten," he muttered between his teeth. "If this man has got any weskits, I'll have a look at 'em."

He lounged into the shop in a leisurely manner, and asked the proprietor of the establishment if he had anything cheap in the way of fancy waistcoats.

Of course the proprietor had everything desirable in that way, and from a kind of grove or arbour of all manner of dry goods at the back of the shop, he brought out half a dozen brown-paper parcels, the contents of which he exhibited to Mr. Joseph Grimstone.

---

1   Made, but implying in a grand and fastidious way; here used ironically.

The detective looked at a great many waistcoats, but with no satisfactory result.

"You haven't got anything with brass buttons, I suppose?" he inquired at last.

The proprietor shook his head reflectively.

"Brass buttons aint much worn now-a-days," he said; "but I'll lay I've got the very thing you want, now I come to think of it. I got 'em an uncommon bargain from a traveller for a Birmingham house, who was here at the September meeting three years ago, and lost a hatful of money upon Underhand, and left a lot of things with me, in order to make up what he wanted."

Mr. Grimstone pricked up his ears at the sound of "Birmingham." The pawnbroker retired once more to the mysterious caverns at the back of his shop, and after a considerable search succeeded in finding what he wanted. He brought another brown-paper parcel to the counter, turned the flaming gas a little higher, and exhibited a heap of very gaudy and vulgar-looking waistcoats, evidently of that species of manufacture which is generally called slop-work.

"These are the goods," he said; "and very tasty and lively things they are, too. I had a dozen of 'em; and I've only got these five left."

Mr. Grimstone had taken up a waistcoat of a flaming check pattern, and was examining it by the light of the gas.

Yes; the purpose of his day's work was accomplished at last. The back of the brass buttons bore the name of Crosby, Birmingham.

"You've only got five left out of the dozen," said the detective; "then you've sold seven?"

"I have."

"Can you remember who you sold 'em to?"

The pawnbroker scratched his head thoughtfully.

"I think I must have sold 'em all to the men at the works," he said. "They take their wages once a fortnight; and there's some of 'em drop in here every other Saturday night to buy something or other, or to take something out of pledge. I know I sold four or five that way."

"But can you remember selling one of them to anybody else?" asked the detective. "I'm not asking out of curiosity; and I don't mind standing something handsome by-and-by, if you can give me the information I want. Think it over, now, and take your time. You couldn't have sold 'em all seven to the men from the works."

"No; I didn't," answered the pawnbroker after a pause. "I remember now, I sold one of them – a fancy sprig on a purple ground – to Josephs the baker, in the next street; and I sold another – a yellow stripe on a brown ground – to the head-gardener at Mellish Park."

Mr. Joseph Grimstone's face flushed hot and red. His day's work had not been wasted. He was bringing the buttons by Crosby of Birmingham very near to where he wanted to bring them.

"You can tell me the gardener's name I suppose?" he said to the pawnbroker.

"Yes; his name's Dawson. He belongs to Doncaster, and he and I were boys together. I should not have remembered selling him the waistcoat, perhaps, for it's nigh upon a year and a half ago; only he stopped and had a chat with me and my missis the night he bought it."

Mr. Grimstone did not linger much longer in the shop. His interest in the waistcoats was evidently departed. He bought a couple of second-hand silk handkerchiefs out of civility, no doubt, and then bade the pawnbroker good-night.

It was nearly nine o'clock; but the detective only stopped at his inn long enough to eat about a pound and a quarter of beefsteak, and drink a pint of ale, after which brief refreshment he started for Mellish Park on foot. It was the principle of his life to avoid observation, and he preferred the fatigue of a long and lonely walk to the risks contingent upon hiring a vehicle to convey him to his destination.

Talbot and John had been waiting hopefully all the day for the detective's coming, and welcomed him very heartily when he appeared, between ten and eleven. He was shown into John's own room this evening; for the two gentlemen were sitting there smoking and talking after Aurora and Lucy had gone to bed. Mrs. Mellish had good need of rest, and could sleep peacefully now; for the dark shadow between her and her husband had gone for ever, and she could not fear any peril, any sorrow, now that she knew herself to be secure of his love. John looked up eagerly as Mr. Grimstone followed the servant into the room; but a warning look from Talbot Bulstrode checked his impetuosity, and he waited till the door was shut before he spoke.

"Now, then, Grimstone," he said; "what news?"

"Well, sir, I've had a hard day's work," the detective answered gravely, "and perhaps neither of you gentlemen – not being professional – would think much of what I've done; but for all that, I believe I'm bringin' it home, sir; I believe I'm bringin' it home."

"Thank God for that!" murmured Talbot Bulstrode, reverently.

He had thrown away his cigar, and was standing by the fireplace, with his arm resting upon the angle of the mantel-piece.

"You've got a gardener by the name of Dawson in your service, Mr. Mellish?" said the detective.

"I have," answered John: "but, Lord have mercy upon us! you don't mean to say you think it's him? Dawson's as good a fellow as ever breathed."

"I don't say I think it's any one as yet, sir," Mr. Grimstone answered sententiously; "but when a man as had two thousand pound upon him in bank-notes is found in a wood shot through the heart, and the notes missin' – the wood bein' free to anybody as chose to walk in it – it's a pretty open case for suspicion. I should like to see this man Dawson, if it's convenient."

"To-night?" asked John.

"Yes: the sooner the better. The less delay there is in this sort of business, the more satisfactory for all parties, with the exception of the party that's wanted," added the detective.

"I'll send for Dawson, then," answered Mr. Mellish; "but I expect he'll have gone to bed by this time."

"Then he can but get up again, if he has, sir," Mr. Grimstone said politely. "I've set my heart upon seeing him to-night, if it's all the same to you."

It is not to be supposed that John Mellish was likely to object to any arrangement which might hasten, if by but a moment's time, the hour of the discovery for which he so ardently prayed. He went straight off to the servants' hall to make inquiries for the gardener, and left Talbot Bulstrode and the detective together.

"There aint nothing turned up here, I suppose, sir," said Joseph Grimstone, addressing Mr. Bulstrode, "as will be of any help to us?"

"Yes," Talbot answered. "We have got the numbers of the notes which Mrs. Mellish gave the murdered man. I telegraphed to Mr.

Floyd's country house, and he arrived here himself only an hour ago, bringing the list of the notes with him."

"And an uncommon plucky thing of the old gentleman to do, beggin' your pardon, sir," exclaimed the detective with enthusiasm.

Five minutes afterwards, Mr. Mellish re-entered the room, bringing the gardener with him. The man had been into Doncaster to see his friends, and only returned about half an hour before; so the master of the house had caught him in the act of making havoc with a formidable cold joint, and a great jar of pickled cabbage, in the servants' hall.

"Now, you're not to be frightened, Dawson," said the young squire, with friendly indiscretion; "of course nobody for a moment suspects you, any more than they suspect me; but this gentleman here wants to see you, and of course you know there's no reason that he shouldn't see you if he wishes it, though what he wants with you—"

Mr. Mellish stopped abruptly, arrested by a frown from Talbot Bulstrode; and the gardener, who was innocent of the faintest comprehension of his master's meaning, pulled his hair respectfully, and shuffled nervously upon the slippery Indian matting.

"I only want to ask you a question or two to decide a wager between these two gentlemen and me, Mr. Dawson," said the detective with reassuring familiarity. "You bought a second-hand waistcoat of Gogram, in the market-place, didn't you, about a year and a half ago?"

"Ay, sure, sir. I bought a weskit at Gogram's," answered the gardener; "but it weren't second-hand; it were bran new."

"A yellow stripe upon a brown ground?"

The man nodded, with his mouth wide open, in the extremity of his surprise at this London stranger's familiarity with the details of his toilet.

"I dunno how you come to know about that weskit, sir," he said, with a grin; "it were wore out full six months ago; for I took to wearin' of it in t' garden, and garden-work soon spiles anything in the way of clothes; but him as I give it to was glad enough to have it, though it was awful shabby."

"Him as you give it to?" repeated Mr. Grimstone, not pausing to amend the sentence, in his eagerness. "You gave it away, then?"

"Yees, I gave it to th' 'Softy;' and wasn't th' poor fond chap glad to get it, that's all!"

"The 'Softy'!" exclaimed Mr. Grimstone. "Who's the 'Softy'?"

"The man we spoke of last night," answered Talbot Bulstrode; "the man whom Mrs. Mellish found in this room upon the morning before the murder, – the man called Stephen Hargraves."

"Ay, ay, to be sure; I thought as much," murmured the detective. "That will do, Mr. Dawson," he added, addressing the gardener, who had shuffled a good deal nearer to the doorway in his uneasy state of mind. "Stay, though; I may as well ask you one more question. Were any of the buttons missing off that waistcoat when you gave it away?"

"Not one on 'em," answered the gardener, decisively. "My missus is too particular for that. She's a reg'lar toidy one, she is; allers mendin' and patchin'; and if one of t' buttons got loose she was sure to sew it on toight again, before it was lost."

"Thank you, Mr. Dawson," returned the detective, with the friendly condescension of a superior being. "Good-night."

The gardener shuffled off, very glad to be released from the awful presence of his superiors, and to go back to the cold meat and pickles in the servants' hall.

"I think I'm bringing the business into a nutshell, sir," said Mr. Grimstone, when the door had closed upon the gardener. "But the less said, the better, just yet awhile. I'll take the list of the numbers of the notes, please, sir; and I believe I shall come upon you for that two hundred pound, Mr. Mellish, before either of us is many weeks older."

So, with the list made by cautious Archibald Floyd, bestowed safely in his waistcoat-pocket, Mr. Joseph Grimstone walked back to Doncaster through the still summer's night, intent upon the business he had undertaken.

"It looked uncommon black against the lady about a week ago," he thought, as he walked meditatively across the dewy grass in Mellish Park; "and I fancy the information they got at the Yard would have put a fool upon the wrong scent, and kept him on it till the right one got worn out. But it's clearing up, it's clearing up beautiful; and I think it'll turn out one of the neatest cases I ever had the handling of."

CHAPTER XXXVIII.

OFF THE SCENT.

It is scarcely necessary to say, that, with the button by Crosby in his pocket, and with the information acquired from Dawson the gardener, stowed away carefully in his mind, Mr. Joseph Grimstone looked with an eye of particular interest upon Steeve Hargraves the "Softy."

The detective had not come to Doncaster alone. He had brought with him a humble ally and follower, in the shape of the little shabby-looking man who had encountered the "Softy" at the railway station, having received orders to keep a close watch upon Mr. Stephen Hargraves. It was of course a very easy matter to identify the "Softy" in the town of Doncaster, where he had been pretty generally known since his childhood.

Mr. Grimstone had called upon a medical practitioner, and had submitted the button to him for inspection. The stains upon it were indeed that which the detective had supposed – blood; and the surgeon detected a minute morsel of cartilage adhering to the jagged hasp of the button; but the same surgeon declared that this missile could not have been the one used by the murderer of James Conyers. It had not been through the dead man's body; it had inflicted only a surface wound.

The business which now lay before Mr. Grimstone was the tracing of one or other of the bank-notes; and for this purpose he and his ally set to work upon the track of the "Softy," with a view of discovering all the places which it was his habit to visit. The haunts affected by Mr. Hargraves turned out to be some half-dozen very obscure public-houses; and to each of these Joseph Grimstone went in person.

But he could discover nothing. All his inquiries only elicited the fact that Stephen Hargraves had not been observed to change, or to attempt to change, any bank-note whatever. He had paid for all he had had, and spent more than it was usual for him to spend, drinking a good deal harder than had been his habit heretofore; but he had paid in silver, except on one occasion, when he had changed a sovereign. The detective called at the bank; but no person answering the description of Stephen Hargraves had been observed there. The detective endeavoured to discover any friends or companions of the "Softy;" but here again he failed. The half-witted hanger-on of the Mellish stables had never made any friends, being entirely deficient in all social qualities.

There was something almost miraculous in the manner in which Mr. Joseph Grimstone contrived to make himself master of any information which he wished to acquire; and before noon on the day after his interview with Mr. Dawson the gardener, he had managed to eliminate all the facts set down above, and had also succeeded in ingratiating himself into the confidence of the dirty old proprietress of that humble lodging in which the "Softy" had taken up his abode.

It is scarcely necessary to this story to tell how the detective went to work; but while Stephen Hargraves sat soddening his stupid brain with medicated beer in a low tap-room not far off, and while Mr. Grimstone's ally kept close watch, holding himself in readiness to give warning of any movement on the part of the suspected individual, Mr. Grimstone himself went so cleverly to work in his manipulation of the "Softy's" landlady, that in less than a quarter of an hour he had taken full possession of that weak point in the intellectual citadel which is commonly called the blind side, and was able to do what he pleased with the old woman and her wretched tenement.

His peculiar pleasure was to make a very elaborate examination of the apartment rented by the "Softy," and any other apartments, cupboards, or hiding-places to which Mr. Hargraves had access. But he found nothing to reward him for his trouble. The old woman was in the habit of receiving casual lodgers, resting for a night or so at Doncaster before tramping further on their vagabond wanderings; and the six-roomed dwelling-place was only furnished with such meagre accommodation as may be expected for fourpence and sixpence a night. There were few hiding-places, – no carpets, underneath which fat bundles of bank-notes might be hidden; no picture-frames, behind which the same species of property might be bestowed; no ponderous cornices or heavily-fringed valances shrouding the windows, and affording dusty recesses wherein the title-deeds of half a dozen fortunes might lie and rot. There were two or three cupboards, into which Mr. Grimstone penetrated with a tallow candle; but he discovered nothing of any more importance than crockery-ware, lucifer-matches, fire-wood, potatoes, bare ropes, on which an onion lingered here and there and sprouted dismally in its dark loneliness, empty ginger-beer bottles, oyster-shells, old boots and shoes, disabled mouse-traps, black beetles, and humid fungi rising ghost-like from the damp and darkness.

Mr. Grimstone emerged dirty and discomforted, from one of these dark recesses, after a profitless search, which had occupied a couple of weary hours.

"Some other chap'll go in and cut the ground under my feet, if I waste my time this way," thought the detective. "I'm blest if I don't think I've been a fool for my pains. The man carries the money about him, – that's as clear as mud; and if I were to search Doncaster till my hair got gray, I shouldn't find what I want."

Mr. Grimstone shut the door of the last cupboard which he had examined, with an impatient slam, and then turned towards the window. There was no sign of his scout in the little alley before the house, and he had time therefore for further business.

He had examined everything in the "Softy's" apartment, and he had paid particular attention to the state of Mr. Hargraves' wardrobe, which consisted of a pile of garments, every one of which bore in its cut and fashion the stamp of a different individuality, and thereby proclaimed itself as having belonged to another master. There was a Newmarket coat of John Mellish's, and a pair of hunting-breeches, which could only have built up the great Poole himself,[1] split across the knees, but otherwise little the worse for wear. There was a linen jacket, and an old livery waistcoat that had belonged to one of the servants at the Park; odd tops of every shade known in the hunting-field, from the spotless white, or the delicate champagne-cleaned cream colour of the dandy, to the favourite vinegar hue of the hard-riding country squire; a groom's hat with a tarnished band and a battered crown; hob-nailed boots, which may have belonged to Mr. Dawson; corduroy breeches that could only have fitted a dropsical

---

[1] Steeve Hargraves' wardrobe is a comical mix of hand-me-downs: hob-nailed work-boots coexist with riding breeches which were originally of a quality to have "built up" (i.e. enhanced the reputation of) Henry George Poole, who from 1832-36 was tailor to many of the crowned heads of Europe.

lodge-keeper, long deceased; and there was one garment which bore upon it the ghastly impress of a dreadful deed that had but lately been done. This was the velveteen shooting-coat worn by James Conyers, the trainer, which, pierced with the murderous bullet, and stiffened by the soaking torrent of blood, had been appropriated by Mr. Stephen Hargraves in the confusion of the catastrophe. All these things, with sundry rubbish in the way of odd spurs and whip-handles, scraps of broken harness, ends of rope, and such other scrapings as only a miser loves to accumulate, were packed in a lumbering trunk covered with mangy fur, and secured by about a dozen yards of knotted and jagged rope, tied about it in such a manner as the "Softy" had considered sufficient to defy the most artful thief in Christendom.

Mr. Grimstone had made very short work of all the elaborate defences in the way of knots and entanglements, and had ransacked the box from one end to the other; nay, had even closely examined the fur covering of the trunk, and had tested each separate brass-headed nail to ascertain if any of them had been removed or altered. He may have thought it just possible that two thousand pounds' worth of Bank of England paper had been nailed down under the mangy fur. He gave a weary sigh as he concluded his inspection, replaced the garments one by one in the trunk, reknotted and secured the jagged cord, and with a weary sigh turned his back upon the "Softy's" chamber.

"It's no good," he thought. "The yellow-striped waistcoat isn't among his clothes, and the money isn't hidden away anywhere. Can he be deep enough to have destroyed that waistcoat, I wonder? He'd got a red woollen one on this morning; perhaps he's got the yellow-striped one under it."

Mr. Grimstone brushed the dust and cobwebs off his clothes, washed his hands in a greasy wooden bowl of scalding water, which the old woman brought him, and then sat down before the fire, picking his teeth thoughtfully, and with his eyebrows set in a reflective frown over his small gray eyes.

"I don't like to be beat," he thought; "I don't like to be beat." He doubted if any magistrate would grant him a warrant against the "Softy" upon the strength of the evidence in his possession – the blood-stained button by Crosby of Birmingham; and without a warrant he could not search for the notes upon the person of the man he suspected. He had sounded all the out-door servants at Mellish Park, but had been able to discover nothing that threw any light upon the movements of Stephen Hargraves on the night of the murder. No one remembered having seen him; no one had been on the southern side of the wood that night. One of the lads had passed the north lodge on his way from the high-road to the stables, about the time at which Aurora had heard the shot fired in the wood, and had seen a light burning in the lower window; but this, of course, proved nothing either one way or the other.

"If we could find the money *upon him*," thought Mr. Grimstone; "it would be pretty strong proof of the robbery; and if we find the waistcoat off which that button came, in his possession, it wouldn't be bad evidence of the murder, putting the two things together; but we shall have to keep a precious sharp watch upon my friend, while we hunt up what we want, or I'm blest if he won't give us the slip, and be off to Liverpool and out of the country before we know where we are."

Now the truth of the matter is, that Mr. Joseph Grimstone was not, perhaps, acting quite so conscientiously in this business as he might have done, had the love of justice in the abstract, and without any relation to sublunary reward, been the ruling principle of his life. He might have had any help he pleased, from the Doncaster constabulary, had he chosen to confide in the members of that force; but, as a very knowing individual who owns a three-year old, which he has reason to believe "a flyer," is apt to keep the capabilities of his horse a secret from his friends and the sporting public, while he puts a "pot" of money upon the animal at enormous odds, so Mr. Grimstone desired to keep his information to himself, until it should have brought him its golden fruit in the shape of a small reward from Government, and a large one from John Mellish.

The detective had reason to know that the Dogberries of Doncaster, misled by a duplicate of that very letter which had first aroused the attention of Scotland Yard, were on the wrong scent, as he had been at first; and he was very well content to leave them where they were.

"No," he thought, "it's a critical game; but I'll play it single-handed, or, at least, with no one better than Tom Chivers to help me through with it; and a ten-pound note will satisfy him, if we win the day."

Pondering thus, Mr. Grimstone departed, after having recompensed the landlady for her civility by a donation which the old woman considered princely.

He had entirely deluded her as to the object of his search by telling her that he was a lawyer's clerk, commissioned by his employer to hunt for a codicil which had been hidden somewhere in that house by an old man who had lived in it in the year 1783; and he had contrived, in the course of conversation, to draw from the old woman, who was of a garrulous turn, all that she had to tell about the "Softy."

It was not much, certainly. Mr. Hargraves had never changed a bank-note with her knowledge. He had paid for his bit of victuals as he had it, but had not spent a shilling a day. As to bank-notes, it wasn't at all likely that he had any of them; for he was always complaining that he was very poor, and that his little bit of savings, scraped together out of his wages, wouldn't last him long.

"This Hargraves is a precious deep one for all they call him soft," thought Mr. Grimstone, as he left the lodging-house, and walked slowly towards the sporting public-house at which he had left the "Softy" under the watchful eye of Mr. Tom Chivers. "I've often heard say that these half-witted chaps have more cunning in their little fingers than a better man has in the whole of his composition. Another man would have never been able to stand against the temptation of changing one of those notes; or would have gone about wearing that identical waistcoat; or would have made a bolt of it the day after the murder; or tried on something or other that would have blown the gaff upon him; but not your 'Softy!' He hides the notes and he hides the waistcoat, and then he laughs in his sleeve at those that want him, and sits drinking his beer as comfortably as you please."

Pondering thus, the detective made his way to the public-house in which he had left Mr. Stephen Hargraves. He ordered a glass of brandy-and-water at the bar, and walked into the taproom, expecting to see the "Softy" still brooding sullenly over his drink, still guarded by the apparently indifferent eye of Mr. Chivers. But it was not so. The taproom was empty; and upon making cautious inquiries, Mr.

Grimstone discovered that the "Softy" and his watcher had been gone for upwards of an hour.

Mr. Chivers had been forbidden to let his charge out of sight under any circumstances whatever, except indeed if the "Softy" had turned homewards while Mr. Grimstone was employed in ransacking his domicile, in which event Tom was to have slipped on a few paces before him, and given warning to his chief. Wherever Stephen Hargraves went, Mr. Thomas Chivers was to follow him; but he was, above all, to act in such a manner as would effectually prevent any suspicion arising in the "Softy's" mind as to the fact that he was followed.

It will be seen, therefore, that poor Chivers had no very easy task to perform, and it has been seen that he had heretofore contrived to perform it pretty skilfully. If Stephen Hargraves sat boozing in a taproom half the day, Mr. Chivers was also to booze or to make a pretence of boozing, for the same length of time. If the "Softy" showed any disposition to be social, and gave his companion any opportunity of getting friendly with him, the detective's underling was to employ his utmost skill and discretion in availing himself of that golden chance. It is a wondrous provision of Providence that the treachery which would be hateful and horrible in any other man, is considered perfectly legitimate in the man who is employed to hunt out a murderer or a thief. The vile instruments which the criminal employed against his unsuspecting victim are in due time used against himself; and the wretch who laughed at the poor unsuspecting dupe who was trapped to his destruction by *his* lies, is caught in his turn by some shallow deceit, or pitifully hackneyed device, of the paid spy, who has been bribed to lure him to his doom. For the outlaw of society, the code of honour is null and void. His existence is a perpetual peril to innocent women and honourable men; and the detective who beguiles him to his end does such a service to society as must doubtless counterbalance the treachery of the means by which it is done. The days of Jonathan Wild[1] and his compeers are over, and the thief-taker no longer begins life as a thief. The detective officer is as honest

---

1 Notorious thief and thief-taker whose exploits are described in Henry Fielding's *Jonathan Wild the Great* (1743).

as he is intrepid and astute, and it is not his own fault if the dirty nature of all crime gives him now and then dirty work to do.

But Mr. Stephen Hargraves did not give the opportunity for which Tom Chivers had been bidden to lie in wait; he sat sullen, silent, stupid, unapproachable; and as Tom's orders were not to force himself upon his companion, he was fain to abandon all thought of worming himself into the "Softy's" good graces. This made the task of watching him all the more difficult. It is not such a very easy matter to follow a man without seeming to follow him.

It was market-day too, and the town was crowded with noisy country people. Mr. Grimstone suddenly remembered this, and the recollection by no means added to his peace of mind.

"Chivers never did sell me," he thought, "and surely he won't do it now. I dare say they're safe enough, for the matter of that, in some other public. I'll slip out and look after them."

Mr. Grimstone had, as I have said, already made himself acquainted with all the haunts affected by the "Softy." It did not take him long, therefore, to look in at the three or four public-houses where Steeve Hargraves was likely to be found, and to discover that he was not there.

"He's slouching about the town somewhere or other, I dare say," thought the detective, "with my mate close upon his heels. I'll stroll towards the market-place, and see if I can find them anywhere that way."

Mr. Grimstone turned out of the by-street in which he had been walking, into a narrow alley leading to the broad open square upon which the market-place stands.

The detective went his way in a leisurely manner, with his hands in his pockets and a cigar in his mouth. He had perfect confidence in Mr. Thomas Chivers, and the crowded state of the market-place and its neighbourhood in no way weakened his sense of security.

"Chivers will stick to him through thick and thin," he thought; "he'd keep an eye upon his man if he had to look after him between Charing Cross and Whitehall when the Queen was going to open Parliament. He's not the man to be flummuxed by a crowd in a country market-place."

Serene in this sense of security, Mr. Grimstone amused himself by looking about him, with an expression of somewhat supercilious wonder, at the manners and customs of those indigenæ who, upon market-day, make their inroad into the quiet town. He paused upon the edge of a little sunken flight of worn steps leading down to the stage-door of the theatre, and read the fragments of old bills mouldering upon the door-posts and lintel. There were glowing announcements of dramatic performances that had long ago taken place; and above the rain and mud stained relics of the past, in bold black lettering, appeared the record of a drama as terrible as any that had ever been enacted in that provincial theatre. The bill-sticker had posted the announcement of the reward offered by John Mellish for the discovery of the murderer in every available spot, and had not forgotten this position, which commanded one of the entrances to the market-place.

"It's a wonder to me," muttered Mr. Grimstone, "that that blessed bill shouldn't have opened the eyes of these Doncaster noodles. But I dare say they think it's a blind, a planned thing to throw 'em off the scent their clever noses are sticking to so determined. If I can get *my* man before they open their eyes, I shall have such a haul as I haven't met with lately."

Musing thus pleasantly, Mr. Grimstone turned his back upon the theatre, and crossed over to the market. Within the building the clamour of buying and selling was at its height: noisy countrymen chaffering in their northern *patois* upon the value and merits of poultry, butter, and eggs; dealers in butchers' meat bewildering themselves in the endeavour to simultaneously satisfy the demands of half a dozen sharp and bargain-loving housekeepers; while from without there came a confused clatter of other merchants and other customers, clamouring and hustling round the stalls of greengrocers and the slimy barrows of blue-jacketed fishmongers. In the midst of all this bustle and confusion, Mr. Grimstone came suddenly upon his trusted ally, pale, terror-stricken, and – ALONE!

The detective's mind was not slow to grasp the full force of the situation.

"You've lost him!" he whispered fiercely, seizing the unfortunate Mr. Chivers by the collar, and pinning him as securely as if he had serious thoughts of making him a permanent fixture upon the stoneflags of the market-place. "You've lost him, Tom Chivers!" he continued, hoarse with agitation. "You've lost the party that I told you was worth more to me than any other party I ever gave you the office for. You've lost me the best chance I've ever had since I've been in Scotland Yard, and yourself too; for I should have acted liberal by you," added the detective, apparently oblivious of that morning's reverie, in which he had pre-determined offering his assistant ten pounds, in satisfaction of all his claims, – "I should have acted very liberal by you, Tom. But what's the use of standing jawing here? You come along with me; you can tell me how it happened as we go."

With his powerful grasp still on the underling's collar, Mr. Grimstone walked out of the market-place, neither looking to the right nor the left, though many a pair of rustic eyes opened to their widest as he passed, attracted no doubt by the rapidity of his pace and the obvious determination of his manner. Perhaps those rustic bystanders thought that the stern-looking gentleman in the black frock-coat had arrested the shabby little man in the act of picking his pocket, and was bearing him off to deliver him straight into the hands of justice.

Mr. Grimstone released his grasp when he and his companion had got clear of the market-place.

"Now," he said, breathless, but not slackening his pace, – "now I suppose you can tell me how you came to make such an" – inadmissable adjective – "fool of yourself? Never you mind where I'm goin'. I'm goin' to the railway station. Never you mind why I'm goin' there. You'd guess why, if you weren't a fool. Now tell me all about it, can't you?"

"It aint much to tell," the humble follower gasped, his respiratory functions sadly tried by the pace at which his superior went over the ground. "It aint much. I followed your instructions faithful. I tried, artful and quiet-like, to make acquaintance with him; but that warn't a bit o' good. He was as surly as a bull-terrier, so I didn't force him to it; but kept an eye upon him, and let out before him as it was racin' business as had brought me to Doncaster, and as I was here to look after a horse, what was in trainin' a few miles off, for a gent in London; and when he left the public, I went after him, but not conspicuous. But I think from that minute he was fly, for he didn't go three steps without lookin' back, and he led me such a chase as made my legs tremble under me, which they trembles at this moment; and then he gets me into the market-place, and he dodges here, and he dodges there, and wherever the crowd's thickest he dodges most, till he gets me at last in among a ring of market-people round a couple o' coves a-millin'[1] with each other, and there I loses him. And I've been in and out the market, and here and there, until I'm fit to drop, but it aint no good; and you've no call to lay the blame on me, for mortal man couldn't have done more."

Mr. Chivers wiped the perspiration from his face in testimony of his exertions. Dirty little streams were rolling down his forehead and trickling upon his poor faded cheeks. He mopped up these evidences of his fatigue with a red cotton handkerchief, and gave a deprecatory sigh.

"If there's anybody to lay blame on, it aint me," he said mildly. "I said all along you ought to have had help. A man as is on his own ground, and knows his own ground, is more than a match for one cove, however hard he may work."

The detective turned fiercely upon his meek dependent.

"Who's blaming you?" he cried impatiently. "I wouldn't cry out before I was hurt, if I were you."

They had reached the railway station by this time.

"How long is it since you missed him?" asked Mr. Grimstone of the penitent Chivers.

"Three-quarters of a hour, or it may be a hour," Tom added doubtfully.

"I dare say it *is* an hour," muttered the detective.

He walked straight to one of the chief officials, and asked what trains had left within the last hour.

"Two – both market trains: one eastward, Selby way; the other for Penistone, and the intervening stations."

The detective looked at the time-table, running his thumb-nail along the names of the stations.

"That train will reach Penistone in time to catch the Liverpool train, won't it?" he asked.

"Just about."

---

1   Beating or fighting with fists.

"What time did it go?"

"The Penistone train?"

"Yes."

"About half an hour ago; at 2.30."

The clocks had struck three as Mr. Grimstone made his way to the station.

"Half an hour ago," muttered the detective. "He'd have had ample time to catch the train after giving Chivers the slip."

He questioned the guards and porters as to whether any of them had seen a man answering to the description of the "Softy:" a white-faced, hump-backed fellow, in corduroys and a fustian jacket; and even penetrated into the ticket-clerk's office to ask the same question.

No; none of them had seen Mr. Stephen Hargraves. Two or three of them recognized him by the detective's description, and asked if it was one of the stable-men from Mellish Park that the gentleman was inquiring after. Mr. Grimstone rather evaded any direct answer to this question. Secrecy was, as we know, the principle upon which he conducted his affairs.

"He may have contrived to give 'em all the slip," he said confidentially to his faithful but dispirited ally. "He may have got off without any of 'em seeing him. He's got the money about him, I'm all but certain of that; and his game is to get off to Liverpool. His inquiries after the trains yesterday proves that. Now I might telegraph, and have him stopped at Liverpool – supposing him to have given us all the slip, and gone off there – if I like to let others into the game; but I don't. I'll play to win or lose; but I'll play single-handed. He may try another dodge, and get off Hull way by the canal-boats that the market-people use, and then slip across to Hamburg, or something of that sort; but that aint likely, – these fellows always go one way. It seems as if the minute a man has taken another man's life, or forged his name, or embezzled his money, his ideas get fixed in one groove, and never can soar higher than Liverpool and the American packet."

Mr. Chivers listened respectfully to his patron's communications. He was very well pleased to see the serenity of his employer's mind gradually returning.

"Now, I'll tell you what, Tom," said Mr. Grimstone. "If this chap has given us the slip, why he's given us the slip, and he's got a start of us, which we sha'n't be able to pick up till half-past ten o'clock to-night, when there's a train that'll take us to Liverpool. If he *hasn't* given us the slip, there's only one way he can leave Doncaster, and that's by this station; so you stay here patient and quiet till you see me, or hear from me. If he is in Doncaster, I'm jiggered[1] if I don't find him."

With which powerful asseveration Mr. Grimstone walked away, leaving his scout to keep watch for the possible coming of the "Softy."

---

1   Used as substitute for profanity.

CHAPTER XXXIX.

TALBOT BULSTRODE MAKES ATONEMENT FOR THE PAST.

JOHN MELLISH and Talbot Bulstrode walked to and fro upon the lawn before the drawing-room windows on that afternoon on which the detective and his underling lost sight of Stephen Hargraves. It was a dreary time, this period of watching and waiting, of uncertainty and apprehension; and poor John Mellish chafed bitterly under the burden which he had to bear.

Now that his friend's common sense had come to his relief, and that a few plain out-spoken sentences had dispersed the terrible cloud of mystery; now that he himself was fully assured of his wife's innocence, he had no patience with the stupid country people who held themselves aloof from the woman he loved. He wanted to go out and do battle for his slandered wife; to hurl back every base suspicion into the faces that had scowled upon his idolized Aurora. How could they dare, these foul-minded slanderers, to harbour one base thought against the purest, the most perfect of women? Mr. Mellish of course quite forgot that he, the rightful defender of all this perfection, had suffered his mind to be for a time obscured beneath the black shadow of that vile suspicion.

He hated the old friends of his youth for their base avoidance of him; the servants of his household for a half-doubtful, half-solemn expression of face, which he knew had relation to that growing suspicion, that horrible suspicion, which seemed to grow stronger with every hour. He broke out into a storm of rage with the gray-haired butler, who had carried him pick-a-back in his infancy, because the faithful retainer tried to hold back certain newspapers which contained dark allusions to the Mellish mystery.

"Who told you I didn't want the 'Manchester Guardian,' Jarvis?" he cried fiercely; "who gave you the right to dictate what I'm to read or what I'm to leave unread? I do want to-day's 'Guardian;' to-day's, and yesterday's, and to-morrow's, and every other newspaper that comes into this house. I won't have them overhauled by you, or any one, to see whether they're pleasant reading or not, before they're brought to me. Do you think *I'm* afraid of anything these penny-a-liner fellows can write?" roared the young squire, striking his open hand upon the table at which he sat. "Let them write their best or their worst of me. But let them write one word that can be twisted into an insinuation upon the purest and truest woman in all Christendom, and, by the Lord above me, I'll give them such a thrashing – penny-a-liners, printers, publishers, and every man-Jack of them – as shall make them remember the business to the last hour of their lives!"

Mr. Mellish said all this in despite of the restraining presence of Talbot Bulstrode. Indeed, the young member for Penruthy had by no means a pleasant time of it during those few days of anxiety and suspense. A keeper set to watch over a hearty young jungle-tiger, and bidden to prevent the noble animal from committing any imprudence, might have found his work little harder than that which Mr. Bulstrode did, patiently and uncomplainingly, for pure friendship's sake.

John Mellish roamed about in the custody of this friendly keeper, with his short auburn hair tumbled into a feverish-looking mass, like a field of ripening corn that had been beaten by a summer hurricane, his cheeks sunken and haggard, and a bristling yellow stubble upon his chin. I dare say he had made a vow neither to shave nor be shaven until the murderer of James Conyers should be found. He clung desperately to Talbot Bulstrode, but he clung with still wilder desperation to the detective, the professional criminal hunter, who had in a manner tacitly pledged himself to the discovery of the real homicide.

All through the fitful August day, now hot and still, now overclouded and showery, the master of Mellish Park went hither and thither, – now sitting in his study; now roaming out on the lawn; now pacing up and down the drawing-room, displacing, disarranging, and overturning the pretty furniture; now wandering up and down the staircase, lolling on the landing-places, and patrolling the corridor outside the rooms in which Lucy and Aurora sat together making a show of employing themselves, but only waiting, waiting, waiting, for the hoped-for end.

Poor John scarcely cared to meet that dearly-loved wife; for the great earnest eyes that looked in his face always asked the same question so plainly, – always appealed so piteously for the answer that could not be given.

It was a weary and a bitter time. I wonder, as I write of it, when I think of a quiet Somersetshire household in which a dreadful deed was done, the secret of which has never yet been brought to light, and perhaps never will be revealed until the Day of Judgement, what must have been suffered by each member of *that* family?[1] What slow agonies, what ever-increasing tortures, while that cruel mystery was the "sensation" topic of conversation in a thousand happy home-circles, in a thousand tavern-parlours and pleasant club-rooms! – a common and ever-interesting topic, by means of which travellers in first-class railway carriages might break down the ceremonial icebergs which surround each travelling Englishman, and grow friendly and confidential; a safe topic upon which even tacit enemies might talk pleasantly without fear of wrecking themselves upon hidden rocks of personal insinuation. God help that household, or any such household, through the weary time of waiting which it may please Him to appoint, until that day in which it shall be His good pleasure to reveal the truth! God help all patient creatures labouring under the burden of an unjust suspicion, and support them unto the end!

John Mellish chafed and fretted himself ceaselessly all through that August day at the non-appearance of the detective. Why didn't he come? He had promised to bring or send them news of his proceedings. Talbot in vain assured his friend that Mr. Grimstone was no doubt hard at work; that such a discovery as he had to make was not to be made in a day; and that Mr. Mellish had nothing to do but to make himself as comfortable as he could, and wait quietly for the event he desired so eagerly.

"I should not say this to you, John," Mr. Bulstrode said by-and-by, "if I did not believe – as I know this man Grimstone believes – that

---

1   On 29 June 1862 a four-year-old boy was found murdered in his home in Road, a town on the Wiltshire/Somerset border. The nursemaid, Elizabeth Gough, was arrested for the crime. She was later released, and the 16-year-old daughter of the house, Constance Kent, was arrested, but later released on grounds of insufficient evidence. She confessed to the crime in 1865 (after the publication of *Aurora Floyd*). The "Road Murder," as it was called, dominated newspapers for the rest of 1862; this chapter of the novel was published in *Temple Bar* in January 1863.

we are upon the right track, and are pretty sure to bring the crime home to the wretch who committed it. You can do nothing but be patient, and wait the result of Grimstone's labours."

"Yes," cried John Mellish; "and in the mean time all these people are to say cruel things of my darling, and keep aloof from her, and – No, I *can't* bear it, Talbot; I can't bear it. I'll turn my back upon this confounded place; I'll sell it; I'll burn it down; I'll – I'll do anything to get away, and take my precious one from the wretches who have slandered her!"

"That you shall *not* do, John Mellish," exclaimed Talbot Bulstrode, "until the murderer of James Conyers has been discovered. Go away, then, as soon as you like; for the associations of this place cannot be otherwise than disagreeable to you – for a time, at least. But until the truth is out, you must remain here. If there is any foul suspicion against Aurora, her presence here will best give the lie to that suspicion. It was her hurried journey to London which first set people talking of her, I dare say," added Mr. Bulstrode, who was of course entirely ignorant of the fact that an anonymous letter from Mrs. Powell had originally aroused the suspicions of the Doncaster constabulary.

So through the long summer's day Talbot reasoned with and comforted his friend, never growing weary of his task, never for one moment losing sight of the interests of Aurora Mellish and her husband.

Perhaps this was a self-imposed penalty for the wrong which he had done the banker's daughter long ago in the dim star-lit chamber at Felden. If it was so, he did penance very cheerfully.

"Heaven knows how gladly I would do her a service," he thought; "her life has been a troubled one, in spite of her father's thousands. Thank Heaven, my poor little Lucy has never been forced into playing the heroine of a tragedy like this; thank Heaven, my poor little darling's life flows evenly and placidly in a smooth channel!"

He could not but reflect with something of a shudder that it might have been his wife whose history was being canvassed throughout the West Riding. He could not be otherwise than pleased to remember that the name of the woman he had chosen had never gone beyond the holy circle of her own home, to be the common talk among strangers.

There are things which are utterly unendurable to some people, but which are not at all terrible in the eyes of others. John Mellish, secure in his own belief in his wife's innocence, would have been content to carry her away with him, after razing the home of his forefathers to the ground, and defying all Yorkshire to find a flaw or speck upon her fair fame. But Talbot Bulstrode would have gone mad with the agony of the thought that common tongues had defiled the name he loved, and would, in no after-triumph of his wife's innocence, been able to forget or to recover from the torture of that unendurable agony. There are people who cannot forget, and Talbot Bulstrode was one of them. He had never forgotten his Christmas agony at Felden Woods, and the after-struggle at Bulstrode Castle; nor did he ever hope to forget it. The happiness of the present, pure and unalloyed though it was, could not annihilate the anguish of the past. *That* stood alone, – so many months, weeks, days, and hours of unutterable misery, riven away from the rest of his life, to remain for ever a stony memorial upon the smooth plains of the past.

Archibald Martin Floyd sat with his daughter and Lucy, in Mrs. Mellish's morning-room, the pleasantest chamber for many reasons, but chiefly because it was removed from the bustle of the house, and from the chance of unwelcome intrusion. All the troubles of that household had been made light of in the presence of the old man, and no word had been dropped before him, which could give him reason to guess that his only child had been suspected of the most fearful crime that man or woman can commit. But Archibald Floyd was not easily to be deceived where his daughter's happiness was in question; he had watched that beautiful face – whose ever-varying expression was its highest charm – so long and earnestly, as to have grown familiar with its every look. No shadow upon the brightness of his daughter's beauty could possibly escape the old man's eyes, dim as they may have grown for the figures in his banking-book. It was Aurora's business, therefore, to sit by her father's side in the pleasant morning-room, to talk to him and amuse him; while John rambled hither and thither, and made himself otherwise tiresome to his patient companion, Talbot Bulstrode. Mrs. Mellish repeated to her father again and again, that there was no cause for uneasiness; they were merely anxious – naturally anxious – that the guilty man should be found and brought to justice; nothing more.

The banker accepted this explanation of his daughter's pale face very quietly; but he was not the less anxious, – anxious he scarcely knew why, but with the shadow of a dark cloud hanging over him, that was not to be driven away.

Thus the long August day wore itself out, and the low sun – blazing a lurid red behind the trees in Mellish Wood, until it made that pool beside which the murdered man had fallen, seem a pool of blood – gave warning that one weary day of watching and suspense was nearly done.

John Mellish, far too restless to sit long at dessert, had roamed out upon the lawn: still attended by his indefatigable keeper, Talbot Bulstrode, and employed himself in pacing up and down the smooth grass amid Mr. Dawson's flower-beds, looking always towards the pathway that led to the house, and breathing suppressed anathemas against the dilatory detective.

"One day nearly gone, thank Heaven, Talbot!" he said, with an impatient sigh. "Will to-morrow bring us no nearer what we want, I wonder? What if it should go on like this for long? what if it should go on for ever, until Aurora and I go mad with this wretched anxiety and suspense? Yes, I know you think me a fool and a coward, Talbot Bulstrode; but I can't bear it quietly, I tell you I can't. I know there are some people who can shut themselves up with their troubles, and sit down quietly and suffer without a groan; but I can't. I must cry out when I am tortured, or I should dash my brains out against the first wall I came to, and make an end of it. To think that anybody should suspect my darling! to think that they should believe her to be———"

"To think that *you* should have believed it, John!" said Mr. Bulstrode, gravely.

"Ah, there's the cruelest stab of all," cried John; "if *I*, – I who know her, and love her, and believe in her as man never yet believed in woman, – if *I* could have been bewildered and maddened by that horrible chain of cruel circumstances, every one of which pointed – Heaven help me! – at her! – if *I* could be deluded by these things until my brain reeled, and I went nearly mad with doubting my own dearest love, what may strangers think – strangers who neither know nor love her, but who are only too ready to believe anything unnaturally infamous? Talbot, I *won't* endure this any longer. I'll ride into

Doncaster and see this man Grimstone. He *must* have done some good to-day. I'll go at once."

Mr. Mellish would have walked straight off to the stables; but Talbot Bulstrode caught him by the arm.

"You may miss the man on the road, John," he said. "He came last night after dark, and may come as late to-night. There's no knowing whether he'll come by the road, or the short cut across the fields. You're as likely to miss him as not."

Mr. Mellish hesitated.

"He mayn't come at all to-night," he said; "and I tell you I can't bear this suspense."

"Let *me* ride into Doncaster, then, John," urged Talbot; "and you stay here to receive Grimstone if he should come."

Mr. Mellish was considerably mollified by this proposition.

"Will you ride into the town, Talbot?" he said. "Upon my word, it's very kind of you to propose it. I shouldn't like to miss this man upon any account; but at the same time I don't feel inclined to wait for the chance of his coming or staying away. I'm afraid I'm a great nuisance to you, Bulstrode."

"Not a bit of it," answered Talbot, with a smile.

Perhaps he smiled involuntarily at the notion of how little John Mellish knew what a nuisance he had been through that weary day.

"I'll go with very great pleasure, John," he said, "if you'll tell them to saddle a horse for me."

"To be sure; you shall have Red Rover, my covert hack.[1] We'll go round to the stables, and see about him at once."

The truth of the matter is, Talbot Bulstrode was very well pleased himself to hunt up the detective, rather than that John Mellish should execute that errand in person; for it would have been about as easy for the young squire to have translated a number of the 'Sporting Magazine' into Porsonian Greek, as to have kept a secret for half an hour, however earnestly entreated, or however conscientiously determined to do so.

Mr. Bulstrode had made it his particular business, therefore, during

---

1   Horse used for riding to the hunting meet or to the covert, where it is exchanged for the hunter.

the whole of that day, to keep his friend as much as possible out of the way of every living creature, fully aware that Mr. Mellish's manner would most certainly betray him to the least observant eyes that might chance to fall upon him.

Red Rover was saddled, and, after twenty loudly whispered injunctions from John, Talbot Bulstrode rode away in the evening sunlight. The nearest way from the stables to the high road took him past the north lodge. It had been shut up since the day of the trainer's funeral, and such furniture as it contained left to become a prey to moths and rats; for the Mellish servants were a great deal too superstitiously impressed with the story of the murder to dream of readmitting those goods and chattels which had been selected for Mr. Conyers's accommodation to the garrets whence they had been taken. The door had been locked, therefore, and the key given to Dawson the gardener, who was to be once more free to use the place as a storehouse for roots and matting, superannuated cucumber-frames, and crippled garden tools.

The place looked dreary enough, though the low sun made a gorgeous illumination upon one of the latticed windows that faced the crimson west, and though the last leaves of the roses were still lying upon the long grass in the patch of garden before the door out of which Mr. Conyers had gone to his last resting-place. One of the stable-boys had accompanied Mr. Bulstrode to the lodge in order to open the rusty iron gates, which hung loosely on their hinges, and were never locked.

Talbot rode at a brisk pace into Doncaster, never drawing rein until he reached the little inn at which the detective had taken up his quarters. Mr. Grimstone had been snatching a hasty refreshment, after a weary and useless perambulation about the town, and came out with his mouth full, to speak to Mr. Bulstrode. But he took very good care not to confess that since three o'clock that day neither he nor his ally had seen or heard of Mr. Stephen Hargraves, or that he was actually no nearer the discovery of the murderer than he had been at eleven o'clock upon the previous night, when he had discovered the original proprietor of the fancy waistcoat, with buttons by Crosby, Birmingham, in the person of Dawson the gardener.

"I'm not losing any time, sir," he said, in answer to Talbot's inquiries; "my sort of work's quiet work, and don't make no show till it's done. I've reason to think the man we want is in Doncaster; so I stick in Doncaster, and mean to, till I lay my hand upon him, unless I should get information as would point further off. Tell Mr. Mellish I'm doing my duty, sir, and doing it conscientious; and that I shall neither eat nor drink nor sleep more than just as much as'll keep human nature together, until I've done what I've set my mind on doing."

"But you've discovered nothing fresh, then?" said Talbot; "you've nothing new to tell me?"

"Whatever I've discovered is neither here nor there yet awhile, sir," answered the detective vaguely. "You keep your heart up, and tell Mr. Mellish to keep his heart up, and trust in me."

Talbot Bulstrode was obliged to be content with this rather doubtful comfort. It was not much, certainly; but he determined to make the best of it to John Mellish.

He rode out of Doncaster, past the Reindeer and the white-fronted houses of the wealthier citizens of that prosperous borough, and away upon the smooth high road. The faint shimmer of the pale early moonlight lit up the tree-tops right and left of him, as he left the suburb behind, and made the road ghostly beneath his horse's feet. He was in no very hopeful humour, after his interview with Mr. Grimstone, and he knew that hungry-eyed members of the Doncaster constabulary were keeping stealthy watch upon every creature in the Mellish household, and that the slanderous tongues of a greedy public were swelling into a loud and ominous murmur against the wife John loved. Every hour, every moment, was of vital importance. A hundred perils menaced them on every side. What might they not have to dread from eager busy-bodies anxious to distinguish themselves, and proud of being the first to circulate a foul scandal against the lovely daughter of one of the richest men upon the Stock Exchange? Hayward the coroner, and Lofthouse the rector, both knew the secret of Aurora's life; and it would be little wonder if, looking at the trainer's death by the light of that knowledge, they believed her guilty of some share in the ghastly business which had terminated the trainer's service at Mellish Park.

What if, by some horrible fatality, the guilty man should escape, and the truth never be revealed! For ever and for ever, until her blighted name should be written upon a tombstone, Aurora Mellish must rest under the shadow of this suspicion. Could there be any doubt that the sensitive and highly-strung nature would give way under the unendurable burden; that the proud heart would break beneath the undeserved disgrace? What misery for her! and not for her alone, but for every one who loved her, or had any share in her history! Heaven pardon the selfishness that prompted the thought, if Talbot Bulstrode remembered that he would have some part in that bitter disgrace; that his name was allied, if only remotely, with that of his wife's cousin; and that the shame which would make the name of Mellish a byword, must also cast some slur upon the escutcheon of the Bulstrodes. Sir Bernard Burke,[1] compiling the romance of the county families, would tell that cruel story, and hinting cautiously at Aurora's guilt, would scarcely fail to add, that the suspected lady's cousin had married Talbot Raleigh Bulstrode, Esq., eldest son and heir of Sir John Walter Raleigh Bulstrode, Baronet, of Bulstrode Castle, Cornwall.

Now, although the detective had affected a hopeful and even mysterious manner in his brief interview with Talbot, he had not succeeded in hoodwinking that gentleman, who had a vague suspicion that all was not quite right, and that Mr. Joseph Grimstone was by no means so certain of success as he pretended to be.

"It's my firm belief that this man Hargraves has given him the slip," Talbot thought. "He said something about believing him to be in Doncaster, and then the next moment added that he might be further off. It's clear, therefore, that Grimstone doesn't know where he is; and in that case it's as likely as not that the man's made off with his money, and will get away from England, in spite of us. If he does this——"

Mr. Bulstrode did not finish the sentence. He had reached the north lodge, and dismounted to open the iron gate. The lights of the house shone hospitably far away beyond the wood, and the voices of some men about the stable-gates sounded faintly in the distance; but the north lodge and the neglected shrubbery around it were as silent

---

1   Sir John Bernard Burke, Irish genealogist, who in 1847 took over Burke's *Peerage* (see 78, n.1) from his father, John Burke, and published it annually. He also published anecdotes about the aristocracy. These are presumably what Talbot is worried about.

as the grave, and had a certain phantom-like air in the dim moonlight.

Talbot led his horse through the gates. He looked up at the windows of the lodge, as he passed, half involuntarily; but he stopped with a suppressed exclamation of surprise, at the sight of a feeble glimmer, which was not the moonlight, in the window of that upper chamber in which the murdered man had slept. Before that exclamation had well-nigh crossed his lips, the light had disappeared.

If any one of the Mellish grooms or stable-boys had beheld that brief apparition, he would have incontinently taken to his heels, and rushed breathless to the stables, with a wild story of some supernatural horror in the north lodge; but Mr. Bulstrode being altogether of another mettle, walked softly on, still leading his horse, until he was well out of ear-shot of any one within the lodge, when he stopped and tied the Red Rover's bridle to a tree, and turned back towards the north gates, leaving the corn-fed covert hack cropping greedily at dewy hazel twigs, and any greenmeat within his reach.

The heir of Sir John Walter Raleigh Bulstrode crept back to the lodge, almost as noiselessly as if he had been educated for Mr. Grimstone's profession, choosing the grassy pathway beneath the trees for his cautious footsteps. As he approached the wooden paling that shut in the little garden of the lodge, the light which had been so suddenly extinguished, reappeared behind the white curtain of the upper window.

"It's queer!" mused Mr. Bulstrode, as he watched the feeble glimmer; "but I dare say there's nothing in it. The associations of this place are strong enough to make one attach a foolish importance to anything connected with it. I think I heard John say the gardeners keep their tools there, and I suppose it's one of them. But it's late, too, for any of them to be at work."

It had struck ten while Mr. Bulstrode rode homeward; and it was more than unlikely that any of the Mellish servants would be out at such a time.

Talbot lingered by the wicket-gate, irresolute as to what he should do next, but thoroughly determined to see the last of this late visitor at the north lodge, when the shadow of a man flitted across the white curtain, – a shadow even more weird and ungainly than such things are; – the shadow of a man with a hump-back!

Talbot Bulstrode uttered no cry of surprise; but his heart knocked furiously against his ribs, and the blood rushed hotly to his face. He never remembered having seen the "Softy;" but he had always heard him described as a hump-backed man. There could be no doubt of the shadow's identity; there could be still less doubt that Stephen Hargraves had visited that place for no good purpose. What could bring him there — to that place above all other places, which, if he were indeed guilty, he would surely most desire to avoid? Stolid, semi-idiotic, as he was supposed to be, surely the common terrors of the lowest assassin, half brute, half Caliban,[1] would keep him away from that spot. These thoughts did not occupy more than those few moments in which the violent beating of Talbot Bulstrode's heart held him powerless to move or act; then, pushing open the gate, he rushed across the tiny garden, trampling recklessly upon the neglected flower-beds, and softly tried the door. It was firmly secured with a heavy chain and padlock.

"He has got in at the window, then," thought Mr. Bulstrode. "What, in Heaven's name, could be his motive in coming here?"

Talbot was right. The little lattice-window had been wrenched nearly off its hinges, and hung loosely among the tangled foliage that surrounded it. Mr. Bulstrode did not hesitate a moment before he plunged head foremost into the narrow aperture through which the "Softy" must have found his way, and scrambled as he could into the little room. The lattice, strained still further, dropped, with a crashing noise, behind him; but not soon enough to serve as a warning for Stephen Hargraves, who appeared upon the lowest step of the tiny corkscrew staircase at the same moment. He was carrying a tallow candle in a battered tin candlestick in his right hand, and he had a small bundle under his left arm. His white face was no whiter than usual, but he presented an awfully corpse-like appearance to Mr. Bulstrode, who had never seen him, or noticed him, before. The "Softy" recoiled, with a gesture of intense terror, as he saw Talbot; and a box of lucifer-matches, which he had been carrying in the candlestick, rolled to the ground.

"What are you doing here?" asked Mr. Bulstrode, sternly; "and why did you come in at the window?"

---

1 See 316, n.1.

"I warn't doin' no wrong;" the "Softy" whined piteously; "and it aint your business neither," he added, with a feeble attempt at insolence.

"It is my business. I am Mr. Mellish's friend and relation; and I have reason to suspect that you are here for no good purpose," answered Talbot. "I insist upon knowing what you came for."

"I haven't come to steal owght, anyhow," said Mr. Hargraves; "there's nothing here but chairs and tables, and 'taint loikely I've come arter them."

"Perhaps not; but you have come after something, and I insist upon knowing what it is. You wouldn't come to this place unless you'd a very strong reason for coming. What have you got there?"

Mr. Bulstrode pointed to the bundle carried by the "Softy." Stephen Hargraves' small red-brown eyes evaded those of his questioner, and made believe to mistake the direction in which Talbot looked.

"What have you got there?" repeated Mr. Bulstrode; "you know well enough what I mean. What have you got there, in that bundle under your arm?"

The "Softy" clutched convulsively at the dingy bundle, and glared at his questioner with something of the savage terror of some ugly animal at bay. Except that in his brutalized manhood, he was more awkward, and perhaps more repulsive, than the ugliest of the lower animals.

"It's nowght to you, nor to anybody else," he muttered sulkily. "I suppose a poor chap may fetch his few bits of clothes without being *called* like this?"

"What clothes? Let me see the clothes?"

"No, I won't; they're nowght to you. They – it's only an old weskit as was give me by one o' th' lads in th' steables."

"A waistcoat!" cried Mr. Bulstrode; "let me see it this instant. A waistcoat of yours has been particularly inquired for, Mr. Hargraves. It's a chocolate waistcoat, with yellow stripes and brass buttons, unless I'm very much mistaken. Let me see it."

Talbot Bulstrode was almost breathless with excitement. The "Softy" stared aghast at the description of his waistcoat, but he was too stupid to comprehend instantaneously the reason for which this garment was wanted. He recoiled for a few paces, and then made a rush towards the window; but Talbot's hands closed upon his collar, and held him as if in a vice.

"You'd better not trifle with me," cried Mr. Bulstrode; "I've been accustomed to deal with refractory Sepoys in India,[1] and I've had a struggle with a tiger before now. Show me that waistcoat!"

"I won't!"

"By the Heaven above us, you shall!"

"I won't!"

The two men closed with each other in a hand-to-hand struggle. Powerful as the soldier was, he found himself more than matched by Stephen Hargraves, whose thick-set frame, broad shoulders, and sinewy arms were almost Herculean in their build. The struggle lasted for a considerable time, – or for a time that seemed considerable to both of the combatants; but at last it drew towards its termination, and the heir of all the Bulstrodes, the commander of squadrons of horse, the man who had done battle with bloodthirsty Sikhs, and ridden against the black mouths of Russian cannon at Balaclava,[2] felt that he could scarcely hope to hold out much longer against the half-witted hanger-on of the Mellish stables. The horny fingers of the "Softy" were upon his throat, the long arms of the "Softy" were writhing round him, and in another moment Talbot Bulstrode lay upon the floor of the north lodge, with the "Softy's" knee planted upon his heaving chest.

Another moment, and in the dim moonlight, – the candle had been thrown down and trampled upon in the beginning of the scuffle, – the heir of Bulstrode Castle saw Stephen Hargraves fumbling with his disengaged hand in his breast-pocket.

One moment more, and Mr. Bulstrode heard that sharp metallic noise only associated with the opening of a clasp-knife.

---

1 i.e. Rebellious Indian soldiers ("sepoys") serving under British discipline in India. Possibly a reference to the Indian Mutiny of April 1857, but since the novel starts in August 1857 and Talbot is still walking with a cane because of his Crimean War wound, this probably refers more generally to rebellion among native soldiers.

2 Presumably Talbot was engaged in the campaigns of the Sikh Wars (1845-46; 1848-49) before he fought in the Crimea, facing the mouths of the cannon at Balaclava in the Charge of the Light Brigade (see 76, n.4). He would have been 20 or 21 in 1845.

"E'es," hissed the "Softy," with his hot breath close upon the fallen man's cheek, "you wanted t' see th' weskit, did you; but you sha'n't, for I'll serve you as I served him. 'Taint loikely I'll let you stand between me and two thousand pound."

Talbot Raleigh Bulstrode had a faint notion that a broad Sheffield blade flashed in the silvery moonlight; but at this moment his senses grew confused under the iron grip of the "Softy's" hand, and he knew little, except that there was a sudden crashing of glass behind him, a quick trampling of feet, and a strange voice roaring some seafaring oath above his head. The suffocating pressure was suddenly removed from his throat; some one, or something, was hurled into a corner of the little room; and Mr. Bulstrode sprang to his feet, a trifle dazed and bewildered, but quite ready to do battle again.

"Who is it?" he cried.

"It's me, Samuel Prodder," answered the voice that had uttered that dreadful seafaring oath. "You were pretty nigh done for, mate, when I came aboard. It aint the first time I've been up here after dark, takin' a quiet stroll and a pipe, before turning in over yonder." Mr. Prodder indicated Doncaster by a backward jerk of his thumb. "I'd been watchin' the light from a distance, till it went out suddenly five minutes ago, and then I came up close to see what was the matter. I don't know who you are, or what you are, or why you've been quarrelling; but I know you've been pretty near as nigh your death to-night as ever that chap was in the wood."

"The waistcoat!" gasped Mr. Bulstrode; "let me see the waistcoat!"

He sprang once more upon the "Softy," who had rushed towards the door, and was trying to beat out the panel with his iron-bound clog; but this time Mr. Bulstrode had a stalwart ally in the merchant-captain.

"A bit of rope comes uncommon handy in these cases," said Samuel Prodder; "for which reason I always make a point of carrying it somewhere about me."

He plunged up to his elbow in one of the capacious pockets of his tourist peg-tops, and produced a short coil of tarry rope. As he might have lashed a seaman to a mast in the last crisis of a wreck, so he lashed Mr. Stephen Hargraves now, binding him right and left, until the struggling arms and legs, and writhing trunk, were fain to be still.

"*Now*, if you want to ask him any questions, I make no doubt he'll answer 'em," said Mr. Prodder, politely. "You'll find him a deal quieter after that."

"I can't thank you now," Talbot answered hurriedly; "there'll be time enough for that by-and-by."

"Ay, ay, to be sure, mate," growled the captain; "no thanks is needed where no thanks is due. Is there anything else I can do for you?"

"Yes, a good deal presently; but I must find this waistcoat first. Where did he put it, I wonder? Stay, I'd better try and get a light. Keep your eye upon that man while I look for it."

Captain Prodder only nodded. He looked upon his scientific lashing of the "Softy" as the triumph of art; but he hovered near his prisoner in compliance with Talbot's request, ready to fall upon him if he should make any attempt to stir.

There was enough moonlight to enable Mr. Bulstrode to find the lucifers and candlestick after a few minutes' search. The candle was not improved by having been trodden upon; but Talbot contrived to light it, and then set to work to look for the waistcoat.

The bundle had rolled into a corner. It was tightly bound with a quantity of whip-cord, and was harder than it could have been had it consisted solely of the waistcoat.

"Hold the light for me while I undo this," Talbot cried, thrusting the candlestick into Mr. Prodder's hand. He was so impatient that he could scarcely wait while he cut the whipcord about the bundle with the "Softy's" huge clasp-knife, which he had picked up while searching for the candle.

"I thought so," he said, as he unrolled the waistcoat; "the money's here."

The money was there, in a small Russia-leather pocket-book, in which Aurora had given it to the murdered man. If there had been any confirmation needed for this fact, the savage yell of rage which broke from Stephen's lips would have afforded that confirmation.

"It's the money," cried Talbot Bulstrode. "I call upon you, sir, to bear witness, whoever you may be, that I find this waistcoat and this pocket-book in the possession of this man, and that I take them from him after a struggle, in which he attempts my life."

"Ay, ay! I know him well enough," muttered the sailor; "he's a bad 'un; and him and me have had a stand further, before this."

"And I call upon you to bear witness that this man is the murderer of James Conyers."

"WHAT?" roared Samuel Prodder; "him! Why, the double-dyed villain: it was him that put it into my head that it was my sister Eliza's chi – that it was Mrs. Mellish——"

"Yes, yes, I know. But we've got him now. Will you run to the house, and send some of the men to fetch a constable, while I stop here?"

Mr. Prodder assented willingly. He had assisted Talbot in the first instance without any idea of what the business was to lead to. Now he was quite as much excited as Mr. Bulstrode. He scrambled through the lattice, and ran off to the stables, guided by the lighted windows of the grooms' dormitories.

Talbot waited very quietly while he was gone. He stood at a few paces from the "Softy," watching Mr. Hargraves as he gnawed savagely at his bonds, in the hope perhaps of setting himself free.

"I shall be ready for you," the young Cornishman said quietly, "whenever you're ready for me."

A crowd of grooms and hangers-on came with lanterns before the constables could arrive; and foremost amongst them came Mr. John Mellish, very noisy and very unintelligible. The door of the lodge was opened, and they all burst into the little chamber, where, heedless of grooms, gardeners, stable-boys, hangers-on, and rabble, John Mellish fell on his friend's breast and wept aloud.

L'ENVOI.

WHAT more have I to tell of this simple drama of domestic life? The end has come. The element of tragedy which has been so intermingled in the history of a homely Yorkshire squire and his wife, is henceforth to be banished from the record of their lives. The dark story which began in Aurora Floyd's folly, and culminated in the crime of a half-witted serving-man, has been told from the beginning to the end. It would be worse than useless to linger upon the description of a trial which took place at York at the Michaelmas Assizes. The evidence against Stephen Hargraves was conclusive; and the gallows outside York Castle ended the life of a man who had never been either help or comfort to any one of his fellow-creatures. There was an attempt made to set up a plea of irresponsibility upon the part of the "Softy," and the *sobriquet*[1] which had been given him was urged in his defence; but a set of matter-of-fact-jurymen looking at the circumstances of the murder, saw nothing in it but a most cold-blooded assassination, perpetrated by a wretch whose sole motive was gain; and the verdict which found Stephen Hargraves guilty, was tempered by no recommendation to mercy. The condemned murderer protested his innocence up to the night before his execution, and upon that night made a full confession of his crime, as is generally the custom of his kind. He related how he had followed James Conyers into the wood upon the night of his assignation with Aurora, and how he had watched and listened during the interview. He had shot the trainer in the back while Mr. Conyers sat by the water's edge looking over the notes in the pocket-book, and he had used a button off his waistcoat instead of wadding,[2] not finding anything else suitable for the purpose. He had hidden the waistcoat and pocket-book in a rat-hole in the wainscot of the murdered man's chamber, and, being dismissed from the lodge suddenly, had been compelled to leave his booty behind him, rather than excite suspicion. It was thus that he had returned upon the night on which Talbot found him, meaning to secure his prize and start for Liverpool at six o'clock the following morning.

Aurora and her husband left Mellish Park immediately after the committal of the "Softy" to York prison. They went to the south of France, accompanied by Archibald Floyd, and once more travelled together through scenes which were overshadowed by no sorrowful association. They lingered long at Nice, and here Talbot and Lucy joined them, with an impedimental train of luggage and servants, and a Normandy nurse with a blue-eyed girl-baby. It was at Nice that another baby was born, a black-eyed child – a boy, I believe – but wonderfully like that solemn-faced infant which Mrs. Alexander Floyd carried to the widowed banker two-and-twenty years before at Felden Woods.

---

1 Nickname.
2 A plug of cloth, tow, paper, etc., used to hold powder or shot in place in a gun.

It is almost supererogatory to say that Samuel Prodder, the sea-captain, was cordially received by hearty John Mellish and his wife. He is to be a welcome visitor at the Park whenever he pleases to come; indeed, he is homeward bound from Barbadoes at this very time, his cabin-presses filled to overflowing with presents which he is carrying to Aurora, in the way of chillis preserved in vinegar, guava-jelly, the strongest Jamaica rum, and other trifles suitable for a lady's acceptance. It may be some comfort to the gentlemen in Scotland Yard to know that John Mellish acted liberally to the detective, and gave him the full reward, although Talbot Bulstrode had been the captor of the "Softy."

So we leave Aurora, a little changed, a shade less defiantly bright, perhaps, but unspeakably beautiful and tender, bending over the cradle of her first-born; and though there are alterations being made at Mellish, and loose-boxes for brood mares building upon the site of the north lodge, and a subscription tan-gallop being laid across Harper's Common, I doubt if my heroine will care so much for horseflesh, or take quite so keen an interest in weight-for-age races as compared to handicaps, as she has done in the days that are gone.

THE END.

Appendix A: Victorian Femininity: The Stable, the Home, and the Fast Young Lady

1. "Fast[1] Young Ladies." *Punch*, 18 August 1860.

FAST YOUNG LADIES

Here's a stunning set of us,
　　Fast young ladies;
Here's a flashy set of us,
　　Fast young ladies;
Nowise shy or timorous,
Up to all that men discuss,
Never mind how scandalous,
　　Fast young ladies.

Wide-awakes[2] our heads adorn,
　　Fast young ladies;
Feathers in our hats[3] are worn,
　　Fast young ladies;
Skirts hitched up on spreading frame,[4]
Petticoats as bright as flame,
Dandy high-heeled boots,[5] proclaim
　　Fast young ladies.

Riding habits are the go,
　　Fast young ladies,
When we prance in Rotten Row,[6]
　　Fast young ladies;

1　See *Aurora Floyd*, 62, n.2.
2　Soft felt hats with wide, limp brims and low crowns.
3　In the 1860s hats rapidly replaced bonnets in women's fashion.
4　On a crinoline or cage.
5　A new fashion, strongly associated with the "fast" set.
6　See *Aurora Floyd*, 280, n.3.

Where we're never at a loss
On the theme of "that 'ere 'oss,"[1]
Which, as yet, we do not cross,
    Fast young ladies.

There we scan, as bold as brass,
    Fast young ladies,
Other parties as they pass,
    Fast young ladies;
Parties whom our parents slow,
Tell us we ought not to know;
Shouldn't we, indeed? Why so,
    Fast young ladies?

On the Turf we show our face,
    Fast young ladies;
Know the odds of every race,
    Fast young ladies;
Talk, as sharp as any knife,
Betting slang – we read *Bell's Life:* [2]
That's the ticket for a wife,
    Fast young ladies!

We are not to be hooked in,
    Fast young ladies;
I require a chap with tin,[3]
    Fast young ladies.
Love is humbug; cash the chief
Article in my belief:
All poor matches come to grief,
    Fast young ladies.

---

1 "That here horse," with the h's deliberately dropped in imitation of a lower-class
    accent, just as the reinforced demonstrative "that here" imitates lower-class gram-
    mar.
2 See *Aurora Floyd*, 100, n.1.
3 Slang: money.

Not to marry is my plan,
 Fast young ladies,
Any but a wealthy man,
 Fast young ladies.
Bother that romance and stuff!
She who likes it is a muff;[1]
We are better up to snuff,
 Fast young ladies.

Give me but my quiet weed,[2]
 Fast young ladies,
Bitter ale and ample feed,
 Fast young ladies;
Pay my bills, porte-monnaie store,[3]
Wardrobe stock – I ask no more.
Sentiment we vote a bore,
 Fast young ladies.

2. "Six Reasons Why Ladies Should Not Hunt." *The Field*, 15 April 1854.

1. A lady in the hunting-field is liable to see sights and hear language used that are not exactly adapted for the drawing-room. Nor is it in accordance with the character of a humane and gentle English lady to enjoy the pursuit of an inoffensive animal, which is urged to flight by all the stimulus that fear can impart; for as the fox lives by hunting, well does he know the consequences of being caught by the hounds.

2. It is not becoming in a gentle and modest Englishwoman to be seen careering across country, surmounting every variety of obstacle that presents itself, with the liability to meet with a fall at a fence, or to have a rent made in her habit by a thorn-hedge, and thus occasion-

---

1 Slang: fool.
2 Cigar (then almost exclusively smoked by men).
3 i.e. Fill up ("store") my purse or pocket-book (*porte-monnaie*) with money.

ing the display of more of her person than is generally considered to be in accordance with the rules of propriety.

3. Ladies may rely upon it that their presence in the hunting-field is anything but agreeable to the gentlemen, however much they may be fond of their society in the drawing-room. Gentlemen cannot observe the courtesies of the drawing-room in the hunting-field, except at the sacrifice of their day's sport; they do not like to gallop past a lady, sending the mud flying about her; and at a fence, if there happens to be only one practicable place in it, and a lady is present, she must of course have the precedence, so that, if the pace is good, and the run straight, adieu to the hounds for that day.

4. There is no doubt but that the company assembled at the meet is the best in point of birth, wealth, and station that the country for miles round can produce; but there are others also whose position and character are very different; and as the only distinction in the hunting-field between the peer and the horse-breaker is the comparative merits of the horses they are riding, a lady is unavoidably liable to be seen jostled, and mixed up at gateways, gaps, and fences, with company which husbands, fathers, and brothers, cannot witness with approbation, or without annoyance.

5. If a lady gets up at the end of a run, her horse is seen distressed and in a lather of sweat, and the frequent application of her handkerchief to her own face, shows that her own exertions have not been trifling. The probability now is that she has to ride her tired horse some miles home; and now that the excitement and emulation of the run are over, ... unless the fair huntress wears a spur, and use it well too, she will have considerable difficulty in reaching home. Is this becoming to a modest, humane, and gentle Englishwoman?

6. The last reason I shall bring forward is this, that lady fox-hunters expose their horses to great risk of accidents, and a numerous class of diseases from over exertion, to which, if ridden as ladies should ride their horses, they are not very liable – as, for instance, curbs, strains,

over-reaches,[1] inflammation, &c., which nothing but firing[2] and other severe remedies can get the better of; and it sometimes happens, that in the morning after a day's sport, which the rider had enjoyed very much, she is told that her pet "has thrown out a curb," or "has got a strain of the back sinew, and is hardly able to move in his stall." If she has any compassion for animals suffering, she must now feel regret at the consequences of her yesterday's amusement; but it is too late, and the best thing she can do is to determine not again to expose her horse to such severe exertion as hunting requires.

In her own case, if the lady meets with an accident, and is laid up in consequence, the general feeling among her acquaintance, though it may not be expressed to her in words, is, "It serves her quite right; she had no business out hunting."

FOXHUNTER.

3. "Muscular Education." Unsigned, *Temple Bar*, December 1861.

[L]et a word ... be directed to those under whose care young ladies are advancing to bear their part in sustaining the honours of the race. Happily the days of back-boards[3] are, we believe, gone, and those frightful instruments of torture by which a young lady was made to keep her feet, or, as the phrase was, "her toes turned out," not in any natural form, but with each foot all but in a line with the other, the heels being kept close together – these "stocks" are also only to be found in the archæology of millinery. The same, it is to be feared, however, cannot be said of those steel-ribbed corselets which for many years were allowed to claim their hecatombs of lovely victims to a fashionable shape, and let loose a whole legion of distortion doctors, with their thousand-and-one artificial spines. Fashion has fortunately

---

1   A curb is a hard swelling on the hock or other part of a horse's leg. An over-reach is an injury caused when a horse strikes one of its fore feet with the corresponding hind foot.
2   Cauterizing.
3   A board held or strapped across the back to produce straight posture.

begun to reform itself;[1] at least it is presumable that while short waists and round waists are in vogue, the heart and lungs must be emancipated to a great extent, although, of course, it is still possible to exercise a severe control over the play of those organs by some insidious ligature beneath the pretty belt and buckle. Still, we are warranted in the supposition that there are signs of a healthy revolt against these most mischievous aids to a style of beauty which emanates entirely from the clever artists of *Le Follet*,[2] and even they must be driven to Nature soon for their models.

It is considered the thing just now to run down dashing horsewomen by fastening upon them the epithet "pretty horse-breaker,"[3] that expression being always used as a term of reproach, often as a sneer; but surely it is not unwomanly to take delight in two such noble and high-spirited creatures as a horse and a dog; or shall we be told it is indecorous for ladies to hunt? The writer perhaps is speaking too much from his own point of view; but to him, and, as he fancies, to many like him, a young lady appears far more natural, more herself, and more interesting, when flushed with the glow of health, and the excitement of a gallop through the fresh, life-breathing air, than when framed in the stiff finery of artificial flowers and full dress to act a part for the evening. Then there is the indescribable charm of health and high spirits, for which we all have so keen an instinct: this is a flower one rarely finds in the hot-houses of society. To admire or to sanction the swash-buckler style of manly young lady, who has been betrayed by silly brothers into talking slang and swaggering, is quite another thing. These are habits, indeed, which are as rarely found to be associated, *au coeur*,[4] with high and noble feelings, as these latter qualities are so generally in one who owns to a passion for horses and dogs, which, being interpreted, generally means love for nature, and not unfrequently the finest sense of the true and the beautiful. After all, though

---

1 The crinoline, which made the waist look small simply by contrast, had the effect of diminishing tight lacing.

2 An illustrated French weekly fashion magazine which ran from 1829-75.

3 A contemporary euphemism for prostitute, punning on the word "whore." It referred specifically to the high-class prostitutes who took to riding in Hyde Park's Rotten Row.

4 Fundamentally.

we may feel a wholesome horror of the strong-minded school, the *figurantes*[1] of social science meetings, the "deep in all the 'ologies," perhaps such little innovations as the most delicately moulded hob-nailed boots, felt hats, and Garibaldi shirts,[2] are really healthy physical signs of the times. Rude health brings with it a sort of irresistible spirit of opposition and independence, that means no harm: like the prancing of a spirited filly fresh up from grass, there's no vice in it, and the pretty creature will soon take to the bit, especially under a light hand, and become invaluable.

But the best argument in favour of riding for ladies is, that it offers almost the only violent exercise open to them; and violent exercise is necessary for strong health. As to dancing, that is violent enough in all conscience, but entirely in the wrong direction; the chest being confined, while the breathing is raised to the highest pitch of rapidity, feeding on air of the hottest and stalest kind, loaded with dust and perfumes, the heart stirred till it beats like that of a frightened bird. All this awful waste of resources, this consuming fire in the system, is made more destructive by choosing the hours which Nature demands for sleep and renovation. If this favourite amusement must be had, and no doubt it is in nature that it must, then we ought to have dancing-rooms as cool and well ventilated as a gymnasium, instead of the quasi Turkish bath to which we have so generally to submit.

The faculty might curse the day, but it would be a real blessing to mothers, if more open-air amusements and recreations could be brought into fashion in which ladies could join.

Of the few good exercises enticing enough to keep their votaries in the field, archery is the best. It has decidedly gained in public favour of late, and deserves to be encouraged in every way; it is a very superior pastime to the new game of *croquet*;[3] indeed, this is too idle a

---

1 Minor role players.
2 A kind of blouse worn by women in imitation of the Italian patriot and soldier Giuseppe Garibaldi (1807-82) and his followers, originally bright red but later in other colours as well.
3 After its introduction in the 1850s, croquet quickly became extremely popular, with rapid growth in clubs and tournaments in the 1850s and 1860s. By the late 1870s, however, its popularity had collapsed: it was seen to provide too little exercise, as this article suggests.

game to be compared with archery, which has a certain nobleness in its associations, and in the skill demanded for success. Neither of these games, however, offers the opportunity for any thing like violent exertion, and they are apt to encourage a disposition to look pretty, and put on fascinating *poses*, rather than to excite the whole energies, as a thoroughly good sport should. Young ladies at school have the great advantage of being permitted to be a little hoydenish; and if we were to speak as a father, it would be to say, that your hoyden is not to be put down as a rude tom-boy. Let her by all means bowl her hoop, skip, and play long-rope to giddy distraction; and even play bat-trap[1] and cricket, with an occasional pull on the lake or river. But better than all is the regular drill and systematic exercise of a gymnasium. Let no one suppose that wielding the clubs,[2] hanging on the horizontal bar, or, indeed, any strain upon the arms, ever makes the hands clumsy; that it ever interferes with the finest needlework, the most delicate drawing; or that that highly-prized quality, the touch of the pianoforte-player, is destroyed by it. It is proved beyond question that the hand becomes more delicate and obedient the more it is used in every kind of exercise; therefore, the excuse we often hear against romping games as "spoiling the hands" has no foundation: even the thick hard skin on workmen's hands is found rather to increase the sense of touch than to diminish it....

Not very long ago a whisper came across the water that England had entered upon her *decadence*; it was suggested that the race was dwindling under the insidious and absorbing power of the merchant and manufacturing interests. The policy of universal compromise,[3] advocated by certain of the philosophical school of would-be statesmen, gave a colouring of probability to the thought begotten by the wish of our enemies; but how do we stand now? The material health

---

1 Popular from the 14th to the late 19th century, bat-trap was a form of rounders or early baseball in which the ball was projected into play by means of a trap rather than being thrown by a pitcher.

2 In the 19th century, so-called "Indian clubs," wooden weights held in the hand, were used for exercise and upper-body toning.

3 May refer to the pacifist views of Richard Cobden (1804-65) and others, who advocated the cause of international arbitration prior to and during the Crimean War.

and prosperity of the nation were never so promising. Sanitary reform[1] has already improved the natural life, and suppressed the life-destroying agents of the crowded cities and "the Black Country,"[2] where coal and iron have banished the flocks and burnt up the pasture. In France, in 1859, there were nearly a million deaths, and 311,385 more people died than in Great Britain; while 23,034 more children were born than in France.

The establishment of baths, and the abundant supply of good water throughout the country, have contributed to this improvement in the condition of the community; and it is satisfactory to see that the use of the bath is decidedly in the ascendant among all classes. The appetite for athletic sports and games is certain to accompany improved health, and an excellent development it would be if public gymnasia on a large scale, with baths of every kind attached, were to be established. There is no reason why they should not be as easily managed as the public baths and washhouses; and the benefit to public health would be incalculable. Next of the Volunteer Movement,[3] which possesses the most important elements of physical education for the nation, the systematic encouragement of athletic exercises in this way should come; and then we can glory still more in the lusty limbs and stout hearts of Old England.

---

1 Following Edwin Chadwick's *Report on the Sanitary Condition of the Labouring Population of Great Britain* (1842), measures were taken to improve public health and living conditions. These included improved water supply and sewers, safer location of cemeteries, and relief of overcrowded living conditions.
2 Parts of Staffordshire and Warwickshire polluted by the coal and iron trades.
3 During the French invasion scare of 1859-60, 100,000 men volunteered for the military under the "Volunteer Movement." This was celebrated as an opportunity for middle-class men to gain military experience and hence manly virtue.

4. "Of Queens' Gardens." John Ruskin,[1] *Sesame and Lilies*, 1865.

"Be thou glad, oh thirsting Desert; let the desert be made cheerful, and bloom as the lily; and the barren places of Jordan shall run wild with wood." – ISAIAH XXXV.I. (Septuagint.)

... I am now going to ask you to consider with me farther, what special portion or kind of ... authority, arising out of noble education, may rightly be possessed by women; and how far they also are called to a true queenly power. Not in their households merely, but over all within their sphere. And in what sense, if they rightly understood and exercised this royal or gracious influence, the order and beauty induced by such benignant power would justify us in speaking of the territories over which each of them reigned, as "Queens' Gardens."

And here, in the very outset, we are met by a far deeper question, which – strange though this may seem – remains among many of us yet quite undecided, in spite of its infinite importance.

We cannot determine what the queenly power of women should be, until we are agreed what their ordinary power should be. We cannot consider how education may fit them for any widely extending duty, until we are agreed what is their true constant duty. And there never was a time when wilder words were spoken, or more vain imagination permitted, respecting this question – quite vital to all social happiness. The relations of the womanly to the manly nature, their different capacities of intellect or of virtue, seem never to have been yet measured with entire consent. We hear of the mission and of the rights of Woman, as if these could ever be separate from the mission and the rights of Man; – as if she and her lord were creatures of independent kind and of irreconcileable claim. This, at least, is wrong. And not less wrong – perhaps even more foolishly wrong (for I will anticipate thus far what I hope to prove) – is the idea that woman is only the shadow and attendant image of her lord, owing him a

---

1 John Ruskin (1819-1900), Victorian prose writer, social and aesthetic critic. In Manchester in 1864, Ruskin delivered two lectures on the respective duties of men and women: "Of Kings' Treasuries" (on men's duty) and "Of Queens' Gardens" (on women's).

thoughtless and servile obedience, and supported altogether in her weakness by the pre-eminence of his fortitude.

This, I say, is the most foolish of all errors respecting her who was made to be the helpmate of man. As if he could be helped effectively by a shadow, or worthily by a slave!

Let us try, then, whether we cannot get at some clear and harmonious idea (it must be harmonious if it is true) of what womanly mind and virtue are in power and office, with respect to man's; and how their relations, rightly accepted, aid, and increase, the vigour, and honour, and authority of both....

Let us see whether the greatest, the wisest, the purest-hearted of all ages are agreed in any wise on this point: let us hear the testimony they have left respecting what they held to be the true dignity of woman, and her mode of help to man.

And first let us take Shakespeare.

Note broadly in the outset, Shakespeare has no heroes; – he has only heroines. There is not one entirely heroic figure in all his plays, except the slight sketch of Henry the Fifth, exaggerated for the purposes of the stage; and the still slighter Valentine in The Two Gentlemen of Verona. In his laboured and perfect plays you have no hero. Othello would have been one, if his simplicity had not been so great as to leave him the prey of every base practice round him; but he is the only example even approximating to the heroic type. Coriolanus – Cæsar – Anthony, stand in flawed strength, and fall by their vanities; – Hamlet is indolent, and drowsily speculative; Romeo an impatient boy; the Merchant of Venice languidly submissive to adverse fortune; Kent, in King Lear, is entirely noble at heart, but too rough and unpolished to be of true use at the critical time, and he sinks into the office of a servant only. Orlando, no less noble, is yet the despairing toy of chance, followed, comforted, saved, by Rosalind. Whereas there is hardly a play that has not a perfect woman in it, steadfast in grave hope, and errorless purpose: Cordelia, Desdemona, Isabella, Hermione, Imogen, Queen Katherine, Perdita, Sylvia, Viola, Rosalind, Helena, and last, and perhaps loveliest, Virgilia, are all faultless; conceived in the highest heroic type of humanity.[1]

---

1 A plethora of Shakespearean references. For Coriolanus, see the play of the same

Then observe, secondly,

The catastrophe of every play is caused always by the folly or fault of a man; the redemption, if there be any, is by the wisdom and virtue of a woman, and, failing that, there is none. The catastrophe of King Lear is owing to his own want of judgment, his impatient vanity, his misunderstanding of his children; the virtue of his one true daughter would have saved him from all the injuries of the others, unless he had cast her away from him; as it is, she all but saves him.

Of Othello I need not trace the tale; – nor the one weakness of his so mighty love; nor the inferiority of his perceptive intellect to that even of the second woman character in the play, the Emilia who dies in wild testimony against his error: – "Oh, murderous coxcomb! What should such a fool Do with so good a wife?"[1]

In Romeo and Juliet, the wise and entirely brave stratagem of the wife is brought to ruinous issue by the reckless impatience of her husband. In Winter's Tale, and in Cymbeline, the happiness and existence of two princely households, lost through long years, and imperilled to the death by the folly and obstinacy of the husbands, are redeemed at last by the queenly patience and wisdom of the wives. In Measure for Measure, the injustice of the judges, and the corrupt cowardice of the brother, are opposed to the victorious truth and adamantine purity of a woman. In Coriolanus, the mother's counsel, acted upon in time, would have saved her son from all evil; his momentary forgetfulness of it is his ruin; her prayer, at last granted, saves him – not, indeed, from death, but from the curse of living as the destroyer of his country.

And what shall I say of Julia, constant against the fickleness of a lover who is a mere wicked child? – of Helena, against the petulance and insult of a careless youth? – of the patience of Hero, the passion of Beatrice, and the calmly devoted wisdom of the "unlessoned girl,"[2]

---

name; for Caesar see *Julius Caesar*; for Anthony, *Antony and Cleopatra*; for Orlando and Rosalind, *As You Like It*; for Cordelia, *King Lear*; for Desdemona, *Othello*; for Isabella, *Measure for Measure*; for Hermione, *The Winter's Tale*; for Imogen, *Cymbeline*; for Queen Katherine, *Henry VIII*; for Perdita, *The Winter's Tale*; for Sylvia [Silvia], *The Two Gentlemen of Verona*; for Viola, *Twelfth Night*; for Helena, *All's Well That Ends Well*, or, less likely, *A Midsummer Night's Dream*; for Virgilia, *Coriolanus*.

1 *Othello* V.ii.231-2.

2 For Julia, see *The Two Gentlemen of Verona*; for Helena, see *A Midsummer Night's*

who appears among the helplessness, the blindness, and the vindictive passions of men, as a gentle angel, to save merely by her presence, and defeat the worst intensities of crime by her smile?

Observe, further, among all the principal figures in Shakespeare's plays, there is only one weak woman – Ophelia; and it is because she fails Hamlet at the critical moment, and is not, and cannot in her nature be, a guide to him when he needs her most, that all the bitter catastrophe follows. Finally, though there are three wicked women among the principal figures, Lady Macbeth, Regan, and Goneril,[1] they are felt at once to be frightful exceptions to the ordinary laws of life; fatal in their influence also in proportion to the power for good which they have abandoned.

Such, in broad light, is Shakespeare's testimony to the position and character of women in human life. He represents them as infallibly faithful and wise counsellors, – incorruptibly just and pure examples – strong always to sanctify, even when they cannot save....

Next, take, though more briefly, graver and deeper testimony – that of the great Italians and Greeks. You know well the plan of Dante's great poem – that it is a love-poem to his dead lady, a song of praise for her watch over his soul.[2] Stooping only to pity, never to love, she yet saves him from destruction – saves him from hell. He is going eternally astray in despair; she comes down from heaven to his help, and throughout the ascents of Paradise is his teacher, interpreting for him the most difficult truths, divine and human; and leading him, with rebuke upon rebuke, from star to star....

Now I could multiply witness upon witness of this kind upon you if I had time. I would take Chaucer, and show you why he wrote a Legend of Good Women; but no Legend of Good Men. I would take Spenser, and show you how all his fairy knights are sometimes deceived and sometimes vanquished; but the soul of Una is never darkened, and the spear of Britomart is never broken.[3] Nay, I could go

---

Dream; for Hero and Beatrice, see *Much Ado About Nothing*; the "unlessoned girl" is Portia in *The Merchant of Venice* (III.ii.159).

1 For Regan and Goneril, see *King Lear*.

2 In Dante's *The Divine Comedy*, the speaker is guided to paradise by the spirit of his dead lover, Beatrice.

3 See Spenser's *The Faerie Queene* (1590-1596). Una appears in Book I; Britomart in Books III-V.

back into the mythical teaching of the most ancient times, and show you how the great people, – by one of whose princesses it was appointed that the Lawgiver of all the earth should be educated, rather than by his own kindred; – how that great Egyptian people, wisest then of nations, gave to their Spirit of Wisdom the form of a woman;[1] and into her hand, for a symbol, the weaver's shuttle: and how the name and the form of that spirit, adopted, believed, and obeyed by the Greeks, became that Athena of the olive-helm, and cloudy shield, to whose faith you owe, down to this date, whatever you hold most precious in art, in literature, or in types of national virtue....

I do not insist by any farther argument on this, for I think it should commend itself at once to your knowledge of what has been and to your feeling of what should be. You cannot think that the buckling on of the knight's armour by his lady's hand was a mere caprice of romantic fashion. It is the type of an eternal truth – that the soul's armour is never well set to the heart unless a woman's hand has braced it; and it is only when she braces it loosely that the honour of manhood fails....

But how, you will ask, is the idea of this guiding function of the woman reconcileable with a true wifely subjection? Simply in that it is a *guiding*, not a determining, function. Let me try to show you briefly how these powers seem to be rightly distinguishable.

We are foolish, and without excuse foolish, in speaking of the "superiority" of one sex to the other, as if they could be compared in similar things. Each has what the other has not: each completes the other, and is completed by the other: they are in nothing alike, and the happiness and perfection of both depends on each asking and receiving from the other what the other only can give.

Now their separate characters are briefly these. The man's power is active, progressive, defensive. He is eminently the doer, the creator, the discoverer, the defender. His intellect is for speculation and invention; his energy for adventure, for war, and for conquest, wherever war is just, wherever conquest necessary. But the woman's power is for rule, not for battle, – and her intellect is not for invention or creation, but

---

1   Refers to the Egyptian goddess Neit, identified by the Greeks with Athena.

for sweet ordering, arrangement, and decision. She sees the qualities of things, their claims, and their places. Her great function is Praise; she enters into no contest, but infallibly adjudges the crown of contest. By her office, and place, she is protected from all danger and temptation. The man, in his rough work in open world, must encounter all peril and trial: – to him, therefore, the failure, the offence, the inevitable error: often he must be wounded, or subdued, often misled, and *always* hardened. But he guards the woman from all this; within his house, as ruled by her, unless she herself has sought it, need enter no danger, no temptation, no cause of error or offence. This is the true nature of home – it is the place of Peace; the shelter, not only from all injury, but from all terror, doubt, and division. In so far as it is not this, it is not home; so far as the anxieties of the outer life penetrate into it, and the inconsistently-minded, unknown, unloved, or hostile society of the outer world is allowed by either husband or wife to cross the threshold, it ceases to be home; it is then only a part of that outer world which you have roofed over, and lighted fire in. But so far as it is a sacred place, a vestal temple,[1] a temple of the hearth watched over by Household Gods, before whose faces none may come but those whom they can receive with love, – so far as it is this, and roof and fire are types only of a nobler shade and light, – shade as of the rock in a weary land, and light as of the Pharos[2] in the stormy sea; – so far it vindicates the name, and fulfils the praise, of Home.

And wherever a true wife comes, this home is always round her. The stars only may be over her head; the glowworm in the night-cold grass may be the only fire at her foot: but home is yet wherever she is; and for a noble woman it stretches far round her, better than ceiled with cedar, or painted with vermilion, shedding its quiet light far, for those who else were homeless.

This, then, I believe to be, – will you not admit it to be, – the woman's true place and power? But do not you see that, to fulfil this, she must – as far as one can use such terms of a human creature – be

---

1   Each Roman city had a temple dedicated to Vesta, goddess of the hearth. Vesta was represented in her temples by the living symbol of fire, which was never allowed to go out.
2   The name of a lighthouse on an island off Alexandria.

incapable of error? So far as she rules, all must be right, or nothing is. She must be enduringly, incorruptibly good; instinctively, infallibly wise – wise, not for self-development, but for self-renunciation: wise, not that she may set herself above her husband, but that she may never fail from his side: wise, not with the narrowness of insolent and loveless pride, but with the passionate gentleness of an infinitely variable, because infinitely applicable, modesty of service – the true changefulness of woman. In that great sense – "La donna e mobile," not "Qual più' al vento;" no, nor yet "Variable as the shade, by the light quivering aspen made;"[1] but variable as the *light*, manifold in fair and serene division, that it may take the colour of all that it falls upon, and exalt it.

I have been trying, thus far, to show you what should be the place, and what the power of woman. Now, secondly, we ask, What kind of education is to fit her for these?...

The first of our duties to her – no thoughtful persons now doubt this, – is to secure for her such physical training and exercise as may confirm her health, and perfect her beauty; the highest refinement of that beauty being unattainable without splendour of activity and of delicate strength. To perfect her beauty, I say, and increase its power; it cannot be too powerful, nor shed its sacred light too far: only remember that all physical freedom is vain to produce beauty without a corresponding freedom of heart....

Thus, then, you have first to mould her physical frame, and then, as the strength she gains will permit you, to fill and temper her mind with all knowledge and thoughts which tend to confirm its natural instincts of justice, and refine its natural tact of love.

All such knowledge should be given her as may enable her to understand, and even to aid, the work of men: and yet it should be given, not as knowledge, – not as if it were, or could be, for her an

---

1   In distinguishing between the negative quality of fickleness and the positive quality of "true changefulness" in women, Ruskin quotes from Verdi's *Rigoletto* (1851). He softens the meaning of "*La donna e mobile*" (Woman is capricious/fickle) to imply flexibility, contrasting it with the next line of the same aria, "*Qual più' al vento*" (like feathers blown before every wind). The quotation from Canto 6, Stanza 30 of Sir Walter Scott's *Marmion* (1808) is also used to contrast types of changefulness. The good woman is not "[v]ariable as the shade," but "variable as the *light*."

object to know; but only to feel, and to judge. It is of no moment, as a matter of pride or perfectness in herself, whether she knows many languages or one; but it is of the utmost, that she should be able to show kindness to a stranger, and to understand the sweetness of a stranger's tongue. It is of no moment to her own worth or dignity that she should be acquainted with this science or that; but it is of the highest that she should be trained in habits of accurate thought; that she should understand the meaning, the inevitableness, and the loveliness of natural laws, and follow at least some one path of scientific attainment, as far as to the threshold of that bitter Valley of Humiliation,[1] into which only the wisest and bravest of men can descend, owning themselves for ever children, gathering pebbles on a boundless shore. It is of little consequence how many positions of cities she knows, or how many dates of events, or how many names of celebrated persons – it is not the object of education to turn a woman into a dictionary; but it is deeply necessary that she should be taught to enter with her whole personality into the history she reads; to picture the passages of it vitally in her own bright imagination; to apprehend, with her fine instincts, the pathetic circumstances and dramatic relations, which the historian too often only eclipses by his reasoning, and disconnects by his arrangement: it is for her to trace the hidden equities of divine reward, and catch sight, through the darkness, of the fateful threads of woven fire that connect error with its retribution. But, chiefly of all, she is to be taught to extend the limits of her sympathy with respect to that history which is being for ever determined, as the moments pass in which she draws her peaceful breath; and to the contemporary calamity which, were it but rightly mourned by her, would recur no more hereafter. She is to exercise herself in imagining what would be the effects upon her mind and conduct, if she were daily brought into the presence of the suffering which is not the less real because shut from her sight. She is to be taught somewhat to understand the nothingness of the proportion which that little world

---

1   In *The Pilgrim's Progress* (Part 1, 1678) Christian battles with Apollyon in the Valley of Humiliation. As Part 2 (1684) makes clear, it is easier for women and children to walk through the Valley: as the Boy Shepherd sings, "He that is down need fear no fall, / He that is low, no Pride." Education, Ruskin suggests, can teach this Christian humility.

in which she lives and loves, bears to the world in which God lives and loves; – and solemnly she is to be taught to strive that her thoughts of piety may not be feeble in proportion to the number they embrace, nor her prayer more languid than it is for the momentary relief from pain of her husband or her child, when it is uttered for the multitudes of those who have none to love them, – and is "for all who are desolate and oppressed."[1]...

I believe, then ... that a girl's education should be nearly, in its course and material of study, the same as a boy's; but quite differently directed. A woman, in any rank of life, ought to know whatever her husband is likely to know, but to know it in a different way. His command of it should be foundational and progressive, hers, general and accomplished for daily and helpful use. Not but that it would often be wiser in men to learn things in a womanly sort of way, for present use, and to seek for the discipline and training of their mental powers in such branches of study as will be afterwards fittest for social service; but, speaking broadly, a man ought to know any language or science he learns, thoroughly while a woman ought to know the same language, or science, only so far as may enable her to sympathise in her husband's pleasures, and in those of his best friends....

Without ... venturing here on any attempt at decision how much novel reading should be allowed, let me at least clearly assert this, that whether novels, or poetry, or history be read, they should be chosen, not for what is *out* of them, but for what is *in* them. The chance and scattered evil that may here and there haunt, or hide itself in, a powerful book, never does any harm to a noble girl; but the emptiness of an author oppresses her, and his amiable folly degrades her. And if she can have access to a good library of old and classical books, there need be no choosing at all. Keep the modern magazine and novel out of your girl's way: turn her loose into the old library every wet day, and let her alone. She will find what is good for her; you cannot: for there is just this difference between the making of a girl's character and a boy's – you may chisel a boy into shape, as you would a rock, or hammer him into it, if he be of a better kind, as you would a piece of bronze. But you cannot hammer a girl into anything. She grows as a

---

1 From the Litany in the Book of Common Prayer.

flower does, – she will wither without sun; she will decay in her sheath, as the narcissus does, if you do not give her air enough; she may fall, and defile her head in dust, if you leave her without help at some moments of her life; but you cannot fetter her; she must take her own fair form and way, if she take any, and in mind as in body, must have always

> "Her household motions light and free
> And steps of virgin liberty."[1]

Let her loose in the library, I say, as you do a fawn in a field. It knows the bad weeds twenty times better than you; and the good ones too, and will eat some bitter and prickly ones, good for it, which you had not the slightest thought were good....

And not only in the material and in the course, but yet more earnestly in the spirit of it, let a girl's education be as serious as a boy's. You bring up your girls as if they were meant for sideboard ornaments, and then complain of their frivolity. Give them the same advantages that you give their brothers – appeal to the same grand instincts of virtue in them; teach *them* also that courage and truth are the pillars of their being: do you think that they would not answer that appeal, brave and true as they are even now, when you know that there is hardly a girl's school in this Christian kingdom where the children's courage or sincerity would be thought of half so much importance as their way of coming in at a door; ...

Thus far, then, of the nature, thus far of the teaching, of woman, and thus of her household office, and queenliness. We come now to our last, our widest question, – What is her queenly office with respect to the state?

Generally, we are under an impression that a man's duties are public, and a woman's private. But this is not altogether so. A man has a personal work or duty, relating to his own home, and a public work or duty, which is the expansion of the other, relating to the state. So a woman has a personal work or duty, relating to her own home, and a

---

14   From William Wordsworth's poem, "She was a Phantom of delight" (1807), lines 13-
14.

public work and duty, which is also the expansion of that.

Now the man's work for his own home is, as has been said, to secure its maintenance, progress, and defence; the woman's to secure its order, comfort, and loveliness.

Expand both these functions. The man's duty, as a member of a commonwealth, is to assist in the maintenance, in the advance, in the defence of the state. The woman's duty, as a member of the commonwealth, is to assist in the ordering, in the comforting, and in the beautiful adornment of the state.

What the man is at his own gate, defending it, if need be, against insult and spoil, that also, not in a less, but in a more devoted measure, he is to be at the gate of his country, leaving his home, if need be, even to the spoiler, to do his more incumbent work there.

And, in like manner, what the woman is to be within her gates, as the centre of order, the balm of distress, and the mirror of beauty; that she is also to be without her gates, where order is more difficult, distress more imminent, loveliness more rare....

And whether consciously or not, you must be, in many a heart, enthroned: there is no putting by that crown; queens you must always be; queens to your lovers; queens to your husbands and your sons; queens of higher mystery to the world beyond, which bows itself, and will for ever bow, before the myrtle crown, and the stainless sceptre, of womanhood. But, alas! you are too often idle and careless queens, grasping at majesty in the least things, while you abdicate it in the greatest; and leaving misrule and violence to work their will among men, in defiance of the power, which, holding straight in gift from the Prince of all Peace,[1] the wicked among you betray, and the good forget.

"Prince of Peace." Note that name. When kings rule in that name, and nobles, and the judges of the earth, they also, in their narrow place, and mortal measure, receive the power of it. There are no other rulers than they: other rule than theirs is but *mis*rule; they who govern verily "Dei gratiâ"[2] are all princes, yes, or princesses, of peace. There is

---

1   See Isaiah 9:6, referring to the Messiah: "his name shall be called Wonderful, Counseller, The mighty God, The everlasting Father, The Prince of Peace."

2   "By the grace of God." The phrase is appended to the formal statement of the titles of sovereigns.

not a war in the world, no, nor an injustice, but you women are answerable for it; not in that you have provoked, but in that you have not hindered. Men, by their nature, are prone to fight; they will fight for any cause, or for none. It is for you to choose their cause for them, and to forbid them when there is no cause. There is no suffering, no injustice, no misery in the earth, but the guilt of it lies lastly with you. Men can bear the sight of it, but you should not be able to bear it. Men may tread it down without sympathy in their own struggle; but men are feeble in sympathy, and contracted in hope; it is you only who can feel the depths of pain; and conceive the way of its healing. Instead of trying to do this, you turn away from it; you shut yourselves within your park walls and garden gates; and you are content to know that there is beyond them a whole world in wilderness – a world of secrets which you dare not penetrate; and of suffering which you dare not conceive.

I tell you that this is to me quite the most amazing among the phenomena of humanity. I am surprised at no depths to which, when once warped from its honour, that humanity can be degraded. I do not wonder at the miser's death, with his hands, as they relax, dropping gold. I do not wonder at the sensualist's life, with the shroud wrapped about his feet. I do not wonder at the single-handed murder of a single victim, done by the assassin in the darkness of the railway, or reed-shadow of the marsh. I do not even wonder at the myriad-handed murder of multitudes, done boastfully in the daylight, by the frenzy of nations, and the immeasurable, unimaginable guilt, heaped up from hell to heaven, of their priests, and kings. But this is wonderful to me – oh, how wonderful! – to see the tender and delicate woman among you, with her child at her breast, and a power, if she would wield it, over it, and over its father, purer than the air of heaven, and stronger than the seas of earth – nay, a magnitude of blessing which her husband would not part with for all that earth itself, though it were made of one entire and perfect chrysolite:[1] – to see her abdicate this majesty to play at precedence with her next-door

---

1   See Othello's speech to Emilia concerning the supposedly false Desdemona: "had she been true,/ If heaven would make me such another world,/ Of one entire and perfect chrysolite,/ I'ld not have sold her for it." (*Othello* V.ii.144-47).

neighbour! This is wonderful – oh, wonderful! – to see her, with every innocent feeling fresh within her, go out in the morning into her garden to play with the fringes of its guarded flowers, and lift their heads when they are drooping, with her happy smile upon her face, and no cloud upon her brow, because there is a little wall around her place of peace: and yet she knows, in her heart, if she would only look for its knowledge, that, outside of that little rose-covered wall, the wild grass, to the horizon, is torn up by the agony of men, and beat level by the drift of their life-blood....

Who is it, think you, who stands at the gate of [a] sweeter garden, alone, waiting for you? Did you ever hear, not of a Maude, but a Madeleine, who went down to her garden in the dawn, and found One waiting at the gate, whom she supposed to be the gardener?[1] Have you not sought Him often; – sought Him in vain, all through the night; – sought Him in vain at the gate of that old garden where the fiery sword is set? He is never there; but at the gate of *this* garden He is waiting always – waiting to take your hand – ready to go down to see the fruits of the valley, to see whether the vine has flourished, and the pomegranate budded. There you shall see with Him the little tendrils of the vines that His hand is guiding – there you shall see the pomegranate springing where His hand cast the sanguine seed; – more: you shall see the troops of the angel keepers that, with their wings, wave away the hungry birds from the pathsides where He has sown, and call to each other between the vineyard rows, "Take us the foxes, the little foxes, that spoil the vines, for our vines have tender grapes." Oh – you queens – you queens! among the hills and happy greenwood of this land of yours, shall the foxes have holes, and the birds of the air have nests; and, in your cities, shall the stones cry out against you, that they are the only pillows where the Son of Man can lay His head?[2]

---

1 In Tennyson's *Maud* (1855), the rich Maud meets her forbidden lover in the garden at dawn; they are discovered by her brother, who is killed in the ensuing duel. Ruskin redirects the reader to a Biblical context in which to consider women walking in the garden at dawn: following the crucifixion, Mary Magdalen went at dawn to the sepulchre where Jesus had been laid, and, meeting the risen Christ, mistook him for a gardener (John 20:1-17).

2 A plethora of biblical references. The flaming sword is set over the gates of Eden (the "old garden") in Genesis 3:24. The next sentence refers to the Song of

Appendix B: Reviews and Responses

1. "Sensation Novels." Unsigned, [H.L. Mansel][1] *Quarterly Review*, April 1863.

'I DON'T like preaching to the nerves instead of the judgment,' was the remark of a shrewd observer of human nature, in relation to a certain class of popular sermons. The remark need not be limited to sermons alone. A class of literature has grown up around us, usurping in many respects, intentionally or unintentionally, a portion of the preacher's office, playing no inconsiderable part in moulding the minds and forming the habits and tastes of its generation; and doing so principally, we had almost said exclusively, by 'preaching to the nerves.' It would almost seem as if the paradox of Cabanis, *les nerfs, voilà tout l'homme*,[2] had been banished from the realm of philosophy only to claim a wider empire in the domain of fiction – at least if we may judge by the very large class of writers who seem to acknowledge no other element in human nature to which they can appeal. Excitement, and excitement alone, seems to be the great end at which they aim – an end which must be accomplished at any cost by some means or other, 'si possis, recte; si non, quocunque modo.'[3] And as excitement, even when harmless in kind, cannot be continually

---

Solomon (6:11): "I went down into the garden of nuts to see the fruits of the valley, and to see whether the vine flourished, and the pomegranates budded." "Take us the foxes ..." is also from the Song of Solomon (2:15). In Matthew 8:20, Jesus says, "The foxes have holes, and the birds of the air have nests; but the Son of man hath not where to lay his head." Finally, in Genesis 28:11, Jacob sleeps with stones for his pillow.

1 Henry Longueville Mansel (1820-71), philosopher, clergyman, and metaphysician. In 1855 Mansel became the first Wayneflete professor of moral and metaphysical philosophy at Oxford; in 1866 he became professor of ecclesiastical history at Oxford; and in 1868 Dean of St. Paul's.

2 Man is nothing but a nervous system. Pierre-Jean-Georges Cabanis (1757-1808), French materialist philosopher and doctor, argued in his *Rapports du physique et du moral de l'homme* (1802) that the brain was analogous to the digestive system, with sensory impressions its food and thought its product.

3 "If possible, by right means; if not, in whatever way possible."

produced without becoming morbid in degree, works of this class manifest themselves as belonging, some more, some less, but all to some extent, to the morbid phenomena of literature – indications of a wide-spread corruption, of which they are in part both the effect and the cause; called into existence to supply the cravings of a diseased appetite, and contributing themselves to foster the disease, and to stimulate the want which they supply.

The sensation novel is the counterpart of the spasmodic poem.[1] They represent 'the selfsame interest with a different leaning.' The one leans outward, the other leans inward; the one aims at convulsing the soul of the reader, the other professes to owe its birth to convulsive throes in the soul of the writer. But with this agreement there is also a difference. There is not a poet or poetaster of the spasmodic school but is fully persuaded of his own inspiration and the immortality of his work....

Not so the sensation novelist. No divine influence can be imagined as presiding over the birth of his work, beyond the market-law of demand and supply; no more immortality is dreamed of for it than for the fashions of the current season. A commercial atmosphere floats around works of this class, redolent of the manufactory and the shop. The public want novels, and novels must be made – so many yards of printed stuff, sensation-pattern, to be ready by the beginning of the season. And if the demands of the novel-reading public were to increase to the amount of a thousand per season, no difficulty would be found in producing a thousand works of the average merit....

These circumstances of production naturally have their effect on the quality of the articles produced. Written to meet an ephemeral demand, aspiring only to an ephemeral existence, it is natural that they should have recourse to rapid and ephemeral methods of awakening the interest of their readers, striving to act as the dram[2] or the dose, rather than as the solid food, because the effect is more immediately perceptible. And as the perpetual cravings of the dram-drinker

---

1   A term coined by the critic William Aytoun (1818-65) to ridicule the Romantic extravagance of poets such as Sydney Dobell (1824-74), Philip James Bailey (1816-1902), and Alexander Smith (1830-67).
2   A draught of stimulant or liquor.

or the valetudinarian[1] for spirits or physic are hardly intelligible to the man of sound health and regular appetites, so, to one called from more wholesome studies to survey the wide field of sensational literature, it is difficult to realise the idea which its multifarious contents necessarily suggest, that these books must form the staple mental food of a very large class of readers....

A sensation novel, as a matter of course, abounds in incident. Indeed, as a general rule, it consists of nothing else. Deep knowledge of human nature, graphic delineations of individual character, vivid representations of the aspects of Nature or the workings of the soul – all the higher features of the creative art – would be a hindrance rather than a help to a work of this kind. The unchanging principles of philosophy, the 'thing of beauty' that 'is a joy for ever,'[2] would be out of place in a work whose aim is to produce temporary excitement. 'Action, action, action!' though in a different sense from that intended by the great orator,[3] is the first thing needful,[4] and the second, and the third....

The sensation novel, be it mere trash or something worse, is usually a tale of our own times. Proximity is, indeed, one great element of sensation. It is necessary to be near a mine to be blown up by its explosion; and a tale which aims at electrifying the nerves of the reader is never thoroughly effective unless the scene be laid in our own days and among the people we are in the habit of meeting. We read with little emotion, though it comes in the form of history, Livy's narrative of the secret poisonings carried on by nearly two hundred Roman ladies;[5] we feel but a feeble interest in an authentic record of the crimes of a Borgia or a Brinvilliers;[6] but we are thrilled with hor-

---

1   A valetudinarian is a person constantly concerned with his/her ailments.
2   From John Keats' *Endymion* (1818): "A thing of beauty is a joy for ever:/ Its loveliness increases; it will never/ Pass into nothingness."
3   So said Demosthenes, when asked to name the three most important qualities of oratory (quoted by Plutarch in *Lives of the Ten Orators*).
4   See Luke 10:42: "But one thing is needful, and Mary hath chosen that good part."
5   Livy (c. 59 BC–c. AD 17), one of the great Roman historians. For his account of the poisonings of 331 BC, see Livy, *History of Rome*, VIII.xvii.
6   Cesare Borgia (1475/6–1507) was portrayed in contemporary propaganda as a monster of lust and cruelty. A number of crimes are attributed to him, but one of which he was clearly the perpetrator was the murder of his brother-in-law, Alfonso, Duke

ror, even in fiction, by the thought that such things may be going on around us and among us. The man who shook our hand with a hearty English grasp half an hour ago – the woman whose beauty and grace were the charm of last night, and whose gentle words sent us home better pleased with the world and with ourselves – how exciting to think that under these pleasing outsides may be concealed some demon in human shape, a Count Fosco or a Lady Audley![1] He may have assumed all that heartiness to conceal some dark plot against our life or honour, or against the life or honour of one yet dearer: she may have left that gay scene to muffle herself in a thick veil and steal to a midnight meeting with some villanous accomplice. He may have a mysterious female, immured in a solitary tower or a private lunatic asylum, destined to come forth hereafter to menace the name and position of the excellent lady whom the world acknowledges as his wife: she may have a husband lying dead at the bottom of a well,[2] and a fatherless child nobody knows where. All this is no doubt very exciting; but even excitement may be purchased too dearly; and we may be permitted to doubt whether the pleasure of a nervous shock is worth the cost of so much morbid anatomy if the picture be true, or so much slanderous misrepresentation if it be false....

Of particular offences, which are almost always contemporary and sometimes personal, undoubtedly the first place must be given to Bigamy. Indeed, so popular has this crime become, as to give rise to an entire sub-class in this branch of literature, which may be distinguished as that of Bigamy Novels. It is astonishing how many of our modern writers have selected this interesting breach of morality and law as the peg on which to hang a mystery and a dénouement. Of the tales on our list, no less than eight are bigamy stories: – 'Lady Audley's Secret,' 'Aurora Floyd,' 'Clinton Maynard,' 'Recommended to Mercy,' 'The Law of Divorce,' 'The Daily Governess,' 'Only a Woman,' 'The

---

of Bisceglie, in August 1500. Marie-Madeleine-Marguérite d'Aubray, Marquise de Brinvilliers (c. 1630-1676) poisoned her father and two brothers and attempted to poison her husband. She was beheaded in 1676.

1 Count Fosco is one of two villains of Wilkie Collins' *The Woman in White* (1860); Lady Audley is the villainess of Braddon's bestselling *Lady Audley's Secret* (1862).

2 This refers to the plot of Braddon's *Lady Audley's Secret* (1862), in which the bigamous heroine pushes her first husband down a well on her second husband's estate.

Woman of Spirit,'[1] all hang their narrative, wholly or in part, on bigamy in act, or bigamy in intention, on the existence or supposed existence of two wives to the same husband, or two husbands to the same wife....

Of our list of Bigamy Novels, some will be noticed under other characters, and some are not worth noticing at all. The two first-named claim a notice as bigamy novels *par excellence*, the whole interest of the story turning on this circumstance. Though both exaggerated specimens of the sensational type, they are the works of an author of real power, who is capable of better things than drawing highly-coloured portraits of beautiful fiends and fast young ladies burdened with superfluous husbands....

Aurora Floyd, as a character, is tame after Lady Audley. The 'beautiful fiend,' intensely wicked, but romantic from the very intensity of her wickedness, has degenerated into a fast young lady, full of stable talk, deep in the mysteries of the turf, and familiar with 'Bell's Life,'[2] – a young lady with large beautiful eyes, and with very little else to command any feeling either of love or the reverse. She runs away from school to contract a secret marriage with a consummate blackguard of a groom –

'A bridegroom, say you? 'tis a groom indeed.'[3]

She separates herself from him after a short and bitter experience of his character, comes home, and deceives her father by assuring him that 'that person' is dead when she knows him to be alive; afterwards, on the report of his death, deceives two worthy men by accepting one and marrying the other without breathing a word of her previous escapade (we are informed that 'her natural disposition is all truth and candour'); and finally deceives her husband again, when she discovers

---

1   See Mary Elizabeth Braddon's *Lady Audley's Secret* (1862) and *Aurora Floyd* (1863); *Clinton Maynyard; a Tale of the World, the Flesh, and the Devil* (1862); Matilda Charlotte Houstoun's, *Recommended to Mercy* (1862); *The Law of Divorce* (1861); Mrs. Gordon Smythies' *The Daily Governess* (1861); Captain Lascelles Wraxall's *Only a Woman* (1860); and *The Woman of Spirit* (1862).

2   See *Aurora Floyd*, 100, n.1.

3   *The Taming of the Shrew* III.ii.152.

that the man she had supposed dead is alive, by making arrangements for sending the obnoxious individual to Australia and retaining the second and illegal spouse as the more agreeable personage of the two. She is inferior to Lady Audley, as a pickpocket is inferior to a thug; but there is this important difference, – that Lady Audley is meant to be detested, while Aurora Floyd is meant to be admired. The one ends her days in a madhouse; the other becomes the wife of an honest man, and the curtain falls upon her 'bending over the cradle of her first-born.' By a fortunate arrangement of nature, which is always at the command of novelists, the birth of the infant is delayed beyond the usual time, till the groom is really dead and a re-marriage has repaired the irregularity of the bigamy. Fortunately also, there is no little pledge of affection[1] born to the Damasippus[2] of her first vows.

Though the moral teaching of the story is more questionable than that of its predecessor, and the interest, on the whole, less sustained, the individual characters are drawn with greater skill. Aurora, with all her faults, is a woman and not a fiend; and John Mellish, the honest, genial, tender-hearted, somewhat henpecked husband, is a portrait superior to any in the more romantic volume. As a companion to [an earlier quotation from *Lady Audley's Secret*] may be exhibited the following description of Aurora Floyd.... The 'stable-man' of the piece is not the one whom she has acquired a conjugal right to chastise, but another of the same profession, by no means so good-looking, but as great a scoundrel: –

'Aurora sprang upon him like a beautiful tigress, and catching the collar of his fustian jacket in her slight hands, rooted him to the spot upon which he stood. The grasp of those slender hands, convulsed by passion, was not to be easily shaken off; and Steeve Hargraves, taken completely off his guard, stared aghast at his assailant. Taller than the stable-man by a foot and a half, she towered above him, her cheeks white with rage, her eyes flashing fury, her hat fallen off, and her black hair tumbling

---

1 i.e., child.
2 In Juvenal (Satires, viii. 147, 151, 167), Damasippus is a fictional name under which the satirist ridicules a noble lover of horses.

about her shoulders, sublime in her passion......She disengaged her right hand from his collar, and rained a shower of blows upon his clumsy shoulders with her slender whip; a mere toy, with emeralds set in its golden head, but stinging like a rod of flexible steel in that little hand.'...

[S]ensation novels must be recognised as a great fact in the literature of the day, and a fact whose significance is by no means of an agreeable kind. Regarding these works merely as an efflorescence, as an eruption indicative of the state of health of the body in which they appear, the existence of an impure or a silly crop of novels, and the fact that they are eagerly read, are by no means favourable symptoms of the conditions of the body of society. But it is easier to detect the disease than to suggest the remedy. The praiseworthy attempts of individual proprietors of circulating libraries, to weed their collections of silly or mischievous works, have been too partial and isolated to produce any perceptible result, and have even acted as an advertisement of the rejected books. A more general and combined attempt in this direction is a thing rather to be wished than expected. Could a taste for the best class of fictions be cultivated in the minds of the rising generation, it might, perhaps, have its effect in lessening the craving for this kind of unnatural excitement; and could any check be imposed on the rapidity of production, it might improve the quality of the article produced....

Even if no remedy can be found, it is something to know the disease. There is a satisfaction in exposing an impostor, even when we feel sure that the world will continue to believe in him. The idol may still be worshipped, yet it is right to tell its worshippers that it is an idol; grotesque, it may be, or horrible in its features, but mere wood or stone, brass or clay, in its substance. The current folly may be destined to run its course, as other follies have done before it; and it must be confessed that there are as yet but few signs of its abating. But the duty of the preacher is the same, whether he succeed or fail. Though we cannot flatter ourselves with the hope that our protest will have the disenchanting influence of 'Dian's bud o'er Cupid's flower,' we are not the less bound to place on record the grounds of our belief, that, when the reading public wakes up from its present delusion, it will discover, with regard to some at least of the favourites of the day, that its affections have been bestowed upon an object not very different in kind from the animal of which Titania was enamoured.[1]

2. "The Archbishop of York on Works of Fiction." *The Times,* 2 November 1864.

The annual soirée of the Huddersfield Church Institute took place on Monday; the Bishop of Ripon in the chair.

The Archbishop of YORK was one of the speakers, and he addressed himself to the following sentiment: – "That Church institutes exercise more or less directly an educational influence on their members, by giving them access to well-chosen books and periodicals".... In order better to understand what useful reading was, he thought he might venture to look at what was useless reading; and he supposed if institutions of this kind were not to guide and supply the want that working men would be likely to fall in, no doubt, with the newspaper for one thing, and also for another with those stimulating narratives which went now by the somewhat barbarous term of "sensational stories." These sensational stories were tales which aimed at this effect simply – of exciting in the mind some deep feeling of over-wrought interest by the means of some terrible passion or crime. They went to persuade people that in almost every one of the well-ordered houses of their neighbours there was a skeleton shut up in some cupboard; that their comfortable and easy-looking neighbour had in his breast a secret story which he was always going about trying to conceal; that there was something about a real will registered in Doctors'-commons,[2] and a false will that at some proper moment would tumble out of some broken bureau, and bring about the *dénoûment* which the author wished to achieve. (Laughter.) This was the sort of food supplied in every kind of publication, from the penny story up to much larger and more important works. For those who

---

1   In *A Midsummer Night's Dream,* Titania (while under Oberon's spell) dotes on Bottom, who has been transformed into an ass. As Oberon releases her from this delusional love, he says, "Be as thou wast wont to be;/ See as thou wast wont to see. Dian's bud o'er Cupid's flower/ Hath such force and blessed power" (IV.i.71-74).

2   See *Aurora Floyd,* 456, n.1.

had no particular object in what they read no doubt these had a great attraction. He would show them what was one cause of that attraction. In the first place, they professed to give a deeper insight into our social system – of course, it was much deeper than anybody by his own observation could possibly discover. (Laughter.) They taught them not to trust to appearances – that there was behind a great world of crime, wickedness, and misery to which they alone possessed the key. Now, it was this claim to superior truth that gave them their first attraction; they satisfied a certain kind of spirit of inquiry. He would show them presently that in point of truth they entirely failed; because, supposing that these histories of great crime had some foundation, they would be at least a very one-sided kind of human nature. There was a much larger chapter of homely sympathies – of pious mothers training little children, of secret prayers offered up to God in the silence of night for those children, of hints and helps to duty strewn in the paths of these children continually – all this was altogether lost sight of and left out of the account, because it was not sufficiently stimulating in its nature, and they were left to believe that the world – bad, no doubt, it was – was a mere welter of crime, misery, and confusion, and that the historian could find nothing else to record. This style of reading was thoroughly false and dangerous for another reason – on account of what he would call its fatalism. Always they would observe in this kind of fiction some great passion was supposed to take possession of a man; it was love, or jealousy, or what not, and it was enough to state that the man was stricken by this passion to be sure that his destruction was settled beforehand by the writer of the fiction, and that there was no possibility of escape. If he was not greatly mistaken, this tone had strongly reacted upon society itself, and in some of the great crimes perpetrated he seemed to see the influence of this kind of feeling. There sprang up in the mind of an ill-regulated young man some great trial from one of these great passions, and he had been told, or had learnt in those his models, that it could not possibly be escaped from, and so he gave himself up to it, and ended his career by a crime which in reality was more terrible than the writer of the fiction had ventured to conceive. And it was also false because of its associating crime with a certain grand strength. It was some great and strong or beautiful person who was the hero or heroine of one of those tales of horror. Something had passed which in itself was horrible, but which they were expected not to abhor, because it was associated with qualities they were apt to admire. Could they suppose anything more dangerous to the young and to the weak and half-fallen than the contemplation of this kind of creation of the writer! It was entirely false. Some of them had read that day the conclusion of one of those tragedies in the conviction of a most miserable man for a most atrocious murder.[1] But there, he thought, there was indeed a moral, for in the first place detection had fallen upon guilt, and in the second place they had had laid before them the weakness and the contemptible folly and misery of such a crime as that of which they had read the history. It would be found invariably, he might say, that crime was the offspring of a broken nature, not of a nature in its strength. (Hear, hear.) He had conversed himself with persons who had had the opportunity of observing the criminal classes, and their testimony was that nothing so destroyed physical and mental power as a course of crime. A man lived a life of dissipation – he lived the life of a hunted beast, and the consequence was that before four or five years were over – he was speaking what he had been told by some of those who had actually observed it – he sank under it and disappeared – that was to say, he died. He (the Archbishop) had now shown, and he had taken some pains to ground himself in the facts, what was the exciting literature which was thrust into the hands of the humbler members of the social body. Depend upon it, it did the utmost amount of harm.

---

1   On 29 October 1864 Franz Müller was found guilty of the murder of a Mr. Briggs. Briggs was bludgeoned on the head and robbed while in a carriage of the North London Railway on 9 July 1864; he was dumped from the train and found alive, but died without regaining consciousness.

3. "Sensation Novelists: Miss Braddon." Unsigned, [W. Fraser Rae][1] *North British Review*, September 1865.

IF the test of genius were success, we should rank Miss Braddon very high in the list of our great novelists. The fertility of her invention is as unprecedented as the extent of her popularity. Month after month she produces instalments of new novels which attract countless readers, and are praised by not a few competent critics. Three years ago her name was unknown to the reading public. Now it is nearly as familiar to every novel-reader as that of Bulwer Lytton[2] or Charles Dickens.

Miss Braddon cannot reasonably complain that, in her case, striving merit has been suffered to fret and pine unheeded. Almost as soon as *Lady Audley's Secret* appeared, it was lauded by distinguished critics, and eagerly purchased and read by an enthusiastic section of the public. Daily newspapers which habitually neglected, or carped at works that fell short of a very high standard of excellence, became conspicuous for the exceptional compliments they paid to this authoress. Even a weekly journal which is noted for lavishing stinging sarcasms on the female novelists in whose works High Church principles[3] are unsupported or scoffed at, has bestowed ungrudging praise on the writings of Miss Braddon. As novel after novel issued from the press, the laudatory epithets were, when possible, more copiously showered upon her. Her triumph has been nearly complete. By the unthinking crowd she is regarded as a woman of genius. The magazine to which she contributes is almost certain to have a large circulation, and to enrich

---

1   William Fraser Rae (1835-1905), journalist, novelist, and reviewer; writer of travel and history books.

2   Edward George Earl Lytton Bulwer Lytton (1803-73), leading novelist and playwright. He wrote bestselling novels in various genres, including those of domestic, occult, historical, science, and "Newgate" fiction. A member of parliament originally for the district of St. Ives and then later for Lincoln, he was secretary for the colonies in 1858-59, and was created first Baron Lytton of Knebworth in 1866. He was a correspondent of Braddon's and a strong supporter of her writing career.

3   Adherents of "High Church" principles within the Church of England embraced the tenets of the Oxford Movement, giving high value to the authority of the priesthood, the saving grace of the sacraments, and, generally, to those points of doctrine which most distinguish the Anglican from the Protestant or Nonconformist churches. On High Church novelists, see *Aurora Floyd*, 216, n. 1.

its fortunate proprietors. She has bewitched so many persons, that those who have the misfortune to be blind to her charms have had small chance of being listened to when pronouncing an adverse judgment....

Now, there is a "faction" which does not think her "sensation novels" the most admirable product of this generation, and considers that, judged by a purely literary standard, they are unworthy of unqualified commendation. To that "faction" we belong. We shall purposely avoid applying a moral test to these productions; for those who apply it are generally prone to condemn that which they cannot praise, chiefly because others think it admirable. On this principle bear-baiting was denounced by the Puritans; smoking is called a vice by the members of the Anti-Tobacco Society; and drinking a glass of beer is considered scandalous by the supporters of the Permissive Bill.[1] A novel which deserves censure from a literary point of view cannot merit high eulogy solely on account of its morality. That which is bad in taste is usually bad in morals: it is sufficient, then, as it is fair, to apply the test we propose to the works of Miss Braddon....

Lady Audley is at once the heroine and the monstrosity of [Braddon's] novel. In drawing her, the authoress may have intended to portray a female Mephistopheles;[2] but, if so, she should have known that a woman cannot fill such a part. The nerves with which Lady Audley could meet unmoved the friend of the man she had murdered, are the nerves of a Lady Macbeth who is half unsexed, and not those of the timid, gentle, innocent creature Lady Audley is represented as being. Whenever she is meditating the commission of something inexpressibly horrible, she is described as being unusually charming. Her manner and her appearance are always in contrast with her conduct. All this is very exciting; but it is also very unnatural. The artistic faults of this novel are as grave as the ethical ones. Combined, they render it one of the most noxious books of modern times. And, in consequence of faults like these, we cannot admit the plea that the story is well told, that the plot is very cleverly planned, that the work is one

---

1 A bill introduced into Parliament several times between 1864 and 1877, designed to give each parish the right to refuse to issue liquor licences.
2 A female devil or demon.

which, once begun, cannot be relinquished before the close. This plea might be urged in favour of the vilest tales. It is not enough that any work should interest, it must be capable of being perused without the reflecting reader being induced to lament the time he has lost over its pages. No discriminating reader ever laid down these volumes without regretting that he had taken them up, and that their authoress should have so misemployed her undoubted talents as to produce them.

The difference between it and *Aurora Floyd*, Miss Braddon's next novel, is chiefly a difference in names and accessories. Archibald Floyd is another Sir Michael Audley. Like the latter, the former, when advanced in years, marries a beautiful but penniless woman. Mr. Floyd's wife "was a tall young woman, of about thirty, with a dark complexion, and great flashing black eyes that lit up a face which might otherwise have been unnoticeable, into the splendour of absolute beauty." This lady did no wrong beyond giving birth to a daughter who commits bigamy and is suspected of being a murderess. Almost at the outset, we are warned against disbelieving anything in this novel. The trick is a hackneyed one. What is notable in this case is the manner in which Miss Braddon introduces her statement. Having to tell us that the lady was not discontented, and loved her husband, she does it in this wise: "If this were a very romantic story, it would be perhaps only proper for Eliza Floyd to pine in her gilded bower, and misapply her energies in weeping for some abandoned lover, deserted in an evil hour of ambitious madness. But as my story is a true one, not only true in a general sense, but strictly true as to the leading facts which I am about to relate, and as I could point out, in a certain county far northward of the lovely Kentish woods, the very house in which the events I shall describe took place, I am bound also to be truthful here, and to set down as a fact that the love which Eliza Floyd bore for her husband was as pure and sincere an affection as ever man need hope to win from the generous heart of a good woman." In addition to considering this as a very round-about way of stating a very simple fact, we regard it as one of those blunders which a true artist would never commit.

Before examining into the details of this novel, we shall indicate the nature of the plot. Aurora, the heroine and daughter of the wealthy banker Mr. Floyd, is first engaged to Talbot Bulstrode, then to John Mellish, whom she marries. Mr. Mellish has a groom, James Conyers, who had formerly been in the employment of Mr. Floyd. With him, Aurora, while still a girl, had fallen in love. He had enticed her away from a French boarding-school, and induced her to marry him. This was her secret, and because she would not reveal it to Talbot Bulstrode, he had broken off the engagement. Before marrying for the second time, she learned, on good authority, that her first husband was dead. When he re-appears as her second husband's servant, she tries to bribe him to leave the country. Terms are arranged between them. She has an interview, and pays him the required sum. A few minutes afterwards he is shot through the heart. Aurora is suspected of having committed murder as well as bigamy. Like Lady Audley, she has been guilty of one crime only. This being satisfactorily proved, she is re-married, and her trials are over. Curiously enough, Aurora has no child by either husband till after the clearing up of the mystery which surrounds her. On the last page but one of the third volume, is the announcement of the birth of a "black-eyed" boy.

The distinctive characteristics of Aurora are her eyes and hair. The former are "like the stars of heaven;" the latter is blue-black. We are told that, "like most young ladies with black eyes and blue-black hair, Miss Floyd was a good hater." This is rather puzzling, seeing that Lady Audley was represented as an excellent hater, although her eyes were blue and her hair red. There must have been something terrible in Aurora's eyes, for on one occasion she is represented as looking at a man "with her eyes flashing forked lightnings of womanly fury." Of course, the possession of such eyes and hair is made the theme of many impassioned paragraphs. The following is a specimen: – "The thick plaits of her black hair made a great diadem upon her low fore-head, and crowned her as an Eastern empress; an empress with a doubtful nose, it is true, but an empress who reigned by right divine of her eyes and hair. For do not these wonderful black eyes, which perhaps shine upon us only once in a lifetime, in themselves consti-tute a royalty?" In another chapter she is depicted "with her coronet of plaits died black against the purple air," and again with "her long purple-black hair all tumbled and tossed about the pillows." Be it observed that her hair changes its colour according to circumstances.

At one time it is simple black, at another blue-black, then dead-black, and lastly purple-black. The last change occurs in the tenth chapter of the first volume. In the second volume the epithets are repeated without much variation. There Aurora is spoken of as "that Egyptian goddess, that Assyrian queen with the flashing eyes and serpentine coils of purple-black hair." She is also represented lying on a sofa, "wrapped in a loose white dressing-gown, her masses of ebon hair unveiled and falling about her shoulders in serpentine tresses, that looked like shining blue-black snakes released from poor Medusa's head to make their escape amid the folds of her garments.... One small hand lay under her head, twisted in the tangled masses of her glorious hair." In this same volume Miss Braddon observes, that "some women never outlive that school-girl infatuation for straight noses and dark hair." Remembering what she has written about Lady Audley's golden locks, we must admit that Miss Braddon is not given to admire any particular hue, and that she evidently loves hair for its own sake, provided that it be abundant.

From a lady novelist we naturally expect to have portraits of women which shall not be wholly untrue to nature. We have seen that Lady Audley is quite as fantastic a sketch as that of any of the male characters. The following example will prove that Aurora Floyd is equally wanting in the traits which constitute a true woman. A half-witted servant having kicked a lame dog of which she was very fond,

"Aurora sprang upon him like a beautiful tigress, and catching the collar of his fustian jacket in her slight hands, rooted him to the spot upon which he stood. The grasp of those slender hands, convulsed by passion, was not to be easily shaken off; and Steeve Hargraves, taken completely off his guard, stared aghast at his assailant. Taller than the stable-man by a foot and a half, she towered above him, her cheeks white with rage, her eyes flashing fury, her hat fallen off, and her black hair tumbling about her shoulders, sublime in her passion.

"The man crouched beneath the grasp of the imperious creature.

"'Let me go!' he gasped, in his inward whisper, which had a hissing sound in his agitation; 'let me go, or you'll be sorry; let me go!'

"'How dared you!' cried Aurora, 'how dared you hurt him? My poor dog! My poor, lame, feeble dog! How dared you to do it? You cowardly dastard! you – '

"She disengaged her right hand from his collar, and rained a shower of blows upon his clumsy shoulders with her slender whip; a mere toy, with emeralds set in its golden head, but stinging like a rod of flexible steel in that little hand.

"'How dared you!' she repeated again and again, her cheeks changing from white to scarlet in the effort to hold the man with one hand. Her tangled hair had fallen to her waist by this time, and the whip was broken in half-a-dozen places.'" – (Vol. i. pp. 273, 274.)

When Aurora's husband suddenly found his wife thus employed, we are told that he "turned white with horror at beholding the beautiful fury." If he had been a genuine man, and not the puppet of a female novelist, he would have turned away with loathing from the sight. An authoress who could make one of her sex play the chief part in such a scene, is evidently acquainted with a very low type of female character, or else incapable of depicting that which she knows to be true. We are certain that, except in this novel, no lady possessing the education and occupying the position of Aurora Floyd could have acted as she is represented to have done.

The same impression of unreality is produced by the other characters. There is Lucy Floyd, who "was very pretty, certainly, with pink cheeks, a white nose, and rose-coloured nostrils," and who gloried in what at one time is styled golden hair, at another "amber tresses." She is a pretty doll. So silly is she that in the matter of dress she is quite ignorant of what will suit her. Indeed, Aurora is obliged to reprove her in this strain: "Why, you silly Lucy, don't you know that yours is the beauty which really does not want adornment? A few pearls or for-get-me-not blossoms, or a crown of water-lilies, and a cloud of white areophane, would make you look a sylphide; but I dare say you would like to wear amber-satin and cabbage-roses."

The gentlemen are, if possible, still less attractive and life-like than the ladies. There is a Talbot Bulstrode who combines in his own person more contradictions than any other man who ever figured in a novel. At thirty-two he had "run through all the wealth of life's excitements and amusements." Yet he was too proud to be either vicious or foolish. Although a "captain of Her Majesty's 11th Hussars," yet he "was fond of scientific studies, and he neither smoked, drank, nor gambled." Once only he went to the Derby, and then he turned away at the exciting moment of the great race. It is said that "those who spoke of him summed him up by saying that he wasn't a bit like an officer." As represented by this authoress, he does not resemble a rational being....

Having now passed in review the long roll of Miss Braddon's personages, what report can we make, what judgment must we pronounce? Have we discovered among them one who thoroughly amuses or interests us; one whom we might be tempted to take as a model, or compelled to admire as the impersonation of anything noble in demeanour and loveable in mind? Is there a single page in her writings from which we have derived any gratification or learned anything new? Have we found her to be a creator of new types, a copyist of living personages, or a creator of unnatural monstrosities?

Applying to her productions the test which we named at the outset, we find that she excels where to excel is no merit, failing utterly in those respects wherein to fail means mediocrity. Of pathos and humour, happy touches and telling sayings, words which depict while they explain, thoughts at once original and impressive, we can discover no traces in her pages. What is conspicuous above all things is the skill with which she groups her materials, and the manner in which she deals with revolting topics, so as to hinder the startled reader from tossing her volume away in sheer disgust. She can tell a story so as to make us curious about the end. Does the power of doing this alone stamp her as a great novelist?

Sydney Smith would have replied, Assuredly it does. When reviewing Mr. Lister's undeservedly forgotten novel, *Granby*, he wrote these words: "The main question as to a novel is, Did it amuse? Were you surprised at dinner coming so soon? did you mistake eleven for ten and twelve for eleven? Were you too late to dress? and did you sit up beyond the usual hour? If a novel produces these effects it is good; if it does not, story, language, love, scandal itself, cannot save it. It is only meant to please; and it must do that or it does nothing."[1]

Now, the reviewers who have lauded Miss Braddon's novels, apply to them only the test employed by Sydney Smith. They tell us that the plots will hardly bear criticism, that the tone is unhealthy, that the views of life are false and mischievous; but they recommend them to us notwithstanding, merely on the ground that each can be read from the first to the last page without our attention ever flagging, or our interest being abated. They are recommended, moreover, as good stimulants in these days of toil and worry, and as well fitted for relieving overtaxed brains by diverting our thoughts from the absorbing occupations of daily life.

Others, again, take different ground. According to them the "sensation tale" is no novelty. They boldly avow that all great novels are as sensational as those of Miss Braddon. If called upon they would cite as examples some of the best works of Scott,[2] and a few of the works of Bulwer Lytton and George Eliot. *The Heart of Midlothian* and *Eugene Aram, Adam Bede* and *The Mill on the Floss*, are unquestionably novels wherein there are incidents as highly coloured as in *Lady Audley's Secret* or *Henry Dunbar*.[3] The difference, however, is far greater than the resemblance. These works are truthful taken as wholes, and even the startling occurrences are not at variance with experience and probability. According to Miss Braddon, crime is not an accident, but it is the business of life. She would lead us to conclude that the chief end of man is to commit a murder, and his highest merit to escape punishment; that women are born to attempt to commit murders, and to succeed in committing bigamy. If she teaches us anything new, it is

---

1   Sydney Smith (1771-1845), clergyman and projector of the *Edinburgh Review*. The quotation is from his review of T.H. Lister's novel *Granby* (1826). See *Edinburgh Review* 43 (1826):395.

2   Sir Walter Scott (1771-1832), whose immensely popular historical novels were published between 1814-31.

3   Both Scott's *The Heart of Midlothian* (1818) and Eliot's *Adam Bede* (1859) feature trials for child murder; Bulwer Lytton's *Eugene Aram* (1832) deals with a gentle scholar who is arrested on his wedding day for the murder of the uncle of his bride-to-be; Eliot's *The Mill on the Floss* (1860) depicts a woman who is compromised when she spends a night with her lover on a boating trip. Braddon's *Lady Audley's Secret* (1862) has a murderous bigamist as its heroine; her *Henry Dunbar* (1864) features an ex-valet who, having murdered his former master, assumes his identity.

that we should sympathize with murderers and reverence detectives. Her principles appear to us to resemble very strikingly those by which the Thugs[1] used to regulate their lives....

Miss Braddon renders all those who are not wicked so utterly ridiculous, that we are tempted to infer she designed to show how mistaken a thing is probity or goodness.

Tested, then, by a purely literary standard, these works must be designated as the least valuable among works of fiction. They glitter on the surface, but the substance is base metal. Hence it is that the impartial critic is compelled, as it were, to unite with the moralist in regarding them as mischievous in their tendency, and as one of the abominations of the age. Into uncontaminated minds they will instil false views of human conduct. Such notions are more easily imposed on the unwary than eradicated from the minds which have cherished them. Miss Braddon makes one of her personages tell another that life is a very different thing in reality than in three-volume novels. She has manifested this in her own works. But the fact of this difference is a conclusive proof of their inferiority. A novel is a picture of life, and as such ought to be faithful. The fault of these novels is that they contain pictures of daily life, wherein there are scenes so grossly untrue to nature, that we can hardly pardon the authoress if she drew them in ignorance, and cannot condemn her too strongly if, knowing their falseness, she introduced them for the sake of effect. The Archbishop of York did not overstate the case when, speaking as a moralist, he said at the Huddersfield Church Institute, in November last, that "sensational stories were tales which aimed at this effect simply – of exciting in the mind some deep feeling of overwrought interest by the means of some terrible passion or crime. They want [sic] to persuade people that in almost every one of the well-ordered houses of their neighbours there was a skeleton shut up in some cupboard; that their comfortable and easy-looking neighbour had in his breast a secret story which he was always going about trying to conceal; that there was something about a real will registered in Doctors' Commons, and a

---

1   A group of professional assassins who travelled through India, strangling and plundering their victims. First described in English travel writing in 1665, they were called "Thugs," "Thags," or "Thegs" from 1810 on, and rigidly prosecuted from 1831 on.

false will that at some proper moment should tumble out of some broken bureau, and bring about the *dénoûment* which the author wished to achieve."[1] Though the foregoing remarks have a general application, yet they apply with crushing force to the present case. It need only be added, as advice to those who either possess or delight to buy such books, that the proper shelf on which to place them is that whereon stands *The Newgate Calendar*.[2]

We should act unfairly if we left on our readers' minds the impression that we do not regard Miss Braddon as an authoress of originality and merit. In her own branch of literature, we hold that she is without a living rival. The notoriety she has acquired is her due reward for having woven tales which are as fascinating to ill-regulated minds as police reports and divorce cases. Her achievements may not command our respect; but they are very notable, and almost unexampled. Others before her have written stories of blood and lust, of atrocious crimes and hardened criminals, and these have excited the interest of a very wide circle of readers. But the class that welcomed them was the lowest in the social scale, as well as in mental capacity. To Miss Braddon belongs the credit of having penned similar stories in easy and correct English, and published them in three volumes in place of issuing them in penny numbers. She may boast, without fear of contradiction, of having temporarily succeeded in making the literature of the Kitchen the favourite reading of the Drawing room.[3]

4. "Miss Braddon." Henry James,[1] *The Nation*, November 1865.

MISS AURORA FLOYD, as half the world knows, was a young lady who got into no end of trouble by marrying her father's groom. We had supposed that this adventure had long ago become an old story;

---

1 See Appendix B.2, 580.

2 The *Newgate Calendar*, published c. 1773, recorded notorious crimes from 1700 to c.1773.

3 i.e. Has succeeded in making the literature of the servant class the favourite reading of the middle class.

4 Henry James (1843-1916), American novelist and critic, who from 1865 on was a regular contributor of short stories and reviews to American periodicals.

but here is a new edition of her memoirs to prove that the public has not done with her yet. We would assure those individuals who look with regret upon this assumption by a "sensation" novel of the honors of legitimate fiction, that the author of "Aurora Floyd" is an uncommonly clever person. Her works are distinguished by a quality for which we can find no better name than "pluck;" and should not pluck have its reward wherever found? If common report is correct, Miss Braddon had for many years beguiled the leisure moments of an arduous profession – the dramatic profession – by the composition of fictitious narrative. But until the publication of "Lady Audley's Secret" she failed to make her mark. To what secret impulse of inspiration we owe this sudden reversal of fortune it is difficult to say; but the grim determination to succeed is so apparent in every line of "Lady Audley's Secret," that the critic is warranted in conjecturing that she had at last become desperate. People talk of novels with a purpose;[1] and from this class of works, both by her patrons and her enemies, Miss Braddon's tales are excluded. But what novel ever betrayed a more resolute purpose than the production of what we may call Miss Braddon's second manner? Her purpose was at any hazard to make a hit, to catch the public ear. It was a difficult task, but audacity could accomplish it. Miss Braddon accordingly resorted to extreme measures, and created the sensation novel. It is to this audacity, this courage of despair, as manifested in her later works, that we have given the name of pluck. In these works it has settled down into a quiet determination not to let her public get ahead of her. A writer who has suddenly leaped into a popularity greatly disproportionate to his merit, can only retain his popularity by observing a strictly respectful attitude to his readers. This has been Miss Braddon's attitude, and she has maintained it with unwearied patience. She has been in her way a disciple as well as a teacher. She has kept up with the subtle innovations to which her art, like all others, is subject, as well as with the equally delicate fluctuations of the public taste. The result has been a very obvious improvement in her style.

She has been preceded in the same path by Mr. Wilkie Collins, whose "Woman in White," with its diaries and letters and its general

---

1   Didactic novels, written to sway their readers' views on a particular issue.

ponderosity, was a kind of nineteenth century version of "Clarissa Harlowe."[1] Mind, we say a nineteenth century version. To Mr. Collins belongs the credit of having introduced into fiction those most mysterious of mysteries, the mysteries which are at our own doors. This innovation gave a new impetus to the literature of horrors. It was fatal to the authority of Mrs. Radcliffe and her everlasting castle in the Apennines. What are the Apennines to us, or we to the Apennines? Instead of the terrors of "Udolpho,"[2] we were treated to the terrors of the cheerful country house and busy London lodgings. And there is no doubt that these were infinitely the more terrible. Mrs. Radcliffe's mysteries were romances pure and simple; while those of Mr. Wilkie Collins were stern reality. The supernatural, which Mrs. Radcliffe constantly implies, though she generally saves her conscience, at the eleventh hour, by explaining it away, requires a powerful imagination in order to be as exciting as the natural, as Mr. Collins and Miss Braddon, without any imagination at all, know how to manage it. A good ghost-story, to be half as terrible as a good murder-story, must be connected at a hundred points with the common objects of life. The best ghost-story probably ever written – a tale published some years ago in "Blackwood's Magazine"[3] – was constructed with an admirable understanding of this principle. Half of its force was derived from its prosaic, commonplace, daylight accessories. Less delicately terrible, perhaps, than the vagaries of departed spirits, but to the full as *interesting*, as the modern novel reader understands the word, are the numberless possible forms of human malignity. Crime, indeed, has always been a theme for dramatic poets; but with the old poets its dramatic interest lay in the fact that it compromised the criminal's moral

---

1   Wilkie Collins's *The Woman In White* (1860) was one of the first sensation novels. Like Samuel Richardson's epistolary novel *Clarissa* [sic] (1748-49), *The Woman in White* consists of a series of documents—in this case, journals, letters, and testimonials.

2   Ann Radcliffe (1764-1823). In her gothic novel *The Mysteries of Udolpho* (1794), the heroine Emily is carried off by the villainous Montoni to the remote Castle of Udolpho in the Apennines.

3   Probably a reference to "The Haunted and the Haunters; or, The House and the Brain," a short story by Bulwer Lytton published anonymously in the August 1859 issue of *Blackwood's*.

repose. Whence else is the interest of *Orestes*[1] and *Macbeth*? With Mr. Collins and Miss Braddon (our modern Euripides and Shakespeare) the interest of crime is in the fact that it compromises the criminal's personal safety. The play is a tragedy, not in virtue of an avenging deity, but in virtue of a preventive system of law; not through the presence of a company of fairies, but through that of an admirable organization of police detectives. Of course, the nearer the criminal and the detective are brought home to the reader, the more lively his "sensation." They are brought home to the reader by a happy choice of probable circumstances; and it is through their skill in the choice of these circumstances – their thorough-going realism – that Mr. Collins and Miss Braddon have become famous. In like manner, it is by the thorough-going realism of modern actors that the works of the most poetic of poets have been made to furnish precedent for sensational writers. There are no *circumstances* in "Macbeth," as you read it; but as you see it played by Mr. Charles Kean or Mr. Booth it is nothing but circumstances. And we may here remark, in parentheses, that if the actors of a past generation – Garrick and Mrs. Siddons – left with their contemporaries so profound a conviction of their *greatness*, it is probably because, like the great dramatists they interpreted, they were ideal and poetic; because their effort was not to impress but to express.[2]

We have said that although Mr. Collins anticipated Miss Braddon in the work of devising domestic mysteries adapted to the wants of a sternly prosaic age, she was yet the founder of the sensation novel. Mr. Collins's productions deserve a more respectable name. They are massive and elaborate constructions – monuments of mosaic work, for the proper mastery of which it would seem, at first, that an index and

---

1 *Orestes* (c. 408 BC) is a play by the Athenian tragic playwright Euripides (c. 480 BC-407/6 BC). Orestes, the son of Agamemnon and Clytemnestra, avenges the murder of his father by his mother and her lover Aegisthus.

2 For Charles Kean, see *Aurora Floyd*, 318, n.1. Edwin Booth (1833-93) was a famous American tragedian and theatre manager. His acting style was restrained, a quality which distinguished it from the excesses of the earlier Romantic school of acting. David Garrick (1717-79), English actor, manager, and playwright, dominated the English stage for over 30 years between 1741-76. His acting style was brilliant, daring and virtuoso. Sarah Siddons (1755-1831) was the greatest tragic actress of her generation. Her acting was marked by her resonant voice and amplitude of gesture.

note-book were required. They are not so much works of art as works of science. To read "The Woman in White," requires very much the same intellectual effort as to read Motley or Froude.[1] We may say, therefore, that Mr. Collins being to Miss Braddon what Richardson is to Miss Austen,[2] we date the novel of domestic mystery from the former lady, for the same reason that we date the novel of domestic tranquillity from the latter. Miss Braddon began by a skilful combination of bigamy, arson, murder, and insanity. These phenomena are all represented in the deeds of Lady Audley. The novelty lay in the heroine being, not a picturesque Italian of the fourteenth century, but an English gentlewoman of the current year, familiar with the use of the railway and the telegraph. The intense probability of the story is constantly reiterated. Modern England – the England of to-day's newspaper – crops up at every step. Of course Lady Audley is a nonentity, without a heart, a soul, a reason. But what we may call the small change for these facts – her eyes, her hair, her mouth, her dresses, her bedroom furniture, her little words and deeds – are so lavishly bestowed that she successfully maintains a kind of half illusion. Lady Audley was diabolically wicked; Aurora Floyd, her successor, was simply foolish, or indiscreet, or indelicate – or anything you please to say of a young lady who runs off with a hostler. But as bigamy has been the cause of Lady Audley's crimes, so it is the cause of Aurora's woes. She marries a second time, on the hypothesis of the death of the hostler. But, to paraphrase a sentence of Thackeray's in a sketch of the projected plot of "Denis Duval,"[3] suppose, after all, it should turn out that the hostler was *not* dead? In "Aurora Floyd" the small change is more abundant than ever. Aurora's hair, in particular, alternately blueblack, purple-black, and dead-black, is made to go a great way. Since "Aurora Floyd," Miss Braddon has published half-a-dozen more

1 John Lothrop Motley (1814-77), historian and the author of *The Rise of the Dutch Republic* (1855) and the multi-volumed *History of the United Netherlands* (1860-67). James Anthony Froude (1818-94), historian and author of another multi-volumed history, the *History of England from the Death of Cardinal Wolsey to the defeat of the Spanish Armada* (12 vols., 1856-70).

2 i.e. Samuel Richardson's massive and elaborate domestic fictions laid the groundwork for Jane Austen's elegant and incisive novels of manners.

3 William Makepeace Thackeray (1811-63), a leading Victorian novelist. His last, unfinished novel, *Denis Duval*, was published in the *Cornhill Magazine* in 1864.

novels; each, as we have intimated, better than the previous one, and running through more editions; but each fundamentally a repetition of "Aurora Floyd." These works are censured and ridiculed, but they are extensively read. The author has a hold upon the public. It is, assuredly, worth our while to enquire more particularly how she has obtained it.

The great public, in the first place, is made up of a vast number of little publics, very much as our Union is made up of States, and it is necessary to consider which of the publics is Miss Braddon's. We can best define it with the half of a negative. It is that public which reads nothing but novels, and yet which reads neither George Eliot, George Sand, Thackeray, nor Hawthorne.[1] People who read nothing but novels are very poor critics of human nature. Their foremost desire is for something new. Now, we all know that human nature is very nearly as old as the hills. But *society* is for ever renewing itself. To society, accordingly, and not to life, Miss Braddon turns, and produces, not stories of passion, but stories of action. Society is a vast magazine of crime and suffering, of enormities, mysteries, and miseries of every description, of incidents, in a word. In proportion as an incident is exceptional, it is interesting to persons in search of novelty. Bigamy, murder, and arson are exceptional. Miss Braddon distributes these materials with a generous hand, and attracts the attention of her public. The next step is to hold its attention. There have been plenty of tales of crime which have not made their authors famous, nor put money in their purses. The reason can have been only that they were not well executed. Miss Braddon, accordingly, goes to work like an artist. Let not the curious public take for granted that, from a literary point of view, her works are contemptible. Miss Braddon writes neither fine English nor slovenly English; not she. She writes what we may call very knowing English. If her readers have not read George Eliot and Thackeray and all the great authorities, she assuredly has,

---

1 George Sand (1804-76), feminist and philosophical French novelist. Nathanial Hawthorne (1804-64), American novelist and short story writer. With George Eliot (1819-80), intellectual and realist British novelist, and W.M. Thackeray (1811-63), satirical British novelist, these represent the leading novelists of their generation and span the field of serious fiction (intellectual, philosophical, and satirical) in France, England, and America.

and, like every one else, she is the better for it. With a telling subject and a knowing style she proceeds to get up her photograph.[1] These require shrewd observation and wide experience; Miss Braddon has both. Like all women, she has a turn for color; she knows how to paint. She overloads her canvas with detail. It is the peculiar character of these details that constitute her chief force. They betray an intimate acquaintance with that disorderly half of society which becomes every day a greater object of interest to the orderly half. They intimate that, to use an irresistible vulgarism, Miss Braddon "has been there." The novelist who interprets the illegitimate world to the legitimate world, commands from the nature of his position a certain popularity. Miss Braddon deals familiarly with gamblers, and betting-men, and flashy reprobates of every description. She knows much that ladies are not accustomed to know, but that they are apparently very glad to learn. The names of drinks, the technicalities of the faro-table,[2] the lingo of the turf, the talk natural to a crowd of fast men at supper, when there are no ladies present but Miss Braddon, the way one gentleman knocks another down – all these things – the exact local coloring of Bohemia[3] – our sisters and daughters may learn from these works. These things are the incidents of vice; and vice, as is well-known, even modern, civilized, elegant, prosaic vice, has its romance. Of this romance Miss Braddon has taken advantage, and the secret of her success is, simply, that she has done her work better than her predecessors. That is, she has done it with a woman's *finesse* and a strict regard to morality. If one of her heroines elopes with a handsome stable-boy, she saves the proprieties by marrying him. This may be indecent if you like, but it is not immoral. If another of her heroines is ever tempted, she resists. With people who are not particular, therefore, as to the moral delicacy of their author, or as to their intellectual strength, Miss Braddon is very naturally a favourite.

---

1 Photography was a recent phenomenon, its technology developed in the late 1830s and early 1840s. Photojournalism and photo-documentation were thus very new in the 1850s and 1860s.
2 Faro is a gambling game at cards.
3 A segment of society which chooses to live in disregard of convention and with irregular habits and morals.

5. "Novels."[1] Unsigned, [Margaret Oliphant][2] *Blackwood's Edinburgh Magazine*, September 1867.

English novels have for a long time – from the days of Sir Walter Scott at least – held a very high reputation in the world, not so much perhaps for what critics would call the highest development of art, as for a certain sanity, wholesomeness, and cleanness unknown to other literature of the same class. This peculiarity has had its effect, no doubt, upon those very qualities of the national mind which produced it. It has increased that perfect liberty of reading which is the rule in most cultivated English houses; it has abolished the domestic Index Expurgatorius[3] as well as all public censorship; it has made us secure and unsuspicious in our reception of everything, or almost everything, that comes to us in the form of print. This noble confidence has been good for everybody concerned. It has put writers on their honour, and saved readers from that wounding consciousness of restraint or of danger which destroys all delicate appreciation. There are other kinds of literature in which the darker problems of the time can be fitly discussed, and, with a tolerably unanimous consent, English writers have agreed to leave those subjects in their fit place. The novel, which is the favourite reading of the young – which is one of the chief amusements of all secluded and most suffering people – which is precious to women and unoccupied persons – has been kept by this understanding, or by a natural impulse better than any understanding, to a great degree pure from all noxious topics.... Our novels were family reading; and the result has been a sense of freedom, an absence of all suggestion of evil, in the superficial studies of ordinary society, which it is impossible to overestimate. "*Nous sommes tous d'un age mûr,*" said an irreproachable French matron to the English acquaintance whose eyes expressed a certain amazement at the frankness of some drawing-room narrative; "*j'espére* [sic] *que vous ne pensez pas que je parlerais*

---

1   George Augustus Sala's rejoinder to this review is reprinted as Appendix B.6, 607.

2   Margaret Oliphant (1828-97), prolific Victorian novelist and short-story writer.

3   Part of the policy of the Church of Rome on works to be forbidden (*Index librorum prohibitorum*) or to be read only in expurgated versions (*Index expurgatorius*). Oliphant suggests that the state of English letters frees the home from domestic censorship.

comme ça devant des jeunes gens."[1] This idea, which is the very heart of French ideas on the subject, is quite foreign to our insular habits. We are accustomed both to read and to speak everything that comes in our way in the presence of *jeunes gens*. The habit has so grown upon us that to change it would involve a revolution in all our domestic arrangements. It would involve us in an amount of trouble which very few could face. We should require three or four packets from the library instead of one. We should have the nuisance of separating our children and dependants from our own amusements. We should no longer be able to discuss, as we do now continually, the books that we are reading and the thoughts we are thinking. This is a necessity from which we have been altogether free in the tranquil past; but it is an indulgence which only habit and the long use and wont of public security preserve to us now.

For there can be no doubt that a singular change has passed upon our light literature. It is not that its power has failed or its popularity diminished – much the reverse; it is because a new impulse has been given and a new current set in the flood of contemporary story-telling. We will not ask whence or from whom the influence is derived. It has been brought into being by society, and it naturally reacts upon society. The change perhaps began at the time when Jane Eyre made what advanced critics call her "protest" against the conventionalities in which the world clothes itself.[2] We have had many "protests" since that time, but it is to be doubted how far they have been to our advantage. The point to which we have now arrived is certainly very far from satisfactory. The English mind is still so far *borné* [3] that we do not discuss the seventh commandment[4] with all that effusion and fulness of detail which is common on the other side of the Channel, though even in that respect progress is daily being

---

1   "We are all mature people ... I hope you don't think I would talk like this in front of young people."

2   In Chapter 12 of *Jane Eyre*, as Jane tries to settle into her routine as a governess, she paces the third storey of Thornfield Hall, swelling with suppressed indignation against the "restraint" and "stagnation" of women's lives. In the *Quarterly Review* (1848), Elizabeth Rigby wrote that Jane Eyre was "the personification of an unregenerate and undisciplined spirit."

3   Narrow.

4   Thou shalt not commit adultery (Exodus 20:14).

made; but there are points in which we altogether outdo our French neighbours. To a French girl fresh from her convent the novels of her own language are rigorously tabooed; whereas we are all aware that they are the favourite reading of her contemporary in this country, and are not unfrequently even the production, with all their unseemly references and exhibitions of forbidden knowledge, of young women, moved either by the wild foolhardiness of inexperience, or by ignorance of everything that is natural and becoming to their condition. It is painful to inquire where it is that all those stories of bigamy and seduction, those *soi-disant* [1] revelations of things that lie below the surface of life, come from. Such tales might flow here and there from one morbid imagination, and present themselves to us as moral phenomena, without casting any stigma upon society in general; but this is not how they appear. They have taken, as it would seem, permanent possession of all the lower strata of light literature. Above there still remains, it is true, a purer atmosphere, for which we may be thankful; but all our minor novelists, almost without exception, are of the school called sensational. Writers who have no genius and little talent, make up for it by displaying their acquaintance with the accessories and surroundings of vice, with the means of seduction, and with what they set forth as the secret tendencies of the heart – tendencies which, according to this interpretation, all point one way. When the curate's daughter in 'Shirley' burst forth into passionate lamentation over her own position and the absence of any man whom she could marry,[2] it was a new sensation to the world in general. That men and women should marry we had all of us acknowledged as one of the laws of humanity; but up to the present generation most young women had been brought up in the belief that their own feelings on this subject should be religiously kept to themselves. No doubt this was a conventionalism; and if a girl in a secluded parsonage is very much in earnest about a husband, there is no effectual reason we know of why she should not lift up her

---

1 Supposed.

2 This probably refers to Chapter 10 of Charlotte Brontë's *Shirley* (1849), where Caroline Helstone reflects on her future as an "old maid": "Is this enough? Is it to live? Is there not a terrible hollowness, mockery, want, craving, in that existence which is given away to others, for want of something of your own to bestow it on?"

"protest" against circumstances. But things have gone very much further since the days of 'Shirley.' We have grown accustomed to the reproduction, not only of wails over female loneliness and the impossibility of finding anybody to marry, but to the narrative of many thrills of feeling much more practical and conclusive. What is held up to us as the story of the feminine soul as it really exists underneath its conventional coverings, is a very fleshly and unlovely record. Women driven wild with love for the man who leads them on to desperation before he accords that word of encouragement which carries them into the seventh heaven; women who marry their grooms in fits of sensual passion;[1] women who pray their lovers to carry them off from husbands and homes they hate; women, at the very least of it, who give and receive burning kisses and frantic embraces, and live in a voluptuous dream, either waiting for or brooding over the inevitable lover, – such are the heroines who have been imported into modern fiction. "All for love and the world well lost,"[2] was once the motto of a simple but perennial story, with which every human creature had a certain sympathy – the romance that ended pleasantly in a wholesome wedding, or pathetically in a violet-covered grave. But the meaning has changed nowadays. Now it is no knight of romance riding down the forest glades, ready for the defence and succour of all the oppressed, for whom the dreaming maiden waits. She waits now for flesh and muscles, for strong arms that seize her, and warm breath that thrills her through, and a host of other physical attractions, which she indicates to the world with a charming frankness. On the other side of the picture it is, of course, the amber hair and undulating form, the warm flesh and glowing colour, for which the youth sighs in his turn; but were the sketch made from the man's point of view, its openness would at least be less repulsive. The peculiarity of it in England is, that it is oftenest made from the woman's side – that it is women who describe those sensuous raptures – that this intense appreciation of flesh and blood, this eagerness of physical sensation, is represented as the natural sentiment of English girls, and is offered to

---

1   A reference to Aurora Floyd's marriage to James Conyers, her father's groom.
2   The title of John Dryden's rewriting of *Antony and Cleopatra, All for Love: Or, The World Well Lost* (1678).

them not only as the portrait of their own state of mind, but as their amusement and mental food. Such a wonderful phenomenon might exist, and yet society might be innocent of it. It might be the fault of one, or of a limited school, and the mere fact that such ravings are found in print might be no great argument against the purity of the age. But when it is added that the class thus represented does not disown the picture – that, on the contrary, it hangs it up in boudoir and drawing-room – that the books which contain it circulate everywhere, and are read everywhere, and are not contradicted – then the case becomes much more serious. For our own part we do not believe, as some people do, that a stratum of secret vice underlies the outward seeming of society. Most of our neighbours, we know, are very good sort of people, and we believe unfeignedly that our neighbours' neighbours resemble our own. It is possible to believe that very fine people or very shabby people are profoundly wicked, but as for the world as represented on our own level we know that it is not so. The girls of our acquaintance in general are very nice girls; they do not, so far as we are aware – notwithstanding a natural proclivity towards the society, when it is to be had, of their natural companions in existence – pant for indiscriminate kisses, or go mad for unattainable men. And yet here stands the problem which otherwise is not to be solved. It is thus that Miss Braddon and Miss Thomas,[1] and a host of other writers, explain their feelings. These ladies might not know, it is quite possible, any better. They might not be aware how young women of good blood and good training feel. The perplexing fact is, that the subjects of this slander make no objection to it. Protests are being raised everywhere in abundance, but against this misrepresentation there is no protest. It seems to be accepted by the great audience of the circulating libraries as something like the truth. Mr Trollope's[2] charming girls do not, now that we know them so well, call forth half

---

1 Annie Thomas (1838-1918), maiden and pen-name of Mrs Pender Cudlip. She began publishing in 1862, and became a most productive writer of romance fiction. (She claimed to be able to write a three-decker novel in six weeks.) Like *Aurora Floyd*, her novel *On Guard* (1865) featured a horse-riding heroine.
2 Anthony Trollope (1815-82), leading Victorian realist novelist, not of the sensation school. His popular series of Barsetshire novels was published between 1855 and 1867.

so much notice from the press as do the Aurora Floyds of contemporary fiction. Is, then, the picture true? or by what extraordinary impulse is it that the feminine half of society thus stigmatises and stultifies its own existence?... Miss Braddon has, without doubt, certain literary claims. 'Aurora Floyd,' notwithstanding its unpleasant subject (though we don't doubt that its unpleasant subject has been in reality the cause of its great success), is a very clever story. It is well knit together, thoroughly interesting, and full of life. The life is certainly not of a high description, but it is genuine in its way; and few people with any appreciation of fiction could refuse to be attracted by a tale so well defined. The 'Doctor's Wife'[1] strikes even a higher note.... Other books of Miss Braddon's have not been unworthy, to some extent, of the applause bestowed upon them. There has been a good story now and then, a clever bit of construction, even an inkling of a character. She is the inventor of the fair-haired demon of modern fiction. Wicked women used to be brunettes long ago, now they are the daintiest, softest, prettiest of blonde creatures; and this change has been wrought by Lady Audley, and her influence on contemporary novels. She has brought in the reign of bigamy as an interesting and fashionable crime, which no doubt shows a certain deference to the British relish for law and order. It goes against the seventh commandment, no doubt, but does it in a legitimate sort of way, and is an invention which could only have been possible to an Englishwoman knowing the attraction of impropriety, and yet loving the shelter of law.... Miss Braddon is the leader of her school, and to her the first honours ought naturally to be given, but her disciples are many. One of the latest of these disciples is the authoress of 'Cometh up as a Flower,'[2] a novel which has recently won that amount of public approval which is conveyed by praise in the leading papers and a second edition. This book is not a stupid book. There is a certain amount of interest and some character in it.... The wonderful thing in it is the

---

1 Braddon's *The Doctor's Wife* (1864) was a rewriting of Gustave Flaubert's *Madame Bovary* (1857).
2 Rhoda Broughton (1840-1920). Her bestseller, *Cometh Up As A Flower* (1867), is narrated autobiographically by the audacious and tough-minded heroine Nell Le Strange.

portrait of the modern young woman as presented from her own point of view. The last wave but one of female novelists was very feminine. Their stories were all family stories, their troubles domestic, their women womanly to the last degree, and their men not much less so. The present influx of young life has changed all that. It has reinstated the injured creature Man in something like his natural character, but unfortunately it has gone to extremes, and moulded its women on the model of men, just as the former school moulded its men on the model of women. The heroine of 'Cometh up as a Flower' is a good case in point. She is not by any means so disagreeable, so vulgar, or so mannish, as at the first beginning she makes herself out to be. Her flippancy, to start with, revolts the reader, and inclines him to pitch the volume to as great a distance from him as is practicable; but if he has patience a little, the girl is not so bad. She is a motherless girl, brought up in the very worst way, and formed on the most wretched model, but yet there is a touch of nature in the headstrong creature. And this of itself is a curious peculiarity in fiction generally. Ill-brought-up motherless girls, left to grow anyhow, out of all feminine guardianship, have become the ideal of the novelist. There is this advantage in them, that benevolent female readers have the resource of saying "Remember she had no mother," when the heroine falls into any unusual lapse from feminine traditions; but it is odd, to say the least of it, that this phase of youthful life should commend itself so universally to the female novelist....

It would be a task beyond our powers to enter into all the varieties of immorality which the novelists of the day have ingeniously woven into their stories. In these matters the man who writes is at once more and less bold than the woman; he may venture on positive criminality to give piquancy to his details, but it is the female novelist who speaks the most plainly, and whose best characters revel in a kind of innocent indecency, as does the heroine of 'Cometh up as a Flower.' Not that the indecency is always innocent; but there are cases in which it would seem the mere utterance of a certain foolish daring – an ignorance which longs to look knowing – a kind of immodest and indelicate innocence which likes to play with impurity. This is the most dismal feature among all these disagreeable phenomena. Nasty thoughts, ugly suggestions, an imagination which prefers the unclean, is almost more appalling than the facts of actual depravity, because it has no excuse of sudden passion or temptation, and no visible boundary. It is a shame to women so to write; and it is a shame to the women who read and accept as a true representation of themselves and their ways the equivocal talk and fleshly inclinations herein attributed to them. Their patronage of such books is in reality an adoption and acceptance of them. It may be done in carelessness, it may be done in that mere desire for something startling which the monotony of ordinary life is apt to produce; but it is debasing to everybody concerned. Women's rights and women's duties have had enough discussion, perhaps even from the ridiculous point of view. We have most of us made merry over Mr Mill's crotchet on the subject,[1] and over the Dr Marys and Dr Elizabeths;[2] but yet a woman has one duty of invaluable importance to her country and her race which cannot be over-estimated – and that is the duty of being pure. There is perhaps nothing of such vital consequence to a nation. Our female critics are fond of making demonstrations of indignation over the different punishment given by the world to the sin of man and that of woman in this respect. But all philosophy notwithstanding, and leaving the religious question untouched, there can be no possible doubt that the wickedness of man is less ruinous, less disastrous to the world in general, than the wickedness of woman. That is the climax of all misfortunes to the race. One of our cleverest journals took occasion the other day to point out the resemblance of certain superficial fashions among ourselves to the fashions prevalent among Roman women at the time of Rome's downfall. The comparison, no doubt, has been made again and again, and yet society has not become utterly depraved. But yet it has come to have many very unlovely, very unpromising, features in it. We are no preacher to call English ladies to account, and we have no tragical message to deliver even had we the necessary pulpit to do it in; but it certainly would be well if they

---

1 John Stuart Mill (1806-73), who, with his wife Harriet Taylor Mill, was a leading advocate of women's rights, especially women's suffrage. In 1866 he introduced the first parliamentary motion to expand the franchise to women.

2 Refers to three pioneering women doctors in England and America: Mary Putnam Jacobi (1842-1906), Elizabeth Blackwell (1821-1910), and Elizabeth Garrett Anderson (1836-1917).

would put a stop to nasty novels. It would be well for literature, well for the tone of society, and well for the young people who are growing up used to this kind of reading. Considering how low the tone of literary excellence is, and how little power of exciting interest exists after all in these equivocal productions, the sacrifice would not seem a great one.

6. "The Cant of Modern Criticism." George Augustus Sala,[1] *Belgravia*, November 1867.

…An anonymous writer in *Blackwood*[2] has thought fit to preach a sermon on Novels; and, with the writer's kind permission, I will proceed to pick his sermon and himself to pieces; to rip him up and shake the bran and sawdust out of him, and to make of his text a stirrup-leather, wherewith, Heaven willing, I will belabour him to my heart's content, if not to his own.

"English novels," begins this sage, "have for a long time – from the days of Sir Walter Scott at least – held a very high reputation in the world, not so much perhaps for what critics would call the highest development of art, as for a certain sanity, wholesomeness, and cleanness unknown to other literature of the same class. This peculiarity has had its effect, no doubt, upon those very qualities of the national mind which produced it…. It has increased that perfect liberty of reading which is the rule in most cultivated English houses … it has abolished the domestic Index Expurgatorius, as well as all public censorship; it has made us secure and unsuspicious in our reception of everything or almost everything that comes to us in the form of print."

The gist of this solemn exordium is, I suppose, that since Sir Walter Scott's days English novels have been "sane, clean, and wholesome." Sir Walter, it may be observed in passing, only wrote three real novels in his life: *St. Ronan's Well*, *The Surgeon's Daughter*, and *Guy Mannering*;[3]

---

1 George Augustus Sala (1828-96), journalist, novelist, and travel writer. Sala contributed articles to a number of magazines and was also a correspondent for *The Daily Telegraph*.

2 This refers to the essay "Novels" by Margaret Oliphant, published in *Blackwood's* in September 1867, reprinted as Appendix B.5, 599.

3 *St. Ronan's Well* (1823), *The Surgeon's Daughter* (1827), and *Guy Mannering* (1815).

and the two former are among his very weakest productions. The immortal series of stories told by the Wizard of the North,[1] and which are popularly known as the *Waverley Novels*, are not Novels in the proper sense of the term, but Romances – romances whose splendour shall never pale while the British name and the English tongue endure. The celebrity of mere novelists, however great it may be, is ordinarily destined to be ephemeral. Who but the Dryasdusts now remember Mdlle. de Scuderi, or Afra Behn, or Patty Fielding? Miss Edgeworth[3] was a novelist properly so called; and but for some valuable scraps of political economy scattered through her admirable books, Miss Edgeworth would be, by this time, completely forgotten. Miss Porter was a novelist pure and simple, and not one reader in fifty thousand knows anything about Miss Porter, or remembers *Thaddeus of Warsaw*,[4] now. Miss Austen was a novelist of the very first rank; but Miss Austen is as completely ignored by novel-readers of the present generation as Mrs. Henry Wood[5] will be ignored by the next. Dirty, droll, old Smollett[5] was a novelist; as humorist scholars still study his works with delight, and keep them locked up from their children; but it is as much as cheap publishers, with catchpenny editions, can do to keep the memory of the lewd old doctor who wrote *Roderick Random*[6], and died at Leghorn, extant among the reading public. Although *Clarissa Harlowe*, as a wonderful analysis of human passion and frailty, still extorts admiration from many "cultivated" persons, the Man Richardson[7] is as dead as a door-nail; only Fielding, who was less a novelist than the author of an astounding philosophical exposition of

---

1 i.e., Sir Walter Scott.
2 Madeleine de Scudéry (1607-1701) was a writer of French heroic romances. Aphra Behn (1640-89) was a playwright, poet, and novelist. Her most famous piece of fiction is *Oroonoko, or the History of the Royal Slave* (1678). "Patty Fielding" probably refers to Sarah Fielding (1710-68), novelist and sister to Henry Fielding (see below). Maria Edgeworth (1767-1849) wrote regional and historical novels, tales based on Irish life, and novels depicting contemporary English society. Her most influential novels are *Castle Rackrent* (1800) and *Belinda* (1801).
3 Jane Porter (1776-1850) published *Thaddeus of Warsaw* in 1803.
4 Ellen Wood (1814-87), author of the sensation novel *East Lynne* (1861).
5 Tobias George Smollet (1721-71), novelist, editor, and satirist.
6 Smollet published *Roderick Random* in 1748.
7 Samuel Richardson (1689-1761). His novel *Clarissa* (1747-48) was extremely popular both in England and Europe.

human nature, still keeps the field of the world with *Tom Jones*.[1]

Sir Walter Scott died, I think, about four-and-thirty years ago.[2] I will try to recollect a few of the "sane, wholesome, and cleanly novels" written since his day. Shortly before his death he addressed a very kind letter to a young gentleman[3] who had been, or was subsequently, in the bookselling line, but who made his literary *début* in a historical romance, the name of which I forget, but which was built on the well-known Scott lines. Emboldened by Sir Walter's good word, this young gentleman, whose name was William Harrison Ainsworth, speedily followed suit with a book called *Rookwood*[4] – a novel whose sensationalism was wilder, ghastlier, and more immoral than had been in the last epoch the craziest screed of Monk Lewis,[5] or the most hideous phantasmagoria of Mrs. Radcliffe,[6] – than the most blood-boultered chronicles of M. Eugène Sue or M. Paul Féval[7] in the present one. The sub-hero of *Rookwood* was Dick Turpin[8] the highwayman; that thief's apocryphal ride to York was – with the exception of the lively passage about the lady buried alive in a sarcophagus – the most exciting episode in the book; and there were several amusing chapters minutely descriptive of the manners of gipsies and the flash minstrelsy of the Romany Rye. *Rookwood* – eminently a "sane, wholesome, cleanly book" – met with prodigious success. Pluming himself for a yet higher flight, Mr. Ainsworth burst upon the age with *Jack Sheppard*.[9] In this astounding rogue's epic –

1   Henry Fielding (1707-54) published his novel *Tom Jones* in 1749.
2   Scott died in 1832.
3   This letter from Scott to W. H. Ainsworth does not appear to have survived. In his journal entry of 17 October 1826 Scott records completing Ainsworth's first (anonymous) novel, *Sir John Chiverton*.
4   William Harrison Ainsworth (1805-82), novelist and editor. His novel *Rookwood* was published in 1834.
5   See *Aurora Floyd*, 151, n.1.
6   See Appendix B.4, 594, n.2.
7   Eugène Sue (1804-57), wrote novels dealing with the criminal world of Paris. Paul Féval (1817-87) wrote French sensation novels.
8   Richard Turpin (1706-39). Turpin, a famous thief, was eventually arrested for horse-stealing and hanged at York. A number of romances and ballads are connected with his name.
9   Ainsworth published *Jack Sheppard* in 1839.

this Newgate pastoral[1] with a vengeance – the principal character was a low, blackguard, gin-drinking burglar and prison-breaker, whose very commonplace trial you may read at large in the Old-Bailey Sessions[2] papers; but, to meet the requirements of "sanity, wholesomeness, and cleanliness," Mr. Ainsworth made out that the vulgar ruffian, who was so satisfactorily strangled at Tyburn[3] for robbing one Kneebone, a draper, was of gentle blood – kinsman to a French marquis; indeed, Mr. Ainsworth would not even allow his hero to pass out of the world in the manner consistent with the historic truth of his story, viz. by the agency of a halter.[4] There was a riot, it seems, at his execution; the military interfered, and a ball from a soldier's musket pierced Jack's heart just as he was about being rescued from the gallows by some masked footman in splendid livery. We all remember how the town went mad over *Jack Sheppard*, and how the book, converted into a "sane, wholesome, cleanly" drama, brought nightly crowds to the Adelphi[5] to see Mrs. Keeley[6] in small-clothes[7] and with a closely-cropped bullet head[8] – very charming did that excellent actress look under the circumstances, – and hear her sing the wholesome and cleanly lyric of "Nix my dolly, pals, fake away!" I know not whether it was the novelist or the dramatist who put into the hero's mouth the immortal ethical proposition, "*Jack Sheppard is a thief, but he*

---

1   Newgate is the principal west gate of London, and its gatehouse was used as a prison from the twelfth century until it was demolished in 1902. A "Newgate pastoral," therefore, is a story which describes and romanticizes the activities of criminals and the underworld.

2   Trials held at the Central Criminal Court in London, called the "Old Bailey" because it stands within the former bailey (outer courtyard) of the City of London.

3   The principal place of execution for criminals well into the eighteenth century. The gallows stood on Tyburn road, which led into London through Newgate.

4   That is, by being hanged.

5   The Adelphi Theatre, located on the Strand, London, was built in 1806 and expanded in 1858.

6   Mary Anne Keeley (1806-99), English actress whose role as Jack Sheppard in 1839 caused such a sensation that the Lord Chamberlain forbade any subsequent play on the subject.

7   Knee-breeches. On a female actor such a costume would show a scandalous amount of lower calf and ankle.

8   Convicts' hair was shaved close to their skulls, giving their heads a rounded, "bulletlike" appearance. This is how Jack Sheppard is presented in the illustrations to Ainsworth's novel, and obviously Keeley adopted the style as part of her portrayal.

never told a lie" – assuredly a most cleanly and wholesome assertion. The sanity and cleanliness of *Jack Sheppard* were completed by the introduction of Jonathan Wild,[1] a thief-taker and receiver of stolen goods; of Blue-skin, a robber and murderer; and of two nymphs from the Hundreds of Drury – two common harlots, called Poll Maggot and Edgeworth Bess,[2] of whom Sheppard was the paramour. In this drama of the Gaol and the Lupanar,[3] Mr. Ainsworth may be said to have reached the apogee of sanity, wholesomeness, and cleanliness.... I am very reluctant thus to dwell on the works which first conduced to the celebrity of a highly respectable gentleman, who since has given to the public many interesting and excellent works; notably *Windsor Castle* and the *Tower of London*;[4] but when canting critics have the assurance to say that the foremost works of English fiction published since the death of Sir Walter Scott have been distinguished for "sanity, wholesomeness, and cleanliness," it is time for the truth to be told, and for those who have good memories to tell what they know.

No Editor of the domestic Index Expurgatorius, I conceive, would venture to banish from the family library such charming, tender, humanising books as the *Caxtons*, as *My Novel*, as *What will he do with it?* or as *Harold*, although I have heard of mammas who forbade their daughters to read either *Pelham* or *Devereux*[5] – both capital novels, but both replete with a degree of sensationalism, which the canting critic of *Blackwood* might well stigmatise as "feverish." The novel author of these works, however, contrived, at about the same time that Mr. Ainsworth was winning his hempen laurels, to produce a number of novels of essentially the same wholesome and cleanly order, and to which I entreat the attention of the Edinburgh preacher. There was *Eugene Aram*,[6] for instance; the apotheosis of a bloodthirsty Yorkshire school-usher, who, actuated by the paltriest motives, murdered a bar-

---

1 See *Aurora Floyd*, 524, n.1.
2 Blue-skin, Poll Maggot, and Edgeworth Bess are all characters in *Jack Sheppard*.
3 Brothel.
4 Ainsworth published *The Tower of London* in 1840 and *Windsor Castle* in 1843.
5 All of these novels were written by Edward Bulwer Lytton (see below). *The Caxtons* was published in 1849, *My Novel* in 1853, *What will he do with it?* in 1858, *Harold* in 1848, *Pelham* in 1828, and *Devereux* in 1829.
6 Novel by Bulwer-Lytton published in 1832.

ber and hid his body in a hole, and, after telling innumerable lies in the dock, was hanged. As the murderer was a good classical scholar, and had even some acquaintance with the Oriental tongues, the noble novelist – then Mr. Edward Lytton Bulwer[1] – made him a Hero, made him the lover of a beautiful and virtuous maiden, and implied that the detestable crime for which he was duly gibbeted had been inspired by his craving for learning and his desire to buy more Greek plays and Hebrew dictionaries. Then there was *Paul Clifford*,[2] another of the sanest and cleanliest novels ever penned. The hero was a highwayman, the bastard son of a judge, who afterwards sentenced his own son to death....

There is less need to dwell on the coarse, brutal, but amusing novels of Theodore Hook[3] (in one of which a gentleman intrigues with his own sister), published between the time of Sir Walter Scott's demise and the era of what the canter in *Blackwood* calls the "feverish" school. The characters of the day were grossly caricatured in *Jack Brag* and *Gilbert Gurney*,[4] and everybody – man or woman – who was not a Tory was foully abused; but Theodore Hook's novels were decidedly laughable. During the same epoch, also, the Countess of Blessington[5] put forth a number of flimsy vicious novels, descriptive of what is called "high life," interlarded with scraps of bad French, and mainly devoted to the intrigues of demireps and chambermaids. Poor old Mrs. Gore's[6] novels may scarcely have come up to the *Blackwood* sermoniser's standard of "cleanness and sanity." They were simply readable, harmless, and silly, and are now very completely forgotten. But for "sanity, wholesomeness, and cleanness" *in excelsis* we must turn to the novels of Mrs. Trollope – to the *Widow Barnaby*, to the *Barnabies in America*, to the *Vicar of Wrexhill*, to *Michael Armstrong the Factory Boy*, and to *Jessie Phillips*,[7] novels undeniably clever and powerful, but so

---

1 See Appendix B.3, 583, n.2.

2 Published by Bulwer Lytton in 1830.

3 Theodore Edward Hook (1788-1841), editor and novelist.

4 Two novels by Hook, *Gilbert Gurney* published in 1836, and *Jack Brag* in 1837.

5 Marguerite Power, Countess of Blessington (1789-1849).

6 Catherine Grace Frances Gore (1799-1861), novelist and playwright. Her two best-known novels are *Mothers and Daughters* (1831) and *Mrs. Armytage* (1836).

7 Frances Trollope (1780-1863) published *The Widow Barnaby* in 1838, *The Barnabys in America* (Sala misspells the title) in 1843, *The Vicar of Wrexhill* in 1837, *Michael Armstrong the Factory Boy* in 1839, and *Jessie Phillips* in 1843.

revoltingly coarse in tone, in thought, and in language, that no publisher of the present day would dare to print them. I had almost forgotten the novels of the Right Honourable Benjamin Disraeli.[1] "Clean" those novels may, without the slightest irony, be declared. Mr. Disraeli has always been distinguished by innate intellectual refinement and delicacy. The "wholesomeness" of *Venetia*, of *Coningsby*, of *Contarini Fleming*, of *Henrietta Temple*[2], is, however, very questionable indeed; but about the "sanity" of the entire series of Disraeli fictions it is difficult to hold two opinions. A recluse student who had been ingeniously left ignorant of the fact that Mr. Disraeli has been Chancellor of the British Exchequer and leader of the House of Commons, and is one of the foremost of British statesmen, could scarcely be blamed if he arrived at the conclusion that the writer of *Sibyl* and *Tancred*[3] was stark-staring mad.

With the exception of the works of Thackeray and Dickens, which stand alone, and cannot be classed in the three-volume, thirty-one-and-sixpence category – with the exception of the nautical novels of Marryatt,[4] who was a kind of salt-water Paul de Kock[5] – with the exception of the mess-table stories of Charles Lever,[6] and the historical romances of G.P.R. James,[7] I have, I think, named all the novelists of note who "flourished," as the saying is, between the demise of Sir Walter and the "coming up like a flower"[8] of such novelists as Miss Brontë [sic], George Eliot, and Miss Braddon. But I say that, with the early novels of Ainsworth, Bulwer, Hook, and Mrs. Trollope, still procurable at a hundred bookstalls, it is the vilest of cant, it is the sor-

---

1   Benjamin Disraeli (1804-81), novelist and politician. He wrote a number of novels before becoming the Member of Parliament for Maidstone in 1837. Disraeli was Prime Minister of England from February to December of 1868, and again from 1874-80. He became an intimate friend of Queen Victoria, who eventually made him the first Earl of Beaconsfield.

2   Novels published by Disraeli: *Contarini Fleming* in 1832, *Venetia* and *Henrietta Temple* in 1837, and *Coningsby* in 1844.

3   Disraeli published *Sybil* in 1845 and *Tancred* in 1847.

4   Frederick Marryat (1792-1848), novelist and captain in the Royal Navy.

5   See *Aurora Floyd*, 76, n.3.

6   Charles James Lever (1806-72) was a popular novelist of military life and of Irish society.

7   George Payne Rainsford James (1799-1860), poet and novelist.

8   Refers to the title of Rhoda Broughton's bestseller, *Cometh Up As A Flower* (1867).

riest of humbug, to speak of English novels as having "held a very high reputation in the world, not so much perhaps for what critics would call the highest development of art, as for a certain sanity, wholesomeness, and cleanness unknown to other literature of the same class."

Do I intend to maintain that the modern, the contemporary novel of life and character and adventure – the outspoken, realistic, moving, breathing fiction, which mirrors the passions of the age for which it is written, is preferable to the silly sentimentalities of Lady Blessington and Mrs. Gore, to the aristocratic highwaymen and intellectual assassins of *Paul Clifford* and *Eugene Aram*, – or to the dead thieves, bullies, doxies, and turnkeys who were galvanised by Mr. Harrison Ainsworth? Unhesitatingly I say that I do. *Jane Eyre* was to all intents and purposes a "sensational" novel, and some fastidious parents might forbid their daughters to read a book in which there is a deliberate attempt at bigamy; in which there is a mad wife who tries to burn her husband's house down; in which the flogging of a girl at school is minutely described; and in which an impulsive little governess sits on a blind gentleman's knee, and pulls his beautiful dark hair about – likening it to the hair of Samson. *Adam Bede* too is clearly "sensational."[1] There is murder, and there is frailty in it. *Lady Audley's Secret, Aurora Floyd, Sir Jasper's Tenant, Henry Dunbar, Rupert Godwin, Eleanor's Victory, John Marchmont's Legacy, Birds of Prey*,[2] are also indubitably sensational. Lady Audley has fair hair, and tries to murder two or three people; Aurora Floyd horsewhips her groom; the adventuress in *Sir Jasper's Tenant* personates her sister. But in all these novels the people walk and talk and act, not like the denizens of some phantom land of anthropophagi,[3] where heads do grow beneath the owner's shoulders, but like dwellers in the actual, breathing world in which we live. If we read the newspaper; if we read the police reports; if we can laugh at such a case as that of the "Honourable Mrs. Geraldine Meurice," or

---

1   See Appendix B.3, 590, n.3.
2   All of these novels appeared relatively early in Braddon's career. She published *Lady Audley's Secret* in 1862, *Aurora Floyd, Eleanor's Victory*, and *John Marchmont's Legacy* in 1863, *Henry Dunbar* in 1864, *Sir Jasper's Tenant* in 1865, and *Rupert Godwin* and *Birds of Prey* in 1867.
3   Literally "men-eaters"; cannibals.

weep over such a one as that of "Augusta Mitchell;" if we have ever troubled ourself about a Yelverton marriage, a Titchborne baronetcy, a Thellusson will, a Road murder, a Cornhill burglary, a gold-dust robbery, a Roupell forgery, a Simla court-martial,[1] we shall take no great harm by reading realistic novels of human passion, weakness, and error. The canting preacher in *Blackwood* insinuates that the language in which modern novels are written is no longer fit to be read by the young, but that we are approaching the verbal license of Sue and Feydeau,[2] and Paul de Kock and Ponson du Terrail.[3] He instances an "irreproachable French matron's" explanation to "an English acquaintance, whose eyes expressed a certain amazement at the frankness of some drawing-room narrative." "*Nous sommes tous d'un âge mûr,*" said the "irreproachable matron;" "*j'espère que vous ne pensez pas que je parlerais comme ça devant des jeunes gens.*" However "irreproachable" in conduct the Scotch preacher's matron may have been, it is certain that her French was not free from reproach. Indeed, he has made her talk like an irreproachable washerwoman. The conversation being among ladies, she would, in the first place, have said, "*Nous sommes toutes,*" and not *nous sommes tous.* But let that pass: the greatest probability is that the matron would not have said anything of the kind. "*Nous sommes tous d'un âge mûr,*" smacks strongly of boarding-school French at two guineas a quarter. "*Mon Dieu! Madame, on est d'un certain âge. On ne parlerait pas de la sorte devant des jeunes gens. Je n'y penserais pas.*" *That* is French.[4] The preacher's Parisian is after the school of Stratford-atte-

---

1   Sala provides a list of sensational crimes and trials. Thus, for example, in 1867 Geraldine Meurice was tried for fraud and conspiracy; the intricate relationship between Major William Charles Yelverton and Theresa Longworth, involving seduction and bigamy, was played out in newspapers and courtrooms from 1858 to 1865; the Thellusson will case of 1859 concerned a dispute as to the rightful heirs of a wealthy merchant who died in 1798, leaving his estate to be divided only when the last of his nine children and grandchildren were dead; and the Road murder, encompassing the death of a four-year-old child, with the possibilty of sibling rivalry or adultery as the motive, held the public's attention from 1860 to 1865.
2   Ernest Feydeau (1821-73), French novelist most famous for his novel of jealousy and adultery, *Fanny* (1858).
3   Pierre-Alexis, Vicomte de Ponson du Terrail (1829-71), French novelist.
4   Sala corrects the *Blackwood's* reviewer's French by pointing out that in the context of several women talking the correct form of usage is the feminine "*toutes,*" not the masculine "*tous.*" His version is indeed more urbane and euphonious than Oliphant's.

Bowe.[1]

It is when our moralist has to advert to the alleged indelicacy of language in modern novels that he comes out in all the full bloom of what Mr. Charles Reade, in a memorable letter to a New-York paper, called "a prurient prude."[2] Prurient prudery is a distinguishing characteristic of modern cant and modern criticism. To be wholly righteous when you assail a celebrated author, you should have the manners of Mawworm and the morals of Tartuffe.[3] Then you can approach in a proper spirit the examination of the author's "language." My own view (not being a Canter) on the subject is, that the best test of the kind of language to employ in a novel is the temper of the public. Occasional coarseness, when it is compensated for by genius and power, the public will suffer.... But the whole question of *les jeunes gens* may be summed up in one dictum – that novels are written for grown people and not for babes and sucklings. If they get surreptitiously what is meant for their elders, let domestic authority look to it. Domestic authority is not yet dead, I hope. That phantom daughter of mine would not be suffered by her papa to study the elaborately-engraved anatomical atlases of Bouchardon and Sue *aîné* and Doctor Fau, the *Proportions* of Albert Durer, or the *Canons Plastiques* of Jean Cousin,[4] which he possesses. I should warn her off the

---

1   A reference to Chaucer's General Prologue to *The Canterbury Tales*, lines 124-25. The Prioresse speaks French learned at Stratford at Bow (a district near London).

2   Charles Reade (1814-84), playwright and novelist. His pamphlet *The Prurient Prude* was published in response to a scathing attack on his novel *Griffith Gaunt* (1866) in the New York weekly newspaper *The Round Table*.

3   Both Mawworm and Tartuffe are characters representing hypocrisy. The first appears in Isaac Bickerstaffe's play *The Hypocrite* (1769), which is itself an adaptation of Molière's comedy *Le Tartuffe* (1664).

4   Edme Bouchardon (1698-1762) was a distinguished French sculptor. Sue "the elder," father of Eugène Sue (see above), was an influential French surgeon who published a number of anatomical studies. Julien Fau's *Anatomie des formes extérieures du corps humain, à l'usage des peintres et des sculpteurs* (1845) was a popular lithographic work designed to help art students visualize the human skeleton and muscles. Albrecht Dürer (1471-1528) was a German painter, engraver, and printmaker. Around 1500 Dürer became interested in developing a scientific method of representing the human form. The resulting series of proportion studies would have been judged inappropriately detailed by most Victorians. Jean Cousin the Elder (1490-1561) was a French painter and engraver. Influenced by Dürer, Cousin's illustrations would also have been too risqué for Sala's "phantom daughter."

police reports. I should gently wean her from a good many advertisements in the daily papers. I should tell her that Voltaire's[1] novels were dull and stupid, that John Dryden's[2] dramas were very dry, that Parent Duchâtelet[3] was quite unreadable, that Cervantes[4] was, though admirable, somewhat too philosophical for her yet awhile, and that *Robinson Crusoe*[5] was better reading for a girl than *Gil Blas*.[6] If she asked me who Casanova[7] was, I should answer Jesuitically, that he was a dreary old metaphysician; and if she wanted to read *Rabelais*,[8] I should declare that his French was too quaint and crabbed for her comprehension. When she came to be one-and-twenty, or got married, I should no more think of dictating to her as to what kinds of books she should read, than as to what kind of stays she should wear – if she wore any at all. *Cela serait son affaire*.[9] But, most assuredly, during her nonage, I should, with equal anxiety, keep her from *Don Juan*[10] and the *Passionate Pilgrim*. For all that, I should not make an *auto da fé*[11] of my books, or discontinue my orders to the newsvendor round the corner. There are books for children and books for grown people.

---

1 Voltaire (1694-1778), pen-name of François Marie Arouet, French philosopher, dramatist, and novelist.

2 John Dryden (1631-1700), poet, essayist, and dramatist.

3 Alexandre-Jean-Baptiste Parent-Duchâtelet (1790-1836), sanitary expert, who wrote on prostitution in Paris, public hygeine, and venereal disease.

4 Miguel de Cervantes Saavedra (1547-1616), Spanish dramatist and novelist, most famous for *Don Quixote*, the first part of which was published in 1605, and the second in 1615.

5 A novel by Daniel Defoe (1660-1731), published in 1719. Although it concerns male characters, the novel was considered suitable reading for girls because the shipwrecked Crusoe focuses on domestic concerns: his domicile, clothes, food, etc.

6 *The Adventures of Gil Blas of Santillane*, published 1715-35, was written by Alain René le Sage (1668-1747). It was translated into English by Smollet (see above) in 1749.

7 Giacomo Casanova de Seingalt (1725-98), Italian adventurer more famous for his amorous intrigues than for his philosophical musings.

8 François Rabelais (1494?-1553), French physician and satirist. The name is italicized by Sala in his original text.

9 "That would be her business."

10 An epic satire by Byron published in sixteen cantos 1819-24.

11 Literally "act of the faith." The ceremony which concluded a session of the Spanish or Portuguese Inquisition, in which unrepentent heretics were burned at the stake. In this context the phrase suggests Sala is unwilling to sacrifice his books to the "cant" of the *Blackwood's* reviewer.

There are books for all ages and both sexes, like *Robinson Crusoe* just mentioned, and the *Vicar of Wakefield*;[1] but we grown-up folks should get into rather an effete and pappy state, intellectually, if we read nothing but about Man Friday, and Moses going to the fair.[2] For all the domestic Index Expurgatorius – and long may it flourish! – there will come a time when our children will know quite as much as we do, and more too; and when they will read all our novels, and, it may be, write novels themselves. I have no fear, because this is the case, for the stability of British virtue, or for the future of the British home. Our daughters will, I have no doubt, grow up to be wives and mothers quite as admirable as their grandmothers were before them. But meanwhile we men and women who live in the world, and have, many of us, lived pretty hard lives too, want novels about That which Is, and not about That which never Was and never Will be. We don't want pap, or spoon-meat, or milk-and-water, or curds-and-whey, or Robb's biscuits, or boiled whiting, or cold boiled veal without salt. We want meat; and this is a strong age, and we can digest it.

I should be content to leave the poor canting creature in *Blackwood* here, but that from the beginning to the end of his sermon – it is twenty-two pages, or forty-four columns long – there is palpably present one guiding and pervading animus. Hatred and jealousy and spite towards one of the most successful novelists of the age – ill-nature and ill-feeling towards the author of *Aurora Floyd* and a dozen more capital novels shine in every page of the lucubrations of this agreeable soul. There is little need for me to take up the cudgels in defence of Miss Braddon: she is quite strong enough and quite cunning enough of fence to hold her own, and to chastise this canting man of Edinburgh town; yet to me there is a kind of pleasure, mingled with sadness, in assailing her detractors in a magazine which she conducts, remembering as I do that it was in a magazine which *I* conducted – in *Temple Bar* – that she reached her first station in the highway of Fame. She very soon shouldered *me* out of the way, I can assure you,

---

1   A novel by William Goldsmith, published in 1766.
2   In *Robinson Crusoe*, Crusoe makes a slave of an indigenous native whom he calls Friday. In *The Vicar of Wakefield*, Moses, the Vicar's second son, attends a local fair in order to sell the family's colt, but is cheated out of the money before returning home.

and the conductor was quite trampled under foot by the youngest and least experienced of his lady passengers. I bear her nor any one else in the world any ill-will; I have had other scissors to grind and other fish to fry; yet I often think with a droll kind of ruefulness of the young lady who came coolly and confidently out of the multitude of "constant readers" and "subscribers from the first," and took her place on the topmost step of the daïs of fiction. I suppose it is because she rose so rapidly, by her own unassisted genius, pluck, and perseverance, that the candid gentleman in *Blackwood* abuses her so. I suppose it is because her pen shows no sign of feebleness that he is so exasperated with her, and that he classes her with "Miss Thomas,"[1] and that he calls her novels "feverish," and that he sneers at "the *Aurora Floyds*" as types of vicious and depraved women. Poor dear Aurora! though she did horsewhip her groom, we all know that she was more sinned against than sinning. I don't think the Scotch gentleman has ever read *Aurora Floyd*; but this would be quite consonant with the cant of modern criticism. To abuse people they have never seen – to vilify those of whom they know nothing – to "cut up" books they have never perused – to accuse scholars of ignorance, and humorists of dulness – to affect a lofty air when they are only writing so much spiteful drivel for a couple of pounds a week – to scoff at passages they don't understand – to throw dirt – to accuse their betters of irreverence and immorality – and finally, to be themselves perfectly inane, ignorant, untravelled, incapable "duffers," who are only permitted to review books because *somebody* must review them, and people who write books are generally too busy or too honest to criticise those of others; – to be and to do all this may be accounted part and parcel of the attributes of a Canting Critic. Without them he would merely be a dunderheaded Libeller.

---

1   See Appendix B.5, 603, n.1.

7. "On the 'Sensational' in Literature and Art." George Augustus Sala, *Belgravia*, February 1868.

Society must have a Cry, and what the cry may be does not very much matter, so long as it be cried loudly enough, and in a manner forced down the throats of people who have not wit enough to cry for themselves, but are content to allow others to do the Town Crier's office for them....

The number of Cries which have been heard in all ages in the history of literature and art would be amazing, did we not remember that artists and men of letters are human, and that humanity must have its howl. It is as the air it breathes. If it have it not, it dies. Now the followers of St. Bernard raise a cry against the followers of Abelard. "Down with the Pagan school!" they vociferate.[1] The "Pagan school" is a good Cry. *Blackwood* gets up a Cry against Leigh Hunt and Hazlitt[2] because they have the misfortune to live at Hampstead or in Tothill-fields. "Down with the Cockney school!"[3] squalls Edinburgh; and the writer of the finest artistic and literary criticisms we possess is termed a "moonstruck idiot;" and the author of *Rimini*[4] is bidden to "go hang himself in his fetid leather-braces."[5] The "Lakers"[6]

---

1   St. Bernard of Clairvaux (1090?-1153) was a French churchman and mystic. Peter Abelard (1079-1142) was a French churchman, philosopher, and teacher. Abelard was a Platonist and believed the methods of logic could be applied to matters of faith. This brought him into conflict with Bernard's emphasis on Christian mysticism, and Bernard attacked Abelard as a "pagan." Bernard, at the 1140 Council of Sens, managed to have Abelard and his teachings condemned, a condemnation that was later upheld by the Pope.

2   James Henry Leigh Hunt (1784-1859), poet, critic, and journalist; William Hazlitt (1778-1830), essayist.

3   The "Cockney School" was a derogatory nickname, meant to imply vulgarity and lack of education, given to certain Romantic writers by John Gibson Lockhart (1794-1854). Lockhart's fierce criticisms in *Blackwood's Magazine* earned him his own nickname of "The Scorpion."

4   *The Story of Rimini*, published by Leigh Hunt in 1816.

5   Between 1817 and 1821 Lockhart published a series of vicious personal attacks in *Blackwood's*, most of them aimed at Hunt, but later ones including Hazlitt (the "moonstruck idiot") and Keats.

6   The "Lake School" or the "Lake Poets" were terms applied to early English Romantic poets because Wordsworth, the leader of the movement, lived in the Lake District of England. The term first appeared in the *Edinburgh Review* in 1817.

had previously had their turn because Wordsworth happened to live at Grassmere,[1] and Coleridge came often to see him.... Dr. Southey,[2] having been laughed at by Lord Byron, thought utterly to crush that noble poet by calling him the chief of the "Satanic school;"[3] and virtuous papas and mammas all over the kingdom sternly resolved not to allow their daughters to read "Satanic poetry." But nine-tenths of what Southey wrote has passed long since into "the portion of weeds and outworn faces;" and Mr. Murray[4] is still making a very good thing, annually, out of Lord Byron's copyrights....

May I whisper in the reader's ear that the agitation against "Romanticism" in literature and art ... was an exactly analogous outcry to that with which we are now deafened in England against "Sensationalism"? But ere I take up that Cry of cries, and strive to show what a hollow, windy, worthless ululation it is, I wish to say a few words concerning a Cry as worthless, which immediately preceded it.

Mr. Charles Dickens has enjoyed European, world-wide fame for thirty years. I have watched his career as narrowly as I have watched it admiringly; and I think I have read every line he has written, and have been enabled to trace with sufficient accuracy the successive phases of development through which his genius has passed, the mellowing of his faculties, the chastening of his style, and their gradual culmination into a splendid but sober afternoon of intellect. He is probably, at this moment, the best-known and the most deservedly popular author in the world; and in the very first number of the very next serial in the familiar old green cover which he might publish, we should probably be constrained to admit that there was something – in the way of character or of description – as good as, if not better than, Charles Dickens had ever done before. Yet, having a pretty retentive memory,

---

1   The correct spelling is Grasmere.
2   Robert Southey (1774-1843), poet, editor, and reviewer. He held the position of Poet Laureate from 1813-43.
3   Southey's derogatory name for the later English Romantic poets, particularly Byron and Shelley. The name was first published in the Preface to Southey's poem the "Vision of Judgement" (1821). Byron's own "Vision of Judgement," published in 1822, is a satirical poem mocking Southey's attack.
4   John Murray (1808-92) inherited the famous publishing house which carried his name from his father, also John Murray (1778-1843). The elder John Murray was Byron's friend and publisher.

and having been all my life more or less intimately connected with what are called "literary circles," I can perfectly well recollect that, in the year 1842 – and we are now, I take it, in 1868 – there was no commoner cry in "polite society" than that "Dickens had written himself out." There used to be a man called Croker,[1] who had something to do with the Admiralty, and didn't know where Russell-square was,[2] and wrote scurrilous articles in the *Quarterly Review*.... In the first bright dawn of Charles Dickens's fame, Croker observed that the author of *Pickwick*[3] had "gone up like a rocket, but would come down like the stick."[4] This was "sack and sugar"[5] to the charitable souls who were so fond of repeating that "Boz"[6] had "written himself out." "Boz" wrote the *Old Curiosity Shop*,[7] and pending the appearance of his next book the charitable souls reported that he had gone raving mad. He went to America, and the charitable souls put it about that he was dead. He wrote *Martin Chuzzlewit*,[8] and the charitable souls declared that there was "a great falling off in his style." He went to Italy, and the charitable souls hinted that he had pawned his plate to raise funds for the voyage. There was no end to the malice of the charitable souls. *Dombey, Copperfield, Bleak House, Hard Times,* the *Two Cities, Great Expectations, Our Mutual Friend*,[9] were all asserted to be infinitely inferior to their predecessors; but somehow the man went on writing, and enlisting fresh tens of thousands of readers with every new book he wrote....

The only wonder is that the charitable souls have failed to discov-

---

1 John Wilson Croker (1780-1857), politician and author.

2 Russell Square lies just to the east of the British Museum in central London.

3 *The Posthumous Papers of the Pickwick Club* (1836-37) by Charles Dickens.

4 Croker's article questioning Dickens' ability to remain popular appears in the *Quarterly Review*, vol. 71, no. 142 (1842-43).

5 *1 Henry IV* II.iv.516. Sack and sugar was a popular drink; the sugar was mixed with the sack in order to sweeten the dry wine.

6 Dickens wrote his earliest works under the pseudonymn "Boz," including his first collection of pieces *Sketches by Boz* (1836-37).

7 Dickens published *The Old Curiosity Shop* in 1840-41.

8 *The Life and Adventures of Martin Chuzzlewit*, one of Dickens' least successful novels, appeared in 1843-44.

9 Dickens published *Dombey and Son* in 1847-48, *David Copperfield* in 1849-50, *Bleak House* in 1852-53, *Hard Times* in 1854, *A Tale of Two Cities* in 1859, *Great Expectations* in 1860-61, and *Our Mutual Friend* in 1864-65.

er that among modern "sensational" writers Mr. Charles Dickens is perhaps the most thoroughly, and has been from the very outset of his career the most persistently, "sensational" writer of the age. There is sensation even in *Pickwick*: the "Madman" and the "Stroller's" story, the death of the "Chancery Prisoner," and the episode of the "Queer Client," for example. The *Old Curiosity Shop* is replete with sensation, from the extravagant pilgrimage of Nell and the old man to the death of Quilp. *Barnaby Rudge*[1] begins with the sensation of an undiscovered murder, and ends with the sensation of a triple hanging and a duel *à mort*.[2] In *Nicholas Nickleby*[3] the end of Mr. Ralph Nickleby and the shooting of Lord Frederick Verisopht by Sir Mulberry Hawk are sensational enough to suit the strongest appetite. And the murder of Tigg Montague by Jonas Chuzzlewit; and the mysterious husband of Miss Betsy Trotwood in *David Copperfield*; and the convict millionaire in *Great Expectations*; and the grinding of the "National Razor" in the *Tale of Two Cities*; and Monks's confession, and the murder of Nancy, and the death of Sykes, in *Oliver Twist*;[4] and finally, the spontaneous combustion in *Bleak House*; and the tumbling down of the house in *Little Dorrit*;[5] and Mr. Carker's death in *Dombey and Son*. Are not all these pure "sensation"? . . .

What is Sensationalism, and who is Sensational? I will strive to tell you. The late Mr. William Shakespeare was an arrant sensational writer. He wrote the play of "Macbeth," which is founded mainly on murder and witchcraft. He wrote "Hamlet," in which there are many murders, a suicide, a suspicion of madness, and a ghost. He wrote "Othello," in which there is jealousy, and also murder. He wrote "King Lear," in which you will find murder, blindness, and madness. He wrote "Anthony and Cleopatra," in which these [sic] is suicide. He wrote "Julius Caesar," in which there is murder and a ghost. He wrote "Richard the Third," in which there are no end of murders and no end of ghosts. He wrote "Romeo and Juliet," in which luxuriate poison, murder, and premature interment. He wrote the "Merchant of

---

1 Dickens published *Barnaby Rudge* in 1841.
2 A duel "to the death."
3 Dickens published *Nicholas Nickleby* in 1838-39.
4 Dickens published *Oliver Twist* in 1837.
5 Dickens published *Little Dorrit* in 1855-57.

Venice," in which there is robbery and elopement, and an attempt on the part of a Jew bill-discounter to cut open the stomach of a Christian gentleman. The late M. de Voltaire highly objected to Shakespeare's sensationalism.[1] He called him *un barbare grotesque.*[2] He preferred murder *à la Grecque,*[3] when you only hear the slaughtered Agamemnon[4] groaning behind the scenes. He liked Peloponnesian adultery, Heracleidan seduction, and Attic incest.[5] Ben Jonson, Beaumont, Fletcher,[6] were not sensational writers. Ben's most sensational play, "The Alchemist,"[7] is made up of the humours of a conjuror, a swindler, and a woman of the town. Desdemona is sensational; Doll Common[8] is not so. Beaumont and Fletcher depicted the "humours" of their age with strength, richness, and raciness; they represented the manners of their time with pliancy, variety, and fidelity; but their plays were plays of Manners, and not of Human Nature. They were plays of Garments, and not of the Life within. So was it with the later comedy-writers. What has become of Etherege's "Love in a Tub,"[9] and Wycherley's "Gentleman Dancing-master,"[10] and Rowe's "Biter"?[11] Where are Shirley, Vanbrugh, Congreve, and Farquhar?[12] Where is

---

1 For Voltaire see Appendix B.6, 617, n.1. His most famous attack on Shakespeare occurs in his *Lettre à l'Académie* (1775).

2 "A grotesque barbarian."

3 Murder "in the Greek mode." Voltaire prefers classical Greek drama in which violence is narrated or implied, but not specifically portrayed. This is in opposition to Shakespeare's "barbarous" (i.e. non-classical) dramatic methods.

4 Agamemnon was king of Argos and leader of the Greek forces at Troy. Upon his return home he was murdered by his wife Clytemnestra and her lover Aegisthus.

5 Sala provides a list of sensational crimes preceded by various adverbs indicating a Greek location. He is implying that such events are acceptable to people like Voltaire as long as they remain tastefully and classically "off stage."

6 Benjamin Jonson (1572-1637), Francis Beaumont (1584-1616), John Fletcher (1579-1625), Renaissance dramatists. Beaumont and Fletcher collaborated on a number of plays between 1606 and 1616.

7 Jonson's *The Alchemist* was first staged in 1610.

8 Doll (or Dol) Common is one of the main female characters in *The Alchemist*.

9 Sir George Etherege (1634?-91?), dramatist. His play *The Comical Revenge, or Love in a Tub* was produced in 1664.

10 William Wycherley (1640-1716), dramatist. His play *The Gentleman Dancing-Master* was first performed in either 1671 or 1672.

11 Nicholas Rowe (1674-1718), dramatist. His play *The Biter* was staged in 1704.

12 James Shirley (1596-1666), Sir John Vanbrugh (1664-1726), William Congreve (1670-1729), George Farquhar (1678-1707), seventeenth- and eighteenth-century dramatists.

Foote[1] even? There is but one play by Massinger, the "Virgin Martyr,"[2] and one by Marlowe, the "Jew of Malta,"[3] that has survived almost utter oblivion. They are both "sensational;" that is to say, they treat of Life and Passion. The Elizabethan dramas of Manners are all dead. Who, save bookworms, reads the "Scornful Lady," or the "Custom of the Country," or the "Beggar's Bush," or the "Humorous Lieutenant," or the "Little French Lawyer," or the "Laws of Candy"?[4] Who knows much about "The Fox," or the "New Inn," or the "Staple of News"?[5] Yet the people who wrote these things were cried up by self-conceited wits and sages as infinitely superior to Shakespeare. Have they kept possession of the stage? Will they ever obtain possession of the stage again? Away from bookmen's shelves, the whole rout of them are as dead and gone as a chandler-shopkeeper's ledger of the year before last.

In the opinion of dolts and dullards and envious backbiters, everything is "sensational" that is vivid, and nervous, and forcible, and graphic, and true. There is no sensation in the wretched daubs of Benjamin West,[6] or the heartless tea-tray varnishing of Mengs;[7] but there is most deleterious sensationalism in Fuseli,[8] and Hogarth,[9] and

---

1   Samuel Foote (1720-77), actor and dramatist.

2   Philip Massinger (1583-1640), dramatist. In collaboration with Thomas Dekker (1570?-1632) he wrote *The Virgin Martyr*, which was printed in 1622.

3   Christopher Marlowe (1564-93), dramatist and poet. His play *The Jew of Malta* was produced about 1592.

4   *The Scornful Lady* by Beaumont and Fletcher was produced around 1613. *The Custom of the Country* by Fletcher and Massinger was written some time between 1619 and 1622. *The Beggar's Bush*, also by Fletcher and possibly in collaboration with Massinger, was produced about 1622. *The Humorous Lieutenant*, written by Fletcher alone, was produced about 1620. *The Little French Lawyer*, written either by Beaumont and Fletcher or Fletcher and Massinger, was produced between 1619 and 1622. *The Laws of Candy* by Fletcher was written around 1619.

5   Three plays by Jonson. *Volpone, or The Fox* was produced in 1606, *The New Inne* in 1629, and *The Staple of News* in 1625.

6   Benjamin West (1738-1820), Anglo-American historical painter. He was a leader of the neo-classical movement. One of the founders of the Royal Academy, he succeeded Sir Joshua Reynolds as its president in 1792.

7   Anton Raphael Mengs (1728-79), German historical and portrait painter. He taught Benjamin West for three years in Italy.

8   Henry Fuseli (1741-1825), Anglo-Swiss painter and draughtsman.

9   William Hogarth (1697-1764), painter, satirist, and engraver. He was most famous for his illustrations of such "sensational" topics as *The Harlot's Progress* (1732) and *The Rake's Progress* (1735).

Goya.[1] Miguel de Cervantes[2] wrote sensationally, but Gongora[3] would have scorned the act. Camoens[4] was sensational, but Lousada[5] was "classic." Wedgwood[6] was a sensational potter, and Flaxman[7] a sensational sculptor. The revival of wood-engraving was a "sensation" as bitterly deprecated by the old admirers of namby-pamby stipple and woolly mezzotint, as vaccination was piously denounced by the advocates of inoculation, or better still by letting the smallpox have its own way. The *Grub-street Journal* and the *Daily Intelligencer*[8] were not sensational papers. The *Telegraph*, the *Standard*, and the *Star*[9] are clearly sensational. Mr. Millais is a sensational painter, so is Mr. Holman Hunt.[10] Mr. Woolner[11] is a sensational sculptor; Mr. Ruskin's art-criticisms are sensational; Mr. Darwin[12] is a sensational philosopher; Mr. Fechter is a sensational actor;[13] Mr. Spurgeon[14] is a sensational preacher; Dr. Cumming[15] is a sensational theologian; so, from another point

1 Francisco José Goya y Lucientes (1746-1828), Spanish painter, etcher, and satirist.

2 See Appendix B.6, 617, n.4.

3 Luis de Gòngora y Argote (1561-1627), Spanish poet.

4 Luis de Camoens (1524?-1580), Portuguese poet.

5 Antonio Jose Coelho Lousada (1828-59), Portuguese novelist.

6 Josiah Wedgwood (1730-95). Best known for his blue jasper ware, a delicate pottery embossed with Greek figures in white.

7 John Flaxman (1755-1826). Designed the cameo-like decorations for Wedgwood's pottery. He was professor of sculpture at the Royal Academy in 1810.

8 Two early newspapers. The *Grub-street Journal* was a weekly literary newspaper published in London from 1730 to 1737. The *Daily Intelligencer* was established in 1643.

9 Three Victorian newspapers. *The Daily Telegraph* was founded in 1855 and was the first daily in London sold for a penny. For a time it had the highest circulation of any English newspaper. The *Standard*, an old Tory paper, ran from 1827-1916. In 1857 it was purchased by James Johnson, who dropped its price to 2d in 1857 and 1d in 1858, doubled its size, and made it a leading morning paper. The *Morning* and *Evening Star* were radical newspapers which ran from 1856 to 1869.

10 Sir John Everett Millais (1829-96) and William Holman Hunt (1827-1910) were, with Dante Gabriel Rossetti (1828-82), founding members of the Pre-Raphaelite Brotherhood.

11 Thomas Woolner (1825-92), sculptor and poet. He was a member of the Pre-Raphaelite Brotherhood and a professor at the Royal Academy.

12 Charles Darwin (1809-82), naturalist. His *Origin of Species* (1859) revolutionized biology by advancing the theory of evolution.

13 Charles Albert Fechter (1824-79), English actor, famous for his interpretations of Hamlet and Othello.

14 Charles Haddon Spurgeon (1834-92), Baptist preacher.

15 John Cumming (1807-81), Scottish divine and popular preacher, most widely known for his interpretations of prophecy. He argued that the "last vial" of the Apocalypse was to be poured out between 1848-67.

of view, is Dr. Newman;[1] so, from another point, is Professor Maurice.[2] As for Mr. Kingsley,[3] as poet, novelist, parson, and historian, he was always sensational. *Belgravia* is a sensational magazine,[4] and Miss Braddon is a dreadfully sensational novelist. M. Nélaton[5] is a sensational surgeon; M. Edmond About[6] a sensational wit; Napoleon III.[7] a sensational sovereign; and Graf von Bismark[8] a sensational statesman. As for Garibaldi,[9] he was never more than a sensational patriot; and it was only General Grant's[10] sensational obduracy that caused the Southern confederacy to collapse.

This is the Cry, this is the yelp, this is the howl, in which the dullards and the dolts and the backbiters revel. Suppose that the sensible portion of society consented just for a season to lay down their arms, their pens, and their pencils, and allowed the non-sensationalists to have their way? No more sensation plays, no more sensation poems – by the way, *Maud*[11] is glaringly sensational, and so is *Enoch Arden*[12] –

---

1 John Henry Newman (1801-90), churchman and author. One of the founders of the Oxford Movement, Newman converted to Roman Catholicism in 1845.

2 Frederick Denison Maurice (1805-72), clergyman and author.

3 See *Aurora Floyd*, 103, n.1.

4 *Belgravia* (1866-99), begun by John Maxwell largely as a vehicle for showcasing Braddon's fiction.

5 Auguste Nélaton (1807-73), Paris surgeon, author of *Éléments de pathologie chirugicale* (1841-61). His clear and precise lectures on surgery were attended by huge numbers of people.

6 Edmond François Valentin About (1828-85), French author.

7 Louis Napoleon Bonaparte (1808-73), emperor of France 1852-70. After a series of failed attempts to gain power he was elected president of the Second Republic in 1848. In 1851 he staged a successful coup d'état, which was ratified by a plebiscite in 1852. In November of that same year a second plebiscite overwhelmingly approved the establishment of the Second Empire, and Louis Napoleon became Emperor Napoleon III.

8 Otto von Bismark (1815-98), German statesman. A leading force in the movement for German unification, Bismark was a dominating influence in that country's nineteenth-century military, political, and economic policies.

9 Giuseppe Garibaldi (1807-82), Italian patriot and soldier. A leading figure in the struggle for Italian unification, his crowning achievement was the conquest of Sicily in 1860.

10 Ulysses S. Grant (1822-85), American soldier and politician. During the American Civil War he was made supreme commander in the West in 1863, and Commander in Chief of the Union forces in 1864. Grant was elected eighteenth president of the United States in 1868.

11 See Appendix A.4, 572, n.1.

12 A poem by Tennyson published in 1864.

no more sensation novels, no more sensation leading-articles, no more sensation pictures, no more sensation sermons, no more sensation speeches. Let us go back to the calmly dull, to the tranquilly inane, to the timorously decorous, to the sweetly stupid. Let some new Macaulay – the old one was a sensational historian – take up the narrative left us by Thomas Babington,[1] and write: "Her most gracious Majesty, Queen Anne, was a very good Queen. She was much attached to the Church of England. Her Consort was called Prince George of Denmark. He was a great donkey, and used to get drunk. Queen Anne was very fond of good eating. She was very clever at making cordials. She had a famous general, whose name was Churchill. The French called him Malbrook. He won the battle of Blenheim for her. Queen Anne is dead."[2] There, if that be not classical, I know not what is. There are very few words of more than two syllables in this non-sensational excerpt. Or let our novels be on the model of the *Grand Cyrus* or *Belisarius*.[3] Let leading-articles begin, "They write from Vienna that the Emperor refuses to treat, and that the Great Turk is likely to give some trouble on the Danube." In lieu of reports of debates in Parliament, let us have "Conversations in the Senate of Blefuscu."[4] Let our Royal Academicians turn coach-painters or cut out profiles in black sticking-plaster;[5] let Mr. Phelps[6] play

---

1   Thomas Babington Macaulay (1800-59), essayist, historian, and politician.

2   Macaulay's *History of England from the Accession of James II* (1849-61) was originally meant to cover the period 1685-1830, but at the time of his death he had taken it only as far as the reign of William III (1689-1702). Much of the *History's* popularity rested on Macaulay's lively and dramatic style, and in this passage Sala mocks a "non-sensational" historian's dull description of the English monarch who followed William, Queen Anne (1702-14).

3   *Le Grand Cyrus* (1649-54), written by Scudéry (see Appendix B.6, 608, n.2), and *Belisarius* (1766), written by Jean Francois Marmontel (1723-99), are both historical romances.

4   Blefuscu is an island kingdom described in Jonathan Swift's *Gulliver's Travels* (1726). The island is a satire on France, and its inhabitants are the sworn enemies of the Lilliputians (the English).

5   The Royal Academy of Arts was founded by George III in 1768, at the instigation of Sir William Chambers and Benjamin West. Its goal was to provide a forum for the development and exhibition of the best in British art. Sala declares that if only "safe" art is to be allowed, members of the Academy will be reduced to such mechanical tasks as painting vehicles, and tracing silhouettes in black to be stuck upon white paper, a common method of portraiture at English fairs.

6   Samuel Phelps (1804-78), actor-manager. Phelps was most famous for his portrayal

Macbeth in the uniform of a captain in the Guards; and the Bishop of London, in a wig like a bird's-nest, preach a sermon in St. Pauls against photography[1] and the Electric Telegraph. Don't let us move, don't let us travel, don't let us hear or see anything; but let us write sonnets to Chloe, and play madrigals on the spinet, and dance minuets, and pray to Heaven against Sensationalism, the Pope, the Devil, and the Pretender;[2] and then let Dulness reign triumphant, and Universal Darkness cover all.

---

of Shakespearean roles, and in 1844 he opened and managed the Sadler's Wells theatre in London.

1 See Appendix B.4, 598, n.1.

2 Representatives of the three great dangers to Protestant England: Roman Catholicism, sin, and the Stuart claim to the English throne. In general the phrase summarizes the threat of religious, moral, and political instability.

8. "Sensation Novels" *Punch*, 28 March 1868.

SENSATION NOVELS.

Mary. "Please. Sir, I've been Looking everywhere for the Third Volume of that Book you was Reading."

Lodger. "Oh, I took it back to the Library this Morning, I——"

Mary. "Oh! then will you tell me, Sir, if as how the 'Markis' found out as she'd Pisoned 'er Two fust 'Usbands?!"

Select Bibliography

1. Victorian Sensation Fiction

Brantlinger, Patrick. "What is 'Sensational' about the 'Sensation Novel?'" *Nineteenth-Century Fiction* 37 (1982): 1-28.

Cvetkovich, Ann. *Mixed Feelings: Feminism, Mass Culture, and Victorian Sensationalism.* New Brunswick, New Jersey: Rutgers UP, 1992.

Flint, Kate. *The Woman Reader 1837-1914.* Oxford: Clarendon, 1993.

Hughes, Winifred. *The Maniac in the Cellar: Sensation Novels of the 1860s.* Princeton: Princeton UP, 1980.

Kalikoff, Beth. *Murder and Moral Decay in Victorian Popular Literature.* Ann Arbor: UMI Research Press, 1986.

Loesberg, Jonathan. "The Ideology of Narrative Form in Sensation Fiction." *Representations* 13 (1986): 115-38.

Miller, D.A. *The Novel and the Police.* Berkeley: U of California Press, 1988.

Mitchell, Sally. *The Fallen Angel: Chastity, Class, and Women's Reading, 1835-1880.* Bowling Green: Bowling Green U Popular Press, 1981.

Pykett, Lyn. *The "Improper" Feminine: The Women's Sensation Novel and the New Woman Writing.* London: Routledge, 1992.

Showalter, Elaine. *A Literature of Their Own: British Women Novelists from Brontë to Lessing.* Princeton: Princeton UP, 1977.

Tillotson, Kathleen. "The Lighter Reading of the Eighteen-Sixties." Introduction. *The Woman in White.* By Wilkie Collins. Boston: Houghton Mifflin, 1969. ix-xxvi.

Trodd, Anthea. *Domestic Crime in the Victorian Novel.* London: Macmillan, 1989.

2. Mary Elizabeth Braddon

Bedell, Jeanne F. "Amateur and Professional Detectives in the Fiction of Mary Elizabeth Braddon." *Clues: A Journal of Detection* 4 (1983): 19-34.

Casey, Ellen Miller. "Other People's Prudery: Mary Elizabeth Braddon." *Sexuality and Victorian Literature.* ed. Don Richard Cox. Tennessee *Studies in Literature* 27 (1984): 72-82.

Hazlewood, C.H. *Aurora Floyd; Or, The Dark Deed in the Wood. A Drama in Three Acts.* London: Thomas Hailes Lacy, [n.d.; first performed 21 April 1863 at the Royal Brittania Theatre].

Schroeder, Natalie. "Feminine Sensationalism, Eroticism, and Self-Assertion: M.E. Braddon and Ouida." *Tulsa Studies in Women's Literature* 7 (1988): 87-103.

Webster, B. *Aurora Floyd: Or, The Banker's Daughter. A Drama, in A Prologue and Three Acts.* London: Webster and Co., [1863? As performed at the New Theatre Royal, Adelphi].

Wolff, Robert Lee. *Sensational Victorian: The Life and Work of Mary Elizabeth Braddon.* New York: Garland, 1979.

3. *Aurora Floyd*: Reviews and Responses

"The Archbishop of York on Works of Fiction" *The Times* (2 November 1864): 9.

"Aurora Floyd." *Athenaeum* 1840 (31 January 1863): 144-45.

Austin, Alfred. "Our Novels (Part II): The Sensation School." *Temple Bar* 29 (June 1870): 410-24.

James, Henry. "Miss Braddon" *The Nation* (9 November 1865): 593-94.

[Mansel, H.L.]. "Sensation Novels." *Quarterly Review* 113 (April 1863): 481-514.

[Oliphant, Margaret]. "Novels (No. II)." *Blackwood's Edinburgh Magazine* 102 (September 1867): 257-80.

"The Popular Novels of the Year." *Fraser's Magazine* 68 (August 1863): 253-69.

[Rae, W. Fraser]. "Sensation Novelists: Miss Braddon." *North British Review* 43 (1865): 180-204.

Sala, George Augustus. "The Cant of Modern Criticism." *Belgravia* 4 (November 1867): 45-55.

—. "On the 'Sensational' in Literature and Art." *Belgravia* 4 (February 1868): 449-58.

"Sensation Novels." *Medical Critic and Psychological Journal* 3 (1863): 513-19.

Untitled Review. *Christian Remembrancer* 46 (1863): 209-36.

broadview literary texts

"This is a series in which the editing is something of an art form."
The Washington Post

"Broadview's format is inviting. Clearly printed on good paper, with distinctive photographs on the covers, the books provide the physical pleasure that is so often a component of enticing one to pick up a book in the first place.... And, by providing a broad context, the editors have done us a great service."
Eighteenth-Century Fiction

"These editions *[Frankenstein, Hard Times, Heart of Darkness]* are top-notch—far better than anything else in the market today."
Craig Keating, Langara College

The Broadview Literary Texts series represents an important effort to see the ever-changing canon of English literature from new angles. The series brings together texts that have long been regarded as classics with lesser-known texts that offer a fresh light—and that in many cases may also claim to be of real importance in our literary tradition.

Each volume in the series presents the text together with a variety of documents from the period, enabling readers to get a fuller, richer sense of the world out of which it emerged. Samples of the science available for Mary Shelley to draw on in writing *Frankenstein,* stark reports from the Congo in the late nineteenth century that help to illuminate Conrad's *Heart of Darkness;* late eighteenth-century statements on the proper roles for women and men that help contextualize the feminist themes of the late eighteenth-century novels *Millenium Hall* and *Something New*—these are the sorts of fascinating background materials that round out each Broadview Literary Texts edition.

Each volume also includes a full introduction, chronology, bibliography, and explanatory notes. Newly typeset and produced on high-quality paper in an attractive Trade paperback format, Broadview Literary Texts are a delight to handle as well as to read.

The distinctive cover images for the series are also designed (like the duotone process itself) to combine two slightly different perspectives. Early photographs inevitably evoke a sense of pastness, yet the images for most volumes in the series involve a conscious use of anachronism. The covers are thus designed to draw attention to social and temporal context, while suggesting that the works themselves may also relate to periods other than that from which they emerged—including our own era.

broadview literary texts: published or scheduled

Mary Hays
The Victim of Prejudice
edited by Eleanor Ty

Eliza Haywood
Eovaii
edited by Earla Wilputte

Eliza Haywood
*The History of Miss Betsy
Thoughtless*
edited by Christine Blouch

Eliza Haywood
Love in Excess
edited by David Oakleaf

Nathaniel Hawthorne
The Scarlet Letter
edited by
John Stephen Martin

Felicia Hemans
Selected Poems
edited by Gary Kelly &
Susan Wolfson

Laetitia Elizabeth Landon
Selected Writings
edited by
Jerome McGann &
Daniel Riess

John Keats
Selected Poems
edited by John Kandl

Stephen Leacock
*Sunshine Sketches
of a Little Town*
edited by
Carl Spadoni

Mary Delariviere Manley
The Adventures of Rivella
edited by
Katherine Zelinsky

J.S. Mill
On Liberty
edited by
Edward Alexander

Christopher Marlowe
Doctor Faustus
edited by
Michael Keefer

Anne Plumptre
Something New
edited by
Deborah McLeod

Amelia Opie
Father and Daughter
edited by John Pierce &
Shelley King

Charles Reade
Hard Cash
edited by Graham Law

Mary Robinson
Selected Poetry
edited by Judith Pascoe

Sarah Scott
Millenium Hall
edited by Gary Kelly

Sophocles
Oedipus Tyrannus
edited and translated
by C.W. Marshall

Mary Shelley
Frankenstein
edited by
D.L. Macdonald &
Kathleen Scherf

Mary Shelley
The Last Man
edited by
Anne McWhir

Mary Shelley
Lodore
edited by Lisa Vargo

Mary Shelley
Valperga
edited by Tilottama Rajan

**Nineteenth-Century Stories
By Women**
edited by
Glennis Stephenson

Bram Stoker
Dracula
edited by Glennis Byron

Mary Ward
Marcella
edited by
Beth Sutton-Ramspeck

Augusta Webster
Portraits and Other Poems
edited by Christine Sutphin

Oscar Wilde
The Picture of Dorian Gray
edited by Norman Page

Mary Wollstonecraft
The Vindications
edited by
D.L. Macdonald &
Kathleen Scherf

bold=already published